"*The finest novel that Rachel Field has yet written.*"

—SATURDAY REVIEW

"*All This and Heaven Too* is the drama of a woman—a city— a nation . . . One lays the book down with reluctance."

—LAURA BENÉT

"Miss Field has succeeded in bringing to quick and appealing life the gifted, high-souled, and much-maligned 'Mademoiselle D.'"

—CHRISTIAN SCIENCE MONITOR

"IN EVERY SENSE A MAJOR EFFORT."

—PHILADELPHIA INQUIRER

# All This, and Heaven Too

### RACHEL FIELD

A Dell Book

Published by
DELL PUBLISHING CO., INC.
750 Third Avenue
New York 17, N.Y.

Reprinted by arrangement with
The Macmillan Company
New York, N.Y.

Dedication: TO ARTHUR PEDERSON

*The title of this book is accredited to Matthew Henry (1662-1714), who wrote of his father, the Reverend Philip Henry: "He would say sometimes when he was in the midst of the comforts of this life—'All this, and Heaven too!'"*

First Dell printing—November, 1963

Printed in U.S.A.

BeTTy Davis - Henriette

# CONTENTS

A LETTER OF INTRODUCTION

*Page 7*

*Part I*

"MADEMOISELLE D."

1841—1848

*Page 13*

*Part II*

MADEMOISELLE
HENRIETTE DESPORTES
1849—1851

*Page 303*

*Part III*

MRS. HENRY M. FIELD
1851—1875

*Page 371*

# A LETTER OF INTRODUCTION

DEAR GREAT-AUNT HENRIETTA,

Although I never knew you in life, as a child I often cracked butternuts on your tombstone. There were other more impressive monuments in our family lot, but yours for some unaccountable reason became my favorite in that group erected to the glory of God and the memory of departed relatives.

Knowing what I know of you now, I should like to think that some essence of your wit and valor and spice still lingered there and had power to compel a child's devotion. I should like to believe that the magnetic force which moved you to plead your own cause in the murder trial that was the sensation of two continents and helped a French King from his throne, was in some way responsible for the four-leafed clover I left there on a summer day in the early nineteen hundreds. But I am not sentimentalist enough for such folly. You had been dead for more than thirty years by the time I came along with my butternuts and four-leafed clovers; when I traced with curious forefinger the outlines of a lily, unlike any growing in New England gardens, cut into the polished surface of your stone.

My forefinger has grown none the less curious in the thirty more years that I have been tracing your legend from that inscription, bare as a detached twig, stripped of leaf or bloom:

HENRIETTE DESPORTES
The Beloved Wife of Henry M. Field
Died March 6, 1875

There it is, almost defiant in its brevity, without date or place of birth; with no reference to Paris; nothing to suggest the transplanting of a life uprooted from obscurity by an avalanche of passion and violence and class hatred.

Half a century ago no memorial was complete without some pious comment or a Biblical text chosen to fit the life and works of the departed. Why should yours be the only one in that group of marble and slate that asks nothing of God or man? Why is there no hint of the destiny which was reserved for you alone out of a world of other human beings? Only you know the answer, and only you could have written the epitaph that was omitted from your stone.

The omission must have been deliberate. I know that as surely as if you had told me so yourself.

"My dear great-niece," I think you would answer me with the wise, faintly amused expression which is yours in the only likeness I have ever seen of you, "some day you will learn as I did to make a virtue of necessity." Then, with that slight Parisian shrug you were able to subdue but never entirely shed, you might add, "Who knows most speaks least."

Still, legends are not easily shed. Silence and obscurity may not be had for the asking. You had your way at the last, and your stone is bare and impersonal; but you could not erase your name from those records of crime, or do away with the files of French and English newspapers for the year 1847. It is your fate to be remembered against your will. You must have waked sometimes in the big Empire bed of polished mahogany that stands now in my room, turning from memories of words spoken and looks exchanged in the Rue du Faubourg-Saint-Honoré; from the din of newsboys calling out your name on crowded boulevards; from the gray walls of the Conciergerie where you walked under guard with curious eyes pressed to the grating. I, too, have lain wakeful in that same bed half a century later, trying to piece together from scattered fragments of fact and hearsay all that you spent so many years of your life trying to forget.

I have grown up with your possessions about me. I know the marble-topped mahogany bureau that matches your bed; the pastel portrait you made of the little girl who became your adopted child; I know the rosewood painting table that held the brushes and paints and crayons it was your delight to use; I know your silver forks and spoons with the delicately flowing letter D on their handles. On my hand as I write is a ring that was yours, and I never take out a certain enamel pin from its worn, carnelian-studded box without wondering if it may not have been some bit of jewelry tendered as peace-offering by the Duchesse after one of her stormy outbursts. Strange that these intimate keepsakes should survive when I have never seen so much as a word in your handwriting.

Your portrait, painted by Eastman Johnson, has made you visible to me as you looked in the years when you were no longer the notorious Mademoiselle Deluzy-Desportes riding rough seas alone, but a married woman of assured position, presiding over the house near Gramercy Park where men of letters, artists, philanthropists, and distinguished visiting foreigners gathered and expanded under the stimulating spell of your presence. I know your calm dignity of expression even as I know your bodice of coffee-colored silk and that single tea rose tucked in the fall of black lace. Yours was a strongly marked face, square of chin and broad of brow. The thick chestnut hair was smoothly parted after the fashion made familiar by your contemporaries Elizabeth Barrett Browning and George Eliot. Your eyes, not particularly large or beautiful in themselves, were keen, full-lidded, and intent above well defined cheek bones and a rather flat nose with a wide, spirited flare to the nostrils. But, of all your features, the mouth was the most dominant, speaking for you from the canvas in eloquent silence. Too large and firm a mouth for the accepted rosebud model of your day, it must have been a trial to you in your youth. Humorous, sensitive, and inscrutable—one could tell anything to the possessor of such a mouth and never know what response might be forthcoming except that it would most certainly be wise and shrewd and worth hearing.

Fragments of your wit and sagacity have survived, like chips of flint left where arrowheads were once sharpened. But the arrowheads themselves, those verbal darts for which you were famous, having found their mark, did not remain for our time. A phrase here, tinged with foreign picturesqueness; a quick comment still vivid with personal pungency; a half-forgotten jest; some humorous anecdote, they make a meager and strangely assorted sheaf for your great-niece to cull.

And I am only your great-niece by marriage. You left no legacy of flesh and blood behind you. Fate played many tricks upon you, yet this was the one you most bitterly resented. You were barren, who should have been the most fruitful of women. To you children were more than amusing puppets to be dressed and coddled and admonished after the manner of the Victorian era to which you belonged. They were a passion, as absorbing as if each had been an unknown continent to be explored and charted. Even your most disapproving censors admitted this power, and your sway over the young Praslins was certainly one of the strongest links in the chain of evidence brought against you. Youth was a necessity to your nature, and so you took a child from your husband's family into your home to be a substitute for your own.

*"Eh bien,"* I can almost hear you saying, "one has not the choice in this world. But to live without a child in the house —that would be tragedy. Is it not so, my leetle Henri?"

Your leetle Henri, who was my great-uncle, agreed, as he agreed in most of your projects, marveling not a little at the Gallic sprightliness and wisdom of that extraordinary lady who had done him the honor to become his wife. A bird of rare plumage had taken possession of his home; a strange blend of nightingale and parakeet was gracing the nest he had vaguely expected to be shared by some meek, dun-feathered wren. He never quite knew how it had happened, but he knew his good fortune in having won you. He was proud of your elegance and wit; of your charm and intelligence, and, yes, of your slightly arrogant ways.

Great-Uncle Henry was small in stature and was your junior by ten years; but there was fire in him, and you knew how to kindle what lay beneath that New England exterior so different from your own. He may have lacked the shrewdness of your judgment, the whiplash of your wit; but his enthusiasm, his warmth and idealism fused with the sterner stuff of which you were made.

I can just remember Great-Uncle Henry as a small, elderly man with a vague smile, whose mind had a disconcerting way of wandering off without warning into labyrinths of the past where a matter-of-fact seven- or eight-year-old might not follow. But that memory has nothing to do with an eager young man, who, for all his Puritanical upbringing and ecclesiastical turn of mind, was born with feet that itched to walk in far places, and an imagination that kindled romantically to the plight of a French governess suddenly faced with the charge of instigating a murder that shook the Empire. He was twenty-five years old when he first heard your name echoing through Paris that summer of 1847. There he stood, fresh from a boyhood in the Berkshire Hills where his father had followed Jonathan Edwards with more hell-fire and brimstone sermons in the meetinghouse that faced the village green. A Williams College valedictory delivered at sixteen, and those first years of preaching sermons of his own from pulpits that only accentuated his boyishness, were behind him. There he stood, earnest and young and unaware that you and he were to spend twenty years together across the Atlantic.

It may be that, like Victor Hugo who described your enforced exercise under guard in the Conciergerie courtyard, Great-Uncle Henry had his first glimpse of you through iron bars. We shall never know. I set down here only what may have happened. Perhaps I have put words into your mouth that you would never have said. My thoughts, at best, can never be your thoughts. I know that, and still I must write them, since you yourself emerge from the web of fact and legend as definite as the spider that clears the intricate maze of its own making. I shall not claim to be unprejudiced, though I shall try to tell the truth as I know it. For the more complex the subject, the more each separate version must vary with the teller. So, each hand that touches the piano strikes a different chord.

Dear Great-Aunt Henrietta, you will never know what I think of you, but here it is—the letter I have always wanted to write; the story I have always wanted to tell.

# Part I

## "MADEMOISELLE D."
### 1841-1848

## *chapter one*

AMONG THE ILL ASSORTED GROUP OF PASSENGERS WAIT-
ing to leave the small steamer that had brought them across
the Channel from Southampton to Le Havre, a woman
stood erect and alone with her luggage piled about her. It
was unusual in the year 1841 for a woman of her age and
appearance to be traveling unaccompanied. Not that she
showed striking beauty, but a certain spirited grace of carriage distinguished her from her fellow travelers.

Late March was not the most propitious time for crossing,
and the English Channel had lived up to its reputation for
choppiness. The night had been rough and rainy, and a general air of limp resignation prevailed in the little group so
soon to be scattered. Curls and once crisp feathers drooped
damply against wan faces; eyes were circled in unbecoming
dark hollows; huddled forms in shawls and steamer rugs
slumped miserably on benches as the edged wind of early
morning blowing across salt water strove with the thickness
of the ship's saloon. The stale scents of food and tobacco
and human occupation mingled with that unmistakable
smell peculiar to all such vessels, a combination of tar and
rope and brass polish, of varnish and smoky oil lamps—
hardly an atmosphere to enhance a woman's charm. But
this solitary female bore up well under the ordeal. She was
young—at least she could not be called old—and she appeared considerably less than her twenty-eight years; she
was vigorous and full of a lively interest in the world and
her temporary companions, and she had learned long before
this how to conduct herself alone.

A shaft of salty air came in with the opening and closing
of doors as men went out into the rapidly thinning dimness
on deck. In response to the freshness her head lifted and her

nostrils dilated as she breathed deeply. Involuntarily she made a half-move to leave the overcrowded saloon; but the impulse was checked almost at once. Much as she would have welcomed fresh air, it would not do to go out and join the men who tramped the damp decks in masculine freedom, untrammeled by billowing skirts of cashmere or taffeta, by yards of petticoat and bonnet strings that were prey to every current of air. Besides, there were all her possessions in the neatly roped bandboxes and bags and the new leather portmanteaus with the brass-headed nails driven into the lid to form the letters "H. D." There was no one to whom she might entrust them.

"Ah, well," she thought, and her shoulders shrugged ever so slightly under the Paisley shawl, folded to display the richly patterned border to best advantage, "it would hardly be *comme il faut* at this hour of the morning, and with so few women about."

It was pleasant to hear the sound of her native tongue again from one or another of the passengers. Though she had spoken English fluently from childhood, and though she had even come to think as easily in one tongue as in the other during the years which she had spent in London, yet she quickened to the familiar accents. Already she felt younger and lighter of heart for the sound. She had been away too long. Yesterday, to be sure, she had shed courteous tears at parting from the Hislop family—especially from the grave and gentle girl who had been her sole charge, and who turned to her with such reverent adoring eyes. Those candid blue eyes had been red-rimmed almost from the moment the matter of a change had been mentioned. It had been affecting to see the child's genuine emotion.

"Come, *chérie*, you have shed too many foolish tears. The time has come when you no longer need a governess. You are a young lady, almost sixteen, and ready to attend finishing school. Why, you will be marrying in a year or two more."

"But, mademoiselle, you have always been so much more than a governess. Papa himself says so, and you know he is not easy to please."

That was true enough. Sir Thomas Hislop expected much of those who served him, especially of the one into whose charge he had given the training of his only child. She had never given him cause to regret the confidence he had

placed in her, and as time went on he had added unusual
household privileges to those customarily accepted as fitted
to the station of nursery governess. As his daughter had said,
Mademoiselle had grown to be far more than governess in
that home, and never once had she overstepped. His letter
of recommendation, on paper bearing the family crest, was
for an Englishman lavish of praise, informing the world in
general and the Duc and Duchesse de Praslin in particular
that Mademoiselle Henriette Desportes had served him for
the better part of eight years as governess and companion to
his daughter Nina, and that, in all things pertaining to deportment, personal integrity, and tact, she had proved herself a model and an ornament to her sex. Her gifts, also, he
had added as an afterthought, were considerable, for besides
being qualified to teach the rudiments of learning she spoke
French and English fluently, was familiar with literature
and the classics, and had a charming talent for flower painting and crayon portraiture.

There had been farewell gifts in token of the Hislop
family's esteem—the handsome shawl which had cost more
than twice what she might have contrived to save out of her
wages; the umbrella with the ivory handle now crooked
over her arm; the beaded bag worked by her young charge's
own devoted fingers. All these were tangible signs of her personal conquest. She smiled with satisfaction, and then
sighed, remembering that these conquests were now behind
her; remembering, too, certain disturbing rumors that had
reached her ears concerning the household which she would
so soon be entering.

"*On arrive,*" a Frenchman was telling his plump wife,
while the sound of chains and churning water and the sudden bustle of landing filled her ears.

It required all her attention to marshal her belongings,
seize a blue-smocked porter, and get herself safely ashore.
No husband or father or brother guided her down the steep
and slippery gangplank and superintended the luggage and
formalities and customs and passport inspection. She awaited
her turn alone, shivering in the pier's half-open shed.

Her passport was duly read and stamped, and the French
authorities thereby informed that Henriette Desportes, aged
twenty-eight years, single woman, native of Paris, parents
deceased, nearest of kin, her grandfather, the Baron Félix
Desportes, former officer of Napoleon Bonaparte, now re-

siding at Paris, was returning to continue her occupation of governess. Port of embarkation, Southampton, England, March 28, 1841.

*"Bien."* Mademoiselle Henriette Desportes tipped the porter as frugally as one dared and settled herself for the train journey to Paris. Just for a moment she had let her mind linger over the prospect of a first-class ticket. But the habit of economy had asserted itself, and she had resisted temptation. The compartment benches were hard and narrow, but she had been fortunate in securing a place by one of the windows. She felt comforted by this and a cup of chocolate and a roll she had hastily secured in the nearest café. From a small package in her bag—labeled in a girlish hand, "Mademoiselle, with the affectionate regard of her devoted pupil Nina H."—she selected a glacé fruit and nibbled it appreciatively as the last whistle sounded and the train steamed slowly out into the early morning countryside.

Even the dirty pane of glass could not altogether dim the effect of sunlight on a world that was dear and familiar to her. She had been so long among smoking chimneypots and houses of brick and chill gray stone that she had almost forgotten walls could show cream-colored or even softly rose where the sun touched their plaster and whitewash. The delicate turrets of a far château pricked out of massed woods. Beside a shallow stream a stooped peasant in sabots and faded blue paused in his turf-gathering to watch the passing train. A woman drove a flock of white geese across a bridge under willows that were already dripping green. Smoke rose blue and wavering from a cluster of thatched roofs. Indeed, everything seemed to swim in a faint blue haze. Always responsive to the picturesque in nature and humanity, Henriette Desportes missed nothing of the passing scene. It filled her with pleased detachment, and she relaxed under the dreamlike unreality beyond the window.

Oh, well, it might look like a patterned world, laid out in prim design, but to those living there it could never be so simple. They were as alive as she: that old peasant contriving to outwit the cold; that woman anxiously counting her comical flock lest one goose escape her vigilance; all those who slept, or toiled, or loved under the low-hung roofs or the sharp turrets. Those people out there, if they caught sight of her own face pressed close to the window pane, might be speculating about her. To them she was part of the pattern of the lumbering train with its trail of smoke and little boxlike carriages. Perhaps they envied her, riding at ease to distant Paris. How little they knew of that! How little she herself knew what awaited her at the end of the journey!

Yesterday marked the end of an era. A cycle of her life lay behind in the dark, well ordered rooms of the Hislop house. She could never recapture that part of herself again. Eight years gone—and what had she to show for them? A letter testifying to her good character; a few English pounds that represented years of patient scrimping; the whole-hearted devotion of a girl who would presently be too submerged in the cares of marriage to need her; a modest wardrobe that fitted easily into the luggage on the rack above and under the seat; some cheap books and trinkets, and certain experiences in self-denial and discipline that had strengthened her character at the expense of her youthful freshness and spontaneity. Twenty-eight was not an advanced age, but is was certainly not youth.

"What chance have I ever had for youth?" she asked herself in a surge of unuttered bitterness. "First the convent without even a summer's holiday free from bells and masses and instruction in books and conduct, and then more lessons—only I am no longer pupil but teacher; and now it will be no different except that I shall be in Paris, where the heart and step should be lightest if one has the means to keep them so!"

Perhaps she had been foolish to come. But the offer had been exceptional. The Hislops had been kind, had urged her to continue in their home till the right opening presented itself; but she knew the signs of change. She could read the writing on the wall and see how soon her young charge would be full-grown. And then this chance to be governess to the children of one of the oldest families of French nobility at two thousand francs and her board and apartment had dropped into her very lap. She could hardly have refused even if she had wished to remain in England, which was far from the case. She knew she had made a most favorable impression upon her interviewer, a friend of the Duchesse who had been commissioned to find the proper guardian for the Praslin progeny. Yes, her credentials were impeccable, and her qualifications obvious. Could she arrange to assume her duties immediately?

In this haste and obvious eagerness, Henriette had sensed something not quite usual, not quite as it should be. She had parried with modest adroitness, and suddenly the positions had been reversed: the questioner became the questioned. The interview was in her hands. Reluctantly she had ferreted out the truth. Governesses seldom stayed long in the Château Praslin. There had been quite a procession in the last two years. That was indeed strange, she had suggested with just the proper shade of pointed naïveté in her manner, since the position was obviously such a desirable one and the salary so generous. Were the young Praslins perhaps difficult and undisciplined? No, she was assured, they were charming and intelligent children. It was only— Well, perhaps a word to the wise would be sufficient. Mademoiselle Desportes was not without experience in domestic affairs, and in this case the Duc and Duchesse de Praslin, though both were from the best families of France and Corsica and their marriage certainly was more than fruitful since it had produced no fewer than nine children in eleven years— Still is must be admitted that there were times when they seemed to be not in complete accord. Of course she must understand this was only a matter of temperament—there was nothing to suggest discord; but the Duchesse, besides having a Corsican inheritance of hot temper, was far from well. She was not always herself, and the Duc was not the sort of man to make compromises with another's moods.

The children were too often witnesses to family disagreements. In fact it was frequently round them that the controversies raged. The Duc had a very deep attachment for his children and very decided ideas about their instruction. The Duchesse, poor woman, resented her husband's interference in such domestic matters—and who could blame her? It required extraordinary tact and understanding on the part of a governess. That was why Mademoiselle Desportes had seemed so particularly fitted for the position, though naturally there were dozens of others as well recommended as she to fill it. Well, there could be no harm in giving the matter a trial. Henriette had evidenced not too great eagerness in her acceptance. She would need a fortnight to prepare herself; that would be little enough time, but she wished to be as considerate as possible. She had promised to report for her new duties upon the first of April.

"And that is day after tomorrow," she reminded herself. "God knows if I shall last long in this ménage!"

Yet she did not dread the thought of entering it. The difficulties it presented would at least be stimulating. One would not perish of boredom in a place where charges of gunpowder might lurk in unexpected corners to explode without warning. She felt oddly exhilarated—almost, she thought, as if she were about to step upon a lighted stage filled with unknown players, to act a rôle she had had no chance to rehearse beforehand. She must find the cues for herself and rely on her own resourcefulness to speak the right lines. Henriette Desportes's heart under the plain gray alpaca basque that was her badge of discreet servitude beat quickly, but with steady self-confidence. She knew she was no fool, though she must not betray such an unladylike knowledge.

Rouen with its cathedral towers and market-place was fair and sleepy under the noon sun. The train stopped there for a quarter-hour, and she made bold to get out and stretch her cramped body. She was the only woman to do so, but her own preoccupation wrapped her in unapproachable dignity. She remembered Rouen from her childhood years because she had gone there with two of the Sisters making a pilgrimage to the Cathedral. The dim, austere beauty of the great Gothic arches and aisles had laid a deep hold upon her young imagination, and the Sisters' pious recital of Jeanne d'Arc's martyrdom had stirred her then, as now. She had veered from the religion those zealous Sisters had instilled into her youth. She was a Protestant now, but the early association and mystic ardor sometimes returned as it did today. Only now it was Jeanne the woman, sore beset and alone, not the saint, who quickened her sympathics.

"You, too," she thought as she returned to the railway carriage, "you, too, were a single woman, defying the pattern of your world. We should have understood each other, you and I."

She settled herself for the second part of the journey and unfolded the English newspaper she had not read the day before. It was a copy of the London *Times*, and already the items she pored over seemed part of another world in which only yesterday she had been an infinitesimal human part.

Lord Palmerston's foreign policy was receiving much comment at home and abroad. It seemed to have excited considerable ill-will in France, where Guizot held the reins of foreign affairs. According to latest reports it appeared that, in spite of Great Britain and Austria taking part with

Turkey against Mehemet Ali, he would be recognized as hereditary ruler of Egypt. The Queen and the Prince Consort had formally opened a new hospital for foundlings at Whitechapel. The Queen's speech was reported in full, and there had been much enthusiasm in token of the recent anniversary of the royal pair's first year of conjugal bliss. Her Majesty not only appeared in excellent spirits but seemed to have improved in health since the birth of the little Princess. The Royal Family had graciously sat for daguerreotype likenesses at the newly opened parlors in Pall Mall. This remarkable process for reproducing the human features was proving a sensation in Paris and London and even in America. Monsieur Daguerre deserved all praise for his invention, which was indeed an artistic achievement worthy of support though as yet too great a luxury to be indulged in by the masses. Rachel, the greatest tragédienne of her day, would shortly cross the Channel to introduce her art and repertoire to London.

Henriette read every word of that last bit of news. To her mind, Rachel was worth all the Royal Families of England and Europe rolled into one. She meant to see that pale face and those flashing Semitic eyes; to hear the vibrant tones of the voice that had shaken all Paris, even the strait-laced bourgeoisie who disapproved of her private life while they wept and marveled at the spell she cast to the most distant balcony seat. "Where I," Henriette told herself as she folded the paper, "shall most certainly be sitting if I am fortunate enough to squeeze myself into the theater at all!"

*chapter two*

MADAME LE MAIRE'S ESTABLISHMENT, ONE OF A ROW OF dingy houses in the unfashionable quarter of the Marais, rue du Harlay, was one not easily defined. Half pension, half school, its narrow, high-ceilinged bedchambers and musty salons had for many years sheltered a procession of students from various shores and other such temporary sojourners to Paris as the extremely elastic proportions of the ménage could accommodate. Madame Le Maire might be said to specialize in female flotsam and jetsam, though she made it a point to be sure of the morals as well as the financial status of her paying guests. Her terms were a week's rent paid in advance and two letters of reference, carefully scanned and verified before the prospective occupant was allowed to take possession. Her reverence for respectability was well known and far outruled the dictates of her heart and sympathies. If tears and entreaties fell upon her gold-ringed ears they left less impression than the drip of rain on the ancient gray slate of her own roof. But Madame Le Maire was not so much hard, as inflexible. She did no favors herself and expected none in return. Her guests received care and simple meals so long as they continued to behave themselves and pay the bills she personally made out every Friday evening in her fine hand that suggested the tracings of a mathematically inclined spider.

"I ask nothing else of *le bon Dieu* and my guests," she frequently explained to all listeners, "than that my accounts should balance to the last sou and the police never darken my door. So far my efforts have been blessed with success."

Henriette Desportes and Madame Le Maire were well acquainted. Henriette had spent six months in the old house the year she had left the convent to continue her studies in art. Since that time she had returned for brief visits. Only the year before, she had spent a month there while the Hislop family were traveling in Switzerland. Madame Le Maire greeted her upon her arrival in a barouche from the boat train with marked approval, if not with the effusive welcome of Pierre the porter.

"Mademoiselle has returned with the spring," the old fellow told her as he shouldered her possessions and led the way through the familiar entrance. "Day before yesterday I heard a songbird in the Bois, and when I returned from my errand Madame is already preparing the Needle's Eye because Mademoiselle Henriette is arriving to occupy it."

"So it is to be the Needle's Eye again." Henriette smiled at mention of the narrow slit of a room under the roof which she knew so intimately. Because of its size and inconvenience and the four steep flights that must be climbed to it Madame Le Maire seldom managed to keep it permanently filled, but whenever occasion warranted, she pressed it into service.

"Well"—Henriette exchanged a knowing look with Pierre—"I can put up with a closet this time since I shall be leaving again day after tomorrow."

"Mademoiselle is leaving, and just as she has arrived—" Pierre's old tongue clicked in affectionate concern.

"Not Paris, Pierre, only the Needle's Eye. I have come back to stay—at least—"

She broke off at sight of Madame Le Maire's erect and tightly boned form at the head of the stairs. The two women did not embrace. They never had indulged in such unbusinesslike pleasantries. They met, as they had always done, on a plane of mutual respect and shrewd admiration each for the other's abilities. Henriette had always known that the older woman favored her above the other feminine boarders. She had never exactly said it in so many words, but the girl knew that this keen-eyed, dumpy Parisienne liked her spirit and good taste in dress and manners. Some of the young ladies had grown deplorably careless in such matters. But Madame Le Maire had always let Henriette know that she knew good breeding when she met it.

"We may have our backs to the wall," she might almost have been saying as the two stood looking each other over after the absence of many months, "but we shall always stand straight, you and I. Yes, our spines will not melt at the first signal of storm."

"Well, Mademoiselle Desportes," was what she really said as they met, "you might have done me the honor of giving me more time to prepare for your arrival. Only by the greatest chance and by considerable shifting about could I find a place for you."

"It was good of you, madame, to overlook the short notice." Henriette was aware of the older woman's self-importance and knew the value of admitting favors and being grateful for them. "The change was very sudden, and I wrote you at once. I hope it is not too inconvenient at this time?"

"No, no," Madame Le Maire was mollified. "I am always glad to oblige if I am able. The only room now vacant is rather small and at the top of the house. You may perhaps remember—"

"I do—very well," Henriette resisted the temptation to smile and call it by name.

Better to accept the poor accommodation without protest. Madame Le Maire's good will was above rubies. She could

afford to puff a little and be cramped for two nights for the
sake of keeping it. There were precious few places in Paris
where a lone woman might find respectable food and shelter
within means of a slim pocketbook. Her tact was rewarded
by the offer of a glass of wine and a wafer in Madame's own
salon. She accepted the invitation and, as her weariness
responded to the delicate glow which stole over her at each
sip of the canary, she and Madame grew less formal.

"So you have left London behind you, mademoiselle?
And are you glad to return to Paris—permanently, it seems,
this time?"

"Very glad indeed, madame; but as to permanence—who
can say? I least of all concerned."

"To be sure, nothing is permanent in this world—nothing
except dying; and that is certainly more my affair than yours
if years mean anything."

"Years should mean very little to one who wears hers so
becomingly." Henriette knew Madame's dread of growing
old. She had always felt inclined to humor, rather than to
laugh at, her attempt to hide the trace of years. The front
hair, so darkly luxuriant and curled in contrast to the scanty
graying strands at the old woman's neck, the pince-nez that
so inadequately did duty for spectacles, the touches of rouge
on her faded cushions of cheeks—all these seemed pathetic,
but commendable efforts. Madame Le Maire, she thought,
was no more brave than the rest when it came to facing what
she really feared. This was her way of showing defiance, as
Henriette had seen children strut and whistle through the
dark stretches of some long corridor leading to bed.

"But"—she returned to her earlier remark after she had
taken another sip of wine and felt the pleasant warmth
slowly lifting the weariness from her body—"when I said
'permanence' I meant only that one can never count upon
certainty in a new position, and this appointment presents
certain new problems."

"Nine altogether new problems if what I hear of the
Praslin family is correct. It is the household of the Duc and
Duchesse de Praslin which you wrote you were about to
enter, is it not?"

"It is, but all the children will not be under my super-
vision. The older boys have a tutor and three of the daughters are at a convent. I shall have charge of three girls and
the youngest boy only."

"I should call that more than enough. Well, you have

good courage and tact. You will need more than your share of that."

Her tone was casual, but opaque dark eyes fixed her visitor with the wise inscrutability of an old parrot. Henriette did not waver under the look.

"I hope I may please my pupils and their parents." She set down her glass, brushed a crumb of wafer from her skirt, and rose. "I shall do my best."

"Naturally." Madame Le Maire made no offer to refill the glasses. "To please is your bread and butter; and if you are clever enough to add a bonbon now and then to sweeten your diet, all the better. But do not acquire the taste for bonbons. A sweet tooth can be dangerous at your age."

"Madame Le Maire, if you mean that I shall grow too fond of luxury—"

"I mean more than that. The household you are entering is certainly luxurious, but it is also—well—let us say difficult. You are young to meet the requirements of such a position, but perhaps you know better than I what is expected of you. A gray head is sometimes placed on green shoulders. But if I may offer one bit of advice—look as much like a governess as possible when you go to your interview tomorrow."

The sharp old eyes took careful survey of the younger woman, lingering significantly over the richness of the shawl, the gray bonnet with cherry ruching and ribbons that brought out the clear color of the wearer's cheeks and lips, the sheen of loosely curling chestnut hair.

"There are times when it is advisable to hide one's light under a bushel. And now you no doubt wish to refresh yourself after your journey. You will find hot water in your apartment, and we dine as usual at half past seven."

Henriette began the long climb, half amused, half annoyed by Madame Le Maire's abrupt dismissal. It was not unpleasant to be warned against her youth, which had of late seemed slipping from her, but she would have liked to get to the bottom of those insinuations. Probably the old woman was merely letting her tongue run away with her; still, she had seldom been so talkative. And the airs she gave herself—calling that hole under the roof an apartment! As for "dining at half past seven"—Henriette knew exactly what the meal would be like, from cabbage soup, whose familiar fragrance followed her up the stairs, to the pyramid of withered tangerines and nuts that would accompany the demitasse.

The Needle's Eye had not changed by one crack less or one piece of furniture more. All was exactly as she remembered. The couch which was converted into a bed only by virtue of necessity and good will on the part of the sleeper, the corner washstand where she had splashed so often with lowered head because the sloping eaves made it impossible to stand otherwise, the row of wooden pegs awaiting their burden of dresses, the shelf which did duty for dressing table, and the mirror above it, perpetually dimmed, so that the reflected face appeared blurred with inexhaustible tears. But beyond the high peaked window all of Paris waited— ancient and ageless in the late March twilight, fair as some hazy though well remembered dream.

Henriette's fingers shook as she unfastened her bonnet strings. Her breath came quickly, as much from emotion as from her hasty climb. She opened the casement and leaned out to the cool air that lifted the hair from her forehead, that seemed almost like a hand laid to her cheek. All about her, other roofs rose, red-tiled or gray, with their smoking chimneys less blackened and less ominous than London chimneypots. Lights were beginning to appear in windows, and an irregular patch of river between buildings shone softly luminous like a bit of polished pewter. The Seine— she felt its presence in the freshened air; in the faint reflection of sky it still held; in the occasional sound of passing boats. Almost she felt that she could distinguish the murmur of its watery flow from that other flow of sound which was the city itself, man-made and more insistent.

"Paris—Paris—Paris," her pulse beat over and over while she leaned there motionless at the casement and twilight dwindled into darkness. It was as if she held the city in her arms and it in turn held her fate hidden—in which corner she could not know.

"Oh, let me be happy here! Let me know that I am alive. Do not let me be old before I have ever been young!"

So, in the dusk of the twenty-ninth day of March in the year of our Lord one thousand eight hundred and forty-one, Henriette Desportes prayed to the city whose streets were to ring to her name six years later.

At half past nine she climbed more stairs—a not too clean or well lighted flight that led to the second floor of an

old stone house just off the Boulevard Montmartre. A slat-
ternly woman answered her ring at the porter's bell and
grudgingly admitted that Monsieur Félix Desportes was in
his apartment. Henriette did not care for the appraising
glances of the old creature and explained her presence in
crisp accents.

"Please announce me to the Baron Desportes. Tell him
that his granddaughter is here. He is expecting me."

But the woman only grinned and shrugged.

"Granddaughter or not," she threw over a lifted shoulder
as she disappeared into the shadows from which she had
come, "it's all the same to me. I ask no questions, and I'm
not paid to announce guests. Be sure you shut the door when
you leave, Mademoiselle—"

"Mademoiselle Desportes," Henriette repeated with annoyance, "and please be so good as to remember it."

But there was no further response and nothing for her
to do but climb the stairs alone, picking her way with care
in the flickering light from a single gas jet at the landing.
She shook her skirts free of dust and paused to steady herself before she knocked. It was not a visit she anticipated
with pleasure, but she was determined to carry off her part
of it to the best of her abilities. Perhaps this time her only
relative might display some sign of affection or interest. The
reunion did not, however, begin with promise.

"Oh, so it's you." There was no welcome in the voice or
in the face that greeted her. "Well, come in since you're
here. I hardly expected you so soon."

"But, Grandfather, I wrote you that I should come at
once. You had my letter?"

"Yes, I had it. It's somewhere about." The tall old man in
a worn dressing gown and slippers shuffled back to his chair
by the grate fire, waving a long, veined hand towards a heap
of newspapers, letters, pens, and sticky glasses that crowded
a near-by table to overflowing. "I knew you would turn up
whether or no."

Henriette felt a sudden chill at his words. The old resentment of childhood flooded her at his unresponsiveness. It
had always been so. Ever since she could remember he had
made her spirit shrink inwardly like a leaf the frost can
shrivel in a single night. Upon their rare meetings in her
youth he had always made it clear that he found her a
nuisance. She had been a plain child, but clever and sensi-

tive. She had hoped that her excellence in studies at the convent might please him, might disarm him into a word of praise or pride. But he had never uttered one. Before each visit of her childhood she had gone to him with hope. Always she had come away with baffled discouragement and a vague sense of actual physical repugnance which both shared. She had hoped that perhaps when she grew older it would be different. But now she knew that a barrier of restraint and even of human dislike must always lie between them.

"You have dined?" The question was perfunctory, and though Monsieur Desportes reached for his own glass of brandy he made no offer to pour her a *liqueur*.

"Yes, at Madame Le Maire's. One of the students escorted me here. He did not wish me to walk so far alone."

"Well, going about alone should be no novelty to you." He eyed her shrewdly from under his bushy, graying brows. "You should be able to conduct yourself without help by this time. You're almost thirty."

Henriette flushed at his look and words. She was not ashamed of her age, but no woman cares to be reminded of it.

"I am only too used to making my way alone," she answered, stretching out her hands to the fire and taking some comfort in their white shapeliness and the flash of a small ring which caught the light. "I only thought you might be relieved to know— But no matter, I am well, and you? I hope your rheumatism has not returned."

The veined hand holding the stem of the brandy glass was not altogether steady, but the denial was instant.

"Rheumatism! I have nothing of the sort. A twinge now and then in the disgraceful damp of this hole they are pleased to let out in the name of comfortable apartments. But when one has come through the campaigns I have and slept with the snows of the Alps and steppes for pillow, one learns to put up with poor fare and hardships. My health need give you no anxiety. Better keep your concern for yourself since, if what you wrote is true, you will have need of it."

"Grandfather!" Henriette leaned forward and laid a hand on his sleeve. "I had hoped you might be glad that I was returning to Paris and even a little pleased and proud at the post that has been offered me."

"Proud—pleased," he echoed her words heavily. Her hand might have been a shadow on his arm for all the notice he took of it. "You have the effrontery to ask me to be glad because you have chosen to cast your lot with the house of Choiseul Praslin that I hate."

"But it is one of the greatest families in France."

"They stand for everything that I spent the best years of my life trying to stamp out of France. This white-livered nobility that feeds on the life blood like some poisonous fungus—that will fasten on us again now that there is no one stronge enough to defy them."

Involuntarily his eyes turned to the souvenirs of his fighting days: his sword and the uniform that hung like a gray ghost in a corner, the portrait of Napoleon in full regalia, his framed commission as officer in the Imperial Guard, his cherished decorations for valor in action and the parchment which had conferred upon him the honorary title of Baron in return for loyal service to his country and his Emperor. As he recognized each symbol of the lost cause to which he would always cling, his voice took on pride along with a more intense bitterness as he continued.

"First you must go to England, to the country that humiliated us and betrayed the Emperor into exile and death. But that is not enough. Now you must choose out of all France those who were the first to hurry back to the side of Orléans when the wind veered in that direction."

"Can I help it if the times have changed?" Henriette answered his accusations quietly, but her color deepened.

"You could help bringing this last insult upon me. Better families than this Praslin tribe have not forgotten past benefits or run so quickly to the side of the King. If the Duc de Praslin has sold his birthright for what favors he can win from this blundering Louis-Philippe let him take what he can get. Let him be made an officer in the royal household. But you need not serve him and his sons and his daughters."

"Grandfather"—Henriette spoke in the firmly soothing tone she would have used to quiet an overexcited child—"I am not royalist in my sympathies. I should like to see France a Republic, but—"

"A fine way to show it then." He broke in testily.

"The Emperor Napoleon is dead," she went on, "and his son is dead. I honor you for your loyalty to the past, but what would you have me do? The past does not buy one food to eat, or clothes to wear, or a roof over one's head. For nearly ten years I have had to think of such things. I cannot afford the luxury of living in the past."

"So!" The old man drained his glass and reached a shaking hand to refill it. "Throw it in my teeth that I haven't provided you with servants and carriages and half the Rue de la Paix to put on your back! This is the thanks I get for educating you above your station!"

"And just what *is* my station?" She stiffened in her chair and faced him squarely across the untidy table with its green-shaded oil lamp. "I would very much like to know. It has never been quite clear to me."

"You need not add insolence to your other faults or reproach me because you are poor and single. I suppose you think I should have added a handsome dowry along with this expensive schooling that has only made you more difficult and headstrong?"

"No, Grandfather, I have never reproached you, and I have not come here asking you for money. But it is not strange that I should want to know something of myself now that I am grown."

"If you know enough to keep out of mischief, that is all I ask of you!"

"But I am asking *you*." His ruthlessness only made her more determined to force an answer to what had troubled her so long. "You have never seen fit to tell me anything of my birth or of my parents. All I know is that I was christened Henriette Desportes and that you are the Baron Desportes."

She was careful not to omit the title he clung to the more tenaciously as it dwindled in prestige.

"I was told at the convent," she went on, "that you were my only living relative; and when the other girls wrote letters to their parents each week I wrote to you with all the affection I had in my heart to give. I was lonely and eager to make you proud of me. Well, I was foolish and sentimental as children will be. I tried so hard, and I hoped—"

"That is neither here nor there, and you are no longer a child." He broke in irritably. "Get to the point, and tell me what you want of me—why you have come here tonight."

"You are still my only relative, Grandfather." She pressed her hands tightly together in her lap. It was hard to go on against the wall of his displeasure, but she had determined to make one final effort to break down his reserve.

"It is not right to go on year after year with such a blank in one's life. If I have anything good in me that was theirs, I should like to know; and if there are faults and weaknesses that have continued in me, it is only fair that I should know these, too, and try to overcome these defects."

"Defects may be overcome without knowing where they were inherited."

"Yes, but it would help me to understand myself. I feel sometimes like those silhouettes artists cut from black paper and paste on a white card—just the outlines of a person standing against nothing. Don't let me be like that all my life."

"I do not propose to rake up the past. Your parents are both dead. You know that already."

"Yes, I know." She sighed uneasily and watched him refill his glass for the third time. "I should like to know that something of passion and love went into my making. I have had little enough of them since."

Her voice had grown low as she forced herself to put the last question. But it vibrated with the intensity of her emotion as a single harp string twangs suddenly in a still room. The old man roused himself. He set down the half-filled glass and leaned towards her. His gaunt, grayish face was only an arm's length from hers, and his expression had sharpened into a hard, malignant stare.

"My name is, unfortunately, yours," he told her levelly, "but only so long as you are a credit to it. If you go against my wishes and take this position which you propose to do, you will forfeit the right to it."

"But, Grandfather, that is impossible. I cannot return to England again, where it might be months before I found another opening. I have done nothing to bring disgrace upon us, and if I needed a good name before, I need it doubly now in this family—"

"Do not mention their name to me again," he broke in. "You have your choice. If you persist in taking this place you must not go as Mademoiselle Desportes."

"But they already know that is my name. If I tell the Duc and Duchesse otherwise they will think it most peculiar."

"What they think is no affair of mine. You accepted this post before consulting me, and if you go to them you need not look to me again for anything. You have no relatives living or dead."

"You cannot speak for the dead." Henriette rose and

gathered her shawl about her. She looked unusually tall in
the dim room, and her face took on a pallor in the green
lamplight that gave it the strength and color of a marble
bust. "You can only speak for yourself, and I can only answer for myself. You need never be afraid that I shall come
to you again. After tomorrow I shall be at the residence
de Praslin in the Rue du Faubourg-Saint-Honoré, number
55, if you should care to know where to find me."

She moved to the door, and though the Baron Félix Desportes followed her with his eyes he did not rise from his
chair. He still held the glass and, as she paused on the threshold to the draughty corridor, Henriette saw him lift it towards the pictured features of his Emperor with the faded
knot of tricolor dangling from the frame. With rage and
pity struggling in her she watched him offering a silent toast.

"Well," she told herself, feeling her way down the dark
well of the staircase, "my only bridge is burned behind me.
From now on I must build them myself or drown!"

*chapter three*

SHE WALKED TO MEET HER FUTURE IN THE FAUBOURG-
Saint-Honoré as if Spring itself were at her heels. The visit
to her grandfather, she put behind her. His words had
shaken her momentarily, but they were, after all, only the
croakings of an embittered old man who resented her youth.
To him her hopefulness was merely one more symbol of his
own declining power. Because misfortune had turned life
bitter for him, he could not reconcile himself to another's
happiness. She regretted the grim interview of night before
last, but it could not touch her. Neither could Madame Le
Maire's pointed insinuations of personal pitfalls take root
in her renewed self-assurance.

She felt equal to anything that morning as she passed the
little stalls with their prints and trinkets and tattered volumes along the Quai. In one of these displays her eye caught
a print of the Empress Josephine, highly colored and fluttering in the river wind, and such was her feeling of confidence
that the Empress seemed almost waving a signal to her.

A blind man, led by his little dog, passed, and Henriette found a sou in her purse to drop into the extended tin cup.

"God bless you, mademoiselle," the man thanked her.

"How did you know that I am Mademoiselle?" she laughed incredulously.

"Ah, that was easy." He nodded. "I heard the rustle of skirts and smelled lavender when you opened your purse. Mignon and I wish you good luck, and may your gift be multiplied."

The pair moved away, the dog full of subdued importance and curiosity, his master unhurried and detached as became one to whom smells and rustles and footsteps determined his own small world. There had been no one else to wish her good luck as she set forth for her interview, and so she cherished his blessing. Better to have one she had earned for herself than to have had none at all.

Flower venders were selling primroses and violets. She hesitated by one basketful, half tempted to buy a small nosegay. But they would be dear so early, she knew. Besides, her previous experience had taught her that such a display might create a poor first impression. Otherwise considerate mistresses did not tolerate jewelry and flowers on the persons of governesses in their households. She would take no chance of offending the Duchesse at their first meeting by even so innocent a lapse of dignity.

When she was within several streets of her destination she hailed a fiacre, telling the driver to take her to the Rue du Faubourg-Saint-Honoré, number 55. Then she settled back to compose herself for the interview.

The hiring of the carriage was a gesture of strategy rather than one of fatigue. For her to have arrived on foot would have been to make a fatal entrance. At best her position was bound to be unpopular with the servants in any household. If it were reported by the footman to his companions below stairs that the new governess had walked up to the door like any nursemaid or milliner's apprentice, she would be treated as less than such. There would be friction enough in preserving her rights without making a misstep at the start. By nature Henriette was independent of spirit. There was little of the snob about her, and at heart she disliked class distinctions. Yet she was practical. She knew that only by demanding the special privileges accorded a governess could she be acknowledged a successful one.

"Please the family, and you offend the servants," she re-

minded herself as the carriage rolled on. "Please the servants, and the family no longer trust you. I must walk the
difficult path between and keep from slipping too far in
either direction. *Allons,* a governess needs the skill of a
tight-rope dancer and the cunning of a fox."

They were drawing up to the entrance of an imposing
residence now. The façade with its long windows, the crest
above the exquisitely wrought ironwork of the gates, and
the clipped trees in their pots made the London house she
had so lately left seem shabby by comparison. Her impulse
was to jump out quickly and pull the bell, but she restrained
herself and sent the grumbling driver to do so for her. When
the porter in livery answered the summons she alighted
decorously, paid the fare and tip and was admitted into an
inner courtyard, round which the wings of the house were
built. Through this she followed the servant into a chilly
reception room. A footman accepted her card on a silver
tray, and she was left to wait alone. She rose and studied
her reflection in a wall mirror, and felt relieved to discover
that the wind had not disarranged her hair, which curled
softly on either side of her face and was drawn into a low
knot behind. She pulled the strands forward a little to suggest more oval contours than Nature had seen fit to give
her. The walk had brightened her color, and her bonnet was
really becoming and at the same time not too dashing for
her rôle. Yes, she was sure the servant had been impressed
by her appearance. If he did not instantly label her as the
new governess, she had at least one point in her favor.

She heard his returning footsteps and had just time to
reach her chair and spread her skirts about her when he
entered.

"The Duc and Duchesse will see you, mademoiselle. This
way, if you please."

She followed him up a flight of stairs and then along a
carpeted hall of vast length with many doors opening on
either side. At the far end they paused, and the servant
raised his hand to knock. As he did so a woman's voice
raised to a shrill pitch of intensity came too distinctly for the
listeners to miss.

"You know my feelings; it's no use pretending surprise.
Everyone in this house knows the pleasure you take in humiliating me—"

The lower, indistinct murmur of a man's voice under

complete control followed, and then the woman's rose again.

"Yes, it is humiliating before the children and the servants, and now you will have a new audience in her. Don't
think I'm fool enough not to know why you've sent for her.
Mademoiselle Maillard satisfied me in every way, but because she was no longer young and attractive—because she
sympathized with me in my misery—you must turn her out.
I tell you I cannot stand another change and more insults.
Every day the children treat me as if—"

Once more the deeper tones broke in, and seizing this
opportunity the servant knocked loudly. As they waited the
word to enter, he turned and fixed Henriette with a significant look. She pretended indifference, but she was quick to
catch its meaning—the sly amusement that accompanied the
almost imperceptible shrug of his shoulders in their green
broadcloth livery.

"Mademoiselle Henriette Desportes," he announced in
formal accents, and left her standing in the doorway.

She was always to remember that room as she saw it in
the spring sunlight with her own senses heightened by anxiety over the impression she hoped to make and startled at
what she had unwittingly overheard. It was a small, intimate
room, evidently the parlor of a woman's suite. The draperies
were deep rose color, the white and gilt furniture exquisitely
upholstered in flowered brocade that repeated the same
shade. Sun streamed in at the long windows, touching the
garlands on the carpet to brightness wherever it fell. Potted
plants bloomed on the window sill—rose and white cycla-
mens with flowers like tropic birds arrested in flight. A small
secretary stood near by with scattered sheets and quill pens
flung down as if some one recently writing there had been
hastily disturbed. She was aware of all this before her eyes
found the man and woman to whom the voices must have
belonged.

The woman lay upon a chaise longue beside a small grate
fire, and even in the loose negligee of crêpe de Chine and
lace which flowed about her voluminously, Henriette saw
that the lines of her body were soft and full, heavy with natural voluptuousness and the wide contours of childbearing.
One was aware of her flesh first and of her features and expression afterward, as one must notice the body before the
spirit in any canvas by the artist Rubens. The Corsican
strain was apparent in the inky shadows of her falling hair,

in the thick dark brows and the startling red lips that showed
in such marked contrast to the pallor of her overfull face. It
was the most sensuous and at the same time unsatisfied
mouth Henriette had ever seen, and there was no smile of
even perfunctory greeting upon it or in the velvet black eyes
under their lazy lids.

"Madame la Duchesse"—Henriette had not expected to
speak the first word, but the silence grew too marked—"I
trust I am not too early, but I understood you would grant
me an interview at eleven."

The occupant of the chaise longue made a vague gesture
with her head, but gave no other sign of acknowledgment.
Henriette took a step forward and looked about for a chair.
As she did so the other figure moved into her view from the
windows. He had been standing close to the hangings, but
now he took shape before her with extraordinary vividness.
She saw that he was in his middle thirties, and that he wore a
gray and green striped dressing gown that accentuated his
fairness and the long lines of his body. His hair and the side
whiskers which he wore trimmed close were yellow as corn
silk, and the skin above them had a warm, healthy glow.
His chin showed prominent and clean-shaven with a deep
cleft under a full lower lip. In contrast the upper one was
short and thin, and when he smiled, as he was doing now,
the effect was youthful despite the high-bridged nose and the
rather tired eyes. Those eyes were far from youthful, however: they were unmistakably those of a man who was experienced, and who could be inflexible as well as pleasure-
loving.

"Allow me, Mademoiselle Desportes." She recognized the
timbre of the voice she had heard from the other side of the
door as she accepted the chair he placed for her near the fire.

"Thank you, Monsieur le Duc," she said, seating herself
carefully so that her skirts might fall gracefully about her.
It was warm in the room, and she let her shawl slip over the
chair back. Her gray alpaca was far from stylish, but it
fitted well; and she drew off the new dove-colored gloves
she had purchased yesterday in an extravagant impulse. She
busied herself with their removal, not wishing to continue
her scrutiny of the Duc and his lady. Except for a heavy
sigh the latter made no attempt to begin the inevitable questions. It was awkward, this silence, broken only by the soft
sound of the fire and the idle drumming of long, well kept

fingers on the marble mantelpiece as the Duc leaned against
the fluted pillars which supported it. Henriette had never
been so openly inspected, but she felt no embarrassment at
the appraisal. Rather a sense of power and strange security
filled her. This luxurious room, this expensive robe of silk
and lace, this family title, and even this handsome husband
might belong to the woman before her; but for all that she
was less at her ease than the governess who waited respectful, and completely self-possessed.

She was just in time to catch a frown and an impatient
motion from the Duc to the Duchesse. It was the wife's
place to conduct such interviews, and she evidently from
annoyance or timidity refused to assume the expected rôle.
Henriette gave no hint that she had noticed the sign; but she
realized that the reins of authority had slipped from her
prospective mistress' hands, and she lost no time in seizing
them. Very well, then; since the other woman had not
availed herself of her rights, the positions would be reversed,
and she must begin the questioning.

"Please allow me to express my gratitude for the compliment you have paid in summoning me to discuss your children's education. I hope my references were satisfactory?"

"The references— Oh, yes—quite so." The Duchesse's
manner did not vary from its irresolute vagueness.

"More than that, they were excellent." The Duc's voice
caught up the unfinished sentence, and he continued to regard Henriette intently.

"There must, of course, be much more that you would
wish to know about me. Many points, that is to say, which
could not be put into a letter. And I for my part, should wish
to know more about my charges before I could assume such
responsibility." Henriette deliberately paused and turned to
the woman on the chaise longue. But she scarcely seemed
to be listening. Her eyes never left her husband's face. "For
instance, Madame la Duchesse specified a very generous
salary, but she did not mention the ages of the children or
the instruction which would be expected of me? It may be
that I am not proficient enough in certain lines to meet the
requirements?"

"The requirements are not taxing, mademoiselle." The
Duc unhesitatingly answered the question addressed to his
wife, and she allowed him to continue without protest, indeed without any effort at entering into the conversation.

"With your experience you will have little difficulty. Our two older sons, as you may already know, have their own tutor, while three of our daughters are attending the Convent of the Sacred Heart. That leaves four who would be your sole charge now: Isabella, our eldest daughter, now nearly fourteen; Louise, just entering her teens; and two much smaller—Berthe, who will be six next month, and our youngest child, Raynald, not yet four. You do not have any objection, I hope, to undertaking the care of a boy?"

"On the contrary," Henriette responded, pleased at the interest he took in his children, "I should relish a touch of masculinity in the nursery. I think it far better when boys and girls mingle, certainly while they are still so young."

"He is a bright little fellow, but I must warn you that he is rather delicate. His health has given me grave anxiety."

She did not fail to notice that he said "me" instead of the "us" she expected to hear.

"I understand," she answered. "Such a child needs particular watchfulness. An overactive mind can so easily exhaust a frail body."

"I am sure we may rely on you, mademoiselle, to instruct without overtaxing his strength. I can see you are sympathetic to the special needs of a high-strung child."

"Raynald is very sensitive like me." The Duchesse spoke suddenly, though she addressed her words towards the fireplace and the man beside it, not to the governess she was ostensibly interviewing. "I was ill and unhappy before his birth, and he will always bear the marks of my suffering."

The Duc gave the fire an impatient kick. Sparks started up from the logs. Henriette was less aware of these than of the intangible sparks of human antagonism which filled the room.

"Have you any preferences," she continued after an awkward period of silence, "as to the language I should use in their studies? I am accustomed to teaching in both English and French."

The Duchesse having dispatched her dart, relapsed into preoccupied apathy and made no effort to answer.

"English, I think, for the two older girls." Her husband again took command of the situation. "They speak it fairly well, but both need practice in writing it. With the younger two, I should leave that to your discretion. I wish them to learn it naturally."

"I think that will come about easily if they are in the room while I go over the lessons with their older sisters. They will unconsciously absorb much of the conversation without realizing that they are doing so."

"An excellent suggestion. I am sure we shall see an improvement in their speech. Mademoiselle Maillard complained of a difficulty in forcing them to use anything but French."

"Certainly they will never acquire proficiency in any language by force," Henriette agreed.

"I have had no fault to find with Mademoiselle Maillard." Once more the Duchesse roused herself, and once more Henriette felt that the conversation had become a tête-à-tête in which she was an unwilling participant. "She has proved her loyalty and her affection, Theo, which you seem to forget all too quickly."

"We are not here to discuss Mademoiselle Maillard, Fanny." He broke in coldly. "Mademoiselle Desportes must in no way be hampered by past methods. I wish her to feel free to handle the children as she thinks best."

The dark eyes in the pale face on the chaise longue took on a sudden gleam, as if a second fire smoldered behind their darkness. "As *you* seem to think best" were the unspoken words she directed towards her husband. Disregarding this mention of her predecessor, Henriette hastened to change the subject.

"I regret to say I am not sufficiently skilled to instruct in the art of music. I play a little on the piano, and I could supervise practicing if that were necessary."

"Their music lessons are already arranged, mademoiselle, and they also have dancing lessons once a week. I see from your credentials, however, that you are gifted in painting. Perhaps you would undertake to develop little Berthe's talent in that direction?"

"Indeed, I should be most happy to."

"You will find her more headstrong than her brother," the Duc went on; "she has spirit, but if you win her affections—well—" He smiled suddenly, showing his fine white teeth and making a slightly deprecating gesture. "You must pardon a father's prejudice, but she is an unusually charming and lovable child."

"You need not apologize for your daughter's attractions, Monsieur le Duc." Henrietta had seldom heard a man speak with such naturalness of his children. She felt the bond which existed between him and them, and it filled her with surprise and admiration. "Never having known a father's interest and affection myself, I can think of no greater blessing than such loving prejudice. They are most fortunate."

The Duchesse sighed heavily. It was the only sign of life from the heap of silk and lace before the fire.

"I should also speak of religion." Henriette felt she could no longer postpone a subject which she knew must be faced, and which she dreaded to open. "I think you already know that, although I was christened and reared in a convent, I have adopted the Protestant faith. I tell you this now, frankly, because I should not wish misunderstandings."

A triumphant gleam appeared in the Duchesse's eyes. "There, Théobold." She spoke before he had time to answer. "You see what comes of sending to England as you insisted upon doing. The situation will be impossible."

"I cannot see why it should be, Fanny, unless Mademoiselle Desportes wishes to make an issue of religion; and she strikes me as being far too wise for that."

"Nothing is farther from my mind." Henriette dared to direct a grateful glance towards the Duc. "I must follow my own beliefs as I wish others to follow theirs. I have reverence and affection for the good Sisters who cared for me in my childhood. It would never cross my mind to interfere in the religious training of your own children."

"Your very presence would be enough to upset their faith." The Duchesse's voice had lost its vagueness. For the first time that morning Henriette caught a defiant note in her accents. "It would be hypocrisy to disregard it."

"That would depend entirely upon Mademoiselle Desportes's attitude, Fanny," the Duc remonstrated. "She says she respects the faith of others, and I see no reason to doubt her assurances. Besides the Abbé Gallard has always dealt with their religious instruction, as he will continue to do."

"It is an insult to the Abbé to allow such a thing."

"I will explain it to him myself if you wish." He turned once more to Henriette and continued in a firm, self-composed manner. "So long as your religious convictions remain your own, I am sure there will be no reason for complaint. I think"—he turned and fixed his wife with a long, meaning look—"that tolerance is a virtue we could all benefit by cultivating."

"Thank you." Henriette allowed the relief to show in her answer. "I am very grateful, and I shall do nothing to betray your trust in me." She waited a moment, wondering if the Duchesse would press the issue. But only the sharp rising and falling of the lace on the soft curves of those ample breasts gave evidence of emotion. "And there is another matter." Henriette pressed her handkerchief tightly between her hands as she summoned courage to mention the other obstacle that she found so difficult to express. "It is rather a personal one which I could not explain in my letter. It is a little favor to ask, but I should prefer to be called by the name Deluzy—Henriette Deluzy."

"This is rather unusual," the Duc answered. "Are we to understand that you are not Mademoiselle Desportes?"

It seemed to her that both pairs of eyes, the greenish gray and the dusky, stared at her with suspicion. Everything, she knew, depended upon the plausibility of her excuse. She disliked telling a lie, but her grandfather had driven her into a tight place. She must stick to the story she had concocted in the wakeful hours following her visit to him.

"I am afraid this must seem like a strange request." She went on in her most deferential manner. "I hesitate to bore you with details of my own life, which has not"—she sighed effectively and pressed her handkerchief to her lips as if to steady them—"been too happy so far."

"That is to be regretted." The Duc covered his curiosity with polite concern. The Duchesse roused herself a little, as if this new turn of affairs renewed her confidence.

"Very few of us are happy in this world." The Duchesse gave another of her deep, meaning sighs. "Have the goodness to explain this mystery of your name."

"Give her time, Fanny. Can't you see that is what she is trying to do!"

Reassured by his tone, Henriette went on, summoning all her skill to touch her listeners.

"No, it has not been easy to face life alone. For a man it must be different, but a woman was not meant by nature to be brave and lonely. I have often felt—" She broke off with just the proper shading of helplessness, and the effect was not lost upon one of her audience of two. The Duchesse moved impatiently, but she refrained from interrupting. "I have been known as Henriette Desportes because the name belonged to my relative—my foster-father who was also my guardian. Out of respect to him I made no protest, but now there is no further need to use it."

"He is dead then, mademoiselle?"

She lowered her eyes with an inclination of the head. It was somehow easier to lie by implication than by word; and after all, she reminded herself, her grandfather had been foster-father to her, and he was certainly dead now as far as she was concerned.

"I am quite alone in the world," she added with resignation and appeal in her voice, "and one turns back to one's own parents, even if there is no memory of them. I felt I could speak of this to you and that you would understand my request because of the great reverence you bear to your own family names. Mine is unknown compared to yours; but it is mine, and I take pride in it."

"Well!" The Duchesse frowned and tapped the floor with a satin slipper. "I must say it seems very strange to me after all these years to shift about so."

"There is no reason why Mademoiselle should not be called whatever she pleases in this house." The Duc swept aside his wife's objections impulsively. "I am glad you did not hesitate to express your wishes. You must always feel free to do so while you are with us—and may I hope that will be for a long time, Mademoiselle Deluzy."

Henriette warmed to the graciousness of his answer. It was impossible not to respond when this man cared to exert his charm as he was doing now in his consideration of her. His masculine magnetism dominated the whole room. Even more than his good looks and vitality, this easy naturalness and unaffected cordiality filled her with delighted surprise. She had expected, if she saw the father of her young pupils at all, to find him formal and detached as became the head of one of the oldest and most influential families of France, and here he was full of concern for his children and eager to put her at her ease. Intentionally or not, he had won her allegiance. Common sense and past experience warned her that it would be far more advisable to keep in the good graces of the children's mother, yet Henriette realized that in all differences—and she felt instinctively after half an hour's association with these two that there would never be any lack of such clashes—she would always find herself and Théobold, Duc de Choiseul-Praslin, in complete accord.

The interview was over. She had won her points, and her

white lie had been accepted. No turning back now. She must answer to the name she had chosen because the initials would match the copper nails on her portmanteau.

It was the Duchesse's place to dismiss her, but when Henriette turned to the woman who was now her mistress she found the heavy lids had drooped over the dark eyes. The plump white hands moved inadequately among the laces of her negligee, and she appeared almost to have forgotten the whole discussion. All her thoughts were centered upon the man who stayed motionless near the fire. He alone existed for her in that room. The more she turned, reaching out invisible arms to hold him, the more he seemed to stiffen and hold her back though he leaned as carelessly as he had before. It was awkward waiting there for her dismissal like a charity child. But it was not the Duchesse who came to her rescue.

"Then we may rely upon Mademoiselle Deluzy to take up her duties tomorrow." He pronounced the name with emphatic clarity. "Does that meet with your satisfaction, Fanny?"

"Whatever you say." The voice had lapsed into injured acquiescence.

There was that in the tone which said far more than the perfunctory agreement. "You will do what you wish in any case, whether you humiliate me or not," was the implication.

Henriette made a move to suggest that she was ready for permission to leave. But the Duc motioned her to remain seated.

"I have sent for the children," he explained. "They will be through their morning lessons at twelve, and I asked Mademoiselle Maillard to bring them here. I thought it might be easier for you to meet now, before you begin your duties."

The Duchesse's heavy brows drew together in a frown. Already Henriette was beginning to know that expression and to dread it.

"You might have told me, Theo. I was planning to dress for a drive before *déjeuner*."

A knock cut short her protest, and the Duc hastened to open the door himself. Henriette turned with sharpened curiosity to face the little group she was to know intimately in so short a time. A spindling, dark-haired boy and a rosy,

fair little girl came first, breaking away from the efforts of a
middle-aged woman of nondescript dress and appearance
who tried to curb their jubilance at sight of their father.

Behind them two older girls clung together in dumpy shyness. Both were brunette, like their mother, and would have
been attractive except for adolescent self-consciousness and
poor carriage. Their merino dresses were an unbecoming
shade of dark blue with white braid edging, fashioned too
childishly for their already maturing figures, and their hair,
though naturally thick and lustrous, was strained back se-
verely from their foreheads and ears. Mentally Henriette
saw them changed before her; saw them moving erect and at
ease, their young bodies responding to softly draped dresses
of crimson or mulberry, their eyes less anxious, their lips
more ready for laughter.

"Isabella—Louise, come and make your curtsies to Mademoiselle Deluzy," their father was urging.

Obediently they went through the painful motions of
presentation—awkward and solemn as two performing
bears being put through their paces.

"We shall change all that," Henriette thought, inwardly
rising to meet their need. "Grace will come when they are
happy and at ease."

Mademoiselle Maillard acknowledged the introduction
with even greater stiffness, though youthful shyness could
scarcely be offered as her excuse. Henriette knew at sight
that the former governess would be a thorn in her side so
long as they both remained under the same roof. But she
did not fear her as a rival. She knew this type too well—
colorless, bitter-lipped, and ambiguous; one who would be
overbearing with servants and those she considered inferior
and would overdo her meeching and humility with superiors. Such a woman resented her position, yet had not the
cleverness or good sense to take advantage of the possibilities it offered. Her narrow, hunched shoulders gave her
away as did her hands. Yellowing, ineffectual hands, Henriette noticed, typical of the gentlewoman who works against
her will and as seldom as possible.

It was only too evident where Mademoiselle Maillard's
allegiance lay. She acknowledged the Duc's casual greeting
with formality, and then overwhelmed the Duchesse with
solicitous inquiries for her health.

"See," her attitude seemed to be saying as she crossed to
a place by the chaise longue, "we must stand together

against this new enemy. Your husband may find me too plain and dull to suit his fancy, but Mademoiselle Maillard will never desert you or let a younger face and figure come between us and our rights."

The two older girls watched her and their mother with anxious glances; but the little boy and girl had eyes and ears for their father, and their father alone. Mademoiselle Maillard's nervous remonstrances fell upon heedless ears.

"Raynald, take care! How many times must I tell you to watch out for the fender. Some day you will fall headfirst into the fire and be burned to a crisp. Berthe, come here. Your slipper is untied. No, no, leave your mamma's desk alone. The ink—*Mon Dieu!* You will upset it."

But her words fell on these two like the drip of distant rain, especially upon little Berthe.

"What a child!" Henriette thought, following the swift, gay grace of the small body; noting the merry glance of those clear, fearless eyes, the fine bright hair that fell about the warmly rounded cheeks.

She was one of those rare children who seem to carry some charm against evil and pain and despair. Their laughter rings clearer and higher; their tears are more tempestuous and must be dried more quickly; their footsteps are more light and sure. Such a little boy or little girl becomes to older eyes less an individual than the very embodiment of all childhood knocking at the doors of an anxious old world. Always they are unaware of the secret that wins them more favors, and more friends than their mates. They never guess the reason till the gift has been lost forever along the thorny, difficult road that lies between childhood and maturity.

Watching the little girl as she moved about the room like some new species of bird or flower, Henriette forgot momentarily the other occupants of the Duchesse's small salon. She looked up at last to find the Duc in turn watching her. He must have caught the softness that lingered in her eyes, for his own turned to her across the room. No muscle of his face moved, but a light filled those eyes staring into hers; and she knew he was touched by her admiration of his child.

"No, Raynald!" Mademoiselle Maillard's voice rose in shrill command. "Come away from there at once. You naughty, naughty boy to pick Mamma's flowers."

She darted to the window boxes, but too late to prevent the catastrophe. Raynald stood rooted in his place, his face awry with dazed guilt; a broken bloom of cyclamen in his hand. Mademoiselle Maillard's discipline broke over his smooth dark head.

"For this you will stay at home today when we drive to the Guignol, and for supper no baba—not one spoonful. Whatever made you do such a thing?"

The large, inexplicable tears of childhood began to rise and pour down his cheeks. "It was for Mademoiselle." Still clutching the forbidden flower, he struggled to explain away his crime: "To put on her dress."

A surprised smile spread over Mademoiselle Maillard's lips, and she could not resist directing a triumphant glance in the Duchesse's direction.

"Oh, that was kind, Raynald. A very kind thought, but you should have asked Mamma's permission first. Perhaps if you do so now she will let you give it to me."

"But—but—" He choked back a sob, and the truth came out in a rush before the next spasm: "I picked it for the new Mademoiselle because she has pink ribbons on her b-b-bonnet."

Mademoiselle Maillard stiffened visibly; the two older girls lowered their eyes, and even the Duc turned hastily to occupy himself with the fire. The Duchesse put her hands to her head as Raynald's sobs broke out afresh, and Henriette stirred uneasily in her chair. Only small Berthe continued her explorations of pens and paper at the desk, oblivious to the crisis which had arisen.

"Well, you may give it to her then, since you have picked it." Mademoiselle Maillard's voice had resumed its dry accents of nursery authority once more. "But you will stay at home from the drive and go without dessert for your disobedience."

With hanging head and heaving chest the boy drew close to Henriette and limply offered the flower that had precipitated so much trouble. She took it from his hand and thanked him politely. A rush of tenderness and pity for his plight and bewilderment, and of pleasure at this early sign of devotion, filled her. But she knew better than to show her gratification. She must be tactful now at the start, and besides Mademoiselle Maillard was the loser.

"I think," Henriette bent low to whisper in the little boy's ear, "I think since it is your mamma's flower it would be nice if you gave it to her."

She turned all her powers of persuasion upon him, while

he hesitated, unconscious of the importance of his response.

"See how pretty it will look in her lace," Henriette continued softly, feeling the silky smoothness of his dark hair and the stubborn set of his small shoulders. "I will pretend I am wearing it when I go out—here." She went through the motions of tucking an imaginary flower in her dress as she urged him.

The bit of play worked. Raynald flashed her a moist smile and ran to offer the flower. His mother took it with an absent-minded caress. Mademoiselle Maillard, slightly mollified, hurried to set the desk to rights, while Berthe ran to embrace her father about the knees.

The servant who had shown Henriette in an hour before now appeared to conduct her to the gates. She rose and made her farewells. The salon door closed behind her first encounter with the Praslin family, but not before she had accepted a grateful glance from the Duc.

## *chapter four*

TO LIE WARM AND UNHURRIED IN THE DEPTHS OF A BED soft with eiderdown and fine linen; to hear the pelt of rain at the windows and know that by merely reaching for the bell-rope beside her she could summon a maid to draw her curtains, light a fire, and fetch hot water: this was a sensation so new to Henriette that even after a week she still marveled at the recurring miracle. No more valiant charges from bed into arctic chillness and determined splashings of cold water while teeth chattered and icy fingers fumbled to fasten buttons and arrange hair. No more standing on tiptoe to peer into cracked or dimming mirrors. Now she sipped her *café au lait* at ease and made her leisurely toilette by a fire, before a mirror that did not distort her features. At half past eight she would emerge, trim and refreshed, to greet her charges and preside over their morning rolls and chocolate at the head of the table where Mademoiselle Maillard sat at the opposite end, gray and furtive, waiting to pounce upon slights and misdemeanors with the avidity of a hawk.

The two ends of that table were identical, and yet from the first morning they had breakfasted there together, Henriette's end had become the head and Mademoiselle Maillard's the foot.

"Mademoiselle Deluzy, Raynald has upset the honey. Quick! It's running into my lap."

"Mademoiselle Deluzy, Berthe ate three crescents, and now there's none left for me!"

"But I tell you I didn't mean to spill the cream. How could I help it, Mademoiselle Deluzy, when Louise tickled me?"

"Oh, Mademoiselle Deluzy! I dreamed last night that Papa took us to the opera—Isabella and you and me and—"

"And me, Louise—did I go too?"

"Of course not, Berthe—you're too little, even in a dream. And, Mademoiselle Deluzy, they say if you dream the same thing three times it always comes true. Do you believe it might?"

Their spontaneous including of her in all their doings, their natural appeal to her as the center of authority, was flattering; but it had its drawbacks. Mademoiselle Maillard's long face grew daily longer and more disapproving. Her air of injured pride wrapped her like an ominous mantle. She brooded on slights real and imagined. Henriette guessed in what light they were duly reported to the children's mother. Secretly elated over her triumph, Henriette determined to give her predecessor no cause for complaint. She made it a point to draw Mademoiselle Maillard into the conversation whenever possible, to take no apparent notice of sniffs and frowns and pointed sighs. But perhaps she would have done better to return the older woman's hostility in kind; to repay envy with an envy she had no need to feel since the welfare of the east wing of Number 55 Rue du Faubourg-Saint-Honoré had now been transferred into the hollow of her hands. It was a spacious wing, this that housed the young Praslins and their staff; but it was not large enough for two governesses to reign equally supreme. Already the servants in their quarters were watching and laying bets on the probable winner.

Mademoiselle Maillard had lasted longer than other governesses, and she was not without her household supporters. Madame Marguerite Leclerc, lady's maid to the Duchesse, and she were on the best of terms. Euphemia Merville, the concierge's wife, frequently invited her in to drink coffee on

her free afternoons. Maxine and Renée, the nursemaids, had
found her an easy superior; for she seldom interfered with
their management of the children. Domestic newcomers
were always regarded as natural enemies till time or some
household crisis proved them to be otherwise; and there was
about Mademoiselle Deluzy a crisp assurance of manner,
a nicety of speech that prejudiced inferiors. Nothing escaped those keen hazel eyes of hers, and they knew it. She
performed her own duties with conscientious and efficient
scrupulousness; therefore she would not be apt to tolerate
any laxness in others. Gone were the easy days when Mademoiselle Maillard reigned, wrapped in her own concerns,
and the children's wing might safely gather a layer of dust
or remain cluttered for days on end without comment.

The subject of the new governess' name had already
aroused curious comment among the staff. Jean the porter
and André the footman, both insisted that they had announced her first as Mademoiselle Desportes; yet here she
was being addressed by all as Mademoiselle Deluzy. In all
such matters Jean's memory was reliable, and it seemed
strange indeed that this change should have occurred without explanation. They were unanimous in feeling that Deluzy was not a proper name for one they considered an
upper servant no better than themselves—much too fanci-
ful and high-flown for their approval; and they resented it
unreasonably.

And then there was the matter of religion. Angèle, who
cared for the rooms in the east wing, had reported that there
was no sign of crucifix or rosary in Mademoiselle Deluzy's
apartment. Only a Bible and a book in English with a cross
on the cover kept them from branding her as an infidel.
Perhaps, Angèle even dared to suggest, she might actually
be one, and these some cunning ruse to deceive the Duc and
Duchesse. Certainly she left the school room during the
Abbé Gallard's hours of religious instruction and remained
apart till he left. Whatever her faith, it was not that of the
Praslin household; and, since the Duchesse was devout almost to the point of fanaticism, this in itself took on the
proportions of eccentricity.

Henriette herself was only half aware of this domestic
disapproval. She expected a certain amount of antagonism
in any household where a governess must keep her difficult
footing in the shifting gulf that lies between drawing room

and kitchen. The social dignity of dinners and receptions was denied her as well as the hearty freedom of a servants' dining room. It was lonely to be slightly more than maid and considerably less than mistress. But she had grown used to loneliness; her training in it had begun early. Experience had taught her immunity to slights and petty jealousies. She knew how far she might safely press her privileges and when to waive her authority, for her technique had been perfected in a hard school. She relied upon her personal magnetism and versatility to hold the affection of her young charges, and upon her tact, reliability, and skill as an instructress to win the parents to her side. Servants might at first resent her; but if they were good ones, they usually came to accept her in time. If they were inefficient they were not apt to remain long enough to cause her lasting inconvenience. But an old governess who must be met and placated at every turn presented an altogether different problem.

"Always a fly in the ointment," she thought, stirring in the green and gilt Empire bed as she prepared to rise and face the last day of her first week in the Faubourg-Saint-Honoré. "More like a spider than a fly, she is—and how she would love to see me packing my bags again!"

In spite of a downpour outside, the rooms seemed positively gay in their gold and green. Yellow draperies lent false sunshine to the small boudoir beyond her bedroom, and the thick carpet lay like green moss under her feet. After years of retiring to some cramped haven of an upper bedroom or an alcove adjoining the schoolroom with its mingled scents of chalk and ink and scalded milk, Henriette had been unprepared for the elegance and charm of what had already become a personal and private small world of her own. Each morning when she woke and each evening when she returned to this sanctuary, those rooms welcomed her with their bright ease till her spirit responded.

"Almost I can feel myself purr like a cat," she told her own reflection in the gilt-framed oval of mirror above her dressing table.

To Henriette the mirror was more a symbol of new-found luxury than anything else in the whole apartment. More than the fire, the thick carpet, the comfortable bed and chairs, more even than the rosewood bureau that could be converted into a perfectly appointed desk, the mirror's flaw-

less glass made her an equal, as it were, with women who
were desirable to husbands or lovers. Heretofore some inadequate square of glass set too high, or dim with age and
imperfections, had been good enough for a governess to
take stock of her appearance. A good mirror need not be
wasted on Mademoiselle, since an inconspicuous neatness
of person was all that any household expected of her. Indeed, to give more was regarded as a distinct breach of taste
and propriety. Years afterward Henriette could summon to
her memory every curve of the gilded scrollwork which
framed that glass. She never mentioned it to anyone else,
but to herself she admitted the part it had played in shaping
her life, in making her a woman first, and a governess
second.

She did not admit that there was a subtle, new incentive
for her to appear her best upon all occasions. Until now she
had not known what it was to feel the approval of a man's
eyes as they rested upon her. Of course there had been a
brief masculine encounter or two, such as passing friendships with the students at Madame Le Maire's. But these had
been casual, and for the most part they had flourished upon
mental congeniality. In London she had been consigned to
the society of women. The Hislop dinners and receptions
were middle-aged and formal, and those at which she had
occasionally been privileged to "fill in" had brought no stimulating male contacts. A curate at the Protestant chapel she
attended had shown her marked favor, conducting her home
discreetly after service while he discoursed upon the varied
trials and inspirations of his calling. But she had not warmed
to his attentions. He was too meek and pallid to please her,
and she found him a decided bore. If she had been less
clever, or more sentimental, she might have endowed the
curate or any other unattached male she managed to meet
with qualities of mind and person supplied by her own
imagination. She might have compromised because of her
own loneliness. But Henriette did not take naturally to compromise and so, for all her shrewdness and intelligence, and
for all her emotional need, she was still heart-whole and untouched as the two Praslin daughters who awaited her in
the breakfast room; as Mademoiselle Maillard who grimly
faced the narrowing horizon of her days. Henriette's heart
might be unscarred, but it was neither youthfully hopeful
nor quiet with mature resignation. For the most part it

obeyed her will, conforming to economic necessity as rigidly as her mind and body had done in those years between the convent and her return to Paris. Only sometimes, unaccountably, she was aware of its power.

"I am like a piano," she told herself sometimes, "a piano in a closed house. There it stands, capable of music, but doomed to silence because no one touches the keys. Who put me in a closed house to gather dust? Why am I lying here at twenty-eight years, alone in a narrow bed?"

Yesterday she had been reminded of her unanswered question. While Isabella and Louise were having their afternoon dancing lesson under Mademoiselle Maillard's watchfulness, she had been reading aloud to amuse the two younger children. Faintly along the corridor of the east wing the notes of a polka had sounded, and her wits had wandered though her lips mechanically uttered the words on the pages before her. The book was a collection of fairy tales, chosen emphatically by Berthe over the protests of Raynald, who had asked for "Aesop's Fables."

"Tomorrow it shall be your turn to choose, Raynald," Henriette had promised. "Now, Berthe, find the story you wish, and listen carefully because tomorrow I shall ask you to tell it to me in English."

They had settled themselves on a window-seat, and she had begun reading absently, half her mind on the distant music, the other half aware of the children's soft bodies pressed close on either side. Then suddenly the words took on reality. The old tale glowed with personal significance:

"And the Fairy Godmother spoke to the Princess and said: 'My child, I have only one gift to bestow upon you. Mark my words well, for once your choice is made it cannot be changed. It is within my power to give you happiness while you are young or happiness when you are old. Which shall it be?'

"The Princess pondered in deep thought: 'It is a hard choice, dear Godmother, but if I spend all my share of happiness while I am young, then I shall have nothing left to look forward to; so let me have my happiness when I am old, and may Heaven send me patience.'

"The Godmother then embraced her. 'You have made a wise choice, and you will not regret it, my dear. Go now with my blessing.'"

Henriette's voice had taken on a deeper note. The children had pressed closer, held by the dramatic intensity of her manner, and so absorbed had the three become in the story that they had not heard a door open and the Duc slip softly across the room to listen.

"And do you agree that she made the right choice?" His voice had startled them, breaking unexpectedly into the words of the book.

"No," Berthe's decisive answer rang out, "I think she was foolish to wait so long!"

"But what could she do?" Henriette had found herself smiling up at the Duc, while she pointed out the seriousness of the problem involved to the two little people beside her. "She had to choose one or the other."

"Couldn't she have asked for a little when she was young and a little when she was old?" Raynald's precise small voice had volunteered as his dark eyes turned from Mademoiselle Deluzy to his father for reassurance.

"Ah, Raynald already shows signs of diplomacy." The Duc had smiled, drawing the frail, serious child close. "But it's not so easy as that, is it, Mademoiselle Deluzy?"

His tone had been light, but she had felt his eyes bent upon her. She had tried not to look up, not to be drawn into the discussion, but she had not been able to keep herself apart. For all his bantering veneer of manner, she had felt a curious persistence behind his question, as if he really wanted to know her answer. When she had raised her eyes from the book, they met his intent gaze. His lips had been gay and smiling, but his eyes had held hers in a look of genuine appeal. She had caught the appraisal behind them, and this made her feel both elated and uncomfortable.

"No," she had answered in all seriousness, "it is not so easy as that. I hope I should have made as wise a choice as that princess, but not many are wise when they are young; and happiness isn't a little cake that can be cut to fit our needs, a crumb here, a slice there."

"If it were I'm afraid our little Berthe here would swallow hers much too fast." He had lifted the child to his lap and stroked the thick fair hair that was so like his own. "Go on, mademoiselle. I find myself as impatient as these two to hear the rest of the story."

He had watched her across the children's heads, his eyes still challenging, still grave above his smiling, red mouth.

She had read on, stimulated by her new audience, giving her voice and mind to the unfolding of the tale. The Princess had suffered and been sorely tried. Thorns and a cruel stepmother had beset her path; her burdens had weighed heavily, and dangers beset her on every hand. The Prince had been long in arriving. Twilight had fallen on the schoolroom before they were united at last to live happily ever after and fulfill the Fairy Godmother's prophecy.

"Bravo, mademoiselle," the Duc had praised when she closed the book. "I shall know how to avoid boredom on other rainy afternoons. Do you know you are very dramatic? I came very near shedding a tear or two for that unfortunate heroine."

"Ah! Now you make sport of me, Monsieur le Duc." But Henriette had felt a pleased glow steal over her under cover of the darkening room.

"Mademoiselle Deluzy reads beautifully, Papa," the little girl's eager voice insisted. "She doesn't read like a mademoiselle at all, does she?"

"That's exactly what I was trying to tell Mademoiselle Deluzy." She felt that he turned to her again, though the room had grown too dim for her to see his face.

"That part where the Princess pleaded her innocence before they threw her into the dungeon would have done credit to the great Rachel herself. You caught the same tragic thrill of voice. It was extraordinary."

"Extraordinary indeed," Henriette had protested; "particularly since I have never heard or seen her."

"You have never seen Rachel?"

"No, Monsieur le Duc. You see I have been away in England, and now that I am no longer there she will pay her promised visit to London. *Eh bien*—so it goes."

"Well, well, that can be easily remedied. She has not crossed the Channel yet—"

The appearance of a servant to light the lamps and draw the curtains had interrupted his sentence.

Henriette had made no further comment. He had spoken impulsively, and there was no reason to expect him to remember his words. Presently Mademoiselle Maillard had returned with Isabella and Louise, and after a few words with them he had slipped away as quietly as he had come.

These unexpected visits of his gave a new zest to the days. At any moment he might appear in the schoolroom,

now in the loose dressing gown that lent such casual in-
formality to his handsome face and figure; or again he might
be in street attire with spotless fawn or dove-gray trousers
strapped to shining boots, a high stock setting off his fairness, and a broadcloth coat of rich blue or green cut in the
latest fashion. Only the night before, he had come in full
evening regalia before he and the Duchesse departed for
dinner and the opera. Henriette and the two older girls had
been alone by the lamp-lit table, deep in the next day's history lesson. He had stood above them like a blond giant in
snowy white and dense black, his silk hat shining and his
opera cloak flowing from broad shoulders. Henriette had
seen such apparitions alighting from carriages or strolling
past cafés on the few occasions that she had been out at the
hour when theaters and opera houses opened or closed their
doors. But she had never been within a few feet of such a
figure of masculine elegance, and the sight was extremely
pleasant to her.

"Papa, are you going to a reception at the Palais Royal?"
Isabella had cried in admiration.

"No, only to dine and then with Mamma to the opera."

"The opera? Oh, Papa, which one, and when shall we be
old enough to go too?"

"Not too soon, Louise. For Isabella in two years perhaps;
for you at least another three." He had smiled at their
flushed impatience and flicked away a bit of lint from his
lapel. "The opera is called 'Norma,' and I must confess I
find it extremely boring. Thank God, most women do not
lose their tempers or tell their most cherished secrets in
high C!"

Henriette knew this comment had been added for her benefit. She would have liked nothing better than to retort with a
smile: "A high C or D is nothing for a woman to reach when
her temper is roused." But she had remained silent while the
two girls surrounded their father with eager chatter and admiring comment.

"A gardenia for your bountonnière," one of them had
cried. "Gardenias are Mamma's favorite flower. She told
me so herself."

"How fortunate!" he had told them. "She is wearing a
wreath of gardenias tonight. Here"—pulling the flower
from his buttonhole, he had tossed it to the two before he
turned to go. "I came to ask about Raynald, Mademoiselle

Deluzy. He did not seem well to me this morning, and I wished to be reassured before we left."

"He complained of feeling chilly at supper, Monsieur le Duc; so I put him to bed early myself and saw that he took his medicine. I think"—she had hesitated before finishing her report—"it would have been better if he had not gone for the drive this afternoon."

"Most certainly he should not have gone. Why did you allow such a thing?"

Henriette had turned her eyes full upon him before she answered. "I was brought word by Mademoiselle Maillard that his mother wished him to go out with her. It was not my place to advise the Duchesse, though I did suggest that with his cough he should not be exposed to this raw wind."

"Next time you will do more than suggest." His voice had boomed at her across the book-strewn table. "I have made you responsible for the children, and there is to be no questioning your authority."

"But, Monsieur le Duc, if the children's mother—if the Duchesse decides otherwise?"

"I will speak to the Duchesse. I will tell her what I have told you. She is sometimes overimpulsive. Her affections run away with her sense. A mother's failing, you understand." His last words had been in the nature of a hurried afterthought.

"Certainly, I understand." Henriette had continued as if the conversation were of a most matter-of-fact sort—the next day's lessons, or a new lamp for the schoolroom. "I will do my best, though my judgment may not always agree with hers, or with yours."

"The children's health and welfare must come before any preferences of my own or their mother's. I shall respect such rules as you may choose to make, mademoiselle. If you feel the need of advice, send for me, and we will consult together."

Henriette left her pupils at the table and followed him to the door.

"And Mademoiselle Maillard?" She had not meant to mention the old governess so soon, but there was no help for it.

"It must be made plain that Mademoiselle Maillard is to take her orders from you from now on."

"I am grateful for your confidence in me, but perhaps

you do not altogether realize that it puts me in a very difficult position."

"And you are afraid to face difficulty?" His fair brows had drawn together as his eyes met hers in direct challenge. "I confess that surprises me."

"I said a difficult position, and I repeat that, monsieur." Henriette had stood her ground, meeting challenge with challenge. Too late, she realized that she had unconsciously omitted to address him by his title. She had spoken to him as a man, rather than as a member of the nobility. But he had taken no notice apparently, and she had continued: "I never said that I was afraid. It would not be true. But you must know that this authority will be resented."

"By Mademoiselle Maillard?"

He had put the question directly, so she had seen no reason for veiling her answer.

"Yes, my presence is already resented by her. It could not be otherwise. I had not meant to speak of this so soon, but I am balked and hindered at every turn; and the children will suffer in consequence. No household can survive two governesses, and I should prefer that you and the Duchesse chose between us."

"But it is not a matter of choice, mademoiselle. That has been already made. I only ask your patience for a little while longer. I ask you simply to go your way and hear nothing, see nothing, and feel nothing."

"That is not exactly a simple request. When one has eyes and ears and feelings— But I will try."

"And I will do the rest. You have my word."

"Thank you, Monsieur le Duc. I will visit Raynald again before we retire to make sure he is sleeping quietly and well covered. Tomorrow he will be himself again, I hope.

He had given her a grateful smile as he turned back to caress the smooth dark heads of Isabella and Louise. The door had closed behind him, and the schoolroom had seemed very empty and quiet after his going. The clock had ticked loudly, and the fire had made its hissing accompaniment to the wind that rattled the casements in the darkness outside. Unconsciously, Henriette and the two girls had drawn closer together about the table with its green baize cover and scattered books. The gardenia lay there, too, incredibly white and glossy-leaved in a pool of lamplight, its fragrance increased by the warmth till it enveloped them all as if a languorous cloud of incense were slowly drugging their senses.

"Well, now to the Wars of the Roses again." Henriette had urged herself and her two pupils back to the interrupted lesson. "Tell me, Louise, which English king could claim both the white rose of York and the red rose of Lancaster for his coat of arms?"

But Louise had yawned, and Isabella's attention had wandered. The confusing royal houses of England had faded into obscurity before the glorious reality of Papa in evening dress and gardenias and hints of the opera.

"Have you ever been to the opera, mademoiselle?" Isabella had broken in.

"Yes, my dear." Henriette had not added that it had been only once and then in a seat under the roof. "But come. We must finish the lesson for tomorrow."

"I can't seem to remember things that happened so long ago and in England, not France," Isabella had complained.

"When I taught a little English girl your age French history, she said the same thing," Henriette had answered with a smile. "She could not believe that anything important ever happened except in her own country. Now listen, and I will explain it again; and you will repeat the little verse after me:

"With this seventh Henry both roses unite,
His own was the red and his wife's was the white.

See how easy it is to remember. The King's coat of arms had the red rose of Lancaster for an emblem, and the Queen's had the white rose of York."

"Just like Mamma and Papa," Louise had remarked unexpectedly. "She had a crest of her own before she married him, only his is better than hers."

"Well, Mamma had the most money," Isabella had hastened to add. "You know what Maxine and Renée said about the big dowry she brought him when they were married."

"Hush!" Henriette had difficulty in hiding the interest she felt. "You must never go about listening to what the servants say and repeating it."

"But, Mademoiselle Deluzy, it must be true. Papa told us once himself that he could not rebuild the burnt wing at

Melun until after he married. He said Grandfather Praslin
couldn't afford to. It's a lovely place with woods and a little
lake with a boat and swans. We'll be going there any day
now."

"There'll be the bluest violets you ever saw, but I like
Olmeto much the best."

"The better, Louise, just as you would say, 'I like blue
better than red,' when you are comparing two of anything.
What do you mean by Olmeto?"

"Oh, mademoiselle, don't you know? It's Grandpapa Sébastiani's place in Corsica, where Mamma lived when she
was a girl. We go there nearly every August to be by the sea.
You can pick up real coral on the beach and the pinkest—or
is it the pinker shells?"

Henriette had closed the covers of the book before her.
There was no use, she had told herself, in trying to continue
with the Wars of the Roses when the flush of remembered
happy experience had come to young cheeks, and young
voices were so eagerly telling her of loved places. So she
had given her whole attention to their recital, and when it
had ended at half past nine she had accumulated a vast number of useful details about life at Melun and in Corsica and
many other bits of information concerning the manner in
which the Duc and Duchesse passed their time in both
places.

"Here, mademoiselle, you can have Papa's gardenia."
Louise, the ever impulsive, had pressed the flower into her
hand at parting for the night. "Only be sure to bring it back
to the schoolroom tomorrow. It smells so sweet."

"And don't touch the petals—because they turn brown if
you do," the methodical Isabella had added.

Henriette had lain awake a long time that night with the
unaccustomed sweetness of the gardenia filling her room.
Incredible that so small a thing should be so subtly disturbing to the chaste formula of her nights. But there it was, and
she could not deny the response of her senses. It made the
lavender sachets in her bureau drawers and her bottle of
Cologne water seem poor and naïve by comparison. Suddenly she knew she had outgrown such simple scents, even
as she had the innocent daisy wreaths of childhood. One
might masquerade in such, but they no longer fitted a woman. Strange to be made so aware of this change in oneself,
and by the fragrance of a single flower.

She had lain there in the dark wondering what it must be like to go to the opera with such a man as the Duc; to know that under all the excitement of footlights and music and such fragrance as this he sat beside one in a box, and later one would not return alone. Well, she would probably never know what that was like. One worked and was thankful for it, she had reminded herself sensibly. One made much of small blessings; one saved one's money against a rainy day and old age. In time one grew less sure of one's position; one faded and became difficult and bitter like Mademoiselle Maillard. Henriette was not given to indulging in such ruthless reveries, but that night she had not been able to disassociate herself from the old governess.

"Have I any reason to expect otherwise?" she had cried in smothered desperation into her pillow.

Sleep came at last to dry her wet cheeks. She woke renewed, and the black mood of the night before had fallen from her. The gardenia stood in a glass on the table, a drooping waxy flower in its cluster of dark green leaves. Only a stale ghost of its sweetness remained to haunt her as Henriette took stock of herself in the oval mirror where no suggestion of Mademoiselle Maillard met her careful scrutiny.

## chapter five

SHE ENTERED THE SCHOOLROOM REFRESHED AND POSItively reckless with good will towards the world. It was well that she did so, for gloom pervaded the east wing. The younger children's nurse, Maxine, reported that Raynald's cold had turned into chills and fever during the night; and Berthe, taking advantage of this complication, had contrived to get herself into her best dress and then stumbled against the grate and smudged the front breadth with black. Her small, energetic figure darted about the corridors while the harassed nursemaid followed hot in pursuit.

"Very well, Maxine." Henriette signaled to the puffing maid to stop the chase. "Leave Mademoiselle Berthe alone. If she wishes to go through the day looking like a little pig, we must let her. Go back to Raynald now, and make him as comfortable as you can. I will be with you soon."

"Mademoiselle Maillard has already gone to notify the Duchesse," Maxine explained.

"In the future, Maxine, come to me immediately about the children." Henriette managed to keep the annoyance out of her voice.

"But we always reported to Mademoiselle Maillard first." The maid's shoulders were set square and stubborn under her cotton dress, and her eyes had a look of resentment that Henriette knew only too well.

"I am speaking of what you will do from now on," Henriette told her evenly. "There must be no more misunderstandings, so please be good enough to remember."

She greeted Isabella and Louise and saw them embarked upon breakfast. Mademoiselle Maillard's place remained conspicuously empty, and Berthe made no move to take hers. Henriette ignored the little girl and motioned the sisters to do likewise, knowing that the high-spirited child would soon tire of a tantrum that won her no audience. In a week Henriette had learned the best tactics for dealing with her four charges. She understood Isabella's cautious, practical mind that responded to quiet reasoning, as she knew that careless, good-natured Louise could be reached only through an appeal to her sentiments. Berthe, volatile and shifting of mood as quicksilver, could be handled by the method of example or outwitted with tactics as clever as her own, while the sensitive Raynald must not be confused by too sudden commands, but rather gently persuaded by appeals to his affection.

She found the little boy flushed and heavy-eyed, protesting hoarsely that he could not swallow even one spoonful of his morning chocolate. Henriette took the tray from Maxine and motioned the maid to set the room to rights while she dealt with the small invalid.

"Never mind about the chocolate, Raynald," she told him. "Here is a tangerine, and when I peel it you must guess how many pieces it has."

"Do you know how many?"

"No, but we'll soon see, and then you can suck the juice." He watched gravely as she peeled the fruit. She felt the dry heat of his hand on hers and noted the quick beat of the little pulse in his delicate neck. "There, let's count: one, two,

three, four, five, six." She spread out the segments for him
to see as she spoke. "Twelve. Try this one first. It's nice and
cool. Just let the juice go down your throat. There, it didn't
hurt much, did it?"

"Not very much." His eyes grew moist with the effort to
swallow.

"Now another," she persuaded gently. "There, you'll have
three down, and then four and then perhaps five."

"My head feels very loose, mademoiselle," he sighed
plaintively, leaning against her between swallows. "You
don't think it will fall off like Berthe's doll that got left out
in the rain and all the sawdust ran out?"

"No, we'll hold it on tight." She brushed back the damp,
dark hair from the moist forehead soothingly. "Besides,
Raynald, your head isn't stuffed with sawdust. Now one
more piece of tangerine, and then half will be gone."

"You eat the other half, mademoiselle, please." His head
drooped against her, and his breath came short and difficult.

To her relief the door opened; but it was the Duchesse,
not the Duc, who entered. Mademoiselle Maillard followed,
and Henriette might have been a piece of the bedroom furniture for all the notice they paid her. Raynald winced at the
sudden violence of his mother's embrace. He pulled away
from the pressure of her arms and burrowed deeper into the
pillows.

"Raynald, my darling," the Duchesse cried, once more
straining him to her. "My poor little boy, you are burning
with fever. Mademoiselle, feel his head and his hands."

The older woman bent over to comply, but the child
pushed her away with all the strength he could muster.

"No, no," he insisted hoarsely, "the other mademoiselle."

Henriette felt a rush of satisfaction at his spontaneous call
for her, but she knew too much to come forward until the
Duchesse gave her permission. She waited quietly at the
foot of the bed, hoping that she might be left alone with the
boy and his mother. But Mademoiselle Maillard had no intention of leaving the Duchesse's side. Her back had stiffened at Raynald's call for Mademoiselle Deluzy, though she
gave no other sign of having heard it.

"Why was I not told before?" The Duchesse, still pressing
the boy to her with frantic and undisciplined affection,
turned accusing dark eyes first upon the hovering Maxine
and then upon Mademoiselle Deluzy. "Do you think I

would have stirred a step from this room last night if I had known? He was ill, and you deliberately kept it from me, his mother."

"I told them he had a bad cough." Maxine hastened to acquit herself. "I told both mesdemoiselles yesterday morning that they should keep him indoors; but of course I'm only his nurse. I'm good enough to dress and undress him and tend him if he wakes; but a governess has to decide whether he's fit to be out in a freezing wind, and then you ask me why he's ill today. He's always ailing, the poor little thing. It's a wonder he's lived this long with that delicate chest of his and the fever he can raise if a summer breeze blows on him, and you think I'm nothing but a cackling hen when I tell you."

"Maxine, in heaven's name be quiet." Henriette's voice cut low and sharp into the nurse's shrill recital. "You will only give Raynald more fever. Yes, you did tell me about his cough, and I advised against his going out yesterday."

"You advised everyone except his mother, Mademoiselle Deluzy." The Duchesse turned black and accusing eyes towards the foot of the bed while the child still struggled to be free of her enveloping arms. "I have no doubt you and the Duc decided the matter between you. In this house a mother is the last to be consulted on matters that concern her children."

Henriette gripped the bedpost with a hand that shook at this sudden outburst. But her voice was calm and even when she spoke. "The Duc noticed that Raynald had a cold," she answered, "when he visited the schoolroom yesterday morning. He came again last night to ask about him."

A triumphant look passed from Mademoiselle Maillard to the Duchesse, but the child's high, plaintive wailing made further discussion impossible. Between his tears and struggles to be free of frantic embraces, the boy was working himself into a state of hysteria.

"Go back to the schoolroom." The Duchesse motioned Henriette away. "The doctor will be here presently."

Raynald's cries grew more frightened at mention of a doctor. She longed to stay and reassure him as she left the room. A fine state he would be in when the physician arrived. Poor little fellow, he was really ill—no doubt of that.

She settled Isabella and Louise at their geography lessons and turned to Berthe, whose earlier tantrum had been forgotten except for telltale smudges on her dress.

"Is Raynald very ill, mademoiselle?" she inquired cheerfully between the sentences she spelled out from an English primer. "Will he die and have to take nasty medicine?"

"Hush, Berthe, go on with your reading. Raynald probably will have to take medicine to make him better, but we don't talk about people dying like that. You've lost your place—here: 'The two boys with the kite are running to the garden.' Now you can go on."

"But, mademoiselle, people *do* die. My white rabbit died, and I loved it more than the brown one that didn't."

"Do you think we can go to Melun just the same, mademoiselle?" Louise put in from her place across the schoolroom table. "Papa said we'd be going next week, but if Raynald is ill—"

"Maybe we'll all be ill," interrupted Isabella.

"What an idea!" Henriette urged them back to the maps they were copying. "Louise, you've been careless and put North America below the equator line."

"Oh, America! What does that matter? It's so far off, and only queer people live there anyway. You wouldn't like to live in America, would you, mademoiselle?"

Henriette smiled at the girl's intolerant shrug.

"Why," she admitted, "I've never given it much thought, but it might not be as bad as you think. I'm not afraid of new places."

She turned back to Berthe and the two boys with their kite. An hour passed during which she tried not to be aware of hurrying footsteps in the corridor and muffled wailing when the sickroom door opened and shut. Presently Mademoiselle Maillard appeared looking glum and important.

"You are wanted"—she flung the order at Henriette without further comment—"in there."

The girls' faces grew sullen as the governesses exchanged places. Berthe flung down her book and tried to follow. Henriette turned her about firmly and shut the door. To her surprise the Duc was pacing the long hall, evidently waiting for her. She was quick to notice a mixture of concern and annoyance in his face as he greeted her.

"Yes," he said without preliminaries, "he is a very sick child. We fear it may be diphtheria."

Another hoarse, hurt cry came from the sickroom. They both winced involuntarily at the sound.

"The doctor's treatments are painful," he told her, "and

Raynald hasn't learned to be brave. Four is too young to
have courage. Besides, he was badly frightened."

Henriette opened her lips to speak, but he cut her short.

"I know," he hurried on, "it was not your doing; but his
mother was alarmed. She is far from well and easily un-
strung. You understand—" He broke off and continued his
quick pacing while the cries behind the closed door broke out
afresh.

"Certainly." She caught the plea he had flung her. "It is
an ordeal to see a child suffering, and if he is your own—
Well, I cannot think how that might be."

He thanked her with his eyes, though his words gave no
sign that he had snatched at her sympathy.

"We must send the others away at once," he was going
on. "We cannot run the risk of three more invalids. They
will leave for Melun this afternoon."

"Very well, monsieur. They will be ready. I will see to
that."

"Good." He nodded, but he still stayed by the door as if
it were a comfort to unburden his mind to her.

"The doctor has forbidden the Duchesse to go in there.
She is not strong, so for her sake and the boy's it would be
dangerous. And Raynald must have absolute quiet and skillful care. More scenes like this morning's might do serious
harm. He will need all the strength he can muster, poor
child."

"Raynald has spirit for all his frailness. He's a reasonable
little fellow, too, if he's not frightened or confused." She
hesitated; then the anxiety in his face moved her to go on. "I
know all about diphtheria, monsieur. There was an epidemic
at the convent years ago. I, myself, recovered from it, so
there would be no risk if I stayed in the sickroom. Of course,
it's not my place to suggest, but I should be glad to do anything in my power at such a time."

"You mean you're offering to stay here with him, Mademoiselle Deluzy?"

"That's what I meant. I may not be a skilled nurse, but I
know how to keep him quiet and amused."

His face lighted suddenly in a relieved smile.

"That's what he needs most. Maxine and others can do
the nursing, but he's taken a fancy to you. He was calling
for you just now. Still it's sure to be a long siege at best, and
at the worst—" He broke off.

"We must not think of the worst, monsieur, only of the best."

His smile answered her—sudden and grateful. At the same moment the sickroom door opened on the doctor and his ominous black bag. Tactfully Henriette stood apart while the two men talked in low voices. She caught fragments from one or the other as she waited for permission to go to the child.

"The throat is badly inflamed. Two days ago we might have kept it from spreading. Now all we can do is continue the treatments every hour."

"They seem to be very painful from the way he resists them."

"It's important that he should resist as little as possible. We cannot afford to have the fever rise. Above all things he must not be frightened as he was this morning."

"You will speak to the Duchesse yourself, doctor? She is very much upset."

"Naturally. Now as to the child's nourishment: his strength must be kept up, but he can only take a small amount at a time."

"And if he refuses?"

"He must be made to take food if we are to fight this infection. I have left instructions with his nurse, but I hardly think she's the person to take charge of a serious case."

"There will be some one who is equal to it."

Henriette felt the Duc's eyes meet hers in quick appeal. She came forward at his summons, and presently all her attention was bent upon following the doctor's directions.

"Yes," she repeated after him. "I understand. The throat must be swabbed every hour unless he is sleeping. The medicine every two hours; food as we can persuade him to take it—milk and sherry, broth and an egg. He must be kept well covered. And if he should be taken with chills, what then?"

"I was coming to that." The doctor eyed her with respect as he continued. "But quiet is the main thing now. These tantrums are too exhausting. Yes, by all means go in and see if you can distract him. I will return later this afternoon."

The two men stared along the corridor towards the other wing and the Duchesse's apartments. Henriette reached for the door knob, but before she turned it the Duc wheeled about.

"Mademoiselle Deluzy!" He stood beside her again. "You

must know the thanks I feel for what you are doing." He
spoke impulsively, with a naturalness that was altogether
disarming. The hand he held out felt warm as it closed over
hers in firm vitality. "When the Duchesse knows of it she
will be grateful, too."

"As to that," she thought, watching him as he rejoined
the doctor in long strides, "we shall see. Her gratefulness strikes me as rather unpredictable; however——" She
shrugged and lingered a moment with her hand on the door,
remembering the Duc's spontaneous gesture. He had not
snubbed her offer or spoken in the impersonal tone, reserved
for maids and governesses, to which she had grown accustomed. He had accepted her help as simply as if she had
been a friend coming to his aid. It was pleasant and stimulating to be treated like an equal. She would prove that his
confidence had not been misplaced. It was grave responsibility, but responsibility was what she throve on. Already
new energy and resourcefulness flowed through her at the
prospect of that small world beyond the sickroom door—a
world of which she had suddenly been put in command.

"No—no—no!" Raynald's hoarse, fretful tones rose
shrill. She roused herself and stepped across the threshold.
"Mademoiselle!" The child's voice grew less complaining at
sight of her. "Why did you go away? They hurt me—see."

He pointed to the bandage about his throat.

"Why, now you're wearing a high stock like Papa's." She
pretended to admire the effect. "Bring Raynald a mirror,
Maxine, so he can see for himself how grown-up he looks.
He'll be getting a cane and a tall hat before we know it."

The game worked like magic. Raynald regarded his image
with satisfaction while Henriette propped the pillows at his
back and drew the covers closer about him. He was flushed
with fever, and his eyes looked enormous and far too bright.
His lips smiled faintly now, but she knew they could close in
stubborn resistance at any moment. It was going to take
infinite patience and all her powers of strategy to deal with
this intricate bit of human machinery.

"Now, Raynald"—she took both his hot, small hands,
noticing as she held them how plainly the blue veins showed
under the delicate skin—"I'm going to stay here with you,
and Maxine will bring your *déjeuner*." His eyes darkened
and his lips opened to begin a protest, but she hurried on.
"*Déjeuner* on a tray, the way your mamma has hers, with a

flower folded in the napkin. Be sure to remember the flower, Maxine," she cautioned the maid. "That's the most important part, because Raynald and I will try to guess what it will be while you're gone. You shall have the first guess, *chéri*. What kind of flower do you think we'll find in the napkin?"

"A rose?" Raynald forgot his objections to food in delighted curiosity.

"Perhaps. But it's early for roses. I guess a lily of the valley. Now, it's your turn again."

"Those yellow flowers in the garden."

"Daffodils? Oh, but they're all gone. Try another."

"A violet?"

"It might be. They're selling violets in the Bois, and primroses. Suppose I say a yellow primrose."

"Pink are nicer. I'll say pink."

And so began those days and nights of tireless maneuvers to keep a four-year-old boy unaware of his own grave plight. Henriette's brain and hands had never been so active; and while she soothed and watched, cut pictures or spun endless tales till her head ached and her voice grew almost as hoarse as the sick child's, spring marched through Paris, taking the city's stone and brick by storm. Beyond the window sills she could feel that heady stir sweep past like a warm tide mounting into summer. She had never been so conscious of a season before; so quickened by unseen natural forces. Because she was shut away from the strong sunshine, she felt its will to renew all life with power. Her own senses responded. Even in a darkened sickroom she felt exhilarated as if a tangible current charged every vein and nerve in her body.

In country places spring was something one saw, a changing miracle before the eyes. But in the city it was something subtly felt. It seemed to her that a different quality crept into the voices of street venders crying their wares through the morning hours; a bustle of hopeful activity that vibrated in the beat of horses' hoofs on those afternoons when smartly fitted carriages took ladies shopping or for airings in the Bois and Champs-Elysées; an added quickness to the wheels speeding to dinner and theater and opera each warm May evening. She came to know the very rhythm of the city, and yet she was no more a part of it than if she and her small charge had been marooned at the bottom of a deep well where pain kept them grim company.

Other people came and went: Maxine and her assistant bringing fresh linen, food, and flowers; the dreaded specter of the doctor with his bag which had become for Raynald the symbol of pain and the signal for tears; the Abbé Gallard in his black robes; the Duchesse hovering on the threshold she had been forbidden to cross, wringing her white hands and weeping ineffectual tears; the Duc, tiptoeing nearer in his shiny boots, his eyes anxious and his arms and pockets full of presents that Mademoiselle Deluzy must unwrap for a child whose hands had grown too weak to hold them.

"See, Raynald," she would hear her own voice trying to distract both the Duc and her patient. "New soldiers. A whole regiment of cavalry with a general on a white horse. They're climbing the Alps where the coverlet's humped over your knees."

Sometimes she could coax the drooping mouth into a smile, and the Duc would answer with a grateful one as he bent over the bed and helped encourage the taking of medicine or food.

"Yes, monsieur, we will show you how the eggnog goes down. This way, *chéri,* the head tipped far back. Now, as the hen drinks. Once more. Another swallow. Ah, that was not so good. The hen forgot to tilt the head. This time it will be better."

She urged the child with praise and playful strategy, but her eyes and the Duc's would meet in unspoken question and answer above the boy's head.

Raynald watched for his father's visits and even stretched out weak hands in welcome. But at sight of his mother he grew restive and hid his face. If she came while he slept he seemed to be aware of her disturbing presence. He would toss feverishly or wake and cry for "Papa" and "Mademoiselle." Henriette came to dread that dark, uneasy shadow that appeared without warning a dozen times in a single forenoon. She spoke to the doctor discreetly, but he only shrugged and raised a professional eyebrow.

"She is his mother," he answered. "It's all I can do to keep her away from his bed. If I forbid her to look in the room she'll work herself into another sort of fever, and there'll be two invalids. I've tended the Duchesse before, mademoiselle."

There came a day when the fever had reached its height

and when no amount of persuasion could force anything down the inflamed throat. The doctor looked grave after his morning visit.

"We can do little now but watch and wait," he told Henriette before he left to report to the parents. "We've done everything in our power for him, and now we shall see if his strength will carry him through the crisis. Yes, I expect a change before night, for better or worse. Keep him quiet and well covered and guard against drafts of fresh air."

"But, doctor!" Henriette followed him to the door. "He complains of the dark and closeness. Surely a breath of sun and air would do no harm if he were not exposed to it directly. He asks about the garden, and perhaps if he saw it had come into bloom——"

"Mademoiselle, have you lost your senses this morning?" The middle-aged medical man regarded her as if she had spoken treason. "He is a desperately sick child; a breath of air might be fatal at this stage."

She said no more, but the staleness of the room seemed even more oppressive as she turned back to it again.

"Sick or well," she told herself, "we were not meant to suffocate in this world."

A screen had been placed about the one window where the shutters were not closed and curtains drawn. Seeing that Maxine was busy rearranging the sickbed, Henriette seized the chance to draw a few breaths of fresh air. Cautiously pushing the shutters wider, she stood in a shaft of May sunshine with the screen between her and the room. She supposed herself hidden when suddenly a step and a voice at her elbow made her turn from the green glimpse beyond the window sill. The Duc stood beside her, and she saw instantly that the doctor had alarmed him. His face looked drawn, and a mask of apprehension had settled over the fair, handsome features she was beginning to know so well.

"Monsieur"—she no longer addressed him by his full title, and she spoke as if he had told her what was in his mind—"don't be too despairing. Raynald will recover. I can't help feeling it. He'll be picking daisies a month from now, and all this will be forgotten."

"You almost make me believe that, Mademoiselle Deluzy"—he attempted a smile as he spoke; "but after what the doctor said just now, and with the crisis coming tonight——" He could not go on.

"It must come some time. Let it be tonight. And you forget that spring is a doctor, too. We cannot resist the spring, monsieur. It finds us whether we will or no. Can you look out there and deny it?"

His eyes followed hers to the half-closed shutters, where the air came up fresh and sunny from the enclosed garden and from the more distant spaces of the adjoining Champs-Elysées. Early green of young leaves and vines and grass blades filled the narrow space, and in the midst of the little square court a flowering almond tree stood up stiff and small, as if it were astonished by the rosy cloud of its own bloom. Perhaps it was because she had been unable to sleep except in broken snatches for the last few nights, and because her eyes had been fixed too long on nearer things, that Henriette felt stirred by that vista of sun and bloom. In one of those sudden flashes which all of us experience without warning, she knew that she would never be able to forget the very shape and color of that flowering bush in its grass plot. It took on a significance all the more keen because she could not explain why it had moved her.

His voice brought her back to the sickroom.

"I don't know why I should have more confidence in your words than the doctor's, Mademoiselle Deluzy, and yet I have. You're not giving me false hope because you have a kind heart?"

"No, I'm too fond of Raynald for that," she told him. "And governesses are seldom reminded of their hearts. You'll find I've learned to keep mine well in hand. I meant what I said just now, only I wish—"

She broke off at the sound of choking from the bed. After the spasm passed Raynald lay back limply among the pillows. His lips moved so faintly that she had to put her ear beside them to catch the whisper.

"No, *chéri*, the doctor thinks not yet. Perhaps, if you are better tomorrow." She turned to the Duc with a little futile gesture.

"What is it he wants so much? Can't we manage it somehow?"

She sighed and shook her head.

"It's against the doctor's orders," she explained in low tones. "Raynald won't believe me when I tell him how green the garden has grown, and that the almond tree is really in bloom. He begs so to look out, and if I had my way I'd let him. After all, the sun and air are good for every other living thing."

They had spoken in low tones, but the child chimed in plaintively as if he had heard.

"I want to see the spring, Papa. Now, please."

His voice was scarcely more than a tiny thread of sound from the bed, but it brought his father closer. Concern and pity spread over the big blond face.

"And you shall see it, Raynald," he promised with sudden decision. "Wait a minute." Once more he turned to the governess as if he were asking for reassurance. "You think it cannot hurt him?"

"It's a very mild day and such a little thing to ask. He'll be satisfied once he's seen the garden, but I couldn't take the responsibility alone."

"Well, wrap the quilt close then. Now, Raynald, lie very still while I lift you. *Mon Dieu*, but he's no weight at all. I might be carrying a shadow."

They moved like a pair of conspirators with the child between them. Neither spoke, and it was only when they reached the window and the square oasis of green was revealed through the half-opened shutters that they dared to exchange a look across the dark head muffled by bedclothes. For a moment Raynald seemed dazzled by the sudden brightness; then, as if some magnet drew him towards it, he stretched a hand to the blossoming tree. In that clear shaft of sunlight he seemed even more fragile. Watching him with solicitous eyes, Henriette was reminded of those pale shoots brought out of dark places to be set in pots on window sills and turned first this way and then that to catch the sun. Gently she took his hand that was like a bird's claw and held it out to the golden warmth.

At the same instant she and the Duc knew that they were being watched. The Duchesse was bearing down upon them with hostile eyes and a defiant rush of satin and lace.

"Theo, are you mad?" Her voice filled the room with frightened accusations. "Do you want to kill him, mademoiselle!"

Raynald buried his head against his father's shoulder as the Duc reached the bed once more and laid him on it.

"Hush, Fanny. I'll explain in a moment. Don't speak so loud. You'll upset him."

"I'll upset him!" the Duchesse's voice vibrated through the whole room.

Henriette, trying to quiet the boy and get him safely back between the bedclothes could feel the tension behind those words. A tumult of bitterness and jealousy and fright began to gather and take shape in a storm of protest which the Duc was trying vainly to quiet.

"Fanny, please, not now, not here!"

"And why not now and here in this room you are all set against my entering? I have a right to know what goes on here. I'm not going to be shut out while my child, my little boy, is helpless in the hands of a stranger."

"But I tell you I can explain. Listen, Fanny! It may have looked strange to you, but it was a fancy he had to see the garden, and when Mademoiselle Deluzy told me, I thought—"

"Oh, it was Mademoiselle Deluzy's idea. I see. She knows more than the doctor. What's one child more or less to her so long as she gets her way in this house? Not a month since she came, and already a mother is nothing but a nuisance to her, some one to be swept out like a broken dish. But I won't stand here and see Raynald harmed before my eyes. The doctor shall hear of this, and if he dies tonight—" Her voice rose shrilly before it broke into wild weeping.

"Fanny, you mustn't say such things. You mustn't blame Mademoiselle. Come, you're ill. You can't stay here now. Maxine, here, help me get Madame to her room."

His voice which had been soothing at first had grown cold. It was as if each word he uttered were held taut. Henriette could almost feel the words straining at some invisible leash. It was impossible not to listen; not to be humiliated for both husband and wife.

"My darling!" The Duchesse broke away and reached the other side of the bed. Henriette saw the large white arms reach out. She saw that the eyes were dark and tortured, that the tears pouring down those cheeks were real. This was certainly no feigned anguish. The Duchesse's full bosom rose and fell with emotion as she strained the little boy to her in a spasm of despairing affection.

"Mademoiselle! Mademoiselle!"

The child summoned all his strength in that appeal to save him from the tempestuous embraces. Tears and lamentations enveloped him. He struggled against them as he might have resisted an avalanche of honey.

Henriette leaned across the bed to answer his appeal. But

as quickly she restrained the impulse and turned to the Duc
with lifted brows. After all, she must take her cue from him.
He met her eyes without flinching, yet she saw that his mouth
had taken on a grim set. There was a half-shamed appeal in
the look which answered hers. He seemed in that moment to
be another Raynald asking her aid, begging her not to fail
him. With a quick gesture he motioned her away.

"Come, Fanny, no more of this." Firmly he began to dis-
entangle the Duchesse from her shrinking child. "Come
with me."

Henriette busied herself at the bureau. She would not
humiliate him by watching their exit. She had seen and
heard enough for one day. The room grew suddenly quiet
again, and she turned to pacify her patient. He soon lapsed
into weary sleep, but she could not rid herself of the vibrant
bitterness of that accusing voice; of the gleam in those dark,
Corsican eyes that had rested on her so jealously.

"She is half crazy with worry," Henriette tried to reason.
"It's only natural she should want to stay with her sick
child, that she should resent my doing for him. If she were
not such a fool with this undisciplined affection, he would
not turn from her as he does. Poor darling, I can't blame him
for that."

She would not own to herself what had been revealed so
clearly. She had felt a clash of temperaments, a suppressed
tension, between husband and wife from her first meeting
with them. Something was wrong there, so seriously wrong
that she dared not let herself think of it. She had a distinct
impression that this other woman was staring at her out of
hell; that those great, anguished eyes distorted whatever they
looked upon. Yes, she had been aware that morning of what
she had dimly guessed before. The Duchesse saw those
about her only in relation to the Duc. He was her world,
and she must already be feeling it slip away from her clutching fingers.

"That woman would be jealous if he caressed a kitten,"
she decided. "I believe she would order it killed or sent
away and if he turned from her to admire a rose, I'm sure
she would trample it underfoot at the first opportunity. God,
what must their nights be like if scenes like this can happen
in broad daylight!"

All through the next hours, while she gave orders to
Maxine, while her brain and hands carried out the intricate

details with which she had been entrusted, the unhappy Duchesse continued to stalk her mind like a violent ghost.

"But there is no reason for her to hate me," she argued inwardly. "I've done nothing to hurt her."

Yet she knew the answer. She, Henriette, had won a child's affection and a father's confidence. That was crime enough to stir the antagonism of an already unhappy woman. The governess had become a symbol rather than a personality. Yes, she was beginning to understand the reason for that word most often used to describe the household Praslin: "Difficult, mademoiselle, very difficult."

Raynald was all too quiet by late afternoon. He could seldom be roused from his apathy. That small, weak body scarcely changed the contour of the smooth bed covers. He might have been the shrunken mummy of a child lying there except for the painful breathing and flushed face. Without protest he allowed the doctor's treatments. Henriette felt her earlier hopefulness waning as she tried not to see how the boy's strength had failed since morning.

Towards twilight she was aware of an unusual stir at the door. Suppressed whispers and hurrying footsteps sounded in the corridor. It was the time of day when the Abbé Gallard had been in the habit of making his visit to the sick child. The appearance of this black-robed spiritual adviser had come to be her signal to retire. Having no part in these prayers, she was free to leave the house and take the air with those who walked the boulevards. So while they called on Heaven in that darkened room in the east wing, Henriette's brief contacts with the world took place. Rather ironical, she had thought, that it should be so, yet she had welcomed these excursions into life and light. She could not help feeling that she brought back something of all that to the child on the bed whether he waked or slept upon her return.

But today she had no heart to set foot on the streets and mingle with unconcerned crowds. She knew even before the Abbé stood at the door in his vestments with the young altar boy he had brought with him, even before she heard Maxine's smothered exclamation and saw her lift reverent hands to cross herself and then reach for her rosary, that this was no ordinary visit. The last rites of the church were about to be administered.

"He is too little to be frightened."

Her first thought was for Raynald who lay staring at the Abbé with glazed, apathetic eyes. But she saw that he made no outcry and seemed hardly aware of the altar being improvised across the room.

"No," she thought, "he cannot know what it means. Perhaps he will like to hear the little bell, and think it's some Heaven-sent toy."

She made her way through the group gathered by the door: the Duc and Duchesse, the valet and lady's maid, and two other house servants. They waited with their rosaries in hand. The Duc's blond head was bent too low for her to see his face as she passed, but his shoulders had a dejected droop. She knew that he despaired of his child's life.

Her feet carried her along the corridor and on down the stone staircase till she came to the door that opened on the garden. She let herself out into the square of green, which seemed greener because of the late light and because her eyes were still accustomed to dimness. Her knees shook as she crossed the flagstones to a bench by the wall, where a jet of water splashed from a bronze dolphin's mouth into a shallow pool below. Now that others had taken the welfare of her charge into their keeping, she felt lost and lonely. A great weariness and fear possessed her in place of the earlier energy and confidence that had been hers since the illness began.

The springing freshness and fragrance of the small garden seemed suddenly a mockery in the face of what she knew was going on in that upper room. Overhead the sky showed bright with gathering sunset. A long flare of rosy light was filling the place with a false glow that would soon fade. The little almond tree stood its ground, still flushed with the fever of spring. But the sweetness of bloom all about her was not strong enough to overcome the incense drifting down from that window above. The hum of life on the Rue du Faubourg-Saint-Honoré could not quite drown out the sound of a ringing bell.

*chapter six*

THE PETALS OF THE ALMOND TREE WERE ALL SCATTERED
by the time Raynald was able to be carried into the garden
each sunny noon. His recovery had been nothing short of
a miracle, for which the doctor, the Abbé, Maxine and
every one who had entered the sickroom took a share of the
credit. Only Mademoiselle Deluzy made no comment beyond thankfulness that it was so. She had no explanation to
offer as she went about her duties. These continued to be
taxing even with the danger well past, for returning health
made the child a lovable but exacting invalid. He needed
constant attendance: he must be kept amused, but not overexcited. The lively brain must not outstrip the energy of the
frail body wrapped in layers of eiderdown. Fortunately
Henriette possessed limitless ingenuity in the art of keeping
children entertained. Each day her crayons conjured up
new pictures to fit endlessly concocted stories. Sheets of
paper became alive for the child as the scissors moved by
her clever fingers shaped people and animals at his command. There were new picture books to be opened and
read aloud; a canary as golden as the cage that held it to be
marveled at; a miniature Punch and Judy show that Mademoiselle could manipulate by concealed strings, and a wonderful Swiss music box that played six tunes. The precise,
gay notes that flowed from the wooden box lent festivity to
the days. It was as if a world of perpetual spring and childhood and tinkling laughter were locked there, Henriette
thought, as she listened.

"What does the music keep saying over and over?" Raynald asked her suddenly.

"Why," Henriette smiled, "I suppose it says something
different to every one who hears it. For me it says: Spring
weather, warm sun, green grass for a little boy to run and
skip on."

"And is that little boy me?" Raynald wanted to know.

"Who else but you?"

She bent to kiss the top of his dark silky head. It was difficult to restrain herself from such demonstrations. She wanted to feel the response of his small live body. Yet she knew she must fight off the growing illusion that he was indeed her own child. This youngest Praslin, so sensitive and appealing in his dependence, had been her favorite from the first. The two older sisters she found pleasant and intelligent companions, and Berthe, with her bounding health, her blond beauty and spirited ways, swept all before her with the Duc's own magnetic charm; but Raynald had crept into a special niche of his own in her affections. The days and nights of anxious care had settled him there too firmly to be crowded out.

There had been no more scenes with the Duchesse. Her visits were less frequent and disquieting. Raynald still shrank from these contacts with his mother, but Henriette by adroit maneuvers usually kept an appearance of dutiful response on the child's part.

"Doesn't Mamma look fine in her new bonnet and dolman?" she would point out tactfully at sight of the Duchesse appearing from an afternoon drive. "You'll give her the hug and kiss you forgot yesterday, won't you? And be sure to tell her you like the talking animal book."

"I told Papa so."

"But your mamma brought it to you. Show her how you pull the strings to make the cow moo. I'll fetch it now from upstairs."

In leisure moments Henriette had had occasion to recall the violent outburst so unmistakably directed at her that day when Raynald had been close to death. She still felt embarrassed by such a display of uncontrolled emotion. She still smarted at the injustice of the accusations hurled at her head. Disciplined as she had been since childhood to holding her own feelings in bounds, she instinctively recoiled from such exhibitions of temper. Children and fishwives gave way to such furies. But one had the right to expect dignity and breeding from a woman in the Duchesse's position. If this cyclone of unreasoning rage had lashed out once without provocation, Henriette knew there would be repetitions. It was inevitable, and the prospect was far from reassuring. She could have coped with the hysteria of a high-strung, pampered woman, whose overwrought nerves gave way under the strain of her child's illness; she could have over-

looked words spoken hastily in anxiety and fear, but she
could not forget the venom that had been flung at her across
the sickbed. She tried to put this from her, yet the memory
laid a chill of restraint upon their meetings.

But in common with most hot-tempered individuals, the
Duchesse had a short memory for her own flare-ups. She
could veer like a weathercock from mood to mood. Suddenly she smiled upon the governess, overwhelming her with
approbation. Henriette could only marvel at the change,
which she found almost as difficult to understand as the earlier hostility. She had learned to be wary of too swift intimacy between women, and now she felt more than ever
baffled for explanation. She felt instinctively that the Duc
was responsible for this new affability, though she had no
actual proof that the tension between them had lessened,
since they seldom visited Raynald at the same time.

"Ah, well!" She shrugged and tried to dismiss the situation. "It's no concern of mine. I should be grateful that she
looks less like a thundercloud without bothering my head
for the reason."

Still she could not help wondering about those two. By
day she knew little of their comings and goings, but once
Raynald had been settled for the night with Maxine in attendance, Henriette had a chance to speculate on much that
went on in the opposite wing across the garden. On several
occasions she had awakened to hear voices in argument. She
could not distinguish words, but the tones were certainly
those of a man and a woman in anything but complete accord. Often, too, she noticed that, though lights burned late
in the Duchesse's bedchamber and in the Duc's private
salon, the small room between, which was hardly more than
a passageway connecting the two apartments, remained conspicuously dark. More than once she had wakened late or
in the early hours of morning to see clearly silhouetted in
the lamplight of a certain window the Duchesse bent over
her secretary, her hand driving a quill pen with tireless
speed. This recurring vision filled Henriette with curiosity.
The Duchesse hardly seemed like a woman to spend her
energies in writing. She appeared more a creature of violent
emotions and of action than one who would weigh words
and patiently set them on paper. She gave little evidence of intellectual accomplishment. She might, like many another
woman before her, have found relief in writing long, flowery

letters. But she seemed to have few women friends, and being an only child she had no scattered brothers and sisters with whom to correspond. True, she had several uncles, and her father, the rich, old Maréchal Sébastiani, adored her. But he had only recently left Paris for Corsica. Even if she had written him full accounts of Raynald's illness these could hardly have occupied her so late and so long.

She was mystified a morning or two later to find on her tray of early coffee a small box and a sealed envelope with an embossed crest and her name in a flowing but immature hand. It bore no stamp or sign of having come by post or messenger. Wonderingly she broke the seal, and while her coffee grew cold she read and reread the words that sprawled across the pale blue sheet of note paper:

Dear Mademoiselle Deluzy

Sleep is denied to those who long for peace and yet feel hostility about them. If in my anguish and fear for the life of my youngest child I may have judged you too harshly I ask your indulgence. I would not wish to wound you for I myself have been too cruelly hurt to inflict like pain upon another, especially to one living under my own roof. You are clever, mademoiselle, possessed of unusual attractions and gifts. It is natural that you should exert yourself to win the Duc's favor and the children's devotion. But not, I am sure, at the cost of a mother's right to be first with those to whom she is bound by the holiest of ties.

I will say no more. A word to the wise is sufficient. From my heart I thank you for your ministrations to my little boy when a mother's care was denied him. From my heart I also earnestly beg your loyal support and tender this small token of my appreciation. May it be a pledge of our friendship and future accord.

FANNY SÉBASTIANI PRASLIN.

The jeweler's box when opened revealed a modest but charmingly designed brooch—a circle of blue enamel whose ends met in a tiny dragon's head of gold. Henriette held it a long time, turning it this way and that between her fingers. Certainly the pin was in exquisite taste, the sort of gift a governess might accept without being under obligation to the giver, but the dragon's head, like the carefully veiled words of the letter, seemed chosen with peculiar significance.

As she dressed, Henriette weighed her response. Twice she went to her secretary and took out pen and paper, but each time she laid them away. Why should there be such formality between them, she reasoned? If the Duchesse had fault to find, or if she honestly wished to make amends, why had she not sent for her and spoken directly what she wished to say?

"No," she decided at last as she put the finishing touches to her morning toilet, "I will not continue this foolish pretense. It will only make constraint between us when we meet. I will go to her now before the day's activities begin."

Madame Marguerite Leclerc, the Duchesse's personal maid, answered her knock a few minutes later. This plain woman of indeterminate years and dress had weathered every cataclysm in the Praslin ménage, thereby strengthening her position into something between companion and domestic. Of all those who served that oddly assorted household, this woman, Henriette guessed, would be her most dangerous enemy. Stolid she might appear outwardly; yet there was a firmness of tread, an uncompromising set to the mouth and a keenness of the eye that Henriette recognized as authoritative. Today Henriette's request to speak with the Duchesse was met with a look of chill disapproval. The maid followed her into the little salon, where she hovered near by, busy with obviously unimportant tasks while in the bedchamber beyond several portmanteaus stood open and waiting to be packed from the piles of feminine apparel overflowing bed and chairs.

"Ah, good morning, mademoiselle."

The Duchesse acknowledged her visitor with a perfunctory greeting. Her dark, lusterless eyes lifted, then dropped once more to a sheaf of fashion plates strewn about the sofa. It was almost, Henriette thought, as if a window blind had been lowered between them.

"Madame"—as usual the other woman's preoccupation forced Henriette to make the first advance—"I hope I am not intruding upon you so early, but I could not begin my duties without first coming to express my gratefulness. I was unprepared for such a gift. It has been happiness enough to see Raynald convalescing and to feel I had a part in his recovery, but I won't deny that this proof of your good will has overwhelmed me." She laid her hand on the enamel pin which fastened the white collar of her printed challis dress.

"Oh, yes, the brooch." The Duchesse spoke absently. "A small souvenir. I am glad if it pleases you." Her voice trailed away, muted and uncertain, almost as if she had not heard the words to which she responded. Henriette had a sudden conviction that this woman, perversely enough, would write in cold black and white what she should better have left unsaid; that she would keep silence when she should make an effort to speak.

Once more a silence fell between them and once more it was necessary for Henriette to take the initiative.

"I see by these signs of packing," she began, "that you are planning to leave Paris shortly."

"For Melun, yes," the Duchesse assented. "You will follow with Raynald as soon as the doctor thinks he is able to travel. We leave this afternoon, the Duc and I."

Only when she spoke that last phrase, "the Duc and I," did animation creep into the dull voice. She lingered over it caressingly, with naïve emphasis which in a lovelorn girl might have been overlooked, but which in a mature, married woman sounded unpleasantly possessive.

"She gives herself away whenever she speaks of him," the younger woman thought, studying the pale, broad face with its discontented mouth and unhappy eyes. "Her very protests would make me guess he preferred to stay here. She's a fool with her affections, but she's desperately miserable in spite of all she has."

"I must not keep you long from your preparations for the journey," Henriette continued, casting a pointed look at the maid who still hovered in the background. "If you could spare me a few minutes—alone, I should be grateful."

At a sign from her mistress Marguerite Leclerc reluctantly took herself into the bedchamber. In the silence that followed they could hear her heavy tread and the thumping of valises. Still the Duchesse waited, her hands knotting and unknotting the sash of her robe. Henriette watched those plump hands twisting the length of rich satin which she could not help knowing must have cost more than any one of the dresses in her own simple wardrobe. She had to look away to keep back a wave of resentment at those careless, idle hands which fumbled aimlessly instead of holding fast to all that fate had placed in them.

"Madame," she went on, summoning all her powers of tactful persuasion, "I was touched that you should have written me as you did. Believe me, I want harmony above all things. I am eager to carry out your wishes for the children, for Raynald in particular, and I beg you to speak frankly. If I have fallen short of my duties in any way I will do my best to remedy the fault."

"I did not say you had fallen short of your duties, mademoiselle. On the contrary, you have been altogether too eager in your efforts."

"I had no intention of overstepping my position. I am sorry if I have. Perhaps if you would be more definite I should know how to conduct myself better in the future."

"The future—ah—who knows?" The Duchesse gave one of her deep, habitual sighs and lifted her heavy lids wearily as if Heaven alone could answer for that.

"I have tried to follow the Duc's directions," Henriette persisted without letting her annoyance at this ineffectual response become apparent. "And I should like to follow yours too, madame, if you will give me any. The Duc has seemed pleased with the children's progress and behavior. At least he has made no criticism."

"I never interfere with the Duc's plans for the children. Their instruction is entirely in his hands."

Another deep sigh made the silken folds rise and fall on the broad bosom.

"But, madame, it should be possible to please you both. A governess has no place in a household where she does not feel the confidence of both parents. In this one month I have grown attached to your children, and Raynald's illness has made him especially dear to me. Perhaps in my anxiety for him I have offended in some way, but you must believe me when I repeat that it was unintentional, that I only meant to spare you such strain as I could and follow the doctor's orders."

"It was not the doctor's order that you and the Duc should expose a sick child to an open window and drafts of cold air. But, no matter, by a miracle he survived, and according to your own notions you have tended him faithfully. We will say no more about it."

"But I still feel your disapproval, madame, and I still want to carry out your wishes if you will give them to me."

"Well, then, mademoiselle, I can only repeat what any

mother has a right to wish and expect—that she should come first with her children. Nothing must come between me and my sons' and daughters' affections—nothing."

"Naturally." Henriette spoke impersonally and disregarded the pointed dart behind those words. "But children grow and reach out to others each year. A mother cannot keep them forever babies at her breast. Your children are intelligent and high-spirited. They respond to affection, but sometimes, if one demands it of them, they are like skittish colts scurrying away at the first sign of a bit—"

She broke off, for it was evident that the other was no longer listening. Her attention had turned from the children to the adjoining apartment, from which a sound had come. The distant rasp of an opening window casement had interrupted their conversation just as it was reaching a climax. Watching this woman before her, seeing the dark head tilt furtively in the direction of that sound and sudden excitement begin to show in every feature, Henriette knew it would always be like this. All reality for Fanny, Duchesse de Praslin, was centered in the magnet of her husband's physical presence.

"No," she thought, still standing there beside the couch, forgotten by the woman stretched upon it, "she does not dislike me for myself. The children and I do not matter to her. We only exist if he notices us."

The interview was over, and she felt more baffled than before it had begun. Plainly the Duchesse was straining to hear further sounds from the other side of the wall. Her whole mind and body waited expectantly for his coming, and there was no use in continuing the subject that had brought Henriette to the small salon.

"Well, madame, I can only say again that I thank you for your gift, and that I hope you will trust me and let me know your wishes. Meantime be happy in the reunion with your daughters and know that Raynald will be well cared for till you send for us."

When the door closed behind her Henriette sighed. Nothing had been accomplished. She felt that her gesture and words had made no more impression than if she had pounded futilely on a feather mattress. But at least there had been no more specific accusations. She would go her way without further attempts to untangle this subtle feud in which she somehow found herself drawn against her will.

"Where is her pride?" she thought. "If I had such a husband and such children, all this as well——"

She shrugged expressively and started back along the corridor, determined to put the whole bewildering business from her mind. After all, those two were man and wife, and she was their children's governess. Let it be so, and forget implications that should not concern her. She would no longer try to solve this Chinese puzzle of human emotions that was far more intricate than she had imagined. Better use all her wits to steer a straight and steady course through unpredictable currents and rough waters that might be ahead. Instinctively she gathered her skirts about her and hurried on.

But passing the Duc's quarters, she stopped short, her eyes caught by what lay almost at her feet. A letter had been thrust under the doorsill in such a way that one corner showed against the carpet. Even in the dimness something about that fragment struck her as familiar. She bent down and recognized the same texture and peculiar shade of blue notepaper that had lain on her own morning tray.

Somehow she could not forget that corner of envelope. It would creep between her and the pages of the stories she read to Raynald. She saw it so clearly before her that when the Duc strolled in after *déjeuner* she half expected to see a triangle of pale blue showing from one of his pockets.

She searched his face for some sign that he knew of her visit to the Duchesse. But if his wife had given him her version of what had taken place in her salon he gave no hint of it in look or manner. He had never appeared in better spirits, nor looked more striking and carefree than in the mulberry coat and dove-gray trousers that set off his strength and height and fairness.

Raynald, now up and about each afternoon, was at first disconsolate at the news of the departure for Melun without him. But between them Henriette and his father cleverly distracted the child. Henriette reminded him that if he should leave that afternoon he would have to miss a visit to the Guignol, and his father assured him that the new duck-pond at Melun would not be ready for another week at least. As a final gesture of farewell the Duc carried the small boy on his shoulders to his own apartments.

"I'll send him back in half an hour," he promised. "He can sit in my big chair and amuse himself while the bags are being strapped, and watch us leave in the carriage."

Henriette heard the bustle of departure as she waited for the child's return. She was relieved to be spared his mother's farewells, and she only hoped that her charge had endured them gracefully. When he was carried back by the porter the little boy's eyes were bright with importance, and he bent intently over a pair of scissors with which he snipped diligently at a piece of paper.

"Papa let me have them," he explained. "They're not sharp like yours, mademoiselle, and I'm making something for you."

"A present? Dear me! I wonder if I can tell across the room what it's going to be."

He held up the cutting for her to guess.

"Why, I do believe it's going to be a heart. Is that right?"

He nodded, satisfied, and went on with his snipping.

"What made you choose a heart?" she persisted, watching the pucker deepening in his soft brows as the effort neared completion.

"Because," he told her gravely, "a heart is the easiest of all things to cut."

"Ah," she thought, "what words from a child! He doesn't know what he's saying, but he's right. Hearts are the easiest of all things to cut."

The gift was finished at last and presented with much admiration on both sides. But as Henriette smoothed the folds of the lopsided and rather ragged object she was startled once more at sight of familiar blue note paper. Turning it over, she was even more startled to see fragments of writing on the other side. Words leaped at her, the more vivid and painful because a child's unconscious fingers had separated them from each other. They seemed alive there in her hands. Tortured, inky things it was inpossible not to read and once having read, impossible to forget:

| My Darl | only a wall |
| separates | yet a worl |
| lies be | I have cried |
| not sleep | Oh, if I had |
| known that | all that once we |
| and shared. | How can I |

With shaking hands she folded and laid the heart away in her workbox before she turned once more to the child.

"Raynald"—she lifted him to her lap and tried to speak casually—"you did not go rummaging in Mamma's secretary to find the paper for my present, did you?"

"Oh, no, mademoiselle. Papa told me I could have anything from his waste basket, and this was the prettiest color I could find."

## chapter seven

"MADEMOISELLE HENRIETTE HAS RETURNED!" PIERRE the porter stood bowing and beaming beside the shiny carriage drawn up before the entrance of Madame Le Maire's. "She went away on foot, and she returns by coach. It's like a fairy tale." The old man blinked at the small crest painted on the door and at the woman who sat on the cushions, familiar of face, yet so elegant in green shot silk and bonnet and veil. "Oh, yes!" he went on, bowing his stiff body in the patched porter's coat. "The sun dances for Mademoiselle. Didn't I predict it? Didn't I say always you were born under a fortunate star?"

Henriette hoped the pawings of the horses drowned out his words. She had no wish for the driver or his liveried mate who held the spirited animals' heads to overhear them. Old Pierre's pride in her was very touching, but he might go too far in his delight at the outward change in her appearance. After all, there was no need for the Praslin servants to know how poor and shabby she had been two months ago. They resented her enough as it was, especially since she had been left in full charge of Raynald and the household at Number 55, Rue de Faubourg-Saint-Honoré. She was wise enough to take no notice of the grudging responses and sullen looks that followed her orders, but she knew well enough that feeling ran high against her in the servants' wing.

"Thank you, Pierre. Yes, I'm very well and happy. The Duc and Duchesse have gone to the country, but young Master Raynald here has been ordered to drive each pleasant afternoon, and I accompany him. I sent a note by messenger to ask Madame to come with us for a little turn today. Tell her we're waiting, please."

When the porter had hobbled off with her invitation, Henriette leaned back against the cushions and stared about her at the dreary familiarity of the street. The strong sunshine only made the houses seem more dingy than she remembered. A blind was missing here, a shade askew there, dead stalks showed in a forgotten window box, and water stains from leaky gutters scarred the walls.

"How was it possible for me to be hopeful or happy even for an hour here?" she asked herself, staring up to find the little, peaked window of the "Needle's Eye" through which she had peered so often. There it was, the casement open and a tattered bit of curtain blowing out like a signal from the past.

"Mademoiselle"—the child's clear voice broke into her memories—"I don't like this street. Why are the houses all gray and sad-looking?"

"Perhaps because they're very old, Raynald. Perhaps because the people who live in them are poor and not very happy."

"Then let's not stay here," he decided quickly. "Let's go to the Bois or the Luxembourg Gardens."

She reassured him. They would only stay till a lady came out to drive with them. The lady was an old friend of Mademoiselle's. She might look a little queer to him, but he must be polite and not seem to notice that her hair was two different colors, or that her face was full of lines and her clothes not like Mamma's or Mademoiselle's. He must say *"Bon jour"* and make his bow and let her sit in the best place because this lady did not often go to ride in a carriage behind two such lively horses.

Madame Le Maire emerged at last in her best beaded black, her bonnet well anchored and her sallow cheeks decorated with two round spots of rouge. The footman held open the door, his face impassive, his shoulders eloquently scornful. Raynald went through his formula and reluctantly yielded the outside seat. The horses clattered over the cobblestones to the admiration of old Pierre and other astonished eyes pressed to window panes.

"Well, well!" the older woman breathed as the carriage swung into broader and smoother lengths of street. "This is a pleasant surprise, my dear Mademoiselle Desportes. Pardon, I forgot you prefer this other foolish-sounding name

which I'll never be able to get out easily. I thought you'd
forgotten all about us in the Rue du Harlay!"

Henriette was full of explanations, though she spoke
guardedly because of the child between them. Perhaps it
would have been wiser to stay away from her old haunts,
but she had not been able to resist the temptation to visit
them while the Praslin horses and carriage and liveried at-
tendants were at her disposal, and before her new costume
had lost any of its crispness. She had needed to see the admiration in old Pierre's eyes and the shrewd appraisal as
Madame Le Maire looked her over from the new bonnet
with its green feather curling against the chestnut waves of
her hair to the trim kid slippers that rested on the foot cushion. She craved such reassurance. After all, one might as
well have stayed poor and shabby, if there were none to notice one's rise to better things. How expect an actress to
play to empty benches?

For more than a week now she had presided over Number
55, Rue du Faubourg-Saint-Honoré. The servants might
scowl and protest behind her back, but they dared not openly rebel. The Duc had left orders that Mademoiselle Deluzy
was to be in full charge. One could afford to disregard slights
and black looks when one held the whip hand as she did.
Yet she was also careful not to overstep her privileges by
making too personal demands. That would be a fatal error
at this time. So she continued to devote herself to her small
charge, not only because he had grown dear to her, but because there must be no possible chance of any laxness being
reported through the elaborate system of domestic espionage
which existed in such establishments.

The departure of the Duchesse had removed, as it were,
the proverbial pebble from Henriette's shoe. It no longer
nagged her at every step. Now she could move freely without feeling that violent, tortured presence always at her
side. The very air of the place lifted, as if cleared of the
sultriness that precedes thunder. Perhaps, she tried to reassure herself, her own fatigue had exaggerated the other
woman's outbursts. Certainly it had been no time to judge
her. No doubt when they met again in the quiet of the country with all the children well and romping through a summer holiday, it would be otherwise. She could have made
herself believe it except for those broken, desperately
penned words on a scrap of blue paper.

*"Au revoir,* Madame Le Maire," she said an hour later as they turned into the Rue du Harlay again. "I am glad you could take the air with us. Any day now we may start for Melun."

As Madame allowed herself to be helped out, a thin young man with an armful of books stopped to peer at the unusual sight of such a handsome carriage. Henriette smiled in recognition and reached out her hand to him.

"Monsieur Remey, have you forgotten me?"

She was pleased by his admiring, incredulous acknowledgment as he stammered his greeting:

"Mademoiselle Henriette, I hardly know you. No, it's not just this—" He waved his free hand towards the horses and footman. "It's you yourself. No need to ask how it goes with you these days."

"And I hope it goes well with you, too."

"I'm still on foot, you see." He looked rather ruefully at his scuffed shoes and tried to hide the frayed cuffs that showed at his wrists. "But I'm very happy. Perhaps Madame has told you of my good fortune? My thesis is to be published, and Marie Aubert and I are betrothed." His eyes grew softly sentimental as he spoke the name of his beloved. "We're to be married in August."

"Like a pair of foolish sparrows," Madame Le Maire broke in, taking the arm the young man offered her. "Two can live as cheaply as one. I know how it is now, and how the tune can change." She shook her head and sighed.

"I remember Marie—a sweet girl," Henriette told him; "and I offer you both my congratulations. You will live in Paris?"

"Where else?" Lines of worry deepened between Monsieur Remey's eyes. Even happiness could not quite hide the anxiety that seldom left his serious, student's face. "I must continue my research if I'm ever to be appointed to a professorship. Meantime I pick up a pupil or two as I can find them. Marie may not bring us a dowry, but she makes wonderful soup!"

"Without bones or carrots or onions, I suppose," Madame Le Maire teased. "If she can make nourishing soup out of love and a kettle of water, she'll be a miracle worker."

"Mademoiselle Desportes, I'm not one to ask favors, but—" Young Monsieur Remey lingered by the carriage, though the driver showed plainly that he agreed with the horses' impatience to be off. "Now that you've gone so far and move in a circle of such wealth and influence, perhaps you'd be good enough to help us. If you should hear of a pupil and if you could recommend me as tutor, it would mean—"

The horses were too restless to be held any longer. His words were lost in a clatter of hoofs and wheels as the carriage moved away. But Henriette caught the appeal in his hesitant words. She turned and nodded and waved an encouraging farewell. Poor, impractical Monsieur Remey in his skimpy clothes and that bundle of books that had worn his coat threadbare where they pressed his arms and side! He had dared to love and to be happy with only the prospect of a couple of rooms up many flights and a girl as shabby as he who knew how to make good soup. Yet she found herself envying those two. That radiance behind his near-sighted eyes had been genuine. She could not forget the way they had shone when he spoke of his good fortune. Somehow the shot-silk folds of her new dress as she smoothed them seemed a poor substitute. Perhaps she might be able to find him a pupil, though why she should trouble about a struggling student and his bride she didn't know. Still, the glow of gathering sunset above the river kept reminding her of the warmth that had taken his face in those few moments. She had a distinct inner conviction that young Monsieur Remey and his bride and she must join hands to keep themselves from slipping into the insecurity that waits to engulf the eager and the intelligent.

"Why did that man carry such heavy books, mademoiselle?" Raynald was asking. "And what makes him wear such queer clothes?"

"He's a student, *chéri*," she heard herself responding, "and students are too busy reading big armfuls of books to notice what they wear or what they eat."

"I'm never going to be a student. Do you think I can have cake for supper?"

The afternoon drive and her reunion with two old friends did not lift Henriette's spirit as she had expected. It was all very well to play Lady Bountiful, but once the glow of that faded she felt lonely and restless. With Raynald settled in bed and her duties done, the evening stretched before her as empty as the corridors and rooms through which she passed. Alone in this beautiful house, she had the distinct sensation of rattling like a dried seed in a gourd.

Though she spread out her portfolio under the shaded lamp on the schoolroom table and dipped her pen resolutely to continue the letter she had already begun to Nina Hislop in England, she could not fix her mind to summon words. The ink dried on the quill tip while she sat staring beyond the lamplight towards the dimness of the open windows above the garden. Down there late lilacs were blooming, giving out a fragrance she did not trust herself to smell at nearer range.

"Fool!" She shook herself firmly and set pen to paper. "What more do you want?"

But she knew, even while she wrote careful and mildly instructive descriptions of a drive in the Bois and an afternoon at the Louvre for her late pupil's benefit, she knew in her heart that one was not meant to be sitting alone on a May evening like this. What good was it to know that lilacs were in bloom and everywhere people strolling together, two by two?

The letter was finished. She shut the portfolio and consulted the clock on the mantelpiece. Ten minutes to nine— for Paris the evening had scarcely begun; for her it might as well be over. This curse of aloneness: what had she done to deserve it?

Among the school books on the shelves was a small green volume of English verse, and without knowing why, she singled it from the rest. Idly she turned the pages, only half aware of the neat rhymes that met her eyes. Polite, well ordered lyrics, they were, for the most part, innocuous garlands of chiming words: love and dove; care, despair, and lady fair; flower and bower. Then, suddenly, words started into life before her eyes. They were no longer gentle and ladylike with the suggestion of clinking cups and spoons about a sedate tea table. They challenged her.

> How should I your true love know
>     From another one?
> By his cockle hat and staff,
>     And his sandal shoon.

> He is dead and gone, lady,
>     He is dead and gone;
> At his head a grass-green turf,
>     At his heels a stone.

She read no further, but her heart beat unaccountably as she thrust the book back into place, and a faint chill crept along her spine. She could not say why they should affect her so strangely.

> He is dead and gone, lady,
> He is dead and gone . . .

Some time she would know the reason why they stirred her like this, though as yet they were but a fleeting shadow of some shape she did not know.

Once more she shrugged free of presentiment and crossed the room to a square piano which had been closed since the older girl's departure. Her fingers stole over the black and white keys as she tried to recall the notes of a waltz she had mastered years before with much pains. As she played the melody came back to her, though she fumbled over the deeper chords.

"Mademoiselle! Mademoiselle!"

So absorbed had she been that she had not heard hurrying feet and voices in the corridor. She looked up to see a tall man's figure standing in the schoolroom door and an eager and disheveled young girl hurrying towards her with outstretched arms.

"Louise!" She returned her pupil's embrace. "What brings you back so late? Monsieur, this is a happy surprise. I hope all is well?"

In a moment the atmosphere of the schoolroom was charged with life. Voices met and mingled in a quick exchange of greetings; the lamp laid a charmed, mellow circle over the three who drew together in its light. A servant hurried in with a hastily prepared tray of food—cold meat and salad and rolls; milk for Louise and a decanter of wine for the Duc.

Henriette listened to the explanations and made occasional replies to questions, but all the time her eyes were on the decanter with its glowing contents and the well shaped hands that carefully filled two glasses. She was struck by their strength and pallor in marked contrast to the rich red of the wine. A drop fell from the lip of the bottle and lay like a splash of blood on the white skin. He brushed it away with his handkerchief and leaned across the table.

"Mademoiselle Deluzy, you will not refuse a sip of port? It is not good to drink alone."

She accepted the glass with a smile. His face took on a new look in the lamplight enveloping them both. The hair on his forehead shone like gilt. His eyes were more green than hazel under their thick lashes. She could not help hoping that the artificial light was as becoming to her. She thought it must be because his eyes lingered on the ringlets at either cheek.

"Yes, the Duchesse is greatly improved by the country," she heard him answering a question she must have asked. "She is busy devoting herself to the poor of the neighborhood."

"I have heard she is much beloved for her good deeds. Louise, *chérie*, what is the matter with your cheek? Why is it so swollen?"

Presently Henriette was hearing all about the painful tooth that would not stop aching and how Papa had decided to bring her back to Paris where he had business to conduct tomorrow.

"You're to take me to the dentist, mademoiselle," Louise explained, "and if it has to be pulled and I'm very brave, Papa has promised a surprise. We planned it coming on the train from Corbeil. You'll never guess what it is?"

"If she guesses, it won't be a surprise, Louise," the Duc reminded his impetuous daughter.

"But the surprise has nothing to do with me," Henriette protested. "It's not *my* tooth that aches."

"Yes, but it's going to be for you, too, mademoiselle. We'll wear our best clothes and sit in a box and not go to bed till midnight. Now can't you guess?"

The Duc gave an amused shrug and raised his blond eyebrows as he lighted a cigar. He regarded Louise fondly while he changed the subject to Raynald and the affairs of the household. Henriette's reports were clear and impersonal. He listened attentively and nodded his satisfaction through the blue smoke that lent such an air of masculine worldliness to the ordered schoolroom.

"I am well pleased, Mademoiselle Deluzy," he remarked as he rose to go to his own apartment. "Your management here in my absence has been excellent. We'll all be returning to Melun in a few days, and it may interest you to know that Mademoiselle Maillard will be leaving in August."

She had only time to answer with a relieved smile before he was gone.

"Mamma didn't want Mademoiselle Maillard to go," Louise confided. "She cried about it, but we didn't. We're glad she's going away, and Berthe even told her so to her face. Mademoiselle, the surprise was Papa's idea because he remembered you'd never been to see Rachel!"

Always she was to connect the great actress with the smell of violets from a bunch in her own lap. A flower seller had thrust his tray into the carriage as they drew up by the lighted entrance to the Théâtre Français, and the Duc had tossed the fellow a coin. One bunch for Mademoiselle and one for an excited and wide-eyed Louise. It was a casual gesture, and the violets were already withering in their own sweetness, but those two purple nosegays somehow became the symbol of that evening of unforgettable enchantment. Louise moved between the Duc and Henriette, her cheeks so flushed that the swelling from her abscessed tooth was scarcely noticeable. She walked on tiptoe in young rapture; her hair fell in shining blackness upon her shoulders, and the soft yellow of the dress selected for so great an occasion brought out her best points. She was still a child, but hints of the dusky, mature beauty which was to be hers were apparent.

"She's like a young leaf dancing in its own shadow," Henriette thought; and she shivered suddenly, thinking of that creeping shadow of age, which lengthens for every living creature year by year.

But she could not give herself long to such thoughts, for Louise's animation was contagious. Even the Duc, seasoned theater-goer that he was, responded to the expectant mood of the guests beside him in the gilded box. Henriette saw him glance with approval at her costume as he helped her lay aside her wrap. It was her old dolman, but the green silk of her dress was becoming even though its lines were not décolleté. She regretted that her white throat and shoulders must be hidden, yet it was some satisfaction to know that the fit of the bodice was faultless, and that the soft green made her skin appear more dazzling and brought out the rich lights in her hair.

"I'm afraid that 'Judith' is hardly the most appropriate play for Louise's introduction to the theater." Her host leaned towards her to lay a program on her lap. "But I had no choice. This is Rachel's last performance before leaving for England."

"I doubt if Louise will be shocked," she reassured him. "Innocence, you know, is its own guard. I believe we find whatever we are looking for in books or plays, monsieur— or in life, for the matter of that."

"Well"—he smiled and shrugged his broad shoulders— "perhaps you're right. At all events you'll have to answer any embarrassing questions Louise may ask tomorrow."

"Papa," the girl broke in, "I want to look through your opera glasses at some people because they're staring at us through theirs."

Henriette followed Louise's glance to one of the side boxes, where four people had just been seated. A dowager and a younger woman were settling themselves on the gilt chairs, while two men leveled opera glasses upon the Duc and his party. He met their stare, bowed stiffly, and turned to devote all his attention to his daughter.

Lights were being lowered all over the packed house. The gas jets that edged the stage flared into magnificence. The curtain became a burnished wall of light while violins and cellos soared and swelled and were suddenly silent. Then hushed whispers and sighs of expectancy ran like little waves from row to waiting row.

Henriette drew a deep breath and leaned forward in her seat. She felt, as always on the few occasions she had attended the theater, almost suffocated with anticipation. Though she continued to feel the chair on which she sat, and though she was aware of the program and violets in her lap and of the dim shapes of the man and girl beside her, something in her was carried out and beyond the great audience till she and the rising curtain became one. Completely severed from her ordinary self, in that moment she knew ecstasy and release.

So the curtain rose on the painted tents of Holofernes' camp. Drums rolled, and bugles shrilled. Figures edged with light moved and spoke stirring words; the very boards of the stage seemed waiting with all that breathless houseful of people for the greatest tragédienne of her day to appear. She came swiftly, more like a wind than like a woman. Soft draperies wrapped her light, almost childish frame as she stood there motionless, holding a thousand people in the hollow of one thin outstretched hand.

"Oh, yes, very good," Henriette was to say many times in praise of this or that actress in years to come. "A beautiful performance; but, of course, if one has ever seen Rachel—"

She never tried to finish that comment. Impossible to find words to describe the power of leashed lightning; for the darkly curved wonder of a wave in the moment of breaking; for the flare of a comet in winter skies. How tell of the vibrancy of that voice, clear as ice and rich as warm honey?

Watching this frail Jewess of barely twenty years, with her pale, oval face and compelling eyes, hearing that unforgettable voice that could chill or rouse or ensnare the listener at will, Henriette knew that the age of miracles had not passed. She herself was witness to one.

It mattered not at all that this woman on the lighted stage was notorious from one end of France to the other for her excesses; that her illicit love affairs were more often tawdry than magnificent. Born in cheapness and squalor, she would never be quite free of that heritage. But even as a ragged child, begging and singing at the doors of saloons and brothels, greatness had claimed her for its own. She had only to lift her dark, proud head, to point one quivering finger, to let words pour out in fiery torrents from her parted lips, and the dream of ancient alchemists became real—the baser metal turned to purest gold.

When the curtain fell for the first intermission and the house burst into a storm of clapping hands and echoing bravos, Henriette sat quiet. One did not hail a rising sun with applause or cry bravo to some blazing meteor.

"Well, Mademoiselle Deluzy"—the Duc's voice brought her back to reality—"does the great Rachel measure up to your expectations?"

"Oh!" She shook herself slightly, as if she were with difficulty accustoming her lungs to breathing different air. "Oh, monsieur, what is there left to say?"

He seemed pleased by her response as he turned to answer some question of the flushed and exuberant Louise.

"Yes." He rose with a smile to take a brief promenade. "I must admit she's a great actress. I know it when I can see how she makes Louise look like a woman and you like a child in your eagerness."

Henriette scarcely knew when he returned to their box, for the curtain had risen again and she had given herself wholeheartedly to the unfolding drama. Holofernes was in the sensuous toils of his love for the spying enchantress, and

Rachel moving with the desperate grace of a panther to the scene of his beheading. Judith had triumphed. Her wiles had overcome the enemy of her people, and the severed head of the general was being borne aloft in her hands. Horror and passion and untamed beauty reached out across the footlights to a breathless audience. And then it was over. The pale heroine of the Apocrypha was gone, and in her place a rather worn young Jewess was being led before the curtain to acknowledge the applause. Flowers rained about her from above and below the stage.

"Mine, Papa, mine!" Louise thrust her violets into the Duc's hand.

For a moment he hesitated; then at the eagerness in the child's face, he leaned over the box rail and threw the little bunch straight at his human target. They fell nearest to her, and though she did not stoop to pick the flowers up, it seemed that the dark eyes were fixed for a moment on the box and the handsome fair man and his two companions.

"Oh, Papa!" Louise was too excited to notice the coat Mademoiselle was trying to wrap about her. "Did you see? She really looked straight at us. I'm glad Holofernes came out and bowed too. He was too handsome to have his head cut off. Didn't you think so? I cried, mademoiselle. See, the tears have made spots on my best dress."

As they left the box the Duc shrugged amiably at his daughter's quick chatter.

"For myself, I prefer comedy," he explained. "It's a sign of growing old, they say; but I can't help it. There's danger and horror enough in the world—and we needn't buy our tears."

His lips closed tightly on those last words. Looking up at the profile of his face in the brilliance of the lighted corridor, Henriette was struck by the grim set of his jaw and the way his eyes took on a sudden blankness, as if to hide something secret and painful.

She did not answer. The crowd milling about the foyer was so great it required all his maneuvering to lead them through. As they moved towards the street Henriette was aware of curious eyes following the Duc's tall figure. She heard his name spoken and caught admiring glances directed towards their little party—glances that included her curiously. Presently she was conscious of particularly searching eyes, and she recognized the group that had scrutinized them with such intentness from the opposite box. Once more the Duc bowed formally, acknowledging a greeting from one of the men. He did not pause as his acquaintances evidently expected, but swiftly piloted his charges out to the pavement where carriages were being called. Henriette kept close to his side. She felt a hot rush of blood creeping into her cheeks because of the way those two men had stared at her in cool appraisal. Their eyes had been hard like glass, like little convex mirrors, she thought, distorting something innocent to the ugly proportions of something evil.

## *chapter eight*

CORSICA IN AUGUST HAD FOR HENRIETTE THE UNREALITY of a feverish dream. A savage beauty lay upon those shores, and a remoteness that chilled her at first sight. She was never to lose an early-morning memory of the Strait of Bonifacio, with distant Corsica and Sardinia rising in peaked magnificence like Scylla and Charybdis on either hand. As the vessel which old Maréchal Sébastiani had chartered to bring his daughter and grandchildren from Marseille for their annual visit drew steadily nearer those sheer cliffs, the strange quality of the landscape overwhelmed her.

They might have been approaching the mountains of the moon, so deserted were the dark heights and hollows; the jutting headlands and deep indentations, with scarcely any sign of life or habitation. Even when Henriette was able to make out a few scattered farms, a cluster of fishing boats in harbor, or some bleak stone church and tiny hamlet in a fold of hills, the impression of somber wildness persisted. She could not shake herself free of dread.

"Ajaccio yonder," a sailor told her as an insignificant huddle of houses became visible. "Napoleon Bonaparte was a boy there."

She looked at the straggling town with new interest. Out of this uncompromising small world of rocky hills and dark harbors had come the consuming genius of the little Emperor whose shadow still lay across the face of Europe. Twenty-one years since he had died in exile. The golden bees that had been the emblem of his glory were scattered now like his lost legions, and the hive had been despoiled. But something of that fierce, indomitable energy which had goaded him on still lingered about these shores. Hidden fires might even then be smoldering under the jagged hills and meager pastures. The glassy waters below those cliffs might suddenly seethe, and the fishing boats rock ominously to the rumble of volcanic thunder.

"Yes," she thought, turning to answer the greetings of Isabella and Louise, who appeared just then from the cabins below. "It is beautiful, this place, but alien. I wish we were leaving, not arriving."

All through those weeks of salt and sun, while the children ran and splashed in unrestrained freedom and grew brown as the kelp drying above the tide line, she felt this sense of being alien to a place. She might sketch the unspoiled wildness in her drawing book, yet even as her pencil set down the bold outlines of crags and the crude rigging of fishing boats something in her drew away in a dread she would not put into words. At every turn she was aware that Corsica and the Duchesse were curiously in accord. The dark, heavy-eyed woman with her shifting moods of despair and frenzy, her sullen broodings, and her violent displays of unrestrained affection belonged here as surely as if in some inexplicable way the island had given her its actual counterpart in human temperament. In the luxurious estate at Olmeto where she was still the pampered only child of a rich and influential old man, with her brood of handsome boys and girls are tangible proof of her fruitful marriage into one of the first families of France, Fanny, Duchesse of Praslin, could afford to patronize Mademoiselle Deluzy.

"She stands on her own ground here," Henriette told herself early in the visit. "Also she means to let me see that she holds the purse strings. No wonder he chooses to stay behind, rather than listen to his pompous father-in-law singing her praises."

Without the Duc's presence to lend her his approval and support Henriette had less authority over the younger children. They remained devoted as ever. No excursion could be complete without Mademoiselle Deluzy; not a day passed

that one or another did not bring her some present—a bit of
coral from the shore, curiously curled shells, pebbles with
lucky bands, the first ripe plum from the garden. But unconsciously they realized their grandfather's indulgence and
took their cues accordingly. She found it almost impossible
to keep to the well ordered routine of nursery and schoolroom with distractions tempting from morning till night.
There was no denying the lure of saddled donkeys waiting
to be ridden into the hills, gayly painted boats with smiling
brown boatmen eager to sail the young Praslins across the
wide bays or up narrow hidden inlets. Each pleasant day
new excursions were planned and led by the old Maréchal;
and Henriette's protests that piano practice must continue
and the weekly letter to the children's father should not be
forgotten, were easily brushed aside. This was holiday time,
the Duchesse and her father would insist.

"They're only young once, Mademoiselle Deluzy," the
doting old man would say, fondling Berthe, who was his
favorite. "Before we know it they'll be betrothed and busy
with homes and husbands of their own. Isn't it so, my
Fanny?"

And the Duchesse would sigh and agree and point out the
Duc's extraordinary ideas about the education of his daughters—as if they needed all these accomplishments when it
would never be necessary for them to earn their own livings.

Henriette held her tongue against such remarks. She was
far too shrewd to take issue with the Duchesse, now that her
powerful ally and supporter was absent. No use putting up
an offensive campaign on enemy soil. Besides, she wanted
to avoid all dissension. There must be no criticism of her
behavior when they returned to Paris. Perhaps, she dared
to hope after certain excursions in which they all joined, or
on days when the Duchesse had seemed more kindly disposed towards her, perhaps they might even come to an
understanding. So she continued to exert all her art of tact
and consideration. The old Maréchal praised her retiring
deportment and congratulated his daughter more than once
upon the superiority of the new governess. Henriette heard
his words on several occasions and modestly protested
against such praise.

"I only seek to serve the children," she told him, "and
hope to please the parents. If I fail sometimes, no one regrets the shortcomings more than I."

"My daughter belongs with the saints of this world," the Maréchal confided to her a few days later on an afternoon when the Duchesse had retired with one of her migraine headaches.

Henriette could not help noticing that the attack had followed the arrival of mail from Paris. She had seen those plump white hands shuffle through a sheaf of envelopes, seize one from the rest, and tear it open in frantic haste. The contents of a single sheet of note paper could not have pleased the Duchesse, for she had crushed it into a crumpled ball and gone immediately to her room. Henriette was thinking of it now as she listened politely to the anxious old man eulogizing his daughter.

"Yes," he went on, "Fanny is generous to a fault. She'd give her very life for those she loves."

"Who wouldn't?" Henriette thought. "It's much more difficult to live and let live."

But she waited in tactful silence while he continued.

"Nine times my poor Fanny has brought forth new life at the risk of her own. She has been blessed with fine sons and lovely daughters, yet I sometimes think the cost has been too great. Each year has taken heavy toll of her strength, and since Raynald's birth she has not been herself."

"And Raynald was four in June. Surely the doctors can find some cure—"

"It goes deeper than that, mademoiselle." The old man sighed. "She suffers cruelly, and what good is my wealth if it cannot lessen her pain?"

"We cannot buy happiness, can we, monsieur—not for ourselves or those we love?"

"True, too true," he agreed, pleased by her interest rather than offended by her curiosity. "She brought one of the largest dowries in France to her marriage," he went on. "Everything smiled on them then, those two—" He broke off with another puzzled sigh.

Henriette made no comment, although she could not help recalling an old saying she had heard in England years before: "A great dowry is often a bed full of brambles."

"Yes," her host went on without noticing her silence. "Time has turned white sugar to white salt before now. Pardon, mademoiselle, if I have said too much, but I beg you not to take offense if my poor daughter sometimes ap-

pears distraught. Humor her, mademoiselle, and your services will not be forgotten."

He left her before she had a chance to reply or learn if
this were a deliberate bribe or simply the effort of a worried
old man to win sympathy for his daughter. How much did
he actually know, she wondered, staring after his sturdy,
retreating figure. How much did she herself actually know
when it came to that? She shrugged and tried to dismiss the
whole baffling matter from her mind. The sun was bright
beyond the windows, and the sea incredibly blue between
the garden cypresses. She could hear the voices of Berthe
and Raynald at play under the grape arbor.

"Mademoiselle," they called, "where are you?"

She turned to go to them, but as she stepped through the
French doors she was not thinking of the brilliance of sun
and sea and the warm gold of ripening fruit trained against
oyster-white walls. She was thinking of tortured, unforgettable words on a scrap of blue paper, and of those adjoining
apartments in the Rue du Faubourg-Saint-Honoré, separated by a few square feet, but with a widening gulf of bitterness and discord between.

"If it is no better when we return," she decided, "I must
go. I must find another place." But she spoke without conviction. It was as if she guessed already that she would not
be able to shed the Rue du Faubourg-Saint-Honoré so easily.

September wrapped the island in a warm, delicious haze.
The mountains took on a softened, remote purple, and the
sharp-toothed shores were less formidable in the mellow
light that quickened the brown grass and meager vegetation
to unsuspected beauty. On the lonely beaches where the
young Praslins played with scantily clad companions from
near-by fishing hamlets, each salt pool was an irregular
mirror of brightness, every wet shell and starfish and polished pebble a fresh miracle of wonder and delight.

Henriette responded to this change. She relaxed in the
heady fruitfulness about her. She gave herself complete to
sun and salt air and the sweetness of ripening grapes in the
small vineyards that clung as they climbed stubbornly up
steep hillsides. She fell asleep quietly with the sound of far
surf in her ears; she woke refreshed to the incredible blue of
morning with a sense of hopeful well-being. Even the Duchesse and her unaccountable moods no longer oppressed
and irritated. She could endure them because she herself
felt equal to life and its exigencies.

Fanny Sébastiani, Duchesse of Praslin, seemed in better spirits than at any time since Henriette had entered the household. Once or twice she had even made timid advances towards the governess, though the brooding apathy prevailed. Still, that was better than the earlier pent-up outbursts. Henriette began to hope that, though perhaps there could never be congenial relations between herself and the children's mother, there might at least be freedom from this suspicion and resentment.

"It's Mamma's birthday Wednesday," Isabella announced importantly one morning. "That's why we've postponed sailing till Friday. Grandpère is giving a banquet for her, and he says Louise and I may come down afterward and listen to the music."

"Yes, and what shall we do for gifts, mademoiselle?" Louise demanded.

"You must finish your crewelwork mat then," Henriette decided. "Fetch your workbag now and let me see how fast you can sew in four days. Isabella, you should have told me before. There's nothing for it but for you to illuminate a poem in your best script. You may use my paints and foolscap if you will be careful."

Mademoiselle's ingenuity must also provide gifts for Berthe and Raynald to present. That was not an easy undertaking with two small people whose minds skipped more foolishly than the island goats, and whose fingers were as yet unskilled. But the problem was solved. Berthe produced a cabbage-leafed rose in lurid crayon crimson and mauve with *"Chère Mama—Souvenir de Berthe"* in crooked letters beneath, while Raynald gathered tiny cockleshells for Mademoiselle to glue into a frame. Both children were overcome with awe by the beauty of this joint creation.

"When will it be your birthday, mademoiselle?" Berthe asked as they wrapped the gift in readiness. "I'll make you a much more beautiful picture."

"Yes," Raynald chimed in, "and I'll give you the piece of coral I found. It's the most precious thing I have."

Henriette smiled and thanked them, but she was relieved these remarks had not been overheard. Their very devotion might be her undoing. Madame Leclerc, the Duchesse's maid, had a way of stealing silently in and out of rooms, and she would be only too eager to repeat such treason.

The old Maréchal spent himself in lavish celebration of

the birthday. Long before daylight the kitchen fires roared in preparation for the feast; the gardens gave up their spoils that the long rambling villa might be transferred into a bower. Choice wines in dusty bottles were brought from the cellars, and all day streams of tenants came with nosegays to pay their respects to the daughter of their landlord. Henriette could see that the Duchesse was touched by these humble signs of good will. To all she was gracious, yet she remained aloof, in a cloud of kindly detachment. It was plain that her heart was not in these festivities centering about her. Even the gifts her children laid in her lap only roused her interest briefly.

"Madame," Henriette ventured in presenting hers, "I have only my own handiwork to offer. I wish that I were more skillful; still, since I give you back the likeness of your charming daughter, I hope you will accept it with my good wishes."

"Your good wishes are more than enough." The Duchesse raised drooping lids and fixed dark, reproachful eyes upon the governess standing before her.

"Madame," Henriette went on, undaunted by the heavy sigh that followed these words and by the other's indifference to the offering, which lay untouched on the table, "the good Sisters at the Convent taught me as a child to count each birthday the beginning of a New Year. I could find it in my heart to hope that you will let today be such between us. If I have made mistakes or failed in my duties I beg you to tell me, to let me know your wishes."

"My wishes," the Duchesse repeated with a note of bewildered irony, "my wishes have ceased to matter. You are more of a fool than I take you to be, mademoiselle, if you haven't noticed that."

"Oh, but surely, madame—" Before she could answer this unexpected thrust, Berthe ran in from the garden.

"Mamma!" The child pointed impatiently to the unopened gift. "You haven't looked at Mademoiselle's present. Here"—she thrust it into her mother's listless fingers—"I sat still as a mouse for hours, didn't I, mademoiselle?"

"Yes, *chérie*, you were a fine subject."

The interruption had been opportune, and when the charming pastel portrait was unwrapped the Duchesse showed genuine pleasure. Henriette had caught the likeness extraordinarily well, and Berthe's fair, round face stared out from the cardboard with wide-eyed candor and innocence. Yet the resemblance to her father was startlingly revealed behind the chubby contours. Too late, Henriette decided, it would have been more tactful to have selected brunette Louise or Raynald, in whose black brows and eyes their Corsican inheritance was more apparent.

But the Duchesse, if she marked the Praslin features, made no comment. Her praise and thanks rang true, and the tension which had filled the room a few moments before was broken.

"Believe me, madame"—Henriette lingered when Berthe returned to her play—"I meant what I said just now. You must believe that I want only harmony between us."

"Perhaps I have wronged you," the older woman spoke wearily, but without the film of bitterness that the governess had come to associate with her words. "God knows I would not hurt another as I have been hurt. But it's not easy to break the habits of doubt and suspicion once they've been thrust upon one. Here in Corsica, where my own carefree childhood walks beside me at every step, I can almost forget the indignities I have suffered. I could almost come to believe again in a world where those we love are not indifferent to us.".

Henriette felt embarrassed by this appeal for sympathy. To confess openly that one was not beloved seemed almost a breach of decency. Yet, in spite of her distaste for such a show of emotion, she recognized that the cry had been genuine. She heard herself answer soothingly, in a tone she might have used to quiet an overexcited Berthe or Raynald.

"Sometimes, madame, we must take affection in other for granted. The minute we doubt, a cloud comes between us and them. Love isn't so much sugar or tea that we can measure and weigh it on scales."

"You seem to know a great deal about love, mademoiselle."

Henrietta gave no sign that the thrust had gone home. She went on speaking steadily.

"I'm alone in the world, madame, and I've learned to take what bits of love come my way and piece them together as best I can to keep me warm. I am reminded of those coverlets patched together from odds and ends of other people's garments." She paused, surprised that she had said so much to this other woman who to all outward appearances possessed everything desirable in life. "Don't begrudge me any stray bits of affection that come my way while I'm under your roof," she went on. "Remember they're very small compared to the whole piece of goods that is yours."

"But even little pieces can leave great holes in time. Don't forget that, mademoiselle, since you are speaking of patchwork."

Henriette found herself recalling their conversation as she stood before the mirror that evening. She resented the Duchesse having had the last word. It had put her at a disadvantage and left them no nearer to the reconcilation she had hoped the birthday might bring. They could never, it seemed, meet on the impersonal footing of the employed and the employer.

"She turns the simplest word into a dart aimed at her sensibilities," Henriette thought, brushing the lengths of her hair about her fingers and letting them fall in smooth ringlets. "No wonder she's unhappy, poor soul, and no wonder all who cross her path hurry to be clear of the shadow she casts."

She hoped Isabella and Louise would appear affectionate and dutiful at the reception tonight. There had been a regrettable scene that afternoon when Raynald had insisted upon remaining at home with Mademoiselle instead of driving with his mother in the carriage. There, her toilette was complete. The folds of her shot-silk billowed green as sea water to her slippered feet. In the fitted bodice her waist looked trim and small and a white triangle of neck showed where the ends of lace fichu met. There was color in her cheeks and the waves of her hair lay softly upon her brow and shoulders. She had not worn the dress since the night they had gone to the theater to see Rachel. As she leaned closer to the glass to tuck a loosened curl into place she found herself thinking of the Duc, wishing that he would be in that company below stairs. Down there guests had been gathering since dusk and now the banquet must be at its height. The sound of bows on taut strings came to her in mounting sweetness from the landing where the musicians were stationed. They were a band of gypsy players from Olmeto. Henriette and the children had watched their arrival in an old cart—three fiddles and two guitars, a tambourine and a crude flageolet. The tunes were strange to her. Listening, she was stirred with sadness and an unrest. She moved to the window and stared at the irregular pricking of lights on the mountain sides, and below the garden and steep terraces to more lights that edged the shore and to still more remote lanterns on the mastheads of anchored boats. She felt far, far from all familiar things, and the music with its sensual rhythm and melody drew out a response from her pulses that made her feel a stranger to herself.

"Isabella, Louise!" She rapped on the door of the room where the two girls waited in their ruffled white muslins and wide sashes of pink and blue. "It's time to go down now. Stand up and let me see if you are ready to make your bows."

Deftly she tightened knots of ribbon and adjusted the smooth dark hair on the young shoulders.

"There, that's better. Remember, Isabella, to keep your shoulders back. And, Louise, don't act as if you'd swallowed a poker. Here are your basket of mottoes to pass."

"What if there shouldn't be enough to go round, mademoiselle?"

"Now, Isabella, when emergencies come we'll face them, not before."

She smiled encouragingly at the overgrown, serious-faced girl.

"But I like to know beforehand what things are going to happen," Isabella protested. "I wish Papa were down there instead of way off in Paris. I think he might have come, don't you, mademoiselle?"

Henriette avoided an answer by hurrying them out into the corridor and down the great staircase. Hundreds of tapers burned, doubling their brightness in mirrors and polished marble. A hum of many voices from the long tables in the hall below rose and mingled with the music that throbbed and swelled as the swarthy players bent to their instruments. They passed close to the musicians, the two excited girls in front clutching their baskets, the governess moving discreetly behind, her face as smooth and taut as the lifted tambourine which echoed the rhythmic confusion of her own heart.

## chapter nine

IN THE PARK ABOUT THE CHÂTEAU DE VAUX-PRASLIN YEL-
low beech leaves made rivers of rustling gold for the children's feet to ford. Oaks darkened to russet and under the
chestnut trees the ground was thick with bursting burrs.
Each noon the fierce October sun melted the ice that coated
pools in the road ruts, but each night the frost laid on a new
film and whitened the wide lawns and terraces. No matter
how early Henriette and her four charges set out after morning lessons and *déjeuner,* darkness always overtook them as
they trudged home to the persistent throb of crickets.

There was, for Henriette, a stirring quality to the landscape at this season, *l'été de Saint Martin.* Always before,
she had been forced to return to city streets and narrow
rooms at the first sign of frost. But now she gave herself to
those afternoons. The clear amber light was all the more
precious because of its briefness. It seemed to her an interlude of mellow completion between the richness of summer
and the bleakness of winter, with the whole round earth a
burnished apple hung in space.

The routine of her days had been smooth and unruffled
since the return from Corsica. They had gone at once
to the château, where the three other daughters had spent a
month's holiday from their convent. Later they had accompanied their mother and father to a watering place in the
South of France where Dr. Simon had recommended the
salt baths. Whether these had benefited the Duchesse or
not, at least her absence had removed the sense of strain and
tension from nursery and schoolroom. The children's lessons were no longer broken by their mother's unsettling
appearances and the inevitable aftermath of hurt feelings
when one or another drew away from her violent embraces
or showed insufficient interest in an avalanche of toys and
sweetmeats. It was far more simple, Henriette found, to
supervise dutiful little notes addressed to *"Chère Mama"*
than to make them respond affectionately to her actual

presence. Isabella and Louise grew noticeably less self-conscious and shy, and Raynald lost much of his nervous intensity during these weeks. There were no shattering scenes to leave him bewildered and hysterical. His sleep and appetite improved till he was able to walk almost as far as Berthe without tiring.

The servants at the château were not a hostile element to balk Henriette at every turn. They accepted her orders without protest, and she did not feel they waited to betray her. For the most part they were peasants not given to the petty scheming of city-bred domestics. They accepted the Duchesse's bounty, her wealth that had restored the Praslin estate to its old impressive stature; they honored her for her religious devotion and for giving the line a new heritage of sons and daughters, but the old feudal instincts of family loyalty persisted tenaciously.

So the days flowed smoothly on with only shortening hours of daylight to mark one from the next. October brilliance would soon slip into the tarnished softness of November.

"It will be All Hallows Eve tonight," Louise announced as they set out for their afternoon walk. "We must hurry back before dark. I shouldn't like to meet a ghost, should you, mademoiselle?"

"Well, Louise, I don't know. There must be good ghosts as well as bad ones. But we're not going to meet any this afternoon," she added quickly as she felt Raynald's fingers tighten in her own.

She was never to forget that afternoon in the woods at Melun. Years afterward she could recall the way the light shifted between huge beech trunks as sleekly gray as mouse skin, and how the brook was a torrent of gold leaf more solidly choked than if Midas had turned it to metal. The sky showed brilliantly blue and polished in gaps between yellow and bronze overhead, but for all its clearness a faint, bitter blue haze drifted. One was always losing and finding it again, like fragments of an old tune. Somewhere leaves were burning with the lovely ghost of summer in every whiff.

They found deep hollows where gold and russet leaves were knee-deep, and Berthe and Raynald played at burying each other in great rustling armfuls. They gathered pocket-fuls of chestnuts, defying the cruel sharpness of prickly burrs to feel the incredible satin guarding the brown treasure. How sweet the kernels tasted as their teeth crunched into the milky crispness! How the squirrels rattled and raged from the boughs above!

They walked a mile out of their way to stop at the old mill and see the mossy wheel turning, turning forever under the press of hurrying water. Leaning over the half-open door, their heads grew dizzy with watching; their ears rang with the rushing din.

The miller and his plump wife came out full of smiles and compliments.

"Mademoiselle Isabella is quite the young lady now. Her own mother wasn't much taller when she came as a bride to the château. And Mademoiselle Louise—what lovely color! Like ripe peaches in the sun. And the two little ones, how they've grown since summer! Berthe here—she's all Praslin, fair like the Duc. Yes, she's her father's daughter and no mistake. And the little fellow isn't a baby any more, though his face hasn't caught up with those big black eyes yet!"

Such praise might be a trifle too lavish, but the friendly meetings with country tenants were good for the children, Henriette decided. She had difficulty in starting them towards home again. The miller advised a short cut through the woods instead of the longer way by the meadows and orchard, and he started them upon it with careful directions. But Henriette had not reckoned on losing the sun so soon. It dropped fast behind the old trees, and shadows turned to twilight all about them.

"We must hurry or we'll lose the way," she told her little troop. "Take my hand, Raynald. Watch for the path ahead, and don't stumble on roots."

"It's growing very dark, mademoiselle," Louise complained. "I wish we'd brought one of the dogs with us."

Henriette wished so, too; but she urged them on confidently, keeping her eyes fixed on the narrow gap between the ranks of trees. Woods where shifting sunlight dappled mossy trunks were romantic places to be lost in, but woods close-packed after dark were an altogether different matter.

"I smell a fire." Berthe stopped short in the path, sniffing and pointing towards a faint, wavering glow. "It's over there."

They pushed on and presently found themselves in a clearing by a small hut. A bent old figure moved about a sunken pit where a brush-fire burned brightly. Henriette stood still with her feet held fast to the frosty ground. She could scarcely believe in the reality of the scene before her —the pagan glare of the crackling fire and the old man heaping more brush upon it as if he were following some mysterious rite, so old that he himself no longer knew the meaning. She was almost sorry when she saw Berthe dart into the circle of firelight and heard voices raised in every-day greeting.

"It's old Loti, mademoiselle," Isabella was explaining. "He gathers wood for our fires and keeps the park trim."

"Yes," broke in Louise, "Papa says he's older than any-thing but the carp in the pond, and they're supposed to be over a hundred."

Henriette could believe that when she saw the brown grooves of his face. He might have been some resurrected mummy except for the brightness of his two specks of eyes reflecting the firelight. His wiry arms and legs were hardly more than thin sticks that showed under his shapeless gar-ments. His hands might have been earth-darkened roots as the gnarled and crooked fingers grasped more bundles of brush or prodded the fire with an iron fork.

"He says he's just going to roast apples for All Hallows Eve," Berthe hurried back to tell the rest. "It's some kind of spell, so please, mademoiselle, can't we stay? He says there'll be one for each of us and you, too."

Henriette hesitated. She knew they should be at home, not here in the frosty twilight. Yet she herself was tempted to linger by the fire. Their strange host, moving with the jerky spryness of an antiquated grasshopper, filled her with curiosity. He might have stepped from the woodcuts of some fairy book she had pored over in childhood.

"It's good luck to eat an apple hot from the fire and wish the dead well tonight," Louise was telling her.

"And he says the moon will be up soon, mademoiselle," Isabella pleaded. "It will be light as day then."

"Well"—Henriette allowed herself to be persuaded—"if Raynald promises to keep warm." She buttoned his jacket and fastened the muffler about his neck. They seated them-selves on a log near the fire while old Loti prepared the ap-ples. This was evidently an important ceremony, not to be carelessly undertaken. First he brought two pans from the house and a bundle of long, pointed sticks. Each apple was scrutinized, dipped first in a pan of water, then rolled in what appeared to be sugar and cinnamon. This done, he pressed the sharpened end of a stick into the core and put the treasure into one of the children's hands. The sticks were long and strong enough to reach over the hottest part of the fire without the heat becoming too great for the holder to bear. He showed them in pantomime how to turn the stick so that the apple should be cooked evenly, not burned black on one side. It was necessary above all things, he told them impressively when they had each been supplied, not to drop the fruit into the fire. That would mean good fortune lost and bad luck for seven long years. When the apples were done they must be eaten, every morsel, but the core and the seeds counted and saved. If you were a girl, he explained, the seeds stood for the number of years you must wait before marriage. If you were a boy they foretold how many children you would have.

"Twelve in mine last year," old Loti chuckled and gave Henriette a sly wink. "But then, who says the age of miracles is past?"

She smiled and shrugged as she accepted the apple he pressed upon her.

"There's no sense in my counting apple seeds," she remarked as she added hers to the others.

"Aren't Mesdemoiselles allowed to marry?" Louise inquired without lifting her eyes from the fire.

"There's no law against it," Henriette answered, "but as a matter of fact they seldom do."

"Why not?" Raynald was curious.

"Oh, usually they're too busy looking after little girls and boys. Careful, *chéri*, your apple is much too close to the flame."

She helped him steady his stick and soon all the apples were bursting their rosy skins. The fire sputtered as drops of hot juice and sugar fell into it. Their faces burned in the heat, but the air at their backs grew frosty with the deepening darkness.

Presently old Loti began to sing in a thin, rusty voice like the chirp of a cricket. His withered lips scarcely moved, so the sound seemed to be less a part of him than some essence of the night and the fire and the apples sizzling in their own sweetness. The song was strange to Henriette, and though many of the words escaped her she made out that it belonged to All Hallows Eve and the restless souls, lighter than dry leaves, who might be abroad.

"Mademoiselle!" She felt Raynald edge closer. "It makes me afraid. Let's go home."

"Hush!" She drew him to her. "There's nothing to be frightened about. It's only an old song. Keep your eyes on the fire and your apple."

The droning old voice sang on, and all at once Isabella and Louise took up the refrain in their high, birdlike trebles:

> "Salt and bread we've set for you
> And we've scattered ash and rue,
> Now we'll say a prayer for you—
> *Requiescat in pace.*"

Listening there in the dim clearing Henriette could almost believe in the superstition. The voices of the living lifted for the dead, in a tune so old and plaintive, made her heart echo like a hollow shell. She would remember this moment always, she knew: the firelight on old Loti, grotesque as some ancient effigy, and the faces of the children, round and rosy as the apples they held to the fire. Pagan or Christian, she thought, what did it matter except that so fair and moving a custom should go on from generation to generation? It was right that on one night of the year the quick should take thought of the dead.

They ate their apples while the great fall moon pushed its way up through the trees. Hot juice burned their impatient tongues; their lips and fingers were sweet with smoky spice. Raynald forgot and dropped his apple core in the fire, and Berthe lost hers underfoot. The older girls tied their seeds carefully in their handkerchiefs to count when they reached home. They rose to start back; but something stirred at the edge of the clearing, and panic seized the little group.

"A ghost, mademoiselle, a ghost!" Raynald buried his head in Henriette's skirts and whimpered.

As she bent to reassure him old Loti chuckled.

"A pretty solid ghost, I must say! Don't you know your own father when you see him?"

"Papa! Papa!"

They all ran towards the figure which had emerged from the trees. Swift-footed Berthe reached him first—excited words about fires and apples and ghosts tumbling pell-mell from her lips. He set her on his shoulder and advanced into the circle of firelight. In the low, pulsating light of the burning brushwood he appeared gigantic and golden as some figure out of a legend, his fair hair brightened to copper, the folds of his long, brown cloak turned to bronze. Even so, Henriette thought, must the early Norse heroes have looked striding from triumphant battle, their proud faces set towards Valhalla.

"I guessed where I should find you." He laughed and showed his strong white teeth as he clapped the old man's bent shoulders. "Loti roasted apples for me when I was no bigger than Raynald here!"

"Take mine and welcome." Loti urged his fruit upon the Duc. "Not a bite have I taken, and who knows but you'll find a surprise or two in the core?"

But the Duc smiled and shook his head.

"No more need for me to count apple seeds, Loti. Nine children are enough for me to manage, thank you! Raynald, it's your turn for a ride. The rest of you keep close behind me, and the moon will see us home."

Following that tall figure, they pressed through the woods in single file, the three girls between and Henriette bringing up the rear. The path showed dim before them, broken by patches of light and shadow. Henriette kept her eyes fixed on their guide as he strode forward, his bare head gleaming pale in the moonlit spaces. Sometimes he looked back and waited for them to catch up to him.

"I forget my legs are so long," he apologized, "and then I know these woods so well. I could walk them blindfolded. I should know if a root or a stump were not in its right place."

"That's a gift, monsieur, almost like a sixth sense," Henriette told him.

"No, it's much more simple. You have only to be young in a place to learn its secrets. Sometimes I think— Ah, well, one is apt to grow sentimental about childhood, particularly one's own."

As they came in sight of the château Henriette noticed that the rooms usually occupied by the Duchesse were the only ones not lighted.

"Madame la Duchesse did not come with you?" she asked politely.

"No, she remained in Paris. I am here for a few days to see how work on the new wing is progressing. It's lonely in the Faubourg-Saint-Honoré without these four, and I confess I wanted a sight of them, too."

"I trust the Duchesse's health has benefited by her treatment at the spa?"

"Somewhat, yes." He spoke guardedly. "But she is far from well and easily upset. The doctors can do little for her, I fear."

Henriette said no more. She felt that he had no wish to continue the subject; and she, for her part, could only feel relief at the poor woman's absence. There would be no trying scenes to meet that night or the next day.

They were very gay about the schoolroom fire. The Duc did not eat alone in the blue and gold salon, but ordered his meal served upstairs with the children's supper. Afterwards they cracked nuts while the fire burned with soft hissings in the grate and the wind outside only increased the sense of warmth and coziness behind drawn curtains. The hours of walking in the open, the hot supper and the warmth of the lighted room filled them all with relaxed contentment. But the Duc's presence charged the atmosphere with festivity.

Henriette sat with her needlework by the table, watching and listening to the little group by the fire. She marveled at his way with the children. Whenever he spoke they hung on his words, and he in turn listened intently to theirs. And how well he understood those four! Stubborn, serious-minded Isabella and impulsive, scattered-brained Louise chattered of their plans and projects like two excited magpies. He knew so well how to keep Berthe's high spirits from turning to arrogance. As for Raynald, the frail child seemed to take on new vigor and assurance whenever he was with his father. "Yes," she thought as she led the two little ones away to their bedrooms, "he is more than just a parent. This gift of his for the young amounts to genius. Lucky he has it, for he needs to be father and mother both!"

When she returned she found the older girls still arguing about the number of seeds their apple cores had contained.

"We're facing a serious problem," he said, keeping a grave face though his eyes twinkled supiciously. "Louise, it seems, has six seeds in her apple and Isabella eight. What shall we do about that, Mademoiselle Deluzy?"

He had never fallen into the easy habit of addressing her by the impersonal title "Mademoiselle." She had grown

accustomed to that wherever she worked, and this acknowledgment that he considered her a personality as well as a
governess was flattering.

"I'm hardly the one to advise," she told them.

"But a younger sister could marry first, couldn't she,
mademoiselle?" Louise persisted.

"Why, yes, I believe it's possible." Henriette smiled as she
spoke. "It seems to me I remember reading in some old
book that if an elder sister dances in her stocking feet at her
younger sister's wedding she'll have a husband herself within the year."

"The first to marry isn't always the happiest." The Duc
wound up the discussion at last. "Off to bed now, you two,
and don't worry your heads about husbands yet. You'll have
plenty of suitors when the time comes!"

He kissed them and stood at the door watching them go
down the long corridor arm in arm. When he turned back
to the fire Henriette saw that a slight frown had deepened
between his eyes.

"It makes a father feel old when his daughters begin to
talk about their husbands. It seems only yesterday I was
being married myself, but I'm thirty-seven. Before I know
it I'll be a grandfather."

"You'll make a delightful grandfather, monsieur. I think
you'll rather enjoy the rôle."

"Perhaps," he agreed. He was silent for a moment before
he went on. "But I might as well face the fact that my
daughters are growing fast. Four, five, six years at the most,
and we'll have to be finding them husbands. Yes." He
sighed and stared thoughtfully into the fire. "It's a barbarous custom—this matter of dowries and suitable mating. I
wonder sometimes if the English aren't more sensible than
we about marriage. But then, what does a girl of eighteen
or a boy of twenty know of love, or raising a family for the
matter of that?"

"The young Queen Victoria seems more than happy in
her choice of a mate," Henriette remarked, sorting out
strands of colored silks from a snarl in her lap. "But I suppose she's hardly a fair example."

He made no immediate response, but settled back into a
chair from which he could stretch his long legs in their polished boots to the fire. She had not expected him to linger
on after the children's bedtime, but since he had lingered it

seemed the most natural thing in the world that he should be there just the other side of the lamp-lit table.

"Mademoiselle Deluzy," he went on after a long pause. "I hadn't thought to speak of this now, but since we seem to be on the subject of marriage I may as well tell you what is on my mind. These next years will be difficult ones for Isabella and Louise. They're maturing fast. Physically they're almost women, though they're children still in their minds and feelings. I want to let them grow easily out of their childhood. There must not be shocks and changes to upset them as there have been in the past. This procession of maids and governesses coming and going in the household, and with their mother's health what it is—well—" He spread out his large white hands in an expressive gesture of helplessness. "What can I say to you that you do not know as well as I?"

"I beg you to go on, monsieur. If I have fallen short in any way I want you to tell me."

"No—no." He leaned forward earnestly and fixed her with anxious eyes. "I have no fault to find, only praise of you and what you have been to my children. You have brought order and peace where all was confusion before."

"I have tried to do my best, but I know I've often made mistakes—"

But he brushed her words aside.

"I had forgotten what peace was," he went on. "But to-night in this room I have found it again. Do you know I think it's years since I felt anything like this—a quiet room, a fire and a lighted lamp, work in a woman's hands, the children going to bed without a trace of tears on their faces."

She was touched by his words, yet embarrassed at the implication behind them. He had broken off abruptly to sit staring before him, his fingers idly plucking at one of the silken snarls that had slipped from her lap. The lamplight shone full on his face, and she saw that he looked tired. In his eyes there was an expression of humiliation and appeal. His mouth sagged at the corners. In that moment, with the barriers of reserve down, she realized that he was not the heroic creature he had seemed in the wood that afternoon—golden, magnificent and equal to all things. She saw him suddenly for what he was—a handsome, unhappy man in the prime of life who reached out to her as helplessly as one of his own children might have done.

"Don't go away!" His voice was tense in its appeal. "Don't take away this refuge you've made in the household for all of us. It's asking a great deal of you. I know that. I know the slights and humiliations you have to put up with. God knows I know them all, and still I ask you to pocket your pride and stay—for all our sakes!"

"I cannot make such a promise, monsieur. You are free to give me notice, and I must have the same privilege if it seems best. Things have a way of changing, almost overnight." He made a queer sound in his throat—half sigh, half groan. She hesitated a moment, then hurried on. "Not that I'm intending to leave. I want to stay. I'm very fond of the children, and I want to please you and Madame—"

She broke off, though it was on the tip of her tongue to add, "—if that's possible."

"I'll make it worth your while," he persisted, "if you'll stay till Isabella marries I'll see that you have a pension. We need not mention it to the Duchesse, but I'll have my lawyer draw up an agreement; so you can feel perfectly assured."

"Why, monsieur, your word would be enough. I need nothing more binding."

"Still," he went on, "if anything happened to me, you would have something beside my word. Mademoiselle Maillard is gone; so there will be no more interfering with your management of the children when you return to Paris. Everything is to be in your hands from now on, and if you need help you can choose your own assistant. You will agree, Mademoiselle Deluzy, so that I need not be afraid every time I see a trunk carried out that you are leaving us?"

It was hard to resist him when he brought the whole force of his personality to bear upon her. But she clung stubbornly to her stand.

"I cannot make a promise I might have to break," she repeated. "But I'll do my best. You can rely on me not to take offense easily. All women in my position must learn to put up with certain slights; and perhaps I've had too much pride, but it's been my only dowry, you see."

He nodded and continued to twist the tangled silks into a more hopeless snarl.

"It will be easier now I know I have your confidence."

Outside, the wind had gathered force. They could hear it among the nearer oak trees and whipping the dried fingers of a vine against the casement. On the nursery mantelpiece the squat marble clock struck ten musical notes. The Duc drew out his own watch with the heavy gold seals, compared both timepieces and rose to take his leave. But he stood for some minutes by the window, peering out between the curtains as if he saw more than the dark pane of glass.

"All Hallows Eve," he said. "I'd forgotten till old Loti and the children reminded me this afternoon."

"It's easy to forget in the city where there's only time for the living," she answered.

"Well"—he turned towards the door—"we won't begrudge the dead their privilege. We have all the other nights of the year. Good night, Mademoiselle Deluzy. I shall see you tomorrow at *déjeuner*."

She heard the sound of his boots descending the stairs, and she continued to hear their echo long after she knew that silence had fallen on the place.

*chapter ten*

THERE WAS NO SNOW FOR CHRISTMAS, 1842, BUT ON THE last afternoon of the year the sun grew pale as a frosty penny and then retired altogether behind a fine curtain of slanting flakes. Henriette stood at her window and watched the wintry garden at Number 55, Rue du Faubourg-Saint-Honoré, take on miraculous whiteness. The bronze dolphin wore an icicle at his open mouth, and the gateposts soon had thick wigs of snow on their round tops. All the bare trees and evergreen shrubbery were transformed before her eyes, and still the streams of flakes fell tirelessly like grains of sand shaken from some inexhaustible hourglass.

"Beautiful," she murmured, "but it will be cold on the streets, and those windy rooms on the Left Bank will be freezing. Well, there's no help for it. I've promised to go, and Marie and Albert will be expecting me."

She had been given a half-day to herself and was to dine with Monsieur and Madame Remey. Madame Le Maire was to join them for the meal, and the occasion had been planned a fortnight before. For six months now Albert

Remey had tutored Isabella and Louise in all their lessons except the painting, which Henriette continued to supervise. This gave her more time to teach Berthe and Raynald and to chaperon the older girls on their visits to museums and theaters and concerts. This choice of an assistant had been Henriette's when the Duc insisted upon her having help in the schoolroom. It had been a successful arrangement. Young Monsieur Remey had proved himself an excellent teacher—conscientious, dignified, and scholarly. Above all, Henriette knew she could rely on his personal loyalty. Intrigues might be brewing under his nose, and he would never scent them. Like the symbolic monkeys of India he literally saw no evil, heard no evil, and spoke no evil.

The Remeys' gratitude to Henriette might sometimes become tiresome, yet it was sincerely moving. Her thoughtfulness in securing the teaching post for Albert had been for her a natural and spontaneous gesture of friendship. But for these two gentle, devoted souls it had been nothing short of a miracle. Because of her, their life together took on the bloom which only small comforts and security can give. She had made possible those four rooms high up in an old house on the Left Bank that were their pride, rooms which Marie's thrifty domestic gifts had transformed into a quiet sanctuary where Henriette was welcomed with warmth and affection whenever she had leisure to visit them.

"They're like a pair of birds in a nest as Madame Le Maire once said," she thought after one of her first evenings there. "Two birds who can be happy in their wisps of straw and dry crumbs."

She might smile at their naïve ways and their tireless enthusiasm for the smallest details of their humble existence, but for all that she envied them the refuge their love for each other had made. It was good to have such simple, loving friends as these; good to feel that she was in a large part responsible for their happiness. For each one of us there must be some one for whom we assume the rôle of Goddess of Plenty. In Albert and Marie Remey, Henriette found this reassurance.

She sighed as she selected her old blue merino dress instead of a new garnet velvet she had planned to wear. When she had so few occasions to go out alone, it seemed a pity that the weather should have thwarted her.

"Ah, well," she thought, taking out her black beaver

bonnet and heavy cloak, "the Remeys won't notice what I have on my back; and, at least, Madame Le Maire will have no reason to remark on my extravagance."

She did, however, permit herself one luxury. The round seal-skin muff she had bought for herself would not be ruined by snow. She lifted it from its box and sank her hands luxuriously in its warm depths. She laid the sleek darkness against her cheek for a moment. Then she blew lightly on the rich pelt, remembering as she did so how years ago the Sisters in the convent had reproved her for doing that very thing to the fur tippet belonging to one of her mates. They had talked in sad seriousness of this unfortunate love of hers for the vanities of this world. A knitted woolen muffler, they had pointed out, would serve the purpose of protecting her from the elements as well. She smiled now, remembering their grave, sweet faces, remembering also that all the while she had stood listening in dutiful silence, she had been inwardly vowing to own just such a muff as the one she now held.

She seldom went empty-handed to the Remeys, and today as she set off she had all she could do to handle the muff and a large basket of fruit in gay wrappings. Besides this bulky gift she carried a box of nuts and bonbons salvaged from the children's lavish Christmas celebration, and in her bag were handkerchiefs for Marie and Madame Le Maire, embroidered by her own hands in the fine convent stitches she had learned. It was difficult to manage all these articles, but she decided against ringing for help. She had learned in that year and a half not to ask favors of the servants. She saw to it that they performed rigidly all duties connected with the children and the east wing, but, knowing their resentment of her position, she was shrewd enough to give them no cause to complain of her demands. The porter would hail a cab for her, or if he seemed surly and there were no public conveyances to be hired near by, she would walk on till she found one for herself.

"Mademoiselle Deluzy!" She had just reached the corridor leading to the entrance when she heard her name spoken.

Turning quickly, she saw the Duc hurrying down the stairway behind her. He ran down like a boy, two steps at a time, his long cape blowing behind him, his hat and cane under one arm.

"Where are you going so laden down?" he asked as he joined her. "Why not call one of the servants to help you? That basket's much too heavy."

He took it from her, weighing it in his own strong hands.

"Oh"—she smiled—"I'm used to getting along alone. I never like to bother any one on my free afternoons. Please, you shouldn't trouble yourself on my account just as you're going out."

But the Duc continued to hold her basket. He did not hand it over to the footman at the door or to Merville the concierge, who hurried out from the gatehouse to be of assistance. By the waiting carriage he stopped.

"I'll see you and your holiday cargo safely to port." He smiled. "This is no day for you to be out on foot."

In spite of her protests she found herself on the cushioned seat with the Duc beside her. A robe was being spread over their knees. The carriage was partly closed, the top protecting their heads and shoulders from snow, but the robe on their laps soon held miniature drifts in its thick folds. On the dark fur of Henriette's muff the white flakes lay without melting, pointed and delicate as tiny feathered stars.

"You're not cold, Mademoiselle Deluzy?" she heard him asking beside her.

Politely she heard herself responding that she was quite comfortable. Comfortable—what a dull, inadequate word it was for the glow and exhilaration she felt as they swung along the familiar street, made suddenly new and strange by snow and this unexpected adventure! They turned into the narrower channel of the Rue de Marengo and from there into the Rue de Rivoli with its glittering shop windows on one side and the open square and vast walls of the Louvre on the other. Although it was not yet four o'clock gas had been lit in the shops, and the windows of jewelers, modistes, and florists took on a detached, yet magnified brilliance through the falling snow.

"If this keeps up," her companion was saying, "we shall need to get out the sleighs."

"And Paris will have more bells to welcome in the New Year," she answered. "Sleigh bells have a holiday sound, don't you think?"

"Yes, but one needs to hear them in the country, coming from a long way off, then growing nearer. I wish now that we had gone to Melun for the holidays. It will be beautiful there in the snow."

There was a deep stillness on the river as they crossed the Pont-Neuf. The tall old houses on the Left Bank showed dim as specters and the vast bulk of Notre Dame rose on its island like an angular mountain, its peaks softened and indistinct.

"I am afraid," Henriette broke the silence with another apology, "that this is taking you out of your way."

"My way," he repeated. "Well, if you must know, it happens to be yours for this afternoon."

"It's more than generous of you to do me this favor." But he brushed her thanks aside.

"The favor's on my side," he insisted. "I was bored, Mademoiselle Deluzy, horribly bored. The children were off with their grandfather for the afternoon, and Madame expected a visit from the Abbé; besides, she has no taste for snow. I thought I should go mad if I sat on at my desk or by the fire in that house which will never be mine."

She looked up startled by his words and tone. His mouth, she saw, had taken on a bitter curve, and his thick brows were drawn close in a frown.

"But, monsieur"—she tried to pass off those words lightly— "surely you don't mean that! It's natural in the holidays when the children are all at home to feel the place is given over to them and their doings. By next week it will be different."

"I did not mean the children. Thank Heaven for what they bring to the place. But it's Sébastiani, not Praslin. Don't you understand? The old Maréchal owns it. He comes and goes whenever he pleases. At Melun, now, it's different."

He broke off abruptly, and another long silence followed. Not since the autumn night at Melun more than a year ago had he spoken so personally. Scarcely a day had passed in all that time when they had not met and discussed matters that concerned the children intimately. Always he had been considerate, generous, and wise in his judgments, but that windy night of All Hallows Eve and this afternoon driving together through softly streaming snow, it was if he had let the reins slip from his hands and given the dark steeds of bitterness and despair their way. Only for a moment now as on that earlier occasion did she feel the violence of the emotion he kept so coolly in check. Almost instantly he had himself in hand and was speaking to her of other matters in casual tones. But she was not deceived. She was herself so accustomed to repressing her own feelings that she had grown quick in scenting others'.

"Yes," she thought, "he's right. It's not his house as the château is. He needed their money, and they needed his title. He was young, and it must have been an excellent match. But whoever marries for money pays for it in this world."

She remembered that discussion in the schoolroom when Isabella and Louise had explained casually that their Mamma had had the money. And yet it could not always have been like this, cold and perfunctory on his part, passionate and turbulent on that of the Duchesse. They must have loved richly and well once. Were not the children living proof of that? She felt her cheeks flushing at her thoughts, and she caught up her muff and laid it to her face, forgetting the snowflakes that stung her with their sudden chill.

"Look!" she said. "It's like fairyland there among the trees."

They were driving by the nearly deserted Gardens of the Luxembourg. About each tall lamp post the spinning flakes glittered like a swarm of tinsel bees, but beyond the lights mysterious white branches and frosted trunks of trees were only half visible in the dimness.

"Why did you smile just now?" he was asking her. "Surely you can share whatever made you look so pleased."

"You'll think it silly, I'm afraid," she explained, turning her face impulsively towards him. "But ever since we began to drive its bothered me—you and I here in the carriage and the snow falling all round us. I couldn't think why it kept reminding me of something I used to know. And just now I remembered. There was a paperweight on a desk long ago—a little round glass globe with figures and a snow scene inside—"

"I know!" His face broke into a pleased smile that made him look suddenly boyish. "My mother had one. You shake it and the snow whirls out of nowhere in a blinding storm."

"Yes," she agreed with a soft laugh. "That's exactly what I meant. Somehow this doesn't seem like a real snowstorm. It's as if you and I and all Paris were caught fast in a little round globe with the flakes going round and round like frozen stars."

It seemed the most natural thing in the world to share

her fancy with him. Only afterwards, alone in her room with the evening spent and another year rung in by all the clamoring bells of Paris, did she marvel at her lack of self-consciousness.

"Here," she said at last, peering ahead to find the familiar street, "this is the corner. The Remeys live in the court behind. Your horses will never be able to turn in such a narrow place, so let me down here."

He insisted on conducting her himself to the door, the basket still on his arm. The rusty bell echoed in the dark hall, but they waited some minutes before the door was opened. As they stood together on the snowy steps she thanked him once more. Then, hesitantly, she asked if he would come in.

"The Remeys would be so honored," she added. "And you've made him happy by your generosity, you know."

But he shook his head.

"No," he told her. "I've an errand to do before I return. Wish them well, and drink my health if you're making New Year toasts."

He touched the top of a bottle that protruded from the basket and looked up with an amused expression.

"I won't forget, monsieur. Happy New Year."

"Happy New Year to you, Mademoiselle Deluzy. It will be 1843 before we meet again!"

She scarcely felt her feet taking the long uncarpeted flights of stairs. Laden down with gifts as she was, she did not have to pause for breath on any landing. She moved, trancelike, through the dingy halls, wrapped in her own warmth and exhilaration. Vaguely she was aware of her host's eager welcome as she surrendered basket and box into his hands, of her hostess' gentle, sisterly kiss on her cheek, and of Madame Le Maire's thorny greeting from the fireplace where she sat drying her damp skirts.

"*Ciel,* but you look blooming!" the old woman exclaimed after a searching scrutiny. "It's plain you didn't come on foot, or your skirts would be more bedraggled than mine."

"No, I was driven," Henriette admitted. But she did not enlarge on that simple fact and quickly changed the subject. "You'd better unpack that box at once, Marie. The cakes crumble easily, and the bonbons will be damp. Take care how you handle that bottle, Albert. It's not champagne, but even so——"

"A bottle's a bottle these days!" Madame remarked, and spread her dress hem nearer to the grate fire.

"Henriette does look blooming tonight," Marie agreed. "If I didn't know better I'd say you had a touch of rouge on your cheeks, my dear, and your eyes shine so. Doesn't she look a picture, Albert, with the snowflakes still caught in her hair?"

"Yes, yes, indeed," Albert responded dutifully, peering at their guest out of his nearsighted, student's eyes. "This spell of cold certainly seems to agree with you."

"Cold—fiddlesticks!" sniffed Madame. "It's luxury she thrives on. Butter a cat's paws if you want to keep it purring by your fireside."

"Now, madame, for shame to tease her." Marie flew to her friend's defense. "You know how hard Henriette works, and how generous she is to us all!"

But Henriette only laughed at the old woman's sly dig. She was in no mood to take offense and rather relished this joke at her own expense.

"Oh," she admitted, laying aside her wraps and bonnet, "I'm not above enjoying a soft cushion and a saucer of cream when they come my way. I'm not unselfish like you, Marie, or a scholar like Albert who can forget himself in his books. If I'm to work all my life I will, but not for scraps and cast-off clothes and the wages of a kitchen maid."

"Hear, hear!" croaked Madame. "I always said you had more than your share of ambition. But remember, we can't any of us go to heaven in a feather bed."

"No, but we can enjoy it before we get there. Here, madame, I've brought you a little remembrance for the New Year."

The handkerchiefs were presented, and the fruit and sweets unpacked, amid exclamations of pleasure and awe.

"Such oranges, Henriette, and hothouse grapes—big as plums; and marrons and little rum cakes to have with our coffee."

She listened with detached pleasure in their happiness. Her own happiness seemed to have retired to a far place within herself. Secret and rosy and almost suffocating, it warmed her with a glow which the mulled wine Marie and Albert had prepared under Madame's instructions only increased. They drank it by the fire, clinking their china cups and pledging one another's health.

"Madame Le Maire—your good health, and plenty of students in all your rooms."

"Marie and Albert—" Somehow it was impossible to toast them separately, those two who thought and spoke and moved as one.

"And Henriette, your health and good fortune."

She stood holding her cup while they drank with the fire-light edging the familiar outlines of their faces, somehow making them new to her in that moment. Snow drove white against the darkening window panes where the candle flames repeated their orange points. On the tablecloth the fruit was a rich pyramid of color, the tin foil wrapping the bonbons she had brought was turned to silver.

"Shall we make one more toast?" she heard her voice saying quietly. "We've drunk to one another, but there's some one else whose health I'd like to propose." Their faces grew curious as she hurried on. She could not forget the favor asked of her on the snowy steps an hour ago. "The Duc de Praslin is responsible for your work, Albert, and for mine. I think we should wish him and his household well before our cups are empty."

"Of course, Henriette." Albert raised his wine. "He's been very generous to us. May he have health and prosperity, and may we continue to find favor in the school-room."

She had planned to word the toast herself, and she would have said happiness instead of prosperity. But no matter, she had kept her promise to him, though no doubt he had not meant his request to be taken literally. It was only after their cups had been drained that Madame Le Maire spoke her usual last word from the fireside.

"It's a queer thing you drink to the Duc and not to the Duchesse as well."

Henriette felt grateful that for once Albert Remey answered for her.

"It may seem queer to you, Madame Le Maire, but Henriette and I both know whom we serve. I don't wish the Duchesse any ill will, mind you, but if we depended on her for our bread and butter we'd be begging crumbs of the sparrows in the Gardens."

"He must be a remarkable man to stir such devotion in you both," the old woman persisted. "I did not guess you were on such intimate terms."

"I'd hardly say intimate," Remey went on, "though I naturally see less of him than Henriette. He makes few comments except where the interests of his children are concerned. A rather cold man, I should say, shouldn't you, Henriette?"

"Perhaps 'reserved' describes him better." She spoke casually and avoided the old woman's eyes. "But he can be cold, yes."

Madame did not drop the subject, though Albert had gone to the kitchen to help Marie serve dinner.

"Handsome, too, I've heard," she observed. "Cold, you both say. Well, don't be taken in by that. There's plenty of fire in the coldest flint!"

Henriette was glad when they were summoned to the steaming tureen of bouillabaisse whose fragrance filled the room. Now Marie, flushed from the fire and her supreme domestic efforts, became the center. She beamed at their words; and her small, plain face grew radiant with loving hospitality as she watched the food disappear.

"You'll spoil me," she told them shyly. "It would have been better if we could have afforded lobster in place of shrimps, and perhaps I put in a pinch too much of saffron."

The roast duck with bursting apple stuffing, the vegetables and coffee—all were praised in turn while the candles burned in four clear points of light, one for each face at the table; and the snow made faint clickings at the window panes. They sat on and on, eating Henriette's fruit and bonbons, cracking walnuts and talking now of the world in general and now of themselves in particular.

Madame Le Maire complained of business. Trade was dull with the court still in mourning for the death of the young Duc d'Orléans. She hoped the talked-of visit from Victoria and Albert to Louis Philippe would materialize next spring or summer. Not that she expected royal guests from across the Channel to fill her rooms in the Rue du Harlay, but it might help. Still, with taxes and the cost of food steadily mounting she would be lucky not to be out of pocket, let alone making any profit.

Henriette and Albert exchanged furtive smiles. They were familiar with Madame's complaints, and they both knew from experience her capacity for paring every franc and sou.

Under Marie's urging Albert admitted that he had been

asked to contribute an article on the Greek philosophers to
a volume in preparation for elementary students. The re-
muneration would be small, but it would be paid upon delivery of his manuscript, and if by working at night he could
finish it by Easter he and Marie might hope for a short holiday together on the coast of Brittany or even in England.
He was anxious to examine some material in the British
Museum.

Presently they spoke of books. Marie opened her soft
eyes wide in astonishment that Henriette should have read
the latest work of the notorious Madame George Sand.

*"Un Hiver à Majorque."* All about her love affair with
the popular composer Chopin. Was it really as shocking as
people said?

"Not particularly, Marie. Daring, one might call it, but
I must confess parts of it seemed dull to me."

Then she was telling them of something else she had read
—a remarkable story she had come across in a recent peri-
odical. It was a translation, she believed, from the pen of
some obscure American writer whose name she had already
forgotten. "The Murders in the Rue Morgue," it was called,
and she had almost missed it because she always shunned
accounts of murder and violence. But this one—well, it was
extraordinary and had kept her broad awake till daylight.

"Really, Albert," she advised, "you should read it. The
way the crimes are detected, and the amazing deductions,
would hold even your academic mind spellbound."

But Monsieur Remey shook his head. Such tales of ghou-
lish fiction were not for him. For a woman Henriette possessed the most stimulating mind he had ever met. It was a
pity to have her waste it on such worthless literature. Still,
why argue with her on New Year's Eve on so trivial a matter? For all her intelligence, she was a woman and could
never hope to go far in lines of scholarship.

Home again through the snow in a hackney coach. It had
been secured with difficulty, and the driver had asked an
outrageous price. But it was New Year's Eve, and any sort
of vehicle brought a premium. Henriette might have hesitated, but tonight she felt above haggling over francs. A mild
recklessness overcame her economical scruples. She felt
warm and in complete accord with the world as she helped
Madame Le Maire in beside her.

"I'll leave you at your door," she assured her. "No, it's

only a little out of my way, and you're not to go floundering about on such a night."

"Well, since you're set on being extravagant I suppose I may as well profit by it. You're generous, Henriette. Yes, I'll say that for you."

Henriette smiled under cover of the darkness. Madame so seldom paid compliments that when she did so her manner became even more grudging and reluctant. She could not help admiring the old woman's spirit. She needed it to cling tenaciously as she did to the small niche she had made for herself. Bargaining and scrimping, week in, week out, to keep her independence in a world of dependent women, Henriette understood her companion because of the stubborn will to succeed which was probably the only trait they shared in common.

"Perhaps," she thought as their carriage crawled along on its difficult course through the snowy streets, "I shall be old and alone as she some day."

But the thought did not alarm or sadden her because she did not believe it. Impossible at thirty, with the blood warm in one's veins and with a new year waiting to be explored; impossible to believe in age and loneliness and death. Other people grew querulous and stiff-jointed and gray; other people died and were forgotten. But somehow you were the exception. You would stay hale and hopeful by sheer force of will.

She was aware that Madame was speaking beside her. Yes, she agreed, it had been a very pleasant evening. The Remeys certainly made delightful hosts, and she was glad to see them so happy. She hoped the article Albert had been commissioned to write would be the first of many.

"They'll always get along somehow," Madame Le Maire said. "You see they believe in ravens."

"In ravens, madame?"

"Yes, when you don't know where to find your month's rent or tonight's dinner, the ravens mysteriously provide. You acted as one when you put that tutoring his way. It's a great gift, having faith in ravens, for they never desert you if you really believe in them. Unfortunately they always knew I was skeptical."

Henriette laughed.

"I've never believed in them either, now I think of it."

"No, you're not the sort to. Ravens like helpless, gentle

people like Albert and Marie. You're much too independent, but you'll get on. Oh, you'll get on in the world. I saw that before we'd exchanged two words."

The driver pulled his horse up sharp and shouted at another carriage which blocked the way into the Rue du Harlay. When the shouts and confusion were over and they moved on, Madame Le Maire began gathering up her belongings, continuing to talk as she did so.

"I've watched plenty of young people come and go. Some of them had looks, and some had brains, and some had both and didn't know how to make the most of either. But you've got what none of them had, and it won't wear out and leave you like a pink and white complexion or a graceful figure." She stooped to find her umbrella on the floor, while Henriette waited to hear final judgment pronounced. "You're like yeast. Put you anywhere and you'll rise to the top. They can't keep you at the bottom, and you couldn't stay there if you wanted to. Well, Happy New Year, whatever it brings to all of us!"

"I'm not sure whether she meant that for praise or not," Henriette thought as she drove on alone, "and I'm not at all sure I like being compared to yeast."

There was only the under porter at Number 55 to return her Happy New Year wishes when she reached the Rue du Faubourg-Saint-Honoré at half past eleven. If the evening had not been stormy she would have been tempted to prolong her drive until the hour struck, but as it was she knew she should be thankful to be safely back in her own apartment. There were worse things than to welcome the New Year in alone.

She turned up the lamp and stared about the little sitting room which now seemed as much a part of her as the gloves she slipped from her hands. Its soft curtains had been drawn, and the fire laid ready for lighting. Potted begonias bloomed in delicate rose, and ivy trailed glossy greenness from a shelf below the window. In the bedroom beyond she could see that the covers of her bed had been turned back. The mirror's curves and her brushes and stoppered bottles gleamed on the bureau below. She thought of the bleak walls and shabby furnishings of that other room in the Needle's Eye, and was well content as she bent to light the fire. This was luxury, and she had earned it for herself. She would never go back to narrow iron bedsteads, to cracked china and dim, distorted-looking glasses hung under sloping eaves.

A knock at the door startled her from her reverie. She answered it, expecting to see Maxine or one of the other maids, and was surprised to find the Duc's valet, standing there. She accepted a small box which he held out to her on a silver tray, and turned back with it to the fire.

There was no mark on the wrappings, though the box bore the name of an expensive shop she had often passed in the Rue de Rivoli. Wonderingly her fingers explored the cotton and felt an object heavy and smooth and round. She had it in her hand at last—a paperweight of clear glass with a little red-cloaked figure inside. At her touch a miniature storm of white flakes rose and whirled about the tiny human replica. She stared fascinated till the snow stopped spinning. Then she set it down on the table and moved to the window. No need to search in the box for the card she knew she would not find.

It was midnight: the first solemn strokes were sounding, from her own clock and others in the great house, from still others throughout Paris. She pushed back the curtains and pressed her flushed cheek to the cold pane. Another year, and all the bells hailing it with their rich metallic din. She knew the clear, musical tones of Saint Roch, swelling near by, and she believed she could distinguish the distant notes of others—even of Notre Dame from its island in the Seine. Such old bells. God only knew how many other years they had welcomed for long dead listeners to hear. And they would go on and on ringing with the same clear solemnity when she was no longer there to listen, to wonder what this New Year would bring in its procession of untried nights and days.

She felt tears gathering in her eyes, and her heart set up an unreasoning beating which she had no power to quiet. She was suddenly afraid of her own heart. It had never betrayed her like this before. Why was she standing there happy and sad, full of questions like a frightened child? But she found no answer. It is better not to ask questions of the heart.

## chapter eleven

THE SPRING OF 1844 FLOWED INTO SUMMER ON CLOUDS of bloom. At Vaux the cherry and peach trees had scarcely flung their last petals to earth and air before the apple orchards put on miraculous white and rose, and their sweetness filled the dark with such subtle fragrance that Henriette woke night after night to a new unrest.

Beauty like this was too much to be borne alone, she thought, and she was glad when heavy rain swept the apple trees bare in an afternoon. Nature mocked her on every hand with its burden of prodigality. She could not shut her eyes to this promise of budding fruitfulness all about her. Even the children seemed aware of the significance. They were continually asking questions that stabbed her anew as she tried to make plausible answers.

"Mademoiselle, will every blossom turn into an apple?"

"No, Berthe, not every one."

"Why not?"

"Well, their branches would break under such a load, and there would not be barrels or cellars big enough to hold them all if every flower were to bear fruit.".

"But who decides, mademoiselle? Who says which shall turn into apples?"

"God knows," thought Henriette, watching Berthe and Raynald skipping before her as gay with spring and new grass as the young lambs in the sheepfold. "God knows the answer to that question!"

And then it was summer again with long, warm days of dappled sunlight on lawns and in the beechwoods. Roses filled the great rooms with sweetness, and the countryside was brilliant with the flames of poppies in fields of wheat. The three Praslin daughters returned from the convent, and the two elder sons and their tutor arrived; but the Duchesse lingered in Paris, to Henriette's relief. The Duc had a way of appearing without warning, for a day or a week, and as usual his coming brought an air of holiday to the entire household.

His old mother had taken up residence in one of the wings of the château, and Henriette found her presence comforting. Besides being an indulgent and devoted grandmother she was a woman of remarkable character—gentle but firm, and with unusual simplicity for one of her position. Henriette came to enjoy the daily visits to her rooms, and before many weeks a genuine attachment had developed between these two women of such varying ages and backgrounds.

Their friendship seemed to please the Duc, and often on his visits he joined them in his mother's apartments. Since that snowy drive on New Year's Eve Henriette had had few opportunities to be alone with him. He took his meals with the children and was likely to turn up in nursery or schoolroom at any time of day without warning. But he seemed absorbed and withdrawn and seldom expressed himself on any subject that did not concern their welfare. Yet always when Henriette saw his height and fairness dominating the room she felt a new animation. Between the visits she found herself storing up remarks of the children, or even observations of her own to tell him at his next appearance. It was reward enough to hear his deep laugh or to see his face light up in pleased response. More and more the stimulation of a masculine audience charmed her; more and more she felt restless and depressed when she was thrown back upon her own resources. At first she would not admit the change. She had always been happy in her independence and self-sufficiency. What had come over her so insidiously? Why was she always straining her ears for the tread of a man's foot on the threshold, for the sound of a deep, resonant voice speaking her name?

"My dear son holds you in high regard," the dowager Duchesse told her more than once. "It was a fortunate day indeed for us all when you came into the household."

As she murmured a grateful reply, Henriette could not help a pang that the words sounded so impersonal. "High regard" certainly should be all a governess could ask, and yet she asked for something less formal.

"Fool," she told herself as she recalled them on those mornings when she woke early and lay fearful of her own crowding thoughts while birds sang with maddening cheerfulness in the branches of the Praslin oaks outside her windows. "Fool, what more do you want?"

All went peacefully and well through the month of June; and even when the Duchesse arrived she seemed less irritable, more calm and pleasant in her dealings with the children.

"She has accepted me at last," Henriette decided. "Perhaps she is happier with him now, and I need no longer walk on eggshells."

But it was a short-lived hope, and presently the château rocked to echoes of dissension. The Duchesse, who had begun by joining the group about the dining-room table in the children's wing, rose abruptly from her place one morning and refused to return. When Henriette brought the two younger ones to their mother's salon at tea time they found her red-eyed and querulous on her sofa. She embraced Raynald with such vehemence that the child struggled to be free and ran to the protection of Mademoiselle. When Berthe, reluctantly following instructions, presented her mother a bouquet of wild flowers, the Duchesse roused herself to a slight show of interest and drew the little girl close.

"For you, Mamma," piped Berthe dutifully, turning her eyes towards Henriette for approval.

"Did you gather them for me all by yourself, my Berthe?"

"Well, it was Mademoiselle's idea. Mademoiselle knows how to fix flowers better than Félix even, doesn't she, Mamma?"

The Duchesse laid the bouquet aside without further enthusiasm, and when the three took their leave half an hour later the delicate ferns and blue chicory were already drooping for lack of water.

"Why doesn't Mamma like you, mademoiselle?" Berthe asked suddenly as they neared the schoolroom.

"Yes," Raynald chimed in before she could answer. "Why doesn't she?"

"Oh, you're wrong about that." Henriette tried to pass off the questions lightly. "Your Mamma is often ill and tired, and perhaps that makes her seem different from other people."

"But I like you when I'm ill and tired," persisted Raynald. "I like you even more if I'm sick."

She bent down and gathered his soft dark head into the crook of her arm. He was growing tall and spindling for his age, but still he turned to her with the same affection of the frail child she had nursed through that dread siege of diphtheria.

"It's nicer when just you and Papa are here." Berthe went on pronouncing judgment in her firm nine-year voice. "I wish she wouldn't go to the fête at Melun."

Of late there had been much talk of the coming festival of Saint Ambrose, an event which meant much to the whole countryside since the old Roman saint was the special patron of the village and neighboring hamlets. The festival was familiar to the older Praslins, but this year Berthe and Raynald had been given permission to attend. There would be services in the old stone church and later merrymaking in the village with traveling shows and gayly decked booths where all manner of knickknacks might be bought. Henriette had heard nothing for weeks past but the wonders in store for them on Saint Ambrose's fête day.

Fortunately the weather stayed cloudless and fine, though so warm that the Duc shook his head over his coffee and said the horses would be in a lather before they were halfway to the village, and he himself would prefer to spend the day swimming in the river with his boys. But no festival would be complete without Praslins in attendance. He would ride ahead with the older boys on horseback and the landau and barouche would be ready for the rest at eleven o'clock.

"Will Madame la Duchesse attend?" Henriette asked as he rose to go.

"Most certainly. The Duchesse has missed only one celebration since the year we were married. That was the summer after Raynald's birth, when she was too ill to attend."

Henriette felt pleased with her reflection in the glass as she tied the ribbons of her leghorn bonnet under her chin. Flat green leaves wreathed the crown and were stitched under the brim. They gave a greenish reflection to her eyes and brought out the sheen of her chestnut hair. Her dress of gray lawn looked cool and crisp with its wide sash and narrower bands of green grosgrain. Hoops, she reflected, were becoming larger and larger, but she dared not go too far in that direction. Governesses were taking up too much room as it was. She dabbed cologne on her handkerchief and stepped out to join the children. They looked like delightful human versions of butterflies, she thought, in their billowing dotted Swiss muslins and sashes of blue and pink and mauve; and Raynald was resplendent in nankeen trousers and coat with scarlet braid.

"How fine you look!" she exclaimed. "Be careful of those

skirts getting in and out of the carriage. You especially, Louise, remember to smooth the folds as you sit down. Stand still, Berthe, while I tighten your sash. Now, my dears"—she faced them with firmness as they trooped about her towards the door—"whatever your Mamma wishes about seating in the carriages, you must do as she says. No protests, please, you understand."

"Yes, mademoiselle," they chorused obediently.

But Raynald kept tight hold of her hand as they descended the stairs. She sighed and hoped they would all keep their promises. Sometimes devotion made difficulties, and she wanted the day to go well.

The carriages were waiting, horses and harnesses decked with green garlands and wild flowers in honor of the day. These already drooped in the intensity of the sun. Even at eleven in the morning the heat was oppressive. Henriette opened her small parasol and tried to keep Raynald under its shade. She dreaded the long drive in the dust and glare for him and the undue excitement of crowds and fair booths. There was a long wait before the Duchesse appeared, large and impressive in lilac silk. Henriette did not envy her the mammoth hoop skirts swelling in fashionable fullness. She was thankful not to be carrying such a decorative load in the heat and close quarters of the carriages. The Duchesse, she noticed was so tightly laced that she moved with discomfort. Her usually pale face was suffused with warmth, and beads of moisture showed on her brow and along her upper lip.

"Ah, mademoiselle!" She paused by the open landau, her face drawing into an annoyed frown. "I did not think you were planning to go with us. Perhaps you did not know that this is a church festival?"

Henriette realized from the tone that this was to be one of the Duchesse's difficult days. She must be careful not to give offense, even though the remark was humiliating before the children and coachmen.

"Pardon, madame," she spoke quietly. "I understood that I was to drive with the children in one carriage, but naturally I will not intrude in the church service. If you wish I can wait with the horses till it's time to return."

She hoped her irony was not lost on the other woman.

"That's impossible," snapped the Duchesse, allowing herself to be helped into the seat. "But, no matter, since I wasn't consulted about plans, you may as well get in." She waved towards the other carriage and singled out the children she wished to have with her. "Raynald," she called, "there's room for you on the seat opposite, only take care not to put your boots in my lap. Berthe, Louise, Isabella and Marie, get in the other carriage."

Raynald clung tightly to Henriette's hand; and his mother spoke more sharply, pointing to the narrow seat behind the driver's box.

"Madame"—Henriette stepped quickly to the carriage —"if you'll let me make a suggestion, riding backwards never agrees with Raynald. You know his delicate stomach, and in all this heat—perhaps Berthe or one of the others could sit there instead."

"Nonsense, mademoiselle, I know how to plan for my children. Jean, lift Monsieur Raynald to the seat, and let's have no more delays and discussions."

There was nothing more to be said. Henriette saw a struggling small boy hoisted to the seat and heard his protests as the carriage rolled ahead of theirs out of the long driveway. It had not been an auspicious beginning for the feast day of Saint Ambrose.

The drive, which usually delighted her with its vistas of river and wood, of farms and fields of ripening grain, seemed endless to her that morning. She scarcely heard the girls' chatter as their carriage followed behind the dusty cloud the other stirred before them. When they drew up by the little church she sent her charges to join the rest while she found a shady spot under a tree at the edge of the enclosure. She was glad to sink down on an old stone bench, to be alone and cool off in body and spirit.

Noon Mass had already begun. She could hear the faint ringing of the bell; the chanting of voices and responses coming from the open doors and windows, all dim and far removed as if they sounded from the bottom of the sea, like that sunken city of legend. If sailors heard that ringing of lost bells under leagues of salt water, they crossed themselves and put back for the safety of shore. Yes, that was the story they told along the coasts of England and Brittany. Perhaps she, too, was being warned all these miles inland.

But she shook herself free of such thoughts. The heat and Madame's unreasonableness were enough to set her nerves on edge. She must try to relax and prepare herself for the ordeal of the traveling shows and booths which she could see had already appeared like mushrooms on the village square. She untied her bonnet ribbons and leaned back, closing her eyes against the glare. But she opened them again almost instantly at a sound of footsteps.

The Duc was hurrying from the church with Raynald in his arms. One look at the child's limp figure told her the story. She sprang up and hurried towards them.

"Lay him flat, monsieur, here on the grass. I know what to do for him. Here, *chéri,* let mademoiselle help you. You'll be better soon."

"I saw him growing paler and paler in there," she heard the Duc saying while she loosened the child's coat and steadied his head through the nausea. "There was nothing to do but get him out quickly. What's come over him since breakfast? He seemed well enough then."

"I was afraid of this," she explained. "The drive was very hot and dusty, and then riding backwards always upsets him. Now, monsieur, if you'll lend me your handkerchief we'll make him more comfortable. Luckily I brought some cologne in my bag."

"But he shouldn't have been allowed to ride backwards. Wasn't there room enough on the other seat?"

"In our carriage, yes, but his mother wished him with her. I tried to tell her it would disagree with him. The excitement of the day hasn't helped either. There, Raynald, doesn't that smell nice? You needn't try to move. Just lie still with your head on my lap."

The Duc said nothing more, but turned quickly in the direction of the village inn. Henriette waited with the child, hoping that Mass would not be over till his father's return. Presently the carriage drew up, and Raynald was being carried out to it. He leaned limply against her, too sick to protest at leaving the feast day celebration.

"I'll manage now, monsieur," Henriette said as the Duc stood uncertainly by the steps. "There's no need to spoil the others' day because of this."

"Well"—he still hesitated, frowning and drumming impatient fingers on the carriage door—"I suppose that's the best plan. The Duchesse and I have always made it a point to appear at this festival, and I shouldn't want the villagers to think anything was amiss."

He gave an order to the coachman to return and stood watching their carriage roll away.

Thinking over his words on the hot drive back to the château, Henriette tried to decide what lay behind them. He had been reluctant to stay. That was plain. But he and the Duchesse must be seen together by all the countryside, ostensibly a devoted husband and wife with their children about them.

"On the feast day of Saint Ambrose they celebrated Mass and went about the village arm in arm, dispensing gifts and going from stall to stall."

That was what the villagers would tell one another afterwards. They would remark on the Duc's strength and good looks and on the Duchesse's pious generosity. Henriette gave a rather wry smile and tilted her parasol to keep the sun out of Raynald's eyes.

Late that afternoon, when the sun laid long golden shafts on the brilliant green of the lawns and the oaks rose tall from their own dark shadows, when a light wind brought refreshing coolness, Henriette went out to walk on the broad terrace. Raynald had fallen into exhausted sleep, and the place was deserted save for the Duc's mother in her wing of the château. Henriette would have liked to pay a call upon the kind old lady, but she feared to alarm her by this early return from the village. So she walked alone, watching the surrounding woods grow shadowy, hearing the birds call with small, watery cries above the plashing of the fountains. She tried to give herself to the greenness and peace about her. But she felt tired. Her head ached from the sultry atmosphere and the long drives, and she dreaded the return of the family.

They were upon her before she realized that the carriages had turned into the drive, the two older boys on horseback beside their father.

"Mademoiselle, wait, mademoiselle!" The girls' voices shrilled above the carriage wheels and horses' hoofs on the gravel. They were out in a swirl of muslin, hurrying to reach her with outstretched hands. Henriette glanced towards the carriages and saw a heavy figure in mauve being helped down. Something about that distant shape filled her with misgivings. Even so far off she felt that the heaviness was not all physical. She hoped the Duchesse would go in at once, but instead she saw her stand quite still, watching the rush of white-clad girls who sped away from her without a single backward glance.

"Yes, Berthe, it's a beautiful handkerchief. Did you really buy it for me at the Fair? Louise, what a pretty chain! And a whistle and knife for Raynald—that will make up to him for missing it."

She heard her voice responding to them, but all the time her ears were strained for something else. She dared not lift her eyes again to the driveway and that other figure.

*"Mon Dieu,"* she thought, "will this day never be over?"

She and the group of chattering girls were halfway up the long staircase when a sound made them all stop short and draw close in a startled group. It rose from below, a terrible mingling of sobs and laughter. Then broken, hysterical words.

"No, no, don't touch me, Theo! Leave me alone. I'm used to that. I've had enough. You'll see I meant what I said!"

Somehow Henriette found herself and the children upstairs in the familiar quiet of the schoolroom. Berthe clung fast to her skirts; and the older girls turned large, frightened eyes upon her for reassurance. Her hands shook as she laid their gifts on the table, though she managed to keep her voice steady and matter-of-fact.

"Now, my dears," she heard it saying, "this has been a long, hot day for you all. Better go to your rooms and make yourselves fresh and tidy. Then we'll have time to read another chapter in our book before supper."

"But, mademoiselle, I'd rather stay here with you, please."

"Mademoiselle, did you hear just now? Mamma was very strange all this afternoon, and she wouldn't speak to us on the way home."

"Well, Isabella, she was probably tired, nothing more."

"Oh, but it was much more! And I heard her tell Papa that she would ki—"

"Hush!" Henriette laid quick fingers to the quivering young lips. "Whatever she may have said, she didn't mean you to hear. Now, go to your rooms, all of you, at once."

Supper was a strangely quiet meal. Instead of eager voices interrupting one another with accounts of the fête day, the girls sat subdued and large-eyed round the table. Even when Henriette opened a box of sweetmeats as an unusual treat, their enthusiasm was perfunctory. She found herself listening unconsciously for sounds beyond the children's quarters.

She knew he would come, but when he did she could

hardly lift her eyes to meet his.

"What long faces here!" He went through the motions of a smile and greetings, pinching Isabella's cheeks and drawing Louise to him with a pretense of gayety. But Henriette saw that his face was grave in spite of the forced smile. She saw, too, that he held his right arm rigid and kept that hand thrust into the front of his coat.

"Mamma has gone to bed with one of her migraine headaches." He made light of the anxious questions. "The heat and crowds were too much for her. She sends you her good night."

After the younger ones had left for bed, Henriette sent the two older sisters into the adjoining room to practice piano and penmanship. She and he were alone at last, though the precise notes of a minuet executed by Isabella's painstaking fingers sounded above their words. The long blue twilight of early summer filled the room, making the Duc's face seem unnaturally pale and strained.

"Oh, monsieur!" She sank down on the window seat and leaned toward him. Their faces were on a level though the table separated them. "Tell me the truth. She did not—"

"No." He shook his head wearily. "She did not harm herself. I don't know how much you heard, but, thank God, you got the children out of the way."

His voice was low and almost monotonous as he told her of the Duchesse's attempt to kill herself; of the Arabian dagger kept as a curio in the drawing-room which she had caught up in her frenzy. Somehow he had managed to gain possession of it. Listening to his brief words, it seemed to her that he dared not let himself speak fully of the tragedy he had so lately averted.

"What has happened to you, monsieur?" She pointed to the hand he still held inside his coat. Her voice, also, was low, but the thumping notes of the piano could not cover its tense concern. "Why do you keep your hand so?"

"Oh, that! It's nothing, but I did not want to frighten the children."

Reluctantly he drew out his hand. She saw that it was bandaged and that a dark stain had oozed through the lint. Her own hand shook as she laid it gently on his. The gesture had been instinctive; only when she felt that live heat under her cold fingers did she realize her rashness.

"Your hand is throbbing and feverishly hot." She wondered as she spoke if he had felt her tremble. "You're sure it's not serious?"

"Only a cut in the palm, but that old blade was sharper than I thought."

He made no move to take his hand away, and she seemed to have lost the power to lift hers. How long they might have stayed so, she did not know; but the piano came to an abrupt stop in the next room, and Henriette roused herself.

"Try the polonaise now, Isabella," she called. "It's not time to stop yet."

When the notes began again, Henriette folded her own hands tightly in her lap before she turned back to the Duc.

"Monsieur," she began, "if anything I said or did was the cause you mustn't try to spare my feelings."

"The cause goes deeper than anything you could have said or done." He sighed and brushed a moist lock of hair from his forehead. "It always comes back to me."

She did not offer more words, but sat quietly, waiting for him to go on.

"I shouldn't have spoken as I did. But, Mademoiselle Deluzy, when I saw the boy suffer because of her petty jealousy I couldn't keep silence; and I said—Well, I hardly know what I said. If it had been one of the other children, not Raynald —but his frailness has always been a reproach to me. I've tried to make up to him for what I hope he will never know—"

He broke off, and she was wise enough to keep silence. But her mind caught at his words. The hesitant, blurred phrases became suddenly open admissions to her now. Raynald, she guessed, must stand for his father as the living symbol of a love that had been revived briefly from cold embers. Almost, she felt, that youngest child had been a last defiant gesture of the Duchesse to prove that she still had power to breathe those embers into flame. So plain was it all to her in that moment that she seemed to see the other woman blowing frantically upon an actual fire. No use to do that now, to stir dead ashes tirelessly day and night. Didn't she know, when love was burned out, it could never be rekindled in such a fashion?

"Monsieur"—she spoke at last with quiet directness— "what's to be done? Things cannot go on this way—for her, for you, for me, or for the children."

A helpless gesture was the only answer.

"It's better that I should go," she persisted. "Perhaps if I leave now she will be happier. You may even become reconciled in time."

"That's impossible!" He roused himself from his absorption, and his voice had the old authoritative note. "What is dead and done can't be brought to life. I'm not pretending to be above reproach. I do not play the martyr. I leave all that to her. If it gives her any comfort to seem the pious, injured wife, I'm not interferring. But the children—they're another matter. They're alive, and I can't make them suffer for what is no fault of theirs. For their sakes and for mine you must not talk of leaving."

"There's an old saying I heard in my childhood," she told him, "and I've been remembering it tonight. To cause trouble between man and wife is like coming between the bark and the tree."

He smiled, but there was a wry twist to his lips.

"When the bark and the tree are no longer one, Mademoiselle Deluzy, when they are miles apart, your saying has no meaning."

"Well, monsieur, I don't pretend to know your heart, or Madame's; but I know she hates me, and the children know it, and sooner or later there will be more tragedy like this that so nearly happened today."

"Even so I am asking you to stay. If you saw some one drowning, wouldn't you reach out a hand to help? Wouldn't you try to free an animal caught in a trap? Well, then remember that I am trapped in a snare of my own making— at least I've had a share in it; and the more I struggle, the tighter it closes round me. You may see me moving freely about, but don't be deceived. I'm in hell, whether you believe in such a place or not."

"Oh, please!" She was moved by his quiet intensity. "What can I say when you speak such words? I only know she loves you, and when she tortures you and others it's because she must be goaded by her terrible need of you. Being a woman, too, I can understand that, though I cannot understand these shocking exhibitions—"

She broke off, fearful that she had gone too far.

"You're right, Mademoiselle Deluzy. Love turned back on itself becomes a disease that corrupts all it touches. I know too well, too well." Wearily he let his head rest in his hands, and the bandage showed white in the gathering dimness of the room. "But I hope you will never understand what is it to be slowly smothered by a love one is no longer capable of returning."

"I shouldn't have presumed to speak of love at all," she apologized. "I've no right, and I ask you to forget it."

"No, don't ask that because it will help if I can remember your sympathy for my plight. Today, when this nightmare was over, I was afraid to be alone. I came here as I have come before when it seemed that I couldn't face the future, not even for another hour."

Though he did not raise his face from his hands, the intimacy, the appeal in his words made her heart set up a wild beating. She dared not trust herself to speak, and presently he went on.

"It seems a little thing to ask for peace in my home. But instead I stand like a bull in a ring, badgered by darts that prick him to fury. Some day one goes in too deep, and then the blood is up. I live in dread of that day."

He rose slowly to his feet, and his great height and strength, his physical presence took possession of the place. She did not herself rise. Her knees felt too weak, and her pulses still throbbed. She sat staring up at him as he stood staring down at her.

"Well," he said at last, "now you know."

"What one knows, it is useful sometimes to forget, monsieur."

Still he loomed above her.

"You haven't said whether you will stay. But you will, won't you? You aren't going to deny me and the children the only sanctuary we have?"

"You make it very hard to say no," she heard her voice answering. "But there are some things in this world its useless to fight against, and one is another woman's jealousy. God knows I've done nothing to earn it except to win the children's devotion and your—your confidence in me. But that's an unpardonable sin in her eyes, and she will never forgive me. If I stay because you ask it—"

"I am asking it of you. You have many gifts, Mademoiselle Deluzy, but none that I admire so much as your courage to face issues."

"It takes courage to live by one's wits. It teaches one to be practical. I'm trying my best to be practical now, though, you make it difficult."

He saw that she was weakening, and he pressed her in her own words. "Let's be practical then," he urged. "There is only one reason to make you go, and there are ten reasons to keep you here."

"Ten reasons?"

"Yes, Mademoiselle Deluzy, nine young Praslins and their father. Shall I count them on my fingers for you?"

He smiled, and she smiled back. But, for all that, their voices remained grave.

"No, monsieur, you needn't trouble to do that." Then, without hesitation, she went on, her voice low and more serious than before. "You have asked this of me, and that is reason enough. If you had tried to bribe or drive a bargain with me I shouldn't have yielded against my better judgment."

He was touched by her response. She knew that even before he spoke.

"We don't drive bargains after we've opened our hearts," he told her. "And remember, to be beloved is above all bargains. Good night, Mademoiselle Deluzy."

He did not wait for her reply, but turned to go to his daughters in the next room. On the threshold he paused and Henriette saw him lift his injured hand and slip it awkwardly into his coat again. The gesture went to her heart.

## chapter twelve

OUTWARDLY NOTHING WAS CHANGED. THE LONG BRIGHT days of summer slid on into autumn. Lessons continued with the regularity of clockwork. The Duc traveled to Paris at intervals and returned, always well groomed and debonair, always thoughtful and generous towards his children, and considerate of their governess. The Duchesse remained aloof from the activities of nursery and schoolroom, making few of those disastrous advances to force the affections of her offspring. More and more she withdrew into herself, and her full face took on a sultry expression of martyrdom that Henriette found irritating, but less difficult than the old unrestrained outbursts.

But Henriette knew herself to be changed. A cycle of her life was over as surely as if she had shed forever some gray, confining chrysalis of youth. It had begun on a spring morning three years before when she had first crossed the threshold of Number 55, Rue du Faubourg-Saint-Honoré, to take her orders, not from a pale, petulant woman on a chaise longue, but from the tall man in a dressing gown who stood beside the fireplace, and it had ended in that twilight schoolroom on the feast day of Saint Ambrose. Since that talk she could never be the same. She only marveled, as she stared at her face in the mirror, that she could find no tangible marks of her new maturity.

She had no explanation to offer to herself, for she had lost the ability to analyze her own feelings. Always before, her mind and heart had been kept as tidy and well ordered as her bureau drawers, the contents carefully sorted and useless or disturbing souvenirs ruthlessly discarded. Now she acknowledged her powerlessness to bring order out of inner confusion. In the year 1844 a young woman of her background and moral standards would not have confessed to interest in a married man; much less would she have dared to admit even the possibility of such love. Henriette did not admit it now. Knowing herself to be an acknowledged spinster of nearly thirty-two years, she felt humble and ignorant upon the subject of love. And it was not natural for her to be either humble or ignorant on any subject. She had spoken truthfully in telling the Duc that life had taught her to be practical. She was trying her best to be practical now, even against this strange new restlessness and elation that possessed her. She felt proud that he had turned to her in his extremity—this man who of all his kind on earth could never be hers. But pride could not completely account for the change in her, for shifting moods of unreasoning despair and sheer, inexplicable delight. Once she had been able to think of the past, painful though much of its lonely striving had been; she had also been able to think ahead, to plan for a future that she would make secure through her own efforts. Now she could not concentrate on past or future. Only the present seemed to count in those timeless garments of days and nights which she put on and off like one walking in sleep.

"But this cannot be love," she reasoned with herself sometimes, and she really believed what she said.

Love was something altogether different if one could go by romantic novels and certain poems of Lord Byron not approved as reading for young ladies. Love couldn't be this urgent unrest, this sense of a volcano about to erupt common sense into fragments. It couldn't be this asking for nothing beyond the quick response of a smile, of a look or words that implied complete understanding, of a jest that had no humor except when shared with the one other person who held the key to its meaning. Love, she was certain, asked much more than this which seemed to be all that mattered to her of late. One ought to feel exalted by love, lifted high above oneself and one's surroundings. Yet here she was, if anything, more acutely aware of every smallest detail that concerned herself and those about her. Why think of love at all? Certainly in that tense, troubled conversation which she returned to again and again she could not find any allusion the Duc had made to it that had not been bitter, except just at the last. "To be beloved," he had said, "is above all bargains." And that might mean so much or so little. Probably, she decided, he was thinking of the children and their devotion to her. One thing only she dared to admit—that he had turned to her for help, and that she would never fail him.

Only when she and the Duchesse met was she conscious of a new assurance in herself. It no longer mattered to her whether she faced approval or disapproval. Tirades of suspicion and accusations might be hurled upon her, but they left her unshaken. Her indifference acted like a goad to the Corsican temperament, but since the night of the Duchesse's attempted suicide Henriette could summon neither anger nor pity for this other woman whose violent exhibitions disgusted her with their lack of pride and personal dignity. She would stand quietly under the furious flow of words and reproaches or the sighs of self-pity—to all outward appearances listening respectfully, but inwardly so chill with contempt that she felt frozen from head to foot. The heavy-lidded dark eyes might flash, the white, ring-laden hands might be wrung, but Henriette would retire unmoved by the spectacle. The servants might be ranged against her. No matter, she would return to her duties with a light step and renewed confidence.

"There's not another governess in Paris or England who works harder or has more obstacles to contend with than

I," she would argue. "In the three years and a half since I entered this house there's not been a word or an act of mine she or any of them could use against me. If she's half out of her mind with jealousy it's because she's afraid to blame herself for losing him; and if the servants have spying eyes and evil tongues it's no affair of mine. I'll go my own way. They shan't humiliate me to please themselves."

She reasoned truly and with conviction, but she left one important factor out of her calculations. The science of mathematics had always been a difficult one for her to master. In algebra she had particularly disliked those problems dealing with X, the unknown quantity. In life, being honest and idealistic and free from a spirit of malice, she reckoned her problem without taking scandal into account. And scandal has a way of catching up with those who disregard its power.

She was therefore quite unprepared when the bolt fell.

They had stayed late at the château that year, returning to Paris for the holidays. After a brief outing at Cannes the Duchesse rejoined her family, refreshed and in better humor than for many months. Christmas had passed off without discord and with elaborate gifts for all, including Mademoiselle Deluzy. The Duchesse had been more affable, and temporarily at least the household seemed calm and the children responding to the more normal atmosphere. Their grandfather, the old Maréchal Sébastiani, was traveling in Spain, and Henriette hoped he would remain away another month, for he was a disrupting influence in the house. His presence always irritated the Duc, and his concern over the Duchesse's health and happiness only made her more difficult and self-centered. As for the children, he spoiled them by all manner of indulgences and upset the carefully planned scheme of their lessons and recreations.

Henriette had greater responsibility now that the three middle sisters were through their convent studies and in her care. These girls, Céleste, Amélie, and Marie, would never be as near to her as the others, with whom she had been so closely associated since her coming. They were pretty and docile, but without the marked personalities of Isabella and Louise and the captivating Berthe. Monsieur Remey continued to instruct all the daughters in literature, grammar, and composition, while Henriette taught them history, painting, embroidery, and superintended their piano practice. She also chaperoned them on their walks and drives and on visits to such places of amusement as were felt to be appropriate to carefully guarded *jeunes filles*. Besides this she continued to teach Raynald his lessons. He was unusually precocious for seven and, though his health had improved greatly, he still needed constant watching. Only Mademoiselle Deluzy could keep him interested and amused without overtaxing his strength. So he remained her most loved and most complex charge.

Isabella, nearing her eighteenth birthday, and Louise, at sixteen, had bloomed into charming young ladies, fulfilling the possibilities that Henriette had forseen under their adolescent awkwardness. The Duc was enormously proud of his two elder daughters with their shining dark hair and eyes and delicately molded oval faces. Already he spoke to Henriette of their future husbands and what manner of men would best suit their different tastes and dispositions. It was strange to her to discuss this with him, and yet she felt pleased and touched at his confidences.

"They must be happy," he would say, following their youthfully rounded figures with a half admiring, half anxious expression. "At least we must see that they have every chance at happiness from the start."

"Well, you know, monsieur, happiness isn't to be bought or given away in prize packages," she would remind him, feeling her heart contract as she spoke of such things to a man who seemed too young to be the father of girls already of marriageable age. "But you're right in making certain that there will be no clash of temperaments. I think Isabella will be harder to please than Louise. She's more decided in her views and less adaptable to circumstance."

"She's stubborn as a Corsican donkey, you mean," he would laugh. "But if she once gives her devotion she's loyal."

"And very methodical," Henriette would insist. "Oh, yes, she can be trusted to take great responsibilities. Louise now will always shed them like water, and she's too careless and easy-going for her own good."

"Yes, Louise will need a firm hand at the check rein. The man who marries her will never know what fancy may take her next; but she'll keep him amused at any rate. Heigh-ho! I must be bestirring myself soon with such pretty daughters. Still, I don't believe in too early marriages."

Always she noticed, he would end these conversations

with some such remark, as if the subject stirred too many personal memories to be continued.

Those weeks after the holidays were crowded with plans and projects. Isabella and Louise especially wanted to go here, there and everywhere. Each day they begged Henriette to accompany them on this excursion or that, rebelling against their own lessons and those of the younger children. One treat, however, had been promised to which she was not invited. The Duchesse had a box at the opera, and Isabella and Louise and the two oldest sons were to attend a performance of the great Meyerbeer's "Les Huguenots." The brothers showed little enthusiasm for this treat, but as the evening approached Isabella and Louise were in a fever of expectation. Their dresses of white net over rose taffeta were laid out in readiness with their gloves and slippers and velvet-hooded cloaks when word was sent down by Madame Leclerc that their mother had been seized with one of her severe headaches and would not be able to attend. It would be necessary for Mademoiselle Deluzy to accompany the party.

Almost as excited by this magnificent prospect as the two girls, Henriette hurried through supper and prepared the best toilette possible on such short notice. She had been especially active that day, but weariness fell from her as she bathed and curled her hair and took out the dress of apricot mull, banded in blue, which she had not yet worn. The neck line was cut lower than any she had owned before, and her throat showed white and almost as youthful as the girls'. She had no jewels, but the dress fitted perfectly and that, she reflected as she took a last look in her mirror, was far more important.

"No one," she thought with satisfaction as she caught up her cloak and hurried to join the waiting group in the schoolroom, "would take me for a governess or a poor relation!"

The girls were more than satisfying in their admiration and seemed almost to have read her thoughts.

"What a beautiful dress, mademoiselle!" exclaimed the critical Isabella. "Doesn't she look lovely, Louise?"

"They'll think you're our sister tonight," Louise impulsively decided. "Let's act as if you were when people stare at us through their glasses."

Henriette quickly discouraged this idea, but as she marshaled them down to the carriage, she could not help feeling flattered at the naïve suggestion.

As they entered, a peculiar air of brilliance and expectancy pervaded the Opera House, and they soon learned from the attendant who unlocked their box and helped them with their wraps that this was to be a great night indeed since the King would attend in person. The Royal box was already decorated, and the young Praslins were enchanted to discover that their own directly faced it. Henriette smiled at their eagerness. It was plain that the stage and singers would meet with a serious rival.

"If Papa only were here," Louise sighed, "it would be much better because he knows the King, and they'd probably exchange bows; and then everyone in the house would be envious of us."

"Ho! I've seen the King," bragged her brother Louis, "and he's not much to look at. You'd never guess he was a king if you didn't know and see all the guards."

The curtain had been up, and the first act was more than half through when royalty entered. Cheers sounded from crowds outside the doors, and the house rustled as if a sudden wind had stirred it while the King and his party were being seated. When the curtain fell and the house blazed with lights once more, the King rose and accepted the applause that echoed from below and from tiers of balconies above. A thick-set, undistinguished man past middle age, he stood smiling in mechanical acknowledgment. Across his chest a broad blue ribbon showed along with other decorations; but except for these he might have been any banker or retired officer occupying an opera box with his faded wife and a group of sons and daughters.

"I wonder which princess that is in blue?" Louise was asking. "Isn't she pretty, mademoiselle? Oh, look! The curtains are moving—some one's coming to our box. Why, it's Papa! What a surprise!"

Surprise indeed. Henriette knew the Duc's distaste for classical music, his preferences for the Opéra Comique and lighter entertainment. But there he was, parting the curtains behind the chair. He tried to stay in the background, but the girls clustered about him as he stood conspicuously tall in his evening dress. Before he could seat himself in the empty sixth seat, their box had become second in conspicuousness to the royal one.

"Papa, the King! Did you know he'd be here tonight? Was that why you came?"

"No, Louise, I needn't go to the opera to see the King. I only wanted to have a glimpse of my daughters in their new costumes sitting in a box."

He nodded approvingly at the four young people and then turned to their governess. Although he paid her no spoken compliment she knew that he also approved of her appearance. His eyes studied her minutely, lingering at the lines of her bare throat and shoulders. She felt her cheeks flush under his glance, and a glow of animation spread over her as it always did whenever he appeared unexpectedly. How fortunate she had decided to christen the new apricot mull instead of wearing the green silk he had seen so often!

"Papa, the King is looking at our box," Isabella told him. "I'm sure he recognizes you."

It was true. Royalty was actually bowing and smiling in their direction. The Duc rose and acknowledged the honor while the crowded house followed this exchange of greetings. But Henriette detected an expression of annoyance on his face.

"I should have waited till the lights were lowered for the next act," he admitted in a low voice under cover of the soaring violins and deeper-voiced cellos and bass viols. "I didn't intend to bring every eye to our box."

"You'll stay to see us home, monsieur?" she asked. "There will be a great crowd outside, and I dread getting to the carriage."

"The King will leave first," he explained, "and I know a side exit. Don't be worried about that."

Those were the only words they spoke together the rest of the evening, but Henriette was conscious of his presence beside her till the curtain fell. To the end of her days she could never give an accurate account of the latter half of "Les Huguenots" though she was perfectly clear about the action of the first act. Driving home in the carriage, they were all crowded close together.

"Like sardines in a box," he laughed, apologizing for crushing the full skirts of mull and net and taffeta.

"Well," he smiled, bidding them all good night at the foot of the staircase, "you must be sure to get your beauty sleep tomorrow after this evening of dissipation. You must see to

that, Mademoiselle Deluzy, for I'm off in the morning for
Marseilles. It's on a matter of business, and I don't relish the
long journey in this cold winter weather."

Henriette gave little thought to this remark. The Duc
was often away on business or pleasure trips, and since the
Sébastiani family controlled certain properties near Marseilles she gathered that he must be attending to his wife's
financial interests there. She missed his visits to the schoolroom those next days, the more so because cold rains kept
them from their daily drives and exercise. The children's
pent-up energy overflowed the rooms; and Berthe, in particular, grew difficult and fractious. She did not seem at all
like her usual, gay self; and Henriette felt her own patience
leaving her under the strain of keeping the child from interfering with the others. It was especially trying that lessons should be interrupted in the middle of the morning by
Madame Leclerc with a peremptory summons: Mademoiselle Deluzy would please present herself to the Duchesse at
once.

Something was amiss. She could tell by the superior gleam
that lingered in the eyes of the lady's maid when she delivered the message. As she hurried along the corridors in
answer to it, Henriette mentally ran through the activities
of the last week, trying to think what offense she could have
given. Usually, with the Duc away, the Duchesse left the
children and their governess alone. Henriette had discovered
that it was his physical presence, above all his preferences of
the schoolroom to his wife's private apartments that brought
on her fits of jealousy. Well, she would soon learn the reason, even if she could not be forearmed.

She found Madame seated at her writing desk by the window and was relieved that her maid was not in evidence. She
had come to gauge this other woman's humor by certain
signs, more or less after the manner of weatherwise sailors
watching for the first storm signals in sea or sky. Instantly
she noted that the plump hands fumbling through a mass of
papers were far from steady, and that the lace and ribbons
of the elaborate negligee rose and fell with each short, almost panting breath. These and the fact that the Duchesse
did not look up at once, though she had told her to enter,
meant trouble.

"She's dangerous today," Henriette decided. "I must be
careful. Perhaps it's nothing really serious."

But when the full lids were raised at last and the dark eyes met hers, she was not reassured. She could have faced flashing sparks of rage better than the glazed intensity of this stare.

"You sent for me, madame," she prompted. Anything to break that look. Let the storm begin, and let it soon be spent.

"Yes, I sent for you. There is something here for you to read. It concerns you, mademoiselle, and all of us."

She held out a sheet of newspaper, and her shaking finger pointed to an item which had been circled in red pencil. Henriette recognized the paper as one she had often seen displayed on news stands. It had an unsavory reputation, and she remembered vaguely hearing that it supplied malicious social gossip to all Paris. But even this meager knowledge did not prepare her for the shock of the printed words in the red circle:

The Duc and Duchesse de Praslin [she read] are in their Paris residence for the winter, but as usual this pair are seldom seen together in public. Lately, however, the Duc had been seen much in the company of a certain lady of marked personal attractions. Night before last at the performance of "Les Huguenots," which was attended by the King, he was observed in his box with four members of his large family and the lady in question, Mademoiselle D——, who we have learned on excellent authority has occupied for some time the enviable post of governess in the household Praslin. The Duchesse, we hear, has not been enjoying good health, but the Duc from all appearances has never been better. He has remarkably fine taste and has been long regarded as a connoisseur in many lines.

The words swam and danced before her eyes as she tried to reread the paragraph. "The lady in question, Mademoiselle D—— . . ." She felt the words sink like leaden weights into her consciousness, and her voice and even her breath failed her as she continued to stand holding the paper.

"Now you know why I sent for you."

She heard the Duchesse's voice muffled and far off like the echo of the sea in a shell. But it railled her nevertheless, and her numb senses began to come to her aid almost before she knew she had summoned them.

"Madame"—she was startled to find that she had not lost all power of speech, though she felt cold from head to foot and could not keep the paper from shaking between her fingers—"Madame, this is as much of a shock to me as it must be to you."

"Mademoiselle, do you realize what such a paragraph means?"

"I am trying to, madame." Henriette felt her knees weakening, but she braced her body against the desk rather than ask for leave to sit down. "If you will give me a moment I can explain about the opera, though I cannot see why such a piece of gossip should have been directed at me."

"You don't see!" The Duchesse's pent-up feelings were already loosed in torrents of furious abuse. Listening, Henriette was at first hardly aware of the words. Then gradually they penerated her mind as she steadied herself against the comforting solidity of that desk.

"Ever since you set foot in my house it's been one insult after another—a deliberate campaign on your part to take all that I love from me—first the children and now my husband. You've been diabolically clever, mademoiselle, far more clever than I. But don't think this smiling, innocent face of yours ever deceived me for a moment. You can pull wool over Theo's eyes, but not over mine. I always knew what you were and what schemes you were laying. But for once you weren't clever enough! Oh, it's intolerable that you should have dared to plan this last insult, that while I lay ill at home you flaunted your hold over him in public for the King and all Paris to see!"

She paused to draw a long, gasping breath; and Henriette seized her chance to speak. Now that she had reacted from the first shock all her years of training in self-control came to her aid.

"Please, madame," she answered with a quietness of manner and clear conviction that was maddening to her accuser, "let me speak for myself. I have that right before you pass judgment on me. I regret this piece of slander as much and more than you. But you must believe I'm telling the truth when I say I had nothing to do with the Duc's appearance in the box that night. I went because you were ill and asked me to take the children. No one was more surprised than I when he joined our party. Your daughters will tell you so, and—"

"My daughters," the heavy voice broke in. "My daughters whose minds you have poisoned against their mother. You stand there and call upon them to repeat lies that their innocence cannot understand. You're a better actress than I thought, but your talents are wasted on me. I'll never fall under your spell as they have."

Henriette laid the newspaper clipping on the desk and clenched her hands so tightly that her nails cut into the flesh.

"We'll leave the children out, madame, please."

"It's impossible to leave them out. Not when you've deliberately taken their affection from me."

"No one can take away affection that does not exist. If your children have turned to me it's because they're afraid of you and your violence. One moment you smother them with caresses, and then if their father so much as touches one of them you resent it. No wonder they're hurt and bewildered. It's as if"—Henriette was speaking her mind at last since there seemed no longer any use in keeping silence —"it's as if you seized upon them because they're fragments of him, like some puzzle you're forever trying to put together. No, madame, I've stolen nothing from you!"

The Duchesse's face had changed from pallor to mottled purple, and she made an inarticulate, almost animal sound in her throat. Henriette pointed to the item in the red circle and continued steadily: "I'll say no more of that, but of this vile insinuation I can only repeat that there's no truth in it except what I cannot deny—that Monsieur le Duc did come to the box and sit with us. I couldn't very well drive him away, could I?"

The Duchesse's lip curled derisively. "I have not sent for you to question me, mademoiselle. But I ask you again: Do you know what this insinuation, as you choose to call it, means?"

"It means that this gossip sheet which I have never stooped to read before, implies that the Duc and I—well, you force me to say it in plain terms—that I am his mistress."

"Exactly. You admit that much."

"I admit nothing, madame. It's impossible. Even if you imagined that I would be capable of such a thing, you must see that, living here as I do with my every move watched and commented upon by the servants, I've about as much privacy as a goldfish in a globe. You must believe facts, even if you won't believe me."

"Well, perhaps there has been nothing actually wrong between you and my husband." The Duchesse was forced to grant that much grudgingly. "But if you have let it appear otherwise to the world you must take the consequences. The public believes that you are what you deny; so for all of us it might as well be so."

"And if it also appears to the world," Henriette continued, "and to this public whose opinion you value so highly that you and Monsieur are not on good terms, does that also become a fact whether there's truth in it or not?"

Henriette's face and voice did not change as she put the question, though she knew it was the only trump card she held in a pack that was already stacked against her.

"You dare to say such a thing to me!"

The Duchesse wheeled about in her chair, and her anger seemed almost visible under the heaving lace and silk that wrapped her body.

"I only spoke, madame, because we were both mentioned in the article. If I have been put in a false position, the same may be true of you."

"Don't go on coupling our names, and stop talking of the true and of the false as if you could tell the difference between them!"

"But I know that there *is* a difference between what we are and what people may think we are. Reputation is one thing, and character is another; and they may be as far apart as the poles. And now, madame, I will go and pack my trunk unless you wish me to stay out the week."

By the time she reached her own room she was shaking so that she could hardly write legibly the note she sent to Monsieur Remey:

Please, my dear Albert, take over all the lessons today and see that the little ones are occupied. I have a slight indisposition and will explain the reason to you later.

H. D.

When the strength returned to her knees and she had warmed her chill hands at the grate fire, she went to the wardrobe and began taking down her dresses. Mechanically she laid them on the bed and turned to the drawers of her bureau. A maid came to inquire if Mademoiselle Deluzy wished *déjeuner* served in her room; but she shook her head and went on with her work.

"I must call the porter to fetch my portmanteau and band-boxes," she reminded herself in the midst of her sorting. "And then there are the children. I cannot go without seeing them. They mustn't be upset, especially Raynald."

Presently she stopped her work and went to the little secretary where she had taken such pleasure in writing and painting. She would leave a letter for him, so he would understand why he would not find her here on his return. It was going to be a difficult letter to write. How could she make clear her side of the ugly story that would be sure to greet him on the instant of his arrival? She had never addressed him in writing before, and she felt suddenly at a loss to tell him of the complexity of feeling that filled her as she sat in that half-dismantled room where she had been so happy for nearly four years and which she was being forced to leave.

How could she tell him without bitterness that the outcome of her standing firm against the abuses of the Duchesse had been disaster with herself the target of malicious gossip? Everything had been against her from the start. She realized that now. The blow had been dealt when he was not there to help her. She knew he would always reproach himself for that and for his impulsive gesture that had been the cause.

Now that her mind was clear again, she knew that the greatest shock had not been to her pride. The Duchesse's words had not really pricked beneath the surface, and the ugly implication of that printed paragraph had not in itself shaken her. But always before she had believed that the boundary of integrity was her own conscience, and now she knew that a clear conscience was not enough in itself. She felt the same helpless futility sweep over her that she had known as a child when she had been powerless against injustice.

Once more she dipped her pen, and tried another beginning to the letter; and once more she crumpled the sheet and added it to others in the waste basket.

"My dear Monsieur," she began simply. "Do not reproach yourself or others for what has happened. It was impossible to keep my promise to you, and so when you return you will find me gone . . ."

But as she sat among her disordered personal possessions, trying to summon phrases to her will, a timid knock interrupted, and Isabella stood beside her.

"Oh, mademoiselle!" she was saying. "Please come at once. It's Berthe: she's suddenly very ill, and Maxine doesn't know what to do. Hurry, mademoiselle—they need you."

The letter was never finished, and the trunks were never brought up to be filled, for by midnight Dr. Simon had pronounced Berthe seriously ill with scarlet fever, and once more Henriette had been put in command of a sickroom.

*chapter thirteen*

DURING THE LONG WEEKS OF ATTENDANCE IN THE SICK-room Henriette had time to consider her situation from all angles, but she reached no conclusion whatsoever because the matter of her dismissal seemed to have been forgotten in the concern over Berthe's recovery. When the child was herself once more, the subject of that newspaper item was never reopened. If the Duc knew of the scandalous bit of gossip he never alluded to it. Several times she gave him a chance to discuss it. But he did not avail himself of the opportunity, and something in his manner kept her from pressing the subject.

With the Duchesse, too, it was as if it had never been. As if, Henriette thought, those harsh and bitter words they had both spoken had been erased by a wave smoothing out ugly markings on a sandy beach. Time and anxiety for the small invalid must be responsible. Yet Henriette could not forget what had passed between herself and the Duchesse. "She said such terrible things to me and I to her," she often thought. "I'm not sorry I said them. I'm glad I stood firm upon my rights, but I can't forget; and if I were in her place I couldn't forget. She's beyond my comprehension—roused like a tigress and then forgetful of what provoked her anger."

No, she could never make the Duchesse out. Whenever she tried to, her efforts ended in a baffled shrug of the shoulders.

But, temporarily at least, the sky was clear of thunderclouds; and spring was in the air once more. The almond tree bloomed in the garden; and first it was primroses, then violets, and then daffodils and tulips in the street flower stalls. Perhaps the Duchesse's habitual cloak of distrust and melancholy had lifted because of the new element of romance that ran like a spring freshet through the entire Praslin household.

Isabella was betrothed. In six months she would marry the son of a rich and important business man of excellent family. She would live in Turin, where her fiancé had been put in charge of certain financial interests. It was the first break in that family group, and with all the rejoicing there was also a consciousness of approaching change and loss. Henriette caught the Duc following his eldest daughter with a loving but thoughtful expression. She knew he was thinking that with her wedding the end of an era would have come for all of them. There was infinite tenderness in his look, too. He seemed to be calling on Heaven to deal kindly with this untried creature whose youth could so easily flower or be blighted by the approaching experience.

"Don't be troubled, monsieur," Henriette told him more than once when she saw his anxiety. "Isabella is ready for love. You've done all you can to find her a good husband. The rest lies with God or Fate or whatever we may call it. You can do nothing about that."

Isabella herself took the matter calmly. She was not a highly sensitive or emotional girl. Her qualities were of a less spectacular sort. She seemed attracted to the well mannered young man with his good looks and handsome clothes who had been provided for her. Perhaps that was all that could be expected, since she had met no other young men except her own brothers. Naturally she responded to the excitement and to becoming suddenly the center of attention; and she bore up remarkably well under her mother's bursts of tearful affection and orgies of lavish buying for her trousseau and household equipment. Only occasionally did Henriette sense any doubt or fear in the girl's mind.

"Mademoiselle," she asked once after she had had a long session with the Abbé Gallard, "I don't always understand what the Abbé means when he talks to me about the duties of marriage."

"What don't you understand, Isabella?"

"Well, he spoke about submission, and—and then almost

the next minute he was talking about my children and how they must be baptized and brought up in the Church. And somehow, mademoiselle, I couldn't see how such things fitted together."

The smooth young brow puckered, and the dark eyes were fixed on Henriette anxiously.

"Don't be worried, my dear," she said. "If you love and are loved in turn it will all come about naturally, and this submission he spoke of will take care of itself. I've never been married, you know; so, if there are things that you want to know, go to your mother and ask for advice."

"Oh, but I couldn't do that!" The girl flushed as she spoke. "I can't talk to her about such things; and when I marry, mademoiselle, I don't want to be like Mamma."

"Isabella, my dear!" Henriette felt it her duty to remonstrate in spite of her secret sympathy. "You mustn't say such things. When you marry you'll feel differently and understand why your mother is often ill and depressed."

"But that's exactly what I meant: I don't want to be ill all the time, and I'd like a few children but not so many as in our family. But from what the Abbé said—"

She broke off uneasily, and Henriette turned away from the question in those candid eyes. Haltingly she explained as much as she could of marriage. It was not her place to do so, and the Duchesse would no doubt be furious if she discovered that a governess had so far overstepped the bounds of propriety. But Henriette was too moved by such blending of innocence and ignorance not to come to the girl's rescue. How could she deal with one and still leave the other untouched?

"Now do not be troubled," she ended her remarks. "Meet experiences as they come. Be generous and think the best of your husband even if this new life seems strange to you at first. Be happy, my dear, for I believe that the greatest good comes out of the greatest happiness. And above all never let what the Abbé or any one else may say, make you anxious and afraid."

"No, I won't, mademoiselle. Thank you very much, mademoiselle." The old schoolgirl manner had returned once more. "And, mademoiselle, do you think I might wear the new cherry poplin when I go with Louise for chocolate with my Sébastiani cousins this afternoon?"

Smiling, Henriette gave her consent, though she felt the

cherry poplin to be inappropriate to the occasion. But Isabella was so young, so young and so touchingly untried.

*"Mon Dieu,"* she thought when the girl had gone off,
humming a tune and holding a bonbon between her fingers,
"they know so little, and they feel so much!"

She sighed and turned back to the next day's lessons she
was preparing, wondering if she had been wise in her advice.
It was all very well to say, "Be happy, and the rest will take
care of itself." But the girl had keen eyes and ears and was
acutely aware of what went on about her. No wonder she
felt qualms at stepping boldly into unknown country where
she must blaze her own trail through the bewildering jun-
gles of the heart and senses.

"Some day," Henriette thought, "it will not be like this.
A young girl will step across the threshold of marriage
knowing almost as much of its necessities as her brothers.
She need not walk into it blindfolded and fearful."

In another month they all journeyed to Melun in time to
see the orchards bloom in drifts of white and rose. May
passed smoothly and June. Raynald celebrated his eighth
birthday in that month, and there was a fête in his honor to
which all the tenants and their children were invited. Henriette was proud of the little boy's looks and behavior on this
occasion, and even the Duchesse expressed satisfaction.

"He does you credit, mademoiselle," she actually remarked when the celebration was over. "I begin to have
hopes that he will some day be as vigorous as his brothers."

"Thank you, madame," Henriette had answered, following the small boy as he proudly collected the gifts that had
been brought him. "He's made great strides in the last year,
and I suppose that means that soon he will be going away
to school, and then my work here will be over. A boy can't
stay close to petticoats forever."

"That is true," the mother agreed. "But they're all growing up too quickly, and he's the youngest, alas!" She sighed
and lapsed into one of her reveries. "Eight years. It doesn't
seem possible it can be so long since his birth. He nearly cost
me my life, mademoiselle. The Duc was beside himself."

"I can well imagine," Henriette murmured tactfully.
"And I, madame, can hardly believe sometimes that it's
over four years since I came here to care for your children."

She did not add that sometimes it seemed far longer than
that, because the years before seemed to have lost all reality

for her. She had been another person then, wrapped in a cocoon of emotional immaturity almost like that which still protected Isabella and Louise. She had rubbed elbows with life, but not until she entered the Praslin ménage had she known the sharp prick of its ecstasies and its despairs.

That summer of 1845 it was Berthe who needed her special care; though she had recovered, the illness had left her ailing. She who had been the gayest one, abounding in vitality and high spirits, was now utterly changed. She had been a rosy and beautiful little girl when the scarlet fever attacked her, and she had emerged from the siege pale and scrawny and listless. She had grown too fast during those weeks in bed, and her childish beauty had vanished. The Duchesse mourned over her child's appearance, and the Duc worried even more over this change.

"Her listlessness is what worries me, monsieur," Henriette told the Duc, "not her lost beauty. That will return in time. She spent all her strength fighting the fever. We cannot expect it to come back all at once."

"I suppose not," he agreed. "And you say her appetite is poor. We must do something about that. When I spoke to Dr. Simon last week he seemed to think she would improve at the seashore, and her grandfather has been urging a visit to Olmeto in August. Well, I will talk to the Duchesse about it if you approve of the plan."

Almost invariably he deferred to her in all matters, not only those which concerned the young people but affairs of the household, and lately even about his own political career. It was flattering to have him turn to her for advice, even more flattering when he followed it. Her suggestions, he had discovered, were both shrewd and wise.

Sometimes they even discussed politics, and she amazed him by her knowledge of affairs in France and in the world. Their views on government and on foreign policies did not always agree, but her opinions were always stimulating and provocative. By birth, inclination and upbringing he was a conservative and an aristocrat, while she was frankly Republican. But more than this she belonged to a minority that defies classification. She was highly individualistic in all her reactions. Like a spirited horse, she rebelled at anything which restrained personal liberty and freedom of expression. Frequently he smiled and shrugged at her arguments because they were his only weapons against her brilliance of speech and her gift for vivid language. Still he held his ground against her, stubbornly though good-naturedly.

"Well, you'll see," she would tell him after some argument in which the King and the House of Peers figured prominently. "Some day you'll see that a Royalist government can go too far. Levying higher and higher taxes and silencing public opinion behind censorship and prison bars has never strengthened a weak party, whether kings or commoners happen to be in power."

"Oh, so we have treason in our midst, Mademoiselle Deluzy!" He laughed at her. "I suppose I ought to report you to the police. But I've noticed that you have no objections to sharing the privileges of this system you so hotly denounce. You don't really want to see the Bonapartes back in power, do you?"

She shook her head.

"Of course I like luxuries as well as you do, but so do the people over on the Left Bank and along the docks at Le Havre and Marseilles, and so do all the little shopkeepers who dread the sight of a gendarme and the tax collector with his new list of levies. No, I'm not a Bonapartist. We can't go back to campaigns that bleed France white. But even the English are more progressive than we. They let a young Queen sit on the throne, to be sure, but they make certain that her ministers keep the upper hand."

"Don't forget their House of Lords is still all-powerful."

"Don't forget to mention their House of Commons, too, monsieur. And don't forget there are Republicans across the water. When I read of them, it seems to me that in America they are at least trying to put into practice an ideal we once were brave enough to fight for, but foolish enough to let slip through our fingers."

"Oh, those Republicans in America! They don't count— a new half-settled country of savages, or at best a stewpot or riffraff from every nation in Europe. You can't take them seriously."

"But they take themselves seriously, and that in time may change the world."

"Well, they bore me." He made a wry face and snapped his fingers as if to put an end to America and Republicans and all such nuisances. "You can be very eloquent at argument, Mademoiselle Deluzy; and I admire you for it, which surprises me since I've always disliked women who talk like men."

"But I never talk like a man, do I, monsieur?" she challenged.

"No, you don't," he admitted. "That's why you're so baffling. You're as inconsistent as any woman alive, and you know it. All these fine convictions of yours, and yet you don't try to follow them. Why not go to America? Answer me that."

"Perhaps I shall some day," she retorted, "when your King Louis-Philippe is no longer in power, and you can no longer afford to keep a governess. Of course"—the fun went out of her voice—"I'm only joking, monsieur. I love France. I wouldn't live anywhere else, and I mean to live and die here; only I do believe—"

"That the King and his peers are a set of rascals, and that their days are numbered—is that it?"

"Well, I believe that a change is bound to come sooner or later."

"That we're a lot of Neros fiddling while Rome burns?" he pressed her.

"In a way, yes. The fire hasn't started yet, and perhaps you and I won't live to hear it crackle; but your sons may."

"You don't mean another Revolution? We're past all that kind of bloodshed and butchery."

"I hope so. It may not be like that, only I know that something stirs in the air of Paris when I walk about and hear what men and women in streets and shops are saying to one another. There have been these attempted assassinations of the King lately. They're all signs that times are changing, monsieur, and we must change with them if we wish to survive."

"So—I shall count on you to tell me in advance when all this is to happen. It will be a comfort when I take my place in the House of Peers to know that Mademoiselle Deluzy will warn me of the deluge."

"You are really going to be made a member of the House of Peers? Of course I had heard rumors, monsieur, but I didn't know it was a fact."

"Yes," he told her with a note of pride creeping into his voice. "It's a certainty. With my father gone and the older peers thinning out it's inevitable that we younger members of the nobility should take over our responsibilities. Perhaps you didn't realize that I took mine seriously." He rose and stood looking down at her with an amused expression. "And now, do you turn from me because I shall so soon be part of the Court you hate?"

She shook her head as she caught his smile and humorously lifted eyebrows. His words came to her as from a long way off because she could hardly keep her mind on what he said. She could only be acutely aware of his strength and vitality. He stood so tall and fair above her, faintly fragrant of bay rum and leather and a recently smoked cigar. Somehow their arguments always ended like this because, when that subtle scent of masculinity which was so much a part of him, overcame her, she could never be completely logical.

The plans for an August holiday in Corsica were all made, and the old Maréchal had chartered a private vessel to carry the party from Marseilles. The two older boys were remaining at the château, and the Duc was to return there after accompanying the others and seeing them aboard the boat. Henriette felt glad that he would be with them on the long journey. The weather was extremely hot, and even luxurious travel was uncomfortable with unforseen delays and crowded accommodations at hotels. She had her hands full enough with the six girls and Raynald and two nursemaids in her charge. Madame Leclerc could be very trying on such expeditions, and the Duchesse's health made travel difficult. With the Duc at hand, Henriette felt she had a powerful ally, and his presence also laid a certain restraint on the servants, who never lost an opportunity to put a governess at disadvantage.

But before Paris was well behind them the rumblings of discord began. The Duchesse refused to continue by train, insisting that it made her ill, and that she would collapse before they reached the seaport. Whether she really was as indisposed as she claimed, Henriette never knew; but the fact that the Duc protested against shifting their plans was enough to bring on one of her worst attacks of combined migraine and hysteria. There was nothing to do but put up the whole party at an inn for two nights and a day. Quarters were crowded, and the children restive. The Duc, to while away the tiresome delay, took Mademoiselle Deluzy and the young people for a day's outing in the country, and unfortunately a broken axle to one of the carriages kept them away until early evening. This incident only added fuel to the already smoldering fire of the Duchesse's injured sensibilities, and for hours the floor occupied by the Praslin party

reverberated with the quarrel which raged. What lightning
would follow the rumblings, Henriette wondered as she
tossed wakefully in a stifling room. She had no doubt that
she figured prominently in the Duchesse's accusations; and
she wished with fervor that the pleasant outing had never
been arranged, or at least that she had not been involved
in it.

Next morning, as she and the children gathered for *petit
déjeuner,* the Duc unexpectedly appeared in his traveling
clothes. He looked worn and grim to Henriette, and he was
unusually quiet through the meal. When the very poor coffee
and rolls had been finished, Henriette ventured to ask what
his orders might be for the day. Was Madame la Duchesse
able to continue with the journey?

"Madame la Duchesse will not accompany us," he told
her briefly. "She insists upon remaining here till she is recovered, and she says she cannot continue to Corsica; so we
must go without her. There has been enough needless delay."
His lips tightened as he spoke. "The ship has already been
kept waiting too long, and there's no reason why one of us
should spoil the holiday for all the rest."

Henriette asked no more questions, and the journey continued by train and carriage. A marked relief showed in the
spirits of the little party. No one except the two servants
seemed to mind the absence of Madame and her maid,
and by the time they reached Marseilles the Duc had recovered his good spirits. They boarded the chartered vessel
that night though the skipper explained that the tide and
difficult harbor conditions would keep him from weighing
anchor until the next morning; no one minded this slight
delay after the longer ones they had undergone. The boat
was far cleaner and more comfortable than the provincial
hotels, and the children revived in the fresh salt air.

"Suppose we take Isabella and Louise ashore, Mademoiselle Deluzy," the Duc proposed after the younger ones had
gone to their cabins. "We'll hear a concert on the Quai and
have a *crème de menthe* at some café."

It was delightful to stroll in the cool darkness of evening
along an esplanade above the harbor with all the anchored
ship lanterns doubling their brightness in black water. The
city's close-packed buildings were honeycombed with luminous streets and innumerable lamp-lit windows; and more
lights followed the curve of the water line, dwindling into

the distance like a string of brilliants on some unseen throat. And still farther away, the single lonely eye of a lighthouse guarded the channel that led to sea.

"How beautiful it is!" Henriette drew a faint sigh of contentment as they paused to lean over a stone parapet. "And by day it seems so sprawling and ugly."

"Yes, coast cities look best after dark," the Duc agreed. "They're like some women in that respect. Gas light and jewels and a certain blurring of features transform them."

She made no further comment as they entered a small park where a band played in a pavilion and tables were spread under the trees. He must know so much of women, she thought. A man of his sort, high-born and rich and handsome—why should he not be a connoisseur of her sex? And yet he seldom made her aware of that. When he looked at her she never felt that mentally he was peeling the clothes from her naked body with the cool appraisal of other men from whose glances she had turned. For all his masculine assurance and vigor and in spite of the physical passion which she had seen flicker like a whiplash across those features she knew so well, she felt him to be instinctively decent, even reticent regarding the temptations of the flesh. The Duchesse, she believed, had offended this personal reticence. That perhaps was the true reason of the widening rift between them.

The band was playing a Viennese air when they entered the little park. The music had a sweet, sad undertone that for her almost obscured the gayety of the melody. It made a catch in her throat as she walked beside him with the two girls following just behind. They threaded their way between the tables, nearly all of which had been taken. People stared at the four as they passed. Henriette knew that the glances were admiring as well as curious, and it pleased her to guess that these men and women probably mistook her for his wife, the mother of the two girls in their full, smartly cut traveling dresses and flower-trimmed bonnets. The waiter was leading them to an unoccupied table some distance off. She would have followed without protest, but the Duc shook his head. With a gesture that was authoritative without being conspicuous he signaled to the head waiter and explained that they must have a better table. As if by magic one was brought and placed to the best advantage. From force of habit she moved to take the seat with its back to the harbor.

But instead he selected the best chair of the four and held it out for her. She accepted it with almost a guilty feeling. Governesses were expected to sit with their backs to a view.

Yes, that was it; that was what made her somehow a stranger to herself in this unfamiliar city. She did not feel like a governess tonight.

"*Oui, oun, crème de menthe frappé pour les jeunes filles.* Napoleon brandy for Monsieur. And for Madame?"

Her cheeks grew hot as she bent over the menu card.

"Champagne cup," the Duc suggested, and she agreed.

It was folly to let oneself believe in the impossible because a waiter had made a careless blunder. Yet how she blessed him for it! What harm could there be to feel for an hour the assurance that one was a *madame* and not a mere *mademoiselle* of indeterminate years? The cool bubbles of champagne slipped deliciously down her throat and tingled in her veins, mingling with other bubbles of happiness and pride that were as transient in their potency.

"*Garçon,*" he called to the hurrying waiter, "*l'addition.*"

She watched him pull a handful of silver and notes from his pocket and lay a generous tip on the china saucer. Once more that easy gesture of assurance enchanted her with its novelty. No feminine fumbling in bag or purse, no counting out change and wondering how small a tip one dared to leave without the humiliation of a waiter's frown or muttered complaint. Quickly she gathered her shawl about her shoulders. Better let the evening be over soon, before the old habits of a woman making her way alone became too difficult to resume.

The music from the pavilion followed them as they started back to the pier, but suddenly it seemed to have lost its power over them. Their feet no longer quickened to a gay tempo. Silence had fallen on the four, and Henriette for one had no inclination to sprightly talk. She dreaded the weeks in Corsica more than she would admit to herself. The old Maréchal would spoil his grandchildren and patronize her; and she would feel as she had felt before on those other visits—an alien in a still more alien land.

"Well, here we are." The Duc led them to the waiting tender which would take them to their boat, whose lights they could barely distinguish from other anchored vessels. Between the pier and those lights inky water lapped, and still farther liquid miles stretched between them and their

destination. A cool wind had risen and blew moist against
their faces as they pressed closer together by the slippery
steps of the landing place. Below them the dark-skinned
sailors waited in the small rocking boat, their hands outstretched to help the voyagers aboard. The moment of parting had come. Henriette braced herself for it.

Seated in the stern of the boat with Isabella beside her and
Louise in front, she looked up and held out her hand in farewell. But the Duc was not bending above them, saying good-
by and offering words of advice for the last lap of their journey. Instead she saw him leap aboard and seat himself in the
empty forward seat as the men bent to their oars.

"Oh, Papa!" Isabella and Louise exclaimed in unison,
their voices shrill with surprise and happiness. "You're coming with us after all instead of going back to Paris. What fun,
and how surprised Grandfather will be! When did you
change your mind?"

"Just now." Henriette heard his voice though she could no
longer see him for the darkness that had closed round them.
"Just a minute ago, to be exact!"

He laughed out suddenly like a boy who has just run away
from school.

"If there are any objections from the stern," he called
again—and there was a challenging note in his voice that
Henriette knew must be meant for her—"I'd like to hear
them now. There's still time for me to swim back."

But the only sound was the creak and dipping of oars in
the darkness. There were no objections from the stern.

## chapter fourteen

HOW THE DUC EXPLAINED HIS PRESENCE AND HIS WIFE'S
absence to the Maréchal Sébastiani, Henriette never knew.
But the old man made no comments to her after their arrival, and he and his son-in-law seemed upon less strained
though slightly formal relations. During the week that he
stayed at Olmeto she had few opportunities to talk alone
with the Duc. The weather being exceptionally fine, the days

were spent much in the open with sailing expeditions and
elaborate picnics planned to amuse the children. But on
the afternoon before he left Henriette found herself alone
with him as they waited for the children and the old
Maréchal to return from exploring some vineyards of which
their host was particularly proud.

They sat in a small arbor, with the sea's vehement blue
stretching before them and the shadows of grape leaves in
the strong, salt sunshine making strange patterns on their
faces.

"How blue the sea is!" she said as one or the other had
exclaimed twenty times before that day. "From here it does
not look flat, but like a curtain hanging there between us—"

"Between us and what?" He took up her words, his eyes
narrowing against the brightness beyond their shelter.

"I don't know, monsieur," she told him. "But tomorrow
you'll be setting off, and it will all look flat and different to
you then."

"Flat, yes." He spoke absently, and his eyes turned from
the water to her once more. "Life is often like that for me
in spite of all I have. Do you ever feel so?"

"No, monsieur, never!" The curls swung warm against
her cheeks as she shook her head. "Life troubles me often,
but I've never felt that it was flat. Always there's something
just ahead that I feel I'm going to meet."

"Ah, Mademoiselle Deluzy," he told her simply, "your
zest for life is contagious. When I'm with you the old
savor returns to me. I envy you this gift, and I hope you'll
never lose it."

Silence fell between them there in the sun-dappled arbor.
Though Henriette could hear men singing as they mended
nets on the shore and the far-off voices of the children calling to one another, it seemed to her that she and her companion were the only two people in the world; as if a circle
had been drawn about them, so that he and she were set
apart in some peculiar intimacy more like transcending contentment than love. She could almost visualize that circle as
if his boots and the hem of her skirt actually touched it.
But another circle came to her mind, a crudely drawn band
or red crayon about words she could never forget. She
sighed, remembering them, and the charm of the interlude
was broken. She knew she must speak to him of less pleasant
matters. There might be no other chance between now and
tomorrow.

"Monsieur," she began, "I haven't liked to spoil this little holiday—" He turned questioning eyes upon her, and she went on slowly. "It's been so happy for us all to have you here, and I've tried not to think of—of the accounting that you and I, too, must give to the Duchesse. I cannot help feeling that you—that we shall pay dearly because you came with us and left her behind."

"I always pay." He spoke evenly, but his brows drew together in a frown. "Sometimes I pay most for what I never had. I've been happy these few days, and at least that's something on my side of the ledger."

"But, monsieur, it was madness for you to come without her. The servants' looks told me that all the way here, and when we return their tongues will say even more."

"So you mind what servants say?"

"No," she answered. "I don't mind. Only it doesn't stop there. I used to feel that it didn't matter what people might think and say of one, so long as one's conscience was clear; but now I'm not so sure. And after that scandal in the paper last winter— Well, monsieur, you must know what they say about us?"

"Yes." He passed his long strong fingers wearily across his eyes as he spoke. "Yes, I know. But ugly words like that can't hurt when we know they're untrue. Besides," he hurried on more casually, "that scurrilous gossip sheet thrives on lies. Everyone knows that. It's famous for sly campaigns against the nobility. I believe"—he smiled rather grimly— "that some of those Republicans you champion are behind it."

"That may be so; but, leaving the Republicans out, gossip is gossip; and there's no end to it once the pebble has been tossed into the pond. The ripples go on and on, spreading and growing larger, and then it's beyond our power to stop them."

The voices of the children sounded more clearly. They were returning and would burst into the arbor in a moment or two.

"Listen to me," he told her. "There have been storms before; and we've weathered them, haven't we? Well, then we'll meet this if it comes. I'm going back tomorrow, and you know what I mean when I say that—suspicion and reproaches and jealous outbursts. You've witnessed plenty of them in nearly five years. And letters! *Mon Dieu,* those letters—always when I return I find one on my desk or under my door. Sometimes they're wet with pleading tears, and sometimes they're the ravings of a madwoman. It doesn't matter which; they're all the same—demanding, demanding what it's not in my power to give. If I lose my reason, too, and they tie me in a strait-jacket some day, you'll know that scribbled words on note paper have driven me to desperation."

He had risen, and his breath came quick and difficult between the words. Usually he was so reserved, so guarded, in what he said that she was frightened by the change that had overtaken him. Before she could collect herself to speak he strode out into the sunshine to meet the group returning from the vineyard. Henriette stared after him, watching his body's indolent strength and grace, and how the sun brightened his bare, blond head.

The children's voices echoed as they hailed their father, and the faint, ghostly repetition of broken words had never been so eerie before. Something prophetic stirred in her at the sound. They would haunt her always, she knew, in the future that seemed to lie behind that curtain of blue sea.

Then they were flocking round her, proudly holding the jug of fresh grape juice they had brought from the vats for her to share.

"Look, mademoiselle!" Raynald was boasting with a boot in either hand. "I treaded the grapes in my bare feet. You can see it's still purple between my toes!"

After the Duc's departure she remained with the children for three more weeks. Berthe was regaining her health and beauty in the salt air and sunshine, but she needed constant attendance. Henriette gave this lavishly to the child, yet all the time her mind seethed in the whirlpool of her thoughts. At night she lay wakeful in her room often till the great burnished sun pushed through a welter of glowing clouds and the sea caught that glory on its wide, heaving waste.

Now that the spell of the Duc's magnetic yet dependent presence no longer held her, she could think clearly and even reason about the problem which each day brought nearer. She had never been one to escape into unreality when issues must be faced. She did not turn now from the inexorable, hard facts. She did not try to blur their outlines with rosy hopes of impossible reconciliations. No, it all came to the same question, no matter how she might shift and sort over the threads that had tangled themselves more tightly about her each year she had remained in the Praslin household. Should she go, or should she stay?

"Go—go now," caution and common sense urged. "The situation will never be better, and it may be much worse. Reputation is a prize you've won for yourself with self-denial and hard work. If you throw it away, what have you left to fall back on? How will you contrive to live without it?"

But the stubborn sense of independence, the high spirits and ambition that were as much a part of her as shrewdness and prudence would always break in.

"You've done no wrong, that you should be forced to leave against your will and in disgrace. You met the Duchesse more than halfway, and whether you go or stay there will always be some one she can find to blame for her unhappiness."

"But she cannot blame you if you are not there. What do you expect to gain by staying?"

"A pension for my old age. But no, that's not really the reason. They need me—these children I love, and a man who is desperate and miserable."

"That's all very well, but children grow fast, and they forget easily. This man, what is he to you?"

"Oh, I don't know. I don't know. There's never been a word or a gesture between us that couldn't have been shared by all the spying eyes in the world."

"But your feelings, can they be shared?"

"My feelings belong to me and to me alone. They're the only personal property many women possess—women born to scrimp and work and rely on themselves as I've done all my life."

And so the debate went on within herself. She was still arguing on that August afternoon three days before the holiday ended when she was summoned to Maréchal Sébastiani's library.

That morning a large sack of mail had been received. Isabella and two of the girls had had notes from their mother, and they had reported her better again and back at Melun. There had also been a paint box for Berthe which her father had promised to send. It had been mailed from a shop in Paris, Henriette noticed. There had been many letters for the Maréchal and large quantities of newspapers. Henriette had hoped that she might have a chance to read some of these, for she was eager for news in this remote place where world events were far less important than fair winds and shoals of fish to be caught in nearer waters.

"Mademoiselle," the old man greeted her after the servant had taken himself off, "I regret the interruption, but it was important that I see you at once. Please sit down."

Though the day was sunny outside, that library was dark in its leather paneling which also seemed to hold and give out accumulated dampness from many seasons of fog. Row upon row of heavy volumes filled the shelves, and the great mahogany desk stood in the center. It was a flat-topped desk, and at each corner a fierce dog's head had been carved. The lifelike expression of their bared fangs was hardly reassuring to Henriette as she seated herself near by. Neither were the bundles of papers the old man had been studying. An open letter also lay under his hands, and it took only a hurried glance for her to recognize the writing. She did not let her eyes linger there, but spreading her dimity skirt carefully about her she waited for him to speak.

"I am not going to mince words with you, mademoiselle," he began in his rather thick, provincial voice. "I've been greatly disturbed by what has come to me in the post."

He cleared his throat and fumbled among the papers before him. As he did so Henriette saw the familiar lines of red drawn about certain paragraphs, and she knew what to expect.

"Isabella had a letter from her mother," she remarked to fill in the pause. She was determined to remain casual as long as possible. "She tells me that Madame la Duchesse is recovering from her indisposition in the country."

"She is at the château, yes; but, far from being recovered, she is apparently in a state of collapse. You will see why when you read what she has sent." He took up the sheaf of newspapers and laid them in her lap. "It has been a great shock to me, a very great shock indeed."

She took the papers up resolutely and began to read. It was very quiet in the room, so quiet that a bee buzzing on the window sill and the distant thud of surf below the headlands made the very stillness hum.

She did not skip a word, though they were ugly words and there were many more of them than in their forerunner. Not one, but several papers carried versions of the latest Praslin scandal. The rôle that Mademoiselle D——, a siren in the guise of governess, had played in carrying the Duc off to

Corsica, into the very stronghold of the abandoned Duchesse, was commented upon fully. Few who read Parisian newspapers could have missed the various maliciously worded items, and this time there were no clever insinuations, but bold statements. What, one paper asked, was the country coming to when a Peer of France could so affront the code of family ethics?

Henriette laid the sheaf down at last and faced the old Maréchal directly. She had turned pale, but that and the beating of the little pulse in her throat were the only signs of emotion. Her voice was low and steady as she spoke.

"If you are shocked by this, how do you think I feel?"

"I don't know, mademoiselle. I am waiting to hear."

She moistened dry lips and spread out her hands in a futile gesture.

"Monsieur le Maréchal," she said, "there's no use in explanations and denials. If you believe in these lies after seeing us here for a week and in Paris also—if you believe that there is more than friendship between the Duc and myself, then nothing I might say could convince you otherwise."

He was unprepared for the simplicity of her answer. Used as he was to the tears and protests and frenzies of his hysterical daughter, he could have dealt better with wild pleas and expostulations than with the calm self-control of this woman who sat waiting for his verdict.

"Mademoiselle," he told her, "in all fairness I must admit that I do not believe these vulgar charges against you. All my life I've been a man of action, and so for me actions speak louder than words. But words like these are very serious, as you yourself must realize."

"I do. It only takes a drop of poison to turn what is sound to something rotten and corrupt. You needn't point out to me that after this my reputation is gone."

"You should have thought of it before, mademoiselle. You should not have allowed the Duc to accompany you and so put yourselves and my poor daughter in such a position. Your indiscretion has laid you open to these attacks, unjust though they may be. And I understand there was a similar one, too, some months ago."

"There was, and I was ready to leave at that time; but then Berthe became so ill I stayed. After all I love your grandchildren almost as much as if they were my own, and I've given them by best always."

"And afterwards?"

"Afterwards they still needed me, and the Duchesse was gracious to me once more. Oh, monsieur, please believe that I tried to go. Many times I have told the Duc that it was best, but he would never hear of it."

"My son-in-law is not always wise in his judgment, mademoiselle. He's impetuous and easily swayed, far too easily swayed."

"When do you wish me to go? Today, tomorrow?"

"Wait." He had risen and was pacing the floor. His stocky, vigorous body seemed charged with energy, despite his white hair and beard and the veined hands that betrayed his age. "We must not be too hasty. No, we must find the best way to quiet these insults."

"I'm grateful for your consideration, monsieur."

His dark, filmed eyes turned upon her with a flash of the Corsican temper she had learned to know so well. For a moment the resemblance between himself and the Duchesse was startling.

"Keep your gratitude, mademoiselle. It's my daughter I'm considering, not you or the Duc. Her welfare is all that matters to me. God knows, it's not in my power to give her much happiness; but I mean to spare her all the humiliation I can. She's had enough to bear."

Henriette pressed her lips firmly together and ventured no further comment. The old man continued his pacing, and it seemed the better part of an hour before he spoke again.

"There's only one way to handle this situation, and that is to seem indifferent to gossip. They expect you to leave the Praslin household now, and the fact that you remain and apparently on excellent terms will help to contradict all this."

"Yes, monsieur." She had not given him credit for so much astuteness. He really had more insight than she had suspected.

"We must go on exactly as usual except, of course, that my son-in-law and my daughter must make it a point to be seen together more frequently in public. You will remain, and we will all return to France day after tomorrow."

"And you will explain to the Duchesse that I stayed at your request? I want her to know that this decision is entirely yours."

"I will make her understand. Fanny has always been reasonable with me. Yes, that will be the best course for us all to take."

He seemed relieved now that the decision had been made. Seating himself once more at the desk, he drew out note paper and a pen and prepared for action.

"I shall write them both at once," he told her, "and dispatch the letters by special messenger to the next packet. They'll reach France before us. The Duc must be made to remember his position, and that he cannot humiliate his wife further. She has been pushed too far, mademoiselle, and as her father I shall find means to bring him to his senses."

His voice grew harsh, and he dipped his pen fiercely in the ink to express his feelings. Watching the hardening of his usually kind old face, Henriette knew that this retired officer still believed in force; that he could still wage campaigns other than those of the battlefields he had known. Gunpowder, she thought, was not the only ammunition at his command. Mentally she could almost see Maréchal Sébastiani tightening the cords of his money bags if his son-in-law refused to comply with his plans.

"Well," she reflected as she made her way from the musty library, "I ought to be leaving, and here I am only more deeply caught. *Mon Dieu,* to see the end, to know what to do!"

Thinking that Berthe and Raynald were in the summer house at the end of the rose garden, she went out to find them. But she paused on her way, arrested by the sound of singing. In the kitchen garden the other side of a high hedge she heard the twanging of a guitar and a girl's voice lifted in one of the plaintive gypsy airs that never failed to stir a responsive chord in her. This was one she had not heard before, and the words came clear and distinct through the thick green that hid the singer:

"I hung my heart on a blackthorn tree,
    For I was young and gay;
 I feared that love would follow me
 And my poor heart betray.
 But who can guess what the end will be?
 Love played me a bitter jest—
 I danced, though my tears fall salt as the sea,
 I sing, with a thorn in my breast."

She stood listening, rooted to the spot as if some invisible warning finger had tapped her on the shoulder. She was trembling long before the song ended. Chill shivers flickered along her spine though the sunshine beat down upon her bare head.

Peering through a gap in the hedge she saw the two musicians, a young stable boy with his guitar and one of the girls from the laundry, bending over some linen spread out to bleach. To her own surprise Henriette found herself addressing the peasant girl who knelt there.

"You were singing just now. No, I'm not scolding. You have a very sweet voice. Can you tell me the name of that song?"

The pair turned from fright to foolish giggles of confusion. Still kneeling, the girl pushed back the red and yellow kerchief that covered her hair and answered shyly.

"It's a very old song, that one—too old to have a name."

"Isn't it rather a sad song?" Henriette persisted by way of accounting for her interest.

The young man and girl exchanged knowing glances. Evidently her remark amused them by its obviousness.

"Well, yes." The girl shrugged her shoulders eloquently. "But why not, mademoiselle? It's always sad when love makes people afraid."

She hurried on along the path, but she could hear those two whispering and giggling behind her.

"When love makes people afraid—it's always sad."

Why had it taken a Corsican peasant girl to tell her what she had fought off admitting to herself?

*chapter fifteen*

IT WAS NEW YEAR'S ONCE MORE; 1846, AND THE PAPERS predicting higher taxes, wider skirts, and further foreign alliances. Across the Channel, Great Britain under Sir Robert Peel's ministry rocked with agitation over a repeal of the Corn Laws, and already the specter of famine stalked over Ireland. Shut away in a London parlor, an invalid poetess named Elizabeth Barrett thrilled to the visits of a certain Robert Browning, with whom she would flee to Italy before the year ended.

In prison at Ham, Louis Napoleon Bonaparte had plenty of leisure to brood upon the late glories of his uncle and to speculate on the future while he waited to regain his freedom. He must be ready to step forward when his supporters should decide that the moment had come to strike at the House of Orléans.

In his palace the tired, aging King of France conferred with his ministers and House of Peers. He missed a certain hearty ring in the cheers that greeted his public appearances, but the band played louder to cover the thinness of lifted voices. They called him Louis-Philippe now, and only a few remembered his old nickname of Citizen King. But he no longer bothered about that. It took all his energy to go through the motions expected of him. At least France was at peace, and her relations with England and the young Victoria and her German consort were extremely friendly. As for the rest, he left them to Guizot, his Minister of Foreign Affairs.

In her room at the château of Choiseul-Praslin, Henriette Deluzy, who only occasionally remembered that the letter D on her brushes and writing case had ever stood for Desportes, welcomed the New Year in alone. She had scarcely been in Paris since the return from Corsica. The old Maréchal had kept his word, and a reconciliation of sorts had taken place. The Duc and Duchesse attended soirées and receptions together and were seen frequently driving and at the theater and opera. All the household, from grooms and kitchen maids up to the Duc's valet, Charpentier, and the inscrutable Madame Leclerc knew this was a mere formality; but at least it gave no further opportunity for items in the gossip sheets.

The Maréchal Sébastiani settled himself at Number 55, Rue du Faubourg-Saint-Honoré, and two of his brothers with their large families resided near by. It seemed to Henriette that they had deliberately closed in round the Duc, that he must literally feel engulfed with Sébastiani relatives. She guessed that his every movement was being watched, and that his father-in-law had laid down his ultimatum. Certainly he seemed worried and preoccupied whenever she saw him. But he never mentioned such matters on the few occasions when they were alone together. She knew that he dared not trust himself to speak of his despair. He had been trapped and humiliated; and there seemed to be no way out but to submit, at least to the extent of keeping up the appearances of a happy marriage.

Henriette could feel a greater tension in him. She did not believe that this outward domestic accord was more than a temporary state. It was only an interlude, like the brief pause that follows the breaking of one wave and the rising of the next. She, too, was caught in this unnatural quiet between storms. It was a strange and lonely time, but she almost welcomed it because of the illusion of peace it gave her. So, she thought, people must live through a siege, glad of sun and green leaves and such happy manifestations of the seasons, while their ears were ever on the alert for the rattle of shells that sent them scurrying for shelter. In a way the Duc's absence was a relief, even though the days seemed savorless without him. She need not be so terribly aware of his every word and glance. She need not strain to catch the personal meaning behind every inflection, or constantly try to give him sympathy without crossing that boundary which separated governess from married employer.

Isabella had been married in October. The ceremony had taken place in the family chapel at the château in order that the Dowager Duchesse of Praslin might be present. The Abbé Gallard had journeyed from Paris to perform the rites. It had been a time of great rejoicing and felicity, and the members of both Praslin and Sébastiani houses forgot their grievances to lavish affection and good wishes upon the young bride and bridegroom. The château overflowed with relatives of all ages; and Henriette found herself not only in charge of the young people but superintending the activities of the household, seeing that new servants were added to the staff, and that all the details connected with so important an event went smoothly. Her genius for directing others had never been given so large a scope, and she rose to the occasion magnificently. Even the Duchesse complimented her, and the Duc's gratitude had been touching.

"It is nothing," she had insisted the day after the wedding when he overwhelmed her with praise. "I love orderliness, monsieur. It hurts me to see disorder in a desk or drawer, and it is even more painful and unnecessary in the affairs of life."

"Yes," he had told her, "you have a passion for order. You've even brought it to the chaos of my own life as well as the routine of my household. It's a pity you can't take over the whole country." He smiled and gave her one of his direct admiring glances. "I can almost see you going about it with your quiet air of pleased determination, sorting out the affairs of state, tidying all Paris as if it were an overturned work-basket!"

"You make fun of me," she had protested. "I'm really a very poor housekeeper. I may tell others what should be done, but if it were necessary for me to build a fire and bake a loaf of bread—Well, we should all go hungry."

But she treasured his praise.

And so it was New Year's again, and she sat alone in her room trying to read from a beautifully bound book on the scenic wonders of America which the Duchesse had sent her as peace offering at Christmas. She turned the pages idly, trying not to think of Paris at this hour with the bells and the lights and the boulevards thronged with revelers, the churches warm with lights and incense where the devout raised prayers for the coming year. Louise, Céleste, and Marie had been privileged to sit up till midnight, and she had gone with them to wish their grandmother Happy New Year. The old Duchesse, grown increasingly frail in the last two years, they had found propped among her pillows, her fingers moving along her rosary beads while she waited for midnight to strike.

When the last note of the clock had sounded she put aside her beads, kissed her granddaughters on either cheek, and called for seed cakes and canary wine.

"Ah, the years!" the old lady had sighed in response to Henriette's good wishes for her health. "For me they are not what they used to be. At my age one is forever walking backward, stumbling over souvenirs of the past, left by those who have already gone. Never pray for a multitude of years, mademoiselle, for it is not meant that we should be ghosts to haunt ourselves."

"You're not a ghost, *Grand'mère*." Louise had broken in with one of her impulsive embraces. "Is she, mademoiselle? It's going to be a wonderful year, and Papa says I shall be betrothed before another."

"Yes, you'll be flying from the nest soon, my pet." Her grandmother had laid her shriveled fingers to the fresh young cheek. "May you be happy, whether or not I live to hear you make your vows. The years come and the years go; so enjoy them while you're young and heart-free."

Fond as she was of the old Duchesse, Henriette could not help agreeing with Louise's impatience at such familiar plaints.

"Mademoiselle," the girl had asked when they paused to say good night, "why do old people always talk as if you could be happy simply because you're young?"

"I don't know," she had answered, "unless it's because we forget grief more easily than joy. Perhaps that's the kindest trick memory can play on us when we're old. But aren't you happy tonight, my dear?"

"Oh, I suppose so, only I miss Isabella; and I keep wondering how she feels now she's a married woman. All the time I wonder how it will be for me. I want things to happen soon; and yet I'm a little afraid, too."

Henriette had been reassuring, and they had parted affectionately. But alone by her sitting-room fire she could no longer fight off dejection and restlessness. The frosty stillness of the country lying behind the rosy, drawn curtains depressed her. She envied the servants the companionship and good cheer they must be enjoying in the château's domestic quarters. She was not given to self-pity—she despised the trait in other people; yet for once it threatened to overwhelm her. Tonight she rebelled at being alone.

"Why should I be cursed with this loneliness?" she thought. "Must I always be caught between two generations without a chance to know my own? If I cannot have love, at least I could take comfort in the companionship of those who think as I think, who feel as I feel."

The tears she so seldom gave way to, rose behind her eyes. She made no effort to check them, but let the salty rush have its way.

"Yes," she told herself, "it will always be this way. Always like tonight, you will stand between the old and the young, listening to sighs for the past and hopes for the future. You belong to the present and yet what good is that to you, caught between what is over and what is waiting to begin—the old Duchesse whispering to dead friends, and Louise with her untried schoolgirl heart?"

After her tears dried, she rose and went to her desk. She could not sleep, and since she longed to be in Paris she would distract her mind by writing to the few friends she had there who might even now be speaking her name—the kind Remeys, cantankerous Madame Le Maire, and another whose interest had lately come to mean much to her. She had met the Reverend Frédéric Monod through the Protestant Church in Paris, which she attended whenever possible. Several times this brilliant writer on theological subjects, this man whose eloquence and faith were as moving as the sure logic of his mind, had preached from that pulpit to a congregation that had been swayed by his power. After listening to one of these sermons Henriette had been prompted to write to the preacher. One of his points, she had felt, might be enlarged further and given a double interpretation. She had written impersonally and scarcely expected to receive a reply. But the Reverend Frédéric Monod had been impressed by her intelligent grasp of his sermon. His response had been cordial, and a meeting was arranged on one of her free afternoons. From his first encounter each had found the other a stimulating personality. She found in him a most unusual type of clergyman for France or any other country. Here was a man of fine physical presence with the intelligence of a scholar and the religious zeal of a prophet. Well born and prosperous, with tolerance for others yet with the highest of personal standards, he was that rare combination—a minister of the Gospel and a man of the world.

He lived simply but with dignity in a large old house where he received Henriette in his study on more than one occasion. Each day except Saturday and Sunday he opened his doors between four and six o'clock to any who might care to come, and for those hours he gave his whole mind and heart to the religious and personal problems of his visitors. Henriette told him little directly of herself and her life in the Praslin ménage. They talked usually of matters he had mentioned in his sermons, or they discussed the unrest and discontent among the people of France, the mistakes of the King and his ministers in their policies. Always his comments were wise and worth hearing, and he had a way of drawing her out to express her own views.

"Ah, Mademoiselle Deluzy," he would caution, "you're much too headlong and idealistic. You must not jump to conclusions so fast, not even if you have read your John Stuart Mill so thoroughly and though you can quote Miss Barrett's 'Cry of the Children' in such perfect English. Of course the world would be better if all the people in it could be well fed and well educated. But remember, there's no way been found yet to pry holes in men's brains and pour the learning in. It's discouraging how many seem to carry a complete immunity to education in their systems."

"That may be," she would retort stubbornly, "but I still say let every one have a chance at it. That's the only way we can ever tell those who, you say, are immune from those who might learn and benefit."

So they would amicably exchange opinions, sometimes arguing their points, sometimes in complete accord until other visitors arrived or coffee was brought in an old family urn that spoke to Henriette eloquently of her host's background and financial independence. Always she left that house refreshed in mind and spirit. She had met his wife only once, and she knew as little of his life and habits as he knew of hers. It was a friendship of the mind that in no way involved the senses, for which, in her inner perplexity and stress, she gave fervent thanks.

So tonight, after she had written notes to the Remeys and Madame Le Maire, she also wrote to the Reverend Frédéric Monod to wish him well in the coming year. It was a courteous, charming note; and she felt in a more benevolent mood towards the whole world when she had sealed it. It was pleasant to let her pen slip over the smooth, expensive note paper provided by the château. Impulsively she reached for another sheet and addressed the greeting to her grandfather. She could afford to be charitable to the harsh old man. After all, he was her only relative, and she would make the gesture of forgetting past differences. It gave her no small satisfaction to slip a hundred-franc note into the letter.

"After all," she thought, "he cannot say that I am ungrateful, no matter what other names he may find for me."

Still she sat at the desk, her eyes fixed on the remaining sheet of note paper. Blank and white it lay under her fingers. There were the pens and ink—so near, yet she might not write the one letter it would have eased her heart to put on paper. A simple Happy New Year addressed to him and signed with her initials might fall under other eyes that would twist the words to mean something ugly and evil. She dared not allow herself even this innocent gesture of good will.

All went smoothly and well in those early months of 1846. The weeks slipped by, serene and uneventful, save for the brief, unpredictable appearances of the Duc. He

spent long hours with his mother and also much time supervising work in the park. The building of a luxurious conservatory to replace an old greenhouse had been started,
and he was full of elaborate plans for raising rare varieties
of plants.

"Why must you have all these hothouse flowers, monsieur?" she asked him once when he was taking her through
the half-finished glass addition, explaining all that would be
blooming there by another winter. "Soon there will be snow-
drops and primroses in the woods, and then summer will be
coming. Of course these artifically raised flowers will be rare
and beautiful, but somehow I think we were not meant to
upset the course of the seasons."

"But that's what pleases me," he told her. "I like to do just
that, to feel I have power over the seasons. And then it's a
distraction. One must have something to do."

Though he smiled and shrugged, she felt the boredom
behind his words. So she said no more about the greenhouse.
It would probably cost, she reflected, more than enough to
support the Remeys for a year, and in less than that time he
would be tired of it. He left her presently to consult some
workmen building one of the great brick furnaces. She
watched him as he stood there, head and shoulders above
them, dwarfing their bodies by the magnificent proportions
of his own. His head was turned sideways, and she was
struck anew by the beauty of his features. In full face he was
a handsome man; but the indolent fullness of lips and cheeks
and the lines about his eyes made him look his forty-one
years. But in profile the proud, clear modeling was accentuated. He reminded her of some sculptured head on an old
coin.

"Oh," she thought, "what a pity he was not born in another age than this! Not in Greece, perhaps—he's too rug-
ged for that—but in the north somewhere. Yes, he's like the
figurehead of some old Viking ship. He belongs to a time
when it was enough for a man to be strong and beautiful.
Now that's less valued than the cunning of a man's mind to
outwit the schemes of other minds."

She had never been deceived that the Duc's mind was
remarkable in any way. His gifts lay not in that direction,
but in his body's vigor. He had been endowed above others
with vitality and good looks. And all this was going to waste
before her eyes. There was no outlet for this power that

possessed him, and some day it would break loose with the very weight of its unused force, and his own strength would be his undoing. She felt this instinctively, as she waited in the half-completed conservatory. It seemed to her only another symbol of the futile extravagance by which he tried to appease his own unrest.

Why must she stand there helpless to meet his need? Time was slipping by them both with every breath they drew, and he played with piles of brick as he must have played with blocks long ago on a nursery floor. There must be something she could do, something she could say. But what? She belonged to a world where people made their own way, living precariously by their wits or the work of their hands. That was not his world. He could never understand what she meant when she talked of such things. He had not been born to understand; and, in a way, that was what she loved in him.

"Come!" He was beside her again. "You must see where I mean to put up the new pavilion by the lily pond next summer."

"Ah, but, monsieur," she began. Then she broke off before she had started to protest.

She could not say simply to him: "Monsieur, a pavilion by the lily pond is not going to make you happy. It will not change your life by so much as a single grain. Face your misery, and find some means to overcome it. Work at something till you ache and the sweat runs into your eyes. Make haste before it's too late and this unused power strikes back at you."

"No, I've been away from the schoolroom too long," she said aloud. "I must go now; besides, I'm cold standing here in this February wind."

"You don't look cold, Mademoiselle Deluzy," he persisted, his eyes disarming her by their scrutiny. "Your lips aren't blue, and your cheeks are positively rosy."

But she did not give in. "I tell you I'm cold," she repeated stubbornly. She hurried back to the château with that queer mixture of glowing inner warmth and conflict of emotions which was more and more the aftermath of her meetings with him. Only now she no longer asked: "Where will it all end?" She acknowledged that she was caught fast in an intricate web not of her own making. In the beginning she had believed she could keep free of its threads. Later she had tried to break away. But now she had given up both these courses. She had no wish to escape.

In mid-February the older girls returned to Paris, and she had good reports of their progress in studies from Albert Remey and of their social doings from Louise, who wrote of theaters and opera and numerous outings with her mother and her Sébastiani cousins. Henriette had more time than she knew how to use, with Berthe and Raynald her only charges. She busied herself with her painting; spent much time reading aloud to the old Duchesse; she read volume after volume to herself in the long evenings; and wrote letters to her scattered friends. Many of those she wrote that winter went to Isabella in Turin and to her other ex-pupil in England, Nina Hislop, who had also been married. These two young women, who differed so greatly in temperament and upbringing, both turned to their governess with affectionate confidences. Their detailed accounts of themselves and their households were hardly as absorbing to her as to the writers of these lengthy and naïve letters. She often smiled over their characteristic outpourings: the English girl's, so shy and conventional, so true to the pattern of domesticity being set by the young Queen; Isabella's less restrained and far more lively descriptions of social activity and domestic bliss. But both were happy; their physical contentment and the secret intoxication of being wives and heads of prosperous households pervaded every letter and seemed almost to leap out between the neatly penned words.

"Dearest Mademoiselle," one posted from Sussex might begin, "your felicitations upon the happy event to which we look forward in midsummer filled me with joy. I pray that I may be equal to the responsibilities in store for me, though I must confess that often I feel very young and not in the least like one so soon to become a mother. But my dear husband is very devoted and considerate of me at this time. He quite spoils me with surprises from his visits to London, and I wish that I might show you his latest one—a rosewood drawing-room set, done in crimson damask. How strange to think that not so long ago I was still a timid schoolgirl, and you were correcting my French exercises . . ."

Or it might be: "Chère Mademoiselle: Your letter was most dear to me. I was homesick at sight of your writing on the familiar château paper, but only for a moment, for though I think often of the old schoolroom I would not wish to return to it. The days fly, and each so full of things to see and do, and my dear husband lavishes every attention he can think of upon me. We dine out often and entertain frequently ourselves now that we are settled in our own villa which I can scarcely wait to have you see. And I am so happy, chère Mademoiselle. It seems impossible that I could ever have entertained those doubts and fears about which you once tried to reassure me . . .'"

She was proud of these two, and their affectionate gratitude was sweet to her. Yet, when the letters came, brimming over with happy confidence, she could not repress a pang. These girls were married women now—secure and beloved and already meeting experiences she had never known, that perhaps she would never know. Each would fulfill the destiny that Nature had intended. Soon one would be a mother, and before long the other would be writing as rapturous an announcement. And here she sat, still a spinster and a governess. A dozen such years lay behind her, and no doubt a dozen more lay ahead. In a few months she would be thirty-four years old. She flattered herself that she appeared considerably younger than her age. Still one could not overlook facts. She had not had the means or the opportunity to marry well. She had only had her youth to offer for a dowry. And now she no longer had that. It had been spent, without stint, on the youth of girls like Nina and Isabella. She did not begrudge it, but sometimes she smiled a little grimly as she put away their letters.

There was never the faintest hint of bitterness in her answers because she loved youth for itself. She had always given herself to it—first from necessity and then because it had become a habit. It was natural for her to reach out to others. She gave freely all that she had to offer, and by the same token she drew from others and was nourished even by experiences she might not share. Like a tree set in meager soil, she drove her roots in every direction, seeking the elements her spirit craved.

The talked-of visit to Isabella in Turin came about, however, far sooner than she had expected.

*chapter sixteen*

IT WAS EARLY SUMMER, AND THE DUC AND DUCHESSE DE Praslin had taken a villa by the sea for the month of June.

Dr. Simon had recommended a watering place for Madame's health after the winter in Paris; and since she had not felt equal to the long journey to Corsica, Dieppe had been chosen. Henriette and the two younger children had joined the rest of the family there a week before, and the reunion had been a happy one. The weather was fine, with sunlight glittering on each wave that broke in rhythmic whiteness on the beach below their windows. At first the Duchesse was almost cordial in her meeting with Henriette, though she still refused to eat at the same table with her.

This had been the first cause of trouble. The villa was far from large, and serving two separate sets of meals simultaneously could not be managed as easily as in Paris or at the château.

The Duc had made the mistake of trying to argue with her, and of pointing out her unreasonableness in such petty matters. At last, when he refused to humor her and even went so far as to take all his meals with the children and Henriette, the old grievances and outbursts began. Through the flimsy walls that separated the young people's apartment from those of their parents Henriette heard the familiar reverberations of that heavy, accusing voice directed not so much against the Duc as against herself. No matter what actually happened to touch off Madame's temper, Henriette knew that it would somehow end by her being to blame. Though she had long ago learned immunity to similar tirades, she could not entirely close her eyes and ears. Once she even begged the Duc to make some sort of compromise.

"Please, monsieur," she had pleaded, "let me eat alone if that will help the situation. Quarters here are small, and we must make adjustments."

"The Duchesse refuses to make any, and I see no reason why the whole household should be upset to satisfy this whim of hers."

"Then, monsieur, I beg you to dine with her. I hesitate to interfere in such personal matters; still, if you could humor her these few weeks for the children's sakes, it would be easier for us all."

But he shook his head, and the old obdurate expression settled about his lips. He shrugged expressively.

"If it's not this, it will be something else," he insisted.

She knew then that matters were no better, but worse, between them. The strain, she guessed, was far greater than before the old Maréchal had given his ultimatum months ago. The very fact that the Duchesse had her husband's company in public, that to the eyes of the world they were reunited, only made his indifference to her in private more unbearable. And she would never let go for an instant, though what she clung to so doggedly must be more merciless in its power to hurt than nettles stinging bare flesh.

"Poor fool," Henriette thought often during those difficult days by the sea, "she's only goading him and herself to desperation. How can she and her father be so blind as to believe that their money can win back his affections? Why can't they see that it only makes him more bitter because it mocks his manhood. *Ciel* I wish this month at Dieppe were safely over."

Outwardly she took no notice of black moods and rebuffs. But under her apparent serenity she writhed at this tyranny imposed by the Duchesse. She seemed bent on infecting the entire household with her own misery. The children felt the tension and reacted according to their dispositions. In a week the long anticipated holiday had taken on the confused unreality of a nightmare.

"Sometimes," Henriette thought, "the weak learn kindness in self-defense; but it's not so with this woman. She must torture others with her own misfortune. It's terrible when the weak are also cruel for then we are defenseless against them."

It was a combination that shocked her. It was as if, when these two elements joined forces, they produced an almost inhuman quality from which she reacted violently. There were times when she had all she could do to keep silence as one or another of their little group suffered. At other times she turned chill with her own contempt for such exhibitions of petulance and uncontrolled temper. The only excuse for them, she told herself, must be temporary madness, and there were occasions when Henriette actually doubted the Duchesse's sanity.

At such times the children's welfare became her first concern, and she maneuvered to keep them away from the villa as much as possible. Louise and the three middle sisters had acquired considerable skill at avoiding their mother's demands. So the two younger ones were most often pounced upon. Almost invariably disaster followed. Berthe was not easily hurt. She had a thick skin and seldom let others prick

below the surface. But this shell of indifference which protected her had a particularly irritating effect upon the Duchesse. Raynald, on the other hand, took his mother's moods
and reproaches to heart. Although he had become sturdier
physically, he could still be nervously upset by any emotional strain, and his mother's shifting moods reacted upon
his whole system. Particularly he resented any slights, real
or imagined, to his beloved Mademoiselle Deluzy. He would
fly like a furious small dog to her defense, and this the Duchesse naturally took as a deliberate campaign on Henriette's part to turn her youngest child against her.

That fortnight in Dieppe grew daily more unendurable.
Between her efforts to appease the Duchesse and her efforts
to make the children respond to unwelcomed affection,
Henriette's usually steady nerves felt frayed; and her patience had never been more tried. She had few chances to
talk with the Duc, for she was more than ever certain that
the servants had been ordered to watch them both. Several
of the old ones had left the Praslin service, and the newcomers were all on the best of terms with Madame Leclerc;
so Henriette knew they would be only too eager to bear tales
to her discredit. She went her way with care and a stubborn
determination to put through the stay without disaster. For
disaster was in the air. She could read the warning signals
altogether too well by now, yet she was unprepared for the
storm when it finally broke upon them.

It had been a glorious, bright blue day, and she had spent
most of it on the sand with Berthe and Raynald while the
older girls went on some expedition with their father. The
water had been warm, and the two children had splashed
and bathed delightedly while she kept watchful eyes upon
them from under the striped umbrella beside their bathing
machine. They had started back by midafternoon, walking
along the promenade where the small shops faced the ocean.
Their progress was slow because of numerous shells and
starfish which Raynald insisted upon bringing from the
beach. When they were not pausing to retrieve these treasures from underfoot, Berthe would be held by some particularly enticing window display. Halfway to the villa, they
met the Duc and the others, and that meant purchases of
toys and sweetmeats. They reached home at last full of chatter and in gay spirits after the hours of salt air and sun. The
villa seemed deserted, and the drawing-room beckoned cool

and pleasant in its soft gray and rose with the glass doors open to the terrace and the blue water beyond. They all drifted in, and presently one of the girls went to a square piano and began trying the keys.

"Oh, here's some music," Louise exclaimed, looking up from a cabinet she had been investigating.

Evidently the former tenants of the villa had not been inclined to classical music. The pieces were all gay and popular, with waltzes and polkas predominating. Polkas had been the rage for the past two seasons, and the girls needed no urging to dance. The drawing-room furniture rocked to the lively tunes and the quick steps of Marie, Céleste, Amélie, and Berthe while Louise's fingers sped over the black and ivory keys. Henriette leaned against the sofa cushions and gave herself up to the infectiousness of dance music and the spontaneity of the girls' delighted response to it. Their young, slim bodies in full ruffled skirts moved with such lightness and spirit. Their cheeks grew flushed, their eyes were starry, and their curls kept time with the quick steps. Up and down the room they went, weaving in and out of furniture, now dancing into patches of brightness by the open doors, now moving into dimmer corners.

With the sea so blue and the music so gay and the young limbs so slim and sure, Henriette felt entranced. The headache she had been fighting off after the glare of the beach left her miraculously. She felt light-hearted and festive, as if the polka had taken possession of her, too, though only her toes hidden under her wide skirts gave her away by discreet tapping. She looked across at the Duc, who stood by the terrace doors. He was watching his daughters with intent appreciation; and his look disarmed her as it always did when she caught him unawares, studying his children. All that was simple and genuine and kind in the man was uppermost then. She stared at him fascinated, while the artist in her tried to fix that image clearly in her mind. She wished that she had the power to paint him as she saw him in that moment of affectionate relaxation.

He looked over in her direction and smiled as their eyes met.

"Mademoiselle," Louise pleaded, "couldn't you play one polka for us? I haven't had a chance to leave the piano. Please do."

Henriette obligingly took her place, and presently she saw

Louise catch her father's hands and lead him into the room as her partner. She had never seen the Duc in this rôle before, though she had always known that he must be a superb dancer. As she saw him begin the lively steps with that easy, effortless grace, she envied Louise, and for the next few minutes she scarcely lifted her eyes from the sheets of music before her. Then, growing more familiar with the notes, she allowed herself to look up and catch glimpses of the reflected scene in a long mirror that faced the piano.

It was in one of these glimpses that she became obsessed by a peculiar sensation—not of arrested motion in space, but rather as if all motion were gathered in that room, embodied in the whirling dancers and her own speeding fingers. She bent to the keys in sudden frenzy. She was possessed with the idea of keeping alive this gayety, this lovely rhythm which would die when she stopped playing as surely as it had been born when the music began. In her ten fingers lay the power to evoke this miracle of motion. This must not end, this must not be over. Quick feet, stepping so surely and freely in unison; warm swaying bodies and glowing cheeks—it was as if she saw them all cold and still forever. But the revelation only spurred her on. She played faster and more furiously, gaining what rest she could on some longer note as it flew past her like the flight of a bird seen from a train window. And always, under the music her hands made, a warning beat in her ears, faint and fine as the imprisoned whisper of sea in a shell: "Some day you will remember all this; some day when time has caught up with these swift feet and all of you in this room are scattered to the four winds."

Over and over she played the tune, her own tireless energy willing the dancers to go on without pause. It was only when a sudden shadow darkened the mirror and Raynald plucked anxiously at her arm, that her hands fell limply into her lap. Unable to rise from the piano bench, she turned and saw the Duchesse standing alone in the doorway. For a moment no one moved, the dancers stood still where they had left off. Then she saw the heavy figure bear down upon them, trailing yards of violet silk as she came.

"So, Theo," the tense throaty voice was beginning, "so I find you at last after hours of waiting! What excuse have you to give me this time?"

"Excuse?" he announced with determined casualness,

keeping his arm about Louise. "Why, Fanny, surely I need no excuse to be here at home, dancing with my own daughters?"

Before she spoke again the Duchesse's glance swept the room and rested suspiciously upon Henriette, who still sat before the mute piano.

"You need not try to mend matters by making light of them."

The dark eyes flashed, and Henriette caught the peculiar reddish luster that she had come to dread in them. It was like an ominous light in the sky that always preceded some cataclysm. The girls shifted uneasily and drew together; Raynald pressed closer.

"Isn't it enough for you to humiliate me at home, without doing it publicly as well? Do you think I enjoyed being made a fool of before them all at the Villa Quelques Fleurs?"

"At the Villa Quelques Fleurs? What are you talking about, Fanny?"

"Where we were invited this afternoon by Signor and Signora Mantino, and where I've been waiting for you to join me for the last hour and a half. Do you think I enjoyed their questions about your absence and the sly looks they exchanged when I had to leave alone? And all the time I made excuses that no one believed, you were here, enjoying yourself—without a thought of me except to laugh and say: 'While the cat's away, the mice will play.' Oh, I know what goes on behind my back!"

"Please, Fanny, be still for a moment." He dropped Louise's arm and stepped in front of the girls. "I knew nothing about this invitation, this appointment that I failed to keep."

"And you care nothing, that's plain. But if you'd taken the trouble to read what I wrote you this morning you'd have known. I left it myself at your door since I'm not permitted to speak to you any longer except when you feel in the mood to grant me a few minutes of your time."

He must have left the Duchesse's letter unread. Henriette guessed that from the way he reddened at mention of it. But he managed to keep his voice cool and deliberate.

"I'm sorry if I caused you inconvenience," he explained. "But I left my room early to take the older girls on a little outing. We've only just returned, and I dare say the letter is lying now unopened on my secretary."

"And I dare say there are many others unopened there

and in your waste basket; or perhaps you and Mademoiselle use them to light the fire. Perhaps she even enjoys keeping my letters for curlpapers. It's the sort of irony that would please her."

Henriette did not hear his response. The Duchesse's attack had been so unexpected that composure left her. The drawing room and the figures in it turned hazy before her eyes. She felt a dull pounding in her ears, but whether it came from the surf on the beach below the terrace or from the blood that mounted in a hot wave to her neck and cheeks and forehead she could never tell. She wanted to rise and lead the children from that room. The Duchesse seemed to fill it with her own distorted imagination. But Henriette could not move. She had no power to make herself leave the piano. The little black notes of music moved fantastically before her eyes, and she could scarcely focus her attention on the flow of words that came across the room. She knew that they concerned her. Out of the vehement torrent of this other woman's rage she caught her own name, recurring again and again, almost like a refrain.

"No, Theo, no! You can't stop me. I've kept silence too long. Let the children know how you torture their mother; how you and this woman have turned them against me. Some day they'll understand, when their own hearts are breaking from neglect and cruelty; only then it will be too late—"

"Fanny, in God's name, I beg you—"

"You may well call on Him, for He knows my sorrows and my tears and my prayers. Yes, God knows what I've suffered ever since you brought Mademoiselle Deluzy here. As if I hadn't been shamed enough before she came. And now I'm ridiculed or pitied wherever I go. I see it in people's eyes whether they humiliate me by words or not. And she sits at the head of my table while I eat alone like an outcast in my own house. You and my children hang on her every word. It's Mademoiselle this and Mademoiselle that till I declare she has more wiles than the serpent in the Garden of Eden!"

Her voice broke, and a second of horrified silence followed before Raynald lifted up his head and answered with a shrillness that brought Henriette back to her senses.

"No," the little boy cried, and she felt his whole frame trembling beside her. "No, Mademoiselle isn't a serpent.

She's good and kind, and I love her. I love her, and I hate you!"

"Hush!" Henriette laid her hand to his lips and tried to quiet the wild sobs that overtook him. "Be quiet, Raynald. Please, *chéri*, please."

"But—but she called you wicked names. Sh-she has no right—,"

"There you see, even Raynald, my baby, takes her part. She's bewitched you all, and I might as well be dead and out of your way forever."

"Fanny, please, you must listen to reason."

The Duc laid a restraining hand on her arm. But his touch only seemed to excite her. Her resentment had been gathering for days, and now nothing could stop the savage force of it, not even her children drawing away from her in a frightened, wide-eyed group. He kept his hand on her arm. Henriette guessed the intensity of his feeling from the way his fingers sank into the plumpness under the violet silk. What a grip he had! His strength must be phenomenal when he was roused. Such a change had come over his face that she recoiled before the transformation. Only a few minutes ago he had been a different human being. Now all that was amiable and pleasant and kind had given way to hardness and cruelty and a positive hatred. The features themselves actually seemed to have altered before her eyes; to have assumed the crude exaggeration of a painted mask.

*"Mon Dieu,"* she thought, "if she should try him beyond the limits of his endurance! I must do something. I mustn't sit here and let this go on."

The Duchesse had begun speaking again, her voice now heavy and accusing, now rising with uncontrolled shrillness. Henriette no longer heard the words she was saying. With an effort she forced herself to rise from the piano bench. Keeping firm hold of Raynald's hand, she moved forward.

"Madame, monsieur." The clear firm tones of her voice silenced the Duchesse's hysterical outpouring for a moment. She regarded Henriette out of eyes that had the glassy stare of a half-crazed animal. "With your permission I will take the children to their rooms."

Raynald shrank against her, his face hidden. The five girls pressed closer. Their stiff full skirts made a faint rustling in the sudden quiet.

"You needn't trouble, mademoiselle." The Duchesse's voice fell like a whiplash upon them all. "Don't think of inconveniencing yourself on my account! No, go back to the piano. Go on with your music. Dance, all of you. Don't give your mother a thought. Let me go, Theo, let me go!"

She shook him off before he could restrain her, and made for the terrace. They saw her disappear down the steps that led to the sea. So abrupt had been her bolt from the room that for a full moment not one of them uttered a sound or moved. Yet they had all caught the desperate note in her voice. There was not a doubt what she meant to do.

"Papa! Papa!" Louise found her voice first. "Don't let her!"

She would have followed her father as he started through the long doors, but he pushed her away. Then he ran hatless towards the water.

Mechanically Henriette heard herself quieting the sobbing Raynald and reassuring the sisters. But all the time she helped them put away the scattered sheets of music and set the disordered room to rights her ears were strained for any unnatural sounds from the beach or promenade. Any moment she expected to hear warning shouts from below; and as time passed she waited for the tread of men's boots on the flagstones as they bore a lifeless form in dripping violet silk between them. But half an hour passed, and the house remained quiet; the waves twinkled blue in the sun and broke in steady rhythm on the hard-packed sand. The tears dried on the children's faces though they still appeared strained and furtive and they spoke in scared whispers. Raynald clung to her as had been his habit years before. He gulped forlornly and could hardly be persuaded to spread his sea treasures to dry in a tray on the window sill.

It was another half-hour before the sound of steps and voices from the next apartment told her that tragedy had been averted. With relief she recognized Madame's voice speaking to her maid.

She did not see the Duc again till they gathered for early dinner. He reappeared just as the soup was being served, immaculately dressed for the evening. Only a faint tension about his eyes and at the corners of his mouth gave any hint of his recent experience. That was plain from his manner and the brief, curt assurance to his daughters that their mother was quite herself again and that he did not wish to discuss what had taken place in the drawing-room. To a timid question from Louise he replied guardedly that Mamma had been badly affected by driving in the strong sunshine. She had taken something to quiet her nerves before retiring.

But the strain of the afternoon had been too great for Raynald. Halfway through the meal, he grew pale, slipped from his chair, and left the table with a hurried excuse. Following him to his room Henriette found the boy struggling against an attack of nausea. She made him as comfortable as possible and sat by his bed till he fell asleep at last, exhausted, and she could return to the others.

The Duc was playing chess with Céleste, but he called Louise to take his place. Henriette found herself following him to a balcony which opened from the room. It did not adjoin the next apartment, so they were sure of privacy there.

"Monsieur," she spoke to him through the darkness, "I must know if she is safe. She did herself no harm?"

"No," he said. "Not this time, though I thought it was the end. Perhaps it might have been better so— God forgive me for what I say."

"Tell me what happened? What did she try to do? You were gone so long I almost went mad listening."

"There was no sign of her on the beach. I ran along it, as close to the water's edge as I could get. People pointed to me. They must have thought I'd lost my mind. Then I decided she must have made for the amusement pier—perhaps she'd even plunged from it already. I kept looking everywhere for that violet dress and I was afraid to ask people if they'd seen her. But as I started back along the Promenade, in one of those little shops, I caught sight of her. There she was, bending over a tray full of knickknacks, talking to the shopkeeper and picking out what she wanted."

"It's not possible, monsieur. How did she seem then?"

"Calmer than I am now. I stood beside her while she made the purchases. Then I called a carriage and made her get in. We drove back, and I left her at the door of her own room."

"Did she have anything more to say?"

"Nothing much. It was exactly as if that scene you witnessed had never been. I was too unnerved myself to bring it up. My one idea was to see her safely indoors."

"What do you make of it, monsieur?"

"I don't know what to make of it except that we mustn't run the risk of another. She's never given way like this before the children. They are not to be subjected to it again."

"They've heard enough today, monsieur. Whether they know what she meant or why she turned on me, they guessed she meant to kill herself. They realize that she hates me. Raynald is ill now as a result. What am I to do? I can't stay on here, that's plain."

"You will take Louise and the two youngest and go to Turin at once. There's a train you can catch to Paris tomorrow noon. Isabella has been begging for a visit, and the change will do Raynald good. Yes, that's the best plan."

He was so close to her there in the darkness on the narrow iron balcony that she could hear him draw a deep breath of relief at the decision he had made. Even without seeing him she was acutely aware of his bewilderment and confusion, of his need of her. They whispered together like two frightened children who had just escaped from danger, but who clung to one another because they knew that even greater danger might by lying just ahead.

"And after Turin—what then?"

She wanted so much to take his hand that she had to keep both her own pressed to the cold iron railing at her back.

"God knows," he murmured. "We'll face that when it comes. Act as if this had never been. Put the children off if they question you, and in a fortnight she'll no doubt be urging your return."

"But I must think of myself, monsieur. You heard her this afternoon. She—she wasn't quite human. That's what terrifies me. I think she's deranged, particularly so where I am concerned. You know I've tried to go before, and now—"

He reached out and laid his hand on her shoulder. The pressure of his strong fingers came hotly through the thin material of her dress.

"And now you will go in and pack your things and get a long night's rest. The train leaves at noon tomorrow precisely."

"But it's no use to bury one's head in the sand like a silly ostrich when facts must be faced."

"I shall see you to the train. Arrangements will be made for you to spend the night in Paris at the Rue du Faubourg-

Saint-Honoré and continue south the day after."

"Please listen to me, monsieur. I've only brought you trouble, though I've tried to do my best for you, for the children."

"And I'd consider it a great favor, Mademoiselle Deluzy, if you would see that Berthe and Louise write their mother from Turin. Perhaps you also would write her a letter with your own impression of Isabella. Such a letter would please the Duchesse, but of course I shall leave that to you. You have excellent judgment in all things—"

"In all but one, monsieur"—she moved away from him towards the room where the girls clustered together in the lamplight—"or I should never let you persuade me against my better judgment—"

"Then you'll do what I ask? Good! I'll order the carriage for eleven tomorrow."

She wavered there on the doorsill, then impulsively turned back to him and the darkness. She felt the warm strength of his great frame behind her, and for a brief moment she let herself lean against it.

"You ask too much." She drew away resolutely. "Do I have to tell you that what happened this afternoon is sure to happen again?"

"There's nothing you could tell me that I do not know already. But if I should tell you what my days and nights have become you'd understand what it means to have you here in my household. One snatches a moment now and then to forget. To be happy—that's why I'm asking this of you, for the children, most of all for myself."

"Monsieur"—she dared not let him guess how the urgency of his appeal affected her—"I'd help you if I could, but there's little enough I can do. I've only brought discord and scandal to your household, at least to the eyes of the world."

"Who cares for the world? I didn't suppose, Mademoiselle Deluzy, that with your courage, your independence, you'd let yourself be dictated to by gossip and convention."

"Perhaps I've been too independent because my own conscience was clear. But I'm beginning to realize that when we break through the shell of convention we can never crawl back into it again. That protection is gone. I've gained many things by staying here with your children, monsieur, but I've lost much also."

"And you'd do it again because you're brave and generous, wouldn't you?"

She was moved by the simple directness of his question. His almost childish trust in her devotion and integrity were more eloquent than any other appeal he might have made.

"I will go to Turin tomorrow," she told him at last.

Bending over her boxes and portmanteau later that evening, she asked herself again and again why she had not held out against him. Where was her spirit that she had not written the Duchesse a letter of resignation before she put out her lamp for the night? What had become of her pride? At what moment in the five years that lay behind her had she let that precious commodity slip out of her keeping?

*chapter seventeen*

THE REUNION WITH ISABELLA WAS SO DELIGHTFUL THAT they lingered in Turin for the rest of the summer. After those days in Dieppe this carefree interlude in new surroundings reacted upon the young people like wine. It was like old times, they all agreed, to be together again.

Isabella's young husband made a most agreeable host, and when it became necessary for him to go to Sardinia on business, he was grateful to leave his wife in such congenial company. She and Louise were inseparable. When the older sisters had plans of their own Henriette took Berthe and Raynald on long drives and excursions. She found distraction in this. It eased her of problems she could never quite shake from her mind. So they visited the Cathedral, the palaces, and explored the outlying regions for relics of early Roman civilization.

"See," she would point out, "this is part of the old wall. The Romans built it before Christ was born, and here we sit and rest ourselves on it in the year 1846. It's strange to think that what men's hands built a thousand years ago can still endure."

In making the past vivid to the children she was often able to forget the present, more particularly the future. But there were other times when she would grow absent-minded in the middle of something she was saying till Berthe or Raynald prompted her politely. This happened once as they were examining some stonework in a chapel.

"Ugh!" Berthe had pointed to a design of leaves and crude but unmistakably carved mice. "Why do they have such horrid things as mice in a church?"

The priest who was showing them about had smiled indulgently.

"It's part of an ancient legend from the East," he explained. "No one knows how old it is or how it found its way into a Christian church. But the story concerns a traveler lost in a far country, who is perishing from thirst. At last he sees a plant growing above a precipice. On its broad leaves is a flower, its cup filled with delicious nectar. The traveler manages by clinging to the stalk to reach the cup, but just as he prepares to quench his thirst he sees below him two mice, one white and one black, nibbling the stem which is his only support. Slowly they are eating it, fiber by fiber. When they meet, the traveler knows that he will be swept away to destruction, but still he puts his lips to the flower's cup and drinks."

"And what then, *mon père?*" Raynald's eyes were wide and dark.

"Well, my son, there's no more to the story. We call it an allegory, and I can only explain it to you in symbols. That traveler stands for all men who have ever lived on earth. The mice are day and night—one white, one black; and they slowly nibble time away from under us. Yet, even in the face of certain death, men still reach for the good things of life and find them sweet to the taste."

The children were not impressed. Already they had found some new distraction. But Henriette lingered by the primitive piece of stonecutting, and when they left she thanked the priest for his trouble and dropped more coins than usual in the alms box. She could not put the legend out of her mind. It seemed to have survived the ages solely for her.

"Yes," she told herself. "I know that leaf above the precipice. I know because I'm clinging to it now, and the mice are eating my days and nights away. But how many of us, I wonder, cling to leaves that hold no nectar?"

She no longer twisted and turned possibilities this way and that. She went from one day to the next, and the old

dread lifted like a fog bank from her immediate horizon.
She would go back to Paris with an open mind and decide
then upon the wisest course. She would talk to Frédéric
Monod, tell him something of her difficulties, and ask his
advice. Autumn would be a better time to seek another position if need be. Here in Turin the problems of the Praslin
household no longer closed in about her. She did not feel
completely surrounded by domestic intrigue and conflicting
emotions from which she could never escape. Almost she
convinced herself that everything might come out right in
the end if she could be patient enough.

This hope was encouraged in late August by the arrival
of a letter from Melun, addressed to Henriette in the Duchesse's own hand. It was in reply to a rather guarded and
perfunctory report she had sent the Duchesse about her
daughters.

Praslin, August 25, 1846

I will not delay a moment further, my dear Mademoiselle, in thanking you for your kind letter which gave me
great pleasure. You apologized for its length, but far from
finding it tedious, I could have wished it to have been twice
as long. It was brought me with Berthe's from the village
post office this evening. Truly I cannot deny that it was
time a letter reached me, for my head and my heart had
been much disturbed by the long silence. But all's well
that ends well.

You can guess how overjoyed I am at all you tell me of
Isabella and her happiness. But I am rather surprised
that you should find her so unchanged by the new life
and experiences. Her letters to me show a great difference,
so much more painstaking and expansive.

I am indeed counting on your kindness in continuing
to send me information about my absent ones. My little
girls here are constantly at my side. On fine days we spend
hours in the Park and often we gather and read aloud
from the works of Molière. There has been an epidemic
of fever in the neighborhood, so we live completely iso-
lated; but, far from being prisoners, my dear daughters
and I are enjoying our solitude.

I was glad to hear that both Louise and Berthe speak
of me often with Isabella, even though you may only

have mentioned this to please me. But in any case the
words brought happy tears to my eyes.

Forgive, dear Mademoiselle, this poor letter, written
from the fullness of my heart. Once more I thank you a
thousand times for your note; and I beg you to write me
further details, as I could never hear enough of them.

                                    FANNY SÉBASTIANI PRASLIN

This letter Henriette read and reread, trying to fathom the
mood and meaning behind its unusual affability. What could
she do but take it in the spirit of good will in which it had evidently been written? She knew the Duchesse was not clever
or subtle enough by nature to assume a rôle she did not feel.
Whatever her faults, she was at least sincere and simple to
the point of primitiveness. Henriette could only hope that
the outburst at Dieppe had cleared the air. Perhaps it took
violent measures to purge so violent a nature of accumulated
grievances. If she regretted her behavior and wished to be
reconciled, Henriette would certainly meet her halfway;
and if the unfortunate attack had passed from her mind
completely, then at least their next meeting would be less
difficult. That, Henriette decided as she put the extraordinary letter away in her writing case, was all she could make
of it for the present.

Looking back to those last months of 1846 and the early
winter of 1847, she was always at a loss to explain why they
should have been so harmonious and uneventful. She returned, refreshed and girded for battle, only to find peace
and reconciliation both at Melun and later on in the Rue du
Faubourg-Saint-Honoré. The scene at Dieppe and the other
stormy sessions she had had with the Duchesse began to
take on the unreality of bad dreams. A sort of tacit understanding, a mutual truce, seemed to have been established
between them. They were not trustful of each other, but
now they could meet without sparks flying. Even the servants, though they continued to range their loyalty on the
side of their mistress, were less hostile to the governess.

Henriette asked no more than that she should be left to
her duties without interference, and the Duc on his part
seemed thankful for even temporary peace in the household.
He continued to take his meals with the children and Henriette, but a slight compromise in this matter appeared to have
eased the situation. The old Maréchal had taken up residence in his quarters, and the Duchesse took her meals with

him. Each day one of the four older girls joined them at *déjeuner* or dinner. Furthermore the Duchesse's health had improved sufficiently for her to attend more theaters and concerts than usual; and Henriette, to her great surprise, was often included in the party. In these invitations she suspected the hand of the Maréchal, who doubtless felt it would be advisable for the governess to be seen in public with his daughter. Henriette did her best not to abuse the privilege. It was strange to find herself in favor again. Often it was difficult to adjust herself to this new state of affairs after the long estrangement. She tried to put suspicion from her, though she still unconsciously braced herself for slights before they came her way. "Take heed of a wind that comes in at a hole and a reconciled enemy" was an old saying that constantly recurred to her that winter.

Just before Christmas, Louise's betrothal was announced, and the household united in celebration. She was to marry a man somewhat her senior, and the marriage would not take place for another year. Between this and holiday festivities it was New Year's again before Henriette realized that another year had gone.

Albert Remey came daily to the Rue du Faubourg-Saint-Honoré to continue his teaching. Henriette took comfort in this and in her visits to these old friends. She went to see Madame Le Maire, too, though her free afternoons were rare. The Reverend Frédéric Monod, she heard preach occasionally, but the chance to talk with him as she had planned did not materialize. Either there were other visitors to his study, or time pressing; so she postponed asking his advice. Sometimes she discussed her difficulties with Albert and Marie, but their own ideally happy marriage and their complete loyalty to her made it impossible for their judgment to be altogether unbiased. In their eyes Henriette could do no wrong. They could only insist that the difference in religion must be to blame for the Duchesse's prejudices. Like Henriette, they belonged to the Protestant faith, and like herself, they knew that this could present serious difficulties. Albert had forfeited several teaching appointments because of his religious beliefs and, as he frequently pointed out, it was only the Duc de Praslin's tolerance in such matters that had given them their present opportunities.

Madame Le Maire, however, gave her opinion gratis and frequently.

"The sooner you get clear of these Praslins, the better,"

the old woman insisted. "That's no household for a girl like you to be in."

"But I'm not exactly a girl any more."

"Well, you're far more dangerous than if you were one. Remember you're just enough younger than his wife and older than his daughters to attract a man like the Duc. And you can be altogether too attractive when you care to be."

"Oh, come now, you flatter me!"

"I'm not flattering. I'm warning you, as I did before you ever took up your duties there; before your name got into print."

"Oh, so you read the scandal sheets, Madame Le Maire!"

"Certainly. I read what all Paris reads, and I can make as much of it as the next one. Apparently you can't, or you'd have sense enough not to sail so near to the wind."

"I'm not afraid of this wind you speak of." Madame's croakings only made Henriette feel more confident in her own ability. "I'm used to steering through rough waters and narrow courses, and I like managing my own boat."

"That's all very well, but wait till your boat capsizes, as it's bound to some day. Then you'll be glad enough to come back to the Rue du Harlay."

Henriette always shrugged and changed the subject at this point. No use arguing with one who always expected the worst of any situation. She wondered, idly, what harsh blows life could have dealt this obstinate old woman to make her so skeptical. She hoped, if she herself lived to be as old, she would not fall into the same mold of bitterness. Still, in her heart, she knew that Madame's cold eyes were more shrewd than either Albert's or Marie's; that she was as wise in her untutored way as the Reverend Frédéric Monod.

The weeks slipped by. Spring blew into Paris once more with its aromatic invitation to the country. But the Praslin family did not accept as usual, for the Duc was to take his place in the House of Peers in April. All that winter he had been much absorbed in matters of politics and had spent more time than formerly at the palace. He had always been a favorite with the King who, feeling the growing dissatisfaction in the country, leaned more heavily for support on the younger peers. Henriette felt relieved at this new interest in affairs outside his personal life, even though she disapproved of Louis-Philippe and his policies. The Duc was more guarded now in his remarks to her upon affairs in the country, and she on her part was careful not to express her

own opinions so freely. He spent less time in the schoolroom
of late, and it seemed to her that he deliberately avoided
opportunities that would throw them together. She missed
the stimulation of their earlier and more frequent meetings,
but she knew it was better for all concerned that they should
meet less often. Yet always she felt the crosscurrents of
restlessness and dissatisfaction in him. She knew he craved
her approval and reassurance whether he asked them of her
or not.

One particular day she was always to remember out of
that spring because he shared it with her; because some fortunate wind of chance seemed to have given it to them without plan or forethought. She had promised to drive to Versailles with Berthe and Raynald on the first fine Saturday
in April; and when the morning came and they were being
stowed into the carriage, the Duc had unexpectedly appeared to join the expedition. He was in excellent humor,
and all their spirits mounted as they left the city behind.
After they reached Versailles the four went on foot in search
of a place to eat lunch in the open. The palace itself did not
appeal to Berthe and Raynald. The fountains were not playing that day, and the children's hearts were set elsewhere.
They wanted to find the remains of Marie Antoinette's
*hameau* with its thatched cottages and barns and dovecots
in half-ruin. They must explore the mysterious rock grotto,
once dedicated to the god of love, and they must eat their
luncheon by the fish pond and the little stream that had
been brought there for a Queen's pleasure, and that still
gurgled among artificially piled rocks that were green now
with more than half a century of moss.

"Here, here it is!" the two children called as they came
on the pathetically romantic little group of buildings. "Look,
Papa, that must have been the mill over there. Mademoiselle, see how the brook tumbles over the little waterfall!"

Their delight in this deserted miniature world was contagious. Henriette could not help thinking that Marie Antoinette herself would have been pleased by this tribute paid
so many years afterward to her favorite toy. The three left
her with the lunch basket while they explored the little
stream and hunted for the hidden Grotto of Love. She
spread a carriage rug on the steps of a tiny peasant cottage
and, seating herself upon it, let the melancholy charm of the
place work its will.

How still it was, and yet alive with the pulses of spring!

The air came fresh and redolent with earthy dampness. The warm noon sun touched her with the same magnetic rays that summoned green grass blades from brown loam; that urged buds to uncurl on bare branches. Nothing disturbed the peace of that small clearing. Not even a caretaker passed on his rounds. Henriette relaxed against the moldering wall, noticing as she did so faint remnants of the paint that had been cunningly laid on to give the impression of worn bricks and plaster chipped away. It struck her as ironical that this subterfuge should remain. No need now, she thought, for the builder to simulate age. It made her think of some child who draws lines on a smooth brow, believing that wrinkles will not leave their marks there soon enough.

And yet she could understand how one might believe that nothing could ever shatter the peace and sunny quiet of this place. She felt glad the mob had not wrecked it in their madness all those years ago. It seemed, in those few moments, almost like a personal refuge for her and for the birds, nesting and flying all about. She reached into the basket for a bit of bread and watched them find it, even as some remote feathered ancestors might have eaten cake crumbs from a Queen's table.

Later, over their luncheon, the four talked of that unfortunate Queen. She seemed curiously real to them all that day, almost as if she were their absent hostess.

"It must have been fun to fish in the pond," Raynald observed. "I wish I had a line now to try."

"I wonder if Marie Antoinette fished here, too?" Berthe added.

"I believe she did," the Duc told her. "At least that's what they say. But she only played at catching them. If one came to her hook, she always made some one throw it back. She had such a tender heart, you see."

"Then why did they have to kill her, Papa?"

For answer the Duc only shrugged his broad shoulders.

"Why did they, mademoiselle?" Raynald persisted.

"Well, the people were poor and hungry. They thought she and the King spent too much money. It cost a great deal to build just this little hamlet, and then there were the palaces and the fountains and the gardens. After all it was the people's money, and they didn't like being half starved and poor—"

"But that's ridiculous—every one can't be rich. Some people have to be poor, don't they?"

Berthe dismissed the whole subject as she flung a crust to the birds.

"Ah, that's another question for Mademoiselle to answer." The Duc gave Henriette a sly smile. "But at least I can see," he added, "you haven't been making them into little Republicans to fit your own views."

"I doubt if Berthe could be made anything but a Royalist," she told him with amusement. "She was born to the purple, monsieur. She and Marie Antoinette would have had much in common."

"They don't cut off kings' and queens' heads any more, do they, Papa?" Raynald inquired a trifle anxiously.

"Not lately," his father answered. "That's as much as any one can say."

Berthe and Raynald went off presently to pick wild flowers. The Duc stretched out his long legs and lighted a cigar while Henriette gathered up the luncheon things. For some time neither spoke. There seemed no need for words in the sunny contentment of the moment. At last he broke the silence, his voice coming slowly between fragrant puffs, his eyes following the children as they moved about under the clumps of old trees.

"It's strange," he said, "that we should be here. I wonder what Marie Antoinette would think of the guests at her *hameau* today?"

"She would think well of you and your children, monsieur, but not so much of me, I'm afraid."

"Why do you say that?"

"Because she would be suspicious of me and the world I belong to, even though she came to understand many things and many sorts of people before she died, poor soul."

"You're inconsistent. You despise what she stood for, yet you say 'poor soul.'"

"I say 'poor soul,' and I mean it. She paid dearly for what she learned too late."

"So do we all." The old bitterness tinged his voice. "We all pay for experience, and then it's too late to make use of it. But I was thinking that you're rather alike in one respect. She was ambitious, Mademoiselle Deluzy, and so are you."

"I used to think I had ambition, monsieur, but now I'm not so sure. It may have been only discontent. They're easily confused."

"And you're not discontented any more?"

"Not often. It's only—" She broke off uncertainly and then went on: "Sometimes it's not easy caring for what doesn't belong to you."

"But once you've cared for a thing it becomes yours."

"Perhaps, but I used the wrong word. I was really speaking of people." She looked up and met his eyes. The directness of the look in them made her turn her own away. "It's not the same, this tending plants whose seeds you haven't sown. Well, that's what it is to be a governess, monsieur." She bent to gather up a crumb from the robe and laughed unsteadily before she could trust herself to go on. "But I never mean to sound complaining—not today of all days, when I'm so happy here in this place."

He smiled and shrugged again.

"I believe you're more sentimental about this place than I for all your fine talk of progress and changing times. Do you know, Mademoiselle Deluzy, I was thinking just now that life, like history, has its quiet moments between revolts."

He seldom spoke so gravely, and she was moved by his words. She felt as if he were trying to tell her that he had accepted his own misery; that he no longer hoped for anything better for himself, except perhaps such brief moments as this, free from reproaches and demands. Resignation always affected her, whether she met it in man or child or beast. She could never bear to see defeat in eyes, or the droop of shoulders bent to any yoke. It was better, she knew, that he should not struggle against his fate. Yet she missed the old rebellion in him.

"Let's hope," he went on after they had both been silent and preoccupied for a while, "that because we've shared Marie Antoinette's happiness here, we need not also share her grief."

"Oh, but, monsieur, I don't believe we can ever really share that. Perhaps it's the reason why we're able to forget pain and sorrow, because we must always bear them alone."

He turned and regarded her intently. "You're right," he said. "Only happiness can be shared with another, and so we remember it, as I shall remember this hour here."

"If only it could last!" She sighed.

"It lasts as long as it's remembered."

He rose abruptly and went in search of the straying children. She watched him move away across the sunny spaces, and his words stayed with her because they were so unlike

his usual manner of speaking. It was the last time she was
ever to talk with him so—quietly, without constraint and
fear, and the dread of spying eyes and ears.

The long drive back was uneventful, but the children
chattered and waved and remarked on a hundred passing
sights. They were late in reaching home; the lamplighters of
Paris were making their rounds; and the windows of 55 Rue
du Faubourg-Saint-Honoré were already alight. As the carriage clattered into the courtyard, Henriette noticed a figure
emerging from the doors. She recognized the tall, black-
robed form of the Abbé Gallard. She saw that he watched
their arrival, though he did not come forward to greet the
Duc and the children.

*"Bon jour, mon père,"* Raynald called out as he spied him
while Berthe curtsied.

"Hardly *bon jour,* my children," the Abbé responded to
their greeting. "The day is already over. I waited till late
hoping to see you and hear your prayers."

"Well, there's tomorrow, isn't there?" Berthe muttered
impatiently.

Henriette hoped the Abbé had not heard her. It was unfortunate enough that he had met them returning together
from the long day's outing without impudence being added.
The Duc greeted their religious adviser rather hastily, she
thought, as she turned to go indoors. Something made her
look back, and through the iron grill work she saw that the
Abbé had not left the courtyard. Retracing his steps, he
followed them into the entrance hall. But he did not continue
up the staircase. Instead she saw him turn in the direction of
the old Maréchal Sébastiani's private apartments. His soft-
shod feet made no sound on the marble floors, and his spare
body in its dark garments moved with a sepulchral, unhurried tread, like a black cat going stealthily upon some
secret errand of its own. An errand, she felt, that in some
way concerned herself.

*chapter eighteen*

IT TAKES ONLY A SMALL SPARK TO SET THE EXPLOSIVE
free, and the dynamite of human emotion is no exception to

the rule. When the charge is ready, the least friction may light the fuse. For six years the feud between Henriette and the Duchesse had been gathering force, but it was June, 1847, before it was ready to be touched off.

The trouble began over a trifling domestic matter, though Henriette had suspected, ever since her return from the expedition to Versailles, that the old Maréchal and the Abbé had joined forces against her. Lisette, one of the two maids in special attendance on the young ladies, happened to be the cause. Lisette had long been a trial to Henriette. She was devoted to the children, particularly to Berthe, but she had an annoying manner of self-importance, and it pleased her to disregard the governess' orders whenever possible. Because she had come from Corsica and was the daughter of an old nurse in the Sébastiani household, a bond existed between her and the Duchesse. Lisette knew herself to be a favorite with her mistress, and the knowledge gave her an assurance which could become insolence with the slightest excuse. Henriette had had more than one tilt with her; but always the maid's violations of orders had been minor offenses, irritating to the nerves and disastrous to the children's discipline, but not worth an issue with Madame.

But when Berthe came down with a slight case of jaundice and Lisette paid no attention to the diet ordered by Dr. Simon, Henriette was forced to take action. Berthe had almost recovered when a mysterious relapse occurred. The doctor was baffled till the invalid confessed that she had persuaded the maid to bring her forbidden delicacies from the pantry. Dr. Simon blamed Henriette for this, and she in turn called Lisette to account.

"Ah, well, I'm not going to see the poor young lady starve," the maid had stolidly maintained. "I don't care what you and the doctor say, she shall have what she wants to eat so long as I'm here to fetch it to her."

"In that case you may not be here to disobey orders," Henriette told her, taking no notice of the defiant look the maid flung at her as she left the room.

She seldom troubled the Duc with domestic problems, and she hesitated to do so just then while he was so deeply absorbed in new political activities. But knowing that Lisette would take further advantage, and that Berthe's recovery would be hindered, she explained the difficulty to him that night.

"She must leave at once," he decided. "It's outrageous. Why, she'll be dosing the child with laudanum next. You should have dismissed her this morning."

"But, monsieur, it's not my place to do that. You know the Duchesse is very fond of Lisette, and I'd prefer you discussed it with her first."

He agreed to that reluctantly, and though the maid departed next day, bag and baggage, the effects of her dismissal were far-reaching. The Duc and Duchesse quarreled violently as a result. The Duchesse took to her bed for a week while the Duc retaliated by keeping to his own apartments and dining out every night. He did not refer to the subject again, but Henriette guessed that the issue had turned upon herself and her influence in the household, rather than upon the servant.

Lisette, however, ran true to her Corsican traditions of revenge. Just as the Duchesse emerged and Berthe recovered and peace had been somewhat restored, a new crisis arose. Lisette, it appeared, had gone directly to the newspaper which had printed the first article about the Duc's affairs, and given her version of the story. She spared no detail that would reflect against Mademoiselle Deluzy. Such unsavory items as she omitted, the editors of the scandal sheet were only too ready to supply; and once more the rift in the Praslin home and the Duc's infatuation for an unscrupulous and scheming governess became common gossip on the Right and Left Banks, at court as well as in shops and cafés. News happened to be dull at the moment the story appeared, and for several days each new edition elaborated on the open scandal of such affairs among the highest nobility. There were hints that the Duchesse had lost her reason through humiliation and harsh treatment, that grief had driven her to enter a convent, that she had been denied the privilege of seeing her own children, that this was not the first conquest of the brazen and beautiful Mademoiselle D., even that the King himself had threatened to interfere if the Duc persisted in this folly.

It so happened that Henriette learned of this latest attack long after the paper that carried it had been read and discussed in the servants' quarters. The blow fell upon Raynald's birthday, when she had been particularly busy. Lessons were hurried through before *déjeuner* so that the afternoon might be free for celebration. Monsieur Remey had been invited to go with them to a matinée of short plays for children in the Passage Choiseul. The big barouche had been crowded with full skirts and high spirits as they set off. The June day was sunny, and the trees everywhere in full leaf, but with no hint as yet of summer dust and heat to mar the fresh green. Flowers were blooming everywhere—in the parks, on flower stalls, in baskets, window boxes, and on ladies' bonnets.

"How lucky you are to be born in the month of June!" Henriette congratulated Raynald who sat beside her in his new linen jacket and trousers and red-topped boots. "Even without presents it would be good fortune."

But Raynald thought presents were very necessary. In fact, on the drive home he decided to share his birthday with Mademoiselle and buy her a gift with his own money. His pockets were burning with francs and ten-franc notes, supplied that morning by his father, his grandfather, and two indulgent Sébastiani great-uncles. Nothing would do but that they stop at a small shop just off the Rue de Rivoli, where they had often watched a jeweler cutting cameos.

Raynald's heart was set on buying a cameo for Mademoiselle, though she tried to dissuade him from such extravagance. Albert Remey was invited to help in the selection while Henriette and the sisters waited in the carriage. The final decision became so difficult that Henriette had to be called into the shop.

"He's found two small ones the shop keeper will let him have for half-price," Albert explained in a whisper. "I doubt if you'll care for the designs, but you'd better let him have his way. It would never do to curb his generous impulse."

It was dim in the shop after the sunny street, and the cameos were very small and finely cut. The elderly jeweler had been explaining their best points to his small customer.

"Now, mademoiselle, it's for you to choose," Raynald urged her with a magnificent gesture.

It was plain that the boy had taken a fancy to one that showed a monk holding a death's head against a brownish background. Raynald had reached the age at which human skeletons were fascinating, and there was no denying that the cameo cutter had been very skillful in his portrayal. No wonder, Henriette thought, that the shopkeeper will let him buy it for half-price. It's hardly a cheerful subject.

"You'll never see one like it anywhere," the jeweler was saying.

Henriette agreed that she doubtless never would, and looking into Raynald's eyes so eager and shining with pleased generosity, she had not the heart to disillusion him.

"What a strange choice!" she murmured to Albert as the cameo was being wrapped in cotton and fitted into a tiny box. "He's the most unpredictable child. I hope it hasn't taken all his money!"

Albert Remey did not answer. She saw that he was bent over a newspaper that lay open on the counter. Something in his expression startled her. His mouth had fallen open, and he looked suddenly pale in the dimness of the shop. Her eyes followed his to the article that held his attention, and in a flash she saw the word Praslin and her own name. The printed letters grew larger and larger before her. She felt for the edge of the counter and gripped it hard. From a long way off she heard the polite tones of the shopkeeper bidding them good day.

"And if Monsieur would care for the paper, I shall be only too delighted to let him take it. I've finished reading."

"No, no, thank you, monsieur," she heard Albert's hurried response, and she felt the distress in his tone and the touch of his hand on her arm.

He was urging her out of the shop, but before they reached the door, the dizziness left her. Quickly she turned back to the counter.

"If you please, I would like to have that paper if you are quite through with it."

Her hand closed over the sheet. She could see the word Praslin under her fingers. With calm precaution she folded it so that the column was hidden. She could not run the risk of the girls' sharp eyes seeing that name.

Mechanically she heard herself answering questions as they drove the short distance to the Rue du Faubourg-Saint-Honoré. Albert sat very quiet in the opposite seat. She avoided meeting his eyes. When they reached the house he made excuse to go back to the schoolroom for some books. As the children started up the stairs he kept at Henriette's side and spoke in a low voice.

"It's dastardly, this attack. How could such foul lies originate? Who can be responsible?"

Henriette clutched the paper more tightly, and as she climbed the stairs beside him she gave a grim smile. Lisette's hatred and vindictive threats at parting had just come to her mind.

"I think I know who is behind this latest piece of slander," she told him. "But that's no help now. Did you read it all, Albert?"

"Practically, though I was so shocked, coming on it there in the shop, the words hardly made sense to me. But I'm afraid it's worse than the others."

"Yes," she said, "I'm afraid so. And even if it were not so serious, Monsieur le Duc has so lately been made a member of the House of Peers that it will reflect greater discredit to him. As for me—well—" She gave a shrug that suggested more than any words she could summon.

"I know; but, Henriette, they see you here every day as I do. They know there can be no truth in these reports that you and the Duc—" He broke off in embarrassment.

"Why do you hesitate to say the word?" she asked bitterly. "All Paris is saying it."

"I know it's a lie, and I'm going with you now to tell the Duc and Duchesse so."

"No, Albert, no! You mustn't be dragged into this. Nothing you might say could help me, and you would only be hurting yourself."

"I'll not keep silence while these insults to your good name are bandied about everywhere. I must do something to prove my trust and friendship."

"You'll have plenty of chances for that," she told him. There was an unnatural grimness in her voice, though her hand shook as she reached out impulsively and laid it on his. "Please go quickly, Albert, and when you return tomorrow act as if you knew nothing."

He stood by the schoolroom door, holding her hand and searching her face with distress and perplexity in the eyes behind his spectacles.

"But, *mon Dieu,* how can I act such a part when you're in such trouble? I hardly know what to do."

"Do what I say, please, and remember you're a scholar, absorbed in your books. You never read newspapers, and you never saw this particular scandal sheet."

Almost without feeling she washed and slipped into fresh clothes. The dress she put on was of pale green challis, strewn with small bright brown flowers the color of her hair. It had been delivered from the dressmaker's only day before yesterday, yet already that seemed ages ago.

"*Bien,*" she thought as she smoothed her hair before the mirror and fastened on the enameled brooch with the dragon's head which had been the Duchesse's peace offering to her that first spring in the Rue du Faubourg-Saint-Honoré. "I look my best tonight, and for what? But I begin to understand why the condemned take such pains with their toilettes when they make their last appearances in public."

Dinner passed off quietly. The young people were so gay and talkative they did not apparently notice her preoccupation. She had feared the Duc might take his place, and she felt grateful that it remained empty. It would have been too difficult to sit opposite him, knowing what she knew, what he must surely know also by this time.

"We'll ask Papa to have your cameo set in gold," Raynald was telling her. "I didn't have money enough for that. And there must be writing on the back. Mamma has that on her brooches and inside her rings. What do you want to have there, mademoiselle?"

"Why, I don't know, *chéri*. I haven't thought."

"They always engrave names and dates," Berthe explained.

"Then we'll have it say, 'Raynald, June 18, 1847,'" the boy decided, "so you'll always remember today."

"Even without that, I couldn't forget the day," she assured him as they admired the cameo under the lamplight.

At nine o'clock the summons she had been expecting came: The Maréchal Sébastiani's compliments, and would Mademoiselle Deluzy please present herself immediately at his apartments? Following the servant along the corridors and down the stairs, she prepared as best she could for the ordeal. They must consider the situation very grave indeed, she decided; otherwise she would have been called to account by the Duchesse, not by her father. Also the Maréchal would have been likely to postpone the interview till morning if he had not felt that matters were imperative. Well, at least she preferred father to daughter.

A door opened. She found herself entering the Sébastiani drawing room, where two old men awaited her. There in one chair was the Maréchal's short, soldierly figure and in the other she recognized the lean and black-clad Abbé Gallard. The Duc and Duchesse were conspicuously absent. A chair was indicated, and she seated herself between them. But as she spread her skirts in decorous folds she knew that she might have been wearing her shabby poplin for all the impression her appearance made.

It seemed to her in the tenseness of the slight pause which

followed, that these two men, who represented as it were
the prosperity of earth and the hosts of heaven, were gathering forces to pass judgment upon her. The Maréchal appeared more than ever like the hard, crude Corsican whose
shrewdness and energy dominated the elegance of his surroundings. But she had less dread of this plain man of action
than of the Abbé, who sat motionless, wrapped in his robes
and his self-imposed aloofness. His face was turned slightly,
and something about his profile struck her as familiar. He
reminded her of some one else as he sat silhouetted against
the yellow-shaded lamp. It came over her suddenly that he
might have posed for the monk's head on her cameo. There
was a pale austerity to the features; the flesh seemed to have
hardened to the same shell-like consistency. She felt that
her distaste for the design had been almost prophetic. He
only needed the death's head to complete the human replica.

So fascinated had she become, studying the resemblance,
that she had to force her mind from the Abbé's profile to the
Maréchal's words.

"You know, mademoiselle, why we have sent for you?
You have seen the papers?"

"I've read enough, yes. They're malicious lies as they were
before."

"Lies they may be," he answered, and a long look of
meaning passed between him and the Abbé; "but this time
they have gone too far. We can no longer sit back and accept such insults."

"You say 'we,' monsieur, and I am glad of that. I hope it
means that you are considering my position in all this."

"Your position has become intolerable to us all." The
dark deep-set eyes flashed threateningly. "The Abbé agrees
with me that there is but one course to take. You must leave
this house at once."

There was complete silence in the room—the stillness
that comes after a thunderbolt has fallen. Henriette felt her
heart hammer at her side, though her body and brain went
numb.

"One moment!" she heard her voice speaking at last. "Let
me remind you, monsieur, that before matters reached such
a serious pass I tried to leave this household of my own
free will. But always I was persuaded to stay. Two years
ago in Corsica you yourself insisted upon my remaining.
You said that would be the surest way to quiet such
rumors."

"Evidently I was wrong. These rumors, as you call them, have grown to alarming proportions."

"But you know as well as I do, monsieur—and Monsieur l'Abbé here also knows—that to send me away at this time will put me in a false light."

"Mademoiselle, there are others who come first in our thoughts." It was the Abbé who spoke this time. He leaned slightly forward in his chair; and his long, colorless hands lay thin and transparent on his dark robe. "I am here as the spiritual adviser of a loving, pious, and devoted mother —a woman who has suffered cruelly because of your presence in her home."

"I've suffered, too." Henriette braced herself against the chair. She knew there was no use in making this last stand, but she was determined to go down with her back to the wall. "For six years I've never known what it was to be trusted or treated with respect and consideration except by Monsieur le Duc and the children. My devotion to them has been turned into something ugly and false. I've been spied upon at every turn, and my words and actions doubted and maligned till I was tried almost past the point of endurance."

"Yes, mademoiselle," the Abbé answered with a faintly sardonic inflection. "I have often marveled at your endurance. It will undoubtedly prove valuable to you in your next situation. But I happen to be more concerned with the Duchesse and her welfare than with your difficulties. I cannot stand by any longer and see her made a recluse in her own home, ostracized by those she loves, who are bound to her by holy ties."

"Holy ties are one thing, and I honor them, but they don't take the place of love that springs from sympathy and confidence. We can't command the love of others; we must earn it, monsieur, as we earn the right to be loved. I'm sorry for the Duchesse. I've honestly tried to make allowances for her ill health and temperament. I'm not passing judgment upon her now. If she is a recluse in her home, as you say, it's because she has made herself so. Her own moods have created the prison walls that keep her dear ones from her."

"Mademoiselle, we are not here to discuss personalities. You have many gifts, but evidently humility does not seem to be one of them."

"Humility doesn't help much when one has one's living to make." Henriette refused to be brushed aside as if she were some annoying fly that had lighted on his brow.

"Be that as it may," the Abbé continued frigidly, "the Maréchal and I are agreed that you cannot remain here."

"Yes, yes, we must be practical," the other hurried on. "It's not only my daughter's distress and the humiliation of this latest attack, but the Duc is now in public life; and such things reflect on the Court and on the King himself. A repetition of such scandal might have very serious effects, and we must think of the future."

"I must think of the future, too. Whether it affects the Court of France or not, it happens to matter to me."

"Certainly, mademoiselle." Her irony was lost on the Maréchal, but not, she hoped, on the Abbé. "That's what I say—we must be practical, and of course I will see that you do not suffer financially."

"But what about my prospects, monsieur? I needn't tell you that a dismissal now will make it almost impossible for me to secure another teaching post in France."

"Exactly. That's why it will be better for you to go to England, where I understand you have influential friends. Surely they will be able to find you more congenial employment than if you remained in Paris. We have decided that will be the best plan, and I am prepared to help you financially if you agree."

"So I'm to be shipped out of the country, like other undesirables. No, thank you, monsieur. You have a right to ask me to leave your house, but not to leave France."

"Wait," the Maréchal interposed, his face flushing purple at her words. "You must hear me out. In view of your services to my grandchildren I intend to provide you with a comfortable settlement."

"Please don't misunderstand me," Henriette broke in. "I was not the one to bring up this matter of money."

"It's not to be overlooked, mademoiselle. By leaving now I understand you will forfeit a pension the Duc promised if you would stay till the older girls married."

"I did not stay because of that. All I ask now is a fair chance to continue my work without prejudice."

"That's why you will do well to go to England, and with an assured annuity from me you should be able to manage comfortably for yourself. Shall we say twelve hundred francs a year?"

"I'm not talking about francs or about England, monsieur. I shall stay in France—in Paris, probably; and I ask for no bribes. I only want the assurance that what has happened while I worked in this house will not injure what means most to a governess—her good character."

"You should have thought of your character before to-night," the Abbé interposed. "I'm afraid we cannot give that back to you unspoiled. It seems to me the Maréchal is being more than charitable in his offer."

"I'm not asking for charity of the Maréchal or any one here. But I do ask the privilege of earning my living where and how I choose. If I could have been allowed to stay the summer out, or until this unfortunate matter died down, it would have been easier; however, that's not for me to say. But a letter from the Duchesse recommending me is very important. I think I deserve that after these six years of service."

"You make it difficult." The Maréchal's thick fingers drummed on the arm of his chair. "Very difficult. I still advise your going to England. You will not consider that?"

"No, monsieur, I prefer France. I've never believed in running away from trouble."

"Well, then, there's nothing more to be said."

"And you will speak to the Duchesse about the letter. Tell her I will be out of the house tomorrow, but I will leave word where it can be sent."

It was horrible to sit there bargaining together as if they were two peasants haggling in some market place. Yet she knew she was fighting for her rights, that her whole future was at stake.

"I will speak to my daughter," he agreed hesitantly, "but I can't answer for her. She's been tried too far."

"The Duchesse is noted for her goodness of heart," Henriette pointed out as she rose. "I'm sure she won't begrudge me a few words of honorable discharge. She might even be generous enough to let it appear that I left for reasons of my own."

"You go too far, mademoiselle," the Abbé once more answered for his friend. "It's not your place to dictate terms with those who have suffered so long from your arrogance and conceit. It seems to me that you protest your innocence too vigorously."

The Abbé's cool denunciation stung her as all the furies of the Duchesse had never been able to do. She flung back her head and faced him directly.

"I couldn't do that, monsieur. I couldn't speak too vigorously against these lies."

"You talk glibly of lies, but let me remind you that there are others than those uttered by word of mouth or set on paper. For these unspoken ones we are also held to account as you will be for the suffering you have caused another—a good woman whose prayers you have turned into a mockery."

The Abbé sighed deeply and raised his eyes—almost, Henriette thought, as if he were enlisting allies from above to his side. She knew she was helpless before the power of this man, yet she was determined to have the last word.

"Monsieur," she said, "you may not know that I, too, am accountable to a father confessor. It happens to be my own conscience, and a clear conscience may also give absolution."

She did not remember bidding the two good night or leaving the Sébastiani apartments. She had no idea if the interview had lasted an hour or a few minutes. She knew only that for her this was the end of an era, and it seemed strange to find the older girls still busy under the lamplight with their books and embroidery and games about them.

"Oh, there you are, mademoiselle!" Louise sprang up as she entered. "Papa was here a few moments ago, but he couldn't stay. He wrote a note and told me not to forget to give it to you. What's the matter, mademoiselle? You look pale, and your hands are so cold."

"Well, I might as well tell you, my dears." She sank down in the midst of the little group. "I've had bad news tonight."

"Oh, mademoiselle, I'm sorry! You're not ill?"

"No." She tried to smile a reassurance she did not feel as she hastily sought for some logical explanation. "I'm as well as usual; but my grandfather is ill, and I must go to him."

"Well," she argued to herself, remembering the Abbé's recent words on the subject of lies, "it's the truth in one way. He is ill, and it's not my place to go into facts. By tomorrow it won't be my place to tell them anything."

"But you'll come back soon?"

She faltered under the searching gaze of those clear young eyes.

"I can't say when—it may be a long time."

"Why, mademoiselle! It's queer I never knew you had a grandfather. You never spoke of him to us before."

"Why should I, my dear? It didn't concern you."

"Oh, but, mademoiselle, everything that concerns you concerns us."

Their sympathy and affection unnerved her more than the shock of the newspaper, more than the interview that had just ended. She had difficulty in restraining their generous offers of help in packing. They wanted to go to her rooms and stay with her till long past their bedtime. They showered her with embarrassing questions about her grandfather, his illness, and the probable length of her stay. She answered them as best she could. But all the time the slim, girlish bodies in full pink and blue and sprigged muslin pressed about her, all the time the quick, young voices buzzed in her ears, she was telling herself that this was the end. They would never be together like this again, gathered round the lamp-lit table where they had refought campaigns of long dead armies and waged more personal wars against columns of figures and the vagaries of irregular verbs. "Going—gone; going—gone," the familiar brown clock ticked like an auctioneer's hammer to Henriette.

She went through the ordeal of good night, set the schoolroom to rights, and reached her own quarters at last. It was only then, with the door locked against possible interruption, that she dared to read the letter Louise had delivered. Except for two or three brief notes giving her impersonal directions about her duties, the Duc had never written her. This was without address, and she saw that the penciled words had been hastily scribbled on a sheet of ruled paper from one of the girls' copy books:

I feel much, and there is nothing to say; nothing that I can do. My hands are tied, and I am powerless to help you, my dear friend, as your support has so often helped me. Misfortune has marked me for her own, and whatever move I make I seem to bring disaster upon others, especially upon you, whom I most wish to spare. It is as you so truly said—we can only share happiness, not grief; and yet I know that I am responsible for the ordeal you must meet alone. But remember, I, too, am alone. Small comfort indeed, but perhaps you can make something of it. You are braver than I. I do not fear for you as I do for myself.

Keep the older girls informed of your whereabouts,

and be sure that we will visit you. Good night, and forgive this poor note.

There was no signature, and her own name had not been written. Even on this last night of her stay there, she guessed that he had not dared so great a risk. The words showed signs of haste and agitation. Some were black and heavy, some light; and the pencil point had broken in one place under the pressure of those strong fingers.

She hesitated by the little secretary, wondering if she should write a discreet answer to his letter. But she decided against that. Even the most politely formal note might be misinterpreted; and, besides, he evidently wished to forestall that impulse, so expressly did he ask her to tell the children where she meant to go. Poor soul, he was afraid of further consequences. She smiled wanly at that. He had deserted her. But she could not reproach him. He could do nothing by taking a stand. He was not brave; as he himself had admitted. He had been like an overgrown boy who had reached out to her because he was afraid of the dark. She had given him her hand, and they had taken comfort in each other's nearness. That was all that had ever been between them. And now that, too, was gone. The time had come for her to go away.

After a little she moved to the window and opened it. Below her the garden lay dark and warm with June fragrance, and from the distance the familiar sounds of Paris came to her—the dwindled hoofbeats and the clatter of carriages on the Champs Elysées, the pulse of the city she was determined not to leave.

She turned back to the room, fetched her night clothes from the closet, and with a quick impulsive gesture blew out the lamp. She undressed in the dark because she did not wish to look about those rooms where she had experienced such varying emotions for six years. She would not sentimentalize about each object that had been part of her life there—the little gilt clock under the glass dome, the secretary, the work table, the vases of fresh-cut flowers, and the mirror that had reflected her face in moments of delight and perplexity and fear. No, she would not brood upon what was over for good and all.

"It's misery enough," she thought as she pressed her face against the cool pillow, "to have once been happy here."

## chapter nineteen

BACK TO THE RUE DU HARLAY; TO THE SLOPING EAVES AND cramped quarters of the Needle's Eye. It seemed narrower and shabbier after the luxurious apartment in the Faubourg-Saint-Honoré, where Henriette had grown used to down pillows and fine linen and upholstered furniture. She had not realized how insidiously such comforts could become necessities. She had steeled herself to meet the loneliness and depression and sense of defeat which she knew would inevitably follow her departure; but she had not guessed the physical repugnance she would experience in the noise and heat and squalor of that dilapidated establishment in the Marais. The fact that she was lucky to have even this refuge did not lessen her gloom, though Madame Le Maire reminded her of it at every turn.

"So," the old woman had greeted her a month before, "here you are bag and baggage, just as I've been expecting you to turn up on my doorstep some day. You held out longer than I thought you would, but it was bound to end like this. I told you so."

"You did, Madame Le Maire." Henriette had smiled wearily. "I'll always give you credit for that."

"And now you're asking for another kind of credit, I suppose."

"Not yet. I've been able to put by a little money. I can pay my way, but of course summer is a bad time to find another place. It may be a long wait, and meantime—"

"And meantime you must live, and there aren't so many pensions in Paris that will care to open their doors to the notorious Mademoiselle D. now she's left the Hôtel Praslin! No, you needn't go into explanations. What I didn't read in those papers I got out of Albert Remey."

Henriette had given her unspoken gratitude to Albert when she heard that he had already been there to intercede for her. He and Marie had begged her to come to them, but she had refused. She would not bring her misfortune into their household, though she had been touched by their offer and their loyal support. As briefly as possible she had told Madame Le Maire of her difficulties. It had been strange to hear herself humbly asking for the privilege of room and board and a chance to teach or chaperon any of the boarders. But she had laid her case calmly before the old woman without asking for sympathy. She would pay her way, and she would work at anything for the present. She asked nothing more than that.

"Well, Mademoiselle Desportes"—Madame had pronounced her old name with peculiar emphasis—"any one else in my place would refuse you. It's not only the scandal which always leaks out sooner or later, but it is you yourself. Things happen to you, and they always will."

"Can I help that?" Henriette had asked.

"I didn't say you could, and in a way it's what I've always liked about you. When I was young they used to say people only threw stones at the tree that was loaded with fruit."

This grudgingly admitted compliment had been Madame's only assurance that Henriette might remain even in the dubious security of that least desirable room. She had made no promises about keeping her, and as the weeks passed and the letter of recommendation from the Duchesse did not materialize the old woman became more insistent. Although there had been no written agreement about this, Henriette had been assured verbally before leaving that it would be given her. She had written the Duchesse reminding her of this and giving the Rue du Harlay address, and she had also mentioned it to the Duc at each of their two meetings.

These had been brief and difficult, and the presence of the tearful children, who clung to her and refused to believe she would not return with them to Melun, had not made conversation easy. Berthe and Raynald would not be reconciled to her absence, and these reunions only left her more exhausted and despairing. She wrote several letters to Louise; letters which echoed her misery, and which she hoped might be shown to the Duc. Not that she counted on his help, but it eased her a little to put her loneliness on paper; to ask for news and reassurance of their affection during those intervals between the unsatisfactory visits. Once she found her emotions carrying her too far, and she left a sentence unfinished that she had begun in a transport of unhappiness. Still she must think of her pupils before herself. Louise was to be married in early autumn, and she must not be burdened with an ex-governess' plight.

On a stifling night in late July, Henriette lay sleepless on her hard bed. Up there under the roof that narrow box of a room gathered heat by day and stayed like an oven till morning. If any breeze stirred in the Rue du Harlay it could hardly have found the gabled window of the Needle's Eye or helped to clear the air of stale smells of past cooking and the faint stench of sewer gas. Henriette pressed a damp handkerchief to her nostrils and tried not to listen as the hours and half-hours struck through the close-pressing darkness. Her eyelids felt hot and swollen, her lips were salty from hours of crying. But she had no more tears to shed, though her breath still came convulsively. She tried to keep it quiet, for two of the maids slept next door, and they had complained that her restlessness and weeping kept them awake. Madame Le Maire was already displeased with her. The old landlady's patience was wearing thinner each day that passed without the arrival of the Duchesse's letter, and that very night at dinner Henriette had further annoyed her by having to leave the table because she had been overcome by a wave of faintness.

The afternoon had not helped her fortitude. It was her second reunion with her former pupils and their father, and each meeting had upset her. That day she had taken Marie, Berthe, and Raynald to the dentist because her presence and encouragement had always helped them through such ordeals. It had been like old times, and she had forgotten her own troubles for those few hours. After the visit to the dentist they had gone to the Luxembourg Gardens. The Duc had joined them, and they had eaten frappés and listened to a band concert under the trees. But it had been an unsatisfactory meeting. He had seemed grim and strained, and spoke little. She guessed that he dared not trust himself to reopen the painful subject of her departure. The King was away from Paris, and the House of Peers did not claim his attention. This was a pity, she had thought, since it gave him too much time to brood on the hopeless tangle of his own domestic affairs.

He had been solicitous for her, commenting upon her paleness and lassitude. He had urged her to take a brief holiday from the city, or at least to let Dr. Simon prescribe for her health. But she had tried to make light of this. It was the heat, she had explained; once the weather grew cooler, she would be able to sleep again—better yet if she could only find some work to absorb her. It was then that she had reminded him of the promised letter from the Duchesse. There had been no sign of it, and Madame Le Maire was becoming more pressing in her demands. There were several young ladies in the pension who wished instruction in English and painting. She had started a small class, but she could not continue without good references from her last position, since the young ladies had been entrusted to Madame's care. She had waited a month now, and she had even written reminding the Duchesse; but no word had come.

He had flushed darkly, his brows drawn into deep lines. It was outrageous that the Duchesse had not kept to the agreement. He would take the matter up with her at once.

"I would not be so insistent, monsieur," she had said, "but I think I have a right to ask that much of her. It's so little for her to do, and it means my whole future to me."

"You shall have your letter," he had promised as they walked together from the Gardens. "Make sure that I shall see to that if it's my last act on earth."

The children had begged her to drive with them to the depot of the Corbeil railway, and she had consented against her will. There had been the inevitable tears when the parting took place at the train gates. She had not been able to keep back her own tears as Berthe and Raynald clung to her.

"Try to be happy if you can," the Duc had said in parting. "It only makes it harder for me to know you are miserable, too."

"I'll try," she had promised. "Night after night as I lie awake I say to myself: 'Why should you expect to be singled out for happiness from a world of people?' And yet, somehow, I go right on believing that it is my right."

He had pressed her hand, and then she had turned away from the little group going down the long platform. The tears in her eyes made everything indistinct. On her way out she had collided with a man hurrying towards the train.

"Pardon," she had murmured.

Looking up, she had seen that he was the Duc's valet, Auguste Charpentier. He had recognized her, she knew, and she wished that he had not seen her crying.

Well, the afternoon was over. The precious minutes had

only been wasted with useless tears and regrets. She would not waste any more. A near-by clock was striking three. She must try to catch a little sleep. She would have need of that to face another day. But the bed was so hard, the room so hot. She turned and twisted endlessly. This was the hour before daylight, when she was trapped by her own thoughts, when hope retreated, and her own vitality ebbed away in the darkness. The little clock that the children had chosen for her one Christmas ticked tirelessly on a shelf she could not see. Time mocked her so, night after night. She was afraid to think of the past or of the future. Both were painful to her now. There was only the present, and what was that that she should cling to it?

After a while she slipped from bed to crouch by the window as she had done through other wakeful hours. But no freshness rewarded her as she leaned at the casement, peering into the hollow pit of the street below where the opposite houses stood dark and lifeless and only a lamp glimmered feebly at the corner. Sometimes a stealthy gray rat sped across that circle of light; sometimes a slow, stooped human figure passed and was gone. Even at this distance such shapes filled her with shudders of pity and disgust. The rats of Paris going upon their secret missions were less repellent than these other night scavengers. Where did they hide themselves by day? How had their shame begun, and where, she wondered, would it end? Where would she herself end, for the matter of that?

Everything came back to that. Every sight and every sound stabbed her with the sharpness of personal futility. She leaned her arms on the window ledge and buried her face upon them to shut out the vision of interminably stretching years. What could they bring but a shifting from post to post? Board and rooms in exchange for the best years of her life; her capacity for love spent on other people's children, and if they loved her in return, only bitterness and hard feelings for reward. She would grow withered and querulous like other aging mesdemoiselles, and in time give herself up to fancywork and tedious reminiscences. She would share with her kind such crumbs of gentility as they could muster. Dullness would be her heritage. All her struggles against it had only brought the specter nearer. She could feel it at her heels. There in the fetid room it seemed actually to have overtaken her.

"Henriette Deluzy. Henriette Desportes, spinster." She

repeated the words with ruthless emphasis on the last one.

Thirty-five years old, and alone. So she might live to be an old woman. Spinsters often did. They had so little to spend themselves upon.

*"Mon Dieu,* never let it be so for me!"

She writhed at the thought, and sweat broke out on her brow and under the folds of her nightgown, though she continued to pant for breath in the closeness of the room.

He had said she had courage. Perhaps she had, but not enough to face that. When life held nothing, nothing that one wanted, where was the harm in letting it go? Not to worry, not to scheme and scrimp, not to compromise with one's self while the eagerness of youth died a slow death in unwanted flesh—that was all that mattered now. God would not be too hard on her. He had created a world of beauty and had given her eyes and capacity to respond to its wonders. He could not have meant it to turn out this way for her. If He really did know the secrets of all hearts there would be no need to explain things to Him.

The bottle of laudanum was in the top drawer of the chest. She knew just where she had hidden it in her handkerchief case. It was a small, squat bottle, but nearly full. Dr. Simon had entrusted it to her care during one of Berthe's illnesses, and he had explained how fatal an overdose might be. Her mind had stored away his words, and now they and the bottle were ready to answer her need. The drawer stuck obstinately under her hands. It seemed to be thwarting her in an almost human manner as she struggled to open it without disturbing those in the next room. She heard the rustle of a mattress as one of the sleepers stirred. Her hands found the bottle, and she stood there holding it close while she made sure that the steady breathing continued from the other side of the wall. Queer to think that so soon those few inches of plaster would divide the living from the dead.

Noiselessly she moved to the washstand under the eaves and felt for the tumbler and pitcher of water . . .

Some one groaned. She was aware of the long, shuddering sound of distress before she realized that she herself had made it. She strained to raise her eyelids, but a blinding light and a blur of faces that looked larger than full moons turned her dizzy again. A wave of nausea overcame the blackness, and sharp odors and still sharper pangs made her conscious once more.

"There now!" she heard Madame Le Maire's familiar voice faintly through a haze of pain. "She's through the worst of it. We need not send Pierre for a doctor. Get downstairs as fast as you can."

Another spasm shook Henriette, and when it passed and she was able to fix her attention on nearer objects she saw that she was still in the Needle's Eye, blinking painfully at the strange brightness of the room. Morning was at the window, its light mingling with that of a lamp on the stand beside her bed.

"Madame," she whispered, "how did you know? Why did you have to come?"

"Why?" The answer came short with annoyance as the old woman rubbed her vigorously with wet towels or pressed smelling salts to her nostrils. "Haven't you given me enough trouble without adding suicide? You might have thought of what a police report would mean to my business. But Jeannette has sharp ears, praise Heaven! She heard you fall and the glass shatter, and we lost no time. Here, lift your arms, and let me get you into a clean nightdress."

In spite of the brusque words and manner Henriette knew that Madame was being very kind as she made her clean and comfortable and later forced her to drink black coffee with a dash of brandy. She lay limp and exhausted, scarcely aware of those who came and went, though she knew that Madame and the maids and even old Pierre, the porter, took turns sitting by her bed, urging her to eat the food they brought and fanning her to keep away the flies. Sometimes she slept, and woke drenched with sweat, beating off the black wings of ugly dreams. Towards evening her head cleared, and the air freshened as a summer shower cooled the streets. She lay back weakly and turned to Madame Le Maire with a faint, apologetic smile.

"Forgive me, madame, for making you so much trouble," she faltered. "I know now that I have been very weak and foolish."

"It's something to admit one's folly. Well, you're alive whether you want to be or not."

"It's no use trying to explain, but I was desperate."

"So I gather. I mistrusted it from the way you looked at dinner last night. You were seeing them most of yesterday. I suppose that accounts for it."

"Perhaps, madame. But nothing happened. They are not

to blame. Only it came over me as it has before, that there was no use in my going on."

"So you tried laudanum. Well, you're not the first. But it's not so easy as all that, Henriette Desportes. Life doesn't mean to be cheated of you."

Tears of weakness gathered in Henriette's eyes. She found it difficult to speak, but after a time she mastered her sobs and went on.

"It was wrong, I know, but there are times when—when tomorrow, even one more hour, seems too much. I couldn't sleep. You know how it is after you've counted every stroke of the clock and your troubles grow like a mountain and you can see nothing else."

"Most certainly I know." Madame wagged her head so vigorously that her fringe of black hair shifted slightly over one eye. "Who doesn't?"

Again they were silent for a time, and only the sounds of venders calling their wares from the wet street below sounded in the room.

"And I felt so alone, you see," Henriette ventured at last. "If there had been some one to turn to, some one for me to lean on."

"Listen to me." The sharp old eyes blinked fiercely out of their nests of wrinkles. "You'll never find that, so stop wasting your time looking for shoulders to lean on."

"But—but other people have that comfort. Why shouldn't I?"

"Because your shoulders were made for them to lean on. You were born a prop and not a vine. You can't go against your pattern as you tried to last night. Believe me, mademoiselle, I know what I'm saying. An oak may not turn into a strawberry plant for the wishing."

*chapter twenty*

IT WAS MID-AUGUST, AND IN THE RUE DU HARLAY MADAME Le Maire's dinner had been over nearly an hour. At least the tables had been cleared; the halls and parlors and draperies were still reminiscent of cabbage and onion, fried fish and coffee. Henriette, seated near a lamp with piles of sewing about her, paused at intervals to wipe the moisture from the needle she forced through the coarse cotton sheets she was hemming. She pressed her handkerchief to her nose, and the sharp fragrance of cologne revived her enough to go on for another brief period of work. She sat in Madame's small parlor, separated by folding doors from the drawing-room where a group of students were trying to while away another dull summer evening. Most of the students were females, and a more nondescript and unattractive lot Henriette thought she had never seen. The three male residents of the pension had gone out immediately upon finishing dinner, and a dispiriting lull had settled down upon the rest. They read or wrote letters, embroidered or gossiped while several more musically inclined took turns at the square piano. But this music failed to enliven the scene. No players were gifted or even very accurate, and the piano needed tuning. Henriette tried to shut the sound from her consciousness; but it was impossible not to wince when false notes were struck, or when some key refused to budge.

Usually she sat with the students, chaperoning or assisting them at their various occupations. But tonight she had been spared that. It was a luxury to be allowed to sew by herself while she waited for the announcement of special visitors. Flies buzzed incessantly about the oil lamp. It was very hot in the small parlor, but she was growing used to that, now the summer had dragged two-thirds through. She had become accustomed to many things that in June had seemed unendurable.

"Well?" Madame Le Maire surveyed her from the doorway. "No sign of your visitors yet? You're sure you made no mistake?"

"No, madame." Henriette looked up from the long hem under her hands. "Louise wrote plainly 'the 17th of August.'"

"I've told Pierre not to keep them waiting. They're to be shown up here immediately. I must speak to the girls next door, but I'll be back directly. It will be less awkward if I'm sitting here with you when they arrive."

The brisk old figure rustled away, and presently her orders were being issued in the next room. Henriette's ears were strained for the rattle of a carriage stopping outside,

for the peal of a bell and the sound of familiar voices on the
stairs. She had faced much in the last three weeks since she
had seen them. The episode of the laudanum bottle had left
its mark upon her spirit, though it had not injured her physically, thanks to the maid's and Madame's prompt action.
But the starch had gone out of Henriette, temporarily at
least. She was even ready to compromise now if need be.
There would be no other way if Madame failed tonight in
her demand of the letter.

All day she had waited, restless and yet in a state of suspended activity, knowing that her fate would be decided
before another day passed. Almost, it seemed to her as she
pushed the needle in and out with precise, even stitches, that
her future had gone out of her keeping. Madame had laid
down her ultimatum, not unkindly, but with a firmness that
Henriette knew would never be shaken. The letter must be
guaranteed. She would speak to the Duc herself since Henriette's efforts had not been successful. There had been nothing to do but agree to this arrangement, must as she disliked
the old woman's meddling.

"Forget those fine stitches you learned in the convent,"
Madame was saying presently. "These sheets will never be
worth the pains you're putting on them. What's the time?
Nearly nine. Well, I must say they might have paid you the
compliment of coming before this."

A quarter of an hour later they heard the sounds of arrival. Before the sewing could be laid aside the children had
run up the stairs with eager cries for "Mademoiselle Deluzy." Berthe and Raynald were first with flowers in their
hands; Louise and Marie came next; last of all came the
Duc, bearing a basket of fruit and one of the famous château
melons. Henriette stood in their midst again, struggling to
keep herself in hand when so much depended upon her
tonight. She took as long as possible with the young people's
greetings before she returned to their father.

When the introductions to Madame Le Maire were over,
they fitted themselves into the parlor as best they could, the
chairs occupied by the adults, the children squeezed close
together on a horsehair sofa. The room seemed suddenly
too small to hold all this influx of life and good looks and
expensive clothes. It was like a pot on a hot stove ready to
boil over in another moment. Henriette felt her head begin
to swim as she tried to answer the eager, bubbling questions

of the young Praslins; to listen to the conversation of Madame and the Duc on her other side, and to keep her eyes from turning in his direction.

"Oh, these roses and heliotrope!" She buried her face in the fragrant bouquets. "Berthe, you remembered how I love mignonette, and this is the first bit I've seen all summer. And ferns from the woods!"

"And the fruit, mademoiselle; we wanted you to have the first peaches, and the grapes grew in the new conservatory. The strawberries are all gone, and the blackberries were too green to pick. But this melon will ripen if you keep it in the sun. It was the biggest on any of the vines."

Over their quick mingled voices she strained to catch what the other two were saying. Had they reached the point yet? Was Madame leading tactfully to the matter of the letter?

"You are pale, mademoiselle," Louise was saying, "and your eyes look——"

"Oh, you've just forgotten how I look," Henriette broke in hastily. They must not ask if she had been crying.

"I've done a study of flowers, mademoiselle: yellow and white lilies and purple iris in a green jar. The flowers were easy, but the jar was hard to do——to make both sides look the same."

"I can't wait to see it, Berthe. Be sure you make a great many more sketches at the seashore——shells and seaweed and ships. The other day I was looking at the ones I did in my old sketchbook at Olmeto, and they made me quite homesick."

Chit chat, chit chat. Flowers and shells and such, when her heart felt as if it were tied fast in a double knot, when her throat was aching and her lips felt dry, holding back all the words of love and homesickness and longing that she must never say.

"Oh, yes, thank you, mademoiselle, the others are all well. At least all except Mamma. She's been poorly since we went to the château. Dr. Simon and Dr. Louis came from Paris to see her. It was their idea to go to Dieppe. But we have a much larger villa than the old one. You remember that other where——"

"Yes, yes, I remember," Henriette once more interposed hastily. "And you're off in the morning?"

"Not till the day after. The others went straight to the

Faubourg-Saint-Honoré, except Mamma and the boys. They were going to the booksellers on the Rue du Coq first. Mamma wants to take some new novels with her."

"I see. And you have good news from Isabella? She wrote me a sweet letter a fortnight ago. Louise, you look blooming. Has your wedding day been finally settled upon?"

From behind the folding doors the murmurs of the boarders sounded with occasional shrill giggles. The piano began again. They could scarcely talk above it. Madame rose, excused herself, and went in to put a stop to that.

"This is a funny little parlor you have, mademoiselle, and where do you sleep?"

"Hush, Raynald, don't ask such questions."

"Oh, never mind, monsieur. It's no secret. This parlor belongs to Madame. She only invites me to share it if I have company, and when I sleep, which I haven't been doing so very well lately, my room is high up among the chimney-pots. The melon will ripen nicely there, almost as soon as if it were in your greenhouse."

She broke off quickly, seeing the surprised pity in the children's eyes and realizing she had admitted too much. She had meant the Duc to hear, and he had. She saw him shift uneasily in his chair.

"Mademoiselle Deluzy"—he spoke hurriedly and glanced towards the hall to make sure their hostess had not returned —"I am greatly worried about you. Your health has suffered. I should have guessed that even if Madame had not told me you have been ill." He looked at her intently, and she knew he must be referring to the laudanum. "You must see Dr. Simon at once, and you must accept my offer to send you on a little holiday. Please let me help you."

There was a note of appeal in his voice, yet once more she could not continue to look into his eyes. What she saw there frightened her. His face had fallen into heavy, listless lines, but his eyes showed his own inner tension.

"Well, monsieur," she sighed and made a little futile gesture with her hands, "there's only one thing that can help me. I suppose Madame Le Maire has already told you."

He had only time to nod before the old woman was in their midst again. Once more Henriette turned to the group on the sofa, and there were further inquiries and answers.

"How is your sick grandfather, mademoiselle? Will he soon be better so you can come back?"

"I can't say, *chéri*. You mustn't count on my coming back."

"Oh, but we do! We don't want any other governess. Monsieur Remey can teach us till you come back—all except painting. He's not very good at that."

Berthe's sudden laughter filled the room with clear, untroubled gayety.

Ten o'clock. A distant clock struck, and the Duc rose to make his farewells. How his height and strength filled the room! The bric-a-brac and furniture seemed nothing but a clutter of flimsy feminine trash by contrast, sticks and straw and bits of china that he could demolish by a single sweep of his hands.

"Good night, madame, and I thank you for the honor you have done me. Come, Louise, Marie, Berthe, Raynald. It's late, and we must make our adieus."

"Good night, Monsieur le Duc," Madame Le Maire peered up at him, looking in her rusty black rather like an aged and scrawny crow. "It was most considerate of you to come tonight, and I hope I've made my situation clear."

"Perfectly clear, madame, though as I said, in case of a slight delay—"

"There's been two months' delay already. It's not that I'm being insistent. You understand how it is when I'm responsible to others and with the circumstances what they are."

"I understand, madame, and all I can say is, I will do my best. Good night."

Henriette followed the five to the head of the stairs. She kissed the soft faces turned up to hers and then stood with her hands on the stair rail, searching his face under the flickering hall light.

"Don't take what she says too much to heart, monsieur," she told him. "I know better than any one else the position you are being placed in because of me, because of this letter."

"I've tried already." His voice was low beside her. "I've done everything in my power, but I play a sorry part in all this."

"Madame la Duchesse has found a way to punish me. She can force me to leave here, and she'll probably end by getting her way."

"She has put you out of the house. Isn't that enough?"

"Apparently not, monsieur. But, please, be careful what

you say. I shall manage somehow."

She turned to go back to the room they had just left, but he caught her hand.

"I will make one more effort," he promised. "Perhaps if I go to her now—tonight, she will listen to reason."

"Don't count on it, monsieur." She could not keep her voice altogether steady as she went on: "Don't go too far for my sake."

"Papa—Papa," the children were calling from below. "Aren't you coming? It's very dark down here, and we can't find the door knob."

"In a moment," he answered. Then he turned to her once more. "Come to the Faubourg-Saint-Honoré tomorrow about two o'clock. I can make no promises, but perhaps by then— Well, we shall see. Good night till tomorrow."

His boots clattered down the stairs.

"Good night, mademoiselle," the young voices called up to her.

"Good night," she called back. "Till tomorrow then, at two."

Madame Le Maire looked up as she returned to the parlor.

"Well?" she asked with that rising inflection whose meaning Henriette knew.

"I'm to go to the Faubourg-Saint-Honoré at two o'clock tomorrow. That's all I know. But I'm not counting too much on that."

She reached for the half-finished sewing and took up the needle and thread.

"He's a very fine figure of a man," the old woman remarked after they had stitched in silence for some time. "I don't wonder the Duchesse wanted to catch him early. He must have been very handsome when he was young."

"He's not so old." Henriette tried to speak casually as she threaded her needle. "Forty-two. That's young to be a grandfather, but he will be soon."

"Grandfather or not, he'd better watch where he's heading." Madame bit off the thread emphatically before she went on. "They're pretty children, and their manners do you credit. I don't envy the Mademoiselle who comes next after the fuss they made over you."

Henriette refused to be drawn into further conversation about the visit. When the sewing was done, she divided her

fruit and flowers with Madame and climbed the stairs to her
room. She felt spent from the evening and yet strangely calm
and settled in her mind as she put the drooping flowers into
water and set the basket of fruit with the melon on her
window sill. The early sun would ripen it in a day or two,
and she would share the delicacy with Albert and Marie.
They had been begging her to make them a little visit, and
she guessed that the time was not far off when she would be
glad to accept their invitation.

The Duc would never be able to secure that letter. It had
been foolish to cling to the hope of it so long. The Duchesse
was taking the revenge she had waited for all these years.
It was consistent with her Corsican heritage that she should
do so, though she would never have been clever enough
to plan so subtly cruel a way. Out of the hopeless tangle of
their lives this power had been put into the Duchesse's
plump, ineffectual hands. Merely by a few pen strokes she
could give Henriette back her independence and good name.
By refusing them she could make her into an exile, and her
future a downhill road. Well, there must be some way out.
There came a time when one could no longer struggle
against difficulties not of one's own making. She had plunged
hopefully into a maelstrom of human emotions. It was not
strange that she had been caught between the fierce crosscurrents of these two lives till she was blind and dizzy, battered by her efforts to keep her own head above water. For
six years she had been part of this dark and dangerous whirlpool, but now she was on land again; she would turn her
back on all that. The ground still felt uncertain under her
feet, but it would grow firmer in time if she could keep her
footing for a little while.

"I mustn't try to hop against the hill at first," she told
herself. "One step after another, and there's less chance of
slipping. And I will not look back."

She hung her dress up with more care than she had taken
since her return to the Rue du Harlay, smoothing its crisp
silk folds with the stripes of blue against the gray background. It was such a pretty dress, yet already it seemed
years ago that she had chosen it—not barely four months
before. Standing presently in her nightgown before the
blurred square of looking-glass she marveled that she should
still be able to recognize herself. Outwardly she had not
changed. Her face showed paler and thinner; but the faint

shadows about her eyes were not unbecoming, and her loosened hair still shone in the candlelight.

She blew out her candle and lay down in the darkness. The air outside had freshened slightly; the Needle's Eye was less oppressive. A great weariness and relaxation overtook her. Better to give up this futile battering at doors that were closed. There must be some way out of her difficulties. Tomorrow she would face them with new eyes. She would write to the Hislop family in England and ask their help. The Reverend Frédéric Monod would return in another week, and she would explain everything to him. Perhaps he could find her work even in France. And meantime she would sleep as she had not slept in many weeks. Already her breath came more easily, and the gentle bliss of unawareness crept upon her.

She scarcely stirred, so deep and dreamless was her sleep. Dawn slipped into Paris, into the Rue du Harley. Milkmen with their carts rattled over the cobblestones, and early venders began their morning rounds. The sun rose red above the clustered chimneypots, touching them to brightness, finding the basket of fruit on the window ledge with the melon waiting to be ripened. But still Henriette slept though, many flights below her, old Pierre hobbled out to answer the insistent jingling of the house bell.

Steps were mounting the stairs to the Needle's Eye, quick hurrying footsteps and heavier ones. Some one knocked sharply at her door. The door knob was frantically shaken.

"Henriette! Henriette, wake up! Please hurry. It's I, Albert Remey."

"Get up, mademoiselle, and let us in before we rouse the house."

Still only half awake, she stumbled to the door and unbolted it. Wide-eyed, she stood there in her long white nightgown, her hair flowing on her shoulders, her feet bare. Madame Le Maire had thrown a heavy shawl over her own nightrobe, and for once her scanty graying knot of hair was unrelieved by the luxuriant black false front. That, more than all other signs of agitation, alarmed Henriette. Madame must be at the last extremity to have forgotten that.

"Shut the door, Albert," the old woman commanded, "and come in. This is no time for worrying about the proprieties."

"But what is it? What are you doing here, Albert, at this hour? Is Marie—

"It's bad news, Henriette. I came as soon as I heard it. Here!" He pulled her to the tumbled bed and forced her to sit down, while he bent over her, his face chalky and twitching. "Sit down. You must prepare yourself for a shock. There's been a murder in the Rue du Faubourg-Saint-Honoré—at Number 55—"

"Murder. Do you understand?" Madame's head jerked like a frightened bird. "The Duchesse de Praslin was found brutally murdered not two hours ago."

"The Duchesse." Henriette stared from one to the other, and though her lips repeated their words her eyes remained wide and incredulous. "But that can't be. I'm to see her at two o'clock today."

"She's dead, I tell you." The old woman's fingers were like claws on Henriette's arm. "Don't sit there as if you were still asleep. All Paris will know it in another hour, and then what will become of us?"

"Hush, madame! Give her a moment to come to her senses. Let me tell her what I can."

Albert took her cold hands and rubbed them between his own, which were a shade less chill. He was speaking to her while Madame continued to babble and jerk hysterically.

"I'd been working all night on that paper for the Académie," he was saying. "I couldn't sleep, so when it grew light I went out to walk. I often do early in the morning to calm my nerves. That was about five, I think. I was going along the Rue du Faubourg-Saint-Honoré, and it seemed to me there was an unusual stir for that hour. People ran past me, and when I came in sight of Number 55 I saw a crowd collected. I thought the family were away at Melun—"

"They were till last night," Henriette whispered.

"I couldn't get near the entrance. The police were already there."

"And they'll be here next," Madame was whimpering. "They'll be pounding on my doors, saying, 'Open in the name of the law,' and all because I took you in."

Albert planted himself between Madame and Henriette and tried to go on.

"I asked a workman what had happened, and he told me the Duchesse had been murdered. Hacked to pieces, he said. *Mon Dieu*, I didn't believe him till I saw they were drawing the blinds of her apartments. They were beginning to call the news in the streets as I came away. I got here as fast as I could. I didn't even stop to tell Marie. I could only think of breaking the news to you before you heard it being shouted under your windows."

Henriette could not answer him. Numbness was creeping over her as she sat in her nightgown on the edge of the bed, staring blankly before her. Madame Le Maire's words of fright and distress fell on her unheeded as rain.

"They'll be coming to arrest us all," she kept insisting. "This is the thanks I get for sheltering you. Oh, that this should happen to me!"

"But, madame"—Albert tried to calm her—"nothing has happened to you. Henriette has nothing to do with this frightful crime. She was here sleeping quietly till we waked her. I only came to prepare her for the shock. There's no reason she should be dragged in."

"But she will be. You'll see. She can't be kept out. I know how it will be, and she mustn't stay in my house another hour."

"Please, madame! You mustn't give way like this. We must find out more of this. I'll go for a paper—"

"And she'll go with you. Take her away before they come."

"But I must be here if I'm sent for." Henriette gathered strength to speak at last in a toneless thread of voice. "The poor children! They'll need me now, more than ever before."

"You'll not be here for the police to find."

The dry, difficult sobs of old age were shaking Madame Le Maire's body under the shawl. Albert looked at her and hesitated; then he touched Henriette's shoulder.

"You'd better come with me," he said. "It will be easier for you over there with Marie. If they send for you, though I can't see why they should, we'll leave word where you've gone. I'll wait downstairs till you're ready."

Somehow he got Madame Le Maire out of the room. She waited till their footsteps sounded faintly on the floor below. Then she got to her feet and began to dress. Mechanically she reached for the clothes she had left folded on a chair. Without feeling, her fingers found brush and comb and sponge; felt for buttons and loops and lacings. Only when she fastened the bodice of the gray and blue silk and adjusted the full skirt did it come over her that she had last put it on in expectation of the Duc's visit.

The household was already astir as she descended the stairs, her cold hands clinging to the railing, grateful for the

solid familiarity of the wood. Albert and Pierre were waiting by the door. The old man had forgotten his coat. He
stood there anxious and unshaved in his coarse blue blouse.

"Don't let any harm come to her," she heard him caution Albert Remey. "She's not been like her old self all
summer." Then as he let them out, he touched her arm, and
his old eyes searched her face. "Maybe it will all turn out a
mistake," he whispered encouragingly. "These papers are
nothing but lies. That's why I never read them. Mind the
steps there. I spilled a jug of milk just now. But no matter,
it will give Madame something else to scold about."

It was half past six as they stepped into the street, which
was still quiet and deserted. But just around the corner they
could hear the cries of the news venders. Even in the distance there was a queer exultant, almost animal note in those
lifted voices, something more than mere shrillness.

"Blood is in their voices," she thought, and for a moment
she turned faint and had to lean heavily on Albert.

"I'll get a carriage," he said.

She shook her head. He must not spend so much money,
and she realized that she had forgotten to bring her own
purse. They walked on without speaking, but they kept
close together. She took comfort from the sense of his kind,
bodily nearness.

Every one they passed held a paper or was in the act of
buying one. Workmen were reading the black-lettered sheets
so avidly that she and her escort often had to turn aside to
escape collision. They alone were empty-handed. But the
words of the news venders followed like hounds at their
heels:

"Murder in the Rue du Faubourg-Saint-Honoré . . .
Murder—Praslin . . . *Catastrophe fatale* . . . Praslin.
Murder."

A man thrust one of the news sheets rudely into her face
before Albert could push him away. But those bold black
letters could not be thrust aside.

"Only a few more blocks," Albert encouraged her. "Don't
listen to them, Henriette, and forget what Madame said.
She lost her senses for the moment, that was all."

"Oh, but, Albert, she's right! I am somehow part of this
—this—" She could not bring herself to say the dreadful
word that was echoing all about them. "Don't ask me how I
know, but I do."

## chapter twenty-one

ON THE ILE DE LA CITÉ THE PALAIS DE JUSTICE WAS A
somber pile of stone against an August sunset. Shreds of
cloud, softly brilliant as flamingo feathers, drifted across the
sky and were reflected in the river flowing between buildings. But the walls of the Conciergerie caught no hint of that
brightness. It stood gray and unshaken by sunsets and sun-
rises, by revolutions and intrigues, by the swift procession of
years and the men and women it had sheltered in the name
of the law. There Marie Antoinette had spent her last night
on earth. Danton, Madame Roland, Robespierre—these and
countless others had passed through the gate on the Quai de
l'Horloge and into the Salle des Gardes. And now on the
18th of August in the year 1847 another pair of feet had
been led across the worn stones of the courtyard; another
pair of eyes stared through one of the barred windows.

Henriette had made no protest when the police had come
for her at eight o'clock that morning. She had been calmer
than the Remeys then. She had even tried to reassure them
as she had left between two guards.

"Don't cry, Marie," she had begged. "It's only a formality. I am wanted for questioning, they say. Please, Albert, don't try to reason with them. You only make it more
difficult for us both. I'll be back again in a little while."

But she had known better than to believe the words she
had spoken. Now it was evening, and still she sat alone in
the small bare room where they had brought her, the latest
comer to the Conciergerie she had so often passed. She had
not guessed what it would mean to be there. The sight of a
cage is only frightening to the bird that has once been
caught. But the sound of a key turning in the door that had
just closed upon her had brought a sharp and sudden sense
of reality. It was as if a trap had been sprung—a trap that
caught but did not kill. In that moment she had known
overwhelming panic, such as she had not experienced since
early childhood. A wild impulse to beat on that door, to

scream in futile protest, had overtaken her. She had needed all her powers of control to make no protest as the footsteps retreated along the corridor.

Twice during the day they had brought her food, and a matron had come with water, and a coverlet for her bed. They asked her if she would care to buy a bottle of wine to drink with *déjeuner*. But she had declined the privilege. She could not bring herself to explain that she had brought no money; she could not venture a question as to why she was confined there. All she knew she had gleaned from one of those early news sheets. It had been under her feet that morning as she reached Albert's door. She had picked it up and carried it with her later. They had not taken it from her, and now in the failing light she pored over the meager account. For perhaps the hundredth time she forced her aching eyes to read the words, forced her mind to believe the reality behind those ink-smudged symbols. This concerned some one she had known, whose home she had shared for the last six years. The phrases were so familiar now she knew them by heart. Still she could not realize them in relation to the Duchesse, to the plump, dark woman whose bounty and bitterness, whose storms of jealousy and spasms of affection she had known so intimately.

The noble Duchesse de Praslin is no more. . . . She breathed her last this morning some time between half past four and five in the family residence in the Rue du Faubourg-Saint-Honoré, Number 55 . . . Little is known as yet of the brutal attack on the person of this wealthy and benevolent member of the nobility, wife of Charles Laure Hugo Théobold, Duc de Choiseul-Praslin, mother of nine children, only daughter of the Maréchal Sébastiani. . . . At the early hour mentioned, people on the street and within the residence were shocked to hear violent screams of agony and the repeated ringing of a bell from the Duchesse's bedroom. According to report three servants—her maid, Madame Leclerc; Madame Merville, the porter's wife; and Auguste Charpentier, the Duc's valet de chambre—rushed to the scene.

Strange to read those names in cold black type when she could summon up the persons behind the letters so clearly; when she had exchanged good morning and good evening with them day after day.

These three tried the doors but found them locked. When they finally effected an entrance all was in the utmost confusion and the unfortunate woman already expiring in pools of her own blood. The Duchesse had evidently put up a fierce struggle against the blows of her assassin, who is believed to have escaped through the garden and into the Champs Elysées. According to the Duc de Praslin, who . . .

Here the paper had been torn at the very place she most longed to read. In vain she tried to piece out the explanation which must have followed. But she could not go beyond the impossible fact that she had not yet been able to make herself believe. Murder did not happen to those we have known intimately in the past, to those we are expecting to meet today or tomorrow. Sensational horror or crime cannot touch us. Other people's lives, perhaps, may be crossed by such violence, but not our own. We are somehow secure against that.

Twilight settled down over the courtyard of the Conciergerie, crept through the identical windows and deepened in the narrow rooms. But for once darkness was not kind. More vividly than ever she saw the pale, full face of the Duchesse with every shifting, unpredictable mood reflected upon it. She saw, too, those luxurious rooms which had been turned into a shambles. She could not rid her mind of pictures those printed words had conjured up before her eyes.

She saw the disordered bed and rich hangings spattered with red stains; chairs and tables overturned; books and bric-a-brac scattered on the carpet with its gay garlands where sinister pools were drying in dark patches. On the secretary between the windows where the Duchese had so often given vent to her grievances, her quill hurrying faster than the bird that had once borne it, unfinished letters might still be lying in confusion. There might even now be one beginning: "To Whom it may concern: I hereby recommend Mademoiselle Henriette Deluzy for those excellent qualities of mind and character which she has maintained during her years of service as governess in my household . . ." Such a letter might have been penned in those last six hours of the Duchesse's life. But Henriette knew that she would never receive it now. It would never be presented to Madame Le Maire or another possible employer.

Some one was unlocking the door. A lamp was being screwed into an iron socket. Once more the woman in charge was speaking her name. She set a bundle down on the cot and went through the contents carefully. Henriette recognized her own Paisley shawl and other articles of her clothing.

"Your friends brought them a little while ago," she was told. "They wanted to see you, but you're allowed no visitors yet."

Marie Remey must have been to the Rue du Harley and have collected these few belongings. No one else would have thought of such personal needs, and Henriette blessed her for that. This simple gesture was all that one woman could offer to another. Yet it comforted Henriette a little to handle the familiar lengths of shawl, to set her brush and comb and handkerchiefs on an empty shelf. She was most grateful to Marie for the handkerchiefs. They smelled faintly of vervain from the gardens at Melun. A dried leaf of it still lay between the folded squares. Strange to smell that fragrance in this place, even stranger to be able to smell at all, to recognize a scent when one felt this numbing paralysis of the senses.

The Conciergerie cot was less hard than hers had been last night in the Needle's Eye; the room was less stifling. Yet she lay, staring wide-eyed into the darkness, listening to the quiet all about her, a quiet so intense that as the hours passed she longed for anything to break the unnatural stillness. It was a relief to hear the hours strike or a footstep echo in courtyard or corridor. Here, in the very heart of Paris, it was as if life were suspended. Whether they slept or lay, wakeful as she, those within these walls were no longer part of the city and its activity. Their lives, their loves, their ambitions, their destinies were for the time being entirely out of their keeping. The idea obsessed her as she waited for morning and the first thin graying at the window.

She forced herself to take the bread and coffee that was brought her. From the guard who came to take away the tray she begged for permission to read a morning paper, but he could not grant that favor. He was a pleasant, talkative fellow, easily persuaded to tell her what he could of the murder.

The papers were full of it, he said. No one talked of any-

thing else. Every café and shop and street corner buzzed
with each new detail of horror that leaked out. That first
rumor about an assassin having broken into the Duchesse's
bedroom was all nonsense. It appeared now that the Duc
de Praslin himself was under suspicion, though it seemed
unthinkable that such a thing could be—a husband guilty
of an inhuman attack upon his own wife. The poor woman
had bled to death from over a score of wounds and had been
brutally beaten beside.

"No, no!" Henriette could scarcely whisper the protest
that interrupted his recital. "That's not possible. Monsieur
le Duc could never— You don't know what you're saying."

But he merely shrugged expressively. He was only repeating what all Paris was saying. At first even the police had
refused to believe it. But they had had to believe what was
all too plain before their eyes. When they had followed the
advice of the Duc's own valet and searched his rooms they
had found plenty of evidence against him. Oh, yes, it looked
very bad indeed for Monsieur le Duc. He was under guard
and they were taking no chances of his escape. No matter
if he was a Peer of France, answerable only to the King,
people meant to see that he paid for murder like any other
criminal.

"And what—do they say of me?" Henriette heard herself
asking faintly.

He answered with another shrug, eyeing her curiously
across the tray with its thick pottery cup and plate. Her
name had certainly been mentioned. He could not deny that.
Some said that she and Monsieur le Duc had been—well,
what men and women often were to one another. There had
been rumors before about the part she had played in that
family. They said there had been no love lost between the
Duchesse and the children's governess; they hinted much
worse things than that. That was why the police had brought
her to the Conciergerie for questioning. They meant to get
to the bottom of what lay behind so ghastly a murder. She
would be answering them herself soon. Then she would
know more than he could tell her. No, he could not say how
long she must stay in the Conciergerie. But she should be
thankful she was here. It would not be safe for her to walk
the streets of Paris just now.

It was not a public courtroom into which they led Henri-

ette, but a smaller, private one where perhaps a dozen men
had gathered. Their faces were so many blank disks to her
as she took her place in their midst and waited for the questioning to begin. The shock of the guard's words that morning had left her numb, with the same incredulous despair
she had felt when Albert Remey had aroused her from her
sleep with the fatal news. She had lost the power to think,
much less feel. It surprised her to find that she could still
walk erectly and without trembling, that she could seat herself calmly on the chair that had been placed for her near
the Judge's desk.

Monsieur Broussais, who was to conduct the interroga-
tion, barely looked up as she entered. His hands were busy
with numerous papers, and he appeared engrossed in conversation with another man, *le Procureur du Roi.* They
talked together in low tones, while the rest regarded her
with undisguised curiosity and made whispered comments
among themselves. Flies buzzed maddeningly; one lighted
in her hair and though she brushed it away again and again,
it always returned. So absorbed was she in trying to rid herself of it that she hardly realized the hearing had begun
until she was being addressed. They were speaking her
name, yet it seemed to belong to some one else, to bear no
relationship to her personally. So began the first examination of Mademoiselle Henriette Deluzy-Desportes, aged
thirty-five years, spinster, governess, native of Paris, resident of the pension conducted by Madame Le Maire at
Number 9, Rue du Harlay, in the district Marais.

The first questions put to her were perfunctory: How
long had she been in the employ of the Praslin family? What
salary had she received? What had been the nature of her
duties? She replied in a steady voice that surprised. But the
next question came in a different tone. Monsieur Broussais
leaned across the desk and fixed her with his enigmatical,
deep-set eyes.

"We have already learned that you were guilty of grave
wrong in this household: that you did not show the deceased
Duchesse proper regard, that you sought to alienate the
affections of her husband and children. Is this true?"

The other occupants of the room also leaned forward in
their places. Henriette felt the slight rustle of excitement
that followed his words, and she knew that the time had
come to give more than a perfunctory answer. All eyes

were upon her as they waited for words from her lips. She summoned them to her as one might call upon a well trained pack of hounds to perform their duty.

"No, monsieur." She spoke clearly and without hesitation. "That was never so. When I first entered the Praslin household, matters were already on a very bad footing. There had been governesses before me, but they left because they found it impossible to get on with Madame la Duchesse. Always there was trouble over the children and their education."

"And what was the nature of this trouble you mention?"

"The Duc wished to direct that himself, and it was understood from the first that I should be accountable only to Monsieur. I was to live and dine with the children in separate quarters. I told the Duc that this was a difficult position for me and great responsibility, and some adjustments were made. But it was not easy. The former governess was still there when I took up my duties, and naturally she resented my presence. From the first she prejudiced the Duchesse against me. Madame continued to interfere with the children's affairs and the results were unfortunate. Monsieur was greatly displeased and expressed himself so to Madame. So we came to live more and more apart, the children and I, though I never consciously tried to win them away from their mother. The disagreements between the Duc and Duchesse continued, and it was beyond my power to change that. Perhaps it was wrong for me to have accepted so extraordinary a position, but I never tried to hurt Madame. If I did sometimes answer her with annoyance it was only because I had been myself unjustly hurt."

"And what," the questioning voice was going on, "were the causes of this dissension you speak of between the Duc and the Duchesse?"

"On the Duchesse's part it seemed to be a desire to dominate the children, and above all her husband. With the Duc it seemed to be a fixed spirit of resistance, though he was less violent by nature."

"Your presence in the intimate life of this family seems to have particularly inspired the Duchesse's jealousy. Was there good cause?"

"I cannot deny that at times Madame la Duchesse showed marked jealousy towards me, jealousy which had no grounds whatsoever. Then at other times the situation between us was less strained. When she was in good humor and treated me graciously I could forget her unjust accusations. There I was, messieurs, without money or friends. I had to try my best to keep the position though often it took all my patience. Then, too, Monsieur le Duc offered me a pension if I had the courage—those were his very words—to complete the education of his older daughters, and I had promised, difficult though that might be."

The matter of the pension had to be investigated: Had it been part of the original agreement when she took up her duties? Had a definite figure bèen set? What could she recall of the conversation concerning it? A long pause followed while Monsieur Broussais made notes on the papers before him. Then he cleared his throat in preparation for his next sally. In the tense quiet of the room that had an ominous sound.

"Is it not true," he asked, "that the Duchesse, particularly of late, believed that intimate relations existed between yourself and her husband?"

So, the old scandal had cropped up again. Henriette had known it must, and she was prepared to face it.

"Never, monsieur, no, never that!" She made the denial swiftly, then she spoke more slowly, weighing her words with care, realizing as she did the significance of the question. "The Duchesse knew that such relations could not have existed. She did not accuse me of them. She may have said so to others, but not to me. Certain libelous articles did appear in the newspapers. Two years ago, while I was staying with the children in Corsica, there was a very malicious one and I wanted to leave at once because of it. But the Maréchal Sébastiani, the Duchesse's own father, persuaded me to stay. For some time the Duchesse did treat me harshly. But then she grew less cold, and all through this past winter she was gracious to me. I had even hoped we might come to a better understanding when two months or so ago I was overwhelmed to be told that my presence was no longer desired."

Monsieur Broussais's expression remained impassive during this recital. When she stopped speaking he reached among the papers before him and selected one which he handed to her. It was written on a sheet of the Duchesse's own note paper, and though it bore no date or salutation she recognized it as one written to her, beginning:

If it is forbidden to go to rest without being reconciled to one's neighbor, it seems to me that a New Year is a still more urgent reason for putting aside all disagreements and forgetting all complaints.

So, she thought, staring down at that familiar writing, they had already been to Madame Le Maire's and rifled the box where she kept her private possessions.

"This letter," she explained, "was written by the Duchesse to me a year ago. It came with a bracelet as a New Year's gift. I remember it very well because it marked a change in her former coldness. She took me to the theater with the young ladies sometimes, and even discussed the subject of their future marriage. She asked me to use my influence with the Duc about his views on this matter, but I had to refuse that. I could not intrude in anything so personal."

When the letter had been returned to Monsieur Broussais's portfolio, more questions followed. These concerned her dismissal, the date of her leaving the Rue du Faubourg-Saint-Honoré, and whether she had continued to see the Duc. There were others, as to how and where she had passed the night of August 17th, how she had first heard of yesterday's tragedy, and why she had not been at Madame Le Maire's when the police agents came for her. It was the next question that brought her to her feet, her eyes wide and panic-stricken as they turned upon her questioner.

"Have you learned of the grave charges against Monsieur le Duc? Do you know that he is believed to have murdered his wife?"

"No, no, messieurs!" She found herself searching the faces one by one in frantic appeal. "Tell me it's only some unfounded rumor. I cannot believe he could have done it. He could never bear to see the slightest suffering of one of his children. Please tell me these charges are not—what you say!"

But no one reassured her; the eyes continued to watch the effect of the news upon her. She knew from their silence that this was more than some wild rumor. It could not be true, and yet if it should be . . . Somehow she must make them understand the part she had unwittingly played in all this. The letter! She must try to explain about it. It came over her now in a lightning flash of conviction that she alone held the key to this horror. That letter of recommendation had been written in the Duchesse's blood.

Her knees were shaking; her hands clasping and un-clasping themselves. She heard herself pleading, babbling broken, incoherent phrases, as Madame Le Maire had done yesterday.

"Please, messieurs, listen to me. He could never have done this dreadful thing . . . but if he should have had any part in it—*Mon Dieu,* then it is I who am the guilty one because I asked too much. . . . I, who so loved the chil-dren, adored them. . . . I was a coward not to accept my fate. I wrote them. You can see the letters for yourselves. I told them how unhappy I was, that I no longer cared to live. I was afraid to face the future. Oh, I was wrong, wrong! I ought not to have let them know my misery. I should have pretended I was resigned, even happy in that bare, small room. I ought to have told them to forget me and think only of their mother. But I was not brave enough for that. I was driven to despair, and I wanted to die. I had a bottle of laudanum, and I drank it. Unfortunately I was called back to life, and life was bitter to me. After six years of such hap-piness among those children I loved and who loved me, the emptiness seemed unbearable. I can see it all now, and now it is too late. He must have gone to her demanding that fatal letter of recommendation the Duchesse had promised me. She must have refused him, and then . . . There, you see, I am guilty. Write it down there in your records—guilty."

Monsieur Broussais's voice cut into her recital, cool and precise and edged with irony.

"It seems hardly possible, mademoiselle, that such a dis-play of emotion, and such lofty sentiments as these you have just expressed, should be applied to children. Was it to these children only that you addressed the despairing letters you mentioned?"

"Yes, monsieur." She raised her eyes directly to his. "All sentiments can be lofty, as you say. Can't you understand that? But I won't deny that when the Duc was so good to me, always so generous and thoughtful, there did not mingle with the love I felt for the children, a genuine affection for their father." She caught her breath sharply, and went on, her voice rising in the stillness of the room. "But I never brought sin into that home—adultery then, since that is in your minds. I could never have held those children close if

I had been guilty of that. They were like my own children, though perhaps I am wrong to use those words for this whole little band. Still, that is how it was. Can't you understand that it is possible to love honestly?"

Question followed question, but she answered without hesitation Monsieur Broussais's bombardment. Now that she had rallied from the first shock, her wits returned, and she was able to meet and turn aside his deft, sarcastic implications. She met the challenge with squared shoulders and a swift, sure fire of words that kept all eyes upon her; that even brought a grudging hint of admiration into the voice of her examiner. She knew he waited like a cat to pounce on any remark that might be misinterpreted, to twist anything that could be turned as evidence against her. She knew how much depended on her answers. It was not enough to speak the truth and that alone. One must be clever as well as honest.

Outside, the noon sun stood high over the roofs of Paris, over the metallic glitter of the Seine parting its watery coil above the Ile de la Cité, about the Palais de Justice and the Conciergerie. Inside the crowded room the air grew heavy, and a merciless glare filled the unshaded windows. Men's faces gleamed with heat. Monsieur Broussais paused often to wipe the moisture from brow and spectacles. Henriette's handkerchief was a limp ball in her hands. She pushed the damp hair from her forehead and accepted a sip of water from a glass an attendant offered. She must not let her mind wander for an instant. No matter how the flies buzzed or how her eyes and head ached from trying to catch the full meaning of the words addressed to her, she must keep on the alert. All her life she had loved words and kindled to them, but now she was in their power. They shot to and fro, like shuttles weaving the threads of some invisible pattern. If only one could know the pattern one wove in that hot room while minutes ticked away into hours!

Ruthlessly as a surgeon dissecting a patient, Monsieur Broussais's questions probed to the very core of that life in the Rue du Faubourg-Saint-Honoré, in Melun, and in Corsica. The quick blade of his irony delicately laid bare the tissues wrapping cause and motive. He must trap her into some unguarded admission of complicity. But she, too, held a blade as powerful as her questioners. She was speaking the truth. She had nothing to hide from him.

At last Monsieur Broussais pushed aside his papers with an impatient gesture. It was plain that he tired of these constant allusions to the Praslin children and the controversies between them and their mother. Here was a crime of unspeakable brutality, the most significant socially and politically he had ever been given to investigate, and this poised, attractive woman sitting before him refused to allow herself to play into his hands. She dared to confound him with answers as crisp as his questions, answers in which he could not find the admissions of guilt he had expected to uncover without much difficulty.

"Come, mademoiselle." He spoke brusquely. "We must keep to the point. We are here to consider, not these suspicions between yourself and the deceased Duchesse, not the jealousy which brought about your immediate dismissal, or this letter of recommendation, the importance of which you have stressed. What concerns us now is a matter of the most serious trouble that can be brought into any household —discord between man and wife. You were supported by the husband against the wife. Can you deny that this was so?"

"In certain matters, true. But how could I know how far it was carried, or how serious the trouble between them actually had become? As to what is evidently in your mind, monsieur, I can only repeat that the Duc de Praslin never showed other feelings for me than friendship and esteem. Again I must protest, and I will not mince words—he was never my lover."

The sincerity of her denial was apparent. But Monsieur Broussais was not through.

"Yet in the brief interval since you left that household," he pressed her, "you have penned letters which you yourself admit you did wrong to write, and you allowed the Duc to pay you visits, three at least. Yesterday you were to have gone to that house to see the Duchesse about this letter, and yesterday she met a violent death. How do you explain all these coincidences?"

"I can't explain them, to myself or to you. I can only say what I have said before. I can only repeat that nothing wrong ever passed between myself and Monsieur le Duc, and there was never any future wrong intended."

She hesitated for a moment, gathering words to answer a question that had not yet been put to her.

"I tell you the children's interests came first with me always. If the Duchesse had died a natural death, and if the Duc had then asked me to marry him, I should not have consented for their sakes to such a misalliance. And I had no idea of any other wrong. If Monsieur le Duc had loved me, there is no telling—I might have sacrificed my life and reputation for him. But as it was I never tried to come between him and his wife. I would not have harmed a hair of her head. I'm telling you the truth, monsieur, and you must believe me. Is there not something in the tone of a voice that can convince you of that?"

Her ability at anticipating questions and turning her answers into direct appeal had scored her several points. The group of listeners could not help being swayed by her eloquence and lack of pretense. Monsieur Broussais was himself amazed. He had never been called upon to examine such a witness. But he could not afford to be lost in admiration. The interview was not over. Once more he brought out a handful of papers for her to identify.

"You have here before you," he interposed, "certain letters. Were they written by you?"

"Yes, monsieur. I sent them to the older Praslin daughters a month or so ago."

"One of them contains an unfinished sentence, whose full meaning is not clear: 'You do not speak of your father. I hope that he is well and continues to keep his courage. It seems to me I should be less unhappy if I were sure to suffer—' Will you please complete the sentence for us?"

Henriette's heart sank. She had regretted that letter ever since it had been dispatched. She had written it impulsively to Louise on a day when it had seemed impossible to go on alone in the Rue du Harlay. Read aloud like this, apart from its context, the sentence certainly took on more significance than she had intended at the time.

"I must have meant to end the sentence with the word 'alone,'" she told them, "or perhaps with the phrase 'for all of you.' I cannot remember why I broke off. Perhaps I decided it would be better not to speak to the young girls of their father."

Monsieur Broussais nodded as he took charge of the letters once more.

"You did right," he commented dryly, "quite right, because it contained expressions of feeling which were not fit for young girls to share."

A quick protest rose to her lips, but the hearing was over. For the present at least Monsieur Broussais and his associates were done with her. A court clerk was already beginning to copy down the notes he had made of those questions and her answers.

"God alone knows," she thought as she passed by that desk on her way from the room, "who will read these words that have gone out of my keeping."

Outside those doors, the spirit that had carried her through the ordeal left her completely. She felt limp and exhausted, as shaken and spent as if she were an old woman. The store of energy that she had called to her aid for the last hour was gone. She was grateful for the guard's arm as she mounted once more to her room in the Conciergerie.

She could not swallow the meal they brought her. She shook her head when they gave her permission to walk in the courtyard for half an hour. So they left her, and she sat on through the interminable afternoon, trying to recall each word that had been spoken at the hearing. Why had she not thought of such and such an answer? Had she made them understand about that letter? What other private papers of hers, of the Duc and of the Duchesse, might not Monsieur Broussais and the police be poring over at that very moment? They all believed the Duc was guilty, and that she was his accomplice in crime. Though she had not slept in the Faubourg-Saint-Honoré that night, they all believed that she had had a part in this horror.

"It's not possible," she repeated as she had repeated that morning. "It's not possible. Monsieur le Duc could never have done such a terrible thing."

She said the words over and over, and yet all the while she was unconvinced. She wanted to believe in that first rumor of the mysterious assassin who had escaped into the garden, but she could not. She was remembering the strained expression of his face as she had seen it last in Madame Le Maire's poorly lighted hall. She remembered how the stair rail had quivered under his grip. She thought of those large, powerful hands that she had seen so often laid fondly upon one child or another or on Berthe's yellow hair. And now they were stained with blood. The sudden recollection of a spring night came to her, the night when he and Louise had surprised her by their return from the country. He had poured out a glass of port, and some of the wine had spilled. She felt faint now, remembering the red drops on his white skin and how fastidiously he had wiped them away. Six years ago last May, that had been . . .

"It's not possible," she kept repeating stubbornly.

Yet she knew too well the truth her lips denied. The daily venom of the Duchesse's jealousy had corroded his self-control. It was as if an oak tree that had defied storms and woodsmen had fallen at last under the incessant hammerings of a woodpecker.

A key clicked in the lock, and the door was opened. She roused at the sound of a familiar voice speaking her name, scarcely daring to believe in the reality of her visitor. Yet there before her stood the Reverend Frédéric Monod. Sobs shook her as they had not shaken her through the long, dark hours of the night or during the hearing that morning. She was no longer alone, and that knowledge overwhelmed her.

"But how did you come here?" she asked when she grew calmer. "Albert and Marie Remey tried, but they were turned away; and I thought I had no other friends in Paris."

He kept her hands in his and spoke reassuringly.

"I am your friend, Mademoiselle Deluzy, Mademoiselle Desportes—it does not matter which name you go by, and I am also your spiritual adviser. They cannot deny you the comfort of your church, no matter what the charges are against you."

"Oh, Monsieur Monod, I hardly know yet what the charges are. This terrible crime, and they say he has done it, and only night before last he came, with the children—" She struggled against her tears at the memory.

"Tell me what you will," he said. "Don't be afraid that I shall repeat your confidences. I know what they are saying of your part in this—"

"You don't believe that I am guilty?"

"No." He shook his head. "But even if I were in doubt I should have come to you here. You would have needed me even more. I was in the country when I read the news. Those first reports made no mention of your name, but I knew you were a member of that household, and I guessed the shock would be too much for you. I did not know you had left. I did not know till I reached Paris this morning that they had taken you into custody."

She managed to tell him all she could of her dismissal, of the Duc's last visit, and the letter which she insisted must have been the cause of the tragedy.

"Yes," he agreed, "it may be as you say. Goliath went down before a pebble from David's sling, and this letter of yours, no doubt, was the final blow. But you must not dwell on that. You have made mistakes; so have we all, though some of us are less ready to admit them."

"Monsieur Monod"—she faced him through her tears as she poured out the story of those six difficult years, while light faded in the courtyard of the Conciergerie—"I ought to have told you all this before—before it was too late. I ought to have asked your advice. But I was so sure of myself. I believed I could manage my own life. Mud might spatter and spoil other skirts, but not mine. Somehow I believed no harm could come to me because I meant no harm to others. I was defiant and proud because I felt too sure of myself."

"You are not the first to make that mistake," he answered gravely. "We all believe our lives are our own till we find we cannot separate them from other lives."

"And I thought," she went on, "I thought, because I committed no actual wrong, that I was above reproach. But now—it's terrible to think that she met this violent death, and that I, too, am being held to account for it. I could never like her. I could never respect her. Even now I can't bring myself to forget her faults and her stupidities, but I can never forget that she might be alive today, poor soul, if I had not insisted on what I believed was my right. Nothing I can do or say can ever change that. She is dead, and God knows what will become of him and of the children."

Monsieur Monod did not try to ease her with trite phrases of comfort. He did not offer to pray for her as other ministers of the Gospel might have done.

"You are too honest to make excuses for yourself," he said. "You are suffering far more than you deserve; for, the greater one's capacity for living, the greater one's capacity for suffering. But remember that the greatest wisdom is to find out one's folly. Keep your courage, mademoiselle. You'll need it, whether Monsieur le Duc is able to clear himself of these charges or not."

She begged for news of the Duc, but he could tell her little more than she already knew—that he had been taken into custody by the police. Each newspaper edition published a more sensational story than the last. Monsieur Monod told her what he could, without attempting to keep other aspects of the case from her. The whole country was aroused, and feeling grew more and more intense. It involved the King and the whole structure of his court.

"Out there," he told her, "the people believe that the Duc is guilty, and they want to see him tried like any other criminal. But, being a nobleman, he is answerable only to his superiors in rank—the King and the House of Peers. If he should be freed of this murder charge, the King is sure to be accused of discrimination; and if he is convicted, that will bring great censure on the court circle. You know the discontent that is in the very air."

Yes, she knew, though she had not thought of that before. Her personal problems had absorbed her completely. But now she sensed what lay behind his words. The King was far from popular, the public ready to pounce on anything that savored of corruption in court circles. This might be the chance the country had been waiting for, to assert its power. It was ironical, she thought, that she should figure in a case involving the House of Peers and the King himself— she, who had championed the cause of a new Republic, who had always been so outspoken in her denunciation of the House of Orléans.

"I know the feeling is against me, too," she said. "One of the guards told me so this morning. He said I was safer here in the Conciergerie than at large in Paris."

Once more Monsieur Monod did not try to soften his answer.

"There are wild rumors going about," he admitted. "Unfortunately your name is coupled with the Duc's. You know the public is more easily swayed by persons than by principles. It's simpler to fasten blame to a man or a woman than to a system of government. Of course no one can guess how this feeling will be from hour to hour. I've seen public opinion shift like a wind and put out the very fire it lighted."

"Or the fire can spread, monsieur, till there's no longer any chance to put it out."

"Well," he told her, "the King is hurrying back to Paris. It's not a simple case of murder that he has to deal with. For that reason it is important that you have a good lawyer at once. You have a right to legal advice, and I shall see that you have the best we can find."

But she shook her head.

"No, Monsieur Monod, I can do without a lawyer. I can answer their questions for myself."

"But you have no knowledge of the law, my child, and you must have help in giving your testimony. Some ignorant blunder on your part, some sudden impulse, might do you great harm."

"I'll take the risk. I'll tell them anything they want to know as I did today."

"You mustn't be hasty in this. If it's the matter of money that makes you hesitate, you're not to give that a thought. I have means enough to help you, and I happen to have influential friends in the law. You shall have the best possible counsel."

"You're more than kind to me," she broke in. "I don't know why you should be when I have no claim upon you. I ask no reason for your generosity, I am only very grateful. But a lawyer would confuse me. The truth is all I have to offer, and I must give it to them in my own way."

He smiled at her in spite of his disapproval.

"Have it your way then," he said.

There was a knock at the door, and a voice warned them that Monsieur Monod had overstayed his allotted time.

"I haven't prayed with you, my child," he said as he rose, "but I think you are capable of making your own prayers. Mine you will have, and those of my household."

"It's good to know that. And you'll come again?" She clung to him anxiously.

"As often as they will let me. Remember, you are not alone. You have friends. The Remeys are waiting for me now. Have you any messages for them?"

"Only my love and thanks. And perhaps if you were to talk with my grandfather—" She told him the address and hurried on. "He has never thought well of me. He opposed my taking this place. That was why I used another name; but still he is my only relative, and at such a time he might be willing to come to my aid."

"I'll see what I can do. I'll go to him with your message at once. Is there anything else on your mind?"

"If you could bring me any word of the Praslin children it would relieve me, especially of the younger ones. And, yes, there is one more thing. Tell Albert and Marie to remind Madame Le Maire of the basket on my window sill. It would be a pity to have the fruit spoil, and the melon ought to be ripe by now."

*chapter twenty-two*

DURING THAT WEEK OF AUGUST 18 TO 24, 1847, ALL France rocked with horrified impatience at each day's revelation in the Praslin murder case. Not only in Paris and Marseilles, but in Brussels, Amsterdam, and Berlin, in London and Manchester, men and women discussed it in shocked voices, avid for more details. They read the doctors' reports on the body of the Duchesse, describing minutely the score of wounds, almost any one of which had been deep enough to prove fatal. They pored over diagrams of Number 55, Rue du Faubourg-Saint-Honoré, following those gruesome ink marks which represented the bloody tracks the victim had left on furniture, floor, and walls during the savage struggle; the red prints of her fingers groping desperately to find the bell cords. They devoured the testimony of the servants who had answered her summons; that testimony which was united in its accounts of domestic discord and in its insistence that the lately dismissed governess had been the chief cause of quarrels between Monsieur and Madame. They read of the valet, Charpentier, and his shrewd advice to the police not to search for the murderer outside the house but to look into his master's quarters.

They marveled at the reiterated denials of the Duc, confronted as he was by such irrefutable evidence as a bloodstained dressing gown and shirt; the charred remains of burned letters and papers in his fireplace, and those unexplained scratches and bites upon his hands. How could he cling so stubbornly to his flimsy story of an assassin in the face of such indubitable proof of his own guilt? How could any man, let alone the head of one of the noblest families in France, do such a deed of violence and brutality, people asked one another on either side of the Channel. The opinion everywhere was unanimous in branding him as the most inhuman criminal of his day. From statesmen to shopkeepers and street venders, it was agreed that no further evidence was needed to condemn him, and no death sentence could be cruel enough for such a man.

And this Mademoiselle Henriette Deluzy-Desportes, the ex-governess whose name and accomplishments figured so prominently in every version of the crime—what of her? She, too, was being torn to shreds in a variety of languages. Always a woman in the case, they agreed, and what a woman she must be! No man hacked a faithful wife, the mother of his nine children, to death unless some other woman had driven him to madness. She must be the most subtle siren on record, yet how could that be possible for a governess in her middle thirties, and not beautiful either according to the papers? But one could never explain such things. The Duc had visited her with several of the children only a few hours before the murder. She had admitted that much and more in a secret hearing. The police had taken charge of her and her belongings. It was well they had done so at once, for with feeling running so high against her there was no telling what a mob might do.

As early as Friday August 20th, the London *Times* was already commenting on the importance of the case in an editorial:

> The Paris papers of Wednesday, received by our ordinary express, contain no political news of any importance. "Even had it been otherwise," says one of our correspondents, "public attention is so painfully absorbed by the murder of the Duchesse de Praslin that nothing short of an insurrection would attract notice."

On Saturday August 21st, Paris papers announced that the Duc de Praslin had the night before been secretly removed under close guard from his residence to the prison of the Luxembourg. There he was said to be suffering from a mysterious illness. His indisposition was considered serious enough to warrant the attention of his personal physician, Dr. Louis, and to delay his examination by Chancellor Pasquier, President of the House of Peers. Alarming rumors began to circulate later that day as to the prisoner's condition, which was said to be growing serious. Meanwhile the Court of Peers gathered to present the arraignment.

No one who reported on the events of that week could actually be sure what new turn the case might take from hour to hour. Information received on good authority might be worthless by the time it had been set in type. The most conservative papers read like lurid gossip sheets, and even important figures in literary circles left their desks to crowd the benches at the first public hearings, setting down their impressions of those concerned in *l'affaire Praslin*. Victor Hugo, writing a day-to-day account in his "Choses Vues," commented on many phases of the investigation. He noted on Sunday August 22nd:

> At the present moment one can perceive, in Mademoiselle Deluzy's window in Madame Le Maire's house, Rue du Harlay, the melon, the bouquet and the basket of fruit which the Duc brought from the country the very evening before the murder. The Duc is seriously ill. People say he is poisoned.

After an account of her position in the family and excerpts from her first questioning, he continued:

> Mademoiselle Deluzy is still in the Conciergerie. She walks about in the courtyard each day for two hours. Sometimes she wears a nankeen dress, sometimes a striped silk gown. She knows that many eyes are fixed upon her at the windows. Those who watch her say she strikes attitudes.

Another writer in *Gazette des Tribunaux* added a more detailed account of her during that period of daily exercise:

> The description of Mademoiselle Deluzy given in ――― is not altogether correct. She is dressed simply, but is not wanting in distinction or grace. Her figure has lost the suppleness of early youth, but her eyes, which are circled with dark rings, have an intelligent expression. Her complexion is pale and shows fatigue; her hair, of rich brown, is arranged with taste. She wore yesterday a nankeen dress, a black scarf, and a straw bonnet with lilac ruching. She walked slowly, her arms crossed on her breast, and her head bent.

So the days passed for Henriette without transition, but with one shock after another in the avalanche of calamity that had overtaken her. Her second examination took place, this one before Chancellor Pasquier. Of this *procès verbal* Victor Hugo made mention, quoting one of his colleagues as saying:

You will see Mademoiselle Deluzy. She is a rare woman. Her letters are masterpieces of wit and style. Her response to questioning is admirable. . . . If you had heard her you would have been astounded. No one has more grace, more tact, or more intelligence. If she wishes to write some day for us, we will give her, *par Dieu*, the Montyon Prize. For the rest she is headstrong and imperious; a woman at once wicked and charming.

Henriette was better prepared for her second ordeal, though the sleeplessness from which she suffered and the strain of waiting had told upon her. She needed no mirror to confirm her feeling that youth had left her forever. The elasticity of hope was gone out of her step and out of her heart. But she met the questions with the same unflinching directness she had shown before. Her answers came without hesitation, each word as direct and well chosen as the Chancellor's own. For hours the verbal tournament went on.

"You did not try then, as you should have tried in every way possible, to bring these children closer to their mother?"

"I tried sometimes, at first, but it was useless; and though the Duchesse did not approve of many of Monsieur Praslin's ideas on their education, she seemed willing to leave that to him. She never gave me any orders about their welfare, except in matters that concerned their dress, and she rarely talked to them. When we were by ourselves, which was seldom, she would talk to me of matters above the heads of children. They grew restless and preferred to be alone with me, and this annoyed their mother."

"Did you not realize," Chancellor Pasquier persisted, "that such isolation from her children must be painful to a mother—that it would cause difficulties between herself and the Duc de Praslin?"

"Quite the contrary, monsieur. I believe on my soul and honor that Madame de Praslin was far more preoccupied with her feelings for her husband than about her children, whom she sent away when their father was present in order to be alone with him. She was constantly trying to divert his attention from them to herself. I have seen her leave the room abruptly if Monsieur le Duc played with or fondled one of the children. She was always showing her jealousy and irritation at such marks of affection. The children realized this and, with the innocent malice of their age,

only redoubled their demonstrations to their father. I saw
the harm that this sort of struggle did them, but it was not
always in my power to prevent the bad effect of it. As time
went on and my love for my pupils grew greater, I could
not keep entirely impartial to all this daily friction. I could
not give back to Madame de Praslin those she had willfully,
or at least imprudently, allowed to slip away from her."

Her explanation left the Chancellor unconvinced. There
was open rebuke in his next words and in the manner of
their delivery.

"From all you say, it is evident that you are trying to
throw the entire blame upon Madame de Praslin. It is hardly
your place to be the judge in such matters, and your words
lead me to doubt that you did all it was your duty to do in
meeting so deplorable a situation between this mother and
her children. It appears from the testimony of others and
from documents in our possession that you exercised almost
absolute power over these young people. We are forced to
believe that you have been far, very far, from conducting
yourself in such circumstances as you ought to have done."

Once more Henriette gathered all her forces to reply.

"I would not for the world be lacking in respect for
Madame de Praslin's memory," she began. "But you ask
the truth of me, and I am bound to tell the whole truth to
the best of my ability. I do not criticize Madame's heart or
her intentions, but her character is another matter. Her temperament was difficult, very irritable and inflexible, which
made her incapable of handling so many children of various ages, minds, and dispositions. She had not the faculty
of winning the heart and confidence of youth. She would
take undue offense over some small matter where indulgence
was needed and then pass over some important issue that
called for firmness. These were the reasons why Monsieur
le Duc insisted upon her not meddling in the children's
education. Unfortunately the Duc's pleasure in his daughters' company angered the Duchesse. We all suffered in
consequence."

"And so it appears that the authority which had disappeared entirely from Madame de Praslin's hands passed
into yours; the affection of the children for their mother
also became concentrated in you. Suppose you did not actually exert yourself to bring this about, you must have seen
how matters were and known that it was your duty to prevent, rather than aggravate the situation. We must therefore

hold you responsible to a large degree for the fatal results
which have followed."

Chancellor Pasquier had shifted from question to direct
accusation, but Henriette had her defense ready.

"I never said, 'I will turn the affections of these children
for their mother to myself.' But I loved them and I devoted
my whole self to them. Their pleasures were my pleasures;
their pain was my pain. Six years I watched over them by
day and by night. They loved me with all the enthusiasm of
their years, and I returned their love. I was without family
ties, without friends, and all my feelings were bound up in
my duties, which were so congenial and pleasant. What
more can I say except to ask you this: Could not any mother
have won her children to her if she had wished to do so?"

This unfortunate ability for turning questions upon her
questioners made her a spirited witness. Like Monsieur
Broussais, the Chancellor found her more than his match
in repartee. But she never went too far in her efforts to justify herself. She clung tenaciously to her points and, though
at times her crispness verged on arrogance, she maintained
a respectful dignity of bearing and speech that was above
reproach. Again she was questioned about her last meeting
with the Duc, and again she gave a full recital of that evening visit to Madame Le Maire's with its fatal emphasis on
the letter of recommendation. Only once did she falter,
when it came to repeating his last words to her: "I play a
sorry part in all this . . . Good night till tomorrow."

"And Monsieur de Praslin said nothing that might have
led you to think he was roused to go to such lengths with the
Duchesse?"

"No, never." She spoke with unusual vehemence. "By all
that I hold sacred in life! I do not know if I am allowed
to mention here certain facts, known to me alone, which
proved that the violence was not always on Monsieur le
Duc's side. I often heard the Duchesse threaten to take her
own life, and twice to my knowledge she attempted to do so.
Once at Melun she tried to stab herself, and the Duc in disarming her wounded his hand. Again at Dieppe, after a
quarrel, she rushed out of the house, threatening to throw
herself into the sea. But with those unpredictable and changing characteristics of which I have told you, she was found
later by Monsieur le Duc in a shop, apparently quite calm
again and making some purchases."

She had hoped to arouse sympathy for the Duc, but it was

evident from the Chancellor's comment that he considered this only another proof of the desperate extremity of the Duchesse. The hearing proceeded much as the first one had done, but with more minute questioning on the daily life and routine of the household. Where Monsieur Broussais had questioned her specifically as to improper relations with the Duc, Chancellor Pasquier seemed more inclined to believe her protestations that no such liasion could have existed. He seemed determined to prove her guilty of a far less obvious crime. His interest now centered upon her undue influence over the Praslin children and the direct results of this upon their parents. It was a clever move on his part to shift the emphasis in order to prove her guilty of a deliberate campaign to estrange the children from their mother. Her own admissions could be used against her in this way. If she tried to justify her hold over her young pupils by explaining their mother's jealousy and indifference, she would be accused of laying the blame upon a dead woman who could not be called upon to clear herself. If she did not account for her sympathy toward the children and their father, she would appear more than ever what the public believed her to be—a scheming serpent whose wiles were behind that tragedy of August 18th. She knew she stood between the two pitfalls. She could only cling, as she had told the Reverend Monsieur Monod she would cling, to the truth. That was her only weapon of defense against these officials in their red robes who sorted and weighed her acts and words as deliberately as if they were actually balancing them on mental scales.

"No," she reiterated wearily as the session dragged on and on. "I did not try to take them from their mother. One cannot steal affections, messieurs; they are given freely or not at all. And you must believe me when I tell you I am not maligning the Duchesse. She was the same to others, often unjust and fault-finding, but she had kind impulses too. One moment she could cut to the quick, and in the next be generous and pleasant. Often in the space of an hour she would be like that, perhaps blaming me because she thought I exerted too great influence over her family and then presently coming to beg me to use it to gain some favor for herself. She would hurt me cruelly or make me some handsome present. One never knew what to expect."

But this seemed to be taken by her questioners as further

proof of the Duchesse's goodness. More questions followed. Henriette's head throbbed with them. The room with all those watching faces swam in a haze before her, and the scratching of pens on paper went on without pause.

"In every answer you make, you insinuate some wrong against Madame de Praslin," the voice rebuked again:

Tears of protest and weariness rose to her eyes. She wiped them away and forced herself to answer in a voice that shook from the long strain.

"I wish sincerely that I need not say what I do. She is dead, messieurs. If I could bring her back to life by giving mine, even by suffering those horrible tortures, I would do so. But I can do nothing now. I knew every turn of her mind in these six years, her every change of mood. No one knows better than I her strange power of shifting from anger to generosity, from disdain to kindness. I have not said a word that was disrespectful or untrue. I do not defend myself. I have only tried to make things clear."

The second examination of Mademoiselle Henriette Deluzy-Desportes was over. They led her back to her room in the Conciergerie.

By that evening of the 23rd of August the rumors concerning the Duc de Praslin's condition had grown alarming, though Henriette was ignorant of them. Across the river in the prison of the Luxembourg is was plain to the doctors that they could do nothing to combat the poison that was steadily gaining possession of their patient. The Duc de Praslin was dying. Only his superb strength had kept him alive with all that arsenic in his system. They agreed among themselves that he must have taken enough to kill half a dozen men, judging by the tortures he suffered. A smaller dose would have proved fatal within a few hours, but the amount he had managed to consume some time during the day he had been taken into custody, was so powerful that he had all but defeated his own end. For nature had reacted to the poison instead of being immediately overcome by it.

He had borne his sufferings at first with stoical indifference, but as the agony increased his half-suppressed groans were terrible to hear. These and the convulsions that shook him at intervals were, however, the only signs he gave to those gathered about his bed.

He had already been questioned, first by the police on the morning of the crime and later by Chancellor Pasquier. The latter had urged him to make full confession, but he had persisted in his denials. From first to last he had clung to the same story, insisting that he had been awakened by shrieks and had hurried to his wife's bedroom. In the horror and confusion that ensued he could give no clear account of himself and his actions. The bloodstains on his robe and shirt must have come there when he had taken the dying Duchesse in his arms; the pistol found near her was his, he had caught it up when he went to her aid. He could not account for the blood and strands of hair upon it. Why had he tried to wash away the bloodstains? To that question he answered that he had done so because he did not wish to frighten his children by such a sight. He made no effort to explain the burning papers in his fireplace. A match must have been thrown there. How could he remember what he had done at such a time, and under such stress? He begged them to spare him further questions till tomorrow. He felt too weak to answer.

But the Chancellor had persisted. It would not take much of Monsieur le Duc's breath to reply briefly "Yes" or "No" to the charges. What about those marks on his hands? The scratches, he explained, he had suffered in the country when he had helped to pack the trunks and boxes for their journey. And the bites? They were not bites. The doctors said otherwise. Well, he could not answer for the doctors, and he felt too weakened to be pressed for details.

"You are always speaking of your weakness, Monsieur de Praslin. No wonder you feel so when you think of your children and of this horrible crime you have committed."

"Crime!" The Duc had roused himself a little. "I have committed no crime. As to the children, they are always in my thoughts."

He had buried his head in his hands and remained silent for some time.

"Were you urged to this act by evil counsel?" His questioner hoped to draw him out in this way, but the prisoner could not be forced into any mention of Mademoiselle Deluzy. His stubborn denials of all part in the murder continued.

"I have had no counsel. People do not counsel such things."

"You are being devoured by remorse. Would it not ease your conscience if you told the truth?"

Again the evasive plea: "My strength fails me today."

"Do you dare to affirm that you have not committed this crime?"

Again no response, and again the question was repeated.

"Your silence gives the answer for you," the Chancellor continued. "You are guilty. Isn't that so?"

"You have come here with a conviction of my guilt. Nothing I might say could change your opinion."

"You can do so if you will give me a reason to believe otherwise. Without further explanations we can only hold you responsible."

"I tell you I am not able to go on. It is beyond my strength."

"Monsieur de Praslin, you are in a state of torture; and as I said to you just now, a simple answer is all I ask of you. Are you or are you not responsible for this murder? Answer yes or no."

"I cannot reply to such a question."

Once more the Duc took refuge in silence which he steadily maintained to the last. The doctors marveled at his vitality. They did what they could to relieve his pangs, but they had been forbidden to administer opiates. He must not be allowed to lapse into unconsciousness while there was still a chance to bring him to a confession of his guilt.

On Tuesday afternoon August 24th, at five o'clock, the Duc de Praslin drew his last breath in the prison of the Luxembourg, just seven days after his arrest. His death and burial were attended with secrecy, and the news kept from the public as long as possible. Of this event Victor Hugo noted:

It would appear that Monsieur de Praslin was a very well made man. At the post-mortem the doctors were much struck. One exclaimed, "What a beautiful corpse!" He was a fine athlete, Dr. Louis tells me. . . . The tomb in which they laid him bears a leaden plate, on which is the number 1054. A number after his death, as convicts have in life, is the only epitaph of the Duc de Choiseul-Praslin.

But others were less restrained in their comment. Once published, the news spread rapidly, and public opinion was united in condemning the government for such negligence.

All officials, from gendarmes to King Louis-Philippe himself, suffered severe censure. The murder had been shocking enough without allowing the obvious culprit to escape from the consequences. Suicide was too easy a way out for such a criminal. The law should have exacted the extreme penalty for this deed, and instead it had been cheated of its victim. Everywhere people grew hot with indignation against a government that had condoned such evasion of justice.

It did not matter to readers of newspapers whether that dose of arsenic had been deliberately smuggled in to the Duc by his superiors, or if he had foreseen his own extremity and prepared for it. One fact, they all agreed upon —this prisoner had not met the fate of an ordinary criminal. If he had not been a close friend of the King, and a Peer of France, he would be alive to face the grave charges against him. What was the use now of all the detailed reports of the examiners? of the carefully tabulated evidence prepared by the police? of the testimony of doctors and domestics?

There was no need now to fill columns of fine type with the pitiful, passionate contents of the Duchesse's journal, or to print those letters the Duc had not burned, anguished appeals for affection that would never be gratified; jealous tirades against "Mademoiselle D." Murdered and murderer were both mute. They could not be called back to life to answer the questions of high officials in red robes. The Praslin murder case had become a dead issue as far as the law was concerned. It was only a skeleton now. But skeletons in royal closets are not easily dismissed, as King Louis-Philippe was to discover all too soon.

Across the Channel a farsighted editor in the London *Times* wrote prophetically of *l'affaire Praslin:*

> Nothing could be more contrary to the interests of the Government than the scandal arising from such an act at the present moment. It is more likely to exercise an unfavorable influence on their fortunes than a systematic sapping and mining of the public liberties for twenty years. The Government had but one chance, to hand the Duc de Praslin over to the public indignation. . . . We foresee that this most injudicious withdrawal of a culprit from justice will be turned against the French Government. We do not mean to attribute any share of the leading people of Paris in this most horrible and revolting

crime. But it would be vain to deny that a profound demoralization does at this moment exist in the very heart of French society. We will not pursue this subject of the suicide of the Duc de Praslin. If the French Government have connived at it, they will soon find cause to repent their error. It is not probable that we have yet come to the end of this disastrous tale.

Henriette may have read these very words, for during those last days of August she was allowed the privilege of newspapers. She still remained in the Conciergerie, still took her exercise in the courtyard each day, and still waited for the law to decide what to do with her. It was a vexing problem. The most careful examinations had revealed nothing that could be used as tangible evidence against her. She had made a remarkable impression upon her examiners during those hours of questioning. Yet the whole country believed her to be a party to the crime. Next to the Duc de Praslin she was most hated, and now that he was dead, she alone remained, the bird in their hands. From being an obscure governess without friends and in search of work, she had become in the course of a single week the most despised and talked-of figure in France.

*chapter twenty-three*

PARIS ROOFS WERE SLEEK WITH NOVEMBER RAINS. THE river flowed in sluggish gray under its bridges, and the tall old buildings on either bank were as drab as the blowing smoke from their chimneypots. The gardens of the Luxembourg and the Tuileries dripped in duns and browns, their benches damp and deserted, even by beggars and sparrows, those most indefatigable city tramps. Only splashing horses and the vehicles they drew moved on the wet streets, or sodden figures under the domes of umbrellas.

In an upper room of a house near the intersection of the Rues de Monceau and Téhéran, Henriette stared through a moist windowpane at a still more moist world. The room was not much larger than the Needle's Eye, though its furnishing showed far more taste and comfort. A table had been drawn close to the window, and a variety of objects littered it—books, sewing materials, a pot of marigolds, a box of pastel crayons, besides writing materials and a portfolio of papers. But her hands were not occupied with any of these; they lay idle and listless in her lap.

A maid tapped at the door and, in response to a "Come in," opened it a crack to deliver her message.

"Madame Monod's compliments, and would Mademoiselle Desportes care to join Monsieur and Madame in the salon for a cup of chocolate?"

But Henriette shook her head. "My thanks to Madame and Monsieur but my headache still prevents my joining them, and I will not be down for dinner."

After the maid had left, Henriette sat without moving while the rain kept up its monotonous drumming in the gutters outside. She had no headache, but one must give some excuse for refusing the kindness of friends. She was under enough obligation to the Reverend Frédéric Monod and his wife without appearing indifferent to their efforts to distract her from the lethargy which she could not shake off. They had been goodness itself, those two, insisting that she make her home with them as long as she cared to stay in Paris. That September day when she had been given her discharge by the law they had made her welcome, and she had been glad to take refuge in this shelter they offered. There had been no other choice except to go to Albert and Marie, for she could not return to Madame Le Maire's establishment, and after the notoriety of the murder no hotel or pension would have dared to take her in. Her grandfather had made no effort to aid her, and she learned from those who had tried to enlist his sympathies that the old man's health and finances were in a precarious state. He lived near Passy, completely under the domination of an unscrupulous old woman. So she could not look to her only relative for help in the difficulties she now faced.

It was fortunate that Monsieur Monod had taken her and her cause to heart. He was a powerful and prosperous ally as well as his two brothers, one a wealthy merchant of Havre. The other, Adolphe, was also an influential Protestant divine who had lately been called to preach at the Oratoire in Paris. The brothers Monod not only believed in

her innocence and admired the courage with which she had
met her ordeal, but they were determined to rally their con-
gregations to her side. Her Protestant faith had been against
her in that Catholic household, and the murder now had
taken on religious as well as political significance. In a Catholic country like France it was inevitable that this should
be so. The Monods knew that even among the minority
which their church represented prejudice against her would
be difficult to overcome. All they could do for her now was
to give her their support and hope that they could influence
others of their faith to do likewise. They knew the violence
of public opinion too well to expect it to be changed overnight. That would take months, even years to alter.

Everywhere people branded Mademoiselle Deluzy-Desportes as the real instigator of the Praslin murder. Since her
release she had become the target of a more intense and
bitter hatred because she was the only living link in that
triangle of domestic tragedy. The press and public still believed her guilty and would have relished nothing more than
to see her go to the guillotine. In her discharge they saw
only another example of legal incompetence and govern-
mental procrastination. Already the Duchesse de Praslin
wore a martyr's halo and was mourned as the victim of a
husband's infatuation for a clever and scheming rival. Everywhere wives and mothers denounced this "Mademoiselle
D." and praised the dead Duchesse as a paragon of virtue,
whose only fault had been to love her husband and children
too well. "Let the women of France lay hands on this governess," was the hue and cry in streets and shops and homes,
"and then she would soon see how we feel about her. All
those fine speeches of hers to the lawyers and Chancellor
would be wasted on us. Let her suffer as she made another
suffer. She has no right to go free!"

It was essential that her whereabouts be kept secret; so
only her few friends knew her hiding place. She must not go
out alone for fear of recognition and the consequences that
might follow. She must use an assumed name if she ventured
beyond that loyal household. Although the subject of future
plans had been carefully avoided so far, it was plain to all
that when she was able to resume her old occupation of
teaching she could not do so in France, where the ghost
of scandal would always follow her from post to post. She
would never be free of it. A spying glance, a whispered

word, an awkward question, and that shadow would fall
upon her. She knew how it would be, though as yet she dared
not speak of that to her generous hosts.

No, her head did not ache. She was past all physical pain.
All feeling had left her; she was held fast in the grip of inertia. Once she had had courage to live and feel, once she had
even had courage enough to die. But now life or death
seemed immaterial. She continued to breathe; to wake and
sleep; to eat and drink what was set before her; to go through
the mechanical gestures of the living—that was all. Whatever was put into her hands to do, she did with her old skill
and efficiency. She helped about the house—sewing, dust-
ing, copying sermons and letters for Monsieur Monod, hearing his children's lessons. She was glad to make herself
useful so long as nothing more was asked of her.

She could even read those newspaper accounts of the
Praslin case without flinching. They seemed not to concern
her now, though the faces of the Duc and the Duchesse, of
the old Maréchal, and each of the children were as clear
as if they still moved about her. Even now, nearly three
months after that morning of August 18th, the ashes of that
tragedy were being raked over and sifted by the press. She
could scarcely pick up a paper without finding some reference to herself and the investigation, and already legends
were springing up. Workmen making repairs on the Duc's
apartments in the château had discovered a fancy dress
costume stuffed behind a loose piece of molding, a scarlet
devil's suit the Duc had worn to a masquerade. The Duchesse's maid had then recalled a dream her mistress had
had earlier that summer. Madame had told her of it and of
the frightening apparition of a devil all in red who had
stood threateningly above her bed. She had screamed, and it
had vanished. They had given the matter no further thought.
But now it took on a sinister significance. Surely so macabre
a premonition was more than a mere dream of the Duchesse. There were stories from Corsica of a gypsy warning
that mentioned danger and blood, and as a bride Fanny
Sébastiani had dared to wear pearls, defying the superstition
that each pearl will mean tears shed in bitterness and grief
later on. Henriette read these fantastic stories unmoved as
she read the dead woman's frenzied and pitiful outpourings
in her published letters and journal:

Do not be astonished, my dear Théobold, at my fear of being alone with you. We are separated forever—you said so; a sad reflection that will ever be attached to yesterday . . .

Wherefore, my beloved, do you refuse to let me share your confidences? You deprive our life of all the charms of affection. . . . Do you deliberately wish to become a stranger to me? . . . You alone know that it is in your power to console me, yet you withhold your consolation. . . . I only wish to share completely your life, to embellish it, and to pour balm upon your wounds. . . . I will blindly obey you. I will no longer torment you by jealousy.

You have deprived me of my children, and placed them in the care of a stranger who has usurped my place in your house . . . It is long since I have written, and my position has since become more and more painful. . . . Mademoiselle D. reigns absolute. Never was a governess seen to assume so scandalous a position. It is impossible to believe that this is only a friendly intimacy between a man of your age and a young woman in her position. What an example to give to young persons!

When I reached here I had hoped for peace, but the illusion did not last long. The carriage steps had not been let down before I saw in your icy, discontented air, in the constrained expression of the children's faces, in those green eyes which appeared behind your shoulder, that I was about to be subjected to the most painful humiliation. . . . Mademoiselle D. must remain at all cost. . . . But why do you, who believe it so simple, so easy to replace a mother, think it so impossible to replace a governess? If you had desired it, she might have been a good governess, but you have changed her functions, her position. . . . How is it possible that her head should not be turned when your conduct says to her every day, even more clearly than words: "I have a wife, but I prefer your society, your attentions." . . . Through love for you I was weak enough to surrender the children to your care, and I have been betrayed. I ought to have died sooner than to have made this sacrifice. . . . You have established a complete separation between us—we are no more than strangers to each other. Things cannot endure in their present state . . . you are weak, and you have reached a point where you are so much under her yoke that you dare undertake nothing without her. You cannot leave her; and your wife, the mother of your children, must live and die alone. . . .

Why will you not read my letters? Why will you not at least accord me your confidence or some explanation? You have too plainly shown that you no longer love me, that you wish all relations to cease between us. . . .

You have a rare and precious talent for poisoning everything. While your conduct only affected my happiness, I kept silence. But you cannot force me to approve in public or in private the conduct of a person I despise. I know well enough that you have not always been faithful, and that it is not solely with her that your life is occupied. But she assumes the attitude. It is this which I have the right to blame. I cannot interfere in your private conduct and affections, but no threats or ill treatment can prevent my repeating, what I have a right to do, that you deceive yourself by putting your children into the hands of a woman who has no regard for her reputation, since she has ceased to respect herself. . . .

If you knew what I suffer, my beloved, by your coldness towards me—I cannot believe that you wish to abandon me thus forever, to deprive us both of our happiness. Life is so short, my beloved, and we have been separated already so long. Soon I shall not dare to make these pleas—always refused, like my caresses . . . your wife will die of grief unless you return. Return, return to her!— My pillow is wet with bitter tears.

Strange to read the broken phrases, the denunciations of herself, the demands that would never be gratified now. Strange to know that the hand that had penned them would never be warm with love or hate again. Light was fading fast in the upper room. The words of the long columns of newspaper print grew dim before her eyes. Yet still she must read the words—her own replies to the questions of the judges; the Duc's last testimony; and letter upon letter of the Duchesse. She could feel nothing as she read those wild and bitter words, though behind the type she could see clearly that familiar blue note paper with its family crest and the heavy, flowing pen strokes she had come to know and dread in the last six years. She remembered so well the first note that had been addressed to her. She remembered how shocked she had been by the discarded one from which Raynald's scissors had snipped a heart. She had felt guilty then to have such intimate revelations put into her hands, and now the whole world was reading them.

A knock sounded on the door. The rap was loud, but it come from lower down than usual, just the height of a child's reach. She put the papers away and turned to greet ten-year-old Théodore Monod. He carried a birdcage in one hand.

"I've brought my goldfinch to keep you company," he announced, setting the cage carefully on the table. "I'm sorry your head aches."

After she had thanked him for the loan of his bird, the boy stayed on, eyeing her in timid fascination.

"You should put cologne on your forehead," he told her. "I can get you some of Mamma's. I know where she keeps it."

"No, thank you, Théodore, it's not the kind of headache cologne would help. How did you get on at school today?"

Even in her state of apathy it was natural for her to take an interest in the child, who was only too eager to respond. He and his older sisters had already fallen under her spell, though they had received strict orders not to disturb their guest.

"I did all my arithmetic right," he assured her, "and the Professor read my composition about the shells to the class, the one you helped me with. But I failed in my Latin. The plural case is so hard. I had to stay after the rest and write *Exeunt omnes* a hundred times. Do you know what that means, Mademoiselle Desportes?"

" 'They all go out,' " she translated. Then she turned from him with a catch of her breath. "Yes, I know what that means."

Presently Monsieur Monod himself appeared, and Théodore was sent downstairs.

"I thought I should find him here." Her host lingered after his son had gone. "You draw our young people like flies to a honeypot, but you mustn't let them impose upon you. My wife and I are sorry to hear you have another of these headaches. We had hoped we could count upon you to help us tonight."

"Tonight?"

"You've not forgotten we are giving a small reception?"

She had forgotten, and the mention of it only made her shake her head and beg leave to stay upstairs.

"No one is coming who might annoy you," Monsieur Monod persisted, studying her with anxious intentness in the failing light. "A few friends besides my brother Adolphe and his family. My niece has promised to sing, and we thought perhaps you might be willing to accompany her on the piano."

"Oh, Monsieur Monod, do not ask me to move among people yet. It's too much for me."

He sighed and laid his hand persuasively on her shoulder.

"The longer you postpone it, the harder it will be. You can't shut yourself away from people forever, you know. I realize it must be gradual, but you will not be subject to the curious tonight. These are friends who sympathize with you—"

"Oh, but that's it," she broke in. "I can't face their sympathy yet."

"You must, my dear Henriette; you have need of all that is offered you. You were so brave during your ordeal, you can't afford to lose your courage now that's over."

"I spent all I had," she told him. "I've no more courage in me."

"You underestimate yourself. I've come to ask you as a favor to me, to join us and our guests this evening."

"I can hardly refuse when you put it so. I'm under too great obligation to you and Madame Monod. But I wish I might be spared."

"If you want to leave after the music we shall understand; but I hope you will feel like staying longer. There will be several Americans, and you know their usual difficulties with the language. Your English is so excellent it would be a comfort to rely on you to act as interpreter. The chances are, they will have no idea of your identity, and I shall not mention your name; so there is no need for you to dread introductions."

"Oh, but, Monsieur Monod, you don't know—"

"I know you will do your best." He smiled encouragingly. "Remember, it's no time to retreat when the battle's won."

At the door, he turned and spoke again.

"Mademoiselle Henriette Deluzy does not concern us now. She belongs to the past. But I have great hopes for a certain Mademoiselle Desportes."

When he had gone she sat a long time in the gathering darkness before she forced herself to light a lamp and lay out her clothes for the evening. She dreaded going to the wardrobe and bureau drawers, where each article she handled kept some painful association. Memories clung to every fold and mocked her as she shook them out. Her linen still smelled of vervain from the château gardens. There was not a dress she owned which did not recall some remark of Louise or Berthe or Raynald, or the approving glances of their father. In the little white jewelry box with the carnelian-studded lid, lay the bracelet and blue enamel pin which had been peace offerings from the Duchesse. The cameo brooch of Raynald's choosing was there, too, with all its poignant memories. It had been mounted according to his own ideas, with his name and the date of his birthday engraved on the gold back.

She turned it over and stared at those letters in the lamplight: "Raynald, June 18, 1847." But even that failed to melt the ice at her heart. She moved in numbness to the wardrobe and selected her best dress, the moss-green moire with bands of russet and small bronze buttons that matched the slippers she took from their tissue-paper wrappings. How Louise had delighted in those bronze slippers the day she had borrowed them to dance the polka up and down the old schoolroom! How gayly she had danced! And now, where were those quick, light feet? Were all those Praslin daughters dressed in mourning? Were the clear eyes red with weeping shocked, incredulous tears, or clouded with dumb bewilderment? What of Berthe, with her father's ways and hair and smile? What of Raynald, sensitive and loving, who had shared his own birthday with Mademoiselle? She would never know how they fared. She would never see them again. Better so, perhaps, since by now their minds and hearts must be poisoned against her. No, she could not have met disillusionment in those young eyes that had always turned to her in love and trust.

"*Exeunt omnes,*" she thought bitterly as she made her preparations.

It was half past nine when she entered the large, old-

fashioned salon where some eighteen or twenty guests had
already gathered. She slipped in unobtrusively through the
adjoining study and joined her host's brother Adolphe and
others whom she knew slightly. As she stood there, speaking
of she scarcely knew what, she caught sight of herself in a
long mirror and marveled that she should look much as she
had looked when she had last worn the green moiré six
months before. She appeared somewhat paler and thinner,
and her face had fallen into graver lines. But these were the
only outward changes she could find. Her hair still curled
and shone on either side of its parting. Her brow was as
smooth and unlined, her mouth wide and full-lipped as ever.
How, she wondered, could it be that she bore no visible
signs of inner blight?

People were being kind—far too kind, she decided after
half an hour had passed. Their determined efforts to be casual embarrassed her more than all the curious scrutiny she
had been subjected to in the Conciergerie. Those she knew
greeted her cordially, but pointedly refrained from addressing her by name. They talked rapidly of the most incon-
sequential matters, and carefully avoided looking her full
in the face. She understood the reason for their feigned
indifference. She had often tried in the same fashion to disregard the sightless eye or scarred cheek of another. Never,
she vowed to herself in the crowded room, would she be
guilty of such obvious kindness again. Better to peer curiously at crippled infirmity or disfigured flesh; better the
frank stare, than the polite, surreptitious glance.

It was a relief to turn her attention to the piano and the
sheets of music spread in readiness on the rack. Fortunately
the airs were familiar, since Madame Monod had lately
prevailed upon her to play many of them for herself and
her daughters. The young singer had a sweet, fresh voice;
and her manners were childlike and modest. She had no
pretensions to soar to the heights of the Swedish nightingale,
who had taken Europe by storm. She knew she was no future Jenny Lind, so she contented herself with pleasing her
family and their friends and keeping on pitch without spectacular tremolos and trills. Henriette took her place on the
bench grateful that the piano was placed so that her back
was to the room which the singer faced. As her eyes followed the notes and her fingers moved over the keys, she
forgot for a little the constraint that her presence had
brought to that roomful of people.

She had planned to make her escape after the musical interlude, but escape from the crowded room was not easy. More people had arrived. She recognized one group, standing a little apart, as the guests from America. There were five of them, two women and three men, less stylishly dressed and assured of manner than their countrymen one saw in shops and on the boulevards. She knew she ought to join them and try to put them at their ease. But somehow, tonight, she did not feel equal to making an effort for these strangers. She felt even a sudden resentment that they should be there at all. Why hadn't they stayed on the side of the Atlantic where they belonged? Why must they come here in their queer-looking clothes, butchering the English language, probably, in their even queerer voices?

She wished they did not look so much like a flock of uneasy, disappointed birds of a feather, huddled on some alien bough. And then, without warning, one of them left the bough. He hurried towards her, his face beaming with frank, pleased curiosity, his eyes looking straight into her own with a sudden light of recognition. She tried to turn away, but even if there had been room to pass the groups of people, something about the eagerness in those eyes held her where she stood. She felt annoyed and furious and yet at the same time compelled to notice this young American who advanced upon her. She did not encourage him by so much as the flicker of an eyelash, but he still hurried on, a small, inconspicuous figure charged with excitement that fairly bristled under a poorly fitted coat the color of snuff. Now he was speaking at her elbow in a voice that surprised her by not being the nasal, high-pitched twang she had come to associate with Yankee visitors.

"You are Mademoiselle Deluzy—Desportes," he began without preliminaries. "I should have known you anywhere, even without the bonnet with the lilac trimmings."

Earlier that evening she had felt embarrassed by the tactful restraint of her acquaintances; now she was experiencing the blunt frankness of an unknown young man. He could be hardly more than some student, to judge from his looks. Still he was old enough to know better. One expected a certain amount of crudity from Americans, but such blundering as this was too much to overlook.

"I see," she responded crisply, "that you read the newspapers."

Her shoulders lifted in a slight shrug, and there was an

ironic edge to her words. But her disapproval made no impression on him. He continued to fix her intently with his candid blue eyes, oblivious to every one else in the room.

"Why, yes, I do read the newspapers," he admitted, and a sudden, disarming smile transformed the plainness of his face. "I can read French better than I'll ever be able to speak it, I'm afraid. The papers were full of you. I read every word, but they never told me all I wanted to know. You see, ever since I landed in France—"

This was preposterous! She would really have to snub him, even if he was an invited guest. She frowned and cut short the eager rush of words on his lips.

"It's quite unnecessary to explain that you've heard of nothing but the Praslin case since you came. Probably you know far more than I do about it."

"I know that you have been brave and steadfast under great misfortune; that you met their attacks with honesty and eloquence. Is it any wonder then that you have—"

"Please!" Again she cut him short. "Please don't say anything more. And now, if you will excuse me, I was just on the point of leaving."

But he did not stand aside politely. He actually came a step nearer to block her path of escape.

"Oh, but you can't do that now!" he went on, unaware that he had been dismissed. "I was going on to tell you that, ever since I landed, you have been so much on my mind."

"On *your* mind, monsieur—"

He nodded an emphatic assent.

"I confess"—she forestalled another rush of impetuous words, and went on quickly—"I confess I see no reason why I should have been there. Haven't you Americans troubles enough of your own without crossing the sea to hunt down more?"

"Yes," he agreed simply, again ignoring her bitterness, "we have troubles of our own, as you say, but yours happen to be very important to me. That's why, when I saw you in the Conciergerie courtyard, and now tonight—"

"You couldn't resist satisfying your curiosity still further! You thought a few questions more or less wouldn't matter after all those I've had flung at me!"

She managed to keep her voice chill as an icicle, but she felt her cheeks flush in angry betrayal.

"I'm sorry," he said, "if I have made you think that. I hoped when I heard you speak such fluent English that it would be easy to make myself clear. But that's difficult sometimes in any language. My trade is in words, you see; so that's why I know they can't always be depended upon to say what we feel."

"You are a writer then?"

She might have guessed there was some such reason behind his persistence. A young newspaper man from America —probably he had been sending back reports of the investigation. Perhaps he meant to write the story of her life with embellishments of his own. The sooner she put a stop to that, the better.

"Only in a way," he was explaining. "I do write articles sometimes when I have time between my sermons."

"Sermons?" It was her turn to stare curiously at the boyish face looking into hers. "You are a minister! But, no, you can't be!"

"But I am," he insisted with another smile. "It's not necessary to look like an Old Testament prophet to preach the Gospel, is it?"

"No," she was forced to admit. "I suppose there must be all kinds, only I never happened to meet a minister like you."

"And I have never met any one like you—so there we are."

"You really preach sermons from a pulpit," she repeated, eyeing him half amused, half admiring. "It's hard to believe that. You look too young."

"I'm twenty-five," he told her, "and I've been preaching off and on for ten years."

"Oh, so they let children preach in America?"

"I was fifteen," he explained patiently, "halfway through college. My father is a minister, too, so I suppose it comes naturally. But"—he turned to her again with that swift smile—"I'll never forget that first experience. It was a little country church where students were often sent to preach."

"And what was the subject of your sermon?"

"On Christ throwing out the money changers from the Temple. I thought when I saw my congregation of farmers and their families that perhaps I hadn't made a very wise choice. But they didn't seem to mind about that, or my not having a robe. You see," he went on confidentially, "my family were very poor, and I usually wore one of my brothers' coats, and they are all much bigger than I. A cut-down

roundabout hardly made me look impressive when I
mounted to that pulpit. It didn't seem so difficult at the time,
but that first sermon did age me. I know, because I had to
pay full railway fare on the trip back, and they had let me
ride for half-fare before!"

He looked so rueful over this early plight that she had to
laugh in spite of herself.

"Yes," he said, studying her with even more pleased intentness than before, "I thought you would look like that
when you smiled."

She made no reply, and he did not seem to expect one.
Other people jostled at their elbows, or brushed by them
with billowing skirts, but they stood quiet together as if they
had made an island for themselves in some hurrying human
stream.

Then it caught them up and whirled them apart once
more. Marie and Albert Remey seized upon her, and presently she must go to help Madame Monod serve refresh-
ments in the adjoining room. For the next hour Henriette
had no chance to talk with the American, though she saw
him now and again, watching her with that air of intimate
expectancy which was so strangely disturbing. She wished
that he would leave, as others were doing, but he lingered
on, a small, determined figure on the fringes of animated
groups of men and women. His quietness made him conspicuous by contrast, although he had so little physical presence to boast of. Perhaps the fact that he did not gesticulate
when he spoke, gave him a kind of dignity. Yet it was more
than just that, she decided. At close range one might be
deceived by plain features, a too naïve eagerness of manner,
or by the queer cut of foreign clothes. But at a distance he
assumed his real proportions, as a certain mountain peak
that has been indistinguishable among others will rise when
viewed in true perspective. The artist in her recognized
this, and the woman in her felt his integrity. He stood out in
that gathering, not only because of a racial difference, but
because of some inner simplicity and sureness of purpose
which possessed him so completely that he was himself
unaware of the power.

"No wonder," she thought, smiling at the memory of his
confession, "no wonder that first congregation of his did
not dare to laugh."

She felt a touch of remorse, remembering how hostile she

had been towards him, mistaking his honesty for crudeness, confusing his enthusiasm with effrontery. She need not have behaved so rudely, trying to snap his head off simply because her own nerves were on edge. But then, she was not used to the headlong exuberance of visitors from America who could be almost indecently personal at first meeting.

The company was thinning out rapidly. She would be able to slip upstairs to her room without much notice now. But there he was coming towards her again with that confident, bright look. She was sure he would outstay all the guests, for he seemed completely unaware of time despite the gold watch chain that flapped on his vest.

"Now we can talk," he began almost before he had reached her side. "I was growing impatient. You were so busy. Now tell me—"

"But first you must tell me something, monsieur—your name."

"Field," he said, "and you'll find my first one simple—Henry. Then Martyn in the middle."

"Henri," she repeated, "Henri, then Martyn in the middle—Field."

"They never made it sound like that at home," he told her admiringly. "They would call you Henrietta over there."

("Field," she thought. "I might have known it would be a short, plain name like that. But it fits him—simple and unpretentious, and yet full of living importance.")

"I like your name, Monsieur Field," she heard herself saying. "It seems right for you."

"It's one of the few things my father thinks his sons should be proud of," he told her. "We're a fair-sized family," he added. "I have two sisters and six brothers."

"Whose clothes you sometimes wear," she prompted.

"Not since I left Williams College." He laughed. "Yes, that's the penalty of being the youngest and the smallest son. I'll tell you how our family goes: David Dudley, Emilia Ann, Timothy Beals, Matthew Dickinson, Jonathan Edwards, Stephen Johnson, Cyrus West, Henry Martyn, and Mary Elizabeth."

He had to pause for breath.

"Don't tell me any more names," she begged. "Henri Martyn is all I can remember tonight."

"I shall be writing them about you," he went on, "by the next mail packet."

"Oh, but, please!" she began, but she could not finish because the two Monod brothers joined them.

"I'm glad you brought me that letter of introduction." Adolphe Monod spoke cordially to their guest. "We should have missed having you with us tonight."

"I would not have missed tonight for all the rest of my stay put together, and I've been in England and Scotland, too."

"And you're off to Brussels in the morning, I hear?"

"Yes, and then on to Germany and Austria, and perhaps as far as St. Petersburg if my money holds out. I've been saving for this, these last five years."

"What globe-trotters you Americans seem to be!" Frédéric Monod smiled wonderingly and shook his head. "He must have been born with an itching foot. Don't you think so, Henriette?"

"He must indeed," she agreed. "I have often wondered, when I've seen tourists tramping about and looking so tired and uncomfortable, what ever made them come so far."

"You should be able to answer that question for her, Monsieur Field."

"Well, it's this way, I think." He grew suddenly serious and pushed back a straight brown lock of hair that had fallen into his eyes. "For most of us one book is not enough to satisfy our minds, and so one life is not enough either. We want to experience more than can ever be crowded into seventy or even eighty years. I am too greedy, perhaps, but I want to catch at the meaning of different lives in different places. I want to find out what goes on under the thatched roofs of cottages and behind the walls of palaces and hotels. I want to walk in old ruins and in new cities. I want to watch people everywhere, whether I can understand the words they are saying or not. It is too much to ask, perhaps, but I want to get behind the faces of men and women and feel what they are feeling." He broke off with a sigh. "Do you understand what I mean?"

"Yes." Henriette spoke before either of the men had a chance to answer. "You've made me understand."

"Some day you must put that all in a book, for those who travel and those who stay at home." Frédéric Monod spoke with approval.

"Yes, Monsieur Field," his brother Adolphe joined in. "You have a true passion for travel, so let us hope you will go far, in more ways than one."

As their visitor turned to leave with the last guests, Henriette held out her hand to him.

"I wish you a fortunate journey," she said, "and a safe return. Good night."

After he had gone the brothers Monod spoke of him to Henriette. A most extraordinary young man, even for an American, they all decided. Perhaps a trifle too eager, but with a good heart and high intelligence. The letters he had presented from friends across the Atlantic all praised his mind and character. They said he was considered a brilliant scholar, a particularly fine student of Greek and Hebrew and philosophy, and that he showed unusual promise in the ministry. His family were of the best Puritan stock, although he certainly had nothing of Puritan coldness and constraint in his make-up. Yes, when one became used to his naïve frankness of manner, one realized that he had a fine mind and largeness of sympathy, even a roughhewn sort of charm—didn't Henriette agree? At all events she had been most kind to devote herself to putting him at his ease. They thanked her for the effort she had made, and hoped it had not been too tiring.

As she climbed the stairs to her room she remembered the unabashed admiration in the eyes of the little American. She had aroused his ardor and idealism, and such was the power of his belief that her sense of futility lifted a little. All these last weeks she had tried to hide behind a wall of her own making, to shut herself away where nothing could ever hurt her again as she had been hurt. Others had respected her wall; even the considerate Monods had only rapped there discreetly. But he had known better. Walls were something to be scaled, and he had leaped over hers in a single bound.

*chapter twenty-four*

IN THE CROWDING POLITICAL EVENTS OF THAT WINTER OF 1847 and 1848 Henriette attached little significance to the Monod reception; yet it marked a distinct transition in her life.

She began to feel once more and to suffer as her numbed senses thawed. Shock and disaster had till then overwhelmed her almost completely; but as strength returns to paralyzed limbs with sharp pin-pricks of pain, so even more cruel stabbings troubled her mind. Whether she woke or slept, she was beset by memories the more bitter because they had once been sweet. Everywhere they assailed her, whether she handled personal possessions or turned some street corner that brought her face to face with the past. Without warning, ghosts would rise up from the very pavement to confound her. A fiddler's tune, a shop window, a playbill announcing the great Rachel's coming performances, the smell of roasting apples, the fragrance of a man's cigar, children with eyes shining above parcel-filled arms, children singing carols, Notre Dame seen dimly through falling snow —she was at the mercy of them all.

Some chance remark of Théodore Monod or his sisters could make her eyes film suddenly or her lips stiffen as the screws of memory tightened at her heart. A man's tall figure swinging towards her with the long vigorous strides she had come to connect with the Duc could keep her trembling long after he had passed. Night after night, she dreamed that he was alive. It was all a mistake—this horror of blood and violence and disgrace that had seemed so real. Then she would wake, and truth would strip her of this brief comfort. She must lie chill and alone, rehearsing the tragedy against her will, ruthlessly recalling every step that had led on to disaster.

> He is dead and gone, lady,
> He is dead and gone.

What was the rest of the song? She racked her brain to remember. At last it came:

> At his head a grass-green turf,
> At his heels a stone.

But, no, even that had been denied him. Somewhere he had been laid away in secret shame. They had not dared to put his name above that spot.

She alone out of all the world did not hate or revile him. "We can only judge another," she thought, "as that person affects us." Whatever had been his passion and weakness, he had never meant to hurt her. Since the day of their first meeting, he had shown her only the best in himself. It was his right to ask that she remember him so. He had been loyal and generous to her always, and nothing should mar that memory.

"I play a sorry part in all this." Those final words he had spoken came back to her now, heavy with meaning.

Only God and she knew what lay behind that last futile act of fury. She knew far less than God, but enough of the life that husband and wife had lived to keep her from passing judgment. She herself was alive. The law had freed her of those charges. But would she ever be able to free herself of his presence when for six years it had dominated her world? She would never know now what he had felt for her. Perhaps it had been love, perhaps merely the need for sympathy of which she had been the human symbol. They had asked so little of each other, and yet that little had been too much. She had not belonged to his world, or he to hers. Some fierce current beyond their control had caught them up and swept them away to certain destruction. Why had she not broken away before they reached the precipice? Why had she not heard the thunder of the rapids in time? That was what she could never answer through those interminable nights and days.

"If I lose my reason some day," she heard him saying again through the hot Corsican sunshine against the blue curtain of sea, "you will know that scribbled words have driven me mad."

Calais—graven forever on an English Queen's heart; Waterloo, on Napoleon's; and on hers, Praslin. Time might blur that name as moss softens the inscriptions on old gravestones, but it had been cut there too deeply to be erased.

The Monod brothers and their wives must have realized something of her state of mind, for they did not press her to personal confidences. They wisely refrained from advice giving, and kept her occupied as much as possible. The hours of copying sermons, helping with fine sewing and the children's lessons, reading aloud, painting, and practicing served to fill part of the days. But her returning energies cried out for better fare. She needed hard, stimulating work as she had never needed it before, especially now that the Christmas holidays were over and the dark, short days of winter stretched bleakly ahead.

The Remeys did all in their power to distract her. She

visited them sometimes, though she could never enter those
rooms without fresh reminders of the tragedy which had
touched all their lives. Albert had secured a few scattered
pupils, but times were bad for such work; and he missed the
security of his teaching post in the Faubourg-Saint-Honoré.
Henriette knew this, and it troubled her to see them anxiously counting every franc and sou. She saw Madame Le Maire
sometimes, and though the old woman had recovered from
her first hysterical denunciations on the morning of the
murder, their meetings were too full of unspoken thoughts
to be comfortable.

Of all the little group there was only one with whom Henriette could talk or keep silence with complete ease. With
old Pierre, the porter, she found herself talking naturally of
what she could not mention to others. He had the simple
directness of those who work with their hands, whose
brains, uncluttered by learning, remain clear and shrewd.
The stubborn devotion of an aging sheepdog looked at her
out of his eyes, and more than once she unburdened her
heart to him in a small café near the Rue du Harlay. It was
a cheap place, but the coffee was fresh and strong, and old
Pierre could leave his post for half an hour of an afternoon
to drink a cup with his favorite mademoiselle.

"You're fretting yourself to fiddlestrings," he would say,
peering at her disapprovingly over his lifted cup. "Didn't I
tell you to get all the sleep you could?"

"Yes, you told me, Pierre," she would admit, "but that's
easier said than done."

"I know, mademoiselle, it's hard when we have the black
dog on our backs."

"The black dog?"

"It's by way of saying everything troubles you. Yes, he sits
heavy on all our backs sometimes; but he will go away. By
spring you will forget he was ever there."

"But spring is a long way off, Pierre."

"My knees have told me that already," he would tell her,
trying to straighten out his stiff old joints. "But no matter,
spring will come, and it will bring you good things. I know
it."

"Oh, Pierre, what good can it bring me after all that has
happened? You know there is nothing for me in Paris, or in
France for that matter."

"Then you will have to travel across the water to find your
good fortune, mademoiselle—as far as America, maybe."

She set her cup down and stared at his seamed old face. He must have read what was in her mind, though she had not spoken of it to another person. She had indeed hardly been willing to consider the idea consciously herself.

"Whatever put America into your head?" She tried to dismiss the subject.

"Because it's the place for you to go," he insisted between gulps of coffee. "There's trouble brewing in Paris. I can feel it, the way I feel a spell of bad weather in my knees while the sun is still shining. You'll see it won't be long."

Queer old fellow, she thought, croaking away like some rusty, rheumatic crow.

"I, too, should go to America," he continued. "Perhaps you will send for me when you have grown rich over there."

"But I tell you I have no intention of going to America; and, if I had, why should you want to go there?"

"Well, I'm an old dog that would be willing to learn new tricks, mademoiselle, new tricks in a new world—or perhaps even my old ones will pass for new over there." He chuckled and dipped his brioche in the syrup at the bottom of his cup. "Put the ocean between yourself and this trouble you've had," he urged her. "Go while you're still young."

"I'm not so young any more," she confessed, "and I'll carry my trouble with me whether I go or stay."

But he shook his head as he rose to go.

"It's a good thing to eat your brown bread first," he said. "Then you'll have plenty of white to look forward to. Don't forget to save a crumb for me, mademoiselle. *Au revoir.* Madame has no doubt been shouting herself hoarse for me these last ten minutes."

She watched him hobble off towards the Rue du Harlay and sighed at the folly of an old man's dreams of seeing a new world. But in February old Pierre's predictions began to be shared by most of Paris. Trouble and tension gathered in the air.

"Power," said Béranger, "is a bell which prevents those who set it pealing from hearing any other sound." So it was with King Louis-Philippe and his Minister of Foreign Affairs, Guizot. The sound of that bell whose clapper they had managed to keep in motion so long drowned out nearer and more ominous rumblings. *"Enrichissez-vous,"* it cried out mechanically with Guizot's own self-assured voice, but even his bourgeois supporters were growing skeptical of the refrain. How could one grow rich under a régime of government inertia and political corruption, with steadily mounting taxes issued under the guise of false prosperity?

The Praslin murder case was not a closed issue. A peer of France had been allowed to evade justice, and that still rankled. It had put the match to public indignation, and once the blaze was started a score of other grievances caught fire. Few guessed, least of all the complacent, seventy-year-old monarch, how briskly the dead wood that had held the Empire together would burn.

Rain had been falling for days; and a thick, smoky fog hung over all Paris. It was the 22nd of February, and since early morning streets had been either deserted or thronged with determined, rain-soaked people. Théodore Monod had been brought home from school at midday in charge of an older student. He reported that crowds had been thick about the Madeleine. Men in smocks and old coats, beggars and gamins and women, too, had been waiting for hours in the downpour, though no one seemed certain what they wanted. Some had shouted, "Down with Guizot," and others had tried to sing the Girondist refrain of defiance. There had even been a bedraggled red flag or two hoisted above the heads, and one particularly ragged figure had worn a placard with something about the "right to work" in letters the rain had almost obliterated.

Monsieur Monod confirmed his son's report when he returned at twilight.

"No one seems to know what is happening," he answered his wife's anxious questions. "But there has been fighting in the Champs Elysées. The Municipal Guard has come out in full force. I saw men burning benches in the streets and tearing down lamp posts. A man told me several shops had been looted. He said he saw one stripped of firearms."

"Then it must be Revolution." Henriette heard herself speaking calmly, almost as if she were making some comment on the weather. She did not realize the meaning of her words till she saw the color drain out of Madame Monod's cheeks and lips, till she saw how that family drew instinctively closer together. Fear was in their faces, and suddenly that word had become a reality to them all.

Troops were encamped round bonfires in the streets that night. Wet and shivering, the mobs scattered for shelter while the rain continued to fall in torrents. The easy-going old King reassured himself that the weather was on his side. The people of Paris, as he remarked to his household, were not accustomed to making revolutions in winter. But by another evening Louis-Philippe had grown less smug. Those hours of falling rain did not dampen the spirit of insurrection that charged all Paris. The crowds were sullen and dogged. Companies of students marched through the streets, denouncing Guizot with challenging cries: *"Vive la réforme!* Down with Guizot! *Vive la République!"*

The ministers and officials of France heard the shouting and waited tensely for Guizot to mount the rostrum and take his stand. It was half past one when he appeared, frail and precise and looking, as a foreign visitor described him, "a cross between a professor of French and an old actor." But he held his head high; he kept his old impelling manner even though he announced his resignation. His words fell like lead on the shocked ears of his supporters. "We have been betrayed," they cried. But the victorious Leftists cheered them down, and the crowds outside hailed the news with transports of enthusiasm.

"The Royalist Government has collapsed," Frédéric Monod reported to his household when he returned late that afternoon. "Guizot has resigned, and God knows who will be his successor. There's been no violence yet, but the National Guard has been called out as well as the Municipal one."

"But the Citizen Militia hate the Municipal Guard," Henriette broke in. "Does that mean there may be fighting?"

"I fear it. Already there is disorder among the regiments."

Few slept in Paris that night. Crowds gathered on the wet and wind-swept streets, ragged coats and military uniforms making strange human patterns under the flare of torches. At nine o'clock the mob grew thicker on the Boulevard des Capucines, where the Ministry of Foreign Affairs was under heavy guard. But when the marchers advanced upon the gates they were met by crossed bayonets. A shot rang out, and others echoed in sharp metallic patter.

By early morning there had been another massacre in the Place de la Concorde. Carts were parading the dead in improvised biers under slaty skies, followed by shouting, water-soaked companies of men and women. Fresh columns of soldiers were being sent out to restore order, but when they reached the Boulevard Bonne-Nouvelle and other im-

portant arteries of the city, they found the way blocked by
rough barricades of mud and stone that had been hurriedly
thrown up in the night. Bedraggled red flags and equally
limp banners of tricolor mingled as one company of soldiers
after another marched out, only to scatter uncertainly.
Everywhere muskets were being reversed. Soldiers broke
ranks and marched with the workingmen they had been
sent to disperse.

The Palace was in confusion. Without Guizot at his side,
the King vacillated like a ship without a rudder. Orders
were countermanded almost the moment after they had
been dispatched. Reform or repression—the King favored
now one, now the other. It was as if, they said of him afterward, "he held out his right hand and shook his left fist."

There was no time to waste in argument if the Palais
Bourbon was to hold its own against the rival government
that was even then being formed in the Hôtel de Ville. At
eleven o'clock on the morning of February 24th, Louis-
Philippe called his two sons and prepared to make his last
royal appearance. He had decided upon a personal appeal
to his subjects. He would review the National Troops on
guard before the palace. They were a picked regiment of
his Citizen Militia whose uniform he wore, and they represented the powerful bourgeoisie on whose support he had
always relied.

But that drizzling day, as he rode along their lines in the
Carousel, no spontaneous burst of cheers rose to greet him.
Only a few half-hearted cries of *"Vive le roi!"* answered his
challenge. The air was heavy about him. He knew that he
had failed. Abruptly he turned his horse back to the palace.
An hour later the abdication had been signed; he had exchanged his uniform for civilian dress and with his family
had turned his back on a Paris that was no longer his capital.

News of the abdication and the flight of the royal family
was not generally known for some hours. In the region about
the Monod home there had been less disturbance than on the
day previous, and Henriette, grown restive from staying so
long behind shuttered doors and windows, had ventured
out upon an errand. Word had reached the household that
a member of Monsieur Monod's congregation was seriously
ill and in need of help. The minister had left some hours
before, and there was no way of reaching him; so she had
volunteered to go to the sick parishioner. It was out of the

question for Madame Monod to leave her children, and besides Henriette rather relished the idea of leaving the house that had held them prisoners for two long, anxious days.

"No, I am not in the least afraid," she had smiled reassuringly from the door. "It seems quiet now, and the rain has stopped."

She reached the stricken home without difficulty, making her way there by back streets. The patient was very ill. She could do nothing beyond reassuring the family that Monsieur Monod would come when he could, and that Madame Monod sent her sympathy. But when she found herself on the street once more she could not resist returning by a different route.

Streets and gutters were still wet, but the clouds had broken overhead. She turned towards the Champs Elysées and made her way along familiar streets. Here there was more activity. People passed her, all moving in the direction of the Tuileries, but in their own haste they took no notice of her, an inconspicuous woman in bonnet and shawl.

It was only when she found her path blocked suddenly by a barricade of mud and cobblestones and a struggling mass of people that she regretted her rashness in choosing that way. Hastily she turned to retrace her steps, only to be met by a crowd that had closed in behind her. Too late she realized she was caught fast between two groups that had met from opposite directions, and that were now mingling like a dark mass of gigantic human bees driven out of a hive. There was nothing to do but keep from falling under the rush of trampling feet. It took all her strength to do that. She had no time to think or feel anything except the immediate necessity not to lose her footing; to hold her own among those swaying, heavy bodies.

All her life, that next hour remained a confusion of sights and sounds and smells without semblance of reality. Sharp detached pictures remained with her always—more like the shifting patterns of a kaleidoscope held to her eyes than an actual scene of which she was part.

*"Vive la réforme! Vive la République!"* voices were shouting all about her—men's deep voices and the thinner cries of women. She had no breath to join in. The sound rolled over her head in dull thunder before it was broken by distinct pattering of gunfire and the quick thud of hoofs on

cobblestones. A company of soldiers bore down the street, and the crowd scattered in panic before the plunging hoofs and bared sabers.

Henriette caught at an arm beside her to keep from falling as the soldiers clattered by. They passed so close that a clod of mud struck her cheek. The man she clung to was a workman. She felt the coarse cloth of his blouse under her fingers. His face was streaked with sweat and mud, and a gash showed over one eye. He cursed thickly and shook his fist at those riders in the uniform of the Municipal Guard. A woman's scream shrilled out above the hoofbeats, and then the crowd closed in about a body that lay sprawled and limp where the riders had cut a path through the crowd.

"Oh!" Henriette gasped to those beside her. "Some one has been hurt, perhaps killed. We must stop. Let me get through."

But no one answered or moved to make way for her. Her lifted voice was like a cricket's chirp protesting the roar of a waterfall.

Up one street and across another to avoid more barricades, more crossed bayonets—it was as if an invisible flood were carrying her along with it. Her feet scarcely felt the ground under them, and her arms were locked with those of a woman at her left side and a man at her right. She felt more like a piece of driftwood than a human being swept along without effort of her own. But she was not afraid. A queer kind of exhilaration quickened her senses like wine.

Somehow, though she never knew how it had happened, they were nearing the Tuileries. The bare branches of trees showed against the sky above the heads of the crowd. Once more the ranks broke about her because a huge bonfire of blazing benches and furniture blocked the way. Henriette smelled the smoke before she could see the flames. Charred wood and sparks whirled up with the blue bitter smoke that choked in her thoat and made her eyes water. She could hardly see where she was going, but she felt some one pulling her away. Presently she found herself in a group of people huddled on some stone steps under the arched entrance of a shop.

"Better stay here as long as we can," a shabby youth who looked like a student told her. "They've broken into the palace, and there will be shooting."

Almost before he had finished speaking she heard again the distant crackle of gunfire, and the pavement about them became blocked with people, retreating in panic at the sound.

They must have been looting the Tuileries. She guessed that from the objects they clutched as they ran past. She saw women, wild-haired and jubilant, clinging fast to some bit of royal finery—a Sèvres ornament, a porcelain vase, a robe embroidered with gold thread dragging in the mud. Men held other incongruous trophies high above their heads. Their pockets were stuffed full. She saw silver spoons fall under hurrying feet, saw them whirl away in the brown water at the gutter.

Shock-headed urchins strutted fantastically in dress uniforms resplendent with scarlet and gilt braid. Men stopped to wrangle over the possession of a bottle. It slipped from between them and crashed against the steps where she stood. She could smell the wine that splashed her skirts.

Her ears rang with a multitude of voices, all lifted together, yet all crying out different words. She made one out now and again: "Guizot—*Réforme*—Thiers—Lamartine —*République*—Praslin!" She felt sure she had heard that name. It could not be merely some echo in herself. "Praslin!" She heard it again, and a man near her spat derisively at the word.

*"Mon Dieu!"* she thought, drawing closer into the folds of her shawl. "If they knew my name! If they guessed who stood beside them, they would make short work of me!"

It came over her then that here she was in the midst of a revolution she had indirectly helped to bring about. She had not chosen to play a part in this fierce storm that had overtaken Paris; the rôle had been thrust upon her. Her own sufferings and the calamity that had struck at the very core of her personal life were bound up with a French King taking leave of his throne, with the fate of these frantic men and women whose ideals seemed lost for the moment in jubilant chaos.

She felt frightened suddenly by the knowledge. How had she ever dared to speak of reform, of revolution, like a presumptuous child prattling of the unknown? She had thought of revolution in terms of a dignified change of power, a transition from one régime to another, not this wild scramble for silver spoons and royal uniforms, not these battered men and women trampling one another down in muddy streets, shouting incoherently for they knew not what.

"Revolution is like death," she thought. "We say the word, but we never quite believe it can touch us."

Somehow she made her way back to the Monod house. When the crowds thinned a little she crept along close to the walls of shops and houses, inching her way towards side streets, and so by slow degrees into quieter channels. Her bonnet had been lost; her shawl hung about her shoulders in tatters; she was pale and mud-splashed, but unhurt by the experience.

She even paused near a small open square to watch a shabby man dividing a loaf of bread with a flock of noisy brown birds. There he stood with outstretched hands in the midst of fluttering wings as if the ground were not shifting perilously underfoot; as if, in spite of all disaster, it were still important to feed sparrows. Henriette felt an overwhelming gratitude for the gesture as she hurried on her way.

The entire Monod household met her at the door with relieved faces. They had heard the distant sounds of shooting and echoes of disturbance, and had feared for her safety. Madame Monod was full of reproaches that she had allowed her to take such a risk alone; and her husband had seen enough violence in other quarters of the city to realize how narrowly she had escaped harm. Between sips of the wine they brought her, Henriette told them what she had seen in the last two hours. They listened aghast to her recital. It was not until later that Monsieur Monod remembered a message he had forgotten to deliver.

"Who do you think I found at my brother's this afternoon, along with others who had taken shelter there? That young minister from America named Field. You remember him, Henriette?"

"The little American who had such a passion for travel? Yes, I remember him. So he's back in time to see a revolution."

"Don't say the word, please," Madame Monod begged. "My heart turns over each time I hear it."

"Well," her husband went on, "he will be able to witness more than most travelers. He wanted to find out for himself what people were thinking and feeling, and now he will have his chance. By the way"—he turned to Henriette—"he sent you a message. He wanted me to tell you that you were still on his mind."

## Part II

### MADEMOISELLE
### HENRIETTE DESPORTES
### 1849-1851

*chapter twenty-five*

ONCE MORE SHE STOOD ALONE IN EARLY MORNING ON THE deck of a vessel and stared at a distant shore whose outlines were beginning to sharpen as the sun mounted. Staten Island, a steward had called it the evening before when the *Celtic* had cast anchor at last after nearly four weeks of salty progress. September, 1849, eight and a half years since that other morning when she had waited impatiently to go ashore with high-hearted confidence in the next adventure. But the port of Havre lay thousands of watery miles behind her now, and she had learned to be wary of adventure. There was trouble enough in the world without running to meet it.

Only a few of the two dozen cabin passengers were astir at that hour. She had left her five female companions asleep in their bunks or busy with packing in the ladies' cabin below. How cramped those quarters had seemed the day she had come aboard! Yet now she dreaded taking leave of them. This compact world of wood and canvas that had plowed unhindered through a trackless waste of gray or blue had soothed her nerves overwrought from the strain of decisions and partings. It was an interlude when time ceased to matter. One might hear the ringing of ship's bells or the call of the watch by night, but there was no past to be reckoned with because that lay far behind the white wake at the stern; no future, because the dripping prow still pointed towards an unbroken horizon.

"I was never able to visualize Eternity till now," she had written in her journal a few days before. "I am not sure that I believe in such a state, but after these weeks at sea I have had a foretaste of what it might be like. One's spirit expands in the strong sunlight and salt air. The fog closes in with the soft chill of infinity. Stars loom large with importance when one knows that one's course is being set by them, and it is strange how differently people move and talk in the middle of the Atlantic. Their voices grow less sharp and hurried. They speak simply and gravely of life and death, even of God sometimes to a comparative stranger."

And now the *Celtic* lay at anchor in the harbor of New York. Her side-wheels no longer churned, and her salt-drenched prow had caught up with the new world. Its busy tempo was already stirring about Henriette. Everywhere hatches were open, bales and barrels being hoisted from the hold to the rattle of chains and the groaning of windlasses. Gulls fought for the food thrown from the ship's galley. Their cries mingled with the activity above and below decks, and from the steerage came excited voices lifted in a medley of tongues.

Henriette could see these immigrants pouring up from their dark quarters like hordes of enormous rats eager to leave the vessel. They packed the small deck space allotted them, crowding to the rail for a first sight of America, jostling, gesticulating and jabbering. She watched them as they waited there, marveling at the almost tangible quality of hopefulness that animated that scene. Expectancy and the early-morning brightness laid a strange radiance upon so many of the upturned faces; faces that had come to be familiar to her during the voyage, and that she had classified as old, ugly, sullen, or stupid until she saw them suddenly transformed before her. Tears filled her eyes at the poignancy of that look. She felt envious of these people. What had they that she had not?

"Faith," she thought, remembering the words of the Epistle to the Hebrews, " 'the substance of things hoped for, the evidence of things not seen.' "

But they kept together in little groups, held apparently by ties of blood, or friendship, or the common bond of language. Vainly she searched among them for any who might be single like herself. She noticed one, who stood apart, a woman of indeterminate years shabbily dressed with a handkerchief over her head and a heavy bundle at her feet. There was something unmistakably French about her, the lines of a peasant in the shape of her body. Leaning over the rail, Henriette attracted the woman's attention and greeted her in French. The other smiled and answered in the dialect of Brittany.

"We have arrived after all the long weeks, madam; and, God be praised, the sun shines."

"You seem to be alone," Henriette ventured.

But the woman shook her kerchiefed head. Only for a little, she explained. Her husband waited for her. No, not in New York, much farther than that. She pointed to a white square of paper pinned to her dress and tried to pronounce a difficult name. Others, Henriette noticed, wore these same badges proudly displayed. There would be some one waiting for them at the end of even longer journeyings.

"*Bon voyage*," she wished the woman, and moved away.

She heard a fiddle playing a lively jig. Earlier on the voyage that same instrument had wailed dismally, and rich Irish voices had sung heartbreaking laments for the shores of Erin. Now the gay tune went rollicking across the water. Tears had dried on the faces of these boys and girls turned towards new shores. But she could not give herself to the spirit of rejoicing. She felt no mounting exhilaration as she stood at the rail. She was alone, more completely alone than in all the thirty-seven years of her life.

The nearer shores stood out clearly now. She could distinguish brown fields and woods of frowzy trees that showed yellow and russet in the morning sun. It had been summer still when she had sailed. Somehow she had expected to find the familiarity of lush green awaiting her across the Atlantic, not this tawny, unkempt landscape dotted with frame houses. Whether these were set close together or stood apart, their flimsy wooden shapes depressed her. She missed the reassuring solidity of stone or brick. There was a sense of impermanence about them that reminded her of Raynald's architectural experiments with packs of playing cards.

"Dear God," she thought with a shiver, "to have come so far—and for what?"

Several of her fellow passengers passed and greeted her. A family group—father, mother, tall son, and pretty daughter—who had sat near her at table paused to say good-by. Their faces were shining with happiness at being so nearly home.

"No place like it," the man said with a broad smile; "and I've seen the best they've got over there. Yes, m'am, give me America any time, and I'll make you a present of all the rest of 'em."

"Oh, now, Papa, that's no way to talk to Miss Desportes," his wife apologized. "But I guess it's only natural to be kind of partial to the place you come from. Don't forget now: if you're ever near Cherry Valley we'd be pleased to entertain you."

How kind they were, these Americans, with their easy offers of hospitality! They seemed like a race of overgrown children to her, with their naïve curiosity in the world, their satisfaction in their native land, and their directness of expression. Perhaps she would grow used to their abrupt ways in time, but to their voices—so high-pitched, so nasal—she would, she felt, never become reconciled. They gave such strange twists to the English language. They bore down upon syllables with such queer emphasis where she least expected it. Where, they asked, would she *lo*-cate in New York? She must kick up her heels a bit and see the sights before she got *swamped* with her teaching. One day they introduced her to sweet-and-sour-tasting preserves called "pickles," and the next day they told her of some mishap that had left them in "a pretty pickle." The precise, pure English she had prided herself upon speaking often brought puzzled looks as she tried to make her meaning clear to American travelers.

"Well, good-by, Miss Desportes. Pleased to have made your acquaintance, I'm sure."

She found herself responding to more farewells as the little group of cabin passengers gathered to watch the arrival of the tender which was to take them ashore. It was a river steamboat with a blackened smokestack and a short blunt whistle that matched its stubby prow.

"Here, m'am." A tall, bearded American with whom she had scarcely exchanged a dozen words on the entire voyage spoke at her side. "You better keep by me, changing craft. I can lug that bag of yours along with mine, and I guess we can all scrouge in this first load."

She tried to smile as she thanked him. American men, she decided, had no manners in the accepted sense of the word, yet they were very polite. They treated women with natural respect, unlike the more sophisticated appraisal of European males. Their speech and dress and bearing might be awkward and unpolished, but they seemed to take it as a matter of course that a woman should be looked out for, whether she traveled alone or not. In France one did not accept the arm of a strange man or let him help and advise one about the transfer of luggage. But here she realized that no familiarity was intended and no unfair advantage would be taken later. She liked this easy kindness in the men of the New World as much as she disliked their fondness for chewing tobacco and then spitting it out like the spray from a rusty fountain.

The wind was fresh as the tender steamed away from the *Celtic*. Henriette's bonnet ribbons began to flap, and her long cloak and skirts to billow. There was nothing for her to do but join the other women passengers in the stuffy cabin. Pressed close to a pane of glass, she had her first sight of Manhattan. A forest of shipping fringed the waterfront, close to docks and dingy warehouses, and beyond that a jumble of brick and brownstone stretched away as the land rose higher. This then was New York, the Queen of the New World. Henriette, accustomed to the impressive buildings and bridges of Paris, to the dark dignity of London, felt a shock of disappointment. Even though these buildings were less flimsy than those on the near-by shores, they seemed hardly more permanent. They, too, had a crude unfinished look, and she peered in vain for parks and green spaces to break the monotony of close-packed streets.

"Only the ships are beautiful," she thought, watching a clipper-built vessel slipping gracefully by; "and they go and come. Why, even Marseilles was more picturesque than this."

It cheered her somewhat to distinguish a number of church steeples rising above the roofs and chimneys. She counted more than a dozen in plain sight as the steamer drew closer, and now she made out a round stone structure resembling a fort with grass and trees at the island's tip.

"Castle Garden," she heard a man explaining to a woman passenger. "It's getting pretty crowded down here, not much like my grandfather's day. Must have been a nice little city then, but now it's too big—six hundred thousand people and still growing. Don't know where we'll end with all these foreigners crowding us off the streets."

"Yes," the other agreed, "they're getting to be a regular nuisance, and I say they'd ought to stay home where they belong!"

Henriette turned away. This was not a cheering conversation to hear on her first morning in America. She had not come over in steerage quarters, but all the same she was only another of "these foreigners." Instead of growing more distinct as they neared the landing place, the buildings blurred before her eyes. In that whole city of six hundred thousand souls there was not one she knew, not a single familiar welcoming face. With all her heart she wished she had stayed at home where she belonged.

But she reminded herself that the country she had left behind had not been eager to keep her. France was still in a sorry state of upheaval after the collapse of the government. The new ruler Louis Napoleon had been hailed with desperate hope, but could he bring order and prosperity out of economic chaos? Could he give work to discouraged and bitter people who had lost their means of support as well as she? Her only chance of work lay here, somewhere in those streets spreading before her in the September sunshine. Some one there had been willing to overlook the shadow of scandal which she would never be free of in her own country. She must hold fast to that one certainty and be thankful for it.

She tried to remember that when she and her possessions were set down with the other entering foreigners in the Immigrant Depot, where she waited to have her credentials passed upon. It was an interval that seemed endless to her. She was never to forget that place with its bare walls relieved only by printed rules and regulations; the throngs of inarticulate men, women, and children grown anxious now under the questions of busy, harassed officials, and just beyond the stonework of the building the jungle of ships' masts and rigging dark against the morning sky.

She felt lost and insecure in all that confusion about her. In vain she looked for a blue-bloused porter to shoulder her luggage. She must wait till help came from some direction. Meanwhile the wood of her stoutly roped chest became a refuge for which she felt grateful. For more than an hour she sat there, clinging fast to a bag that held her credentials, her small amount of American money, her letter of credit on the banking firm of August Belmont, and the letter assuring her of employment. The familiar shapes of her belongings only accentuated the strangeness of the world into which she and they had suddenly been projected. They seemed pathetic bits of wreckage from her own past—the umbrella, the bandbox with the label of the milliner's shop in the Rue d'Antin, the flowered carpetbag, the portmanteau with her initials in brass-headed nails. It looked battered now, the corners rubbed, the brass tarnished. She bent down and laid her hand to the worn leather, almost as if it were something alive, an aging pet dog that had followed her into exile. The years they had shared had taken toll of them both. Together they must adapt themselves to new ways.

Through that hour of waiting she tried to recall the encouragement of the friends she had left behind. Albert and Marie had been so devoted, so steadfast in their belief in her ability to make a new start across the Atlantic. Madame Le Maire, too, had forgotten past differences and had actually wept at parting. Old Pierre had wept, too, drawing his rough blue sleeve across his eyes while he assured her he envied her the chance to go to America.

"You will find your fortune over there, Mademoiselle Henriette," he had insisted. "It's walking to meet you even now."

And the Monod brothers—without their help and practical plans where would she be today? They had sent out appeals to influential friends on both sides of the sea to secure for her another position. They reiterated their belief in her innocence, and they called upon their Protestant associates to come to her aid. It had seemed a hopeless undertaking, but their confidence had never wavered; their efforts in her behalf had only been redoubled. And when the miracle happened and the offer came for her to teach in a select finishing school for the daughters of rich New Yorkers, the brothers Monod had arranged everything for her comfort on the long journey.

She had clung in sudden panic to Frédéric Monod's arm as he helped her into the railway carriage that last day. She had hardly been able to see his kind, strong face through her tears. But his words at parting remained the more clear.

"You will be valiant, Henriette," he had said. "It will always be so, for you were cast in a brave mold."

"I shall try," she had faltered, "but I do not feel brave. Somehow it was easier to face the charges in the Conciergerie than this going so far away—alone."

She had struggled to master her tears, but he had not blamed her for them.

"'Those who sow in tears shall reap in joy,'" he had reminded her. "I hope I shall live to see your harvest, Henriette. It will be a good one wherever you go. Yesterday when I was helping my boy with his Latin I found a motto worthy of your own particular coat of arms. Say it over after me. You will remember it better in the Latin: *Qui transtulit, sustinet*—'He who transplanted still sustains.' Never be afraid to send your roots deep into that new soil. I think you will grow there and be happy in time."

He had written the Latin words on his card and slipped it into her hand before the train moved away. She had repeated them to herself many times on the voyage, and now on the doorstep of the New World she repeated them again: *Qui transtulit, sustinet.*

She was free of the building at last. She and her possessions were being stowed into an open hackney coach that presently was clattering over the cobblestones. The driver, with good-natured volubility and a rich Irish broque, was determined that she should miss nothing. He continually turned on his box to point out with his whip this or that sight of interest.

City Hall Park surprised her by looking like a well kept English square. The Hall itself had fine proportions and a cupola that rose above the few shade trees. Across the Park the Astor House boasted six stories. Its broad steps and marble pillars were impressive, and the shops on its ground floor showed glittering window displays. Barnum's Museum and Stewart's Dry Goods Store, a huge marble building, both adjoining the Park, were pointed out by her guide, who continued to bombard her with information as they rattled along a busy thoroughfare called Broadway. It was crowded with vehicles at that hour. Often their horse must be pulled up short to avoid collision; often they were caught fast in a snarl of omnibuses, smart carriages, lumbering drays, of other public conveyances. The unevenness of the cobblestones made the hack sway and lurch with a motion that was far more trying than that of a small ship in rough water. Mud splashed from gutters and worn hollows in the pavings. Henriette felt dizzy and deafened by the confusion of motion and sound.

A medley of impressions had taken over her mind before that drive ended. She was struck by the compactness of these streets. Only an occasional vacant lot broke the solid ranks of brick and brownstone as one narrow, high building dovetailed the next with scarcely a foot to spare. Signs were displayed on nearly every one, huge boards proclaiming wares of every description. They added to the unfinished look of the city—as if, Henriette thought, children had built it haphazard to suit their changing tastes, and then plastered their handiwork with naïve embellishments in the way of pictures and printed signs. Then there were markets and hand-pushed carts loaded with vegetables and fruit. She marveled at such careless profusion; she marveled, too, at the sense of sturdy independence and activity which charged the very air she breathed. Even to the casual observer there was less contrast among those who crowded the pavements. Beggars were not so much in evidence. There were fewer fashionably dressed strollers. All appeared bent on some definite purpose, and they moved at a brisker pace than Europeans going about their business. "Time is money" seemed to be a motto that Americans took for granted.

Churches, shops, hotels, and theaters—she tried to fasten names and façades together as they were pointed out by her guide. But most of them—Niblo's Garden, the Bowery Theater, the Astor Place Opera House, the American, the Irving, the St. Nicholas, and the Prescott hotels, all ran together in her mind. Union Square, looming between handsomer buildings, with its benches and flower beds, its trees and tall flagpole, was a relief after the commotion of the bustling thoroughfares. Then presently they turned into a quieter side street of comfortable, unpretentious homes set about a small enclosed plot of grass and trees where nurses were watching their charges at play.

"Gramercy Park," the driver turned to announce with a flourish of his whip, and Henriette welcomed the reassuring name.

The horse was tied to a hitching post before a row of brick houses each with a flight of steps leading up to a white-trimmed doorway where brass knobs and knockers shone prominently. Henriette peered once more at the letter in her bag to verify the numbers. Ten—yes, there could be no doubt that the house next to the church on the corner marked the end of her long journey. A neat brass plate on the door left no doubt as she read the words: "Miss Haines' School."

She followed a housemaid into a long, cool parlor, shaded from the glare of the street by drawn blinds. The half-light gave a thin watery look to everything as if she were suddenly at the bottom of the sea, and the subdued sounds from the street in the hushed stillness of the house only intensified the illusion. She had barely time to note that the room was furnished in austere but excellent taste with heavy mahogany pieces. Sofa and chairs were still sheathed in summer dust covers, and a light matting lay on the floor.

Then she rose to take the extended hand of Miss Henrietta Haines.

"Ah, Mademoiselle Desportes, you have arrived in good time and I hope in good health. Did you have a comfortable voyage on the *Celtic?*"

As she responded, Henriette found herself pleasantly impressed by the middle-aged lady in the primly cut gray dress, relieved only by white collar and cuffs and a black taffeta apron. She liked the fastidiousness of person and the refined manner of speech of this schoolmistresss. There was quiet authority in the voice and in the direct glance of those eyes that were somehow youthful in spite of the wrinkles about them. This woman had traditions and spirit which Henriette recognized at once. There would, she felt, be no need of subterfuge between them.

"I am naturally a little tired and confused after the long journey," she was assuring her new employer; "but you must know how grateful I feel to be here, especially under obligation to you for your lack of prejudice in giving me this opportunity to work."

"You must not feel under any obligation to me personally." The other smoothed her apron and continued to sit erect as the proverbial poker in the opposite chair. "I came to the decision after long thought and considerable investigation."

"I am thankful that you know all the facts of—of the tragic episode in which I was so unfortunately involved. It will make things less difficult if I need not rehearse them to you again."

"Yes, I am fully acquainted with the Praslin case. Our own newspapers here were full of the affair, and then from our pastor I learned further details of your plight. After the letters he received from the Monod brothers I felt certain that you had been the victim of circumstance. From the Monods and other members of our faith I also learned that you had suffered because of your religious convictions. That was what really decided me to help you. Some of my own forefathers settled here to escape religious persecution— on my mother's side there was a French Huguenot. I remembered that when we heard of you."

"I shall do my best," Henriette promised, "so that you will never regret your decision."

"Well," Miss Haines continued, "I did not arrive at it without prayer and trepidation. You had such excellent qualifications, and you were so highly recommended; but still in a school like this, where the daughters of the city's best families are entrusted to my care, your coming seemed perhaps to present too many difficulties. I had my own reputation and responsibilities to the parents to consider."

"I know. I have taught long enough to understand all that."

"It was really providential for you that young Mr. Field should have come to me as he did—"

"Mr. Field?" Henriette repeated in bewilderment. "I did not know that he had anything to do with my coming to America."

"Why, yes, our minister brought him to call on me soon after his return from Europe. His personal account of you convinced me more than all the letters of recommendation. Such high praise coming from a young man of his standards, and family, naturally carried great weight. He made it plain"—a faint suggestion of a smile hovered about her lips as she spoke—"that, besides filling every requirement, you would be an ornament to any situation you might fill."

Henriette felt her cheeks flush. She had almost forgotten the eager admiration of that persistent little American, and now she found him responsible for her fresh start in the New World. One chance meeting a year and a half before, yet it had brought her across all the watery miles to this cool, impersonal parlor. She had been rude to him that night, and he had repaid her in this fashion. How strangely things came about, past the power of reckoning! We meet; we exchange words; we part; we are caught up in separate currents of activity, only to be brought together again, to have the whole course of our lives changed by a word from the other— spoken, or left unsaid. She had never expected to encounter that young minister with the candid blue eyes and impetuous manner again, yet here he was, bound up in the pattern of her very existence.

"I am afraid," she ventured with a slightly deprecating shrug, "that Mr. Field may have been somewhat prejudiced by his own enthusiasms. Did he tell you that we met but once?"

"Once seemed to be quite enough for him; and now, Mademoiselle Desportes, let us discuss your duties before we go upstairs. School will reopen next week, so there will be plenty of time for you to rest and accustom yourself to our ways."

Miss Haines had very definite ideas about how a school should be conducted, but Henriette found them sensible. She was to have all the French classes and instruct an older, more advanced group of girls in painting. Henriette and two other resident teachers were expected to supervise daily walks to relieve the strain of too long work at desks, and there were other duties outside the classrooms for half a dozen girls were boarding pupils. Miss Henrietta Haines, however, assumed most of the executive tasks herself.

"And now I am sure you wish to rest and unpack." The schoolmistress rose, and the first interview was over satisfactorily. "Our noonday meal is over, but I will order some refreshment sent to your room. We dine at half past six and only Fräulein Schmit, who teaches German and mathematics, will be with us. I believe a letter came for you yesterday. I will have it sent up with your things."

Once more Henriette found herself in a small room up several flights of stairs. The school filled two adjoining houses which had been thrown together. The kitchen, servants' quarters, and dining room occupied the basement, with parlors and classrooms directly above. Miss Haines had her own apartments on the top floor of one building, while the resident teachers and boarders had smaller rooms in the other. The one assigned to Henriette had two windows that faced the little park and the brick row beyond. It was a pleasant outlook over the trees, and a cool breeze stirred the crisp white muslin curtains. The furnishings were plain, but the place was immaculate, and everything had been arranged for her comfort.

Still, it had a precise, unadorned look that reminded her of the old convent days. She sat down on one of the stiff, straight-backed chairs and tried not to give way to depression. The varying emotions of the morning, the confusion of a new city—all this had left her suddenly spent. She felt, as she often did when great weariness overcame her, utterly detached in spirit. She saw herself, sitting alone and friendless on her own wooden chest in a corner of the cheerless Immigration Depot. She knew exactly the way her cloak had fallen about her drooping shoulders, how small her belongings had looked about her. Always that picture of loneliness at the gates of a strange land would stay with her.

Some day, she knew, she would put that scene, that woman's figure, those few possessions, and the flapping printed rules and the gray walls on canvas or paper. Her brush or crayons would make it a remembered reality. But just now she must try to forget how very real it had been.

When her luggage had been brought up, the room took on a more personal look, and presently a maid appeared with food on a tray and a letter. Henriette held the light square of paper in her hands and studied it curiously. It was too soon to have news from France, and besides the stamp was as unfamiliar to her as the writting. There must be some mistake, yet there were the letters of her name and the address set down plainly in strong, flowing penmanship. "St. Louis, Missouri": she made out the postmark and was further mystified.

My dear Mademoiselle Desportes [it began]: May I be the first to greet you by letter on the day of your arrival in a country where I hope you will be very happy?

From my kind friends Adolphe and Frédéric Monod I learned of your plan to resume your former occupation, and it was also my privilege to speak of you to the good lady in whose school you will teach. I am sure that this association will be mutually pleasant and I envy the young minds fortunate enough to be inspired by your own.

I regret the distance that makes it impossible for me to welcome you when you land for the first time, but as you see I am many miles away from New York. My father and brother Stephen and I were united in London this past summer, but I sailed before them and it seemed best that I should return to my old pastorate here for a few more months. My brothers Cyrus and David are both living with their families in New York and have urged me to make headquarters in their homes, so, my dear Mademoiselle Desportes, it is my hope to call upon you there before long.

I have not forgotten our conversation together, nor could I forget you if I wished to do so, which is far from the case. Your welfare means much to me and I find myself impatient to hear of your safe arrival and how you find yourself in the new situation.

Soon you will count many friends on this side of the Atlantic, but I trust you will remember that I welcomed you here even before you set foot on these shores.

May I remain, dear Mademoiselle Desportes, with pleasant remembrances of our first and even more pleasant anticipation of our next meeting,

Faithfully yours,<br>HENRY MARTYN FIELD

She paused later in the midst of unpacking to read the letter through a second time. How characteristic it was! The impulsive gesture of friendliness and admiring good will under the slightly formal phrases; the simple directness with which he took their next meeting for granted; the appealing way he hoped that she would be happy in his country.

"But, mademoiselle," she remembered how Louise had carelessly dismissed this country and its inhabitants, "only queer people live in America. You wouldn't like to go there, would you?"

Strange how the words came back to her after so long. "*Eh bien,* queer or not, they have taken me in," she reminded herself as she laid her first American letter away to be answered. "It is good to have a friend here. I like this little minister—this Henri Martyn-in-the-middle Field."

## chapter twenty-six

SIX TIMES ROUND GRAMERCY PARK, THEN NORTH ON Lexington Avenue as far as the paving continued smooth, and back again: Henriette dreaded that mid-morning exercise period with the thirteen girls in her charge. They were in the difficult middle teens, and though she had favorites among them individually, collectively they tried her patience. These daily promenades were what she most disliked in the school routine. She was supposed to keep them walking in step at a brisk pace; to see that they did not lag or behave conspicuously. Above all, she must make sure that they did not attract the attention of any passing male, young or old. This was not easily managed, but Miss Haines insisted upon strict observance of a rule drawn up according to the school's best standards of deportment: "Young ladies are urged at all times, but especially during exercise periods, to maintain an erect carriage, proper decorum of manner, and to pay no attention to extraneous objects."

"Extraneous objects," Henriette soon discovered, had come to be a phrase with double meaning in Miss Haines' School. It covered the entire male species, but more especially the young men of the neighborhood, who delighted to congregate and watch these daughters of Manhattan's most prosperous families put through their paces. Henriette walked in the center of her little group, and if by farsighted strategy she managed to maneuver the three first couples past masculine obstacles, the set behind her would invariably lose composure. If she turned her attention to her rear guard, then those in advance might be guilty of some breach of etiquette.

On a certain day of February, 1850, she set off with her charges, feeling particularly low-spirited. She had been disappointed at having no letters on recent ships from France, and the weather was bitterly bleak and depressing. There had been heavy snow in January and then a thaw, followed by an intense cold that crusted streets with ice. Raw winds blew in from the rivers, chilling to the marrow when one ventured out. Indoors it was not much more comfortable. Those who sat near the grate fires in each classroom grew flushed and stupid from the intense heat, while those a few feet off shivered with numb fingers and toes. Extra woolen stockings and layers of flannel petticoat helped somewhat, Henriette found, but they weighted her down as she moved among her pupils, trying to keep their wits from wandering. They had plenty of ability, these select young ladies of New York, but little application; and it took all her energy to drive them to their work. Lately, among the girls in the older group she had detected more than ordinary signs of restlessness and suppressed excitement. They whispered more frequently and passed little three-cornered notes from hand to hand. She found them studying her with furtive curiosity and then exchanging sly glances full of personal significance. This had been going on for over a week now, though she had been careful to take no notice of the phenomenon.

Now, as she marshaled them down the steps of Number 10 Gramercy Park, she felt more than ever aware of secret activity. In some way she knew it concerned her. They had been restless and difficult before, but she had not been the sole object of their attention. Something had turned them against her. She could feel an almost tangible hostility as the little procession formed.

"Marianna Van Horn, you will please walk with Kate Delancy; Isabelle Lorillard with Agnes Brevoort; Rebecca Jay with Ellen De Peyster." She tried to pair them discreetly, separating the more lively spirits. "Louise Jumel will please accompany me part of the way, and Lucy Schuyler will change places with her on our return. The rest take your places behind us. Emily Delavan, please to fasten your tip-*pet*."

Ordinarily she would not have minded their amusement when she accented the wrong syllable, but today the muffled giggles annoyed her. A sharp retort rose to her lips, but she kept it back. She would order them all to speak in French during the walk, and that would restrain them somewhat. Again she racked her brain for some explanation of their behavior, but she could think of nothing to account for their antagonism.

"But I tell you I *am* sure," a lowered voice came from behind her. "Mother's maid Céleste kept all the papers, and I read them. Imagine, he was a Lord or Duc or something, and he killed——"

Henriette lost the next words as a sleigh went gliding past on smooth runners with bells jingling. She forced herself to make polite comments in French to the girl at her side while her ears strained to catch more conversation from the rear.

"You mean she's all mixed up with a murder? Oh, Emily! If it's true it's the most exciting and romantic thing I ever knew, and she's right here in Miss Haines' School."

"It certainly is true. I borrowed the papers, and Ellen and Louise are stopping to see them on the way home. I don't think it's so romantic, and I guess Mamma won't either when she gets back from Baltimore next week and she finds out the kind of French teacher we've got."

"Hsh, Emily, she's turning round—speak French to me, quick! *Qu'est-ce que c'est, s'il vous plaît?*"

*"Oh la, la, prenez garde de tomber ici. Cet* icy— What's French for sidewalk? There, that's enough to satisfy her, but you just wait and see, Rebecca Jay, what I've got to show you. You'll be surprised. Of course, I don't intend to make trouble, but if she starts correcting me for my accent again before the class, I'm going to look her right in the eye and ask her a few questions myself."

"Oh, Emily, you wouldn't dare!"

"I would so. I'll ask her how to pronounce P-R-A-S-L-I-N and C-O-N-C-I-E-R-G-E-R-I-E, and we'll see how she acts then!"

Henriette separated the two girls on the walk back. She took Emily Delavan for her own companion and placed Rebecca Jay directly in front. Temporarily, at least, she had silenced the whispers; but she knew that soon every girl in the school would have heard some garbled version of the story. Later, as she moved about tidying her classroom, she found a folded bit of paper under a desk.

"Just wait till you hear the awful thing Emily has found out about Mademoiselle D.," she read in an immature girlish hand.

That use of the initial must have been unconscious; yet if they had tried to be malicious they could not have devised a more cruel way to hurt her.

"Mademoiselle D.," she thought bitterly. "So she has crossed the Altantic also. I had hoped she was left forever in France."

That evening she asked Miss Haines if she might see her upon a rather important matter. She found her settled before a coal fire in the small sitting room, busy with books and correspondence under the lamplight.

"I hope that you are happy with us, Mademoiselle Desportes." Miss Henrietta Haines laid down her book and studied her visitor keenly. "You have seemed a trifle tired these last few days. I hope you are not finding our American winters too severe?"

No, she assured her employer. What she had come to discuss with her had nothing to do with weather. She reiterated that she enjoyed her classes. Group teaching had been new to her, but she found it stimulating. Until lately she had felt that she and her pupils were in complete accord, but for the last week a change had come over the older group of girls. This had puzzled her until today, when she had discovered the reason. Briefly she repeated the fragmentary conversation overheard on the walk, and she produced the crumpled note.

"Emily Delavan," Miss Haines remarked thoughtfully. "That is unfortunate, for she is a leader, and her family are influential. Still, I suppose, this was bound to happen sooner or later."

"I suppose so," Henriette agreed. "I have been trying to think of the best way to meet it. I did not wish to take any steps without consulting you."

"Several of the parents already know of your connection with the Praslin tragedy," Miss Haines continued. "I consulted them before offering you the post. They agreed with me that old scandals should be forgotten in your case. I had hoped that, since you were referred to oftener by the name Deluzy in accounts of the trial, you might escape notice as Mademoiselle Desportes."

"I had hoped so, too, but girls are clever at spying out secrets."

"Yes, I know. We must be prepared for trouble and perhaps complaints from parents. I shall take your part, of course, but I must say I should not relish a visit from the Delavans or the Van Horns, or Mrs. De Peyster."

"They are a very spirited group of girls," Henriette agreed, "particularly this Emily Delavan. But she has a good heart, and so have the rest. I believe, if I could tell them exactly what happened——"

"You mean give them all the sensational details of the murder and your—your connection with it?" Miss Haines was openly shocked and incredulous.

"By tomorrow they will all have read those old newspapers," Henriette went on. "They will know all the scandalous details, as you say. But if I tell them in my own way I think I can still keep their respect. I should like to have you give me leave to try."

"And suppose your method fails. What shall we do then, mademoiselle?"

"In that case I will not embarrass you by staying. You will find another teacher of French, and I will try to find another place. I see no other way to keep this trouble from spreading."

"Perhaps you are right; but it seems rather strange to

confide your story to a group of young girls who lead such carefully sheltered lives."

"But they live and breathe; they will love and suffer in a few more years. I think it will not hurt them to know the truth. It is better that they hear it from me than that they magnify the words of servants and newspapers to mean what is false. With your permission I will trust myself to these girls, tomorrow, and take the consequences."

"It seems rather rash." Miss Haines hesitated.

"Perhaps, but one must be rash sometimes. If I did not take these girls into my confidence, always between us there would be this barrier. We could never work freely together."

"Well, Mademoiselle Desportes, since you are ready to take the risk—"

"Thank you. Tomorrow then, during the ten o'clock French conversation, I will tell them my story."

"You will be very circumspect, please?"

"You can trust me. And if I fail you need not feel under obligation to keep me here. Good night."

That night she lay wakeful long after she had finished correcting exercises in French grammar and blown out her lamps. It was intensely cold. The wind from the East River tugged at the window shutters, and wheels and hoofs sounded sharply from icy streets below. In spite of all the comforters and a hot brick at her feet she stayed stiff and shivering as she planned tomorrow's campaign. She felt lonely and middle-aged. Exactly, she reminded herself, as a spinster school-teacher nearing thirty-eight should feel. Yet she faced the future calmly, though she knew how much depended upon her handling of a delicate situation.

"I have been through too much," she thought, "to care so desperately what others may think of me. I shall never make compromises with myself for others again. I shall say what I think and feel from now on. That is what I learned in the Conciergerie. One cannot go through blood and tears and disgrace and not be changed."

She dressed with special care next morning. It was not fitting for a school-teacher to wear the flowing curls of Paris boulevards. She had already made that discovery, but she brushed her hair to gleaming softness on either side of her face and put on a blue cashmere dress that was especially becoming. At the collar she fastened the enameled pin with the gold dragon's head. She had worn it through so many

All This, and Heaven Too

days of stress since the Duchesse had presented it that she had come to feel an almost superstitious attachment to the piece of jewelry. Yes, she felt ready to meet the enemy on its own territory.

Her first class was for the youngest scholars, and all through that hour her mind kept looking ahead to the next. Plans and phrases raced through her mind as she copied out simple poems and heard the children recite them.

> *"Je suis le petit Pierre*
> *Du Faubourg Saint-Marceau*
> *Messager ordinaire,*
> *Facteur et porteur d'eau . . ."*

Their strange high-pitched voices droned after her in singsong unison. It was torture to hear their pleased mispronunciations. But how sweet they looked—round and rosy-cheeked, with such innocent clear eyes, such small perfect bodies in full dresses and starched aprons! One little girl with yellow hair reminded her of Berthe, and Berthe had looked so much like her father.

*"Merci, mademoiselle, je vous remercie."*

*"Au revoir, mademoiselle,* and please, I've lost my handkerchief!"

*"Votre mouchoir, chérie,"* Henriette corrected, and offered a fresh one from her desk.

They had gone, and the advanced French class was filing in. She watched them from under lowered eyelids while she pretended to be busy over some papers. An undeniable air of bravado was stirring in the room. Those thirteeen girls were fairly bursting with importance as they took their places. Emily Delavan's black curls quivered excitedly. She whispered to Marianna Van Horn, and they nodded in complete understanding.

Henriette continued to study the little group, fascinated as she always was by the different racial inheritances that cropped out in spite of dominant Americanism. These daughters of early settlers showed their stock. The Dutch Van Horns, Brevoorts, Schuylers, and De Peysters were sturdy, placid, and blond. The English DeLanceys, Jays, and Wards were also fair-skinned, but with more delicate features. The spirited, dark French strain showed plainly in the Lorillards, Jumels, Delavans, and De Rhams, descend-

ants of Huguenot families. How the types persisted in spite
of transplanting!

*"Bonjour, mesdemoiselles,"* she began when the clock
struck the hour and they were settled in their seats before
her. "Our lesson will not be conducted in French today. You
may lay aside your books, for it is to be entirely oral. All I
ask is that you give me your whole attention, and that you
will do your part faithfully when I shall call upon you for
comments. I am going to tell you a true story, and it is important that we understand one another perfectly. Are you
ready that I should now begin?"

An uneasy rustle followed this announcement. Puzzled
looks were exchanged. Something in Mademoiselle Desportes's manner let them know that this was to be no ordinary recitation period. The classroom had grown very still
during this pause. Blue, brown, and gray eyes were turned
expectantly toward the teacher's desk.

"Well, then, we shall go to Paris, to a large and beautiful
house in the Rue du Faubourg-Saint-Honoré, the residence
of a noble family named Praslin—"

Again an uneasy presentiment stirred the classroom.
Emily Delavan shifted in her place and glanced sheepishly
towards Rebecca Jay.

"This Duc and Duchesse de Praslin had many children,"
the quiet voice continued, "sons and daughters of various
ages; so it was necessary that they employ a governess. It is
of this governess that I shall tell you."

Once she was well launched into her recital, there was no
more restlessness. The girls sat without moving except for
an occasional long-drawn breath or a rustle of skirts as they
leaned forward absorbed and intent. A pencil fell to the
floor, but no one thought of picking it up. There must be
no interruption. From the first Henriette had their undi-
vided attention. But that was not enough. She must have
their sympathy, too, and to this end she brought all her
gifts of eloquence and persuasion to bear. She called words
to her command as she had summoned them under the
questionings of Monsieur Broussais and Chancellor Pasquier in the courtroom. It was more difficult, however, to
make herself clear in English and to remember her promise
to Miss Haines that she would be circumspect. She was
nearing the most difficult part of her recital.

"And so"—she leaned towards them across the desk, and

her voice grew even more low and vibrant—"and so, just when she thought there was more harmony in that household, just when she hoped there would be no further lies printed about Monsieur le Duc and his attentions to his children's governess, there appeared another article in the newspapers—a much more slanderous one than before. She was ordered to go, and she could do nothing but pack her things and leave that house where she had been so happy."

"I call it a shame, a regular shame!" Agnes Brevoort's cheeks were scarlet as the words burst from her involuntarily.

"Hush!" the other girls whispered in hasty rebuke.

"It was not easy for her to find other work." The voice was going on. "You yourselves must know how careful your mothers are about the characters of those who serve them. Without a letter of recommendation from the Duchesse de Praslin, what could she do? And that promised letter, it did not arrive. A month she waited, and her despair —you cannot think how great it was. But worse was yet to come. Oh, very much worse!"

The schoolroom clock had struck the half-hour, and still they hung on her words. Their ears were strained to miss none, and no one giggled at strangely misplaced accents.

"The investigation, it was ended. The law declared her innocent, and she was allowed to leave that prison, the Conciergerie. But where to go? What to do? So horrible a crime had shocked the people of France, and many still believed her guilty of having a part in it. She was without friends, but a kind family took her into their home. She must hide there for many months since it was not safe for her to go among people even though she had partly changed her name. She was very miserable in those long months. She wished to die, but that was not possible. God must have meant that she should endure. But how was she, then, to live? Where, then, was she to go?"

"To America!" This time the exclamation came from Lucy Schuyler.

"Ah, yes, but suppose the terrible things that this governess wished so much to forget should follow her to America? Suppose even were she able to pay her passage across the ocean and find work to do in a strange city; suppose even then she might not be allowed to leave her troubles behind her? People can be as cruel in one country as in another.

They can find copies of old newspapers and stir up what is best forgotten. They can exchange sly glances and whisper; and though they perhaps mean no harm, the ugly story spreads and grows till there is no peace for her—not even in America."

"Oh, mademoiselle, please don't go on." A smooth brown head went down on folded arms, and a girl's sobs broke out suddenly in the stillness.

"One moment, please, and I shall say no more."

Henriette had risen to make her final appeal. The intense quiet of the room was broken only by a stifled sob or a telltale sniffle. All eyes, even the most tearful, were fixed on her face as she began to speak.

"It is for you to tell me the end of my story. But first the question I shall put to you, which I beg you will answer truthfully: Do you, mesdemoiselles, think that this governess deserves to suffer the rest of her life, or do you think that she has earned the right to continue her work without prejudice in a country where many before her have sought refuge?"

Their response was overwhelming. Rachel herself, though facing far larger audiences, had never been more compelling; and she had certainly never received a more spontaneous ovation. Between tears and vehement protestations they rallied to her side.

"Oh, mademoiselle, it was wonderful! I mean, she was, to stand up before them all and plead her own case."

"Of course, she shouldn't have to suffer any more, and any one who ever mentioned it to her ought to be, to be— Well, they ought to be put a stop to!"

"Goodness me, but she was spunky! Excuse me, mademoiselle, but I mean she certainly had a lot of grit."

"Of what, Lucy? What word is that you are saying?"

"Well, anyway, you can count on us never to breathe a word."

Henriette smiled as they flocked about her. "I thank you all from my heart. But you, Emily Delavan, you have said nothing. That surprises me. I thought you would be the first to ask me a question."

The girl's dark head lifted. Her usually bright, defiant eyes were clouded as they met Henriette's.

"I haven't any question, mademoiselle." She faltered, and her lips quivered suspiciously.

"What! You do not wish to know the name of that governess I am quite ready to tell you."

"No." The dark curls shook emphatically. "You needn't tell us any more. I guess you know how we feel. We're just —just plain skunks."

"Why, Emily Delavan!" The others opened their moist eyes in shocked surprise. "If Miss Haines ever heard you use that word she'd send you home for good and all!"

"Well, it's what we are, and I don't care who hears me say it. I'm going to burn every single one of those old newspapers when I get back, and I'm never going to mention a word of this to any one as long as I live. Here, let's all cross our hearts and hope to die and be cut in little pieces if we do!"

"Oh, but please, no," Henriette interposed hastily. "That is far from necessary. I shall trust you, and you must trust me. We shall have understanding now. That is all we need, I think. And tomorrow we will resume the exercise in French conversation that you prepared for this morning. This hour has not been lost since it has shown me how wise it was that I crossed the Atlantic Ocean to find new friends. Make haste now, *mes chères*, it is already time for our walk."

Once more the procession set off on its daily round. Snow was in the air, and the sky a dull gray above the leafless trees in Gramercy Park. But a new harmony possessed the little group. They moved as one, united by a common enthusiasm. Mademoiselle Desportes was a heroine. Before, she had been only their French teacher, correcting accents and grammar and supervising these tiresome walks. Now, though she walked beside them in the same brown cloak and beaver bonnet she had worn yesterday, she moved in a romantic haze. They saw her now as one of those who gather legends to themselves. Jeanne d'Arc, Marie Antoinette, Charlotte Corday, and Portia—their ordeals were as nothing compared to the sufferings and triumph over injustice of their own Mademoiselle D. She had taken them into her confidence, not as children but as contemporaries. She had shared her secret with them, and they would never betray that sacred trust.

Henriette felt the reflected glow of this new enthusiasm as she walked in their midst. She was exhilarated by her conquest, yet deeply touched by their loyal response. Young championship was very sweet and also very affecting. They

chattered eagerly about her, drawing her into their conversation continually. "Don't you think so, too, mademoiselle?"
She could hardly answer all the questions in French and
English. She smiled into those bright, admiring eyes and
thanked God that she had not lost the power to quicken
young hearts.

*chapter twenty-seven*

SPRING REACHED MANHATTAN EARLY THAT YEAR. THE
last remnants of dingy snow had hardly melted before unsuspected green appeared between brick and brownstone.
Buds swelled wherever a tree or shrub could manage to
grow, and in Union Square and Gramercy Park delicate
tassels and soft dottings that would soon be leaves lay like
mist on brown branches. Everywhere window boxes
bloomed with pansy, hyacinth, and geranium plants. Fresh
paint brightened blinds and doorways, and in all well conducted houses east and west of Fifth Avenue violent orgies
of spring cleaning began.

By late April the girls came to school in fresh new dresses
of gingham and poplin, gay with stripes and plaids and
sprigged patterns. They looked as fresh and charming as the
bouquets they brought to her desk—daffodils and tulips and
the first apple blossoms from their families' country places
at Spuyten Duyvil or Harlem or suburban Bloomingdale. It
was hard to pay strict attention to the classwork with these
flowers filling the schoolroom with distracting fragrance.
They made Henriette homesick for the gardens and lawns
and the woods of Melun. Sometimes on a Saturday or Sunday she would be invited by Emily Delavan or Rebecca Jay
or Lucy Schuyler to drive out to their country places. She
enjoyed these outings, and found the region beyond the
city full of a simple and prosperous beauty. The houses
pleased her by their rambling and unpretentious style. She
had come to like these estates set along the Hudson and the
East River. Their white wooden walls and neat pillars fitted
into the landscape, set among orchards and groves of fine

trees with lush lawns sloping down to the water where small craft anchored in sheltered coves.

Now that the days were longer, she often walked about the city with Fräulein Schmit or another teacher. Women could go safely without male escort until darkness fell and the lamplighters began their rounds with ladders and torches. After that the ladies of New York did not go abroad unaccompanied, though they sat at their open windows or high front stoops, greeting neighbors and watching their children at play. Henriette had a passion for exploring the byways of Manhattan. Fräulein Schmit enjoyed these excursions except when Henriette's curiosity carried them beyond the limits of propriety, as in the exploration of Dutch Hill.

Dutch Hill turned out to be a crazy-quilt village of board and mud shanties cluttering a section of the East River on that northerly outpost of the city, East Forty-second Street. Henriette had been fascinated by this squatter community of picturesque squalor, with its nondescript barking dogs, its rooting pigs and goats, its swarms of ragged, exuberant children. She was eager to talk with them and with the untidy women picking over great heaps of rags, bottles, and bones they had salvaged. But Fräulein Schmit was shocked by this spectacle.

"It iss scandalouse!" she had exclaimed in horrified accents. "Come at once away, Mademoiselle Desportes, lest we the cholera catch!"

Fräulein Schmit preferred sedate promenades in the fashionable Stuyvesant Square quarter where they passed the handsome pillared homes of many of their wealthy pupils. Or if they had a whole free afternoon and the day was especially fine they might turn south and stroll down Fifth Avenue as far as Washington Square. North on Fifth Avenue to the city limits at Forty-second Street was another favorite promenade where they usually made the huge stone pile of the Croton Reservoir their objective. Going and returning, they always paused by the Waddell suburban villa on the corner of Thirty-eighth Street with its gardens and miniature Gothic lodge, its impressive brick and sandstone mansion set behind smooth lawns and shrubbery. Fräulein Schmit considered this place the only elegant one in New York, but Henriette did not admire its ornate imitation of foreign architecture. She found Fräulein Schmit's con-

ventional opinions more tiresome than the provincial preferences of the Americans she had met. She longed for more
adventurous companionship through that first spring in
New York, and at last the wish was granted.

On a mid-May morning with the last school term ending in
a fortnight, she received two letters that affected her various-
ly. One came from Paris, bringing news of her grandfather's
death. He had died without being reconciled to her and,
though Henriette's legal representative had put in a claim for
her as his only heir, the woman with whom he had taken
shelter had managed to gain possession of his small estate.
Times were still very precarious in France, the letter told
her. There was almost as much confusion in the government
as before the new régime under Louis Napoleon had been
established. She had done well, it seemed, to find refuge with
the Republicans across the sea, since the French Republicans were steadily losing power; and it appeared that the
formation of a second Empire was inevitable.

The other message, from Henry Field, told her that he had
finished his duties in St. Louis and was on his way to New
York. He expected to be there almost as soon as his letter.
He would visit his brother David Dudley and would call
upon her at the earliest opportunity. She laid the letter away
with mingled feelings, for she both dreaded and anticipated
this meeting. To see this young man who was so bound up
with the most unhappy year of her life would be difficult.
Wounds that were healing could so easily be reopened. Yet
she welcomed the thought of his companionship. She had
met few men in New York, and she wearied of female society with its narrow, domestic chatter. During that year
she and the little minister from New England had corre-
sponded frequently. His letters convinced her that besides
being well read and scholarly he possessed a flexible and at
times brilliant mind. With all his learning he had kept the
capacity of response to the world about him. He shared her
curiosity and enthusiasm for people. She had been impressed by his fine discrimination and by a natural gift for
expressing all that he felt and believed.

He came one warm May evening, and she knew at once
that she need not have dreaded their reunion. He was
twenty-eight now, but only a trifle less eager and boyish
though his travels abroad had given him more maturity of
outlook. She had forgotten the blue directness of his eyes

and the way his plain face kindled to his thoughts. She had forgotten, too, his absent-mindedness. He sat for half an hour holding a bunch of lilacs he must have bought from some corner vender for her. It took a good deal of sly maneuvering on her part to remind him of the intended gift.

"Ah, yes!" He smiled suddenly and handed them over. "I knew there was something I had left undone. Lilacs are not so fragrant here as our country ones. Our Berkshire bushes will not be out for another fortnight. You will like Stockbridge, Mademoiselle Desportes, and find many things to paint there."

His easy assurance that she would visit his old home amused and touched her. She had met American hospitality before, but this was something more. He wanted her to share his own enthusiasms, which included an appallingly wide range of subjects. He had much to tell her of his brothers: of David Dudley, whose legal opinion was becoming rapidly the most respected in the country; of Cyrus and his financial success in the wholesale paper business. Cyrus was only thirty, but already he headed his own company. And then Stephen J.! He was bursting to tell her of this brother's adventures across the continent on the Western Coast. Stephen had studied law and been partner in David's firm, but when gold was discovered in California he had gathered his resources and set off by sailing vessel for the Isthmus of Panama. From there by long and difficult stages he had reached the Pacific and sailed for San Francisco. Only lately the family had received letters from that far-off frontier.

"No, Stephen has staked no claim," he told her. "Panning gold didn't appeal to him. He wanted to be one of the first lawyers in California. He landed in San Francisco with ten dollars in his pocket; but he writes that his shingle was hung out at once in Marysville, where he's had plenty of cases. They pay in gold out there."

"And is it true what I read, that they answer arguments with their pistols?" she inquired.

"Stephen didn't say, but he's got plenty of the fighter in him. He writes that California is the most beautiful place he has ever seen, with high mountains like the Alps in some places, and that the Bay of San Francisco with its islands reminds him of Greece."

"He has been to Greece?"

"Oh, certainly, and to Turkey. My sister and her mis-

sionary husband took him with them when he was a boy.
Stephen speaks Greek fluently. He keeps his journal in
Greek so he will not grow rusty. But just now his heart is
set on drawing up a legal code for the state of California.
There will be confusion till that is done, and he thinks they
could not do better than to adopt David Dudley's code for
New York."

"So this Stephen, he believes in keeping laws all in the
family." She smiled. "What brothers you are, one for another!"

"Well"—he joined in her laugh—"we all had to stick together when we were young. And now, I am perplexed.
Stephen wishes me to come to California, where there is
also a great need of preachers, and I have just received a call
to a church in New England. I should like to ask your advice, Mademoiselle Desportes."

"But how is it that I should advise you? I have met you,
to be exact, only once. We have exchanged letters—true,
but I have not heard you preach."

"Day after tomorrow you can hear me," he told her. "I
have been asked to fill the pulpit of Dr. ——'s church on
East Ninth Street. My brother David Dudley and his wife
will be pleased to call for you at a quarter to ten, and it will
make me proud and happy to know you are in the congregation."

She was waiting in Miss Haines' parlor in her best green
poplin, black silk dolman and bonnet with black lace and
bunches of green and purple grapes. It was not a new costume, and the hoops in her skirts were considerably smaller
than fashion decreed. But she had brought it from Paris,
and it had, she knew, "a certain air." She felt sure that the
tall, distinguished Mr. Field, who helped her into the open
carriage, and his handsomely attired wife were favorably
impressed by her appearance. They eyed her with well-bred
interest on the drive down Fifth Avenue, and exchanged
polite questions and answers.

"Henry has told us so much of you, Mademoiselle Desportes." The blue eyes that were larger and infinitely keener
than the younger brother's were bent upon her. "We have
been anxious to make your acquaintance. We should have
called upon you earlier in the winter, but my practice has
taken me often from the city."

"And I, too, have been busy," Henriette answered. "It is,

I think, better that your brother Henri should himself make the introduction."

"You are younger than I pictured you," Mrs. Field remarked. "You're not in the least what I expected."

"What you mean, perhaps"—Henriette reacted at once to the appraisal behind these words—"is that you would not at once mistake me for a school teacher, and perhaps you also wonder that I do not bear the marks of the ordeal I suffered in Paris."

"Oh, no!" Mr. Field answered quickly. "That was not what my wife meant, but according to Henry—"

"Yes." She broke in with a smile. "I can imagine that his enthusiasm, as you say in America, 'ran away with him.' Henri must be always the champion of some cause or some person—is it not so?"

She sat in the corner of their pew and watched the stylishly dressed women in their billowing silks and taffetas and poplins rustle up the aisle beside frock-coated men. A group of girls from an orphanage filled one section, and there were shabby individuals scattered here and there; but for the most part it was a representative gathering of the city's most conservative and prosperous families. She wondered what Henry could have to say to them. She tried to picture his youthfulness in that high, mahogany pulpit.

But when she saw him climbing the steps and taking his place on a tall Gothic chair she was struck by his dignity and unselfconsciousness. He was no novice to his calling, and there was authority in his manner when he rose and announced the opening hymn.

> "Awake, my soul, stretch every nerve,
>     And press with vigor on;
> A heavenly race demands thy zeal,
>     And an immortal crown-n,
>     And an *immortal* crown."

The words were new to her. She pronounced them carefully, trying to keep her accent like the voices that rose about her in a great surge of sound.

> "A cloud of witnesses around
>     Hold thee in full survey.
> Forget the steps already trod,

And onward urge thy wa-ay,
And onward urge thy way."

Singing that stanza with the rest she was startled by the
personal significance of those words. They might have been
written for her and for her alone. Had Henry chosen them
for her peculiar benefit in all that congregation? She lifted
her eyes from the hymn book to find that his were fixed
upon her face. It was no time or place for an exchange of
smiles. Neither he nor she moved a muscle, but they answered each other across the pulpit and intervening pews.

A cloud of witnesses around
Hold thee in full survey—

And then her head was bowed in prayer. She could hear the
tones of his voice, but his words were lost in those of the
hymn. "Cloud of witnesses"—the accusing faces of the Paris
courtroom came before her with such clearness that she
trembled in her corner of the pew. Only he and she in all
that congregation guessed what that phrase could mean,
what it had meant in her life.

Forget the steps already trod,
And onward urge thy way—

A wave of thankfulness flowed over her. It was not easy to
go on one's way without looking back. No, it would never
be easy, but somehow she felt it was not going to be so
difficult from now on.

The collection plates had been passed, another hymn had
been sung, and the congregation settled itself for the sermon. Henriette felt a sudden anxiety for that young minister
towards whom all the eyes were turning. He looked very
small behind the high desk with its great open Bible, small
and boyish. His serious beardless face was lifted in earnest-
ness from the page before him. His voice came clear and
vigorous as he took his text from Paul's First Epistle to the
Corinthians:

Though I speak with the tongues of men and of angels,
and have not charity, I am become as sounding brass or
a tinkling cymbal.
And though I have the gift of prophecy, and under-

stand all mysteries, and all knowledge; and though I have all faith, so that I could remove mountains, and have not charity, I am nothing.

She had long been familiar with the verses, but as he spoke them on that warm spring Sunday, they took on a new and personal meaning. He seemed to have chosen them, like the hymn, for her alone out of that congregation. She had begun by watching and listening with critical anxiety, hoping that he might create a good impression, yet preparing herself to make allowances for his youth and for crudities of delivery. But from the first she recognized, beside his gift of expression and his sincere and scholarly interpretation of the Scriptures, a latent power that commanded respectful attention. He had a way of illuminating passages rather than distorting them to fit his points, and he was not given to overstressing and elaboration. Eloquence, in the accepted sense of the term, was not his, but his lack of affectation and his own simplicity and goodness gave weight to his words. Hearing him preach, she thought, was like looking through the clear water of some deep and quiet pool where nothing on the surface marred what lay below.

But long before he was through she had given up analyzing his ability. Almost she forgot that he was her friend. She lost the circumstances of their acquaintance in what he had to say. Charity had never seemed a virtue worth cultivating until then. She had looked down upon it as a weak and negative quality. It was something that made one the object of patronage, that laid one at the mercy of others. Now he made her see how wrong she had been. She knew suddenly that charity in its highest sense might be stronger than all the more obvious virtues she had admired and tried to cultivate. She, who had been so proud and arrogant, so sure of herself and her own actions and opinions, she had lacked this greatest of all attributes. She had asked charity of others, but had she been willing to give it in return? She had prized her own independence, her sense of honor and the gifts with which she had been endowed, but she had not prized charity. She had not given it a thought. If she had there might have been no such tragedy in the Faubourg-Saint-Honoré.

She and the preacher of that sermon had little chance to talk together after the service or later at his brother's home, where Henriette had been invited for dinner. The David Dudley Fields lived in a large house between Fifth Avenue and Stuyvesant Square, and the other brother, Cyrus, and his wife had come for the meal from their near-by home. Henriette studied with interest these three members of a New England family. The brothers were so completely different in appearance and tastes, yet closely bound by inheritance and family loyalty. She had seldom seen so strong a clan spirit in three men of such varying personalities. Unquestionably David Dudley, the oldest brother, had the most original and brilliant mind of the three and by far the widest range of interests. He talked with ease and authority on matters of international importance. She found his knowledge of European affairs more stimulating than anything she had heard since her landing in America. She had been hungering for just such talk, and his response to her eager questions soon dominated the conversation about the dinner table.

Cyrus, she found less intellectual; but he also was a thoughtful commentator upon affairs outside the provincial limits. He had traveled extensively in Europe and had much to say upon political and social changes across the Atlantic. But his interests were more centered upon business affairs. He was shrewd, stubborn, and intensely practical. Like David Dudley, he had a commanding presence, and his height, aquiline features and red hair and beard made him noticeable. His eyes were not blue, but gray and deep-set under prominent brows. He gave the impression of hawk-like keenness, and he seemed to be charged with some inexhaustible fund of energy. There was an indomitable quality to this brother; a fierce and unshakable determination that Henriette sensed from the moment he entered the house.

"I should not like to cross his will," she thought. "He could be very ruthless. He is like the man who, once having put his hand to the plow, cannot turn back. Yes, he is more what I believed these Yankees to be—hard-headed, as they say, but also, I think, farsighted. Henri is not like either of these two. They are more shrewd and dominant than this youngest brother. He must take care that they do not overshadow him."

It fascinated her to study and compare their traits and resemblances. Henry was like a smaller, less toughly bound family edition. His features were not so sharply cut, his eyes milder, his mouth more generous but also less firm. Their minds and energies had already determined their characters and achievements, but Henry was still flexible, like half-formed clay.

"They are devoted to Henri," she decided. "They are helpful and loyal to him because he is their flesh and blood, but I think they do not quite take him seriously yet. To them he is still the little brother going to college in their made-over suits. But he will show them what he can do. He *must* show them."

Watching him across the table, she was filled with a great determination to see this youngest brother develop to the utmost all the gifts she knew he possessed, different gifts from the assured successful pair who were deep in discussion of the development of the Far West and its resources. She guessed his power, and she also guessed his weaknesses. This boyish modesty was charming, but it must not grow into lack of self-confidence. This enthusiasm for the minds of others must not make him neglect his own. He must not step back and let them pass him because he was so trusting and idealistic. Yes, she decided, he was at that stage in his career where he could easily be drawn up or down. He had not the flinty determination of these brothers. He had been endowed with a remarkable mind, but he lacked their practicality, their will to achieve. Still, he could be made to achieve. It ran in the blood. She felt it in him though he was himself unaware of it.

"I could make him succeed," she thought. "He needs a wind pressing behind his sails to drive him on the right course."

She flushed, embarrassed at her thoughts, and turned from them hastily.

After dinner she found it dull to sit with the two wives while the Field brothers retired to talk in the library. She would have infinitely preferred their conversation to the domestic duet of the sisters-in-law. Their interests seldom ranged from household activities, and their talk of clothes, meals, house furnishings and of the rising cost of wages bored Henriette since she could contribute nothing. It did not seem a major tragedy to her that the price of bed and table linen had risen, or that an Irish maid fresh from the steerage had the presumption to expect two dollars a week as well as board.

She felt instinctively that these wives regarded her with

suspicion and pity. They disapproved of the active part she
had taken in the dinner table conversation. Women should
rule their homes absolutely and leave international affairs
to their husbands. If they had no husbands they should be
especially careful to maintain a self-effacing manner, and
avoid laying themselves open to the accusation of unladylike behavior. How much Henry had told them of her past,
she could not guess; but they had evidently made up their
minds not to include her in the intimate circle of their completely feminine world. If she had been a spinster sister,
living in some sheltered home, at the beck and call of parents, married relatives, and nephews and nieces they would
have accepted her as one of the less fortunate members of
their sex. But she showed too much spirit in speech and
dress, and far too much independence in earning her own
living, to be altogether trusted.

It was a relief when the gentlemen rejoined them, and
Henry at last suggested that he see her home to Gramercy
Park.

It was too pleasant to ride in one of the crowded stages,
and though her escort offered to call a carriage, she convinced him that she preferred to walk. They took their way
with other Sunday afternoon strollers along the shady side of
Stuyvesant Square and north up Second Avenue with its
large houses and handsome doorways. The fine spring
weather had brought out more carriages than were usual on
Sunday in Manhattan, and the clatter of hoofs and wheels
broke into their talk. But they felt happy to be walking together. They responded to the sun and nimble air and to the
pleasure of each other's company. Henry's sermon was behind him, and he felt pleased with the impression Mademoiselle Desportes had made upon his brothers. Despite his
usual preoccupation with deeper matters, he was not unaware of her distinction and grace. To him she possessed
beauty, the provocative beauty of the unexpected. He could
not have told what she wore, but she knew he could not take
his eyes from her as she moved in a cloud of swaying green
and black, with dark lace making a shadow about her face
and clusters of artificial grapes bobbing against her hair. He
only knew that it filled him with secret elation to be there
beside her.

"I liked your brothers," she told him, "but most of all I
liked your sermon."

He flushed under her praise and looked so pleased that

she half expected to see him snatch off his high Sunday hat
and toss it in the air like a schoolboy.

"I'm glad," he said. "It seemed good when I wrote it; but
when I stood up and began I felt unequal to my subject,
almost as if it were presumptuous of me to interpret the
words of the Apostle Paul."

"You did not spoil them," she insisted. "It moved me,
what you said about charity, for you made me know my own
lack of it."

They had reached the gates of Gramercy Park, yet somehow neither he nor she went on towards the door of Number 10. Only a few people were in the small inclosure. The
old man who tended it opened the gate and greeted Henriette. He knew her as he knew all in the neighborhood who
shared this privilege. They found a bench under a horse-
chestnut tree, and the five-fingered young leaves made delightful patternings on her outspread skirts.

"There is a difference of opinion regarding various in-
terpretations of that chapter of Corinthians," Henry was
going on to explain. "I cannot quite decide myself whether
'charity' or 'love' is the more exact meaning. Even in the
original Greek it's hard to tell. 'Love' is, of course, a more
comprehensive term, and yet for that reason I hesitated to
use it. And then it has come to mean—" He broke off in
confusion at having become involved in so difficult a defini-
tion.

"Yes," Henriette answered without taking apparent notice
of his embarrassment. "It has come to mean much that
Saint Paul did not perhaps intend."

He smiled at her gracefully and laid his hat on the bench.
Somehow it seemed the most natural thing in the world to be
sitting in this sanctuary of green shade discussing love in the
abstract, while above them city birds were interpreting it in
terms far more shrill and personal.

## *chapter twenty-eight*

MAY WAS OVER, AND SCHOOL WAS OVER FOR THE LONG
summer holiday. The girls had departed with their families

for suburban retreats from the noise and heat of the city, and Miss Haines' establishment on Gramercy Park suddenly became very large and still, with echoing, empty schoolrooms. Only Miss Haines, Fräulein Schmit, Henriette, and the servants were left to fill it. Henriette was free to spend the summer there if she wished, and she planned to do so except for brief visits to several of her pupils' country places. But these would not be till August. June and July stretched before her with long uninterrupted days to spend as she pleased. She had looked forward to this time. It would be a chance to catch her breath after the busy winter of confining work. She would resume her painting again, she decided, and write her long neglected journal besides long letters to the friends across the sea. Yet the summer was slipping by, and she had done none of these things, for during those weeks the youngest Field brother had been a constant visitor.

He had been filling several pulpits in the city while he made up his mind whether to go West and join his brother Stephen or accept the call to duties nearer home. He, too, had plenty of time on his hands, and at first there were frequent excuses for his dropping in at Number 10 to ask Henriette's opinion on a variety of subjects. Of late he had discarded even these flimsy pretexts. He appeared each afternoon as regularly as clockwork for the simple and altogether too evident reason that he could not stay away. Sometimes they rode as far north or south as the stages could take them; sometimes they explored the half-settled regions along the water fronts or in the rocky, half-cleared squatter communities beyond the Reservoir; sometimes on excessively warm days they went no farther than the little Park or the quiet parlors where shutters dimmed the glare from the streets. Often Miss Haines pressed him to stay for supper and the evening, and Henriette could not very well discourage such invitations from her hostess. She approved wholeheartedly of Mademoiselle Desportes's friendship for this young minister. He supplied the masculine element that had been lacking in Number 10 and a new animation crept into the meals as the four gathered about the table on those long summer twilights. Perhaps, too, Miss Haines was more romantically inclined than she would have cared to admit to herself or her pupils. Certainly she was sympathetic to this visitor's absent-minded lapses when he heaped mustard on

hot biscuits instead of butter, or sprinkled salt on strawberries while his eyes remained fixed on Henriette sitting
where the slanting light brightened the soft frame of her
hair. She heaped his plate and refilled his cup as if she were
supplying the needs of a growing boy. But she asked his
opinion on many subjects and listened to his comments with
respect.

"A most unusual young man," Miss Haines often remarked after such a visit. "Really it's a comfort in these
days when so many are rushing off to the West with nothing
but gold and land speculation and making money on their
minds, to find one with good manners and principles left."

Henriette did not disillusion her about the possibility of
his also starting for California, though they discussed the
advantages and drawbacks to such an uprooting when they
were alone. In those weeks their conversation ranged far
and expanded like the balls of dried ferns that unfold to
miraculous greenness in a bowl of water. It was amazing,
they continually told each other, that they should feel so
alike upon nearly every subject under heaven when no two
people had ever been born and reared under such different
circumstances.

"I knew you would agree," Henry would nod with satisfaction, whether they discussed Louis Napoleon and French
politics, slavery in the Southern States of America, or a
mutual dislike of dandelion greens. "I knew before you
spoke exactly how you would feel!"

They had come a long way since the May Sunday when
they had first sat together on the bench in Gramercy Park.
Henry had left off comparing "love" and "charity" in the
Greek of St. Paul's Epistle to the Corinthians, for he was
revising his own version of love. This personal revelation
that looked out of his eyes had begun to disturb Henriette.
She had at first refused to notice certain signs. She made
excuses for the frequent calls, the eager confidences, the
sense of completeness in each other's company. She told
herself that he was lonely, that he had few friends with
congenial tastes, that he had known few women outside his
family. This was true enough, yet it did not explain the
growing conviction that lighted up his face each time they
met. She was afraid of love, and she had resolutely turned
her back upon it. She wanted to keep this new friendship
that had flowered so amazingly; she did not want to lose it

just when it had become satisfying and necessary to her. So she maneuvered conversation away from the dangerous channels of sentiment. She tried to overlook what she had no wish to see and hear. She threw out occasional subtle hints which she hoped would discourage ardor, without destroying congeniality. But her efforts were not successful. In fact Henry Field took no notice of them whatsoever.

"It is incredible that I should find love waiting to trap me on this side of the Atlantic, where I thought to be secure from it," she would sigh after he had left and the house was still. "I must put a stop to it at once. I would not for the world hurt him, and I cannot afford to let him hurt me."

But when tomorrow came, and when her visitor came with that look of secret exhilaration and complete faith in her understanding, she had not the courage to keep to her resolutions. One more day together shot through with this magic current of shared happiness could do no harm, she would reason. Tomorrow she might be able to break this thread that she felt drawing them closer together. For she, too, was happy, though not as she had been happy before. The wild clamor of startled ecstasy; the terrible restlessness and delicious pain no longer stirred her. What she felt now was something steady and strong and quiet that had crept upon her so gently she had not guessed its presence till too late to arm herself against its force.

"This cannot be love I feel," she argued. "It is too kindly and simple for that. *Mon Dieu*, if I had the right to keep it always! But no, for him it would not be enough. He is so young and inexperienced, and I know too much because I have been through the fires."

She saw herself suddenly as the burned-out shell of a house. The blackened walls remained. In time vines and weeds might cover them with green, but that was all one could hope for. The house would be empty. Yes, she told herself, it must stay empty. That was the penalty of fire and ruin.

And then, in July, he announced that he was going away —not far, he explained, but to spend a few weeks with his parents in Stockbridge; and he hoped that she would come for a visit. She shook her head and tried to make excuses which did not in the least convince him.

The afternoon was warm, but a breeze stirred from the East River as they walked up the familiar lengths of Fifth

Avenue. It was almost deserted in Croton Cottage, a small restaurant that faced the Reservoir and the Paupers' Burying Ground that lay behind the huge stone pile. They found a secluded table and ordered root beer and seed cakes while they rested before starting the long walk back.

"Why do you put me off with these excuses?" he asked her, resuming the subject she had hoped he would drop. "Why do you say it's impossible for you to come to Stockbridge when you know I want it above all things?"

"But it is impossible, Henri." She sighed and gave her little Parisian shrug that always enchanted him. "Why do you insist that I force myself upon your parents? You will return in a few weeks, yet you behave as if you were setting off for California—no less."

"Whether I go to California or not depends entirely on you." He leaned across the table to search her face. "Everything depends on you," he added in sudden intensity.

"Oh, but, Henri, how can you say that?"

"Because it's true, and I must say it. I have been trying to for weeks now. Surely you must have known. You must have guessed."

She felt a chillness creep over her though the heat was oppressive. It had come, then, all in a moment. Now there was nothing she could do to put him off. He had said the words, and more were coming—the hesitant, half-articulate phrases of love that she had waited so long to hear. Too late, she told herself; they had come too late. Yet they fell upon her like rain on parched earth, and the deep roots of her loneliness and need responded in spite of all the doubts her reason could muster. Love was all the more miraculous and dear because she had never expected to find it here, speaking its own language with alien accents.

"You are everything to me." The eyes across the table would not let her turn away. "Everything that has ever seemed good and beautiful and desirable in this world or— or the next—"

"Oh, Henri, please! Even you know nothing of the next world, but I know so much more than you do of this one. I cannot let you go on because each word you say only— only makes it more difficult."

Tears rose and filled her eyes. They came between her and his face, but she felt his hand, warm and urgent on her own. She ought to draw hers away, but she had no power to do so.

"Look at me, Henriette."

She felt herself answering his quiet command.

"Yes," he said. "I knew how you would look with tears in your eyes though I never saw them there before. Now I have seen you in every mood, and I love you in every one."

Long ago on the night of their first meeting she had known this same sensation; this feeling of completeness with another. They had been among many people then—now they were alone; yet it was as if they were close together on an island of their own making. She must wrench herself free while she could still command her feelings. She must resist the terrible temptation to answer his love with love.

"Henri." She spoke with all the ruthlessness she could summon. "You must listen to me. You are not practical, so I must be practical for us both."

How it dogged her always, that word! "I am a very practical person," she had insisted years ago with the Duc's eyes on her face. "We must be practical, messieurs." She could hear the very tones of her voice answering the old Maréchal and the Abbé. And now at another crisis of her life, the fatal word rose to her lips.

"You have given me too much already, Henri," she was going on, "—help when I most needed it, your loyalty and friendship, and now your love. You ask me to be your wife, and a man can offer nothing more to any woman. You overwhelm me, so that I can hardly say what I must. But, Henri, what you wish is not possible, not after all that has happened to me."

"What happened to you is also responsible for our being here together today. Don't forget that because the past was bitter. Oh, my dear, if I could make you feel what I feel you would not think the price had been too great to pay."

But still she shook her head.

"I am thinking of the price you also would have to pay. I need not rehearse my story to you. I thank God that you know every part of it. But there will be others who do not know, and who will find it out. It will always follow me wherever I go, and by whatever name I am called. You do not realize the difficulties, Henri, even though you are generous enough to share them with me."

"*Ad astra per ardua,*" he murmured. "To the stars through difficulties."

She smiled, thinking how natural it was for him to drop

into Latin even at such a time. But still she shook her head.

"We are not alone in the world," she pointed out; "at least you are not. We would have no right to bring my past troubles upon your family."

"My family will love the woman I love. I can count on them."

"Perhaps—you are very closely bound together. But family ties cannot be stretched too far. I come of a different race from yours; and, though you and I might learn to forget that, they never would. And then, there is another reason—"

"I shall not listen to it," he broke in.

"It is there, whether you listen or not, and it is a matter of mathematics." She tried to smile, but failed miserably in the attempt. "Women dislike mathematics, especially where their ages are concerned. Still, I must remind you, if you have forgotten what you must have read in Paris newspapers, that there is a difference of ten years in our ages."

"As if years had anything to do with us!"

"Ah, but they have when they happen to lie in the wrong direction. If those ten years were on your side it might be another matter."

"Hearts are more important than calendars. Do I have to tell you that?"

"We can never cheat time," she persisted. "We should be fools to think we could, and whatever else you and I may be, Henri, we are not fools. You are just twenty-eight and that means I am nearing forty. Your best years are all ahead, and, as women go, mine are not." She found it difficult to keep her voice steady. "It is not easy for me to remind you of this. But you have the right to wish for a marriage that will bring you all a man desires, and it might be that I could not give you that—" She broke off, then forced herself to go on. "I mean children, Henri, have you thought of that?"

He reddened at her words and shifted uneasily in his chair. No unmarried American or English woman would have thought of mentioning the possibility of unborn children as anything but impersonal gifts from heaven. He was taken aback, yet at the same time curiously stirred by her Continental frankness. He saw that her eyes swam with more tears, that she could not speak because of her deep emotion. He cleared his throat awkwardly.

"I can think only of being with you always," he reassured her, "as long as we both live and feel what we are feeling now."

She gathered herself for further protests, but he would not listen. A new quality of possessiveness had taken him. He seemed suddenly older and more determined as he refused to be shaken in his resolve. He would not insist upon her answer yet. He begged her for the present to put aside all her scruples and preconceived ideas on marriage. All he asked was that she give herself to her own feelings and let them guide her. He would accept the verdict of her heart, but not of her head. In the meantime he urged her to make the visit to his parents before she came to a definite decision. At last he persuaded her, though she agreed with some hesitation.

"Give me a week to prepare myself, Henri," she told him. "It will be best that you go to them first. Tell them all that they do not already know of me. Do not soften the story of my part in the Praslin tragedy because of your own feelings. Tell them that we have seen much of each other, but that we have as yet no understanding as to our future. And, Henri," she suggested tactfully, "the waiter looks discouraged. Perhaps he would like you to settle the bill."

It was a week since that afternoon and now she had almost reached the end of her long and dusty journey into New England. She had set off at eight in the morning, exchanging her place in the rumbling horse-drawn stage for another in one of the steam trains at the railway terminus uptown at Thirty-fourth Street. The heat had been intense from the start, and by noon the cars were like ovens, with smoke and cinders pouring in at open windows. Henriette shifted on the hot seat and tried to forget her discomfort. She unfastened the ribbons of her straw bonnet and wished that she might discard more than her lace mitts and shawl. She could not sleep because of the noise and jolting motion of the train and the annoyance of flies that lighted on her face. At first she had found diversion in the landscape beyond the window, a world that grew steadily greener and more pleasant at they puffed into less populous country. But at last the glare became too strong for her to stare steadily at rolling meadows and farms and woods, at busy small towns and quiet villages clustered about pointing white steeples.

Her head ached with the throbbing vibrations of the engine and her own anxiety that had increased with each day and night of that week. She was no nearer the answer that Henry expected, and she dreaded this ordeal of family as much as she had dreaded other more spectacular ones.

"Oh, why is he not alone in this world?" she thought under the grinding rumble of wheels on endlessly stretching miles of track. "Why must he be one of nine children, and these brothers with their wives and their ambitions? And his father—a Puritan of the old school, no doubt, who will believe the worst of me. I wonder if love can surmount these difficulties?"

She knew now that she loved him. Yet she was not sure that this would be enough for marriage in the New World. She had managed to regain her lost foothold on life after misfortune had struck her down. She had fought to win back her old independence and pride, and though she was sure of herself again in the capacity of teacher, she knew that the responsibilities of marriage were great and completely unknown. She loved this impetuous, idealistic young man too much to run the risk of failing him. Once she would have been as eager as he to plunge headlong into the wonder and excitement of this experience. But now she was older and wiser, and her wisdom had been painfully acquired. Yet she longed for marriage, all the more because she had faced the impossibility of it for herself.

"Only the heart knows its own boundaries." She had read that once, it did not matter where. They were comforting words to remember. Perhaps, she thought, even a heart could not measure its own capacity for love.

She left the train in midafternoon and changed to another that branched from the main line in the direction of Stockbridge. Henry had promised to meet her part way in the family carriage. He had explained exactly where and when to look for him, and the conductor seemed to know all about the plan as he helped her aboard with her bag and bandbox. Only a little longer, she told herself, before she would see him waiting for her with that look on his face that she both dreaded and longed to see.

The air was fresher now, and as the train rumbled on into the rolling ups and downs of green country she revived. So this was the New England from which Henry and his brothers had come! Even in that first meeting she had felt that his roots were here, and now she was more than ever certain of it. He belonged to these wooded hills; these rocky half-cleared pastures where cattle grazed among fern and juniper; these fields that sloped to quiet streams or made rough patchwork of green and brown in the distance. The

farms were smaller than she had expected, the houses boxlike
and plain beside the great red barns that dwarfed them. But
she liked their uncompromising simplicity of line, their
square chimneys and neatly stacked woodpiles. She liked
their sturdy orchards and small gardens bright with sun-
flowers, phlox, and delphinium, the morning-glory and scarlet bean vines about their kitchen doors. It was a hard-won
land, where even in the lushness of summer a hint of frost
lingered like some minor chord that haunts a melody.

It was the haying season. Everywhere men moved with
their scythes in long, swinging strides, or tossed and piled
the hay in yellowing heaps for old blue wagons to carry from
field to barn. The air was strong with sun and fragrance.
Henriette drew deep, contented breaths and waved to a
group of children as the train slowed down at a country
crossing.

She alighted at the appointed place—a country depot with
bales piled on a wooden platform. An old horse and buggy
were tied to a hitching post and Henry stood beside them.
They greeted each other with shy restraint, conscious of
curious glances from the train. Even after it had rumbled
on, they found it difficult to speak. There was so much to
say after seven days of separation. He stowed away her
things and helped her up, spreading a homespun coverlet
over her lap.

"To keep off the dust," he told her gravely as he settled
himself beside her on the seat and took up the reins. "Gid-
dap, Boney."

"Boney?" she questioned as the white horse turned into a
side road and set off at a surprisingly brisk jog for one of
such apparent age.

"It's really Bonaparte," he explained with a smile. "She
was named that before she came to us, and it hardly seemed
appropriate. Boney suits her better, don't you think?"

"Much better," Henriette agreed. "She is no longer in her
first youth, but she appears very wise."

"There's not a road hereabouts she doesn't know. When
Father used to drive out to visit church members, he could
sit back and think out his next sermon on the way home.
She always brought him back safe and sound, and it was a
great comfort to mother. Boney has traveled all over Connecticut, too; but since father gave up the church in Haddam she has got about less than she used to."

"Your father does not preach each Sunday now?"

"No, though he often fills neighboring pulpits when there's need. Now that he has retired and David and Jonathan and Cyrus have put the old parsonage in order, he has leisure to revise his sermons. Several have already been published, and more will be. By the way, I've finished an article on certain aspects of the Catholic Church. I want to read it to you and ask your advice before I submit it to the *Evangelist*."

"And your book on the Irish Rebellion. You have not laid that aside?"

"No, but I was moved to set down certain arguments for and against the Catholic Faith. It seemed the right time to express something of my feelings. I hope it may be published. See!" He broke off and pointed with his whip. "That's Bear Town Mountain over there. You will be glad to know the bears have all gone."

"How beautiful it is, this country! You did not tell me it would be so green, or that it would smell so sweet."

"It always does in haying time. I helped my brother Jonathan pitch hay in the back meadow yesterday. It's four years since I've done that, and I'm rather stiff today in consequence. Mary Elizabeth warns me I shall grow fast to a desk if I'm not careful."

"Mary Elizabeth—she is your younger sister?"

"She's just a year younger than I, and the only one left at home now. But Jonathan and his family live a little way up the street, and David and his family are in their cottage near by for the summer. You'll meet a lot more of us here in New England."

"New England," she repeated. "It is more like England, certainly, than France. Yet I feel that I could be happy here."

He pressed her hand. The hopeful urgency stirred so strongly in him that it was contagious, though they were still reluctant to give words to what they felt. It was enough happiness for the time being to be riding together in the creaking buggy behind the old horse. Late afternoon light slanted in long golden fingers across hillsides and fields and between tree trunks when woods closed about the road.

"Are you tired, my dear?" he asked after a long silence. "Was the journey too long?"

"Very long, but now I could wish this part of it would be even longer." She leaned back with a soft sigh. *"Je suis très contente."*

*"Moi aussi,"* he responded with a fervor that made up for his accent.

Near another farm they passed a lanky youth driving cows home from pasture.

"Evening, Henry," he hailed them.

"Evening, Seth," Henry answered, waving the whip. "One of the Wells boys," he explained. "An old friend of mine."

"I should hardly call him an old friend, Henri," she protested; "rather, I should say, an early friend."

"You're right." He smiled. "I stand corrected."

The sun was setting behind the hills that enclosed the Housatonic valley as they turned into the village street under great arching elm trees on either side. At the far end the slim white tip of another steeple rose above more trees; and nearer by, the substantial houses with their lawns and gardens were all warm with reflected brightness from the western sky. A far clock was striking six, and the delicious smell of freshly baked bread met them even before they came in sight of the square brick parsonage.

Boney quickened her pace from a jog to spirited trot. They rattled into the yard almost before Henriette realized that she had reached the end of her journey. In the reunion with Henry, in the beauty and sense of complete well-being that had taken possession of her as they traveled those miles together, she had forgotten her weariness and all her doubts and misgivings. Now they rose to engulf her as she faced the meeting upon which so much depended. For herself, she did not mind if this family disapproved of her. She had met far too much antagonism in the last few years to be easily dismayed. But for Henry's sake she cared to make a good impression upon these people. His eyes were so loving and anxious she must not fail him.

A girl in a blue cotton dress was bending over a flower bed; but at the sound of wheels she set down her watering can and came hurrying with outstretched hands. She was young and fair, with broad brows under smoothly parted hair and clear, thoughtful eyes that lighted in eager responsiveness.

"She is kind and intelligent," Henriette decided after the introductions were over and they walked together up the flagstone path between orange lilies and phlox. "We shall be friends."

Submit Dickinson Field, mother of seven sons and two daughters, stood in the doorway, a small woman nearing seventy in a plain cotton dress and lawn cap and kerchief. She had been beautiful in her youth, and in age she was still lovely to look upon with the fine features and color only a little dimmed by years of activity and fulfillment. Her eyes were soft and kind in their framework of delicate wrinkles, and her lips kept a half-smile even in repose. "I have given my best to life," that radiant old face seemed to be saying unconsciously, "and it has given its best to me in return." Henriette felt the warmth behind the greeting in the hand that closed over her own.

"Come in," she said with cordial scrutiny. "Come in and rest you. My, but you're a little body to have come across all that water!"

"But I did not swim the Atlantic, you know," Henriette responded with a smile.

"My boys and girls are all travelers, too," the pleasant old voice was going on. "Emilia Ann lived ten years in Turkey; Stephen's in California; David and Cyrus and Henry and Mary Elizabeth here are all back from far parts; and Timothy—"

She broke off and turned away. She could never speak of this second son without tears, for Timothy had been lost at sea somewhere off the coast of South America fifteen years before.

"Yes," she went on, "they all want to see far places but me. I've been content to stay at home and let them see the world instead."

"They have brought the world to you, madame," Henriette told her while Henry beamed upon them both.

("So far, so good," Henriette thought as she put on a fresh dress and brushed her hair. "But I have not met his father.")

The room she had been given was simple to the point of bareness, but the curtains and bed linen were snowy white, the homemade rugs and blankets woven in plain, soft colors. The bed, the chest of drawers, the washstand, and two chairs were of cherry and maple. She liked the variation from the mahogany, walnut, and rosewood of city houses. There was no wardrobe, merely a row of wooden pegs for her dresses, and the mirror was very small. Evidently the matter of feminine adornment played little part in this household. Yet both mother and daughter had been appropriately and freshly dressed, and one of them must have taken pains to arrange the glass vase of flowers on the chest. She fastened a tea rose in the ruffles of her green and white muslin before she answered the ringing of the supper bell. Henry waited at the foot of the stairs to conduct her to his father. The pressure of his hand was reassuring, though she also felt that he was bracing himself for the meeting.

The Reverend David Dudley Field had a presence that filled the house with Old Testament dignity, though he was less tall and commanding than she had expected. As he rose from his chair to greet her, Henriette was struck by the spare erectness of his figure and by the angular beauty of his features. The silver-white hair that almost touched his shoulders grew away from the high dome of forehead that dominated the whole face. The eyes were deep-set and searching. Later she was to discover that they were blue and capable of kindness as well as intensity, but on that first meeting they appeared dark and almost fanatical under jutting gray brows. For the rest, his nose was long, large, and straight; the cheek bones, high; the chin, sharply prominent, and the mouth, tight-lipped. A somber austerity wrapped him like a mantle, and behind that stern old face the flame of the spirit was almost visible. So, Henriette thought, the prophets of old must have looked—Isaiah, Ezekiel, and Jeremiah. He would never falter in performing whatever the Lord might call upon him to do. Almost, she believed him capable of sacrificing a son or a daughter to the Will of God, as Abraham had been called upon to offer up Isaac.

Yet he turned fond eyes upon his two children and spoke grave words of welcome to their guest.

"Mrs. Field"—he addressed his wife as formally as if they were not nearing the completion of fifty years of married life—"let us go in to supper now, for Henry and I must uncover the young melon plants before dark."

Henriette stood with bowed head at her place while he delivered the blessing before their meal. He seemed, she thought, to be speaking with an intimate Presence to whom he was used to confiding the simple details of garden and barn as well as more complex matters of the spirit.

Supper, in this New England household, delighted her with its simple perfection. Fresh bread and butter and cottage cheese; a platter of cold meat; a pitcher of milk and a bowl of strawberries were spread on the table with its white cloth and willowware china. A country girl who helped in the kitchen took her place among them as a matter of course and was included in the family conversation.

"Jonathan raised these strawberries," Mrs. Field explained with pride. "He's promised us a mess of early peas soon. I expect you've had them for weeks in New York. The season's later up here in Berkshire. Jonathan's very pleased with his garden. He'll want to show it to you, Miss Desportes."

Mary Elizabeth was almost as eager as Henry to talk of world affairs. She had traveled with Cyrus and his wife and showed unusual gifts of observation and insight in her questions and comments. Besides studying the classics under her father's instruction, she had attended a female academy in Albany. Like Henry she expressed herself well, and Henriette discovered that she had already contributed a number of articles to newspapers upon her foreign experiences. It was pleasant to compare personal reactions to European cities, and to discuss the latest news from France, Italy, and England. Between Mary Elizabeth and her father a peculiar bond existed. Though he seldom joined in the conversation, Henriette noticed that he listened with interest and watched this youngest daughter with tender regard. Once only he addressed their visitor directly, and she was startled by his reference to Paris and by his giving the French pronunciation to her name.

"I found Paris a beautiful city, Mademoiselle Desportes," he remarked. "There were great extremes of poverty and vice as against ostentation and luxury, but no more than in other capitals, and the French people impressed me by their buoyancy and thrift and by their good manners."

His son and daughter exchanged amused glances.

"We never worried about Father wandering the streets of Paris by himself," Henry explained. "Stephen told me that some one always brought him back to their hotel if he lost his way."

Henriette thought that such a remarkable old face would have awed any Frenchman into respectful solicitude. Yet she felt before him something of what she had felt when she had faced the Judge and Chancellor in the courtroom. It was as if his austere goodness made others turn inner scrutiny upon their own shortcomings. One felt this Minister of the Gospel not only had been chosen to exhort the faithful, but also had been endowed with an almost supernatural power to wrestle with the hosts of Satan. Her own worthiness was about to be tested by unflinching standards. Woe to her if she should be found wanting in his eyes.

They rose from the table. Henry and his father went out to the garden; Mary Elizabeth and the helper went into the kitchen to wash and wipe the dishes, while Henriette and her hostess repaired to the parlor. An overflowing workbasket was brought out, and Mrs. Field drew close to the window to make the most of the failing light. Henriette watched her bent over yarn and knitting needles as a woolen sock lengthened under her busy old fingers.

"Yes," she looked up and smiled, "I can knit socks with my eyes shut, all but turning heels. My sons still like to wear the kind I make. I used to be a good hand at spinning wool and flax when I was younger, but with the mills turning out such good cloth it hardly pays to do your own weaving nowadays. I make my husband's shirts still, and I always wash and starch them and his socks myself. These socks are for Stephen in California," she added, holding out the half-finished piece of knitting, "but dear knows how long it will take to send them so far!"

Henriette offered to help with some mending, but her hostess would not hear of it.

"No, no, you sit and rest yourself. This first evening it's your privilege to be idle. Tomorrow you can lend me a hand with a quilt I'm patching if you've a mind to and Henry makes no objection. He'll want to take you calling, maybe. He's told every one on both sides of the street all about you."

"Henri is too kind and generous, madame," she ventured. "I am sometimes fearful that he does not see faults in those he——" She broke off, not wishing to commit herself too far.

"Yes, I know, he believes the best of every one. All Henry's geese were swans when he was little, and now he's a man it's the same way. Not that I mean you by that," she added with her wise, disarming smile.

"Henri has—has told you of me?"

"There, I can never get used to your saying his name in French. Makes him sound so outlandish some way, but I guess he likes to hear you do it. Yes, whatever you do and say suits him. I've known that a long time now. He's told us plenty about you and your troubles, too. You've had more'n your share, but I hope you've seen the last of 'em."

"Thank you." Henriette was touched by the genuineness of the old woman's sympathy. "My troubles seem very far off here in your house where it is so serene and comfortable. I do not wish to bring them into your midst, for I have respect for a family such as yours, and though it would be an honor to become a part of it, perhaps I have no right— after what has happened. There are many who believe the worst of me, madame, things that I could not even speak about to you. To the day I die this tragedy will be with me. I cannot unravel the tangle of my life and knit it over again as you might unravel that yarn in your hands."

"I guess there's not a one of us but would like to pick up a few dropped stitches," the kind voice answered as the needles clicked on in the gathering twilight. "No, you're not the first to wish you could make over the past, and you won't be the last, if that's any comfort. But I say, never put the past between yourself and the future. If Henry loves you and you love him, that's for you both to decide."

"Oh, madame, your life has been sweet and good and beautiful with no dark places to mar it. I can see that, and so perhaps you do not know what evil things the world can say and think. Suppose, for argument's sake, that I had commited grave wrong. Would you wish your son to marry such a woman then?"

"I'd rather see a son of mine married to a woman that loved him—" The needles stayed poised in stillness before the voice went on in soft conviction: "Yes, I'd rather he did, even if she might have fallen from grace, than to have him marry without love. There, don't you ever press me so hard again, and never let Mr. Field hear me say such a thing. It's heresy, maybe, but women know some things that men can never fathom for all their learning."

Mary Elizabeth came in just then, and their conversation ended. After she had set an oil lamp on the table, she brought a large Bible which she laid in readiness.

"Father and Henry are through in the garden," she told her mother. "They're washing up in the kitchen and will be ready for prayers in a few minutes."

Presently the two men and the young household helper appeared and took their places about the table. Mrs. Field laid down her work and joined them. It was absolutely still in the cool parlor, except for the fitful, sleepy calling of birds in near-by trees. The lamplight threw a warm circle about the reverent small group and a heavy sweetness from rose bushes laden with bloom came in through the open windows.

"Let us turn to the Book of Proverbs for our evening lesson." The Reverend David Dudley Field took up the Bible and began to turn its worn leaves. Deep and compelling as the tones of a bell, his voice reached out to the farthest corners of that quiet room.

*"Who can find a virtuous woman? for her price is far above rubies. The heart of her husband doth safely trust in her, so that he shall have no need of spoil. She will do him good and not evil all the days of her life. She seeketh wool, and flax, and worketh willingly with her hands. She is like the merchants' ships; she bringeth her food from afar. She riseth also while it is yet night, and giveth meat to her household . . ."*

Henriette kept her eyes fixed on the folded hands in her lap. She dared not raise them to the face of the preacher, or to Henry, whose look would have been too hopeful for her to bear. She could only listen with the blood throbbing at her temples, knowing that she had been singled out for this particular challenge.

*"With the fruit of her hands she planteth a vineyard . . ."* The words continued. *"Her candle goeth not out by night. She layeth her hands to the spindle, and her hands hold the distaff. She stretcheth out her hand to the poor; yea, she reacheth forth her hands to the needy. She is not afraid of the snow for her household . . ."*

A great gray-green moth fluttered close to the lamp. But the voice did not falter. Henriette looked up and saw the hand that brushed it away. In the light that long forefinger made her think of those solemnly pointing New England steeples. She was struck by the resemblance.

*"Her husband is known in the gates, when he sitteth among the elders in the land. . . . Strength and honour are her clothing; and she shall rejoice in time to come. She openeth her mouth with wisdom; and in her tongue is the law of kindness. She looketh well to the ways of her household, and eateth not the bread of idleness. Her children shall arise up, and call her blessed; her husband also, and he praiseth her. Many daughters have done virtuously, but thou excellest them all. Favour is deceitful, and beauty is vain; but a woman that feareth the Lord, she shall be praised.*

*Give her of the fruit of her hands; and let her own works
praise her in the gates."*

Long after prayers were over and they had gone their
separate ways for the night, Henriette lay in the darkness,
hearing the echo of those verses from Proverbs. They mingled strangely with the faint guttural of frogs in some far
meadow and the chirping of crickets like summer's own
throbbing pulse. Yes, she knew why Henry's father had
chosen that passage. She and he understood each other all
too well, though gulfs of age and tradition and differing
beliefs separated them.

"Seach your heart, O strange woman," were the words he
had been asking her, "and see if you can do all this for my
son."

## *chapter twenty-nine*

THE DAYS IN STOCKBRIDGE WERE A REVELATION TO HEN-
riette. She was revived by the clear, enlivening air with every
breath she drew, and no less revived by contacts with the
remarkable personalities gathered into this narrow valley
folded in by the Berkshire Hills. She had not yet heard the
principle of "plain living and high thinking," but she felt it
here in the homes to which Henry brought her. He beamed
with undisguished pride as he conducted her from house to
house along that elm-shaded street or drove her to outlying
homesteads in the pleasant countryside. Everywhere hospitable doors were thrown open, and the Dwights, the Can-
nings, the Williamses, the Sedgwicks, and other neighbors
made her welcome, first because the son of their former pastor had seen fit to bring her with him, and later because a
congeniality of mind and interests had sprung up instantly
between them.

They knew the world, these New England men and
women, who had read and traveled widely, and who were as
well informed upon the latest news from the Continent as
upon country doings. She knew that they must be aware of
her identity and of her connection with the Praslin case.

Many perhaps disapproved of her part in it, yet there was
no hint of this in their cordiality. Some dropped into French
with her, and the sound of her native tongue spoken in so
different a setting was a continual amazement and delight.

There was a memorable all-day excursion to Monument
Mountain with a dozen congenial spirits. They drove as far
as the road could take them, then climbed the last steep
stretch on foot and ate lunches from baskets. Half the countryside lay spread out below them, looped and laced by the
pale thread of the Housatonic. There was an adventurous
trip to the sunless depths of Ice Glen, where the ladies of the
little party squeezed through the narrow rock caves in their
full skirts with considerable excitement. There was another
outdoor luncheon on the shores of the Stockbridge Bowl
at which particularly lively conversation flourished. The
Charles Sedgwicks came from Lenox, with Miss Catharine
Sedgwick, the author of "Hope Leslie" and "The Linwoods"
—those picturesque novels of domestic life in New England.
Henriette found this plump, plainly dressed woman in the
sixties stimulating company with her shrewd and witty
comments on matters foreign and domestic. They discussed
Thackeray's latest work, "Pendennis," and compared their
reactions to Elizabeth Barrett Browning's newly published
"Sonnets from the Portuguese." Both were admirers of the
poetess, but Henriette was forced to confess that she had
not read the works of Mr. Nathaniel Hawthorne, the novel-
ist from Salem, who ranked, to Miss Sedgwick's mind, with
the foremost fiction writers of Europe. With the sister-in-
law, Elizabeth Sedgwick, she exchanged views on educational methods, for this woman's Berkshire School for girls
had won an enviable reputation.

She listened intently to Judge Sedgwick and David Dudley Field taking opposite sides on points of legal controversy. She prompted Henry tactfully when he held forth on
those days of Revolution in Paris when barricades had been
set up and the palaces stormed. And then there was the visitor from Boston, a lawyer named Sumner, whose words
struck like sparks when he spoke of slavery in the southern
states. They could not long avoid that subject, for agitation
over Henry Clay's Fugitive Slave Act was in the very air
they breathed. Henry had talked of it, but it was Sumner's
eloquence that kindled her indignation. Compromise, he insisted, could never be effective. To have admitted California

as a free state was only a concession to northern sentiments. It could never compensate for this greater concession to the South—the Fugitive Slave Act that not only prohibited aiding escaped slaves, but required citizens of free states to capture such fugitives and return them to their slave owners. Who could keep such a law to the letter, he asked them, and not be guilty of committing a crime against all their principles of liberty and the rights of man—white or black? His fiery appeal stirred her as she had not guessed she could be stirred by the politics of these unknown United States.

The party broke up in the late afternoon, still arguing, discussing, and comparing views.

"You did not tell me, Henri"—Henriette turned to him with mock reproach before the group scattered—"that I should find here a new Parnassus, and drink at the Castalian spring!"

They were pleased to have her compare their mountain and countryside to the ancient abode of the Muses. Her enthusiasm was contagious, and even those who had been prejudiced and skeptical of her before found themselves disarmed by her quick comments and by the unexpected facets of her mind. They responded to her wit and repartee, and if they were slightly startled, not to say shocked, when she raised her skirts higher than propriety allowed to scratch a mosquito bite, they reminded one another that Mademoiselle Desportes was French and therefore to be allowed certain liberties.

"These mosquitoes," she remarked with a vigorous slap to emphasize her feelings, "they do bite my legs!"

Henry saw nothing out of the way in her naturalness. In his eyes her every move and word were perfection. He moved at her side in a blissful trance or waited impatiently for her coming when they were separated. Pride and wonder in her filled his days and nights, making him more absent-minded than usual. His mother smiled and his sister shook her head over his lapses, but his father took no part in their tolerant amusement. His presence was a shadow that lay long and disturbing across the sunny greenness of those days. Henriette knew that, for all his polite hospitality, this stern old man was not reconciled to her presence.

In a way she liked him better for that. His reserved and unflinching standards were in keeping with the strictness of his own moral code. He had more power and strength than all his vigorous family, and because she had learned through adversity to be strong and uncompromising herself, Henriette understood and honored him. Sometimes, when his lips tightened and that sudden flame lighted behind the clear gravity of his deep-set blue eyes, she was conscious of strange conflicts beneath the quiet exterior; conflicts that rose from the core of his being like stirrings of a hidden volcano. He had not won his peace without struggle. She still suspected him of wrestling with the Devil and all his hosts. No, she did not smile at the hell-fire and brimstone convictions which her more liberal generation could not share. She did not condemn him for hardness, since hardness was something she had come to respect. She did not think of this old minister as narrow or bigoted, but rather she recognized him as one who had set up more exacting rules and obligations for himself to follow in the game of life. He had not yet accepted her into the circle of those who carried on the heritage of his flesh and bones. She would have to convince him of her right to belong there, and so he quickened the challenge she had come prepared to meet. Until he gave the signal she would wait. And she must keep Henry waiting although his urgency was growing pathetic.

Jonathan Edwards Field lived in a low wooden house halfway up the street with his children. His wife had died a year before, and already it was rumored that he would marry again. This brother, Henriette found genial and easy to know. Like the older sons he was large-framed, with reddish hair and ruddy skin. He had studied law in David's firm, had practiced it later in Michigan, and he now took part in county politics. But his heart was in the land that had called him back. Henriette went almost daily to this home, helping to gather berries and vegetables in the garden, making friends with his two sturdy sons and pretty daughters.

David Dudley lived on the Hill, a steep shoulder of green that rose directly behind the village street. His acres were impressive in beauty and richness of growth. Trees old and young grew about the large, rambling house that was in marked contrast to the more compact, older dwellings in the Valley. His son and daughter were there, back from college and European travel, eager to exchange views and experiences with a former resident of Paris.

This oldest brother and his wife were less formal in their

country home than in the New York atmosphere. Henriette pleased David Dudley by her appreciation of the scenery he loved. Nature was this busy lawyer's relaxation and delight. Henry saw trees as vague mounds of green foliage, but to this brother each leaf and twig, each peculiar marking of bark and branch took on vital significance. He pointed out every variation to Henriette, praising her artist's eye that was quick to learn names and shapes, that never mistook maple for elm or confused birch with ash and beech. On a corner of his property stood a small frame house, square and weathered but with crude dignity to the carving about the door. This was the Mission House that had been built more than a century before from oaks hewn in what was then a wilderness. It had housed John Sergeant, man of rare gifts and learning, who had answered the call to bring the Gospel to the Stockbridge Indians. As long as he lived, David Dudley Field told her, it should be preserved, a tangible reminder of the spirit that had first blessed the Valley.

"Yes," Henriette had agreed, laying her hand on the solid wooden door, and bending to peer at the worn sill over which the feet of white and red men alike had passed. "The spirit lingers here. One feels if good or if evil has been done in a place. I could ask nothing better than to live in such a house."

From there she and Henry often walked along the crest of the hill where the road ran between pasture and steep fields that sloped to the clustered houses of the village.

"If there is a more beautiful prospect than this," he told her on one of their visits to the Hill, "I have not yet seen it. Perhaps it is because most of my childhood is bound up with this place that I feel as I do. When Father used to read of the Holy Hill I always pictured it something like this."

Later he pointed out to her a great granite boulder that rose high on the crest and commanded a wide view of the Valley, the nearer green hills, and the more distant purple ones. Some ancient cataclysm had split the rock almost in half, and in that deep cleft a maple tree had taken root and grown in vigor.

"I used to come and sit for hours here," he confessed shyly, "and think all the things that boys think. I learned the Greek alphabet under this tree, and once when I was very young I preached a sermon standing here all alone with my bare feet braced in that crack. A family of robins nesting near by were my only congregation, and I'm afraid they were not greatly impressed by my theology."

She turned to him in quick response, smiling fondly at the picture he drew.

"Ah, my little Henri," she said, "you were young to feel the call! I should like to have known you then, but I can almost see you so, like a child St. Francis. Come, let us go down to your first pulpit."

They sat for a long time on the boulder with the stubborn-rooted maple shading them from the afternoon sun. Shadows deepened in the green hollow of fields below. The delicate silver coil of river was bright and smoke rose, blue and faint from the chimneys of houses that already she had come to know and call by name. At the far end of the street the white steeple of the old meetinghouse dominated the scene. It must, she thought, have marked Henry for its own long ago, though he had been unaware of it.

"What are you thinking of, Henriette?" He leaned towards her with his loving, serious face that still seemed boyish to her as on the occasion of their first meeting, though now she knew every characteristic change of expression that could take him. "You have grown so silent."

"I was thinking of you, Henri, and a little of myself, too, and how strange that we should be here together. I am almost afraid when I think of it, and I must believe that it is not by mere chance that we have come to this place, to this stone that is older than any living thing, that will be here long after we are both gone. It is like—like a sign to us—"

She broke off and laid her hand caressingly on the rough lichened surface beside her, warm in the sun.

" 'A house built upon a rock.' " Henry's hand closed over hers, and he drew closer. "Ours must be like that. No, my dear, it was not chance that carried me so far to be near you in your time of trial, and it was not chance that brought you across the water to me. We must never be afraid to think of it, even though it is beyond our understanding. Only fools could be so blind as to doubt a Divine Providence, and this rock shall be our sign, as you say."

"But, Henri, to think that Divine Providence should single us out of a world of people! It is too much for me—"

"Yes," he echoed simply, "it is too much."

He dared to kiss her then for the first time with the familiar hills and valley, the gray boulder, the maple tree, and the ghost of his boyhood for witnesses. She closed her eyes and let past and present and future mingle in a daze of incredulous delight. Over the warm response of her senses the air blew fresh and fragrant with the spices of summer. In her ears the hum of unseen insects was clamorous as the louder beating of her heart, of that other heart so close to her own.

He had been a boy to her till that moment, but now the pressure of his lips and arms told her that he was a man, needing her as she had despaired of ever being needed. The long, lonely years of waiting fell away like dried forgotten fruit crowded from orchard boughs in the miracle of spring bloom. She did not question the miracle in herself though it had come out of its appointed season. The sweet unused sap of her youth rose the stronger in her because it had retreated before treacherous frosts. In sudden wonder and thankfulness she knew that early blight had not killed, but only deferred her blossoming.

They hardly felt the road ruts under their feet as they descended the hill with an orange sunset flaring before them. They did not speak till they came in sight of the Parsonage.

"You will let me tell them tonight?"

"No, Henri, not yet."

"But why? Whether we speak or not, they will feel our happiness."

Still she shook her head.

"Your father," she reminded him. "He is not yet ready for this. No, do not say that he is. I know better."

Reluctantly he agreed, though it was difficult for him to contain his feelings.

They ate supper hurriedly, for they had been invited to attend a gathering at the Sedgwick home in Lenox and would drive there with David Dudley and his family. The reception was to be in honor of the great actress Fanny Kemble, who spent her summers in a cottage near by. Henriette dressed with particular care. In a happy trance she put on her best cream-colored mull with bands of moss-green trimmings, made over a green underbody. The neck was, perhaps, cut lower than village standards allowed, so she added her black lace scarf and let her hair fall in ringlets at either side of her face. Peering in the square of looking-glass before she went downstairs to join Henry, she was startled by her own reflection. It was not merely that her eyes were brighter and her cheeks more flushed than usual. A new softness, an inner radiance had taken her features, so that they seemed strange to her. She had seen this in others, but she had never hoped to see it in herself.

Henry looked his best, too, she thought, as she slipped her arm in his and felt the swift, possessive touch of his hand closing upon hers.

The five-mile drive through the fragrance of early evening was a delight. She hardly knew what others said or what she answered as the horses trotted on and on. Henry was silent beside her, but it was a silence that they continued to share. As darkness deepened about them they touched hands now and again, not for reassurance so much as for the sheer delight of feeling that incredible response. The lights of the Sedgwick house streamed out to meet them, and guests were already arriving on foot or alighting at the broad stone carriage step by the hitching post where a lantern hung in festive anticipation of the evening.

And what an evening it was, from the moment they crossed that threshold till the last carriages clattered off through the quiet of the sleeping countryside! The Sedgwicks welcomed their guests with such gracious ease of hospitality, making as much of townsfolk as of their more distinguished visitors. Henriette found herself talking with animation not only to Mr. Charles Sumner, whom she had already met, but to the Boston lawyer Rufus Choate, to President Mark Hopkins of Williams College, and to an older poet and editor, William Cullen Bryant, with a handsome bearded face that reminded her of a Michelangelo head. Henry had spoken with awe of this Massachusetts-born poet and of the great power he exerted as part-owner of the *New York Evening Post;* but Henriette was not in the least awed by his appearance or the weight of his editorial influence. She found him friendly and eager to listen to her comments.

"Mademoiselle Desportes," he had said at their introduction, giving her a long look of interested approval, "I have long wished to take you by the hand."

"Here it is, Monsieur Bry-*ant*," she had said, smiling up into the dignity and benevolence of his face. "I am happy to take the hand that could pen 'To a Waterfowl.' You did not know, perhaps, that my pupils in France once ordered me to translate it from English into French. That is how I came to know how great a poet you are."

"Repeat it to me, mademoiselle," he had urged.

"No, not here with so many people. But I will write it down for you if you will promise not to be critical."

He promised, charmed by her vivacity and her quick Parisian shrug.

"You express yourself in English far more easily than I speak French," he confessed. "I can read it, but the accent!" He smiled and sighed. "My spirit is willing enough, but my tongue is weak."

They laughed together, and then he went on more seriously.

"I meant what I said just now, mademoiselle, from my heart. I have long wanted to tell you of my admiration for the way in which you conducted yourself in that terrible calamity. As a newspaper man I followed your testimony to the smallest detail, and now that we meet I know that my respect was well deserved. I only hope that America will not disappoint you in the future it offers."

"I thank you," she acknowledged his praise. "You will understand, since you already know so much of my past, why I wish only to live in the future, and in the present," she added with a quick smile of appreciation, "which it seems to me could not be improved upon."

They talked for some time together. He, too, had spent his youth in New England, he told her, and he often returned to Great Barrington, where he had studied and practiced law in his twenties, snatching such leisure as he could to write poetry. He was eager to hear her impressions of America; to draw out her comparisons between Paris and New York. By the time Henry joined them she and this poet-editor were already friends.

"I believe you know him better in ten minutes than most people would in ten years," he whispered fondly. "He's considered very grave and dignified, but he laughed at something you said just now. Come this way. Catharine Sedgwick tells me Mrs. Kemble will give her reading in the back parlor, and you must not miss a single word or expression."

Henry had already heard the great actress give one of her readings, but Henriette had not been able to attend the performances in New York the winter before. It seemed extraordinary to have journeyed to this remote village to enjoy

the privilege of meeting this famous daughter of England's
most famous theatrical family. But here she was—a superb,
glowing creature whose very presence made a stage of the
floor boards on which she stepped, whose voice seemed to
vibrate with the lost tones of her aunt Sarah Siddons. One
forgot a certain heaviness of feature in the spirited flash of
brilliant dark eyes; in the sensitive quiver of lips and
nostrils.

"She is more than beautiful," Henriette whispered to
Henry as they watched her take her place at a small table
by the bay window. "She shines like that 'rich jewel in an
Ethiop's ear.' "

She was most curious to see this woman to whom she felt
drawn by the bonds of common misfortune. Both had
shared scandal and censure and weathered the storm of personal shipwreck. Henriette, like all the others gathered
under that roof, knew Fanny Kemble's tragedy and the
courage with which she had surmounted it. They were all
aware of her early meteoric rise to the position of foremost
actress of her day on both sides of the Atlantic; of her re-
tirement from the stage at the height of her success to marry
the prominent Philadelphian, Pierce Butler, whose clash with
her views concerning marriage and slavery on his Georgia
plantation had ended in a humiliating divorce case and enforced separation from her two daughters. She, too, had
met slander alone. She had stood in the ruins of all that she
had built her hopes upon, and had not been crushed by the
weight of its collapse. Overbearing, generous, tactless, and
inspired by turns, Fanny Kemble the vivid and unpredictable raised her proud, dark head, and a hush fell on those
sedate New England parlors.

Only the art of Rachel had moved Henriette to such answering emotion. Tonight, with her senses keyed to the highest pitch of intensity, she missed not a single shade of meaning, not one exquisite inflection of that compelling voice.
Now it was Titania conjured up before them, the symbol of
all foolish, deluded womankind; now it was blundering Bottom; and now Ophelia, wringing all their hearts. "There's
rosemary, that's for remembrance . . ." The eyes and voice
of another woman stirred Henriette to old pain even in the
warm security of new joy. She knew that she, too, must
carry rosemary with her to the grave.

And then it was Macbeth who appeared before them,

waylaid by the Weird Sisters on a Scotch heath. Henriette felt Henry shift uncomfortably beside her as the murder approached. She saw Miss Sedgwick look anxiously in her direction and several guests exchange meaning glances. She kept her composure, knowing that her kind hostess and Henry must be wishing that Fanny Kemble had not selected this play out of all the rest.

> "Duncan is in his grave;
> After life's fitful fever he sleeps well;
> Treason has done his worst; nor steel, nor prison,
> Malice domestic, foreign levy, nothing
> Can touch him further."

The past rose suddenly to overwhelm her. She forgot the friendly faces all about, the crickets chirping in the peaceful country stillness beyond the windows. She was back in Paris with the cry of "Murder" ringing in her ears.

> "Canst thou not minister to a mind diseased,
> Pluck from the memory a rooted sorrow,
> Raze out the written troubles of the brain
> And with some sweet oblivious antidote
> Cleanse the stuff'd bosom of that perilous stuff
> Which weighs upon the heart?"

She trembled, hearing that cry that might once have been her own.

Later in the evening she was presented to Fanny Kemble. "Ah, Madame Kemble," she said, "there will be many to praise you tonight, but only I of all who are gathered here can perhaps know the true greatness of your art, for I have lived some of the drama you interpreted. I shall not trust myself to your 'Macbeth' again."

She did not sleep well that night. The varying emotions of those hours had been too much for her, and when the sun brightened the eastern window she rose and dressed herself. This was to be the last day of her visit, and she knew it would be filled with activity. She wished to make some gift to Henry's parents before her leave-taking, and she had decided upon enlarging a drawing of the house. She would go out and work upon it now before the household was astir. With her crayons and sketchbook in hand she stole downstairs. No doors were locked in the village. She slipped out alone into the morning freshness.

Dew brushed her ankles in chillness as she moved across the grass. The knobs of half-ripened apples fallen under an old tree were silvered with wet. Only robins marked her coming as she spread out her work on a bench under a tree near the vegetable patch. From here she liked the angle of the square brick house among its trees. Her hands moved with swift skill, outlining and blocking in flat color masses, preparatory to shading. She had been busy for some time before she heard the village clock strike six. The sun grew warmer on her shoulder and the parsonage chimney sent up a fresh blue feather of smoke. Some one must be astir in the kitchen, though the family would not gather for morning prayers and breakfast till seven. By that time she hoped to have finished her little study.

Just then a figure emerged from the house, and she recognized the spare frame and white hair of old Dr. Field. He carried some gardening tools and a basket as he came towards her between the rows of potatoes, beans, and peas. His eyes were fixed on the hillside beyond, and when he was within some fifty yards of where she sat, she saw him set down his implements, fold his hands, and bow his head. His lips moved in what she knew must be prayer though if he uttered words she was too far off to hear them. He was almost at her side before she startled him with a greeting.

"Yes, a beautiful day," he agreed. "I have just thanked God for it. I see that your hands are already busy with your gift of delineation. That is good. One who greets the early morning as a friend will not squander the future."

"Are you always up at this hour, Monsieur Field?"

"I find it the best time to work here in my garden," he explained gravely, "for it is after all a small counterpart of the world and one must labor without ceasing that good may overcome evil."

"Is it that you mean by evil these armies of weeds that wou'd choke your plants and vines?"

"Weeds, yes, and caterpillars and potato bugs—surely instruments of evil, if I may be permitted to say so."

Grimly he bent to capture one of the invaders on a potato plant. Such a remark from another would have sounded ludicrous, but this old patriarch lent dignity even to garden pests.

"But, monsieur," she persisted, "the caterpillar and the bug are not doing evil in their own eyes. How do you justify that in your destruction of them?"

He gave her the faint suggestion of a smile.

"The laws of life are hard to explain," he said, "but we must believe that we have greater potentialities for good than the insect in the grass."

She laid down her work and looked into his eyes with sudden directness.

"There is another question, Monsieur Field," she began, "one which I have wished to ask you ever since I came here to stay in your home. You do not accept your son's love for me or my love for him. Is it because you believe I am not all that a woman should be?"

"Why do you ask me what only your own conscience can answer?"

"Because that is not enough. I have come to see that such a family as yours is like a living tree whose branches may reach out in different directions but are all bound to the same roots. I would never wish to separate you from your son, for that would be striking a blow at both the root and the branch. I must know from your own lips today whether you are reconciled to a marriage between us."

"I know that you have undergone great suffering." He seated himself on the bench beside her, but his voice was still grave and detached. "Henry has told me of the evil that engulfed you, and that you proved your innocence."

"But unless I can prove that to you I am still guilty in your eyes."

"I see that you believe me a harsh man." His eyes searched her keenly from their deep sockets. "Perhaps I am. Yet I continually remind myself: 'Judge not, that ye be not judged.'"

"Let me put my question differently then. Suppose, on some path where I walk, I dislodge a pebble from its place and a flood is loosed in consequence. Do you believe that the hand or foot that moved the stone is responsible for the calamity? Must we pay the penalty for great evil that has come through some act of carelessness or omission?"

He shook his head.

"You seek an answer that would try the wisdom of Solomon, Mademoiselle Desportes; and I, alas, am not Solomon."

A long silence fell between them, broken only by the call of robins and the distant lustiness of a village rooster.

"Shall we pray here together?" he spoke at last.

"Yes, please."

She folded her hands and closed her eyes and heard his voice as if it were part of that summer morning.

"O Almighty and Merciful God, who knowest the secrets of all hearts and whether there be good or evil therein, look upon this Thy servant and this Thy daughter as they call upon Thee in the shadow of Thy hills. For Thou hast seen fit to bring her from afar through the troubled waters of grief and humiliation. Free her of old doubts and bitternesses, that she may in strength and joy use the gifts Thou hast bestowed in the new life opening before her. Bless her and keep her and him whom Thou hast also blessed. May their deeds be acceptable in Thy sight, and may Thy Spirit move them all the days of their lives. Amen."

He rose, but still he lingered by the bench, obviously struggling to say something more. It was far easier, Henriette guessed, for him to express himself in prayer, than in the more casual words of daily speech.

"I should like to feel that I had your blessing also," she ventured.

"It is yours." He took the hand she held out to him. Then, still holding it, his firm lips relaxed into a smile, and he added: "I think you are quite capable of answering your own questions, my daughter."

"Oh!" Her voice was a little tremulous with relief. "Do you call me that because you are a Minister of God, or because you are Henri's father?"

His eyes were gentle as they met hers.

"Henry's father and the Minister of God will always be one and the same man, I hope," he reminded her as he turned back to the potato patch.

*chapter thirty*

ON A BLEAK GRAY DAY IN THE AUTUMN OF 1851 THE REV-
erend Henry M. Field led his wife to the door of their new
home in West Springfield, Massachusetts. He was jubilant
as he pressed her arm in a surge of affection while they
stood together in the empty hall.

"Ours, my dear," he whispered. "Our first home, and you
will make it beautiful."

"Yes, my little Henri." Her hand was cold in his, and she
hoped he would not notice the shiver she could not suppress
under the folds of her cashmere shawl. "I will try, but you
must not expect a miracle."

"You have made me expect them."

His face still glowed, and he continued to see her rather
than the narrow hall with the four rooms opening from it in
somber bareness. They had been married since May, and the
summer had passed swiftly. They were still incredulous of
their joy in each other; of the wonder of days and nights together without dread of parting; of the revelation of shared
thoughts and intimacies.

Henry had managed a leave of absence from the church
duties he had assumed in this Connecticut River community
during that winter of waiting for Henriette to finish her
classes in Gramercy Park. After their quiet wedding and
some weeks of travel they had been glad to accept David's
offer to spend the summer in the Mission House on the Hill.
Life had been simple and idyllic there with the days and
nights unfolding before them like the soft procession of
flowers in meadow and garden.

It had been easier than Henriette expected to be part of
this large and dominant circle. The Field brothers, and more
particularly their wives, had not been enthusiastic, she knew,

over her entrance into the family. But once Henry had convinced them of his determination to marry this woman of
foreign speech and ways and rather too great notoriety, they
had accepted the inevitable and had been kind. If they regretted the marriage in private, they were loyal in public;
and between the old minister and his French daughter-in-
law there was complete accord.

The summer had been happy, even on certain days when
Henriette could not help reminding herself that there must
be many advantages to marrying an orphan. But she liked
the companionship of young nieces and nephews, who appeared at strange hours with strange requests of their new
relative, who had instantly been adopted as "Aunt Henrietta." She had enjoyed the excursions to remotely situated
friends and relatives; the little parties in her honor, and trips
to the city to choose furniture for the new home. Then there
had been the excitement of letters from abroad, overflowing
with felicitations. The Monod brothers were overjoyed by
the marriage for which they claimed to be responsible. Albert and Marie sent good wishes by every other ship and
across the Channel her old pupil, Nina Hislop, extended invitations to visit her in England. But the response from the
Rue du Harlay had been most unexpected of all.

Henriette had written Madame Le Maire of her good fortune and had enclosed a letter to Pierre. From time to time
she had contrived to send the old man small drafts of money,
and in a sudden burst of gratitude and affection she had dispatched fifty dollars from her savings. Henry had not criticized her generosity, and they had both discussed certain
comforts it would procure for the aging porter who could
not hope to continue much longer at his post. They had
given little thought to his response, knowing that letters were
not part of his stock in trade. And then, one hot day in midsummer, word came from Miss Haines in New York that old
Pierre had arrived. What to do with him? The newly wedded
pair had stared blankly at each other and met their first domestic problem.

"But how could I know that he would spend the money to
buy a passage to America?" Henriette had sighed. "Nothing
was farther from my mind."

"Well, poor fellow, he probably thinks you have married
a rich man. To a French porter all Americans are rolling in
money. Don't be upset. I will write to have one of the clerks

in Cyrus' firm see him safely on the boat for Hudson. We can borrow Father's horse and drive there to meet him."

"And then what? Oh, Henri, I do not believe he knows a dozen words of English, and with his rheumatism he will be less help than hindrance. I told him to use the money to go to a place in the country where old soldiers are cared for. Even if we do not pay him wages we cannot afford a man servant."

So old Pierre had made his appearance, considerably stiffer in the knees and more stubbornly devoted than he had been in Paris. His pride in "Mademoiselle" as he persisted in calling her, touched their hearts even though his presence became an increasing problem as the summer passed. Henriette's fears were justified. He spoke no English, and his hearing was beginning to fail so that there was little hope of his acquiring a passable vocabulary. Save for service in Napoleon's army he had spent his entire life in city streets, and was hopelessly ignorant of country ways. Vegetables and berries were foodstuffs to be purchased from shops and carts, not weeded and watched over. He could not milk cows or help with haying. His hands were clumsy at carpentry and tinkering of all sorts. If he was set to scare off crows from the cornfields, he trampled more young stalks than he saved; if they entrusted a patch of lawn to his care he invariably broke tools against rocks or cut down some favorite bush or plant. All he wanted was to stand guard in his blue coat with the worn braid and fling the door wide to possible visitors. But since most doors stood open in summer, and visitors walked in unannounced in that quiet community, old Pierre soon became a decided inconvenience. He christened himself *valet de monsieur,* though he knew even less of valeting than of gardening. Henry was long-suffering, but others were far from patient; and before the summer was over Henriette was at her wits' end.

In vain she had reasoned and advised the old man, suggesting as tactfully as possible his leaving for France when cold weather began. Stubbornly he refused all offers of a return passage.

"I always told them you would succeed in America," he maintained, "and now that you have done so I only ask to serve you the rest of my days. A corner by the stove, a crust of bread, a little wine and coffee—my wants are simple, mademoiselle, now that my dearest wish to come to America has been granted. You and Monsieur have need of old Pierre, and in time your children will need him too."

No matter how firmly she resolved to be ruthless, the trust and admiration in his eyes always disarmed her. She could never forget his devotion during her dark days, and so she made small tasks to keep him occupied and hoped that some way might be found to rid her of this unexpected burden. It was a comfort to talk with him in their native tongue, though she was continually reprimanding him for faults and urging him to be less intolerant of American ways. Still his shrewd French comments upon people and places often so perfectly matched her own that she could hardly hide her amusement. Above their protests he had insisted upon coming to West Springfield; even now he was dropping boxes and bundles and generally getting in the way of the men unloading furniture from a hay wagon.

Henriette was always to smile and sigh, remembering her arrival in that little town on the banks of the broad Connecticut River. Stockbridge by comparison seemed like a cosmopolitan community, more than ever dear as she stared at the frame houses along this other New England street. In summer greenness they might not have looked so plain and forbidding; but rains had swept the trees bare of leaves, and the gardens and lawns were everywhere brown and frost-nipped. She tried not to let Henry see how empty and dismal she thought it, or how much she wished that the square parlors on either side of the hall had not been painted a depressing yellow-green that would clash with the claret-brown of her chairs and sofa. She wanted to cry at the ugly iron stove that jutted into the middle of the dining room, crooking an elbow of pipe to the ceiling its smoke had already blackened; at the chilly bedchambers above the long uncarpeted flight of stairs.

Calamities beset her at every turn during those difficult days. First there had been the unfortunate episode of Pierre and the currant bushes. To get him out of the way while she directed the men unloading furniture, Henriette had told him to busy himself outside the house. Pierre, thinking to rid the yard of some dead-looking shrubs, had attacked them with a pruning knife. But his attempt at improving the landscape was short-lived. He had hardly cut one bush down and started on the second before a group of agitated women surrounded him. They protested in their language, and Pierre

even more volubly in his. Words flew like missiles, and the
old man brandished the knife and stood his ground as stubbornly as the massacred Swiss Guard on the staircase of the
Tuileries. It had taken Henriette's most emphatic French
to dissuade him from further destruction, and all Henry's
tact and persuasiveness to placate the ladies of his parish.

"But, Henri, how were we to know that these sad-looking
bushes were so greatly cherished?" she had sighed after the
disgruntled group had finally left.

"Of course you couldn't know, my dear," he had comforted, "but, you see, they depend on these currants. I suppose they saw their next year's jelly disappearing before
their very eyes."

"Ah, but they did look so grim and desperate, and now I
have made a bad start, just when for your sake I most
wished to please them."

Henriette's own efforts had proved even less successful
than Pierre's, and all because these new neighbors did not
share her sense of humor. She had been prepared for a
steady stream of callers those first days, but not for the donations of pie that filled kitchen and pantry shelves to overflowing. No visitor came empty-handed, and some brought
two and three varieties of this popular fare. Apple, mince,
pumpkin, squash, custard, and lemon meringue pies were
supplemented by every possible combination of berry. Henriette received these gifts with mystified gratefulness at first,
then with grim fortitude, since Henry explained that the ladies meant to be kind. After three days she was ready to
scream instead of expressing thanks at sight of a familiar
round shape wrapped in a napkin. And still they came.

"Oh, Henri!" she exploded in desperation. "Is there no
end to these pies? They descend upon us like one of the
plagues of Egypt!"

Henry laughed at her dismay and ate all he could. But
even his New England heritage failed him when it came to
having pie served for breakfast, dinner and supper.

"I don't wish to seem disloyal to the good ladies of my
congregation," he pleaded at last, "but I would be grateful
if Cassie Sampson could make us a rice pudding for supper."

Cassie Sampson had joined their household as "accommodator," and though Henriette found her so far unresponsive
and disapproving she had been thankful to place all kitchen
activities in her capable hands. Cassie had been recom-

mended as smart and thrifty, but Henriette wished that she
looked less like one of the pear trees by the back door
dressed in shapeless calico. She had arrived on their first
morning while Henry struggled with a smoking stove and
Henriette stared at two eggs cooked to the consistency of
bullets.

"You will please tell me what is wrong with these eggs,"
she had besought the newcomer. "I boil them and boil them
and they will not be soft!"

It had not been the best possible introduction. Cassie had
set to work with a will, but her eyes were shocked and her
lips grim. They had remained so ever since. In vain Henriette had spent her charm upon this nimble-fingered, silent
woman with ageless face and angular body who made her
own efforts seem awkward and childish by contrast to her
swift accomplishment. Cassie Sampson, she felt sure, would
not approve of wasting these dozens of pies; and yet something must be done about them.

The solution came to Henriette as she stood by the gate
after watching Henry leave with the doctor to visit a stricken
family some miles away. Her eyes had been drawn irresisti-
bly towards the eaves of the house and a narrow ledge that
ran along just under a small half-moon of window. In a flash
the remembered the picture in an almost forgotten book of
her childhood—gingerbread cakes in a frieze under the
peaked gable of a cottage. Why not try the effect? There
were certainly plenty of pies to be sacrificed, and Cassie was
hanging clothes to dry in the side yard; so no explanations
would be necessary. It would have been pleasanter to share
the experiment with a young conspirator. How Raynald or
Berthe would have entered into the spirit of it, or one of her
newly acquired nephews! She missed clear, impetuous young
laughter and the adoring looks she knew how to bring into
children's eyes.

The attic stairs were narrow and steep, and her billowing
skirts and petticoats were a decided inconvenience. But
with persistence and loaded trays she managed to transfer
eighteen pies from the pantry. The tiny window that looked
like a Cyclops' eye, stuck fast. She was showered with dust
when it finally yielded to her efforts. Her arms ached, reaching over the sill, and twice she almost lost her balance plac-
ing the pies upright. But the beam below held them well,
and she took pains to vary the design—now a thick crusted

top, now one with a crisscross pattern of pastry. At last they were all in place, and she went to her room to remove dust.

Foolish, she thought, standing before her mirror, to have wasted a morning in such childishness. Yet she felt young and gay as if she had been engaged on some secret adventure of her school days. Her eyes were bright as they stared back at her from the glass. Her cheeks were warm and glowing, and her hair had strayed from its smooth bands. Thirty-nine years old, she reminded herself, and she still felt young, almost younger than in the twenties that lay behind her. Once her fortieth year had seemed the farthermost boundary of life, the end of the road stretching before her. But roads seldom ended. They only dipped behind hills or branched in new directions leading into the unknown. Years were nothing when one felt strong and full of vitality. She loved and was beloved. Disaster and shame lay so far behind that only rarely now did their shadow overwhelm her. She had come to a strange world with grim determination to make the best of a ruined life, and suddenly the best of life had come to her, with all that she had ever hoped for laid in her hands. Well, perhaps, not all—it would be terrifying to have everything. But so much, so much where once there had been so little. She pressed her hands to her heart because there were moments like this when happiness seemed to swell through her in a warm, sweet tide of well-being.

Henry's socks met her eyes in an accusing heap in her sewing basket. She ought to sit down and darn them and mend the pocket of his second-best coat, and there were tablecloths to be hemmed, and napkins and towels. But no, she was too happy to give herself to such humdrum housewifely tasks. She ran to her little rosewood painting table and opened the lid. Inside, her cardboard sheets and brushes and crayons cried out to be used. She would paint a picture for the parlor wall to hide that ugly water stain—a little vase of flowers such as she had loved to bring in from the Stockbridge garden—a moss rose with fuzzy leaves, a pansy or two, dark as velvet, white clematis, misty against the blue background she loved, and a single drooping crimson spray of fuchsia. She would have it finished by the time Henry returned. She would tell Cassie Sampson not to disturb her for dinner. Almost, she believed, she could force herself to eat another piece of pie, she felt so charged with the urge to make her own happiness tangible on paper.

Henry returned that afternoon to find a cluster of out-
raged ladies gathered before his home, and he spent the rest
of the day in visits of apology. His wife was a stranger and
an artist, he explained with pride that still overcame his annoyance. They must not take offense if she brought strange
customs with her. The appeal in his eyes and voice helped to
assuage the insult. But Henriette was never quite able to live
down that frieze of pies which continued to haunt her eaves
long after their removal.

But even such mistakes and difficulties could not dim the
bliss of those first weeks together in their own house. Henriette had a genius for arranging and rearranging furniture
till the perfect combination was found. She could make a
room take on unsuspected beauty merely by the addition of
a picture, a mirror, a lamp or a bright square of cloth laid
over a table. She turned a cheerless upper bedroom into a
studio for herself, and one of the square parlors became
Henry's study, a wonder to callers with its mahogany secretary and leather-padded chair, its shelves of books that
reached to the ceiling, its clock shaped like a church, and
the Franklin stove with brass fittings where a wood fire was
always ready to be lighted. Pierre preferred charcoal, but
so long as firelight could be summoned Henriette did not
complain. Nothing mattered on those evenings when there
was no midweek prayer meeting to conduct, no sermon to
prepare, when with the crimson curtains drawn against the
chill darkness she and Henry had their coffee together from
the new flowery and gilt cups of French china.

Even the grimness about Cassie Sampson's lips could not
spoil their pleasure in this ritual.

"You and your foreign furbelows!" the stiff set of her
shoulders seemed to be saying as she carried in the tray.
"Why can't you drink your coffee at the supper table like
sensible folks?"

Henry remained blissfully unaware of this disapproval,
and Henriette did her best to ignore it. Cassie, she had decided, might rule absolute in kitchen and pantry, but elsewhere she must not intrude.

"Henri," she would chide fondly as he reached towards
the sugar bowl. "I beg you will stir your cup, for I have already put in three spoonfuls of sugar."

And he would smile at the reminder and settle back in
his chair. He had never known that such contentment of the

body could be combined with the mental stimulus she brought him. Even her mistakes lent an air of uncertainty and charm to each day. This Continental custom of coffee served by the fire delighted him, though noon dinner had been eaten hours before. No less than she, he was incredulous of their happiness. He marveled that this woman who had from the first so stirred his imagination should be here beside him, sharing his hearth and his home. Her presence in his life lent new importance to each thought, each act, each intimate small detail, for she charged whatever she touched with a zest and color peculiarly her own. He loved to look up from his desk and see her in the lamplight, bent over a piece of needlework or turning the pages of some book—like any other wife, he would tell himself, when all the time he knew there was not her like under the sun.

He loved an excuse to question her, whether it happened to be upon some problem of the world in general or of themselves in particular. She had a way of giving her whole attention to the matter, weighing it gravely with a slight tilt of her head, like a thoughtful bird. Her response might be a smile, curving the generous fullness of her wide mouth, or that little French shrug that never failed to enchant him, or perhaps she would speak with that swift discernment of thought, like an arrow speeding from the taut bowstring of her brain.

He could never make her understand what he felt that first Sunday when he looked down from the pulpit and saw her sitting in the pew reserved for the minister's family. He had served this congregation for several months the year before, but that pew had always been empty, as his life had been empty till she had taken possession of it. Such a wave of thankfulness and elation overcame him as he felt the reassurance of her eyes meeting his from under the gray bonnet with the cherry velvet trimming that he wanted to rise and read Solomon's Song of Songs instead of the less exuberant text from Ecclesiastes he had already selected.

"Ah, my little Henri!" she was thinking from the pew below. "How young he looks, and how good, much too good for this world and this very cold church!"

Outside, the ground was already frozen solid as iron, and though it was not yet November an edge of snow sharpened the air. Inside, the congregation's breath mounted visibly with their voices, raised in the opening hymn:

> "Must I be carried to the skies
>     On flowery beds of ease,
> While others fought to win the prize,
>     And sailed through bloody seas?"

How little, she thought as she tried to sing through chattering teeth, how little do they know about beds of ease! She was remembering in a flash the gilded scrolls and horns of plenty, the seductive cupids and garlands on a certain bed in the Faubourg-Saint-Honoré. She shivered, recalling its magnificence and the blood and violence that had sprung from it. What would these good people lifting up their voices about her think if they knew she had been part of all that? For a moment old panic seized her and she wanted to throw down the hymnal and run out through the white doors and down the church steps. But the momentary panic passed. The blur cleared before her eyes as she lifted them once more to the high pulpit and Henry's face.

She was sure of Henry and his love, and she had been sure of so few things in her life till now. Nothing should ever come between them, certainly not the past which she had put aside like a worn garment.

*chapter thirty-one*

"BUT, HENRI, THIS CANNOT BE POSSIBLE! YOU COULD NOT have understood what they said."

Henriette pushed the half-written letter to the Monods aside and regarded her husband with a puzzled expression.

"I'm afraid there's not the least doubt about it. Deacon Judd and Dr. Willard wouldn't have told me unless it were true, and I hurried back as fast as I could."

Once more he was telling her what he had learned by a chance meeting with two sympathetic members of his congregation—that this afternoon some twenty or more ladies of the parish would appear at the door without warning and expect to be supplied with a bountiful tea. This barbarous custom of discovering whether the latest arrival in the community could prove herself equal to such domestic emergencies had long been in practice. Henry, during his years of bachelor preaching, had naturally been spared this ordeal since it was an entirely feminine affair, arranged in strictest secrecy. If the unexpected guests were well received and ushered out to a loaded table, then the surprised hostess was the object of respect among her neighbors. If, however, she failed to rise to the occasion, if more particularly there was plain or scanty fare, she had failed miserably in that first requisite of a New England wife, which was to be a good provider. Fortunately two husbands had discovered the plan in time to warn the minister and give Henriette an hour's start.

"It's kind of a mean trick, I say," the doctor had added when he and the deacon had broken the news to Henry. "But you know how women can be about such things, and your wife wouldn't be expected to know our ways yet; so we thought we'd tell you what they're up to. You tell Mrs. Field to expect 'em round about four and then you take my advice and clear out. A tea-squall's no place for a man. And whatever you do, don't let on we told you!"

For once Henry's absent-mindedness left him. He realized that this was a crisis: one in which he could do little to help. The village clock was striking three as he hurried towards home feeling like Paul Revere with the British at his heels. He was breathless when he burst into the quiet of Henriette's upper room, and it took some minutes to explain the situation.

"But why should they come here when they have not been invited?" she questioned, mystified and annoyed. "Have they not plenty to eat and drink in their own homes?"

Henry had to confess that the logic of the surprise tea party was altogether beyond him. But he felt sure she would know how to meet the emergency. Henriette felt anything but sure as she rose to go downstairs.

"Well, first of all we're short on cream. The Reverend will have to go over to Blodgetts and see what they can spare us. Here!" Cassie rose and held out a jug to Henry. "You can talk 'em into letting you have some if anybody can do it. Hurry right back."

They knew she had taken command. By the time Henry had left, Cassie was moving from woodshed to stove, from pantry to table with the precision of a general marshaling his resources in preparation for the enemy advance. Orders issued shortly from her lips as she sifted flour, broke eggs, and measured sugar into mixing bowls.

"You tackle the china closet. I've got no time for that. Here's a dish towel. You better wipe every last one of the cups and plates and glasses. If there's a speck on anything it won't be overlooked. I'll need those two cake stands you put on the top shelf and all the preserve dishes you can muster."

"But if we have no preserves, what good are dishes?" Henriette faltered from the door.

"You leave that to me. I've been expecting this, but I did think they'd be considerate enough not to select a Monday with half the linen soaking-wet. Well, it can't be helped. Here's a piece of flannel for the silver. We won't have time to give it a polish, but you can kind of shine it up!"

Henriette found herself following directions meekly without further questions. She recognized the creative fire in Cassie Sampson's eyes. She felt awed by the power that emanated from this woman, willing the fire to burn, the cake batter to assume golden smoothness and hidden stores of preserved peaches and pears to appear from dark corners.

"I fetched them from my sister's last week," she answered Henriette's incredulous look. "Thought they'd come in handy some time, though I didn't count on it this soon. Better bring the tea and coffee pots out here, and I'll need another dish for butter."

"Oh!" Henriette sighed as she filled the orders. "If I had not been so foolish with all those pies! I begin to see now the reason for such presents."

"Don't you fret about them. 'Twouldn't do to serve folks back their own baking anyhow. Now you get that big platter for the cold ham."

"Ham, Cassie?" This time Henriette felt that she certainly could not believe her ears.

But there it was when she returned, a large boiled ham falling into thin pink slices.

"Where—how?" Henriette gasped.

"I've been keeping it," was all Cassie would admit as she sliced, "against some rainy day. I guess this is it, and no mistake."

Henriette did not question further. If the Angel Gabriel had come down to her kitchen and exchanged his horn for a wooden spoon and set to work, she could not have been more grateful.

"It's half past three," Cassie told her. "Time you went up-stairs and got spruced up. Let's see now——" She swept a strand of limp brown hair out of her eyes and surveyed Henriette critically. "Won't do for you to look too dressed up or they'll know they was expected. That green silk's your handsomest, but I guess you better put on that printed challis with the blue braid and be on the safe side. You can kind of make excuses for it when they come."

"A lace collar, do you think, or would a plain one be best?" Henriette meekly sought further advice.

"Well, maybe the lace looks a little mite too fancy. Stick to the plain one, but there's no harm in a breast pin and some cologne on your handkerchief."

As she went to her room and took out the dress Henriette marveled anew at Cassie Sampson. She had not guessed that she noticed, much less cared for clothes. Yet apparently she knew and speculated upon every article of her wardrobe. For the first time in those three weeks since Cassie's coming as accommodator, they had talked as woman to woman, not as mistress and maid. Cassie did not really disapprove of her, and she need not meet this dreaded avalanche of unbidden tea drinkers alone. Together they would contrive to meet the crisis and emerge triumphant.

"*Bien!*" She commended her reflection in the glass before she hurried downstairs again. "Cassie has chosen well. I should never have thought of the challis."

"Well, now you look as if you'd come right out of the top drawer," Cassie praised. "I just dusted the parlor and filled the woodboxes. You hung up everything in your room, I hope, for they'll manage to snoop the house through."

Strange words were falling from the lips that had re-mained sealed so long. Henriette listened as if she were hear-ing an unfamiliar language in those last frantic minutes be-fore the knocker sounded. Cassie's natural genius had far outrun her vocabulary, but. they understood each other as only two women united against desperate odds can under-stand and move in complete accord.

"I put the extra leaves in, and they'll be room for ten each side and one at each end," Cassie was saying from the din-ing room. "If more turn up we'll squeeze 'em in some way. Here, just give me a hand with this cloth, will you? It's a mercy you've got one big enough."

But when its smooth damask folds were spread out upon the lengthened table they stared at one another in dismay. A large rust mark showed prominently. How it had happened, Henriette could not explain, but there was no disguising it. All the other cloths were too small or already in the wash-tub, and no amount of maneuvering could bring the stain to the center where a pot of fern or a dish of apples might have hidden it. Even Cassie's resourcefulness failed her momentarily.

"We shall have to manage with a bare table," Henriette sighed, "or perhaps two of the smaller cloths put together."

But Cassie shook her head emphatically.

"Might's well serve tea without sugar and cream," she decided, "as do anything like that. Why, you'd never hear the last of it. No, we'll just have to brazen it out between us some way!"

Henriette ventured no further suggestions as they set the china and silver in place. Pierre was called in from the barn and given instructions about opening the door. He was to make no remarks in French or English, and he was to bow with restraint and make a good impression upon the ladies he had so incensed by attacking the currant bushes. Pierre beamed with approval and clicked his heels. At last the occasion he had been waiting for, but why had not Mademoiselle told him that morning in time to wax his mustache and give his blue coat a thorough brushing?

Henriette left him peering through the narrow glass panels beside the door in anticipation of the first arrivals while she returned to the kitchen.

"It is almost time," she said. "What are we to do about the tablecloth?"

Cassie drew a pan of perfectly browned biscuits from the oven before she answered. She stood by the stove, where the kettle rocked on a red-hot lid. Through the clouds of steam that rose about her, Cassie's plain moist face wore an ageless look, like a moon on the wane, but still holding its own against the elements. She rested her weight squarely on her two large feet and wiped her hands on the all-enveloping apron of horizontal blue stripes. So, Henriette thought, some ancient soothsayer might have looked above her sacred brews, and so she might have issued her warnings.

"Now you listen to me," she ordered as she shifted stove dampers. "You do same's I tell you to, and everything'll be all right. The sugar bowl's set over that spot now and when the time comes to move it you've got to act all put out and provoked. Yes, you've got to make a regular fuss so's they all stop talking to listen. You turn on me and point to it and say real sharp: 'Cassie Sampson, what do you mean by disgracing me in front of everybody with a tablecloth that isn't fit to be seen?' That'll be your part and you've got to sound mad's a hornet."

"But, Cassie, it was not your fault. I cannot have you taking all the blame."

But Cassie Sampson stood her ground.

"Don't you worry about me," she sniffed. "You got plenty on your mind without that. Just remember to make a big fuss when the time comes, and for the love of heaven get out of my kitchen 'fore you spill something on your dress and we have to explain two spots away!"

Henriette did as she was told. The spiciness of Cassie Sampson's baking cakes filled her nostrils, and her heart and eyes overflowed with gratitude. Her resentment at such outrageous spying of neighbors into the privacy of one's home faded before this evidence of unsuspected devotion. Where but in America, she asked herself, could such things be? Still, one could forgive America its crudities when they were compensated for by such loyalty.

The surprise tea party passed off without mishap, and the impromptu scene over the tablecloth was managed with real finesse. Cassie threw herself into the spirit of the occasion, and Henriette's reproof rang out with a dramatic zeal that would have done credit to the Comédie Française. The guests were decidedly impressed and discussed the incident before they separated at the gate to go their various ways in the chill November dusk. Everything, they agreed, had been above reproach, and she certainly set a good table if that tea was any sample. If it hadn't been for the tablecloth they would almost have thought she had got wind of their coming beforehand. But she had seemed so upset over that accommodator putting on a spotted cloth they felt sure the surprise had been complete. No wonder she had been embarrassed! My, but she had worked herself into a state over it, and the way she had lit out and scolded with those funny foreign words and gestures thrown in had been a caution, they all decided as they compared notes on the episode. They guessed the Reverend Field could have done a lot worse for himself as long as he had seen fit to take a wife from far parts.

It would have shaken them considerably to see their recent hostess fly to the kitchen with outstretched arms when the last guest was safely out of sight.

"Ah, my Cassie, but you are an angel from heaven!" she cried. And in a burst of gratefulness she reached up and kissed her impulsively, French-fashion, on either cheek. "You were *magnifique!* There is no other word. And the biscuits and the cake—did you see how they ate each little crumb? Did you hear how they praised the peaches and the spiced pears?"

"Well, you don't need to go into hysterics now it's all over," Cassie reproved in embarrassed pleasure. "You keep out of here in that good dress. I just see the Reverend sneaking back, so you go let him in. Tell him I've saved out enough for his supper. You can fetch it in to his study on a tray while I get the table cleared."

But Henriette lingered because she must somehow make this other woman understand the thankfulness she felt.

"You were so generous about the tablecloth. All the time I was feeling such gratefulness, and yet I must make myself say those harsh words to you."

"Shucks, that was nothing! Kind of like playing a game nobody but us knew. You certainly made things hum when you got under way. Had me scared for a minute or two there."

"Perhaps Henri will think we were wrong to do it. After all, I suppose, we did tell a lie."

"Don't you say a word to him. I guess women have got some privileges of their own in this world. We paid 'em back in their own coin and I'll take the consequences right up to Judgment Day! But you see what I mean 'bout a ham coming in handy."

"Oh, yes, yes! You are right. I shall leave all such matters to you in the future. I should have been taught to mix flour and eggs and sugar as well as to mix paints and crayons and play the piano."

But Cassie thought otherwise.

"There's nothing to cooking," she insisted. "Look at all the women that can do it. I'd swap the stove for a piano any day, but much good it would do me."

She stared at her large hands and sighed.

"You wish to play the piano?" Henriette tried to hide her astonishment. "But why did you not tell me this before?"

Cassie flushed to the roots of her thin brown hair and turned back to the crowded sink.

"I expect you never heard the saying, 'If wishes were horses, then beggars would ride'?" she volunteered sheepishly. "Guess I better let well enough alone, but I'd be satisfied if I could just play one piece."

"Why should you not play one? I will teach you. You shall have your first lesson this very night if you are not too tired."

Henry was sympathetic when she told him of the plan, and later in the great mahogany bed upstairs they laughed and sighed over the day's happenings.

"This eating and drinking—why should it be so important?" she demanded. "Food is necessary, and we should not spoil or waste it. But why must there be all this ceremony, all this fuss about it?"

"And yet, my dear, the French are the finest epicures in the world," he reminded her.

"It is considered an art in France, not a moral virtue. I do not condemn one who has no ear for music. Why should they think the less of me if I serve plain bread and tea or even no tea at all?"

Henry smiled in the darkness and was forced to confess he had no answer.

"But," he added, "we must not forget the miracles in the Bible that concerned eating and drinking—the water turned into wine; the feeding of the multitude from the loaves and fishes."

"Ah, miracles!" She caught at the word. "That is a different matter altogether. What I tire of is this petty vying from one kitchen to another."

"But you forget, my dear, because you have lived so richly and because your talents have brought so much to fill your mind, how little most women have beyond the world of their own kitchens."

"You are right, Henri, and I have been wrong," she told him in one of those swift, unpredictable changes of mood that were for him one of her chief charms. "I have been stupid not to see before that these pies and cakes and preserves are no less masterpieces than the works of Raphael and Michael Angelo because they vanish so quickly down people's throats. And it is a miracle to do what Cassie did this afternoon. What the flour and butter and eggs and sugar would have been in my hands—I do not like to think!"

"I prefer your gifts," he assured her.

"Ah, my little Henri, that is fortunate." She drew closer and sighed, a sigh half of contentment, half of apology. "But I am too often impatient of their looks and ways that are so strange to me. Yet I must be even as strange to them. Only this morning I misjudged Cassie Sampson. I thought her like those plants you call thistles—all stiff, sharp points. And tonight I find that the wish of her heart is to play 'The Last Rose of Summer.'"

## chapter thirty-two

IT WAS GOING TO BE A SEVERE WINTER. EVERY ONE PRE-dicted it and remarked on certain infallible signs. The squirrels were unusually active in their nut hoardings; the wild geese had started South ahead of schedule; and all the village cats were growing extra-heavy coats of fur. Frost had come early, and snow fell before Thanksgiving.

Henriette watched that first snow from the window of her improvised workroom and felt the stirring of old ecstasy and pain as the flakes began to whirl. Snow was the same wherever it fell, whether it dimmed the outlines of Notre Dame and the gray buildings along the Seine; whether it whitened the roofs and red barns of a New England landscape. Each year while she had eyes to see and a heart to remember she would dread that first sight of falling snow, not for the long months of cold it promised, but because a storm of memories would rise to envelop her even as the flakes swarmed in stinging whiteness. She would feel caught once more, like some traveler who finds himself walking backward through a storm he has already weathered; like the figure in the glass paperweight that had come with her across the Atlantic.

The few possessions she had brought from France were displayed on bureau and mantelpiece—all but this souvenir of the Faubourg-Saint-Honoré and a snowy New Year's Eve. That was too poignant a momento to be kept in sight or even to be shown to her husband. Some day, perhaps, she might trust herself to look at it unmoved; but that time had not yet come. Today, however, she felt a need to hold it in her hands again. Her fingers shook as she lifted the little globe from its wrappings and at her touch the miniature snowstorm began to envelop the small red-cloaked figure in a white flurry.

"*Mon Dieu*," she thought, "that this should be all that remains of those years which were so sweet and so bitter! This frail bubble of glass is still whole in my hands, though the giver of it—"

She broke off. After four years she could not think of the Duc de Praslin as dead. Impossible to believe that one who had been so alive and vigorous, so strong and good to look upon should be lying, hated and shunned, in a numbered grave. Even his children, whom he had so dearly loved, must have learned to forget their father's disgrace.

"And even I," she told herself, "who perhaps knew him better than any, even I have been forced to put an ocean between that past and this present. It is as if I, too, had died had been raised from the dead!"

At such moments, when crowding memories overcame her, she would feel a curious conviction that she had actually died and been born again. She would stand as she stood now, holding some trinket that had been intimately associated with the old life, and marvel that together they had survived those years of uncertainty and despair.

Old Pierre was coming up the stairs. She heard his slow, heavy steps that paused hopefully as they neared her closed door. It was an annoying habit he had formed, this method of telling her that he was lonely in this place where he did not matter to any one but herself; where only she cared or understood what he might say. His utter dependence upon her was growing increasingly difficult, the more so since he grew daily stiffer in his knee joints and more unyielding in his mind. Each night she and Henry discussed the problem of what could be done with Pierre, and as yet they had found no solution that would not be too painful to his feelings.

"*Entrez*, Pierre." Henriette could not resist the unspoken plea from the other side of the door.

"*Regardez—la neige!*" The old porter burst in, pointing to the windows with his chapped hands. "*La neige, mademoiselle.*"

She nodded and returned to her easel and the sketch she

had begun from memory of a bookstall on the Quai with the arch of the Pont-Neuf and the Ile de la Cité in the background. He hobbled to her side and regarded it intently.

*"C'est bon, bon,"* he praised after a long scrutiny. "I know the exact spot. You have caught the very look of the Quai. I can almost smell the river damp and hear it flowing under the bridge. Ah, yes, I marvel at your gift!"

He sighed and continued to stare as she laid on a pale blue wash for sky and mixed colors for the foreground. Presently Henriette laid aside her brushes and turned to study his face. She was struck at the way he had aged since his arrival. There was a dejected droop to his mouth, and his shoulders sagged. His hands hung forlornly at his sides, and his legs were bowed with rheumatism. She had seen bewildered peasants look just so as they waited in strange depots far from their own provinces. Pierre had come too far from home, yet he would never admit that to her, or to himself.

"Pierre!" She reached out impulsively and took his stiff old fingers in her warm ones. "I am not the artist you think me. No, do not protest. I know my own limitations. You fill in these outlines of mine with the longing that is in your heart. Your homesickness is mixed with my paints—isn't that so?"

"No, no, mademoiselle," he protested. "You are a true artist. You bring Paris back to me on that piece of cardboard. I will not deny that I often think of it and wonder how it goes in the Rue du Harlay and those boulevards where I used to walk. But you must not think for a moment that I wish to return. I am not complaining of this place, though it seems to me that you and Monsieur might have done better to remain in the city."

She repressed a smile and tried a different method.

"It is not a crime to miss one's own country, or to return to it," she went on. "See how the snow falls out there. It will be like that for many months, Pierre, only the drifts will grow deep and the cold will be more bitter than you have ever known. I should miss you if you left us, but I should be happier knowing you were in Paris where you belong."

"I belong to you." He clung stubbornly to the old refrain, but she saw his eyes remained on her easel.

"There is a old saying," she persisted, "that 'the heart's letter is read in the eyes'; and your eyes tell me what you will never bring your lips to say. You are lonely here. Tell me the truth: is it not so?"

"Can you tell me that you also are not lonely sometimes?" he asked her in turn.

"Perhaps I am. But, for me, love is here, and that is all that really matters to a woman. Love can take the strangeness out of any land, Pierre. For you, it is different."

"You mean—" He frowned to cover his emotion and looked away. "You mean that the old dog is not able to learn new tricks?"

"That dog should not be ashamed because he is faithful to his old ones," she comforted.

And so Pierre was persuaded to return. Henriette used the last of her savings to buy him a third-class passage to France, and she dispatched a letter to the Monod brothers asking them to take the old man in till he could be enrolled in a comfortable pension for retired soldiers near Passy. She missed her old friend more than she would admit to Henry or to herself. There was no one now to understand her French outbursts; no one to call her "mademoiselle" and remind her of Paris. He had been a blundering and difficult charge, but when he went he took with him another link with the old days.

Gradually she was beginning to know and sort out the various members of Henry's congregation. The men she found easy to classify and much less formidable than the women. There were so many more of the latter, for one thing: wives, widows, grandmothers, spinsters, and a few unmarried daughters. These were the first with whom she made friends, for youth continued to respond to her. The older women kept their reserve, and the wives were smug and suspicious and completely absorbed in their own households. If she tried to please them, they resented her efforts and decided among themselves that the minister's French wife was bold and gave herself too many airs. If she remained aloof and waited for them to make the first advances, she was criticized as being superior and stand-offish.

"They are so stiff in their ways," she would sigh to Henry after an afternoon of parish calls. "Their manners are like the horsehair furniture in their parlors, and they hoard their smiles as the squirrels do their nuts."

"Don't be discouraged," he would reassure her. "In time they will show you where they keep them."

Henry was right, but it took patience. He made few suggestions, though it was through one of these that she made her next conquest after Cassie Sampson.

"Dr. Willard tells me that Ora Newton is poorly again," he told her one day at dinner. "Her mother is a member of my congregation, and the daughter a poor conscience-stricken young thing. I think perhaps if you visited there you could do more for her than I."

Ora Newton, Henriette learned further from Cassie, was the only child of a widow who lived at the far end of town. They had a difficult time making ends meet by sewing for the village and frequently had to be tided through the winter by more prosperous neighbors. Ora was sixteeen and the apple of her mother's eye, but already she bore the signs of consumption.

"She was headed for it from a child," Cassie explained with professional relish. "You can always tell, some way. That Bates young one has got the look already. You mark my words, they'll never raise her to marry. Yes, you go see Ora this afternoon. Put on that plum-colored cashmere if you've a mind to, and carry your muff. She needs to have her mind taken off the next world now and then."

Henriette was shocked and curious.

"But surely, Cassie, this poor young girl does not know that she is going to die?"

"Oh, my, yes! She don't think of much else, and you wait'll you hear her go on about her sins. Here, I'll put up a basket of food for you to take along. Most any contribution comes in handy over to Newton's."

Henriette set out with vague misgivings. She had followed Cassie's advice and put on her plum-colored dress and matching bonnet. But in spite of her warm dolman and seal-skin muff she was chilled through before she reached the edge of town. Winter was at her heels. She felt its frigid finger upon her as she hurried over the frozen ruts. The road was still open enough for wheels, but the distant hills, the pastures and nearer lawns were already whitened with light snows. The Connecticut River below its banks was icy except where the open water of the main channel showed like the steely length of some gigantic coiling snake. Along its shores the willows strained in the wind that whipped Henriette's fashionably full, hoop skirts. She was thankful when at last she came in sight of her goal, a small red house behind two dark, symmetrical hemlocks.

With the coming of winter she began to understand why New England farmers chose red paint for their barns. It

answered the need for color in their lives through the long,
bleak months that stretched ahead. Mentally she made a
note to remind Henry to suggest that the ladies' sewing circle
dye the new material for pew cushions a rich crimson. Coming from him, the suggestion might be adopted, whereas if
she made it the ladies would probably decide on a service-
able brown, as dull as the old covers.

Mother and daughter welcomed her with open arms. She
found herself expanding under the warmth of their greeting
as she had not done in any home since her arrival. They
hung upon her words, and not the smallest button or ruffle
of her costume escaped notice. While they talked, the fingers
of her hostesses were active—the mother's over a skirt hem
she was binding, the daughter's with tiny scallops on a flannel sack. Ora helped with the light sewing when she felt
able, and her pale, almost transparent fingers were deft.

"Let me show you a stitch the Sisters in the Convent
taught me to do," Henriette offered, taking up a piece of
flannel. "See, like this. And when you join the chain, it
makes a pattern of roses."

The two were enchanted. Under Henriette's guidance
they soon mastered the stitch.

"Well, that beats all!" the widow Newton exclaimed. "I
never knew nuns gave a thought to fancywork. Now, long's
you're here to keep Ora company, I'll just run over to
Weeks's with this dress. I was hating to leave her here all by
herself."

The mother hurried off, leaving Ora and her visitor in
the kitchen together. Seeing that the girl looked flushed and
feverish, Henriette took the piece of sewing from her hands
and went on with the scallops. The kettle on the stove hissed
with a comforting sound, and the clock ticked away on the
shelf by the door. Ora lay back on the pillows that propped
her up in a large rocker and regarded her guest hopefully.
Henriette felt that something important was expected of
her, and for once was at a loss for conversation.

"My Henri has told me of you," she began, "and he
wished me to say that he will soon be coming himself to see
you. He has gone to Springfield this afternoon, so I came in
his place. Do you like to crochet as well as to sew?"

Ora nodded and continued to regard her visitor.

"In that case I will bring you some wool to make a shawl
for your shoulders. It is red," she went on, though without

receiving encouragement. "I think red is a pleasant color for winter, and it would become you."

Yes, she thought, red would be a great improvement on the gray wrapper that only accentuated the false brightness on those prominent cheekbones.

"I can't see as it makes much difference," the reply came dishearteningly. "I'll be going where it don't much matter what I wear 'fore long."

"I do not wish to hear you speak so. You are much too young not to—to care for color and pretty clothes."

Ora eyed her with surprise and picked at the afghan fringe uncertainly.

"You talk awful queer," she said at last. "I expected different."

"And what did your expect of me?" Henriette questioned with a directness that seemed to startle the girl.

"Well, I figured you'd come to discuss my spiritual state. You being the minister's wife, it's only natural you'd want to talk about my soul."

Aghast, Henriette laid down the work and faced her.

"I leave such matters to my husband," she said. "And to tell you the truth I know very little about this state you speak of."

The girl's eyes widened in shocked surprise, but Henriette paid no heed to that disapproval. With a quick, impulsive gesture she leaned forward and touched the fair hair strained back unbecomingly from the pale forehead.

"You have such pretty hair," she said admiringly. "It is the color of yellow primroses, and it would curl charmingly about your face with even a little encouragement."

"I haven't got much time left to think about curling my hair," Ora reproved. "When your days on earth are numbered—"

Henriette cut her short.

"That is all the more reason to look your best, to make your mother forget you are not well. Do you think God would have put beauty into the world if he did not wish us to enjoy it?"

"Well," Ora hesitated, "I don't know about that. But the minister we had before Mr. Field thought I ought to consider my spiritual state first, and it's not as if I could ever hope to get married."

The wistful appeal that crept into her voice touched Henriette. She rose and brought a brush and comb from the adjoining bedroom, and without further comment began to rearrange the soft hair.

"You see," Ora continued, though she submitted to the hairdressing without resistance, "I haven't experienced religion yet, and if I shouldn't 'fore I die—"

Once more Henriette broke in firmly.

"Ora," she said, "must you talk always of dying? Can you not think of something else for a few minutes?"

"But I'm going to die. I've known it an awful long time."

"We are all of us going to die"—Henriette stepped back and studied the side of hair that she had curled—"every one of us here in this world; so I do not see why you talk as if you alone had been chosen."

"Well the doctor from Springfield told Ma he'd be surprised if I got through the winter."

"Hush!" Henriette emphasized her command by a flourish of the brush and comb. "I will not listen to you. I am going to curl the other side now, and then I shall bring the mirror and let you see yourself."

Ora remained silent for a few minutes, and the work continued.

"I guess you must be same's they all say—frivolous," the girl spoke at last.

"Bien!" Henriette set the last strand in place and nodded approvingly. "So they say I am frivolous. Ah, well, there are worse things than that in this world. A woman should not be vain, but she should not neglect her appearance. Now, tell me if you are not pleased with your reflection?"

She brought a small mirror from the next room and held it up before the girl.

"Why"—Ora's anxious expression relaxed slightly—"I wouldn't hardly know it was me, but—"

"Now no more of these buts, if you please. I shall expect you to wear your hair exactly so when I see you next, and I shall tell Henri to report to me if you have not curls when he comes to call."

She seated herself once more and resumed the sewing. Her heart ached with pity for this frail, troubled child, but her spirit also rose in wrath at the stern doctrines that had taken such hold upon her. It was cruel enough that her life should be cut short by this fatal disease without her mind being haunted by morbid fears and confused ideas about her soul's salvation. Henriette could see that the time was indeed short. That was all too apparent on the innocent, plain face. But it made her the more determined to put what she could of youth and light-heartedness into the months that remained.

"I must distract her from these fears," she vowed to herself. "If I can only make her smile and forget the shadow of death for a few minutes, that will be all that I can do."

Twilight was beginning to creep across the snowy fields, closing in about the small house and the kitchen where they sat and talked. Their two voices wove a pattern of sound, with the steady ticking of the clock beating its relentless rhythm under their words. Henriette listened and responded, but she felt a strange, almost primitive sense, of holding some intangible presence at bay by the very power of her own will. She was more than twenty years older than this girl, yet Ora was already marked as Cassie had said. The shadow had fallen upon her while she was still hardly more than a child.

"It's not that I'm scared of being dead," Ora was confessing; "only when I think about dying, nights I can't sleep——"

A pang stabbed Henriette at those words. For a moment she felt almost suffocated by memories of a narrow upper room in the Rue du Harlay. Yes, she knew the panic of lying awake with nothing but blackness ahead.

"I guess I'm not very brave," the girl sighed.

"I was not brave, Ora, when I had to leave my friends and all that I knew behind; when I had to cross those miles of water alone and come to a strange country." She took the girl's hands between her own, as if she could somehow let her own vitality flow from palm to palm. "I do not think it will be so very different," she went on, "for that was almost like dying. I did not know what I should find on the other side of the sea where people would not speak as I spoke or perhaps even feel as I felt. But I found happiness in America after a while, and I can tell you not to be afraid, even when you cannot sleep at night."

"You mean"—the girl turned to her hopefully—"that maybe heaven will be like America?"

"I should not be surprised if it were. But you must ask Henri about that," she added hastily.

"Maybe I won't go to heaven." Ora's fears seldom left her for long. "You see, I've been such an awful sinner, and I haven't experienced salvation yet."

Impatience overcame Henriette's pity, and she faced the girl once more with brisk protest.

"Ora, you must not keep saying such dreadful things. You are not a sinner."

"Oh, yes, I am! Mrs. Field, you don't know how wicked I've been."

For a moment Henriette felt hysterical laughter on her own lips. She thought of newspapers, black with the inky horror of murder and her name; of the accusing eyes and voices of judges uttering words she could never forget; of those dark pools of scandal she had struggled through alone. And here she sat in the security of a New England kitchen listening to this poor child who insisted that she was a sinner in doubt of heaven.

"But what wrong could you possibly have done?" she heard herself demanding. "How can you be a sinner, Ora, when you have never been out of this little town?"

Afterwards, making her way home through the chill December dusk, she felt that she had been too hasty. What had the confines of a town to do with this searching of the secret places of the heart?

Lamps were being lighted in the plain, square houses along the village street. She could see into kitchens where women bent over stoves and families gathered for supper. Men hurried home carrying pails or bundles, and by the general store a group of loungers laughed at some jest—the low, throaty chuckle of men exchanging some sally not meant for women's ears. A horse and buggy jolted over the icy ruts, and she recognized Dr. Willard's huddled shape on the seat. He was heading away from town, from those lamp-lit windows, out into the bleak countryside where pain must be fought, as it was being fought in Paris, in West Springfield, and in houses the world over.

Passion, violence, love, hatred and sacrifice—she felt them all striving about her there in the gathering dark. They raged and flowered behind those frame houses she passed. Her neighbors' kitchens held them all, and those unlighted windows above that would later be pale oblongs of lamp or candle light—what could not lurk there of the bitter and of the sweet? Those chill upper bedrooms—might they not hold the beauty of fulfillment in their four walls? Might they not hide secrets, dark as those of the Conciergerie?

"Fool!" she called herself as she quickened her steps and

hurried towards the church and the familiar shape of her own house. "Fool, to think that good and evil are a matter of geography!"

## *chapter thirty-three*

You ask, dear friends, the views of Henri and myself upon this much discussed question of slavery.

HENRIETTE DIPPED HER PEN AND EMBARKED UPON AN-other sheet of the thin paper she kept for her foreign correspondence. It was the first opportunity she had had for many days to answer the last letter from the Reverend Frédéric Monod and his wife, and her pen moved steadily on over the pages she filled with the French words she so seldom heard nowadays. The parsonage was very quiet, and since Henry had left to attend a Congregational Conference in Hartford the day before, she had settled herself at his desk and indulged in the luxury of a fire. He would be back late that night, full of news to tell her and probably with a present in his bag—a new book, perhaps, or a pair of gloves. One could never tell what object his glance might light upon to admire and bring back for her pleasure or adornment. He had urged her to accompany him, as he had on several trips to Springfield, where he introduced her with pride to old friends and the most casual acquaintances. She would have enjoyed the visit to Hartford, but such journeys were expensive and already Henriette had taken charge of the household expenses and knew that extravagances must be carefully considered and resolutely curbed.

Yes, I suppose we might be called Abolitionists since we side most ardently with those opposed to the institution of slavery [she wrote]. You will understand the term better when you read the copies of speeches by Mr. Sumner and Mr. William Lloyd Garrison which I will also send you in a separate packet. Ever since my arrival in America the most vital topic of discussion has been the passing of the Fugitive Slave Bill, which has aroused much feeling in the North and particularly here in New England. Can you imagine being forced to turn from your doors an escaped negro who perhaps still bears the marks of chains and blows upon his unfortunate body, black though it be? Not only does this law deny one the right to shelter such a fugitive, but it further requires that one return him into slavery. How, one asks, can such injustice be sanctioned in a free country? I know that I could not find it in my heart to keep to the letter of the law were I personally to be put to the test, which I most earnestly hope I may never be.

Yet, as my little Henri admits, it is not so simple a matter as this. The runaway slave is but the symbol of something far more complicated and intangible, which involves the constitution of this Republic and the whole structure of the economic system of the South. The latter, Henri believes, is at the bottom of the trouble, and he grows very grave when I ask him what the end of it all will be. For, as you know, cotton is needed in France and in Great Britain, and it appears that only with slave labor can the supply keep pace with the demand. So what is to be done? The Abolitionists feel that there is but one course to take—free the slaves, even if in so doing the South becomes bankrupt. The Southern States refuse to be dictated to and even threaten to withdraw from the Union, and already there is a great agitation over this newly settled territory of Kansas, whether it shall be admitted as a slave or a free state. Each side claims the right to it and I can only say that it seems to me rather like a bone which two stubborn dogs are each determined to possess. A sorry state of affairs.

You have doubtless read of the arrival of Kossuth on these shores. He is the popular hero of the day, and there is much talk of the cause of Hungarian patriotism. I rejoice that he has found refuge in America even as I and other enforced exiles have done.

Do you smile at this championship of my adopted country? Do the agitations that rock this New World seem relatively unimportant to you who witness the present crisis in France? Louis Philippe is dead, and already the Revolution through which we lived, and of which we hoped so much good might come, is forgotten in this new imperialistic régime. It is hard for me to believe all that you write. So Thiers's influence is failing and this new

Napoleon's eyes are fixed upon another throne! I do not
know what I feel when I think of all that has happened in
less than five years. My head reels before the shiftings of
parties and persons.

She rose and lit the student lamp, laid more wood on the
fire and drew the curtains against the sudden darkness of
mid-December. She need not be interrupted by a summons
to supper. Cassie had gone to see her sick sister and would
not return till late. It was good sometimes to be alone, without demands, without the relentless procession of small
doings. She was grateful for such activity, for all that bound
her to Henry and the life he had chosen. She stood smiling
by the desk, thinking of his return, of his step outside and the
eager rush of words on his lips, the reassurance of his eyes.
Once more she took up the pen, and her thoughts began to
flow in the rhythm of French which lay behind her consciousness, ready to rise like a hidden spring of water.

Here I sit, secure and content [she wrote on], in a world
you do not know, while the Paris of which I was once a
part is shaken by new reverberations. First Revolution
and now, if what you predicted in your last letter comes
to pass, a Second Empire. Like you I have grave misgivings. I am too much of a Republican at heart to rejoice in
the return to imperialism. My grandfather would have
died happy if he could have known that another Napoleon
had been recalled to France. Yet I do not trust what I hear
of him. He is neither an aristocrat, nor an inspired peasant. He is, it seems to me, merely a stupid fellow upon
whom opportunity has smiled.

Ah, my dear, dear friends, how changed is the Paris we
shared! It is as if time had reversed our positions, for you
seem to live in a strange world, not I myself who have
journeyed.

You ask after my health and happiness. It is easily told
in the small space that remains. My little Henri is all
generosity and affection, and I can only say that he has
multiplied all that was good in life a hundred times over,
and he shares my difficulties with me. Already his influence grows in religious circles, though, between ourselves,
I feel he is destined for a wider scope than one church can
afford. His gifts are inclined to writing, rather than to

preaching. I notice that he is more happy and absorbed at a desk composing his sermons than when he stands in the pulpit delivering them. But for all that he has won the respect and devotion of his congregation.

As for my part, often I fail; but Henri is my unfailing prompter, and I try to be unobtrusively adequate. I attend all religious services and church gatherings, and return the calls of the ladies of the congregation. I visit the sick and take my place in the sewing circle and missionary meetings

*"Ciel!"* She dropped her pen and left the unfinished letter at a sudden recollection. "The 'Little Season'—I did all but forget it!"

With relief she saw that the hands of the clock pointed to a quarter past six. She had remembered in time to save herself the embarrassment of arriving late at the home of Mrs. Adam Weeks, where the affair was to be held. The invitation had come several days ago, and she had forgotten to mention it to Henry before his departure. It was unfortunate that he would not be able to attend. She sighed, thinking how she would miss his presence beside her, for social functions in West Springfield were still a little baffling and unpredictable. But she would go. She would take special pains with her toilette and array herself with the best her wardrobe had to offer, exactly as if she were going to the opera or an evening reception. Never should it be said of Mrs. Henry Field that she did not make the most of whatever Society had to offer!

Though her teeth chattered in the chillness of the bedroom, she hummed as she set the lamp on her bureau. This "Little Season" had a festive, almost Continental sound, she thought as she began to rearrange her hair. Seven o'clock did seem a rather strange hour, too early for a soirée, and there had been no mention of supper. But she no longer questioned the times at which her neighbors ate and rose and retired. It was unfortunate that she had not thought to ask Cassie what to expect of a "Little Season," for Cassie's advice had proved invaluable on more than one occasion. It was a pity, too, that Cassie should miss this first appearance of the bottle-green taffeta, with its low-cut bodice and black lace overdrapings on the skirt that boasted more yards of crinoline stiffening than any other in town. Cassie had almost worshipped that dress as it hung waiting for an opportunity to be worn.

She had forgotten how becoming it was! The brilliant color and luster of the silk set off her best points. It intensified the whiteness of her bare neck and arms, the sheen of her hair which she had brushed from smooth bands into curls, and greenish light into her eyes. The black lace gave an elegance and grace to the wide bell-shaped skirt that pleased her as she caught glimpses of it in the tilting pier glass that had been transported from New York at such peril of being shattered. She snapped on a pair of black enamel bracelets, sprinkled her handkerchief liberally with vervain toilet water and hurried down the stairs. She sighed at the necessity for galoshes and mittens, and for a woolen shawl to cover her head; but these would soon be discarded as the butterfly sheds its cocoon of dull protective wrappings.

Her spirits continued high as she left the dark house behind and started on her way. She felt exhilarated, walking abroad after dark with only the far sound of sleigh bells and the crunching of snow under her hurrying feet to break the quiet. These winter skies of America thrilled her with their high, unhindered clearness. The deep blue dome, she often thought, seemed arched to fit a race of giants. She knew where to look for Orion and the Pleiades, for the Big Dipper tilted above the pale steeple of Henry's church. The stars were particularly brilliant tonight, almost as sharply pointed as the tinsel ones she used to help Berthe and Raynald fashion to hang above the carved *crèche* at Christmas. But those two would be past all that now. They were no longer the children who had pressed close, whispering holiday secrets in her ears. Berthe was no doubt betrothed, probably married, and Raynald would be a tall young student with a man's deep voice.

The thought of the approaching season warmed her with joyful anticipation, for this would be like no other she had ever known. Christmas with Henry in a home of her own! Soon the house would be filled with spicy fragrance from Cassie's kitchen. She would ask the freckled children with whom she had begun to make friends, to take her to the woods to gather greens and those shining scarlet berries that grew by the frozen swamp. She would fasten these in sprays at her windows and door, and she would herself make a beautiful wreath to hang below the pulpit. There would be Christmas hymns, not the familiar noels of her childhood, but others that also echoed "Peace on earth; good will to-

ward men." And Henry would open the great Bible and read
in his earnest voice of Wise Men and Shepherds and of a star
over Bethlehem: "And this shall be a sign unto you: Ye shall
find the babe wrapped in swaddling clothes, lying in a
manger."

She caught her breath sharply at the miracle behind those
words; at the miracle of new life that assailed her everywhere. If only she could know that before another Christmas . . . She longed for a child so deeply that often she
prayed in secret as those other wives of the Old Testament,
Sarah, Rachel, and Hannah, had prayed before her. Their
tears had been rewarded, and surely she had a right to hope
that the miracle would not be denied to her and to Henry,
who hoped no less than she. She had only to watch his face
when a child was put into his arms for baptism to know the
thoughts with which he would never reproach her. But tonight all things seemed possible as she hurried through the
cold in her handsomest dress, warm with self-confidence and
the knowledge that Henry would be proud of her upon his
return.

As she neared the Weeks house she overtook several
neighbors—Mrs. Asa Deane and her daughter Rebecca;
Miss Annie Stillwell and her sister Jane; Mrs. John Holden
and her two daughters, Hattie and Ruth. It surprised her a
little to notice that they were without male escort but she
decided that perhaps this was not so strange since the Misses
Stillwell were unmarried and Mrs. Holden's husband suffered from rheumatism. Mrs. Deane was a widow of substantial stature, the mother of many married sons and daughters,
who clung to this remaining child with a tenacity that puzzled Henriette. She had already noticed a number of such
sturdy older women leaning upon frail young daughters.

"Poor things!" she thought now, watching Rebecca's girlish figure piloting her mother up the path. "They are like
vines trying to support trees. I do not think it is according to
nature, but perhaps there will be some young men to divert
them at the party!"

The ladies paused to greet her and remark upon the unusual coldness of the weather.

"We most always have a white Christmas, but we don't
count on it getting below zero much before January. Still,
you might's well get used to it early."

"I do not mind the cold," she assured them. "When it is so

clear and fine it makes me feel gay. I had my first ride on a sled day before yesterday. Your grandson, Mrs. Deane, was most gallant and lent us his sled. My Henri wished to give me the experience."

"Yes, we heard." There was a world of disapproval in the the three words.

Henriette felt it and hurried on.

"There is as much and sometimes more of the boy than of the minister in Henri," she explained. "Your grandson was astounded that he had not forgotten how to take a sled down a steep hill. I am sorry," she added as they reached the doorstep, "that Henri could not come tonight, but he is still away at the Conference. It is a thousand pities he should miss such festivity."

She saw a mystified look upon their faces in the light from the open door, and puzzled glances passed from one to another at her words. What had she said that was wrong? She had only made apology for her husband's absence. Ah, well! She gave an inaudible sigh and followed them into Mrs. Weeks' hall. It was a large house, for their hostess had been left in comfortable circumstances by her late husband. She was one of the pillars of the church and helped liberally in its support. Her donations to the sewing and missionary circles did much to relieve the financial strain of the parish, and she had been particularly thoughtful of Henry during the months he had preached there in his bachelor days.

Henriette moved eagerly towards her hostess, a woman as solidly built as her house, dressed in a severe gray alpaca with bands of black. She returned Henriette's greeting with a subdued smile and inclination of the head. From the parlor beyond there was no reassuring buzz of conversation.

"It is strange," she thought as she laid aside her wraps; "they speak in whispers, almost as if there were a death in the house. But I should have known if it were a funeral. They would have sent for Henri."

She saw that the guests were being motioned towards the parlor, and she hastened to follow them. But as she removed her dolman a button caught in the lace of her dress and by the time she had disentangled it those who had arrived with her had already gone forward to join the rest. She followed them, the crisp crackle of yards of taffeta sounding about her as she went. The parlor was chill as a vault from disuse. Its cold smote upon her bare shoulders as she crossed the threshold, and she shivered involuntarily. She had expected a cheerful blaze of firelight and the glow of tapers in a candelabra, but instead the high-ceilinged room appeared cavernous, lit as it was by one oil table lamp and a pair of candles. She paused to take stock of her surroundings and as she did so she was aware of a distinct stir about her, an audible gasp from a simultaneous intaking of breath. A score of women stiffened in their chairs, and the hush that followed her entrance was more ominous than a thunderclap.

"Oh, Ma!" she heard young Cora Weeks whisper faintly in the silence. "Oh, Ma!"

Somehow Henriette found herself in one of the chairs that had been set in a large circle about the room. As her eyes became more accustomed to the dimness, and the shock of her own surprise grew less, she realized that the room was entirely given over to women members of the church. Without exception they were soberly clad and their hands were folded decorously in their laps while they waited in silence. Their eyes kept turning upon her, large with curiosity and disapproval, only to be lowered once more to their folded hands. It was disconcerting, Henriette thought, not knowing whether to disregard or meet their glances, and it was certainly not according to the school of social etiquette in which she had been trained. Their hostess moved at last to the center of the room, where the lamp burned on a round, cloth-covered table.

"A séance!" It came to her suddenly that this must be the solution. "Ah, in that case they should have explained to me. But at least it will be diverting!"

Séances had been quite the vogue in Paris before she left. She had attended one once with the Remeys, and though naturally unsympathetic to the macabre she had been rather impressed by certain phenomena and the fragmentary messages received. She had not suspected that her neighbors were interested in the occult, but that showed how she had misjudged them. And Henry had certainly never warned her of this particular trend. She rather doubted that he would approve. Well, she could do nothing about that at the moment. Mrs. Weeks had taken up a small black book and was about to speak.

"We are gathered together tonight," she began solemnly, "as has long been our custom, for a Little Season of Prayer."

There was a light in the study window as Henriette came in sight of the parsonage two hours later. Henry was back! She felt for the icy doorknob and flung herself upon him in a whirl of taffeta and shawl fringes.

"Oh, my little Henri!" Her cheeks were cold against his, her lips warm and tremulous. "Oh, my Henri, such an evening! And you were not here and I did not know. Again I did not know, and all the ladies—"

He had been troubled at not finding her there. And now to have her appear, a vision of color and vehemence, pouring hysterical phrases into his ears, went to his head like champagne. They clung together as if they had been parted for years, and it was only after much questioning that Henry was able to reconstruct the evening.

"What is this you say, my dear?" He could hardly listen to her words, she was so vividly alive and beautiful in the green and black dress, with her bare white shoulders and her curls in warm showers about her tingling cheeks. "You have been —where? And what is this you keep saying about a Little Season?"

"Oh, Henri! At first I thought it would be a soirée, and so I put on my best for it. For your sake I did it, and I did not think about the neck."

"The neck—Yes, it is a little low, but very becoming. Go on."

"And then when they sat in that dim room and all so still —I thought it must be a séance. But it was not. They prayed. Oh, Henri, we have prayed and prayed! It was—I cannot tell you—"

Her eyes were wide and tragic, her arms flung out in a dramatic gesture of appeal, yet the corners of her mouth twitched like a child's, uncertain whether to laugh or to cry.

"Tell me," Henry urged with tender curiosity, "why you are so upset. Perhaps your costume did startle them somewhat. But surely the prayers did not trouble you?"

"Oh, Henri, it was for *me* they prayed! Each one of the ladies in turn. First they got down upon their knees and they prayed for many things, but before they said 'Amen' they prayed for me."

"But that cannot be possible, my dear. What makes you think so? What did they say?"

"They prayed for that poor heathen that had come amongst them. No, I am not mistaken. I listened and listened before it came my turn—"

"Your turn? You also prayed, Henriette?"

"What could I do, since it was expected of me?"

Henry's throat felt dry with apprehension. But his heart was divided between resentment at these women and a sudden flood of loving protectiveness. He had been to many Seasons of Prayer, and he could visualize the scene as if he had actually been present. Henriette rustling to her knees in yards of taffeta, her bare shoulders gleaming in the subdued religious light, her clear voice with its unexpected accents, ringing out authoritatively in what he dared not think.

"And what did you say?" he pressed her gently.

"I prayed for that poor heathen, too," she told him simply.

He stared at her helplessly for a moment before his own lips began to twitch. Then a spasm of laughter suddenly overcame his anxiety. Only Henriette, he reflected with pride and a host of misgivings, would have taken up the challenge and carried it through.

"But, my dear," he sighed when they had both regained their composure, "if only you had asked me about the Little Season! It seems impossible that you should not have known what to expect."

"Ah, my Henri!" she protested. "Here in America you have seasons in the year and you season your food. How was I to know?"

## chapter thirty-four

ALWAYS WHEN SHE THOUGHT OF THOSE YEARS ON THE banks of the Connecticut River, Henriette was to remember the very tones of the bell that summoned worshipers to the old white church; the clatter of wheels and hoofs over the long bridge to Springfield; the voice of Cassie Sampson lifted in song above the pleasant activities of kitchen and pantry. She was to remember the revelation of spring, when ice broke and floated down the river and water overflowed the lower meadows in sheets of quicksilver. There was the early wonder of pussywillows the neighbors' children brought her in preparation for the greater wonder of bloodroot and hepatica and arbutus hiding its incredible pink and white under last year's leaves in the woods behind the town.

Henry had brought her the first bunch, but even he had been unprepared for the reception she gave this fragrant symbol of New England.

"Henri," she had said, bending over the rosy buds and starry white flowers he put in her hands. "It is the strangest, sweetest perfume in the world—cool like snow, yet sweet as spice. There is—how shall I say?—a wild innocence about it that makes me wish to cry!"

There were many things that made her wish to cry because they moved her by their strangeness and unexpected beauty. There was the sudden yellow of cowslips fringing brown rushing brooks and dandelions like gold coins in the new grass. There was delicate shadblow in the woods when she drove with Henry on his parish calls, or when she went exploring with some young neighbor and returned with wet shoes and draggled skirts and a basket of ferns or violet plants to set out in her border.

"We have seen a bluebird," she would call to him through the study window. "It moved in the sun like a flash of pure cobalt-blue. Katy and Jane Whitcomb tell me it is good luck to make a wish upon the first bluebird of the spring. Did you know that, my Henri? No? Ah, well, I did so for us both."

Her wish was invariably the same. It lay upon her heart even as she knew it lay upon his, whether they made mention of it or not. Her candor in expressing a wish for children startled her more reticent women neighbors, though her open envy of large families and her appreciation of their own spring was disarming.

"It's tempting Providence to want young ones so bad," Cassie reproved her sometimes. "The surest way to get 'em is not to hanker so. But there, who am I to talk?"

"Ah, Cassie, I cannot but feel bitterness when I see women who have so many more than they want."

"I know, it goes against the grain."

"I spent my youth on the children of others, and now when the time comes to hope for my own—"

"Well, it's pain if you have 'em and pain if you don't. It's the pattern we're cut on—women, I mean."

She found herself turning to Cassie Sampson often in

those first years of her marriage. They talked for hours sometimes, and Cassie told her many things—how to keep jelly from clouding and the best way to wash woolens, and now and again of her meager childhood and the hoarded secrets of her own heart. She came to know, little by little, why Cassie had never married.

"He was all set to marry a girl in his home town before he came to help his uncle in the mill," she explained. "I was working in the place where he boarded or I'd never have got to say good morning to him even. He had lovely manners, always spoke soft and pleasant, not rough and loud-mouthed like the rest, and you wouldn't have wanted to see a handsomer man when he was dressed to go to church. I've had my chances since, but somehow he spoiled me for taking 'em. Well, it's something to know what love is even if it don't get you anywhere is this world."

In those recurring seasons of orchard bloom, of green summer warmth and autumn brilliance, of winter whiteness, she came also to know her neighbors and to share certain experiences with them. When Ora Newton was failing fast and poor Mrs. Newton grieved that she could not afford the luxury of a daguerreotype likeness, Henriette made a crayon portrait of the girl for the mother to keep. When Will Hardy's house and barn burned to the ground she took the Hardy twins in for a month till another house could be found for the family. She gave lame Ellen Riggs lessons in painting and fine needlework and let several of the older girls practice on her piano. When "Uncle Tom's Cabin" came out and she owned the only copy in town, she did not keep it to herself. Any one could borrow it for the asking, and when it was returned at last with the pages dropping from between the covers and with thumb marks and tear blisters all over it she did not complain of the damage.

"Books were written to be read," she had said. "I am sure it would gladden Mrs. Stowe's heart to see this copy."

Yes, they all agreed she was generous and meant well once they grew used to her queer ways. And she in turn came to recognize, if not to understand, their reserves. It was a small world, but as she became part of it the same currents of life and death, of marriage, success, and calamity, swept her along with them as surely if not as fiercely as they had done in Paris years before.

Then there were visits to Stockbridge and New York; to

Williamstown where Henry had spent his college years; to
the old home at Haddam and other Connecticut River towns.
There were frequent trips to Westfield and across the river
to the thriving near-by city of Springfield, which seemed
busy and almost cosmopolitan compared to the smaller
community. Here she could attend an occasional lecture or
concert, and here she was included in much social activity of
an informal sort. The *Springfield Republican* was a newspaper of distinction exerting a powerful influence, and its
editor, Samuel Bowles, entertained a wide and unusual circle
of friends. Henry Field and his vivacious French wife were
made welcome here, as they were in the home of J. G. Holland. This rising poet and essayist soon became a particularly congenial host and friend. He delighted in Henriette's
apt comments, her humor and Gallic charm. She expanded
in this atmosphere of culture and hospitality. They knew the
world beyond the Connecticut Valley, these New England
men and women. They recognized the quality of her mind
and the shrewdness of her quick response. They listened
when she had an opinion to offer, and she snatched eagerly
at all they had to say upon matters foreign and domestic.
Now it was of the restoration of the French Empire under
Louis Napoleon of which they talked; now the forthcoming
inauguration of the Democratic President Franklin Pierce,
or the all-absorbing topics of Slavery and Secession. Their
words wove to and fro like shuttles across the long dinner
tables while food cooled on the plates before them. Some of
these new friends and acquaintances, Henriette guessed,
were fully aware of her story and of her part in the Praslin
murder case, but there was no trace of curiosity or constraint
in their meetings. They accepted her on her own terms as the
wife of a neighboring friend and minister for whom they
bore deep affection and high regard.

In summer when the weather was fine she often accompanied Henry if he exchanged pulpits with neighboring
ministers. These expeditions pleased her. She delighted in
the drives behind a hired horse. It was so pleasant to ride
along unfamiliar roads through the rich farming country
that Henry knew and loved. Even when he grew absent-
minded discussing some new article or his next sermon and
they found themselves miles from their destination, it was
adventurous, and farmers and their families were always
kind and hospitable. Once they drove to Amherst and Henry

preached to the college students, a broad-shouldered, long-legged group that moved Henriette by reason of their youth and earnest expressions. Raynald, she reminded herself, must have reached this age by now. What was he like? She seemed to see him in every thoughtful, dark-eyed face that passed.

Later they were entertained for dinner by the post prominent citizen of the town, a distinguished lawyer named Dickinson. Henriette was impressed by the dignified atmosphere of that home with its large, beautifully proportioned rooms, its shelves of books and handsome furniture and also by the arresting grace and spirit of his elder daughter, a girl in her early twenties named Emily. Her hair and eyes were the rich russet of oak leaves in October, and her skin as white as the rose she pressed upon Henriette at parting. She was never to forget the gesture or the haunting beauty of this girl, though years afterward she heard it whispered that Miss Dickinson had turned remote and shy, flitting through the rooms of that house and across the lawns in her dresses of white dimity like some pale moth. Strange, she thought, remembering how vivid the girl had been that day and how intently she had listened when Henriette spoke of Paris.

And so the months passed. It was 1853, and she and Henry were well launched into their third year of marriage. In Stockbridge the Reverend David Dudley Field and his wife Submit would celebrate their Golden Wedding in October, and their children and grandchildren would gather in the old parsonage to honor them. It would be a great family reunion, and Henriette did not look forward to it. Not that she would have stayed away. The old parson and his wife were dear to her, and she knew she held a place of her own in their affections. But she would always be an outsider in this close family circle. She had made friends with the brothers and their wives, and she was fond of Emilia Ann Brewer, who had returned with her missionary husband from the Far East to live in Connecticut. Mary Elizabeth and she were congenial, and now this youngest daughter had been married for more than a year and was expecting a child the coming winter. Matthew was still an unknown quantity, but he and his family were back from several years of bridge building in the South. Only Stephen, prospering in California, and the lost brother Timothy, would be absent. No, what she dreaded was the thought of the grandchildren who would fill those rooms with promise, with the healthy din of their young activity. How could she bear to meet that press of new life, knowing that she and Henry could claim none of it for their own? How could she harden herself to meet the ordeal?

She tried not to let Henry guess her thoughts as they set off together on the journey. He was eager as a boy on a holiday. Almost he seemed to have slipped away from her, he was so full of the long anticipated reunion. At such times she was more than ever aware of the closeness of these family ties. It came over her, as upon her first visit to the Stockbridge home, that no matter how far this group of brothers and sisters might scatter and disagree they were still branches of the tree that bore them. She did not begrudge this deep-rooted strength that she felt in them. Yet she was after all a grafted branch. Only if she were fruitful could she truly be part of the growing whole. It made her feel lonely and even a little sad, knowing how it would be as she sat among them all tomorrow.

"If only Stephen could have come," Henry sighed regretfully at intervals in the seat beside her. "I know he will be thinking of us, though when the sun reaches California tomorrow the Golden Wedding will be half over. I hope the new room David and Cyrus are building on the parsonage will be done in time. Did you remember to pack those books I promised to lend father, my dear? I laid them with my sermon in the study, but I am not sure—"

"Yes, Henri, they are at the bottom of the valise; and I also put in the last two numbers of *Harper's*. Your mother enjoys them."

"Good. I should have forgotten. You seem quiet today, my dear. What makes you so silent?"

"I am listening to you instead, my little Henri." She smiled and laid her hand on his with one of her quick demonstrative gestures. "You are happy hurrying home to your parents. There will be so many of you it makes me feel a little—well, a little like a bird of a different feather when I see how you all flock back to the old nest."

Henry laughed.

"It's not that I want to leave our nest," he reassured her, "—at least only for a few days and because this is a great occasion. Think of being married for fifty years and living to see your children and grandchildren gather from every direction to be with you."

"Yes," she answered quickly, turning to the train window that he might not catch the glint of tears in her eyes. "I have thought how it must be, and I rejoice for your father and mother."

"Fifty years," she repeated to herself as the train rolled on through the glory of scarlet and gold and russet of New England in October. "I am over forty now. Henri and I shall be lucky if we have half that number together."

She moved instinctively closer to his side, and the words he was saying mingled with the grinding of the train wheels. They mattered less than his presence. Years in themselves meant little or nothing. It was what one shared in them that counted.

They had an hour between trains at a country junction. Presently the little station was deserted save for themselves, and a nondescript dog stretched out in the sun. A distant mill whistled the noon dinner hour, and from the houses across the tracks the fragrance of food on stoves mingled with the dusty sweetness of summer's end—wild grapes, goldenrod and asters, apples and bonfires. They found a shady bench under a near-by maple and spread out the lunch they had brought. About their feet crickets were clamorous in the burnt grass and above their heads the sun came warmly through matted gold. Now and again a yellow leaf let go its hold and spiraled down to fall on their laps in noiseless surrender. Henriette reached for one and held it between her fingers.

"It goes in beauty, now its season is over," she said, "like your parents, Henri, in golden fulfillment. I think that must be what Nature intended for people as well as trees."

"Yes," he agreed, "it should be so. May I borrow your words for the reunion tomorrow?"

She gave him one of her swift smiles.

"My little Henri, when we are together like this I hardly know which of us thought or spoke, we are so close and the world is so beautiful—almost too beautiful sometimes to bear."

But before he could answer her their attention was attracted to the figure of a man striding towards them along the tracks. He was a tall man, well over six feet, with broad shoulders and a powerful frame under the loosely fitting gray coat. He carried his hat and a shapeless carpetbag as if he had forgotten them, and his hair was thick and burnished

red in the noon sun. At sight of him Henry sprang to his feet
with an eager hail.

"Matthew—it's Matthew!"

"Henry!" The answer came deep and vibrant as the long
legs quickened their pace.

This then was the brother of whom Henriette had heard
much; the self-taught engineer and inventor who had been
busy with his bridge building in the South. She watched the
two as they met on the wooden platform.

"Ah, these Field brothers!" she thought, smiling at the
warmth of their greeting while she waited for Henry to
remember that he had left his wife sitting under a tree. "How
strong is the bond between them!"

She felt sure she would have known Matthew for a member of the clan wherever she had encountered him. There
was a marked family resemblance, though in some peculiar
way he seemed a composite of them all. He had Jonathan's
build and ruddy skin; Cyrus' bushy red hair; a look of David
about the brows and a smile that was frank and illuminating
like Henry's. As they came towards her, this older brother
towering above the younger, she felt that he belonged more
to the earth than the rest. His big feet moved as if he were in
accord with the laws of gravity and magnetic forces. When
he lifted his eyes to the sun one knew that he was on friendly
terms with it and needed no instruments to measure its
course. The elements had marked him for their own. All
that he knew he had somehow acquired by natural keenness of eye and intuition. He must, she felt as she studied
him, have been born knowing how to build bridges and dam
streams, as beavers know their craft without consulting
books. It was in keeping with the pleasant simplicity of this
man that his boots were in need of polishing, his coat worn at
the seams. She felt his easy kindness in the direct glance of
his deepset eyes, in the friendliness of his handclasp. But for
all his powerful frame and tawny color she felt that he lacked
the relentless mental force of David, the driving energy and
will power of Cyrus.

"I like this brother," she decided, "though he will never
make his mark in the world. I think he will always remain
pleasant and shabby and hopeful."

As he shared their lunch Matthew answered Henry's questions and alternated between schemes for his next business
ventures and accounts of his family. Yes, he explained, they

were back for good from Kentucky and Tennessee; his wife, Clarissa, hoped they could settle down again and have the children all under the roof of the old farmhouse in Southwick. They had been scattered too long, and the new baby, born in July, was a fine little boy, but not robust. All this junketing from pillar to post and malaria and mosquitoes were bad for children.

"Wait till you hear the young ones talk," the father laughed. "They learned from the darkies, and I doubt if father and mother will make out half they say. They all went to Stockbridge yesterday. Caty is old enough to help tend the baby. But Clarissa's got her hands full this winter wherever we go."

Later in the train they listened to his talk of conditions in the South. You couldn't condemn slave owners wholesale, he admitted. It was like everything else in the world, some good and some bad in it. But it was no place for a New Englander right now. Feeling had been growing bitter these last few years, and this book "Uncle Tom's Cabin" had stirred up a perfect hornets' nest of trouble. Clarissa had tried to buy a copy of it on a visit to Charleston and had been nearly run out of the city for mentioning the name. Well, he had built his bridges at Nashville and Frankfort, but he didn't fool himself they would last long. Bridges and railroads were the first things to go when there was any fighting, and he'd seen and heard enough to know they were heading for that.

"We won't live to see it maybe," he told them, "but my boys will; and it'll be war between the States and no mistake."

Henriette listened and joined in the questioning. But she could not make herself believe in even the remote possibility of war. It seemed, in that golden, glowing countryside through which they traveled, that security and fruitfulness must be the only realities in so fair a world. Indian summer had taken the valley of the Housatonic. The familiar hills were softened in a mellow haze, the trees everywhere were arrayed like Solomon in all his glory. Her eyes ached with the brilliance, and her heart sagged under the weight of external beauty that had been laid upon it.

"There they are!" Matthew shouted as they came in sight of the old parsonage and an eager group hurried out to meet them. Henriette recognized Matthew's three older children, two boys and a girl, for they had been left to attend school in the North the last few years. The others were strangers to her. Matthew's wife, Clarissa, was a slight woman with a worn, sweet face. She held a baby in her arms, and two young children pressed close to her skirts. One of these was a boy of seven, redheaded and sturdy like his father, the other a little girl with hair that matched the late-blooming marigolds in the border by the door.

"Ah, *la belle petite!*" The words rose involuntarily to Henriette's lips at the child's beauty. "It is too much, too much," she sighed, "a world and a child like this—all in one day."

She was hardly more than a baby, not much over two years, yet all the innocent perfection of childhood seemed centered in her. Not since Berthe had danced gay as a young leaf into the room in the Rue du Faubourg-Saint-Honoré, not since Raynald had beckoned her with imperious trustfulness, had Henriette been so drawn to a child. She saw that under the tawny curls, the eyes were clear as brown brook water, the tiny features firm and delicately cut for all their softness. Such tender confidence, such directness of gaze—Henriette trembled before them and could not look away. So they continued to regard each other with grave understanding while the babel continued on every side.

Then, almost as if some inner signal had passed between them, the small fingers loosened from the skirt folds they had been clutching. Henriette made no move but waited while the little girl came steadily and surely towards her across the grass. She felt her throat contract and her breath grow painful as each step brought her nearer. She tried to steel her heart to meet that advance, yet she could not resist it.

"This is Clara," she heard someone saying presently.

But she had no notion who spoke the introductions for she was only aware of the warm reality of that small hand in her own. The family group about them retreated in a blur, and the tightness that had held her in its grip all day also retreated in that moment to which she would return in memory all the remaining years of her life. Together they followed the others into the house and together they celebrated the Golden Wedding next day.

The day was a long one of reunion and rejoicing. Emilia, David, and Jonathan's families were there; Cyrus, back from

months of travel in South America with his. Neighbors came
bearing gifts; letters were opened and read with moist eyes;
the noonday meal was eaten with rows of faces on either
side turned towards the two who had spread and blessed
that board fifty years before. Apples and pumpkins and ears
of Indian corn heaped the center in a rich pile, like the early
symbols of plenty, cherished by all such households, time
out of mind. Even the daguerreotype artist who had been
brought from the city to commemorate the event by his skill,
rose nobly to the challenge. Somehow he managed to crowd
all the sons and daughters and grandchildren about the frail
old couple in his picture. The sun shone on all the heads; the
crickets shrilled under the tumult of eager voices, and the
parsonage doors stood open to all who came and went. It
was a great occasion with something of Old Testament dignity and magnificence about it.

And Henriette, who had dreaded the day, found herself
moved by the sight of these generations that filled the rooms
with a great press of life. Here, she thought, past accomplishment and the promise of greater accomplishment met and
paused for a brief moment. Tomorrow they would all be
scattered again; today they lifted their voices in the Doxology
and bowed their heads as the old minister rose to give them
his blessing.

"And His truth endureth from generation to generation."
The voice of the preacher and the voice of father and grandfather were one as he spoke the words with solemn pride.

And always Henriette was aware of the little girl who
stayed close at her side; whose small body relaxed drowsily
as the long festivities ended and Henry rose to offer evening
prayers. She sat at the edge of that group, yet she did not feel
apart from them as she had expected to be. She was proud
of Henry, standing erect in his best black coat with the late
afternoon light lending radiance to his face. All the fullness
of his heart was in his voice as he read from the family Bible.

" 'The lines have fallen unto me in pleasant places; yea, I
have a goodly heritage.' "

She lifted the sleepy child to her lap and settled the head
that was so heavy for all its softness into the crook of her
arm. The fine bright hair lay warm against the silk of her
dress; the small chest rose and fell with the intricate rhythm
of life.

"Let us pray together," Henry's voice was saying across
the room.

She heard him faintly through a sudden tide of happiness that overwhelmed her. Yesterday she would have slipped to her knees as the rest were doing, but for once she belonged with those other women who bowed their heads without disturbing the children in their arms. This was the ancient pattern for which women were fashioned from the beginning of time. Perhaps it did not matter that the child was not one's own.

That night she and Henry slept in the upper bedroom that had been his in boyhood. They talked late of the Golden Wedding and all the goodness which had flowed to and from that home for half a century. But they had been silent a long time before she ventured to speak of what concerned her more personally.

"Henri," she began, "I have been guilty of a sin today. I broke a commandment."

He turned to her mystified, but she cut short his protest.

"Oh, yes, my Henri! You know the one I mean. I have coveted thy brother's child."

He felt her tremble beside him in the darkness.

"There are laws of nature that go back even farther than those of Moses," he reminded her, "and I think you were following them today. And as for breaking a commandment it seems to me that you were fulfilling another. To love thy neighbor as thyself also means thy neighbor's child."

"Oh, Henri, you are comforting. You make goodness not a difficult virtue but a simple pleasure."

And then, as if the inspiration were entirely his own and not an answer to a question she had not asked, he suggested that it might relieve Clarissa and Matthew at this time if they took the little girl back for a visit in West Springfield.

## chapter thirty-five

HENRY'S SERMON BARREL IN THE HALL CLOSET WAS FULL to overflowing, but still he spent longer and longer hours at his study desk. It had taken only a little urging from Henriette for him to recast certain of his discourses into more literary form and send them off to various newspapers and religious periodicals in Springfield, Boston, and New York. Few of these carefully copied manuscripts in his flowing, legible hand returned to him. In fact there began to be requests for more, and even small drafts arrived to be added to the funds deposited in a Springfield savings bank. Henriette took charge of these and the family finances, for though she lacked skill in cooking and other domestic arts she had been born with a passion for thrift. Under her shrewd management the household was run comfortably and with a margin of profit on Henry's small salary.

"We must think beyond the Connecticut Valley, my Henri," she would remind him when they discussed finances. "You were not meant to stay a country minister all your life. There will be larger work for you to do, and we must be ready when that time comes. I think it would be well that you remind the editor who published your article on 'The New Rome' that you have as yet received no payment."

Such letters were more difficult for generous, absent-minded Henry than the writing of half a dozen such articles. He was simple enough in his own tastes. Books and travel and an occasional indulgence in the matter of presents for her were his chief extravagances. But money in itself meant nothing to him except that it disappeared mysteriously from his pockets. Time and again Henriette had to curb his impulse to give away more than they could afford.

"One of us must be prudent," she would tell herself. "It seems that I have been elected to that office!"

It was at her suggestion that he brought out the journal he had kept during his European travels of 1847 and 1848. Together they read and relived those months of change and upheaval. Strange to read his entries about the Praslin case, his earliest mention of Mademoiselle D., the remarks concerning her in her imprisonment at the Conciergerie and his burst of spontaneous enthusiasm written after their first meeting at the reception.

"Sometimes," she told him, raising her eyes that had filled with tears to his, "sometimes I cannot believe that this woman you mention could ever have been I."

"I am changed, too," he said. "You have given me so much of yourself."

As they read those closely packed pages evening after evening, she was more than ever struck by his ability to put into words not only the very look and color and atmosphere of a place, but the character and temperament of the people in it. She was amazed by his power of analysis as well as by the vividness of his descriptions. He was not only a born traveler with an extraordinary knowledge of history and the classics; he had a human understanding that made him see with the eyes of a simple man as well as the mind of a scholar. To Henry the past was always showing through the immediate present. He was able without apparent effort to link the two so that neither lost its identity.

"Henri," she told him with conviction, "this journal of yours must not lie gathering dust in a desk drawer. You should take out what is significant and join it with the events that have followed. In time you will have enough sketches to make a book. Ah, how is it that you miss nothing of any scene or chance conversation, yet you never notice if your pocket is being picked or your umbrella forgotten!"

He smiled and admitted his inconsistency, but her words had set the machinery of his mind in motion. He began to see possibilities in the journal, and all through the winter he reshaped and wrote again many of its passages in the light of recent events and greater maturity of vision.

*"Non, chérie."* Henriette would lift a warning finger as small Clara started for the forbidden study door. "Uncle is busy writing. We must not disturb his pen."

Clara's visit had lengthened from week to week. First there had been difficulties in settling the farmhouse in Southwick, and then one or another of the children had been ill. Matthew had many business schemes afoot which took him often to Springfield, to New Haven, Boston, and New York. He often stopped on these trips, and upon each visit Henriette feared he would announce that the time had come for the child to return. But when he left her with them she would draw a long breath as if she had been granted a reprieve. She tried not to become too possessive in her growing love for this third member of their household. Clara, she reminded herself a dozen times a day, had been lent to them for a little while; that was all they might expect. She talked to her daily of her father and mother, of her sister and brothers. "Aunt" was as near as she would let herself come to "Mother." Yet when she dressed and undressed that round, small body, when she watched the widening eyes and heard new words uttered in the surprising accents of childhood, she felt renewed. Young life quickened the rooms again, and while

Cassie cut out gingerbread men and women in the kitchen she fashioned miniature garments and cut down her old sealskin muff to set off the sheen of copper hair and the warmth of frost-brightened cheeks.

Clara, even at that tender age, had a character and mind of her own. Not only did she bear a marked family resemblance in features and coloring, but the traits of determination, independence, and impetuous affection were already noticeable. No child could have differed more from the young Praslins than she in gifts and temperament. With the ease of early childhood she understood whatever Henriette might say to her in French. But when she answered it was always with a firm New England accent, that sounded more like Cassie Sampson's each day. Even Henry smiled to hear her and remarked on the family likeness. She was all Field, he told Henriette with pride in his discovery.

"Yes," Henriette admitted, "and she has the spirit that goes wth her hair. She had need of it yesterday when the children next door set her on their sled and she went down that steep hill alone. She will not repeat the little French noel I am trying to teach her for Christmas; but she was so devoted and quiet yesterday when my head ached, and she runs with open arms to all who come to the door, even the tin peddler with his ferocious black beard."

Christmas had never been so beautiful as that year with pine boughs sending their spice out into the warm rooms, with red berries from the woods and bare feet hurrying from bed in the early hours of morning. There was a chair of the exact size to fit a three-year-old waiting by the fire, and in it a wonderful rag doll with the most lifelike of painted faces. Henriette had executed it with all her best skill and oil paints, and Clara's delight when she saw it was reward enough.

It was late January when Matthew stopped unexpectedly one evening to break a journey from New York. The cold was intense, and he had been delayed by snowdrifts before he reached their door. He was tired as he stretched his big boots to the study fire and drank the coffee Henriette poured. But his tawny hair vibrated with inner energy; his eyes had a peculiar light, and his whole presence charged the room with a sense of excitement.

"Matthew has another invention on his mind," Henry had warned his wife after they had welcomed him. "I know all the signs."

Certainly he was full of something of tremendous importance. He could not keep it suppressed for long, and presently he had launched into his subject.

"I met Gisborne in New York," he began. "Pure chance that we ran into each other in front of the Astor House, and a lucky thing for us both."

"Gisborne?" Henry questioned vaguely.

"Yes. An Englishman and an inventor. I suppose you wouldn't know about him, but he's accomplished a lot in his line. He knows electricity and more about the telegraph than any one except Morse himself. He'd come down from Newfoundland where he's been working on new telegraph lines. Well, we got to talking, and that's how the scheme hatched. I tell you it's going to revolutionize the whole world if it works, and I don't see why it shouldn't. Funny thing is, I'd sort of been playing with the notion myself lately; so it didn't take long for us to put our heads together."

Henry leaned forward in his chair, and his coffee grew cold as he listened. Henriette laid aside her cup, but she made no move to take up her basket of sewing. Matthew's voice rose and fell in the quiet room, and each word seemed winged with a conviction that held them spellbound. The whole village might have been burning up beyond the drawn curtains, and not one of the three would have been aware of it.

Matthew was a practical man. Whatever else might be said of him, that was certain. When he built bridges there was no guesswork about them. Their spans were true, and they were built to last. When he laid railroad lines they fulfilled all requirements. His enthusiasm was great, but it had never run away with his common sense before. Yet what could they think, what could they do except gasp and look at each other incredulously when he was telling them that if a telegraph could operate successfully on land there was no reason it could not also be laid under the Atlantic ocean?

"It's as simple as that," he was saying. "Morse has proved it by land. We'll prove it by sea. If you don't believe me, ask Cyrus. He's all steamed up about it."

And so he went on to explain. Gisborne had taken concessions to extend telegraph lines in Nova Scotia and Newfoundland. Part of these must be laid under water with the wires protected by waterproof cables. The work was well under way, but he had had to stop when his funds gave out.

That was why he had been in New York trying to raise more. Matthew had been convinced that it would be a sound investment and had immediately thought of Cyrus. Cyrus had sold out his paper business at a large profit and had plenty to invest. He was spoiling for some new enterprise to undertake. So, he and Gisborne had gone to Cyrus' new house in Gramercy Park and talked for hours. At first Cyrus had been indifferent to the idea. He was after all a business man and a capitalist, not given to science and inventions. No, he had not been much impressed by the Newfoundland telegraph project. It was later on that the real possibilities of the idea had taken hold of him. Why stop with a short cable line between some northerly islands? Why not an Atlantic cable between Europe and America?

"Yes," Matthew went on, his voice full of pride and generosity, "I've got to give all the credit to Cyrus, for Gisborne and I weren't seeing much beyond our own noses—neither of us could afford to," he added with an apologetic smile.

"But, Matthew," Henry put in mildly, "even if the theory is sound, how could it ever be put into practice? Surely Samuel Morse has carried the telegraph as far as it can go."

"Not by a long shot, he hasn't. And Morse is all in favor of this. He said years ago it could be done, but that's as far as any one went. Well, you know Cyrus when the sparks begin to fly!"

"I thought I knew Cyrus, but this—this wildcat scheme hardly sounds like the hardheaded business man of our family."

"You wait till you hear him. Cyrus has got to do things in a big way or not at all. Nothing picayune about him. I wasn't too hopeful when we left the house round midnight; still I figured I'd hang around New York another couple of days just in case anything happened."

The logs in the Franklin stove had burned down to a handful of dwindling embers. The room had grown so chill that Henriette shivered suddenly and pointed to the woodbox. Matthew paused long enough to replenish the fire before he continued.

"I was right. Cyrus was on my trail first thing the next morning. Seems he sat there in his library after we'd gone, turning that big globe of his round and round when the notion took him, all in a minute. He walked the floor, he said, all alone in the middle of the night, knowing a telegraph line was going to be laid between two worlds and he was going to put it through."

But even Matthew had been astounded by his brother's response. He had not guessed that any one could start a ball rolling so fast. Before another day passed Matthew and Gisborne were putting all their engineering experience at his disposal. He had begun immediate negotiations for scientific advice from Morse himself, the Secretary of the Navy, and Lieutenant Maury of the National Observatory. They had responded at once and favorably. It all came down to the problem of financial backing, but already Cyrus was talking in sums that paralyzed the rest of them. David Dudley had been called in as legal adviser. There must be no chances of possible claims and lawsuits later on when a company was formed.

Henry gasped and shifted in his chair.

"David, too," he murmured, "and Cyrus talking in figures. That means business. But, Matthew, it's beyond my power to believe in such a colossal possibility. Two hemispheres joined by a coil of wire thousands of miles long—"

"That's what it is—colossal." Matthew caught eagerly at the word. He usually bowed to Henry in matters of vocabulary. "And that's only the half of what it's going to mean. Think of it, in an hour we'll know what's just happened over there in London and Paris!"

"I cannot think." Henriette spoke for the first time. "It is wonderful and it is also terrible."

Matthew's voice grew deeper and more jubilant. "I tell you it's going to revolutionize the world! No more waiting for news that's dead and done with by the time we get it."

"Ah, but bad news also travels fast."

The brothers both laughed at her dismay.

"That's like a woman," Matthew reproved her. "Cyrus' wife made almost the same remark when she heard about it, and I'll miss my guess if Clarissa won't, too, when I tell her. Can't you see any farther than your own front yards, you women?"

"Ah, it is not that. I am not against this great invention," she tried to explain. "Only it frightens me when I think of all it can mean."

She felt her cheeks flush, and she could not go on to tell them what was in her mind. She realized that she had left the two men in the quiet parsonage study and had gone back across the years to Paris and the voices of news venders, crying murder and her name. In an hour's time, Matthew had said, such things would be known round the world. Well, that was over. What had she now to fear of this live coil that would carry the pulse beats of the universe under restless salty miles?

With a smile she rose and turned to them both.

"We do not serve strong drink, as you know," she said to her brother-in-law; "but this is no ordinary night, and we must commemorate it. Do you think, my little Henri, that we might drink to the future of this deep-sea monster in some of Cassie's cherry syrup?"

They were still engrossed in talk when she returned from the pantry with three small glasses and seed cookies.

"About how big will it be?" Henry was questioning.

"Oh, maybe the size of my fist, maybe smaller. There will be many interwoven strands of wire in the cable."

Henry made a faint, incredulous sound in his throat and stared at his own fist as he closed it.

"We must drink our toast standing," Henriette decided. "It would not be fitting to remain seated when we propose the success of so great and perilous an enterprise."

"Now you're talking the right way, Henrietta!" Matthew beamed at her as he got to his feet. "I'll leave the toast to Henry. Words are his line."

They lifted their three glasses, and the homemade cherry bounce showed ruby-red in the lamplight. Henry's face was very serious as he wrinkled his forehead in thought.

"We cannot call it a telegraph," he said. "What name is it to go by?"

Matthew shook his head.

"I guess Cyrus hasn't got that far yet," he admitted. "Call it whatever you want to, Henry, but be sure you get in the Atlantic Ocean."

"And it is this 'cable' that you say will carry it," Henriette added.

"Well, then"—Henry's face had grown uplifted—"to the Atlantic cable."

The little glasses clinked, and it seemed to Henriette standing between the two that the air quickened and hummed about them in some prophetic way.

"We shall remember tonight always," she told them gravely. "It is somehow a most solemn occasion."

Midnight was striking as they climbed the stairs. They tiptoed across the landing, that the little girl who slept might not be wakened.

"Matthew will have a part in this new project," Henry confided to her when they were alone in their room. "When the plans are made and the company organized his engineering skill will be needed. He tells me he thinks Cyrus will send him to work at the Newfoundland end."

She caught a note of wistfulness in his voice. It was as near as Henry would ever come to expressing envy. Swiftly she went to him.

"Look at me, Henri," she commanded. "No, do not try to hide your feelings. I can read your thoughts too well. You wish to have a part in this even as your brothers. Why should you not wish it?"

He smiled in sheepish apology.

"I must remember that I am a man of words, not of actions. But tonight as I listened to Matthew I could have wished it might be otherwise."

"You will have your own part in it," she told him with conviction. "I am certain it must be so."

"Perhaps, but after all this is still a dream of theirs, not yet under the ocean."

"Yes, but when such a thing takes possession of men's minds, of a man of such indomitable will as your brother Cyrus, it already exists by the very power of his belief. It may take years, but I feel that we shall live to see it, you and I."

"Yet you seemed against it at first," he reminded her.

"Not against the invention," she told him. "But it came over me suddenly how different my life might be now if this living wire, this Atlantic cable, had brought you news of that tragedy in the Faubourg-Saint-Honoré before you had set out upon your travels. I could not help thinking that if you had known you might not have come——"

He drew her close as she broke off.

"My dear!" His lips were warm with reassurance against hers. "Don't you know that I should have come to you all the sooner?"

## chapter thirty-six

CHANGE STIRRED IN THE AIR ALL THROUGH THAT SPRING of 1854. Pussywillows and skunk cabbage had hardly showed in the woods behind West Springfield before Henry celebrated his thirty-second birthday. In honor of this he and Henriette paid a week's visit to New York, her first in many months. They stayed with David Dudley, whose large new house adjoined the one Cyrus had taken on the northeast side of Gramercy Park. A door had been cut between the two homes, and the brothers and their families moved intimately from one to the other. There was much activity, and the talk was all of the absorbing new enterprise, which had progressed far since the night Matthew had talked of it. Peter Cooper, another Gramercy Park neighbor, had been won over by Cyrus' eloquence. He was not only one of the richest men in the country, but New York's most important citizen philanthropist. With his support and that of other prosperous friends—Moses Taylor, Marshall O. Roberts, and Chandler White—and with the aid of David's legal knowledge and the scientific cooperation of others, Cyrus was beginning to organize his own deep-sea telegraph company and preparing to sail for the bleak coast of Newfoundland as soon as the weather would permit. He was impatient to see for himself how the land lay at this northerly base and how far the telegraph line there had been extended.

By the time Henriette and Henry returned to the Connecticut Valley they had acquired an amazing fund of information on the subject. But their days in New York were important in other more personal respects. Henry visited the editors of several publications to which he had been a contributor. Among these was the *Evangelist,* a religious weekly that had published some of his articles. The paper had been growing steadily in quality and influence and was beginning to be read widely. A new editor was needed, a man of Presbyterian background, literary ability, and liberal outlook. Henry's age and tastes, his experience and broadminded views were ideal, and the editorship was offered him. He had all qualifications but one: It would be necessary for him to buy a controlling interest in the paper.

He had smiled regretfully as he told Henriette about the offer. If only he had the means to take over such a post! But of course, he must not consider the possibility. It would take more funds than they could muster to meet such financial output, and the salary would be small till the paper had justified its new policy and enlargement. New York was an expensive place to live in compared to a small New England village. No, Henry did not feel he could accept. Yet he was loathe to refuse. Such a chance might never come his way again, and it was so exactly the work that he longed to do.

"But certainly you will accept!" Henriette had flung out her arms in one of her unguarded Gallic gestures. "You did not refuse it? *Bien*, it is a gift from heaven. No, do not keep murmuring these foolish *buts!* When do they wish to make the change? At once?"

Impractical though he was by nature Henry had all the details at hand. The present editorial policy and staff would continue through the summer. He need not begin duties till September. That would allow time for his resignation from the West Springfield church, and for the parish there to find a successor. He could contribute articles and editorials by mail before he assumed full responsibility. That part of it was not difficult; but the money—how could that ever be managed?

But Henriette had no uncertainty. There were times to take risks; times to borrow money if the cause justified it. She knew that he stood at a significant parting of the ways. She saw more clearly than he that all his success and happiness in life would be determined by the decision.

"Henri," she told him with a decisiveness that swept away all objections, "you will take this post. It is right, and you will make a good editor because your heart is in it. I have known for a long time that you needed a larger scope. We have no children of our own. It is not in our power, it seems, to change that. But this we can do. Have no fears. Be happy in this opportunity that has come because you are so well fitted to take it, and leave the rest to me."

The Sunday following, Henry read his resignation from the pulpit of the old white church. Before he began, he gave one swift glance towards the pew where his wife sat. Her eyes reassured him as he made the announcement that would bring such a change into their lives.

"This decision has not been entered into hastily," he was telling his surprised listeners. "I am not severing the ties that bind me to you, to this church or others where it has been my privilege to interpret God's word according to the faith that has been mine and my father's before me. I seek a larger congregation, not a better or more devoted one than this which I have served for nearly three years. It is not as if I were leaving to enter a different field. My service will only, I trust, be further enlarged, and my pen reach beyond the range of my voice."

Henriette felt the sincerity behind his words. She was moved with greater love, greater pride in him, as she listened. Later, standing at his side on the church steps, she was touched by the expressions of regret that came from various members of the congregation before they scattered to their homes in the early spring sunshine. Some she knew had been critical of him, and perhaps justly so. Although he was above reproach in matters of principle, and although he had tried to deal justly and wisely in all problems concerning this church, she knew that he had sometimes made mistakes in judgment. He as well as she had offended some members. His duties had often been irksome, and perhaps she had not helped him to meet these parish controversies as might a wife who had come from such a small community. But this chapter was nearly ended. Henry had served these men and women honestly and well. They were sorry to see him go.

In the months immediately following his resignation, Henriette gathered all her resources to meet the challenge she had accepted. Henry had double work to do, carrying on the church activities till another minister had been chosen to fill his place and at the same time writing his weekly articles for the *Evangelist*. Henriette must meet alone the strain of their financial problems and the transplanting to New York at the end of the summer. She took minute account of their resources and found that with what they had been able to put aside under her management and a loan, based on personal integrity rather than tangible assets, the necessary stock in the paper could be secured. Once this had been done, she set about reducing their household expenses to the lowest possible basis of operation. She drew up a long list of domestic necessities and questioned Cassie for hours upon how the best results might be achieved at the smallest expenditure. Cassie gave valuable information on purchases and economies of all sorts. She was only too eager to be helpful, but when the departure was mentioned she invariably broke down at the thought of leaving those three she had come to love with an almost fanatical devotion.

"It's bad enough with Clara gone to her folks for the summer," she would sigh over stove or sink. "I can't look a ginger cooky in the face or go by the door of that little room without getting all choked up; but when I think there'll be another minister and his family in this house just's we've got it all fixed so nice, and you and the Parson off in the big city without me to look after you—well, I could just sit right down and give up. I declare it's on my conscience not to pack up and go too."

But Henriette had to discourage her generosity. Cassie Sampson would, she knew, be as unhappy in New York as a duck set down in the Sahara Desert. Even if this had not been so there was a married sister in poor health who needed help frequently in her own large family. Though she was tempted more than once to bring Cassie with her for the settling at least, she resisted the impulse and was firm.

"No, Cassie." She would shake her head and try to lighten the woebegone face before her. "We must be sensible. Change comes to us all, and I have been fortunate that you were sent to share these years with me. I cannot think how I should have done without your gifts and your advice to guide me. I hope I shall be a credit to your teaching. You will find some one who needs you as much as I did."

"I won't find no one like you and the Reverend." Cassie dug her big knuckles into the bread dough she was kneading and turned her face away with a suspicious sniff. "I guess I won't have the heart to play that piece you taught me even if I do ever get another piano to practice on."

"Oh, come! That is not fair to your teacher," Henriette reminded her gently. "No, you must play it whenever you can and think how happy we have been together. I believe that certain people are sent to be our friends at times in our lives when we have most need of them. I know it is true, Cassie, for there have been times when I could not have gone on otherwise—"

She broke off and stood quite still for a moment staring

through the window past the thick-starred syringa bush where the bees clustered and hummed. In that moment her mind left West Springfield and turned back upon itself down a strange vista of years peopled with figures grotesque in their variety. They passed before her there—the tall Duc, handsome and graceful, with his children about him; Albert and Marie Remey, gentle and affectionate, moving hand in hand; Frédéric Monod and his brother, coming to her aid; Madame Le Maire, sharp-tongued and shrewd; old Pierre in his faded blue porter's blouse; Miss Haines welcoming her to the school on Gramercy Park; and Henri—ah, but Henri was a whole procession of love and loyalty and understanding in one.

She returned once more to the kitchen's immediate present and the admiring curiosity in Cassie's face.

"When you stand and look like that," she said, almost as if she guessed what had passed in Henriette's mind, "I know you're kind of figuring things out. Your being here, I mean, from such a long ways off. You've been through plenty. I always knew that. But first time I ever set eyes on you I said to myself, 'She's one that'll land right side up.' Well, as I was saying yesterday you'd better leave me put up a lot of bread and butter pickles, and soon as the early peaches come along we'd better lay in plenty. You'll need all the jars of preserved fruit you can fetch with you to New York. They'll help out come next winter."

Henriette had written of their plans to Miss Haines and had received a prompt and encouraging reply. She was delighted at the prospect of having her once more a neighbor. A French teacher had already been engaged for next year; but pupils were always requiring special lessons to keep up with the classes, and once the school opened there might be a group of older girls who wished to continue their French conversation and more advanced instruction in literature and painting. She would use her influence to send them to such an able teacher. Continuing with her practical advice, Miss Haines further suggested that she had lately received inquiries from out-of-town parents who wished to send their daughters to the school if they might be cared for in some near-by home. The school had no facilities for admitting more boarding pupils, but if Henriette could find a house in the neighborhood and felt like taking these paying guests she would be well repaid.

"But, Henri, we must consider it," she had met his first

reluctance at the idea. "I, too, prefer that we need not share our home; but it will only be for a year or two, and it will mean our security and comfort. I confess I should dread older guests, but you know I am used to the responsibility of young girls. It will seem like old times to me, and I will let nothing interfere with your work and with our life together."

It was not easy to find a house that answered the requirements of proper location and small rent, but she discovered one after days of discouragement. She had come to the city with Henry in the last stifling heat of August, but he had returned to his church, leaving her at David's home to continue the search. More and more families were moving from the old streets below Washington Square to this neighborhood which had been almost rural a few years before. The rows of houses had grown fast and were beginning to be in demand. She could not afford one that fronted the little green park, but she was determined to be within easy distance of it and the school. There was nothing to distinguish those in a long block on East Eighteenth Street from one another. All were brown and narrow, built on the same pattern with basements and high stoops and three stories, each containing three windows at front and back. Only the numbers and an occasional variation in the matter of door and shutter paint gave individuality, but once the landlord had named a monthly rent within the range of possibility Henriette had taken mental possession of number 102. There were certain undeniable drawbacks. The stairs were steep, and the kitchen dark and inconvenient. All the grates were rusty, and many broken. Such sanitary conveniences as had been installed were badly out of repair, and plaster on the upper floor gave mute evidence of a roof that leaked. But there were long parlors with folding doors and fireplace mantels of white marble that lent dignity even to the empty rooms, and there was a small room that could serve as Henri's study. She saw them all with fresh paint and plaster even before she wrung a promise of these from the landlord.

I shall remain to see that he keeps his word [she wrote Henry that night after a jubilant account of her find]. Once that is done, I shall hasten back, and we can begin the great upheaval. Miss Haines approves the situation and has written to a family in Chicago who wish to place their daughter with her. Cyrus returned to the city from one of his recent business trips in connection with his project. He looks worn and shows the effects of his grief in the loss of his little boy. His earlier elation has, I notice, settled into a dogged determination. He read me Matthew's most recent accounts of his labors with the telegraph lines at the Newfoundland base, and it appears that a more bleak and difficult spot could not have been chosen. But there is no turning back. I could not but think, as we sat in the library and Cyrus talked with his hand upon the globe, that the same gleam of accomplishment must have lighted the eyes of Columbus before he set out to prove that the world was round!

The heat is still oppressive, but I bear it better now that a roof has been found to shelter us for the winter. May it prove tight is my fervent prayer as I argue with the owner and go about armed with yardstick and pencil.

Yesterday in a shop window on Fourteenth Street I paused to look at an engraving of the Empress Eugénie. Her elegance and beauty are undeniable, and she carries herself with proud assurance of her own worth. They make a strange pair, this royal couple. One cannot but wonder how the Second Empire will fare under the rule of this branch of the Corsican peasant tree and his Anglo-Spanish bride. In the same shop I secured a copy of Victor Hugo's remarkable pamphlet "Napoleon le Petit" which I am eager to discuss with you.

The papers here commented at considerable length upon your friend Beecher's sermon in Brooklyn last Sunday. He delivered another stirring appeal to keep the territory of Kansas free of Slavery. I wish we might have heard him. You have done well to win his promise of a series of articles for the *Evangelist*. Perhaps it will even be possible for you to secure others by his sister Mrs. Stowe. What a feather that would be in your editorial cap!

Good night, my little Henri. Continue to miss me as I miss you, but let your mind be at rest about the winter. We shall be busy and happy in our new home, and may the door that will soon bear your name upon its plate be open to men and women of wide vision and inquiring minds.

Your most loving
H. D. F.

Those words hurriedly penned on a sultry late summer night were more in the nature of a prophecy than a wish. That narrow brownstone house on East Eighteenth Street became almost at once the accepted gathering place of a variety of friends and visitors to New York. It was not chance that the phrase "inquiring minds" had been set down by her pen. She cared little for other traits in those she met. Integrity of thought, flexibility of mind, and a consuming curiosity concerning the world and its occupants were the touchstones to her friendship. Whether she happened to find these in some struggling gifted youth or in some person of recognized achievement, her response was equally sincere. The sensitive antennae of her own sympathy and human awareness reached out in a roomful of people and unerringly found minds to quicken hers, talents to match her own. She loved wit, but not at the expense of wisdom. She delighted in good company and the exchange of talk, yet she was seldom deceived by mere superficial brilliance.

"Ah, yes," she might agree if Henry or another tried to draw her out upon some rather too voluble person. "He has been so busy collecting the best opinions that he seems not to have found time to have any of his own."

The years of discipline had tempered her impatience at duller minds and less quick wits. Her own misfortunes had taught her tolerance, had brought her a deeper sense of human values than it was given to most women of that time and place to know. Facing scandal, ruin, and hostility as she had done had intensified her natural independence. She was too dominant to be capable of compromise once her convictions were established. But her husband's love and the generosity and largeness of his views had made her gentler, more indulgent of others.

"This is my belief," she would wind up some devastating comment upon a subject under discussion, "but Henri says I do not paint the picture in fairness. He thinks that I mix my colors with prejudice, and it may well be so."

"But you still believe you are right, my dear," Henry would smile with indulgent pride across the long table about which more and more guests gathered.

Entertaining as a means of social advancement meant nothing to either of them. "Society" was a word that made them smile and shake their heads. They had nothing in common with the lavish receptions and dinners of that select

circle of wealthy and aristocratic matrons who fancied themselves New York's social mentors. Sympathetic as Henriette
might be with human inconsistencies and shortcomings, she
could never hide the deep-rooted scorn she felt for those
who considered themselves superior because of wealth or
position.

No, Henry and she had come to that house on the edge of
a good neighborhood without social ambitions and with no
thought of formal entertainment. That he should give his
best to the new work, that the paper should expand and
prosper under his editorship, and that they should keep their
heads above water financially was all that occurred to them
in those first years. Under Henriette's touch the house took
on personality. Its inconveniences remained, but its comforts and charm increased. Those who came there remembered the easy intimacy of chairs drawn close to the fireplace, the vases of French porcelain, and the mirror above
reflecting the red curtains, the pictures and books on the
shelves. They forgot, if they noticed, the worn places in the
carpet, the unevenness of floor boards, and the faded wall-
paper.

Few who stayed for supper in that house remembered the
steep, dark stairs that led to the basement dining-room,
where the table with its fresh linen and fine silver and china
was spread under a softly shaded hanging lamp. They could
usually recall the conversation about that table, but they
were seldom aware of the plainness of the food some young
Irish girl set down for their hostess to serve. They usually
began with a tureen of steaming soup. After that a platter
of cold meat might follow, or perhaps fish with a French
sauce that disguised humble cod or haddock. Vegetables
were invariably potatoes, onions, carrots, or winter turnips,
though there might be a special treat of preserved fruit in
small glass dishes or a plate of thin sugar-sprinkled cookies.
But there was always coffee, enough to fill cups again and
again. The fragrance came like a tantalizing preface long
before the pot appeared.

"It should be so with coffee," Henriette would make
simple acknowledgment of the praise that was sure to follow its arrival. "One should feel as one raises the cup the
same expectation that precedes the rising of the curtain at a
play, or the cutting of the first page of a new book."

No, she did not take her housekeeping duties as seriously

as other women of her acquaintance. She refused to waste half her time considering meals and fretting over the ineptness of Irish immigrant help. She learned to market in the smaller shops far to the east where women with shawls and baskets haggled over the price of eggs and sugar and butter. Two mornings a week she went with a small boy from the next block to carry the baskets home. If she managed on a little less than the sum laid aside for expenditure, the balance went into the bank as a matter of course. She taught the raw young immigrants fresh from landing what she had learned from Cassie Sampson and her own limited domestic experience. She explained the simplest principles of service and let the training end there. She understood these girls and their homesickness, their bewilderment at strange ways. She made allowance for mistakes, but not for waste or disobedience. They came and they went after the order of their kind— good natured and willing for the most part, but eager to marry or move on to higher wages in more prosperous households.

It amused Henriette in those first years when she must practice such strict economy; when without the French lessons she gave privately or the boarding pupil who occupied their most comfortable bedroom—it amused her to hear other women rattle on for hours about their domestic difficulties. They took such problems so seriously, as if it mattered in the scheme of creation whether one served boiled fish with an egg sauce or drawn butter. She felt like reminding them that the sun had risen as usual and the stars remained in their courses even if yesterday's pudding sank in the middle or Sunday's roast had been tough. When her sisters-in-law or some inquisitive friend expressed surprise at the number of distinguished guests she and Henry entertained, she would smile and shrug.

"But they do not come for what is put upon their plates," she would point out in all honesty. "Do you think that Mr. Bryant's mind is upon the beef stew when he and Henri are quoting the Greek of Homer to one another?"

These other housewives could not understand her casualness, but the fact remained that more and more important men and women came to that house off Gramercy Park. Now that Sunday had changed from being Henry's most arduous to his most restful day, he had fallen into the habit of asking friends and visitors to the city to drop in towards the end of the afternoon. He was the most hospitable man alive, and it was inevitable that they should be invited to remain for a light supper. As the months passed and their circle of friends widened, these impromptu Sunday evenings became something to be reckoned with even by so informal a hostess. She did not overlook the importance of food; she knew that good conversation flourished about a dining-room table. Her problem was to provide the essentials of hospitality for the least possible outlay of money and effort. Once again she fell back on Cassie Sampson's advice about keeping a ham on hand. By practicing strict economy during the week she was able to afford generous platters of cold sliced ham when Sunday came round. Potato salad had not yet become generally popular in New York; but in France its value was known, and it could be stretched to meet the emergencies of unexpected guests or late arrivals. Pans of biscuits could be heated on short notice. Relays of fresh coffee appeared and disappeared. By giving the maid of all work the unheard-of luxury of a whole weekday to herself, Henriette was able to enlist full support on Sundays, and she was lenient in allowing dishes to be stacked and washed the following morning.

She never knew beforehand how many would gather. It might be a night of rain or sleet or snow with only a half-dozen about the lamplit table, or it might be that the brass knocker kept up a steady rapping and those who had already finished supper rose and gave their places to newcomers, lingering near by to continue the topics in which they had become engrossed. Sometimes they sat on about that table for hours while controversies raged, or they all stayed spell-bound as some guest warmed to a subject and poured out his best to sympathetic listeners. Henriette was wise enough not to disturb a group that had fallen into congenial conversation, not to break the frail thread of mental intercourse. She had no patience with hostesses who felt called upon to re-arrange their guests during the course of an evening.

"It is most barbarous," she would protest vigorously, "this custom of shuffling and dealing out one's visitors as if they were so many cards in a pack. If I desired to play whist I should certainly not do so with my guests."

Henry agreed; he loved people. Human beings renewed him in some deep inner way that only Henriette understood. He demanded less of people than she, was less discriminating in his appraisals. Not for nothing had his family smiled at his enthusiasms and reminded one another that "all Henry's geese are swans." But somehow with experience and his wife's shrewder judgment he made fewer mistakes in human equations, and his writing expanded and took on new ease and sureness under the stimulation of these contacts with the most intelligent minds of his day.

With her it was different. She was always a gracious welcoming hostess; always an attentive listener; but unconsciously she was also the center of their domestic stage. She had been born with an oversupply of creative energy, and it found its best outlet in her genius for friendship. In a group of people her mind took on an uncanny power, like the hazel-wood divining rod that in certain hands will tug and turn at the presence of water. In the same instinctive way she was always seeking thirstily the hidden springs of other human minds and hearts. Consciously or unconsciously they all responded to her: Peter Cooper, the eccentric millionaire, from his great house across Gramercy Park; William Cullen Bryant, poet, philosopher, and editor; Samuel Morse, artist-inventor; the Beechers, brilliant preacher and famous sister; Bowles and Holland and Gilder; Fiske, the historian; Youmans, the scientist; Bayard Taylor; Edmund Clarence Stedman; Eastman Johnson, the painter.

So they flocked to the house on East Eighteenth Street or to others that succeeded it. Wherever she and Henry might move in those years before and during and immediately after the Civil War, the door knocker would begin to be active; chairs would be drawn to the fireplace; plates and cups would be set out in readiness on the dining-room table, and the fragrance of fresh coffee would begin to climb the stairs. Some of the men and women whose feet passed over that threshold had a part in the shaping of events, political, scientific, literary, and artistic; some of them lived and died in obscurity. But years after, when they were scattered and that house was only a memory, it still served its purpose of friendly introduction.

"Didn't we meet one Sunday evening at the Henry Fields'?"

It was like a password, one that would have warmed Henriette's heart as she had warmed theirs.

## chapter thirty-seven

RACHEL HAD LANDED IN NEW YORK! UNDER THE BRASS
blare of P. T. Barnum's superlatives she would make her
début in Corneille's tragedy "Les Horaces" at several New
York theaters that autumn of 1855.

Henriette read the announcements heralding this forthcoming event with feelings that she could not share, not
even with Henry. No, she could not explain to him why she
had stood in the relentless glare of noon sun on busy Fourteenth Street devouring each word of the theatrical handbills
displayed before the new Academy of Music entrance. The
familiar French names stirred her mind as if they had been
so many pebbles flung into the still depths of her consciousness to spread out in disturbing ripples. In a few weeks
Rachel would be playing here, too, at this theater only a half-
dozen city blocks from her own door.

How long it was since the night she had sat with the Duc
and Louise in that luxurious box! How little had they
guessed, listening to the magic of that voice, watching the
play of feeling that illumined those features like flashes of
summer lightning—how little they had guessed the tragedy
that would descend upon them, too! Fourteen years since
then, yet even now Rachel's name on a cheaply printed playbill could set Henriette's heart pounding with echoes of lost
emotions.

She turned from the announcement at last. But before she
moved on, her eyes began searching curiously for the door
which admitted players to the theater. "Stage Entrance"—
she read the inconspicuous sign and peered through a grating set in a door that gave upon a dark alleyway. The contrast of those two entrances struck her poignantly as she
turned away. Perhaps it was symbolic, she thought, that
those whose destiny it was to kindle fire in others must
grope their way first through such narrow tunnels as this.
But Rachel must be used to dark stage doors by this time.
She wished her well in this venture.

This Yankee, Barnum, was a genius in the art of show-manship. There had never been his like for exploitation, whether he made the diminutive General Tom Thumb a national character overnight or roused the American public to such heights of frenzy over Jenny Lind that they cheerfully fought their way to hear the Swedish Nightingale warble at ten, twenty, and even thirty dollars a ticket. P. T. Barnum for all his shrewdness was capable of mistakes. General Tom Thumb had been a droll freak of nature, a human being cast in miniature to be marveled at in frank curiosity. A voice like Jenny Lind's soared to the farthest gallery seat unhampered by barriers of language. But Rachel's art was far less simple and direct in its appeal. It required a response. And how could there be answering emotion when only a fifth of those beyond the footlights found the words intelligible? In vain the great actress summoned her best gifts for this public she had traveled so far to conquer. She called upon every ounce of her strength, every dramatic mood within her range. The brilliant passages of Racine and Corneille fell like pearls cast before—not the proverbial swine, but bewildered and dwindling audiences. A meager group of theatrical enthusiasts hailed her greatness, it was true, and the papers praised her power as a tragedienne. Henriette took some small satisfaction in this, though she felt humiliation at New York's indifference and at Mr. Barnum's crude methods. His announcements that Rachel would be loaded down with jewels valued at some two hundred and forty thousand dollars and presented to her by many different admirers, was certainly in the worst possible taste. Yet she read eagerly any and all comments upon the actress and her troupe. She sprang to her defense at the first hint of criticism.

"Well, I must say, Mrs. Field, I couldn't see anything to brag about in her," some casual acquaintance would volunteer. "If they like her so much in France I don't see why she didn't stay over there. Fanny Kemble may have been a Britisher, but at least you could understand what she was saying."

"An actress is hardly responsible for the minds of her public," Henriette would point out with spirit. "It is their misfortune if her art is lost upon them. I suppose to a deaf-mute Jenny Lind must have seemed no more than a blonde woman beside a piano opening and closing her rather large mouth."

So through that month of September Henriette fought off the impulse to see Rachel act again. It was not that Henry would have disapproved. Unlike many of his profession he had no prejudice against the theater. He would have taken her gladly if she had expressed a wish to see her great compatriot. But she could not bring herself to mention it to him, though as the days passed the longing to hear her own language in those unforgotten accents became an obsession.

She might, perhaps, have continued to control it if the engagement of the French troupe had not begun at the nearby Academy of Music the same week that Henry left for a short trip to New England. His mother's health had been poor of late, and he wished to see her and attend to certain commissions connected with the paper. He was eager to go to Concord and meet Ralph Waldo Emerson, who was at work upon a new series of essays, "The Conduct of Life." On the way back he would stop in Southwick and visit Matthew's family. Clara had spent the summer there with her mother and brothers and sister, but she would return to New York with Henry for the winter. Without actually planning that the arrangement should be permanent, the child had grown more and more at home with her uncle and aunt. The months she spent with her family circle were more in the nature of long visits, and it could not be denied by the generous Matthew and his wife that the child benefited by the advantages they could not give her.

"Be sure you do not mislay Clara's belongings on the way back," Henriette cautioned Henry as he set off for the week of travel, "and do not let the child out of your sight when you wait between trains. Give your parents my affection, and Clarissa also. I hope Matthew will soon be home from the North. I shall have time to write you once, and perhaps you will send me word too along the way."

After he had gone she kept herself as busy as possible that her thoughts might not stray too often in the direction of Fourteenth Street. She called upon Miss Haines and discussed the requirements of three pupils who were behind in their French classes, and she gave the first evening to helping their young school boarder from Chicago rearrange her room. Next day, having an unusual amount of leisure on her hands, she began a water-color sketch which had long been haunting her. It was to be a study of an immigrant girl with her few possessions, waiting for entrance to America. Although she had no intention of making it a self-portrait, she could not help visualizing herself and her feelings in every line. Once she would have been too close to the subject to snatch at the essentials and transfer them to paper with her brushes. But now the time had come to make that homesickness and hope tangible in the slumped figure waiting as she had once waited with those souvenirs of the old life about her and with the masts and prows of shipping in the background.

"It is good," she said as light faded and she rose from her easel. "I think I have caught the attitude and feeling. Tomorrow I can finish the final washes of color."

Mr. Peter Cooper dropped in after supper to see Henry, but he stayed to talk with Henriette for more than an hour. They spoke of the cable project and of the latest difficulties which Cyrus must meet. She had brought the unfinished sketch into the parlor to study it by lamplight, and his eye fell upon it with interest. He thought it good and said so after his own blunt, emphatic fashion.

"No reason at all, my dear," he said, "why most of the interesting work in the world should belong to the men. Not that I hold with all this women's rights nonsense. If a woman's made the way she should be, she'll get her rights and more. But I'd like to see boys and girls, too, with talent have a chance to put it to some good use."

She nodded and listened with intentness as the eccentric, benevolent old millionaire warmed to his theories of youth and labor. People admired him because of his wealth and vision in industry, but they laughed at his peculiarities and independence of thought and speech. He had seen the possibilities in the development and manufacture of iron and made a fortune in it and in glue. His own inventions ranged from locomotives and lawn-mowers to a contrivance to rock a cradle, keep off flies and amuse the occupant with music-box tunes. But Henriette never smiled behind Peter Cooper's back at his extraordinary schemes. She found him a most stimulating man, a most generous friend.

"I mean to found a school," he was telling her, "according to my own notions, and it won't be all mixed up with the classics. Not that there's anything wrong with them for men like your Henry and others. But this one I have in mind will be for a different sort of young man and young woman. It'll teach them to use their hands along with their brains. How'd you feel about helping me plan it and maybe teach painting to girls that show any knack at it?"

"Of course," she had agreed. She would be most happy to help. She believed there was a great need of such an institution in New York. Where, certainly, were there so many young people growing up in poverty and squalor with the gifts and traditions they had brought from their native countries all being wasted and forgotten in the struggle to live on this single, overcrowded island of Manhattan?

"Well, then, you promise to help me," he had said as he prepared to walk home round Gramercy Park and see how the new trees he had set out there were flourishing. "I'm mulling it over in my mind along with a few dozen other schemes."

But she did not take him too seriously. After he had gone she went upstairs to bed, missing Henry and trying not to think of the lighted doors of the Academy of Music and of that smaller entrance from which a woman's cloaked figure would soon be stepping.

She kept well occupied till the third evening of that week, when her resolutions not to give way to her desires suddenly left her. Rachel was to play Phèdre, her most famous rôle. Temptation was no longer to be resisted. Henriette hurried through an early supper and helped the young pupil with next day's French. Then, instructing the Irish maid to remain on duty before locking the house at ten o'clock, she hurried upstairs. With careful, swift fingers she made herself ready, putting on fresh linen and curling her hair before the pier glass. At the wardrobe she surveyed her dresses and weighed the advantages of her new plum-colored poplin and her made-over green taffeta with the black lace drapings. The poplin was more fashionable in cut, but it was not décolleté. She selected the taffeta, feeling that the occasion demanded full evening dress.

"I must honor Rachel with a costume worthy of her art," she decided as the shimmering folds rustled about her.

She felt grateful that her dark wrap was inconspicuous, and that it could be fastened close to her chin. A scarf of black lace covered her head, and she carried a small beaded bag as she closed the front door behind her and set off alone upon this adventure. Respectably married women did not walk alone after dark. She was well aware that in doing so she was defying neighborhood conventions. Not that she felt any timidity, but she hoped to avoid those who might expect some explanation. Luck was with her, and presently the bright lights of Fourteenth Street beckoned and the

Academy of Music loomed before her like some brilliantly illumined cave.

Traffic was heavy on that thoroughfare. She had to wait some moments before she could cross between the carriages clattering eastward towards the theater. Men and women in evening dress were alighting upon the crimson carpet that Mr. Barnum had had laid from curb to entrance. Henriette took her place in line before the ticket window, the only woman in that crowd of men and boys. Their curious stares meant nothing to her as the line moved steadily nearer the grille-protected opening behind which a man's fingers exchanged bits of cardboard for silver and paper currency. She relaxed somewhat, once her hand held a ticket and she could move on into the lighted lobby. She paused to slip back her scarf and open the fastenings of her wrap. As she did so her attention was drawn to the ticket collector beside his little box and an excited old man who gestured and protested in French.

The ticket taker refused to let him in because the one he held entitled him to a gallery seat. He must go outside again and climb the stairs that led from the street. The old fellow could not understand him. He believed his ticket was not being honored, and his face was a puckered study in bewildered despair that reminded her of old Pierre. Henriette turned on the attendant in reproof for his shortness and then in swift French made the situation clear.

*"Merci, madame. Je vous remercie."*

The old soul poured out a torrent of thanks and blessings, and the familiar words fell refreshing as dew. She had been missing the sound of her native tongue more than she had realized.

"Good night and enjoy yourself, monsieur," she answered in French as they parted. "The great Rachel will at least be sure of two across the footlights to understand her words."

The incident put her in an even more expectant frame of mind, though she wished she might have afforded to buy another orchestra seat for the old man. Her own was a little to the side, though no pillar interfered with her view of the stage. The gilded boxes were not all filled, and a few rows at the back were empty; but it was a better house than she had expected from reports of former receipts. And it was apparently a well mannered, well fed, and well dressed audience. It pleased Henriette to see so many men in formal black and white, so many women in silk of various hues with their bare necks and arms gleaming under the brilliance of gas light. It pleased her to hear the rising chatter of voices all about her. Venders of English versions of the play moved up and down the aisles, doing a thriving business with their sales. Every one, it seemed, but herself was preparing to follow the play by means of these texts. An elderly man at her right was studying one as if his life depended on it, and the young girl in blue satin with the heavy-scented bouquet of tube-roses who sat on her left kept fluttering the pages between bursts of conversation.

"Mamma was very set against my coming," a shrill girl's voice was proclaiming behind her. "You know what she thinks of actresses, and she was shocked when she read about Rachel having so many admirers and dear knows what beside!"

"Ssh, don't mention it so loud or Cousin May will make us leave before the first act. I only teased her into taking us because I said it would improve our French. Oh, look, the Vandercamps are just coming in to that second box. I wonder if Ellen really is engaged to Will Leonard. He's sitting next to her and they look sort of—"

To Henriette's relief the orchestra cut short this conversation. Violins were mounting, high and sweetly singing to the roof, with cellos and piano keeping the melody anchored to earth and the orchestra pit. There, she recognized the tune! It was a polka, so infectious, so much a part of the old life that Henriette could scarcely breathe remembering the grace of young girls in summer dresses and a tall blond man dancing to it in a drawing room by the seashore.

Now the footlights grew bright, the curtains were parting on the rather bare stage which had already drawn unfavorable comment from New York theatergoers. Henriette cared nothing for elaborately painted scenery. She waited tensely for the first words to be spoken that should transport her across time and space. When they came even from the lips of those less important members of the troupe she could have burst into tears at the perfection of accent, at the beauty and rhythm of the dialogue. About her the audience stirred restlessly, and at regular intervals the actors' voices were drowned out by the rustle that rose from all parts of the house at the simultaneous turning of some thousand pages. But she forgot even this irritation as the play unfolded, as the moment for Rachel's entrance approached.

At last she stood before them in the flowing Greek robes that fell from her shoulders, the white folds accentuating her pallor and the darkness of her eyes and hair.

"Ah, but she has aged!" That was Henriette's first reaction as she applauded till her palms tingled. "We have not grown younger with the years, Rachel and I!"

She saw that those features had sharpened subtly as if a cameo cutter had been too diligent with his instruments. The eyes appeared more brilliant because of the deep sockets that held them. The exquisite oval of the face was a shade too angular, and under the flattering draperies the frame was more gaunt than she remembered. But that voice! Though Henriette was aware that the tones were less resonant and full than they had once been, what flexibility and power still charged it as the words flowed out with the old magic!

Long before the curtain fell for the first intermission Henriette had surrendered to the spell. She had been stirred before by Rachel's art, but not as she was moved tonight sitting alone in that alien audience on Fourteenth Street. She had been young and untried then; now she was a woman of middle age and bitter experience. The more one suffered and lived, the more one had known of joy and grief, the deeper the response must be if an artist were great enough to summon it. She leaned forward in the dimness, scarcely daring to breathe lest she miss a single glance of those eyes, a single syllable from those lips.

Rachel was giving out her best. But for one member of that audience it was more than a magnificent theatrical performance. It was for Henriette a renewal of her very self through the art of another. Every gesture, every look, every inflection of that voice brought back lost ecstasy and lost despair as if the actress had known and evoked them. So the present slipped from Henriette, forgotten like the lace scarf that had fallen from her bare shoulders.

"Bravo, bravo!" she cried out as the curtain fell.

She was oblivious to the curious glances that her enthusiasm drew from those about her. As the girl in blue satin rose to promenade with her escort during the intermission, her bouquet fell at Henriette's feet. In a daze she rescued it.

"You have dropped your violets, mademoiselle," she said.

It was only the astonished look on the girl's face that brought her back to reality. She had spoken in French and called tube-roses violets! Yet the memory of a little purple bunch that had lain fragrant on her lap all those years ago, had returned stronger than the living flowers between her fingers. Could any actress ask a greater triumph than this, she wondered.

So the evening continued until as the play neared its climax Henriette was so completely under its spell that she would hardly have responded if her own name had been shouted through the theater.

She trembled as Phèdre poured out her anguish to Hippo-lyte:

Miserable! et je vis et je soutiens la vue
De ce sacré soleil dont je suis descendue . . .

She was shaken to the core with answering emotion.

Wretch that I am! I live and still must
Endure the sight of the sacred sun.
I have for ancestor the father of the God,
Heaven and all the Universe is full of my ancestors.
Where can I hide myself?

When the final curtain fell tears were streaming down Henriette's cheeks. But she did not pause to wipe them away. With her hands lifted high she was responsible for at least two curtain calls.

"Oh, to tell her that I heard and felt as no one in all this city could have done!" she thought as she joined the audience that crowded the aisles.

If Henry or any member of his family had been beside her she would have curbed the impulse that followed this thought. But she was alone. There was no one to remind her that she had been rash enough to come here unaccompanied without seeking out an actress of Rachel's reputation.

Somehow she found herself at the stage entrance, where several men stared at her appraisingly.

"Who do you want, m'am? What's your business here?" one of them asked her bluntly.

"I wish to see Mademoiselle Rachel," she announced in a voice that surprised her by its calmness. "Here is my card, which you will be good enough to present her if you will lend me your pencil, monsieur."

He handed her one without further questions. There was something in her manner that impressed him. Women of her type seldom appeared at the back doors of theaters. This woman spoke with authority and a French accent. It was against his orders, but he would let the actress' brother deal with this visitor.

"Mrs. Henry M. Field," the calling card was neatly engraved; but below this the hasty penciling read: "Née Henriette Deluzy-Desportes."

Presently she was following the man down the dark alleyway. He led her into the wings, where she was vaguely aware of dangling ropes and properties that had a strange yet familiar look because she had so recently seen them across the footlights. She stumbled against an artificial orange tree and the bench upon which Phèdre had wept her tears of bitterness. A dark, rather too conspicuously dressed man received her. She disliked his scrutiny and self-importance, but his French was excellent when he introduced himself as Mademoiselle Rachel's brother and her manager.

"A beautiful, a superb performance," Henriette hastened to assure him. "As a compatriot I could not resist the desire to offer my praise."

"My sister will see you," he explained as he led her across the darkened stage. "She is not at all well," he went on, "and far from happy at her American reception."

"I know, Monsieur Félix, and I regret it. That is why I ventured to express my gratitude tonight as I should not have done in Paris. But if she is too tired after so exacting a rôle I will not intrude upon her."

"No, no, she has expressed a wish to meet you."

He gave her a look of such obvious curiosity that she lowered her eyes and waited without speaking while he knocked at a door. A maid appeared behind it. The two spoke in low tones together before they both stood aside to let Henriette enter alone.

Her first impression was of disorder. The small room seemed overflowing with costumes and baskets of flowers whose fragrance mingled with the scent of powder and pomades. Then she became aware only of the woman who dominated it. Rachel lay on a divan wrapped in a cloak of crimson wool. Under her make-up she looked utterly spent and no flecks of light stirred in the somber darkness of her eyes. Seen at such close range there was no disguising the worn lines of that face, the hollows that showed too prominently at cheeks and throat. But the full red lips curved into a smile as a long transparent hand was extended in greeting.

"You are Mademoiselle Deluzy-Desportes?"

The question came almost in a whisper. Rachel was evidently saving her voice from all possible strain.

"I was," Henriette answered simply.

She had not until that moment given a thought to what she should say to the great actress. Now that their paths had crossed in this cluttered dressing room across the Atlantic, her composure for once deserted her, though she continued to speak in the French that rose so naturally to her lips.

"You have brought her back to life tonight," she was explaining. "Tomorrow she will be gone again. But it seemed only right that she, that I—that we should thank you in person."

"It is incredible," Rachel answered. "Of all strange meetings this is surely the most strange. That we should both be here so far from home—"

"This is my home now," Henriette reminded her. "I have been fortunate to find happiness and peace in the New World. Here the tragedy in which I was forced to play a part is forgotten."

"Ah, madame!" Rachel gave her a long, intent look. "You also have known tragedy. Drama has come to us both in different ways. Compared to what you have lived, my rôles must seem like the charades of children."

Henriette acknowledged the common bond. "Drama has marked both our lives. For me it took the form of a yoke; for you—wings."

Rachel sighed.

"This long journey was too far for those wings. I feel that they are failing me."

She made a futile gesture and the cloak fell back. Under its vivid folds Henriette could not help seeing how frail that body had grown.

"Good night, Mademoiselle Rachel," she said. "I salute your genius."

The interview was over. She sped along the dark alley and deserted streets, a woman hurrying to the security of her own home. For an evening only she had entered this world of artifice where even the make-up was more pungent than the scent of living flowers. She felt for the latchkey in her bag. As she climbed her doorsteps, the present reclaimed her, and once more she shed the past.

## chapter thirty-eight

LOOKING BACK TO THOSE YEARS OF 1855 TO 1858, HENRIette realized how the Cable, or Atlantic Telegraph as it was still called, dominated their thoughts. Not only Cyrus, completely in the toils of his electrical sea serpent; not only Matthew battling the elements of the Newfoundland coast—not only these active brothers, but scholarly Henry too was obsessed by this dream of joining two worlds.

"It is perhaps fortunate," Henriette thought as those months of suspense lengthened into years of grim effort, "that Henri and I have not the means to invest in this enterprise, or we should long ago have been ruined."

Cyrus, it began to be rumored, was on the verge of bankruptcy. All his business assets, real estate, and personal properties were pledged to the support of the company he headed. The original capital of a million and a half dollars which the first little group of backers had subscribed had been swallowed up almost immediately—a mere drop in the bucket. Land extensions of the line alone had cost more than a million, and of this Cyrus had contributed over two hundred thousand. No wonder his wife looked anxious as thousands followed thousands to meet new demands and one unforeseen setback after another. There were times when Henriette regretted her impulsive toast to the adventure.

But Henry remained steadfast in his belief. Cyrus could accomplish the miracle. It was merely a question of time. He had set himself the task of recording the progress of the undertaking from start to finish. His part would be less spectacular, but when the goal was accomplished he would have his history ready to give to the world. Tirelessly he prepared notes on all that Cyrus and Matthew told of their activities; patiently he copied and filed away all letters and documents that might have future bearing upon the work. Besides this, he had himself been an eyewitness to the first experiment in cable laying between Newfoundland and Nova Scotia. A party which included, besides Cyrus and Henry, Peter

Cooper, Samuel Morse, and others concerned in the expedition had set off by steamer from New York harbor. But the attempt seemed doomed almost from the start. The captain of the steamer was not experienced enough for such an undertaking. He grew stubborn and seriously bungled the delicate operation of towing the bark which was to pay out the miles of cable. Halfway across the Gulf of St. Lawrence a violent gale had threatened to sink both ships. The heavily loaded bark and the steamer that towed it were in such danger that it had been necessary to cut the cable. Forty miles had been laid, and nothing to show for the attempt but loss and discouragement. The party had returned in a far less confident mood than it had set out.

"Yes, it was a bitter blow when the order was given to cut the cable," Henry had admitted. "But perhaps the experience was needed since it proved to Cyrus beyond a doubt that sailing vessels are unfitted for the work. He realizes now that the cable must be paid out from a steam-propelled one where speed and smoothness can be regulated."

Yet even Henry's natural optimism had been somewhat shaken when the Telegraph Company confronted the losses of this disastrous experiment. It meant a year's delay at the least, for months would be required to make a new cable, which could not be safely laid until the following summer. New funds must be raised, and a cable of more and heavier wire strands manufactured. Without hesitation Cyrus set off for England to undertake these responsibilities.

Through most of the year 1856 he remained there, conferring with British scientists and financial backers. Brett, who had laid the first cable across the English Channel, and Bright, another pioneer in ocean telegraphy, gave him their advice and support. But such cables had been short, barely a hundred miles in length, and the proposed line from Newfoundland to the coast of Ireland must be reckoned in thousands. The general opinion in Great Britain, as in the United States, was that Cyrus Field was an impractical visionary. His scheme would never work, and those who were fools enough to believe him deserved to lose their money at the bottom of the Atlantic.

It was not comforting to hear what people thought of Cyrus in those days. Henriette came almost to dread the mention of his name. Not that she had lost faith in him or in the great undertaking; she still believed in the driving force

of his energy and in the indomitable will power that was
strong enough to remove mountains. But she dreaded the
effect upon Henry of the doubting headshakes, the easy ridi-
cule and biting criticism. These instantly roused Henry to
his brother's defense. For all his mildness and tolerance
Henry had his share of the family spirit. He could cling as
tenaciously as Cyrus to the idea of the invention and its
practicability. He spent himself trying to convince skeptics
till Henriette feared that his writing and health might suffer
from the strain. The *Evangelist* had grown and prospered
under his editorship, and his weekly editorials had begun to
be quoted and watched for. He must keep his family loyal-
ties and personal views separate from his work, she had to
remind him frequently when his enthusiasms mounted.
Often she must restrain him from penning a sharp reply to
some article that charged Cyrus with wasting millions on
what was obviously a fool's dream.

"Uncle Cyrus isn't crazy, is he?" the child, Clara, asked
anxiously as she returned from playing with a group of
neighborhood children on the front steps.

"Most certainly not," Henriette hastened to reassure her.
"What put that into your head, *chérie?*"

"They said so, just now. I told them 'No,' but Mary and
Sam and Lucy wouldn't believe me. They said they heard
their father tell their mother he was because he's got crazy
notions in his head."

"You must not listen to what they say, and you must never
repeat such things to Uncle because they make him very
unhappy."

"I promise. But when I told them that my father was
helping Uncle Cyrus they all laughed and they tapped on
their foreheads, like this."

Her plump fingers gave an eloquent imitation.

"Think no more of it," Henriette told her. "Get your bonnet and you can come with me to Third Avenue, where I am
going to Mrs. Pope's shop to buy more cinnamon and raisins
and perhaps a bag of peppermints, since you and Uncle
enjoy them so much."

"And Mr. Bryant, too," Clara added as they set off. "He
ate four the last time."

"Ah, it is not polite to notice how much a guest eats,"
Henriette impressed upon the child. "And the last time Mr.
Bryant came you failed to make your curtsy. I fear you
forgot your manners."

"I hate manners." Clara spoke cheerfully at her side, avoiding the cracks between the pavings.

"You will like them better some day, *chérie*. Why do you jump so from stone to stone?"

"Because it's a game we made up, and one of the rules is never step on a crack."

"Well, then, manners are a game, too. I am only telling you the rules of politeness so that you will play well and not make mistakes when you are grown up."

"Is politeness like checkers?" Clara was very definite once her interest had been roused. "My brothers play checkers on a red and black board."

"A little like checkers, yes—more perhaps like a difficult game called chess. Now be sure to be very polite the next time Mr. Bryant or any of Uncle and Aunty's friends speak to you. I shall let you select the peppermints."

Henry smiled later when she told him of this conversation.

"It is hard to discipline Clara," he said. "Her natural friendliness defies rules."

"Yes, I must admit she has a gift for people, but she must learn now without conscious effort the social formalities. Politeness should be a matter of course."

"I seem to remember a certain occasion when politeness deserted you, my dear," he reminded her with fond amusement in his look. "If I had not overlooked it as I did—who knows—"

"Ah, my little Henri, I believe you actually treasure my rudeness to you that first evening! Can you not be charitable and forget that lapse now that we have been married for over five years?"

Henriette came to dread the arrival of mail from across the Atlantic in those months. Cyrus' family had joined him abroad, taking Henry's sister Mary Elizabeth with them. She had been left a widow soon after her marriage, and her health was failing. Her death in Paris shocked and saddened the whole family group. But Cyrus must push on with his negotiations. He could not take time for grief just when he had persuaded British officials to furnish ships for another experiment in cable laying and to promise a government subsidy for official messages if the venture succeeded. England had responded to the practical possibilities of his Atlantic Telegraph more readily than his own country. A new company was being organized, he wrote home with confidence in every stroke of his pen.

This time it was to be upon an infinitely larger scale. Three hundred and fifty shares of stock had been issued at a thousand pounds a share. Queer, Cyrus added in a postscript to Henry, that he, a dyed-in-the-wool Yankee, should find himself heading a company that had turned out to be predominantly British.

It was Christmas Day when he landed in New York with the second venture before him and over sixty shares of undisposed-of Atlantic Telegraph stock standing in his name. If Congress could be persuaded to follow England's example and support the enterprise, he was certain of success.

"He's off to Newfoundland again, and in such weather!" Cyrus' wife sighed as she shook the snow from her bonnet and shawl and drew closer to Henry's fireside.

"But he'd promised to keep New Year's with you and the children, Mary," Henry protested. "He told me so only day before yesterday."

"Well, he didn't like the sound of those reports in the letters that were waiting. I kept them from him as long as I could. I don't know what another rough voyage will do to that cough of his. He'll never give up, no matter what."

"No, he'll never give up." There was pride in Henry's voice though he, too, shook his head anxiously. "Not if it kills him."

"Hush, Henri, please, that is no comfort to Mary," Henriette put in. "If this deep-sea demon could kill him it would most certainly have done so before now!"

She had never been congenial with Cyrus' wife. They had little in common except family matters. But Henriette gave credit where credit was due, and she admitted that Mrs. Cyrus was meeting the strain with fortitude.

"Well," their guest said later as she rose to go home, "it'll be 1857 before we know it, and what the new year will bring I don't even let myself think."

"All that Cyrus hopes for," Henry reminded her. "We must pray for it with all our hearts."

"Oh, Henry, I'm so worried all the time I'm afraid my prayers won't do much good. You don't know what it's like," she said, turning to Henriette, "—and I hope you never will —to have people shake their heads when your husband's name is mentioned, or have your friends take you aside and say his mind's affected and he ought to—to be put away somewhere."

Henry's face was grave when he returned from seeing his sister-in-law to her door.

"Poor Mary," he said, "her endurance is being tested. I wish Cyrus were not heading into these northern fogs, but he'll find himself in thicker fogs when he goes to Washington to talk congressmen into voting the appropriation he needs."

"Yes," Henriette agreed, "of the two evils I should choose Newfoundland."

Henriette was to remember the year 1857 with peculiar vividness. In the far West Stephen Field, the brother she was yet to know, was elected to the Supreme Court of California, while in Washington Cyrus, overwrought from illness and anxiety, began his campaign for a congressional subsidy of seventy thousand dollars. He roamed like a restless ghost through the Capitol lobbies, trying to convince Senators and Representatives of the reasonableness of the proposed bill. If England, he pointed out, had voted such an appropriation, the United States should be willing to assume an equal share in the support of his enterprise. But everywhere he met opposition and indifference. Political machinery balked him at every turn. From his downtown editor's desk Henry followed the progress of the bill, hardly daring to believe it had a chance to win.

"The Atlantic Cable," Henry was to write later of this critical stage, "has had many a kink since, but never did it seem to be entangled in such a hopeless twist as when it got among the politicians."

Congressmen and Senators wrangled. Spokesmen from the South with their minds on States' Rights and matters of more immediate economic pressure opposed it, but Cyrus' few supporters, headed by Mr. Seward, the influential Senator from New York, were determined that it should not be lost in the last sessions of Congress. It was mid-February when the bill passed the House by a slim majority.

"We've got the President on our side," Cyrus assured them on one of his hurried visits home. "Now if we can get it past the Senate we can start work again this summer."

Henry repeated Cyrus' words to his wife that evening.

"Do you think there is a chance?" She put the question directly.

"With Senator Seward behind it, yes, I think so. Still there's a bare fortnight to do it in."

It was March 4th before they knew that it had passed the

Senate through fierce hostility and won by a single vote. President Pierce had signed it a few hours before he left office.

That was the spring that Henriette saw a young actor named Edwin Booth give a remarkable performance of "Richard II" at the Metropolitan Theater. Henry had complimentary tickets, and they had gone, knowing little of the chief player save that he came of a famous theatrical family, that his father was Junius Brutus Booth.

"He is young, and this is to be his New York début," Henry had warned her as they waited for the curtain to rise. "I believe he has had some experience with a traveling company, but we must not expect too much."

They had sat incredulous in the not too crowded theatre before the miracle of genius that wrapped a slender, dark-eyed man of twenty-four in the mantle of dramatic authority. When the curtain fell for the first intermission they turned excitedly to each other.

"Oh, Henri," she exclaimed. "This young Mr. Booth is already a great actor! He speaks with the tongue of men and angels. What a Hamlet he will be some day!"

All that summer through the heat of July and August a sultry sense of uncertainty hung over the country, though the storm of financial panic did not break until September. Henriette was glad when Henry proposed that they go to Stockbridge for part of August. The old parson and his wife had failed greatly since the Golden Wedding celebration. They showed the effects of their youngest child's death and the strain of waiting for letters from Matthew in the north and Cyrus in English waters on the latest cable-laying expedition.

It was in the tranquillity and green beauty of Stockbridge they waited with impatience through those late summer days, knowing that the second attempt to link two worlds was in progress. This time Cyrus was to start from the coast of Ireland in the screw-propelled ship *Niagara*.

"Now they must be well on their way," Henry said again and again, as he consulted Cyrus' last letters and the most recent British newspapers.

" 'Their line is gone out through all the earth, and their words to the end of the world,' " old David Dudley Field murmured, pacing under the elms along the village street with his thoughts those thousands of watery miles away.

It was three weeks before they knew that once more disaster had overtaken the expedition. Four days out, with nearly four hundred miles laid on the ocean bed, the cable had parted without warning. On board the *Niagara* Cyrus and his men had stood helpless as half a million dollars and the work of two years sank to the bottom.

"Once again—failure." Henry could say no more when he brought back the news.

"It cannot be possible he will have the courage to try again," Henriette said later when they were alone. "There must be an end to Cyrus' money if not to his confidence."

But Henry shook his head.

"I don't know how he will do it," he insisted, "but I know he will."

Two days later they returned to a city where new fears already crept up from the congested streets about the Stock Exchange, through the long channels of Broadway and the avenues into the prosperous security of Stuyvesant Square and Gramercy Park. The glorious bubble of Western expansion, of speculation in railroad stock had burst. The Ohio Life and Trust Company was the first bank to close its doors, and five thousand others were to follow its example as if a cyclone had struck them. Panic was everywhere—in New York and New England, in Philadelphia, in the cotton centers of the South and the newer cities of Ohio and Kansas, in the ports of the Great Lakes and as far west as San Francisco.

"No," Henriette told her Irish servant patiently again and again that autumn, "we will not preserve peaches and pears this year. Times are hard, so be saving with butter and eggs and molasses. We do not know what to expect."

Henry remained calm. He understood little of stock markets and overexpansion. But, like Henriette, he knew what it meant when banks closed their doors; when presidents of old firms and heavily capitalized railroad lines disappeared or shot themselves rather than face their creditors; when the best houses in the neighborhood suddenly stood empty with "To Let" or "For Sale" signs on their walls. They shivered and crept closer together when ragged men marched by the house, tramping east towards Tompkins Square to the hunger meetings of the unemployed.

"It was like this in Paris—just after—" Henriette faltered to Henry more than once in those first damp, chill weeks of

November. "Where will it end, my Henri, for the world—
for us?"

## chapter thirty-nine

IT WAS EARLY JUNE OF 1858. THE YEAR OF STRESS AND
anxiety they had somehow weathered lay behind them, and
the green beauty of England beckoned across the bows of
the steamer *Amazon*. Henriette strained her eyes for the
loom of the Old World as nine years before she had strained
her eyes for sight of the New. In spite of financial panic
and uncertainty they were to have the summer holiday in
Europe that they had planned and hoped for since their
marriage. Not quite all holiday, Henriette reminded herself
as she found a sheltered spot where the land breeze would
not play quite such furious havoc with the yards of blue
mohair in the fashionably stiffened skirt of her new traveling costume. No, Henry was to furnish a series of travel
articles for his paper and several others, and he would also
contribute his editorials and comment upon affairs in European capitals for his American readers. The *Evangelist* had
survived the hard times. It would never compete with
*Harper's* or the *Atlantic Monthly* in popularity, but it had
gained steadily in its following under Henry's editorship.
His business associates were trustworthy, and he had proved
a wise and scholarly commentator with a liberal outlook on
the religious and political affairs of the day. Henriette's predictions had been fulfilled, and now his gifts for travel and
writing were to be combined as she had hoped they might
be.

She watched his small, vigorous figure pacing the decks as
impatient and eager for the voyage to be over as he had been
for it to begin. His appetite for travel could never be satisfied. And his enthusiasm! It flowed out to everyone he met,
whether that person happened to be a distinguished foreign
statesman, the ship's captain, or some weather-beaten sailor
on watch. How boyish he still looked, swinging towards her
with quick step and a smile spreading across his face!

"Yes," she thought fondly, "my little Henri hardly looks his thirty-six years."

She did not resent this quality of youthfulness in him, even though it might, in time, accentuate the difference in their ages. She was not without her personal vanities. She faced her mirror deliberately, marking as she did so the lines that had deepened at the corners of her eyes, the contours of cheek and chin and throat that were no longer softly rounded. But her hair was still thick and richly brown, her large mouth as full and generously curved. A few months are more and she would be forty-six. Ah, well, if years were crowded with activity, with friendship, and with love they were not to be dreaded. She would not have Henri look older than his age because it might be more flattering to her.

"Good news, my dear," he was telling her. "The pilot has just come on board and reports that the *Niagara* is still off Falmouth. We shall be in time to see Cyrus before he sails."

His arms were waving like a windmill's, and his coat blowing. She half expected to see him take leave of the deck, blown out to sea under his own power.

They landed in Plymouth, and Henriette longed to linger in that harbor town of clean, white and gray houses sunk into the lush green that flourished even where the sea beat so near on the great sea-scarred cliffs. But Henry was set upon Falmouth, seventy miles away where Cyrus was supervising the final preparations for his next expedition. They found him at the Royal Hotel deep in discussion with the directors of the company. Instantly they were drawn into the bustle of preparation as he welcomed them and launched into explanations that left them breathless. Suspense quivered in the air of that little English inn, and in the harbor the "wire squadron" waited orders for departure.

"We can't fail this time," Cyrus was assuring them. "We've profited by past mistakes and we know our problem better. This trip the *Niagara* and the *Agamemnon,* each with escort, will carry the cable to a rendezvous in mid-ocean. We'll splice the lines there and then start in opposite directions. I'll be on the *Niagara* heading for Newfoundland and the *Agamemnon* will make for the Irish coast. This new device for the release of the brakes works automatically and relieves any sudden strain. If we'd had it a year ago the break wouldn't have occurred. And then we've increased the weight of the cable."

He drew a bit of the coil from his pocket and laid it on the

tablecloth between them. His lean, nervous fingers played
with it lovingly as he pointed out the strands of copper wire
which would be the living core in that protective covering
of interwoven hemp, iron wire, and gutta-percha.

Henriette could not suppress a feeling of awe and unbelief as she took it into her own hands.

"But it is so little!" she exclaimed. "No, it cannot be possible that this can stand the fury of the sea and the weight of
miles of water!"

"It's tougher than it looks, Henriette," Cyrus was going
on with almost parental pride. "This new one weighs three
times as much as the old. Not that mere weight matters; it's
strength and flexibility that count when we start to pay out.
Our tests show it can carry eleven times its own weight in
water, and we figure a depth of about two and a half miles
on the course we've picked. Allowing for that, it's more than
equal to the strain."

"Ah," she thought as she watched Cyrus' worn flushed
face and heard his tense voice, "but will the man be equal to
the strain as well?"

He was, as she had said before, possessed of a demon. He
scarcely seemed to eat or sleep; and a fierce, half-fanatical
light showed in his gray, deep-set eyes.

"I cannot look into his eyes," she told Henry. "They
frighten me. It is as if they also were charged with this
electrical current."

They visited the cable-loaded vessels and attended a ship's
service the Sunday before the sailing. The officers and crew
stood with bare, bowed heads while Henry prayed and repeated the familiar, significant words of the 107th Psalm:

"They that go down to the sea in ships, and occupy
their businesses in great waters; these men see the works
of the Lord: and his wonders in the deep."

Henriette could not see for tears as those men's voices
were lifted together.

"O hear us when we cry to Thee
For those in peril on the sea."

Her eyes were still blinded with them as men's hands
helped her into the tender.

"Don't you load us down with those tears, m'am," a pleasant voice cautioned her. "We'll ship enough salt water before we get our lady passenger spliced safe and sound. She's like all the rest of you, needs plenty of humoring."

And then she and Henry were in Paris! It did not seem possible, but there they were with the familiar streets and signs, the sounds and smells and the rhythm of her native tongue on every side. She wept, and she laughed, and she sat silent under such a press of memory that she hardly knew what Henry said in English beside her. He had chosen a new hotel, not too near the Faubourg-Saint-Honoré and yet close enough to the old scenes to please her. Their parlor and bedroom windows faced the green of horse chestnut trees, the walks and carefully tended flower beds of the Tuileries Gardens.

"Oh, my Henri!" she told him again and again through the wonder of those first days. "It is too much for me to be here once more and to be happy in my return."

"I had hoped it might not be too difficult, and yet I was half afraid that certain memories—"

"But no," she hastened to reassure him, "I see Paris through your eyes, and so even the past has no power to hurt me."

Some of the old friends were no longer there to welcome her. Pierre and Madame Le Maire had gone, and Adolphe Monod's recent death had left a gap in that hospitable circle. But Frédéric Monod and his wife embraced her as if she had been a long absent sister, and their affection for Henry had doubled. Night after night they talked in those rooms with the furniture exactly as she remembered it—the sofa set between the long windows, the gold and onyx clock ticking on the mantel under the mirror, the silver coffee urn shining in its old place on the sideboard. There was a sense of reassuring permanence about these inanimate objects that had remained unchanged, as there was reassurance in this reunion with old friends. They talked for hours on end, and whether it was of now or of then that they spoke there was sure to be the same refrain. "Do you remember"—those three simple words held them close and would keep them so always.

With Albert and Marie Remey it was the same. They were as serene and content in their modest prosperity as they had been in the old precarious days. Marie had grown plumper, and there was gray in her hair; but her eyes were as soft and dovelike as they had been when she was a bride. Albert stooped more and wore heavier spectacles; otherwise he seemed unchanged, though he now lectured to crowded classes, and his scholarly theses were praised by the academic world where he had found his own niche. They lived in comfort now and could afford the luxuries of a pleasant apartment nearer the Sorbonne and a maid to help in the kitchen.

"But I would not trust the soup or the sauces to her on such an occasion as this," Marie confided when they gathered about the table. "See, we have kept the basket you brought that snowy New Year's and filled it with fruit once more. And here is the cake dish you gave us on our first wedding anniversary. I always wash and dry it with my own hands."

These souvenirs, cherished because she had presented them long ago, brought the past back to Henriette with almost too great vividness. She stared at the forgotten shape of the basket, remembering also the shape of the strong, fine hand that had lifted it from the carriage through falling snow. Those incredibly plump, pink roses were bright on the china dish, impervious to Revolution and change and the rising fortunes of a new French Empire. Memories that even Henry and her kind hosts could not share, crowded upon her in those moments like a flock of unseen birds.

"Only see, Monsieur Field," Marie was going on, "she made this sketch in Corsica, and this pastel of flowers she did in the château de Vaux Praslin—"

Confused, she broke off at mention of the Praslin name. Albert hastily changed the subject, but later Henriette drew him back to it.

"Tell me all you know of them, Albert," she asked when they spoke together and Henry and Marie were viewing the city from the balcony. "I long to hear what has become of those children."

He told her what he could, though all he knew had been gleaned from hearsay and meager newspaper items. The eldest son had inherited the title. All the daughters were married. Sometimes he read the announcement of a birth in that family circle.

"And Raynald." Her face grew tender and remote as she spoke his name. "He must be a young man now. We could pass one another on some street, and I should not know him.

It is strange and a little sad to think that when he was so dear to me."

"Yes," Albert agreed, "but his childhood will always be yours. You made it happier for your presence. Never forget that, Henriette."

"I like to think that he and Berthe will remember the old days with less bitterness than the rest. Send me news of them when you hear it."

"I will," he promised. "I had thought it might be painful for you to be reminded of the old days."

"No, I am past all that now. Oh, Albert, it is good when we can face our bitterest memories and find that the sting has gone out of them."

But for all that she did not linger by certain personal landmarks. She felt her knees shake once as she passed the small jeweler's shop where the cameo had been bought on Raynald's birthday, where that fatal newspaper had lain on the counter. She looked the other way whenever they were in sight of the gray pile of the Conciergerie. She did not regret that in his remodeling of certain sections of Paris Napoleon III had demolished part of the Rue de Harlay. She was glad that shabby house and the window of the Needle's Eye were gone forever.

It was on her last afternoon in Paris that she had her first sight of the new Emperor and Empress. She was returning alone from a shopping tour. Her arms were full of gifts for the relatives in America, and she glowed with the zeal of feminine accomplishment as she neared the hotel. She had just crossed the Rue Castiglione and was continuing along the Rue de Rivoli when she heard a distant commotion— cheers and the clatter of hoofs. Mounted guards, brilliant in the palace uniform, were clearing the way for royalty.

"Vive l'Empereur! Vive l'Impératrice!"

Scattered shouts mingled with hoofbeats and the grinding of wheels as the royal carriage came to a halt beside the curb where Henriette stood, curious and bundle-laden. In that brief pause while the street was cleared of other vehicles she found herself staring straight into the faces of Napoleon and Eugénie. She was so near that she thought she smelled the perfume that rose faintly about the Empress, who bent and bowed her acknowledgment of the crowd's cheers. Napoleon seemed less impressive in the flesh than in the various portraits displayed in shops and stalls. He looked sallow and dyseptic, and his limp goatee and heavy lids gave him a sleepy expression. But Eugénie surpassed any likeness of herself. Only the German artist Winterhalter had been able to put any hint of her spirit and beauty on canvas.

"Yes," Henriette decided, noticing the pure, proud cut of those features, "she is all Queen whether she is the Spanish upstart they call her, or not."

Everything about her was perfection—the grace of her body under the billowing blue folds of skirt and tightly fitted bodice, the burnished bronze of her hair beneath the small feathered hat she had made fashionable that season, the brilliance of her complexion and of her eyes. Their glance rested on Henriette for the fraction of a second. Cool, impersonal eyes, she thought, but blue as gentians.

A cracking of whips, and the carriage with its Imperial crest began to move again. New cheers broke out as it rolled on towards the Tuileries. As she stood staring after it Henriette could not help remembering those very different cries that had rung in her ears ten years before while the palace was looted and another royal family made its escape through barricaded streets. Napoleon III had been an exiled prisoner then with few political prospects, and Eugénie had been only an exceptionally pretty girl with a title from her Spanish father that meant little and an ambitious Scotch mother. Ten, eleven years ago, who could have guessed how it would turn out?

"But for the Praslin case," people still speculated on Louis-Philippe's disastrous exit, "there might have been no Second Empire."

Henriette knew what they said. A murder in the Rue du Faubourg-Saint-Honoré had touched off fires of discontent that might have smoldered for years and come to nothing. Sometimes on such an occasion as this she asked questions that had no answers. If she had stayed in England, if some other governess had taken her place, would an exquisite woman in blue and a thickset man of Corsican stock have been acknowledging those cheers on the Rue de Rivoli? What would they have thought, those two in the royal carriage, if they had known the identity of a woman with parcels in her arms who had watched them pass? Ah, well. She gave a quick shrug and hurried on. Mrs. Henry M. Field must not keep her husband waiting. They were dining out that evening, and tomorrow they were starting for Denmark.

"See!" As she bent over the packing late that night, Henriette held out an engraving of the actress Rachel. "I could not leave her likeness to flap to tatters in that stall on the Quai. She has been dead six months now, and already Paris seems to have forgotten her. Oh, Henri," she added, "I have felt today a little homesick."

"Well, perhaps that is only to be expected," he comforted. "Of course you will be homesick for Paris now you have seen it again—"

"Mais non, not for Paris," she corrected him quickly. "It was for America the feeling overcame me."

"I believe you think of it more often than I." He smiled as he drew her to him from among their unpacked possessions. "Nothing you might have said could have made me so happy."

"I did not know how I should miss America," she went on. "It may not be the country from which I came, but it is a country I have shared. No, Henri, you belong to that soil, and I, too, have somehow taken root there with you. I shall not be sorry to return when the time comes."

They were in Switzerland in August when the news reached them that the Atlantic Cable was laid. Henry could not speak for his emotion, and at first they scarcely dared to believe in the truth of the rumor. But it was true. There had been delays and another break in the lines on the earlier start. The ships had crept out of harbor a second time that summer almost without notice, so weary and skeptical had even the loyal British public grown of the enterprise. The lines had been spliced in mid-ocean, and the ships had steamed in opposite directions, uncoiling their miles of cable to eastward and westward. The *Niagara* with Cyrus on board had reached Trinity Bay, Newfoundland, without mishap. The cable had been joined to the telegraph base on shore, and contact established with Ireland where the *Agamemnon* had successfully completed her course. Live currents ran from Europe to America on that August morning. From Stockbridge to San Francisco word of the miracle sped. Boston fired a salute, and New York set off fireworks; factories and ships whistled, and schoolboys rang bells and lit gigantic bonfires. London, Paris, Berlin, and Rome confirmed the report of the triumph. At last Queen Victoria's message of congratulation crossed the Atlantic, and President Buchanan returned her felicitations. Almost overnight Cyrus had become an international hero.

"Listen, listen, Henriette. They're all talking of Cyrus and the cable!"

Henry's face was radiant in those days. Wherever they went, they heard the familiar name. In French, in Italian, in German they heard it spoken with every conceivable accent and intonation.

"Oh, to be at home now!" Henry sighed at each fresh burst of jubilation.

Even his love of travel could not make up for missing New York's demonstration in his brother's honor. Having shared in the preparations and discouragements only to be absent when success came was almost more than he could bear. He would have hurried back on the next westbound ship if Henriette had not restrained him. It was impossible, as she pointed out, to reach New York in time for the celebration; and he could not afford to shift his plans and give up the remaining articles he had undertaken. Besides, she reminded him, his part was to write the history of the Atlantic Cable; and Cyrus would be too deluged by this first frenzy of rejoicing to give him accurate details of the final accomplishment.

So they continued their journey, and it was three weeks before they learned that while the official celebration to the promoters of the enterprise was at the height of its glory, the cable signals had suddenly grown faint. Engineers at the Newfoundland and Irish coast bases had worked frantically, but all their efforts had failed. The spark had flickered fitfully for a time and then gone out.

"The Atlantic Cable is dead!"

They heard it as they boarded the ship at Havre that was to take them back to America. Public reaction was only too apparent. Sullen looks and sneers took the place of recent elation. "People were ashamed of their late enthusiasm," Henry was to write years later of that aftermath, "and disposed to revenge themselves on those who had been the object of their idolatry."

Henriette touched her husband's arm and tried to urge him away from a group clustered about the latest editions of French newspapers that had been brought on board just before the ship left dock. The dejection in his face smote her as she saw him reading the headline that confirmed this new failure. She was thankful the talk was in such swift French that Henry could not follow it as well as she.

"No," he insisted when she tried to distract him, "tell me what they are saying."

"Please, Henri," she begged, "do not make me repeat it."

"But I must know."

"Well, then," she told him reluctantly, "they say that the undersea telegraph is dead. It has ceased to operate."

"Suppose it has—temporarily! It will work in time. What has been done once can be done again. But tell me what they're saying of Cyrus. I caught his name just now."

"Oh, Henri, they are saying such terrible things! They say it is a gigantic 'hoax' and that Cyrus speculated with his shares, selling them when the messages were coming through successfully. Now that the line is dead, they say he has abandoned it. Of course we know that is not true, but, Henri, do not press me to go on. I beg you not to protest. Come to the other side of the ship, where we can have another sight of France. Our summer holiday is so nearly over. Give me these last few days. You will hear the truth soon enough."


*chapter forty*


HENRY STAMPED THE SNOW OFF HIS BOOTS AND SIGHED contentedly as he shed his hat and overcoat and found the fire lighted in his study. Snow had been falling all day, and the horsecar that had brought him from his downtown office had been hampered by wind and drifts and other struggling vehicles. He felt chilled and tired, and he hardly heard the greetings of nine-year-old Clara, who rushed to meet him. It had been a difficult day, and he was weary. His eyes ached from finishing his writing by gaslight in time to reach the printers' hands, and there had been a long and difficult conference of the editorial staff and owners to discuss new contributors and the paper's policy in the forthcoming presidential election. Even a religious weekly, it seemed, could not keep altogether clear of politics when they were so bound up with the very life of the nation. No one who read or thought at all could help being aware that the issues were very grave and were growing graver each day. All the men whose opinions he respected—Bowles of the "Springfield Republican," Bryant of the "Evening Post," Greeley of the "Tribune," Peter Cooper, Henry Ward Beecher, his brothers David and Cyrus across the Park, and Stephen in the far West—agreed that the Union was threatened with perhaps the most serious crisis since its formation. There were even those who predicted that the country was on the verge of war. That, of course, was carrying pessimism too far, but no one could deny the existence of this rift between North and South; no one could deny the situation called for a President of the caliber of Washington and the farsighted genius of Jefferson if the country was to weather the next four years. And where was such a man to be found?

Henry dropped into his leather chair by the fire. It was good to relax in the warmth without taking up the evening paper he had bought on his way home. He gave another sigh and stretched his feet to the fender. Times were growing too strenuous and uncertain for him. Once, he reflected, a minister need concern himself only with the welfare of human souls. But now, whether one preached or wrote, religion could not be kept clear of politics. It was no longer enough to believe in God and to live according to Christian standards and try to love one's neighbor as oneself. Neighbors across the Mason and Dixon line wanted no love, and certainly gave none in return. That brutal attack on Charles Sumner in the Capitol had proved how high the feeling ran.

> "John Brown's body lies a-mould'ring in the grave,
>   John Brown's body lies a-mould'ring in the grave,
>       His soul goes marching on.
>       Glory, glory, hallelujah."

Clara's young voice was lifted as she came clattering down the stairs; every word rang out, clear and thoughtless and sweet. Poor, fanatical John Brown and his raid on Harper's Ferry! Henry did not like to be reminded of that misguided martyr.

> "Glory, glory, hallelujah—

"Uncle!" She stopped in the middle of the line.

"Yes, Clara. But please sing another song. You know how I feel about that one."

"Oh, I forgot. Aunty said to tell you she'll be right down. Dinner's nearly ready. It's early tonight because you're going to the meeting."

"Meeting? What meeting?"

But Clara was gone without hearing his question. He hoped the child had made a mistake. This was not Henriette's evening to teach the art class she had undertaken at Peter Cooper's new school, and she had given up taking pupils in the evening now that debts were paid and his salary was enough to cover their needs. He wanted an evening alone with her by the fire, with snow dulling the noise of hoofs in the streets and no interruptions from a too complex world. Perhaps he could finish that remarkable new book "Adam Bede" that had been recommended as deserving of a review. Henriette had been so impressed by its dramatic power and by the depth of its human sympathy that she had urged him to make an exception in his policy of leaving fiction reading for her.

"Henri!" He heard his name and the soft rustle of her skirts as she hurried to him across the hall. "What a night! You are not chilled from the cold ride?"

"No, my dear, I am almost thawed out; but it's been a trying day, and I'm rather tired. I've been hoping all the way home for the luxury of an evening here by the fire with you."

But she shook her head as she bent to kiss him.

"Have you forgotten that tonight we go to hear this Westerner speak? The one your brother David and Mr. Greeley regard so highly."

"Must we go on such a night?"

"You promised Mr. Bryant. He sent the tickets this morning, and he will introduce the speaker. The name is a strange one—Abraham Lincoln." She stressed the last syllables in the French fashion she could never overcome.

Henry laughed in spite of his weariness.

"I guess 'Honest Abe,' as they call him out there in Illinois, would be surprised to hear you giving a French accent to his name. Well, it's certainly the last thing I feel like doing tonight, but I'd never dare to face Mr. Bryant if we stayed at home."

"Or David. He promised to call for us on his way to Cooper Union. We must not keep him waiting, for he will escort this Westerner to the platform."

"Yes, David's supporting his platform in more ways than one," Henry told her. "He thinks the man has a fair chance of being nominated by the Republicans for the Presidency next summer. It seems an odd choice; but David heard him debate against Stephen A. Douglas two years ago, and he never forgot it. There must be something about this Lincoln if he can get David and Greeley and Bryant behind him."

"But not Cyrus," Henriette put in. "The Field brothers have very different opinions on our next President."

"Well, you'd expect Cyrus to favor Seward," Henry reminded her. "Without Seward the Cable appropriation bill would never have gone through, and if he's elected Cyrus can count on his support again. It's hard," he went on, "being pulled in two directions. Of course I'd like to see Seward in the White House when it means so much to Cyrus and his plans for raising the cable. But David and Bryant both want what's best for the country, too. Nothing to do, I guess, but give up our evening at home and hear this Rail Splitter for ourselves."

"Rail Splitter?" she questioned, puzzled. "You cannot expect me to know these political terms."

Henry smiled in amusement as they went in to the dinner table.

"It has nothing to do with politics, my dear. This Abraham Lincoln, it appears, spent his youth cutting logs into fence rails out there in the backwoods. He's completely self-taught, if one can believe what's said about him. He picked up what education he could for himself. Learned law by practicing it mostly. I doubt if you've ever met his type in America, and he's probably never seen an eastern audience like the one he'll address tonight."

"If there *is* any audience for him in such a storm. Listen, Henri, to the snow ticking on the windowpanes. I am thankful David will take us. There will be few cabs out for hire."

Cooper Union, towards which they were soon moving in the comfort of a private closed vehicle, had materialized from the vague scheme that Peter Cooper had outlined four years before. The large, red bulk of a building partially filled an irregular piece of property that had been redeemed from an unsavory open space formerly used as a slaughtering place for cattle. It stood on Seventh Street, bounded by Third and Fourth avenues and the district known as the Bowery. Their capitalist neighbor had personally supervised its construction and had spent many hours at the Henry Field home discussing his architectural and educational theories. In

Henriette he had found an appreciative listener and a shrewd adviser. He consulted her particularly in matters connected with the department to be devoted to the instruction of young women. Woman's place, he firmly contended, was predestined to be in the home. But Mrs. Henry Field was one who could combine a home with creative work, and he adopted a number of her practical suggestions. Her sympathy in the undertaking had endeared her to him, and he had appointed her principal of the institution's Female School of Art. He liked nothing better than to drop in and discuss the problems of this pet project, this "Union of Art and Science" for which he had set aside six hundred thousand dollars of the fortune he had made in glue and iron works. He liked, too, to roam through the building that bore his name.

"I wonder if Mr. Cooper will be here tonight," she said as they drew up before the great building, its gas-lit windows magnified by the falling snow.

"Not many seem to be going in." David looked anxiously about as they entered.

"It's still early," Henry reminded him as they scanned the half-empty auditorium which was the founder's special pride. "I recognize some faces among those present. Colonel Harper, the publisher, just went in, and that looks like Beecher over there; and I see our Twentieth Street neighbor Mr. Roosevelt."

"Numbers count less than faces, perhaps." David tried to sound cheerful. "However, it's a pity we have such a night. This first eastern speech may make or lose the nomination for Lincoln. But we can gauge his chances better tomorrow from the newspaper reports. Well, I must go now to join Mr. Bryant and our speaker. I'll want to hear later how he impresses you."

Their seats were in the middle section, well forward, and gave excellent opportunity to watch the audience that straggled in. It was late in arriving and almost entirely masculine though a few women, like Henriette, had accompanied their husbands. In the warmth of the hall damp coats gave out a faint steam, and there was a continual stamping of snowy boots and flapping of wet mufflers.

"How many do you think are here?" Henry asked a young newspaper man of his acquaintance who stopped to speak on his way to a front seat.

"Well over a thousand, I'd say. Not a bad turnout, considering the weather. Most of them seem to have bought tickets, too, and it's not all Republican party. I see plenty of Democrats are out to size up this Abe Lincoln and his chances for the nomination. Looks as if he might be matched with Douglas again."

"What do you know about him?" Henry questioned.

"Not much; but I'd hate to be in his shoes tonight. It'll be a hard audience to win over. He's a good way from the home folks back in Illinois."

His words and the half expectant, half hostile atmosphere of those about her roused Henriette from indifference to curiosity. She had come, almost in complete ignorance of the speaker, merely because David and Mr. Bryant had seemed so insistent upon their attendance. But now she found herself impatient to see and hear this western Rail Splitter, this self-taught debater who had somehow managed to draw a surprisingly large number of influential men there on a night of snow and sleet. What would this Abraham Lincoln be like, she wondered. What would he have to say? Did he appreciate the honor that the author of "Thanatopsis," one of New York's most revered newspaper editors, was doing him by making that introduction? Did he realize what it meant to have Henry's brother David act as his escort? Did he guess that Henry Ward Beecher, the most inspired master of words in the country, might even be there to hear him?

A buzz of voices swept through the hall as the men took their places on the platform. She had an impression of some one dark and of immense height and thinness between her brother-in-law and Mr. Bryant. Then they sat down, and her view was broken by those in front. David looked unusually distinguished, she thought, in his black, well fitted clothes. He had grown gray though he was only in his middle fifties; but it set off his fine features, his strikingly blue eyes and fresh color, and lent dignity to his erect, strong figure. Mr. Bryant was rising now with his benevolent poet's face, his full beard and impressive dome of forehead. His words were, as always, well chosen and delivered with calm precision. There was no doubt of his sincerity, his admiration, from the beginning to the close of his introduction:

"I have only, my friends, to pronounce the name of Abraham Lincoln, of Illinois," he was saying, "I have only to pronounce his name to secure your profoundest attention."

Henriette moved in her seat to make sure of an unimpeded view of the platform. But she need not have done so, for the figure that rose was tall enough to be visible above any interfering head. It seemed to her in the hush following the patter of applause that a grotesquely lengthened shadow rather than a man dominated the platform.

"Henry was right," she thought. "I have never seen anyone like this before."

Her first impulse was a desire to laugh at the ungainly apparition. Then the very incongruity of that ill contrived shape filled her with a sense of pity. She braced herself mentally against the titters she expected. To her relief none came. People, she decided, must have been startled into silence even as she had been.

He did not hurry to begin. In spite of his strange, shambling walk he balanced his great frame squarely on his incredibly long feet, and when he stood still, looking out across his audience, the pause was deliberate, not hesitant. Studying the stark black and white of that gaunt face, she marked the power of the jaw, the glint of the eyes under their heavy brows, the nose that had the flinty strength of some outcropping of granite rock in a pasture. She found herself suddenly reminded of such bold natural outlines that defied even summer's softening of green.

She smiled, too, remembering those figures set in cornfields to frighten crows—angular frameworks in the guise of men, whose garments hung as limp and shapeless upon them as did this man's. A scarecrow, yes, but somehow touched with a sad magnificence as she had seen them transformed sometimes by the setting sun.

He was speaking now, and at first she found it hard to follow him because of the strange twang of his speech, unlike any she had ever heard. The voice was not what she had expected. It was not deep and resonant, such as that great frame might have produced; it was not hoarse or rasping, which might have been in keeping with that thinness of body. It was low and gentle though it carried his words to the farthest seats. He spoke as if he were not on a platform, rather as if he were leaning across the counter of some country store, talking to a customer about the state of the nation.

As he went on, Henriette lost the man and his voice in his words. Then she became less aware of the words than of the thoughts that transcended them. Without conscious effort his mind and hers were fused into one. Issues and policies that had seemed beyond the range of her understanding emerged clear as a pane of glass washed clean of confusion and perplexity.

He spoke of the South, of those states upon whom the permanence of the Union rested. Fearlessly, quietly, and without bitterness he reviewed the cause of dissension between North and South. It was as if a wise and ruthless surgeon laid his hand at the root of a dread malady.

All the heated, fierce arguments for and against slavery that Henriette had heard in those last ten years; all the controversy over states' rights and free states, the inconsistencies that had confused her as she tried to reconcile them with her own personal views suddenly crystallized in the sure simplicity of his words, in the tolerant conviction that made them significant:

> Wrong as we think slavery is, we can yet afford to let it alone where it is, because that much is due to necessity arising from its actual presence in the nation. But can we, while our votes will prevent it, allow it to spread into the national Territories and to overrun us here in the free states? If our sense of duty forbids this, then let us stand by our duty fearlessly and effectively.

He waved no oratorical banners from that platform. No figurative eagle screamed ill advised war cries in the name of patriotism.

Henriette sat, scarcely aware of herself, of Henry at her side, of the whole tensely listening audience about her. Without fanfare he finished what he had come there to say:

> Let us have faith that right makes might; and in that faith let us to the end dare to do our duty as we understand it.

Henry and she found themselves moving automatically with the rest towards the doors. They stood together, waiting for David, as the crowd departed. But they were too moved to heed the comments about them. Mechanically they acknowledged the bows of acquaintances who passed.

"Well"—Henry spoke faintly as if he had just wakened from sleep—"what did you think of Abraham Lincoln?"

"I could not think," she answered, "not after he began to speak. Henri, he is America."

"You mean," he corrected her absently, "that he is an American."

"No." She shook her head. "I meant it the way I said—he *is* America. I would cast my vote for him if I were a man."

*chapter forty-one*

ON A SUNDAY EVENING JUST BEFORE CHRISTMAS OF 1860 the talk that flowed through the house on East Eighteenth Street was particularly animated. Guests had never been more varied or congenial. Peter Cooper and Mr. Bryant had both dropped in. Henry's publisher friend George Putnam was there, and a young man named Charles Scribner also with publishing ambitions. David Dudley Field had brought his colleague William Evarts the lawyer. Edward Youmans had arrived with John Fiske, who had come down from his Cambridge lectures. The two had scarcely stopped their discussion of Darwin's theory of evolution long enough to remove their hats and overcoats and greet their hosts. J. G. Holland had appeared early to ask Henriette's opinion of a new poem, and there were visitors from New England who happened to be in the city—President Hopkins of Williams, Charles Sedgwick of Lenox, and Professor and Mrs. Calvin Stowe from Andover, Massachusetts.

"Yes," Henriette answered the question of the artist Eastman Johnson, in whose work she saw great promise. "That is indeed the authoress of 'Uncle Tom's Cabin,' Mr. Beecher's sister. You will have no doubt of it if she feels in a mood to talk of her experiences with that book or of her travels in England. But she may prefer to listen, for she is at work on another novel to follow 'The Minister's Wooing.' Her husband is less well known but he has a most stimulating mind. Mr. Henri finds his knowledge of Greek and Latin amazing, and he is an ardent spiritualist. Do not encourage him to talk of his messages from beyond, or our evening will turn into a séance."

But they were all too busy with the affairs of the present-day world to talk of the next. One subject after another held them about the table and later round the parlor fire. Once Mr. Youmans embarked on the works of Darwin, Huxley, and Tyndall it was not easy to stop him.

Then there was so much to discuss of other books and authors. Mrs. Stowe's comments were well worth hearing, and she spoke from personal experience—of Dickens and Thackeray whom she had met in England. From the latest works of Carlyle and Ruskin and William Morris they ranged to Tennyson, Kingsley, Matthew Arnold, and the Brownings, and nearer home to Emerson, Longfellow, and Holmes. Henriette even dared, in that advanced circle, to mention the name of George Eliot, whose unorthodox union with George Henry Lewes had been causing as great a sensation as her latest novel, "The Mill on the Floss."

"I care nothing for what is said of her personal life," Henriette flung out in quick championship of this woman who had also become the butt of scandal. "She has written a great book. There is more honest religion between its covers than in twenty volumes of narrow-minded sermons."

"It would surely surprise her to hear a minister's wife say such a thing," some one ventured.

"She knows what I think of her and of her books," Henriette assured them. "I have already written and told her of my admiration."

Henry added his approval.

"With Henriette, to feel is to act," he said. "She must respond to whatever has moved her. It would not have surprised me if she had journeyed out to Chicago to tell Abraham Lincoln of her satisfaction when he was elected."

"Ah, Lincoln!" Instantly the pulse of talk quickened at the mention of that name. "What state will the country be in next March when he takes the oath of office? Will there *be* a United States by then, the way we're heading?"

"South Carolina means to show Old Abe and the rest of us she won't be dictated to. She's the first one to talk back, but there'll be others. They're only waiting for their chance—"

"Plow them under, I say. Plow them under." A cool New England voice startled the room with unexpected intensity. "Might as well do it now as later. They've got their dander up, and we'll have to show them we've got our share of that, too."

They were off, and Henriette knew it. Words had left the safer channels of books and theories. The "Origin of Species," the singing of that girl prodigy Adelina Patti, the possibility of resurrecting the Atlantic Cable, the wonder of the pony express that would bring mail from California in ten days or even less—all these topics were forgotten once those names had been spoken: Abraham Lincoln, South Carolina.

"But Lincoln can't hope to abolish slavery. He came right out and said so—at Cooper Union."

"Who said it's a question of slavery? Though how he can take that solemn oath to support the Constitution of the United States and not know what it's going to mean if he keeps to the letter of it—"

"But I tell you he's against war. He's got to keep it from coming to that."

"Remember his nomination speech in Chicago?" One of the younger men had taken the floor. "I can't forget that part about 'a house divided against itself.'" The speaker's face flushed as he repeated the words: "'I believe this government cannot endure permanently half-slave and half-free. I do not expect the Union to be dissolved—I do not expect the house to fall—but I do expect it will cease to be divided. It will become all one thing, or all the other.'"

"That's all very well, young man," a skeptical voice cut in; "but he wrote that speech over six months ago, and South Carolina has voted to secede. What's he going to do about that?"

"God knows! God knows what we're heading for in another year!"

Henriette looked from face to face. Old friends, most of them there in the firelight, and yet tonight they seemed unfamiliar. Fear, uncertainty, confusion, and doubt had made strangers of them. Insecurity was a tangible presence in the room. A year ago she had hardly heard the name Abraham Lincoln and now she, like the others there, knew that the fate of the country and all their small, cherished destinies were in his keeping. "A house divided against itself cannot stand." How terrible those words were, how beautiful and true! How had he known with such sure instinct where to find them in time of need?

"I've been called many names." Everyone had stopped to listen because the author of "Uncle Tom's Cabin" was speaking. "And a good many were uncomplimentary. They say I must be an Abolitionist because I wrote as I did about slavery. I'm against slavery, of course, but I'm against violence, too. As my father put it: 'Abolitionists are like men who burn down their houses to get rid of rats.' "

"Meaning certain southern states, Mrs. Stowe?" some one asked pointedly.

"She means nothing is worth a war that would cripple free states as well as slave ones," Henry interposed. "I'm in complete agreement on that. I can't help feeling that this gesture of defiance on South Carolina's part will blow over. It's only a small section of the country—"

"Small, yes," a voice interrupted, "but so are wasps. It's been a little wasp from the beginning!"

The talk grew more heated. It seemed to Henriette that it quivered and twisted about her like flames. As the actual fire in the grate dwindled, this verbal one flared higher. It ignited them all as they listened or flung out questions and answers. Opinions leaped from every side; opinions that met and mingled and changed hands in that room while the oil lamps flickered out and only the gas jets on the walls burned blue with orange cores. Even when their last guest had left, she and Henry could not stop talking. They must go on, recalling opinions, hopeful or pessimistic; comparing this remark or that, wondering which predictions and warnings might prove to be prophetic by the end of another year. The first milk wagon was jolting by in the stillness of early morning when they fell asleep.

Christmas came and went. Bells everywhere rang in the year 1861, and New York drank to it in eggnog, Madeira and champagne. Washington warned South Carolina that Fort Sumter was Union property and would be defended to the last extremity. New York was in the grip of winter. It thought first of keeping warm and second of national difficulties. Chimneys smoked with tons of burning coal from the Battery to the less populous region above what the City Fathers had taken over to be developed into a park. People hugged grate fires and stoves. In Gramercy Park Peter Cooper's pet trees stood whitened with snow or dark with cold rains. Horses slipped on the icy streets that tilted towards the rivers; streets venders carried buckets of burning charcoal to keep their hands and feet from freezing. Clara Field and the neighbors' children, the young Putnams and Roosevelts, slid on the pavements going to school. They sang "John Brown's Body" till their breath froze and stiffened the mufflers round their necks.

Each evening Henry returned chilled by the long horsecar ride from his office, carrying an evening paper that brought little comfort in its news and editorials. By March faces, as well as days, were growing longer. South Carolina was not alone in her rebellion. Mississippi, Alabama, Louisiana, Georgia, and Florida had joined the scramble to secede, and Texas was preparing to follow suit. They were a close-knit group of Confederate states, and they meant business as even the most complacent northern newspapers were forced to admit. They held a congress of their own and elected Jefferson Davis president. The day Abraham Lincoln was inaugurated in Washington, a new flag with seven stars and three stripes was raised above another capital at Montgomery, Alabama.

There was a Confederate Army now with General Beauregard taking command at Charleston. He had made formal demand for the surrender of Fort Sumter. That was going too far, most Northerners said, and yet there were others, even a Mexican War veteran like General Winfield Scott, who thought it should be evacuated. But Major Anderson and his seventy-five Union soldiers were there, awaiting orders and the relief ships that had been dispatched.

In those days Cyrus moved feverishly between New York and Washington. The winter had broken his buoyancy, but not his belief that his cable could save the country from war. He was sure he could prove that, if only he had a chance to ressurrect it from the bottom of the Atlantic. He had met bankruptcy that last December. The mercantile firm he had bought and operated had felt the strain of the recent financial panic and had been forced to suspend business along with others in the city. Cyrus had paid his creditors what he could by mortgaging his personal property. He was carrying a heavy burden in loans, and everyone with the exception of himself considered his shares of stock in the New York, Newfoundland & London Telegraph Company worth less than their weight in paper. But Seward had been appointed Secretary of State in Lincoln's Cabinet, and Seward believed in Cyrus and the project. With the Government behind him again he could organize a new company and begin work at once. Congress must listen to him before another summer was wasted. If only he could make Washington listen! He knew he could convince them from the new President down to the most indifferent representative. All this talk of war only spurred him on. His cable was the surest way to head off trouble. It would never come to a war between the states if England and France knew what was happening in America from day to day and could take measures to prevent serious trouble.

"Lots easier to stamp out a bonfire before the house and barn catch on," Cyrus was insisting one April evening when he had stopped to see his brother and sister-in-law and report on the progress he was making. "Not that we've got to the bonfire stage yet, but there's no telling when we will be."

"I see your point, Cyrus," Henry agreed. "Still, I'm not sure things haven't gone too far for even such an invention as the cable to help. I wouldn't have said so last year or last month even; but now you'll have to mend a break in the whole country as well as in those undersea lines of yours. I'm afraid that's beyond any human power."

"But it stands to reason——" Cyrus was on his feet, moving about the room restlessly. His face showed strain and lack of sleep, and he was so charged with nervous tension that Henriette watched apprehensively as her mantelpiece ornaments quivered in response to his pacing.

"Please sit down, Cyrus," she begged. "You are not a lion in a cage, though you often remind me of one."

"I feel like one these days," he admitted with an apologetic smile. "Sometimes I think I'll go crazy if I can't push through the bars they've raised around me. You see"—he turned to Henry again—"it all comes down to a question of dollars and cents."

"Your cable—most certainly, and far more dollars than cents."

"No, Henry, not the cable alone. I mean the situation we're in. You never did understand finance, and why should you? But I'm a business man, and I know it takes more than flags and bunting and a lot of cheers to start a war and see it through. The South can get money raising cotton, and England's her best customer. There you have it in plain words. England and these Confederate States, as they please to call themselves, are partners. They raise the product, and she manufactures it. Great Britain, if she knows in time, isn't going to see them leave their cotton fields to go to war. I said *if* she knows in time—that's the crux of the matter."

"But if England should support the South the country would be more divided than ever," Henry argued. "It might mean another war with Great Britain for all we know."

"England's got trouble enough right now with her colonies and her sepoy rebellions. All she wants is to make sure that Manchester and some of her other big industrial centers don't have to stop spinning. I know what the feeling is over there."

"Cyrus." Henriette broke into the discussion once more. "How soon could you start work on the cable if you had the Government behind you?"

"Tomorrow!"

His reply was instantaneous, and the old excited glint that she knew so well leaped into his eyes.

"For two years now," he was going on, "this committee of investigation has been making tests and experiments, and they all show it can be raised and spliced, or, what would be best, a better line laid. There's a new ship, the *Great Eastern*, that would answer my purposes exactly. I went over her while she was building, and she's large and steady enough to lay it in half the time and with half the risk. Just give me the summer, and I'll prove the Atlantic Cable is alive, not dead!"

"I would most gladly give it to you if I could," Henriette sighed as she laid down her sewing.

*     *     *

She was at her desk writing letters to go on the weekly steamer for Europe, and listening to make sure that Clara did her full half-hour of piano practice, when she heard Henry's voice at the door. Even in fine spring weather he seldom returned before half past five or later. This was the day the paper went to press, and that usually delayed him. But here he was, coming up the stairs at a quarter past four. She knew from his step that something was wrong. He did not call her name as he usually did the instant he closed the front door. Her heart began to pound even before she caught sight of his face. She had not seen him look so stricken since they had heard the news of that last cable failure.

"Henri, what is it?" She hurried to him, searching his face in alarm. "You are ill?"

"No, my dear. I did not mean to frighten you by coming back early."

"But something has happened. I know it from your look. The paper has failed? We are ruined?"

"No, at least not yet. But I thought you'd be hearing soon. The papers are beginning to be full of it, but we heard the news first downtown. It's Fort Sumter—"

He broke off because his voice failed him. She took the paper he had brought, and spread it on the desk. Her hands were shaking. The headlines were large and in fresh black ink that smudged her fingers as another hurriedly printed news sheet had done years before. Then it had been "Murder" that the letters spelled. Now it was "War." She read them with the same sense of unbelief.

Fort Sumter had been fired on off Charleston Harbor. Major Anderson had stood by his orders and refused the demand to surrender, and Confederate guns had begun their bombardment. The relief ships were too late in arriving, and the Fort had been forced to lower the flag in surrender. It was war now. Nothing could prevent that. The country only waited to hear the President's proclamation.

Clara ran up the stairs, calling that she had finished her practicing. Pale mid-April sunlight slanted across the room, so dear, so familiar, where she and Henry had been so secure in their love, in each other, in the hope that somehow the worst could not happen to this world of which they were a part.

*chapter forty-two*

TWICE IN THOSE FOUR YEARS HENRIETTE WAS TO STAND with Clara at her side, while flags and marching troops went by that she could not see for the blur of her tears.

Marching figures in blue uniforms with packs and muskets became an everyday sight to New York after Lincoln's proclamation that followed the firing on Fort Sumter. He had called first for an emergency militia of seventy-five thousand, and the response had been immediate. Union or Confederate, every state must answer the call to join one side or the other. No dodging the issue now—one must stand by Lincoln or Jefferson Davis. Virginia's choice was inevitable with Robert E. Lee in command of her forces. Texas and North Carolina, Arkansas and Tennessee were added to the southern cause. But Lincoln had the North and his own Middle West solidly behind him. Regiments from New England and up the Hudson poured into New York on their way to

Washington and points south. By June Henriette scarcely went out upon an errand without hearing the sound of fife and drum corps and the steady tread of men's boots on city streets. She would look up to see some passing company with a banner that proclaimed they had responded from Rhode Island, Connecticut, Maine, New Hampshire, Vermont, or Massachusetts. Once she read the name Hampden County on a flag and thought as she did so the neighbors' boys in West Springfield who would be old enough to enlist.

Matthew's two older sons had both joined—nineteen-year-old Henry with the 34th Massachusetts volunteers and Heman with the 71st New York Regiment. Heman was twenty-three now, a tall, friendly, fun-loving young man who worked in Cyrus' firm. He was going to war in a new uniform that he displayed with pride to his uncles and aunts and to his admiring ten-year-old sister. He had answered the first call for "Ninety-Day Volunteers," and now he was leaving for the front. Perhaps he would cross over one of those suspension bridges his father had built ten years before. But that was unlikely. Matthew had prophesied his Tennessee and Kentucky bridges and railroad lines would be the first to go in wartime.

"You'll come to see us leave tomorrow, Aunt Henrietta," the young soldier had begged on a mid-July day when he had come on leave to say good-by. "Mother and Father won't be able to get down from Southwick, and Uncle can't leave his office to wait for hours on a street corner, but I'd like for you and Clara to be there. If you stand on the corner of Twenty-third Street and Fifth Avenue I'll be sure not to miss you."

"Most certainly we will be there. At what hour will you pass?"

But he could not be sure of that. He was not sure of anything except that the regiment was to move south the next day.

Though they had been expecting the change for some weeks, they could hardly realize the finality of the order. Matthew's oldest son was going away into this something they called war. Tomorrow he would have left these rooms where his laugh echoed Clara's and his feet in their new army boots tripped up the corners of the best rug.

"It is not possible," Henriette thought as she watched him consuming coffee and gingerbread in hearty gulps. "No, it is not possible he is going away to kill—to be killed perhaps."

They stood with a crowd at that busy corner of Fifth Avenue. They had been there since an early breakfast, and now it was nearly noon. The July sun blazed down fiercely on their heads, and heat almost as intense rose from the pavements. About them men, women, and children wilted as they waited. One division of the brigade that was leaving had already passed on its way to entrain, but there were long gaps between the battalions. Clara peered as far as she could see down the lengths of Fifth Avenue and inquired once more when the 71st Regiment would appear. Henriette envied the child's endurance, her cheerful responses to those about her. Everyone within hearing distance knew that they were watching for her brother's company, that he would be on the lookout for them, that she had brought a package of lunch to give him, and that she hoped he would surely be on their side of the line.

"Some other soldier will be glad of the food if you cannot reach him," Henriette had pointed out, to forestall possible disappointment.

"But it's got his name on the paper, Aunty. They'd give it to him, wouldn't they? I'd hate for him not to have the gumdrops I picked out."

"Maybe you'd better eat 'em yourself, Sissie," a man at the curb suggested. "You might get hungry before that brother of yours comes by."

But Clara refused to think of such a thing. "I must get it to him some way," she insisted.

Henriette and the man exchanged weary smiles. Argument was useless, they saw. The child's face was flushed and eager under the straw bonnet with its blue ribbons. There was a determined expression that her aunt had come to recognize when she met it on the faces of that family whose name she answered to.

"Now they're coming! Listen, Aunty, you can hear the music! I'm praying God to make it the 71st Regiment."

More drums were rolling out their mock thunder, challenging pulses to quicken, urging feet to keep pace with that primitive beat. One long blue line was swinging after another through the dazzle of noonday. Henriette felt the hot press of bodies behind her, crushing the crinoline of her skirts, knocking her bonnet askew in eagerness to see over her head. Clara strained forward, calling out the numbers and names on banners that perspiring color bearers held high. Cheers rose, now for this company, now for the next.

For herself, Henriette had given up trying to distinguish the marchers. The nephew who had sat in her parlor yesterday was swallowed up like a single drop of water in those heaving blue waves that were men's bodies moving in unison. They had no reality in their uniforms and visored caps, and yet they were real. Their feet and legs moved steadily, their arms swung and carried muskets; and sometimes she saw eyes move and lips smile. Some were tall, some were stocky, some were dark, some were fair—except for that they might have been one soldier infinitely multiplied. Under the shining mask of sweat they all wore, age, features, and individuality were lost. She was grateful for the tears that shut them from her sight.

"He saw us!" Clara cried out jubilantly above the noise of feet. "Did you see him smile? He was way in the middle, but I guess he'll get the package. I gave it to the man on the end."

Somehow they made their way through the crowd and began to walk east. A few shops had awnings out, and Henriette made for these patches of shade wherever possible. She scarcely heard Clara's remarks at her side.

"Violence," she thought. "I cannot escape it. It follows me from France to America."

"What's the matter, Aunty?" Clara was asking. "You cried when the 71st marched by, and now you're walking ever so slow and you look—queer."

"I am tired, chérie," she said. "If I walk slowly it must be because my heart is heavy with the weight of this war."

"Uncle's too old to go, I guess," the child comforted her, "and besides he's a minister and wouldn't know how to fire a musket. Heman says you have to learn to be quick on the trigger or some other fellow'll get you."

"Clara, please! You do not know what you are saying."

"But *he* said it, Aunty. I'm only—"

"I know, but do not repeat such words."

Henriette thought suddenly of her grandfather who had fought through Napoleon's campaigns. She could not remember the Battle of Waterloo, but her childhood had been passed in the ebb tide of its aftermath. She had witnessed revolution, had even been a part of it herself. But that, it seemed, was not enough. The ruthless cycle of war was to be repeated, and she was helpless before the forces behind those marching troops. No wonder the elasticity had gone out of her step; no wonder her heart felt like one of those lead bullets whose power she knew. It was a signal of age when one thought and felt like this even though one had no son to wear a blue or a gray uniform.

"Well," she reminded herself, "why should you not feel old? You are forty-eight years old, within sight of forty-nine."

Years had always meant little to her, but now for the first time in her life she felt her age.

"Listen," Clara urged, "you can still hear the music. They're playing 'John Brown's Body.'"

\*       \*       \*

A military band was playing it on another morning when she and Clara stood with a larger, quieter crowd at the same corner. It was April, 1865, and in those four years the tune had come to be whistled or sung as naturally as breath was drawn. "Dixie" in the South, "John Brown's Body" in the North—those two melodies were forever part of the struggle that had ended at Appomattox Court House less than a month ago.

"Mine eyes have seen the glory of the coming of the Lord;
 He is trampling out the vintage where the grapes of wrath
  are stored."

All about them people were singing new words that fitted the old tune.

"He hath loosed the fateful lightning of his terrible swift
  sword:
        His truth is marching on.
        Glory, glory, Hallelujah . . ."

The men's voices sounded husky; the women's trembled as they joined in; only the children's rose clear and unconcerned by the significance of those words, by the solemn rolling of muffled drums, by flags at half-mast. Across the Avenue façades of buildings were draped in black crepe. Hardly a house they had passed but had worn some sign of mourning. The dark knots were soggy from yesterday's rain.

Clara stood quiet beside her, a tall, half-grown girl of fourteen. Her eyes were serious under the hat brim that partly hid her long bright curls. "Copperhead," her playmates had teased her through those years while she had protested her loyalty in furious defense.

"Aunty!" She pressed closer and spoke in awed tones. "I never saw men cry before. I didn't know they could."

The first divisions of the military escort were passing—veterans of Bull Run and Shiloh, of Vicksburg, Antietam, and the Battle of the Wilderness. They marched with a difference now. Their steps were surer, more wary. Their faces were marked by experience no less plainly than the banners they carried, faded or bullet-riddled. There were carriages for some who could not march. Limp blue sleeves were pinned against the chests of others.

If Matthew's sons had come home like that! But thank God they were both safe. Heman had been honorably discharged from service, though Henry was still with his regiment in Texas.

People pressed thick behind Henriette, but no one jostled to gain a better place. There were no cheers, only low murmurs as the divisions filed by. A hush of waiting hung over them all. It was as manifest as the fresh wind that spread the flag folds in the thin April sunshine. Somewhere in the crowd a name was spoken, and a bitter oath answered. Clara turned with a shocked expression.

"Oh, Aunty!" she whispered. "They swore at Mr. Booth's brother. Isn't it terrible?"

"Hush, we must not speak of it here. We must remember that Edwin Booth is a great actor; nothing can change that, whatever his brother may have done. If Edwin Booth ever plays 'Hamlet' again we will go to show that this makes no difference to us."

"And will he come into the box afterward in his costume and talk to us, the way he did before?"

"Perhaps. There, I think I hear the Funeral March in the distance, and men are removing their hats."

It was coming at last, the strong slow-stepping horses with their burden under black covers.

"'Death is swallowed up in Victory.'" Henriette found herself remembering those words.

That was from the burial service. They were glorious words. Surely Abraham Lincoln deserved them more than any man who had ever lived. But she must think, rather of his own words that she had heard his living voice say on a night five years before: "Let us have faith that right makes might; and in that faith let us to the end dare . . ."

She could recall the very tones of his voice. She could have sketched his large hands in charcoal on paper, so vividly had their shape remained with her. Hands like roots, she thought, roots that hold the earth in its place when storms threaten. She had seen them cling tenaciously to the soil even after the tree had been felled.

## *chapter forty-three*

HENRIETTE WOKE EARLY ON THAT JULY SUNDAY OF 1866. The dimity curtains scarcely stirred though the air was still fresh from night dew and darkness. It would be another warm day, and the Stockbridge robins and finches and orioles had been clamorous ever since sunrise. She slipped from bed, wrapped a shawl about her nightdress, and left the bedroom without disturbing Henry. No one was astir in the house but herself. She paused at the foot of the stairs, as she often did when she was alone, reaching out to those quiet rooms in a rush of possessive affection. Sometimes, in such moments, it seemed to her that the walls and all the familiar furnishings responded to her happiness in them.

"It is our own," she reminded herself and Henry again and again. "We shall return to it each year to renew ourselves in this country that I, too, have come to love."

They had bought the place a year before when they had learned that these acres on the hill and a small frame dwelling were for sale. The house had been little more than a flimsy shell set on the foundation of an older one. But it faced the hills and the valley with its houses and church steeple. The bright thread of the Housatonic wound below through meadows and wooded green. And if one stood on the doorstep, as she was standing now, that tilted field with the gray boulder and rock maple tree showed plainly beyond the road. That landmark had been too much to resist. Henriette knew they must not hesitate.

"It cannot be meant that this land should belong to others who might perhaps cut down your tree or remove that stone where you preached your first sermon, and where I first knew that your life and mine must go on together."

She met the wish in his face with immediate decision.

"It does not matter," she hurried on, "that the house is small and ugly. We will change that. Hills and trees and a rock to remind us each day of your youth and of our love are far more important. Is it not so, my little Henri?"

And he had agreed, knowing that this miracle also would be accomplished.

So many years of her life had been passed in cities that she quickened to this renewal of acquaintance with the earth. Each foot of their land she came to know intimately from the patch of woods that closed in behind to the sloping field across the road where the grass was fragrant with hidden wild strawberries and with sweet clover and buttercups and daisies white as sea foam in the sun. She would not let them be mown down. Scythes might cut a narrow path from the road to the boulder, but that was all. And after the daisies passed there was the wonder of Queen Anne's lace, delicate as hoar frost and later the splendor of purple asters and goldenrod at the first hint of fall.

The house conformed to no school of architecture, and therein lay its charm. "A little brown teacup of a house," Henry had said after their first inspection. "We will give it a handle and saucer," she had decided, "and then it will fit our needs." With an added wing, dormers for the upper rooms, and a veranda that faced the valley, the teacup took on an air of rambling comfort among its clumps of trees with the ground about it gradually turning into a lawn. Flowers and vines began to prosper under the care and encouragement she and Clara gave them.

"Often I feel the urge to pin back my skirts and dig and hoe," she told Henry. "The woodcutters on the road beyond us are so wasteful it pains me to see how they leave twigs and branches strewn about. If it were not that I feared to shock some of our neighbors I should make bundles of faggots and carry them home for our fires. Yes, Henri, now that we have acres of our own I could easily become a peasant. Did you bring from New York the last numbers of *Blackwood's* and *Harper's Monthly?*"

Henry had smiled at her inconsistency, and she smiled now on this Sunday morning as she weighed the advantages of dressing to go out and weed her flower border, or writing letters before the day's activities began. She decided upon letter writing, for Henry could take them with him to post in New York. Every other Monday he journeyed to his office to spend several days over business affairs; and when he returned to Stockbridge he continued his editing from the upper study that overlooked the valley.

Here, as well as in New York, friends gathered on Sunday evenings. In fact, at all hours and on all days of the week they climbed the hill on foot or by carriage. In pleasant weather the door stood open for any visitor to enter without the ceremony of knocking. Henry brought strangers and friends with him from the city; neighbors appeared from all over the country; David and Jonathan Field and their families came and went. Henry's father wandered up from the village to sit for hours looking off at the valley which was so bound up with his own life and the life of his children. He liked to talk to Henriette of the past—of his wife who had been gone now for five years, of the son who had sailed away to sea and never returned, of his youngest child, the daughter whose death he could never reconcile. His mind wandered through its maze of experience and sometimes lost the way. But she did not confuse him by trying to help sort out the happenings of eighty-five years. He had the right, she thought, to remember or to forget what he pleased. The dignity of his fine old face, the lonely detachment that enveloped him touched her deeply.

"Henri," she had said to her husband only the night before, "your father has failed in these last few months. When I see him with his white hair I am reminded of the dandelions just before they go to seed. Sometimes I am fearful he will blow away before my eyes as they do."

"What do you mean, Henriette?"

"I do not know exactly—only there is a look of waiting in his face whenever he sits alone."

A clock struck eight. The smell of freshly ground coffee came from the kitchen. Henriette folded the letter she had written as Clara hurried downstairs fastening the sash of her dotted Swiss muslin.

"*Bon jour,* Aunty. Did you see the morning-glory by the fence is out at last? And there are more sweet peas and mignonette, and I'm sure that bud on the yellow rosebush must be open. I'll have time to pick some before breakfast if I hurry."

Henriette watched Clara speed over the lawn, past the clump of white birch trees that stood in the shade of their own foilage. Then she rose from the desk and her letters. Henry was moving about in the room above. She heard the sound of drawers being pulled open. Probably he had forgotten his Sunday clothes had all been laid out on a chair last night. She must hurry, or he would have every drawer turned upside down just when she had finished tidying them.

"Henri," she called, "wait a moment. I am coming."

She had forgotten to date those letters she had left unsealed. What day was it? She glanced at the calendar in the hall to make certain. Sunday July 29, 1866, she read without knowing that she would have reason to remember it always. The world beyond the windows might look as it had looked yesterday, but for all that it would never be the same world made up of smaller worlds separated by salty miles of ocean; worlds going their own separate ways in insular self-sufficiency. The Atlantic Cable had been successfully laid at last, though it was high noon before they heard of it.

David had driven them to church. She and Henry and Clara had sat together in the high white pew with its mahogany rail, conscious that when the minister prayed for "those of this congregation whose hopes are fixed upon a distant son and brother" he had referred specifically to Cyrus and the latest cable expedition and the news they awaited. But they had heard nothing for the last fortnight, and in those ten years of suspense and disappointment they had learned to take both prayers and congratulations calmly.

The service was over. They moved with the rest down the aisle to the open doors and the steps leading to the shadow-and-sun-splashed green. Old Dr. Field stood bareheaded among his sons and daughters and their children, answering the greetings of the churchgoers. Another minister might preach the sermon, but he still looked with grave kindliness and concern upon those who had come to worship at his former church.

"Father." David touched the old man's arm. "You'll come back with us for dinner. I've a letter from Stephen to read you."

"From California? They come fast nowadays."

"No, Father," Henry reminded gently. "Stephen's been in Washington for three years. You forget Lincoln appointed him to the Supreme Court."

They had started towards the waiting carriage when the

sight of a man running down the village street, shouting as he came, made them pause and peer curiously. No other figure moved in the quiet of that Sunday noon; and there was something arresting about the way he came on, waving a piece of paper and gesticulating. Too breathless by the time he arrived to speak, he flung himself upon the group about the old minister. David took the paper he held out. He scanned it quickly, then handed it to Henry. No one spoke for the moment it took to read those words. But in another moment the decorous Sunday stillness had been shattered.

"It's laid—the Atlantic Cable's laid!" The messenger from the telegraph office had found his voice again.

No doubt of it this time. The *Great Eastern* had come to anchor off Newfoundland with her task well done. Her burden of wire was all paid out safely, and living words were already speeding under the Atlantic.

"This message is for you, Father." Henry put one of the papers into the thin old hands. "It's from Cyrus at Trinity Bay."

Henriette had given up trying to speak or listen in that babel of excited voices. Everyone about her was talking, crying, or shouting in jubilation. Henry's hat had fallen to the ground under their feet; David's urban clothes and manner were shaken as he tried to hear questions and give replies.

"Yes," she heard him say, "it's been working for two days, but the news just got through. Damage to the land wires this time, not the cable. They'd about given up hope and didn't keep the line in repair after last summer's failure. Cyrus must have been wild when he had the line to Europe working and had to send his New York messages by vessel. But that's a small matter now. Cyrus says—"

The church bell from the steeple above their heads drowned out his words.

Henriette pressed Henry's arm in the din and tried to keep her embroidered shawl in place. She had lost sight of the old minister, but she saw him presently moving alone across the green grass. She knew why he was hurrying away from the ringing bells and the crowd of rejoicing neighbors. She knew where he was going even before she saw him cross the village street and pass through the gates of the burying ground.

" 'Lord, now lettest thou thy servant depart in peace,' "
she thought as she watched that spare figure in Sunday black
go its solitary way. " 'For mine eyes have seen the glory—' "

"Where's Father?" Henry was asking.

"I know where he is," she said, pointing across the road.
"No, Henri, wait. Give him a few minutes there before you
bring him back."

It was late that night before she and Henry were alone
again. They could hardly speak for their weariness after the
hours of rejoicing. Message had followed message, and
friends had flocked from every direction as the news spread.
Their ears still tingled with the ringing of bells; the smoke
of a huge bonfire still hung in the air though the valley was
dark and quiet at last.

"It's true this time," Henry said as they blew out the light.
"Cyrus has changed the present and the future. He'll go
down in history the way they're all saying. What a day to
remember!"

"What a day!" she echoed. "And your father has lived to
see it."

"Yes. I shall never forget his face, when he heard that his
son had joined two worlds."

"He has other sons, too," she reminded him. "David's a
great lawyer, and Stephen sits in the Supreme Court; and
you, my Henri, are—"

But he cut her short.


*chapter forty-four*


ONLY NOW WHEN SHE WAS A WOMAN IN HER FIFTIES DID
Henriette understand fully the truth of a saying she had
heard in her childhood: "Rue and thyme both grow in one
garden." Cassie Sampson's shrewd reminder to "take the
bitter with the sweet" also came back with a personal ring in
those months that immediately followed the cable's success.
At first it had been thrilling to be included in the celebration;
to be a part, though vicariously so, of such fame. But long
before the return to New York she felt irritated by the ava-

lanche of acclaim; revolted by the exhibitions of bad taste and unabashed emotionalism that had been given free rein.

America, with characteristic fervor and an unbridled talent for enthusiasm, completely lost all sense over the new marvel of the age. The nation rocked at such sensational achievement and promptly took Cyrus to its heart. He was the darling of the gods, the hero of the hour; and no praise could be too extravagant to do him honor. The fact that his own country had been skeptical of his Atlantic Telegraph of late years, only made the demonstration more violent. Great Britain and her capitalists had shown greater belief in the enterprise, had risked more in giving it financial support; and this knowledge rankled a little in Yankee hearts. They must vie with the old country in their appreciation. An American had been the promoter of the undertaking. Now that it had succeeded that was enough for his countrymen.

Parades and processions, bonfires and bells went into action from Maine to the Golden Gate. The South was distracted momentarily from bankrupt bitterness; the prairie states of the Middle West responded in lusty ardor. Superlatives gathered momentum as they sped. It was as if the entire country became another P. T. Barnum, hailing its hero as the greatest man on earth. Cyrus W. Field had become a name to conjure with, synonymous with glory and renown. He was "the Columbus of his time." "Our Field is the Field of the World," they said of him, and "The Old Cyrus and the New. One conquered the world for himself, the other the ocean for the world." Rhymes flourished:

> Let nations' shouts, 'midst cannons roar,
> Proclaim the event from shore to shore.

Poetical pens were dipped into the ink of jubilation. John Greenleaf Whittier was not above composing a "Cable Hymn," slightly more restrained and dignified than the jingle revived from an earlier *Harper's Weekly* of 1858:

> Bold Cyrus Field, he said, says he,
> "I have a pretty notion
> That I can run a telegraph
> Across the Atlantic Ocean."

From platforms and backwoods schoolhouses the stanzas were rendered with appropriate emphasis:

> And may we honor evermore
> The manly, bold and stable,
> And tell our sons to make them brave,
> How Cyrus laid the cable.

By October Henriette felt that the subject, even though it warranted the highest possible praise, had been thoroughly exhausted. She grew weary of such harping upon a difficult task achieved. Even Henry found it a little trying to be bombarded with questions and requests for anecdotes of his distinguished brother, to be introduced wherever he went as "the brother of the Atlantic Cable promoter." He was too generous and admiring to begrudge the world-wide acclaim that had come to Cyrus. But neither he nor the other brothers had realized the proportions it would assume. It had never occurred to them that this would effectively dwarf their own lives and achievements.

"One would think," Henriette had remarked to her husband in private, "that there had been only one Field since the creation of the world. Almost," she had added with spirit, "one would think, to hear people talk, that Cyrus had created two worlds as well as joining them!"

Henry had reproved her, but more gently than he might have done several months before.

"Cyrus isn't to blame because people have lost their heads," he reminded her. "He said yesterday that if he had to hear another recitation of 'How Cyrus Laid the Cable' he wouldn't answer for the consequences."

"He likes it nevertheless," she had insisted. Then she admitted honestly: "It would not be in human nature not to respond to the honors even though one may tire of the banalities. No, I am not holding him responsible for those who make fools of themselves. I cannot but remember in the old days how they said Cyrus would hang himself with his own cable; and now it seems to me it will be the death of us all."

Her endurance had begun to wear thin under the added strain of Cyrus' return from England. In August he had headed another expedition to raise and repair the earlier cable. Now that this had been accomplished and two ocean telegraph lines were in operation, an orgy of feting and feasting began. It irritated her that Henry should so often be an unofficial spokesman at these functions whether or not he was invited to attend. Henry could never say no to any family call for help and Cyrus could not keep up with the demand for appropriate responses to toasts and after-dinner speeches. So Henry continually laid aside his own work to concoct these for his brother. The sight of them reprinted in newspapers all over the country next day was particularly trying to Henriette.

"Cyrus wants me to give him a few notes for a speech next week," Henry would apologize as he went to his desk after a long day of editing. "He stopped in at my office on his way to Washington on company business."

"But, Henri, you have scarcely had a free evening in a fortnight, and if you must work so late there is your own manuscript to finish. You know Mr. Scribner is holding the presses in readiness."

"I know." Henry sighed. "He spoke to me about it again yesterday. He says the demand for my 'History of the Atlantic Telegraph' is urgent."

"Certainly, and with all the material you have been gathering you could have finished it last month except for these interruptions."

"Well, but, Henriette, I can't refuse to help Cyrus out when he's so pressed with business matters."

"You have spent years on this history already, and as Mr. Scribner told you delays now will affect your returns. You have put your time and your skill into the cable as well as those who invested their money in it. You have a right to your small share of the returns."

"Yes," he admitted, "but without Cyrus there'd be no profit for anyone. He must give all his attention to these matters of reorganization now that the different cable companies are to be consolidated. There's friction between the English and American backers, and he's the only one who can straighten that out and start dividends paying."

"Please, Henri, make haste with your book and let the speeches go."

But she knew her words were wasted. Those brothers, though they might disagree, though they might even know the pangs of envy, would always come to one another's aid. In legal matters connected with the cable David Dudley was well versed, but only Henry had the incidents of each attempt, the letters, the documents, the most minute newspaper item concerning its accomplishment at his finger tips. Cyrus could trust him down to the smallest detail.

"Ah, well." She watched him spreading out his notes and papers. "You will be working late. I can see that, and when you read the words you have prepared it will not matter to you that your name is not signed to them. No, do not begin to explain to me again that you must devote your evening to what profits you nothing. I suppose"—she bent and kissed him as she turned to leave—"I suppose I should not be your wife to stand here and scold you for it if you had been made otherwise."

No, she could not always master the resentment she felt in that aftermath of cable furore. Henry was too much of a person; he had accomplished too much in his own right to be dismissed merely as "Cyrus Field's brother." There were times when she could not keep her annoyance to herself.

There was, for instance, the occasion when she had been forced to attend a large reception without Henry. She had hoped to the last moment that he could go with her. But no, she had left him at his desk with another assignment to be finished before morning. The evening was spoiled for her from the start, and though the guests were particularly congenial and there were visitors from Europe she had wished to meet, she took little pleasure in the occasion and prepared to leave early. It had been unfortunate that she encountered Cyrus' wife at the foot of the stairs.

"And is not dear Henry here tonight?" she had asked as they greeted one another.

"No." Henriette had been powerless to keep back the crisp reply though she had not expected it to carry quite so distinctly in a sudden lull in the conversation. "No, dear Henri is at home writing the speech for dear Cyrus to give at tomorrow's banquet!"

She had felt no contrition at the time. She even relished her little sally when she confessed it to Henry on her return. But when her words went the rounds of New York and Brooklyn she wished she had been less outspoken.

"But, Henri, our sister-in-law asked for the truth," she protested, "and it was indeed the truth that I gave her. There, forgive me for being so hasty. If you will only copy the last chapters of your book I promise to keep my tongue under lock and key!"

The house on East Eighteenth Street with all its associations of their first years in New York had passed to other tenants. That winter they took temporary quarters in the Fifth Avenue Hotel since Henriette was to accompany a party of friends to Europe in the spring of 1867. She had been reluctant to go without Henry, but it was impossible for him to leave America. The task of editorship had grown heavier, and his father's health was too precarious for him to be so far away. But he urged her to visit France again and at the time of the great Paris Exposition. It was nearly nine years since their last trip abroad. Already other links in the friendships that held her to the past were broken. Frédéric Monod would not be there to welcome her. He had been dead for over three years now. But his family begged her to come to them once more. Henry had set his heart upon her going now that his "History of the Atlantic Telegraph" was in print at last and bringing in fair returns.

"Adieu, my little Henri." She clung to him as the gong of the *Péreire* sounded the warning for visitors to leave the ship. "Now that the moment has come, I could find it in my heart to wish to stay with you on this side of the Atlantic."

"You will find it in your heart to go," he told her, "and be happy in all that you see and do in France and England."

He was gone, leaving her alone in the stateroom he had been so happy in providing for her. It was still winter outside. The Hudson was filled with floating ice as the *Péreire* moved out to sea. But the morning was clear and fine, the shores and all the shipping glittered in the sunlight.

"Cher Henri." It seemed impossible that she should be writing him from Paris, only twelve days later, but so it was. And at that the ship had been delayed by a terrible storm that threatened to send them all to the bottom of the Atlantic to join the cable. She was safe and had wished for him beside her on that trip from Brest through the ancient, beautiful province of Brittany that once had been as large as his own beloved state of Massachusetts. They had reached Paris comfortably. How inadequate words were, she thought as her pen hurried on, flying across the paper to Henry in New York:

"As we arrived by the left bank of the Seine, our course lay through the Faubourg-Saint-Germain, where every street, every house, was familiar. Nothing was changed. As we rode along, I recognized every spot, and was in a constant revery, until the carriage drove into the courtyard of the Grand Hotel. . . . I have a charming little room on the second floor, looking out on the new opera house which is in the process of construction. Here, for the first few hours, I give myself up to my thoughts. My heart is too full to go among strangers, or even to go among friends. This is my native city, and is dear to me by a thousand associations. . . . And now as I sit at my window and look into the street at this evening hour so many forms go floating by in the twilight; memories, sweet, sad and tender, come back upon me, —memories that I shall cherish to the last hour of my life . . ."

Yes, it was good to be back. She laid down her pen and leaned her cheek on the window frame. Good to be back in the most beautiful city she knew. Yet—what hour was it now in New York? Was Henry just boarding an omnibus to bring him home from his office? Was Clara happy at school in Massachusetts? And did they both miss her as she was missing them? In two, no, perhaps not two, but surely in four days she could hope for mail from America.

"The Americans, like summer birds," she was writing in her next letter, "have been flying southwards, to sun themselves during the winter months on the shores of the Mediterranean. It is said that there are eight hundred at Nice alone! Our countrymen swarm also in every city of the peninsula. Of course they will all flock to Rome for Holy Week, and then return slowly northward over the Alps, winding up at Paris for the Exposition. Such was the program of my friends who left last week and who pressed me to go with them. But that would have taken me still farther from home. It is not merely the added distance, but that when traveling, you are almost as a soldier would say 'cut off from communications.' Letters follow you about from city to city, perhaps not to find you after all."

Friends, she added, were constantly calling to see her. She had attended the last reception at the American Embassy. General Dix, the new minister, was making a most favorable impression. He seemed admirably fitted for the post. She had enjoyed the evening and had been surprised to find so many acquaintances from New York in Paris. Professor Morse and his family were there, but she had just missed Mr. Bryant who had left for Spain.

Everywhere one met Americans—in cafés and hotels, in the Louvre, at the theatre, and if one stepped into a shop.

"Our young countrywomen flit about here and there," she wrote, "like humming birds, in search of pleasure, shopping extravagantly by day; glittering at balls and operas and theatres by night."

At every turn the changes in the city amazed and delighted her. It had grown in size and beauty since their visit nine years before. Now that the rains were over, the sun brought all Paris out of doors. How she had longed for him yesterday afternoon when she had driven to the Bois de Boulogne! "All the chairs on the sidewalks along the Champs Elysée were filled; all the carriages were open and instead of the riders being wrapped in shawls and cloaks, parasols were raised to protect them from the sun." The Emperor and Empress and the young Prince had been taking advantage of the fine weather. She and her friends had a clear view of the Imperial carriage.

"The Emperor looks older; he has grown stout and has a duller, heavier look. Cares of state have visibly worn upon him; but he has the same impassible, emotionless countenance. Time has not spared even the Empress,—though still beautiful, she is no longer young. At one moment our carriages almost touched and we were staring royalty in the face. I know some people think Kings and Queens are like public monuments, set up only to be looked at, yet I cannot but feel the rudeness of staring at anybody, king or commoner. But for an instant curiosity prevailed and I could not help gazing at one I had seen years before in the dazzling beauty of her youth. No one could mistake that face; the high arched brows giving it a peculiar expression."

The Empress had bowed pleasantly to their little party. She showed great tact and grace which she was obviously exerting to the utmost, hoping to charm away the opposition to her husband's rule. The pair were not so popular as they had been. There had been little cheering from the crowd that waited to see their majesties pass—evidently more of curiosity than of enthusiasm in the response.

Driving back along the boulevards just at evening, she had been overcome by the magic of Paris: the softly budding trees, the dim outlines of familiar buildings and bridges, the lighted cafés and the throngs sitting before them. "Thousands of people," she told Henry, "all *jabbering* as you used to say, and only as Frenchmen can!"

She dispatched sheets of finely written notepaper to him

telling of the extraordinary impression that the preaching of Père Hyacinthe had made upon her—Père Hyacinthe, whose challenge to Paris to shake off its apathy and turn once more to the true religion of the spirit had reached across the Atlantic. She knew how Henry longed to hear this man, and so she had waited for hours in Notre Dame with a congregation that overflowed even that vast cathedral. He had come at last in the long brown robes of the Carmelite Order, with sandals on his bare feet and a white cowl thrown back from his strong pale face. Mounting the steps of the pulpit, he had knelt in prayer. Then he had risen, erect and majestic. With the light falling full upon his shorn head he had for some moments regarded in silence those gathered to hear him.

It was the Lenten Season. He had announced his text in a firm voice, first in Latin, then in French: "Agonize for your faith; combat for your soul." He had begun to preach, and as she had fallen under the spell of his words she had almost believed that she was listening to Savonarola thundering against the vices of the age. "Merely to repeat his arguments and illustrations," she wrote Henry, "could give you no impression of his power, for it lay in the man, in his eye, his gestures, and his voice. In true eloquence there is something which escapes analysis, a power beyond words, a magnetism which penetrates like lightning, which cannot be described."

It was no retiring, fleshless ascetic who spoke to Notre Dame that Sunday. Henriette felt certain of that. In the brilliant, powerful man whose words had flowed out in tender or fiery torrents, she detected a struggle. The senses and the spirit wrestled for mastery. He belonged to the world, though he had deliberately put its pleasures aside. He belonged, she had decided, to that heroic company of the old confessors and defenders of the faith. Yet, no less than Henry Ward Beecher crowding Plymouth Church to the rafters, Père Hyacinthe possessed that inexplicable gift of holding his audience in the hollow of his hands.

Of the great Exposition Universelle she hardly dared to write. Her pen failed her in recounting its marvels, and many of the buildings and exhibits had not yet been completed. What would the city be like, she wondered, with the added magnificence of its full illumination glowing through the dark like those fabulous jewels of Aladdin's Cave? Already on the boulevards one saw representatives of all nations who had come to bring their treasures and pay their respects to the Second Empire. It was amusing to pass prosperous Turks in incongruous fezzes; to see grave, small Orientals peering in shop windows; to watch swift-stepping Arabs in their flowing white robes, and turbaned princes from India. Blue-eyed Norsemen and bearded Russians mingled with uniformed officers of Prussia and Italy, of Austria, Greece, and the British Isles. It pleased her to hear so many different tongues, and yet—what were these men saying of one another as they passed? Peace should be the keynote to the Exposition of 1867, yet she could not feel that peace was in the air.

"One feels little permanence," she mourned in her last note from Paris, "in all this lavish display of art and science and the cunning of men's minds. To me it suggests rather some exquisite replica of a castle fashioned by children from shells and sands. In the night it will all be leveled and lost. Perhaps it is because I have lived through the passing of another reign, top-heavy with magnificence and sham, that I can detect the almost invisible signs of change about me. I feel a queer presentiment that the end of an era is in sight. For one thing the army is much more in evidence than on our earlier visit. Martial music and military atmosphere chill me when I think of our own years of war so recently ended. They say that all this is to impress the Prussians and their Chancellor Bismarck, who will attend the Exposition in person, it is rumored. But the blue blouses of busy workmen and the contented faces of shopkeepers and their families would be far more impressive to me if I were gauging the strength of a country.

"Cher Henri, this will be my last letter from Paris. In the morning we leave for Calais, then Dover and our stay in London. I can scarcely believe that so soon I shall see my little English pupil Nina and her tall sons, and perhaps even be privileged to meet the author of 'Adam Bede.' "

And then she was writing him of that very happening. She had been invited to the house near Regent's Park.

"Come, sit by me on this sofa," George Eliot had beckoned warmly to the visitor from America who had dared to disregard public prejudice and exchange letters through years of social ostracism.

Henriette had marveled that the massive head with its rich auburn hair should belong to one of such ordinary proportions. It was impossible to feel a stranger as they talked intimately together. All distance seemed instantly removed between them. "To me her welcome was the more grateful as that of one woman to another. There is," she had added, "a sort of free-masonry among women by which they understand at once those with whom they have any intellectual sympathy. A few words and all reserve was gone. Can you imagine what it was to sit at her side for an hour—to talk and to listen to that voice, so low and soft that one must almost bend to hear?"

And London, and the English countryside in April! She had forgotten that wonder, it was so many years since she had seen it unfold sheath upon sheath of vivid green. She could not resist the flower sellers who held out golden daffodils and nosegays of forget-me-nots, violets, and pale primroses wherever she went.

"I stood at my hotel window overlooking Green Park where nurses and children were out in the sun when your cablegram was put into my hands. Oh, Henri, how strange that this first message you have sent me by the wires which Cyrus gave ten years of his life to lay, should have been the word of your father's death! Do you remember long ago how you and Matthew reproved me for thinking first of the bad news that might travel across the Atlantic as well as of the good? Almost I think I must have known how it would be.

"And so your father will not be there when I return to Stockbridge. I shall miss him for he had grown dear to me. I am filled with thankfulness that he lived to see his children prosper; that it was given him to know and share in Cyrus' achievement. He rejoiced in his sons' accomplishments, but he took no glory to himself. 'My sons are all good men,' he told me once. That was as near as I ever heard him come to uttering pride.

"It is difficult for me to be so far away from you at this time. But I have taken passage on the next ship for America. Like the birds I shall hasten back, and I shall reach you before the American spring is passed and the Stockbridge dandelions have gone to seed. Do you think our lilac bushes will bloom for us this year? Already you see that my heart has crossed the Atlantic."

## chapter forty-five

"GOOD-BY," HENRY AND CLARA CALLED AS THE CARRIAGE rolled out of the Stockbridge driveway. Henriette waved back, but she did not rise from the sofa by the open French windows. Her eyes followed the two figures on the seat with affection—the young woman's in light muslin, the man's that had settled into lines of middle age.

"My little Henri," she thought. "The years do not change him greatly. They may take his hair a little and put a few lines in his face, but he will never look old. He will never be old, whatever his age."

Yet he had passed his fifty-second birthday that spring of 1874. It was August now. The hills across the valley were hazy with heat; the Housatonic was hidden by dense green except where it flowed through the meadows beyond the church in lazy, glittering loops. The air felt soft and deliciously warm. She drew in summer with every breath. The fragrance of her own particular flower bed of mignonette, heliotrope, and lemon verbena came from below the windows.

"Lemon verbena." She smiled to herself as she repeated that name which had seemed so much less lovely than vervain when she had first tried to say it. Now it came naturally, though there were times when she and Clara gathered and dried those aromatic leaves to lay among the linen, or when she picked a sprig and crushed it between her fingers—moments when the past was stronger than the present. Vervain meant Vaux Praslin to her. She found herself recalling the old days more frequently of late. Perhaps it was because of the sorry state of her native country crushed under the disaster of the Franco-Prussian War and the fall of the Second Empire. Perhaps it was only that she had more leisure now to remember.

She had not been well that winter and spring. It had seemed an effort to dress to go out to theaters and lectures and receptions, even to friends' homes. Once she was there, however, the exchange of talk, the magic of human communication revived her, as it was sure to do on Sunday nights or whenever friends gathered about her own table. But there were sudden seizures of pain and weakness, headaches that came without warning.

"No, chérie, it is nothing," she would reassure her niece. "It will pass, but perhaps we had best take a carriage home. The omnibuses look crowded, and it seems to me that they jolt more than they used to do."

She could afford to drive now, though she resented the necessity. Henry had hired the horse and carriage for her special benefit that summer, and Clara liked nothing better than to drive her over the familiar Berkshire roads. But she preferred the cool parlor or a wicker chair on the veranda. Today they had been disappointed that she had not gone with them to take tea in the village and then to meet the train which was bringing guests from New York. But there had been a reason why she wished them to go without her. She glanced at the clock and saw that the hands pointed to four. The doctor would be arriving any moment now. She had asked him not to come before that time.

"Asleep, Mrs. Field?"

She roused herself at his friendly voice.

"No, I was resting only," she told him. "It has been so warm today. If you sit there between the windows you will catch whatever breeze there is. You did not meet Henri and Clara on your way here? Good. I do not wish them to know that I sent for you."

She saw that he was studying her with professional intentness as he listened.

"Our doctor in New York did not wish to alarm me," she was going on. "But he told me to be wary of certain signs. He hoped that these would not recur, but I must tell you that they have. Lately I have felt more discomfort, and the pain—here—"

She laid her hand lightly on the folds of her dimity dressing gown.

His hands were gentle; his questions more keen and direct in their probing. He was a good friend and neighbor as well as a skillful physician. She trusted him and he knew it. That made the half-hour more difficult for them both.

"Yes," she said when she had answered all his questions, "I can see that you agree with the doctor in New York."

"You make it hard for me." He bent and fumbled in his bag. "Of course we cannot say with certainty, and yet from what you tell me—"

"I understand. There can be little doubt," she prompted him. "That is why I asked you to come when my husband and my niece would not be here. They must not know—yet."

"I think it would be wise for me to talk to Henry. In fact, if any woman except yourself had asked me for an opinion I should have tried to put her off."

"You could never have deceived me. I know these signals of pain. I am not fool enough to believe that my body is invulnerable. How long do you think I have to live?"

She waited quietly as she had waited years ago for another verdict. His eyes answered her first with a plea that she would not press him; but when he saw that she meant to repeat the question he spoke hesitantly.

"It's impossible to say. Every case is different, and you are an unusually vigorous, strong-willed woman. With care and drugs to ease you it might be a year or even longer."

"I see." There was another pause before she went on. "Now let us be practical. We know the truth, you and I. That is enough for the present. I should like Henri and Clara to have their summer without sadness. These drugs you mention will help?"

Again his face showed the doubts he felt. Once more he protested the ethics of his profession.

"But you have yourself said that every case is different," she reminded him. "Make this exception for me. Henri and I have been married for twenty-three years. You must believe that I know what is best for us. Let me be the one to tell him."

After he was gone she lay without moving, and her body felt so light and at ease that it seemed she and the doctor must have been discussing some one else. There was no reality to pain when it left one, though while it held one fast all other realities faded.

The clock struck five, and she rose at the sound. She moved about the room, straightening the sofa cushions, putting books on the shelves and turning the bowl of roses so that the sun from the western windows would light their petals. In the mirror above the mantel the green lawn outside and her favorite clump of white birch trees were reflected as she delighted to see them. When every chair was in its accustomed place and each ornament where it should be, she stood back and surveyed the room. From being merely familiar objects they had suddenly become animate, bound up as they were with all the essential intimacies of life. She and Henry loved these possessions that had accumulated with their years together. What was it he had said to her only day before yesterday about the house and this very room?

"All this, and heaven too!" The words had arrested her at the time, and they came back to her now with new poignancy. "All this," she repeated as her eyes went round the room and its furnishings once more, and on through the open windows to vistas of sun and green shade. No, she could not go on with the phrase. It had suddenly come to have too literal a meaning.

She went upstairs and exchanged her dressing gown for the embroidered mull with lilac bands at the neck and sleeves and waist. Her reflection in the mirror reassured her. There was scarcely a trace of gray in her hair; her throat was still full, her forehead showed surprisingly few lines. She did not look her sixty-two years.

Once more she went downstairs. Through the hall to the veranda and on down the drive she moved. Then she crossed the road. No one was in sight. She had the hillside and all the outspread valley for her own. Clover and daisies were past, but Queen Anne's lace rose tall about her skirts as she took the rough path down the sloping field. She stooped and picked one of the frothy flowers, scrutinizing it as if she were about to put its shape on paper. She could scarcely bear the complexity of that frail pattern, each minute tip of bloom adding its whiteness to the perfect whole her hands held. And that single jewel of garnet in the center! It seemed to her that she had never really looked at Queen Anne's lace until that moment.

"Ah," she thought, "if I had died without truly seeing it!"

Henry's rock was warm in the sun. She sank down in one of its worn hollows, grateful for the enduring stone. The maple tree in the cleft had been struck by lightning one year, but new shoots were flourishing about the shattered trunk. Their leaves gave her shade from the glare.

"Nearly a quarter of a century," she reminded herself, "since we sat here together that day."

How long a quarter of a century seemed when one thought of it; how brief it actually was when one lived it! She had been half afraid to trust herself to love that other summer afternoon. Yet it had not betrayed her. Many things had been difficult in the years she and Henry had shared, but love had been easy always. Still, she had never taken it for granted. She was as incredulous of the miracle now as she had been then.

Down in the valley a far whistle sounded. That would be the train bringing mail from the city, and their guests. She could linger only a few more minutes on the warm stone. It was the time of day she loved best, when the hills retreated in the late light. Who could have guessed that this scene of all those she had known and loved would have come to be the most dear, the most familiar?

Yes, she had survived her transplanting even as Frédéric Monod had predicted. If only she might have been fruitful also. But perhaps it was enough that the plant had taken root in alien soil without bearing seed. She took comfort in that as she climbed the rise of land that had never seemed steep to her before that summer.

Her breath was short as she reached the house. She was thankful to have gained the veranda before Henry's return. He must not see how quickly she tired.

Now the carriage was turning into the drive. She could see Henry pointing out the view and the trees and the house to their guests. She caught the tones of his voice and smiled fondly at the pride and happiness he could never manage to keep out of it on such occasions. For a moment she lingered where she had paused to regain her breath. Then as the hoofs and wheels crunched nearer on the gravel she felt herself responding to the summons of hospitality. Words rushed warm to her lips as she went forward with her welcome.

# Author's Acknowledgment

FOR THEIR ASSISTANCE IN PUTTING INCIDENTS, ANECDOTES, and other related material at my disposal I am indebted to:

Clara W. Herbert for her special co-operation in the loan of family portraits and possessions, and for much valuable information.

The late Clara Field, whose personal reminiscences of her youth in the Henry M. Field family formed the nucleus of this book.

For recollections, anecdotes, and other data and for the loan of books and letters, I am indebted to the following:

Katharine C. Atwater,
Elizabeth C. Field,
Lucy A. Field,
Mr. and Mrs. Theron R. Field,
Mrs. Wells L. Field,
Miss Frances Fowler,
Miss Rosamond Gilder,
The late Edmund Lester Pearson.

And for special help in research I am indebted to:

The Stockbridge, Massachusetts, Library,
Cooper Institute, New York City,
The Museum of the City of New York.

It is difficult to list and classify all the books and articles that have been written on the Praslin Murder Case; but among these may be briefly mentioned:

INSTIGATION OF THE DEVIL by Edmund Lester Pearson
THE WICKED DUKE OF PRASLIN, article in *Vainty Fair* by Edmund Lester Pearson
CAUSES CÉLEBRES DE TOUS LES PEUPLES by Armand Fouquier
REMARKABLE TRIALS by Dunthy and Commings (?)

NOTED MURDER MYSTERIES by Mrs. Belloc Lowndes

LUCILE CLÉRY: WOMAN OF INTRIGUE (published in England under the title FORGET-ME-NOT) by Joseph Shearing

THINGS SEEN by Victor Hugo

ASSASSINAT DE MADAME LA DUCHESSE DE PRASLIN. PROCÈS-VERBAL DES SÉANCES RELATIVES À CETTE AFFAIRE (record of the French Court des Pairs).

Other books relative to the period which I have read are:

CYRUS W. FIELD, HIS LIFE AND WORK by Isabella F. Judson

RECORD OF THE LIFE OF DAVID DUDLEY FIELD, HIS ANCESTORS AND DESCENDANTS (privately printed, compiled and edited by Emilia R. Field)

THE LIFE OF DAVID DUDLEY FIELD by Henry M. Field

HISTORY OF THE ATLANTIC TELEGRAPH by Henry M. Field

SUMMER PICTURES: FROM COPENHAGEN TO VENICE by Henry M. Field

HOME SKETCHES IN FRANCE, AND OTHER PAPERS (a privately printed memorial to the late Mrs. H. M. Field)

GARRULITIES OF AN OCTOGENARIAN EDITOR by Henry Holt

STOCKBRIDGE, PAST AND PRESENT by Electa F. Jones

RACHEL, THE IMMORTAL by Bernard Falk

SAINTS, SINNERS AND BEECHERS by Lyman Beecher Stowe

LIFE AND LETTERS OF CATHARINE M. SEDGWICK

A SAGA OF THE SEAS: THE STORY OF CYRUS W. FIELD by Philip B. McDonald

ABRAHAM LINCOLN: THE PRAIRIE YEARS by Carl Sandburg

VALENTINE'S MANUALS OF OLD NEW YORK edited by Henry Collins Brown

BROWNSTONE FRONTS AND SARATOGA TRUNKS by Henry Collins Brown

FORTY-ODD YEARS IN THE LITERARY SHOP by James L. Ford

THE STORY OF GRAMERCY PARK, 1831–1921 by John Buckley Pine

FANNY KEMBLE by Margaret Armstrong

FANNY KEMBLE by Dorothie Bobbé

# BELLE DE JOUR

## BY JOSEPH KESSEL

### AUTHOR OF THE LION

**A DELL BOOK**                                          **50c**

**DORIS MILES DISNEY'S**

*magnificent suspense novel*

# NO NEXT OF KIN

The suspense-filled novel of a beautiful woman whose secret past left her prey to violence, blackmail and murder.

"Exciting, skillfully written"

　　　　　　　　—*St. Louis Post Dispatch*

"This book will grip the reader to its end. Congratulations, Miss Disney!"

　　　　　　　　—*East Hampton Star*

Doris Miles Disney is one of the outstanding mystery writers of all time. "The roster of Disney novels is astonishing both in its variety and in its sustained high quality."

　　　　　　　　—*The New York Times*

A DELL BOOK　　　　　　　　60c